"DARK VISION OF THE FUTURE."

In the time
when there are no nations on Earth,
only mutually hostile power blocs,
suddenly a new inhabited planet
is discovered:
JEM

Bantam Books by Frederik Pohl

JEM
MAN PLUS

JEM

•

FREDERIK POHL

BANTAM BOOKS
TORONTO · NEW YORK · LONDON · SYDNEY

RL 8, IL age 12 and up

JEM

*A Bantam Book / published by arrangement with
St. Martin's Press, Inc.*

PRINTING HISTORY
*St. Martin's edition published April 1979
Literary Guild edition September 1979
Parts of this book appeared in Galaxy Magazine.*

*Bantam edition / April 1980
2nd printing . . . . April 1980
3rd printing . . . . November 1980
4th printing . . . . . February 1982*

*Bantam Books are published by Bantam Books, Inc. Its trade-
mark, consisting of the words "Bantam Books" and the por-
trayal of a rooster, is Registered in U.S. Patent and Trademark
Office and in other countries. Marca Registrada. Bantam
Books, Inc., 666 Fifth Avenue, New York, New York 10103.*

PRINTED IN THE UNITED STATES OF AMERICA

13 12 11 10 9 8 7 6 5 4

ONE

●

WHEN DANNY DALEHOUSE first went to Sofia he did not know it for the first stage in a much longer journey nor that he would meet some of his future companions. He had never heard of that larger destination, which bore the unattractive name of N-OA Bes-bes Geminorum 8426, or for that matter of the people. Their names were Nan Dimitrova and Captain Marge Menninger. The occasion was the Tenth General Assembly of the World Conference on Exobiology and the time was not in any way bad for any of them. It was a springtime season, and for a moment there all the world seemed to be budding into sweet and friendly life.

There were three thousand people in the Great Hall of Culture and Science for the opening session, so many of them political that the five or six hundred scientists who were actively involved had trouble finding seats. Even the translators were doubled up in their booths. Handsome, hoary old Carl Sagan delivered the opening invocation, looking like a spry octogenarian instead of whatever incredible age he really was. He was already wheeling forward to the rostrum as Dan Dalehouse squeezed into a seat at the back of the hall. Dalehouse had never been in Bulgaria before. He had been drawn to the sunny parks, and he promised himself a look at the museum of centuries-old ikons under St. Stephan's Cathedral, a few blocks away. But he didn't want to miss Sagan, and the first plenary session was a tutorial on tactran reports. Some of the stuff he had never heard before. That was probably Sagan's work, he thought. Even as honorary joint chairman, Sagan passed the whole program through his nonsense filter. What was left was sure to be worth hearing. Sagan spoke briefly and cheerfully, and rolled away to a standing ovation.

Because the keynote speaker had been an American, the chairman of the tachyon-transmitter tutorial had to be from one of the other blocs. That was international etiquette. He was an Englishman from Fred Hoyle's Cambridge group. A few of the dignitaries from the Fuel Bloc stayed to hear him out of group solidarity, but most of the other political people left as inconspicuously as they could, and Dalehouse was able to move up to a better seat on the center aisle. He settled himself to tolerate the chairman's opening remarks, lulled by the scent of flowers coming through the open windows—Bulgaria made even less use of air conditioning than the United States.

Since Food and Fuel had already been heard from, protocol required that the next space go to People. So it was a Pakistani who read the first paper, entitled "Vital Signatures Reported from Bodies Orbiting Alpha Draconis, Procyon, 17-Kappa Indi, and Kung's Semistellar Object."

Dalehouse had been half drowsing, but as the title came through his earphones he sat up. "I never heard of some of those stars," he remarked to his neighbor. "Who is this guy?"

She pointed to her program and the name: Dr. Ahmed Dulla, Zulfikar Ali Bhutto University, Hyderabad. As Dalehouse leaned over, he discovered that the flower scent was not coming from the windows but from her, and he took a closer look. Blond. A little plump, but with a solid, good-natured, pretty face. Hard to tell the age, but maybe about the same as his, which was mid-thirties. Since his divorce, Dalehouse had become more aware of the sexuality of women colleagues and chance-met females in general, but also more wary. He smiled thanks and sank back to listen.

The first part was not exciting. The reports on the probe to Alpha Draconis had already been published. He was not greatly interested in hearing again about the photometric measurements that established the presence of photosynthetic "plant" life in a reducing atmosphere. There were plenty of planets like that around that had been scanned and reported by the tachyon probes with their cargoes of instruments—the whole thing no bigger than a grapefruit, but miraculously capable of leaping interstellar distances in a week. The Pakistani seemed intent on repeating every word of every one of the reports, not failing to comment

on the number of other reducing-atmosphere planets discovered and the apparent generally low level of evolved
life on them. The Procyon probe had lost its lock, and the
reports were at best ambiguous. Mercifully, Dulla did not
dwell on the instrumentation. The data on 17-Kappa Indi
sounded better—an oxygen atmosphere, at least, although
the temperature range was bad and the signatures were
sketchy—but the real prize was at the end.

Kung's Semistellar Object was not much larger than a
planet itself. As stars went it was tiny, barely big enough
to fuse nuclei and radiate heat, but it had a planet of its
own that sounded like fun. Hot. Humid. Dense air, but
about the right partial pressure of oxygen to be congenial
to life—including the life of a human exploratory party, if
anybody cared to spend the money to try it out. And the
signatures were first-rate. Carbon dioxide. Traces of meth-
ane, but only traces. Good photometry. The only parame-
ters missing were radio wavelengths; otherwise it sounded
a lot like Miami Beach.

The Pakistani then went on to explain how Kung's Star
had been discovered by the big fixed radio dish at Nag-
chhu Dzong, in the Thanglha hills, and that the discovery
had come about as a direct result of the wisdom and
example of the late Chairman Mao. That was not in itself
very interesting except to the other members of the People
Bloc, who were nodding grave concurrence, but the planet
seemed pretty strange. The translators had trouble keeping
up with the Pakistani, and it wasn't Dalehouse's area of
special interest anyhow, but he made out that only a part
of one hemisphere was covered in the biotic study. Funny!
Nor was he the only one fascinated. He looked up at the
bank of translators, each in their individual glass cages,
like nail clippers and pocket combs behind the windows of
a vending machine. Each booth had its draped scarlet
curtains tied back with a gold sash, very Slavic and
incongruous, and behind them the translators looked like
astronauts in their solid-state communications helmets.
One of them was a young girl with a sweet, plain face,
leaning forward to stare at the speaker with an expression
of either incredulity or rapture. Her lips weren't moving;
she seemed to be too entranced to function.

Dalehouse borrowed a pencil from the woman next to
him and made a note in the margin of his program:
Invstgt Kung's Star, posbl survey grant. He didn't name

the planet. It didn't have a name yet, though he had heard some of the Peeps refer to it half reverently as Son of Kung. It would be called other things, and worse.

What can be said of someone like Danny Dalehouse? Grammar school, high school, college, graduate school; he got his Pretty Heavy Diploma at twenty-six and jobs were scarce. He managed to teach freshman biology for a year, then a year on a grant in Tblisi and more than a year of post-doctoral studies, so that he was past thirty before he caught on at Michigan State's new exobiology department. The marriage that had survived a year of living on cheese and white wine in Soviet Georgia began to dissolve in East Lansing. He was medium height, viewed charitably—about one seventy centimeters in his shoes—and slim. He wasn't particularly handsome, either. What he was was smart. He was smart enough so that in three years at Michigan State he had made himself one of the Food Bloc's top experts in reading the telemetry from a tachyon-transmitter probe and translating it into a good guess at how much life the signatures represented—even what kinds of life. Then he was smart enough to figure out that a telemetry interpreter who got to be nationally known for his skill was going to look too valuable where he was to be risked on a manned expedition to one of those fascinating, remote worlds. So he tapered off on the interpretation and resharpened his skills at mountain climbing, sailplaning, and long-distance-running. You never knew what kind of athletic qualities you might need if you were lucky enough to be one of the fewscore people each year who got tossed to another star.

Being divorced was probably a plus quality. A man without much home life would be judged better able to concentrate on the job than someone mooning over wife and kids fifty light-years away. Dalehouse hadn't wanted Polly to leave. But when she did pack up and go, he was quick to see that the divorce wasn't all bad.

That night in the Apertif Bar he ran into the blond woman again. He had gone to listen in on the headliners' news conference, but the crowd at that end of the bar was pretty thick, and most of them seemed to be actual reporters he didn't feel justified in shoving aside. Between their heads and cameras he caught glimpses of Sagan and Iosif Shklovskii sitting together in their life-support chairs at one end of the narrow room, having their picture taken, and passing smiling comments and an oxygen mask back and forth to each other. They rolled away toward the elevators, and most of the crowd followed them. Dalehouse opted for a drink and looked around the bar.

The blond was drinking Scotch with two small, dark, smiling men—no, he realized, she was drinking Scotch; they were drinking orange juice. The men got up and said good night while he was looking for a place to sit down, and he perceived the opportunity.

"Mind if I join you? I'm Danny Dalehouse, Michigan State."

"Marge Menninger," she said, and she didn't mind his joining her at all. She didn't mind letting him buy her another Scotch, and she didn't mind buying him one back, and she didn't mind going out for a stroll under the fat Bulgarian spring moon, and she didn't mind going to his room to open his bottle of Bulgarian wine; and, altogether, the day when Danny Dalehouse first heard of Kung's Star was a very successful and pleasurable one.

The next day, not quite so good.

It began well enough, in the early dawn. They woke in each other's arms and made love again without changing position. It was too early to get anything to eat, so they shared the last of the bottle of wine as they showered and dressed. Then they decided to go for a walk.

It had rained a little during the night. The streets were wet. But the air was warm, and in the lovely rose glow of sunrise, the Maria-Theresa-yellow buildings were warm peach and friendly.

"The next thing I want to do," said Dalehouse expansively, slipping an arm around Marge's waist, "is take a look at Kung's Star."

Marge looked at him with a different kind of interest. "You've got funding for that?"

"Well"—coming down—"no. No, I guess not. MSU launched four tractrans last year, but we've never had a grant for a manned probe."

She butted her head against his shoulder. "You're more of an operator than you look."

"What?"

"You don't come on real strong, Danny-boy, but you

know what you're doing every minute, don't you? Like last night. Those two Ay-rabs weren't getting anywhere trying to put the make on me. Then you just eased right in."

"I'm not sure I know what we're talking about."

"No?"

"No, not really." But she didn't seem about to clarify it, so he went back to what really interested him. "That planet sounds pretty great, Margie. Maybe even industry! Did you get that part? Traces of carbon monoxide and ozone."

She objected thoughtfully, "There were no radio signals."

"No. Doesn't prove anything. They wouldn't have heard any radio signals from Earth two hundred years ago, but there was a civilization there."

She pursed her lips but didn't answer. It occurred to him that something was troubling her, perhaps some female thing of the sort he had never considered himself very good at comprehending. He looked around for something to cheer her up and said, "Hey, look at those fellows."

They were strolling past the Dimitrov Mausoleum. In spite of the hour, in spite of the fact that there was no other human being in sight, the two honor guards stood absolutely immobile in their antic musical-comedy uniforms, not even the tips of the long curled feathers on their helmets quivering.

Margie glanced, but whatever was on her mind, sightseeing was not part of it. "It would be at least a two-year hitch," she said. "Would you really want to go?"

"I, uh, I think I'd miss you, Margie," he said, misinterpreting her point.

Impatiently, "Ah, no crap. If you had the funding, would you go there?"

"Try me."

"That Pak was so flaming pleased with himself. He's probably already got it all lined up with Heir-of-Mao for the Peeps to send a manned probe there."

"Well, that's fine with me, too. I don't want to go for political reasons. I don't care what country meets the first civilized aliens; I just want to be there."

"I care," she said. She slipped free of him to light a cigarette.

Dalehouse stopped and watched her cup her hands around the lighter to shield it from the gentle morning breeze. They had had a good deal to drink and not very much sleep. He could feel a certain interior frailty as a consequence, but Marge Menninger seemed unaffected. This was the first time he had gone to bed with a woman without the exchange of several chapters of autobiography. He didn't know her at all in his mind, only through his senses.

The other thing in Dalehouse's thoughts was that in the 10:00 A.M. session he had a paper to give—"Preliminary Studies toward a First Contact with Subtechnological Sentients"—and he wanted enough time to add some comments about the planet of Kung's Star.

He sneaked a glance at his watch: 7:30—plenty of time. The city was still quiet. Somewhere out of sight he could hear the first tram of the morning. Far down the street where they walked he could see two city gendarmes strolling hand in hand, their batons swinging from the outside hand of each. Nothing else seemed to be happening in Sofia. It made him think of his own home in East Lansing at that same promising time of day and year, when the university was running at half-speed for the summer sessions and on decent mornings he walked or biked to his office to enjoy the peace. And, of course, since the divorce, to get out of his empty house.

To be sure, he reminded himself, Sofia was not in the least like East Lansing: flat and urban, where his home was hilly and carpeted with solid quarter-acre split-levels. And Marge Menninger was not in the least like absent Polly, who had been dark, tiny, quick, and easily bored. What exactly was Marge Menninger like? Dalehouse had not quite made up his mind. She seemed to be different people. Yesterday in the Great Hall of Culture and Science she had been another academic colleague; last night, exactly what every all-American boy would like to find in his bed. But who was she this morning? They weren't strolling with their arms around each other's waists anymore. Marge was a meter away and a little ahead of him, moving briskly, smoking with intensity, and staring straight ahead.

She seemed to reach a decision, and glanced at him. "Michigan State University, Institute of Extrasolar Biology. Daniel Dalehouse, B.A., M.S., Ph.D. I guess I didn't tell you that I saw a preprint of your paper before I left Washington."

"You did?" He was startled.

"Interesting paper. Makes me think you're serious about wanting to go. Danny-boy, I might be able to help you."

"Help me how?"

"With money, dear man. That's all I've got to give. But I think I can give some to you. In case you didn't notice my name tag when you were taking my clothes off, that's what I do for a living. I'm with SERDCOM."

"Praise COM from whom all blessings flow," Danny said fervently; it was the annual grants from the Space Exploration, Research and Development Commission that kept Dalehouse's institute green. "How come I've never seen you when I go to Washington with my begging bowl?"

"I've only been there since February. I'm vice-secretary for new projects. Job didn't exist till the first of the year, and I wangled it. Before then I was teaching the stuff at my alma mater . . . among other subjects; we didn't have much of an extrasolar department. It's a small school, and it fell on hard times even while I was still an undergraduate. Well? What about it?"

"About what?"

"Were you creaming? Or do you want a grant for a manned trip to Kung's Star?"

"I do! Christ, yes, I do, I do."

She took his hand in one of hers, patted it with the other. "You may regard it as settled. Hello, what's this?"

"But—"

"I said settled." She was no longer looking at him; something had caught her attention. They had come to a large park, and off to their right was a mall leading up to a monument. Flanking the entrance to the mall were two heroic groups of bronze statuary.

Dalehouse followed her toward them, feeling dazed as well as hung over; it had not sunk in yet. "I suppose I ought to submit a proposal," he said tentatively.

"You bet. Send me a draft first before you put it through channels." She was examining the bronzes. "Will you look at this stuff!"

Dalehouse inspected them without interest. "It's a war memorial," he said. "Soldiers and peasants."

"Sure, but it isn't that old. That's a tommy gun that soldier is holding . . . and there's one on a motorbike. And look—some of the soldiers are women."

She bent down and inspected the Cyrillic lettering.

"Damn. Don't know what it says. But it's the workers and peasants welcoming liberators, right? It has to be the last of the Big Ones—World War Two. Let's see, this is Bulgaria, so that must be the Red Army chasing the Germans out and all the Bulgarians bringing them flowers and hearty fraternal-solidarity handshakes and glasses of clear spring water. Wow! Jesus, Danny, both my grandfathers fought in this war, and one grandmother—two on one side, one on the other."

Dalehouse looked at her with amusement and fondness, if not full comprehension; it was strange to find anyone who took such an interest in actual foot-slogging fighting these days, when everyone knew that war was simply priced out of the market for any nation that wanted to survive. "What about your other grandmother? Some kind of slacker?"

She looked up at him for a moment. "She died in the bombings," she said. "Hey, this is fun."

The bronzes were certainly military enough for any war fan. Every figure was expressing courage, joy, and resolution in maximal socialist-realist style. They had been sculptured to fit in foursquare oblong blocks, with all the figures fitted into each other to conform; they looked a lot like a box of frozen sardines writhing around each other. Margie's interest in the sculpture was itself attracting interest, Dalehouse saw; the gendarmes had reached the end of their beat and were passing nearby on the return, watching benignly.

"What's so much fun about soldiers?" he asked.

"They're my trade, dear Dan. Didn't you know? Marjorie Maude Menninger, Captain, USA, late of West Point, or late of the practically late West Point, as I sometimes say. You should see me in uniform." She lighted another cigarette, and when she passed it to him for a drag he realized she had not been smoking tobacco.

She held the smoke, then exhaled it in a long plume. "Ah, those were the days," she said dreamily, gazing at the bronzes. "Look at that prunt holding the baby up in the air. Know what he's saying to the other soldier? 'Go ahead, Ivan. I'll hold the kid while you rape her mommy; then you hold the kid and it's my turn.' "

Dalehouse laughed. Encouraged, Margie went on. "And that young boy is saying, 'Hey, glorious Red Army soldier,

you like my sister? Chocolate? Russki cigaretti?' And the
WAC that's taking the flowers from the woman, she's
saying, 'So, comrade! Stealing agricultural produce from
the people's parks! Make no mistake about it, it's a long
time in the camps for you!' Course, by the time the Soviets
got here the Germans were finished anyhow, but—"

"Margie," he said.

"—still, it must have been pretty exciting—"

"Hey, Margie! Let's move on," he said uneasily. He had
suddenly realized that the gendarmes were no longer
smiling, and remembered, a little late, that all the munici-
pal police had been given language lessons for the conference.

TWO

●

WHAT ONE COULD SAY about Ana Dimitrova was hardly necessary to spell out, because it was apparent on first meeting: she was a sweet, cheerful girl with a capacity for love. Sometimes she had the grinding tension headaches that were typical of the people whose corpora callosa had been cut through, and then she was disoriented, irritable, sometimes almost sick with pain. But she excused herself and bore them in private whenever she could.

She woke up early, as she had planned, and stole into the kitchen to make tea with her own hands. No powdered trash for Ahmed! When she brought it in to him he opened those heartbreaking long lashes and smiled at her, crinkling the dark brown eyes. "You are too good to me, Nan," he said in Urdu. She set the cup down beside him and bent to touch his cheek with hers. Ahmed did not believe in kissing, except under circumstances which, while she enjoyed them, were not included in her present plans.

"Let's get dressed quickly," she proposed. "I want to show you my good monster."

"Monster?"

"You'll see." She escaped his grasp and retreated to the shower, where she let the hot water beat on her temples for a long time. The solid-state helmet often brought on the headaches, and she did not want one today.

Later, while she was drying her long brown hair, Ahmed came in silently and ran his fingers along the narrow scar in her scalp. "Dear Nan," he said, "so much trouble to go to to learn Urdu. I learned it for nothing."

She leaned against him for a moment, then wrapped the towel around herself and scolded gently. "There is no time for this if we are going to see my monster in the dawn light. Also, it was not to learn languages that I had my brain split. It was only to be able to translate them better."

11

"We would not do such a thing in Pakistan," he said, but she knew he was only being dear.

Outside the bathroom door, listening to him squawk and grumble as the cold water hit him, Nan thought seriously about Ahmed. She was a practical person. She was quite willing to sacrifice a material good for a principle or a feeling, but she preferred to know clearly what the stakes were. For her love game with Ahmed, the stakes were pretty high. Bulgaria, like the Soviet Union, was among the most People-tolerant of the food-exporting nations, but the lines of international politics were still clear. They would be able to see each other only seldom and with difficulty unless one or the other of them renounced citizenship. She knew that one would not be Ahmed.

How deeply did she want to be involved with this dear Pakistani? Could she share a life in the crowded, slow cities of the People Bloc? She had seen them. They were charming enough. But a diet of mostly grain, a nearly total lack of personal machines, the inward-turning of the People Bloc minds—were they what she wanted? Congenial to visit, pleasant and quaint for a day or a month ... but the rest of her life?

She dressed quickly without deciding the issue. One part of her mind was on what she was doing, the other on rehearsing her plans for that day's work at the conference; nothing was left for Ahmed. She made the bed while he was dressing, put away the washed dishes and glasses, and almost tugged him out the door.

The sky was bright pink, but the sun was just appearing; there was time if they hurried. She led him down the stairs—no waiting for the tiny cranked elevator—and out into the courtyard, then quickly away from the university to an intersection of two boulevards. She stopped and turned around.

"There, see?"

Ahmed squinted into the sunrise. "I see the cathedral," he grumbled.

"Yes, that's it. And the monster?"

"Monster? Is it in the cathedral?"

"It *is* the cathedral."

"St. Stephan's is a monster? ... Oh! Yes, I think I see. Those windows up high, they are the eyes? And those windows lined up underneath. They are the teeth."

"It's smiling at us, do you see? And there are the ears, and the nose."

Ahmed was not looking at the cathedral any more, but at her. "You are such a strange girl. I wonder what sort of Pakistani you would make."

Nan caught her breath. "No! It's too much. Please don't talk like that." She took his arm. "Please, let's just walk."

"I have not had any breakfast, Ana."

"There's plenty of time." She guided him through the small park to the university, and down toward the larger one. She laughed. "Have you forgiven me for translating you so badly into Bulgarian?"

"I would not have known how bad it was if you had not told me."

"It was bad enough, Ahmed. I was looking at you when you were talking about this Kung's Star, and I forgot to translate."

He glanced at her cautiously. "Do you know," he said, "Heir-of-Mao is personally interested in this planet. It was he who chose the name for the quasi-stellar object. He was there at the observatory when it was discovered. I think—"

"What do you think, Ahmed?"

"I think exciting things will happen," he said obscurely.

She laughed and lifted his hand to touch her cheek.

"Ana," he said, and stopped in the middle of the boulevard. "Listen to me. It is not impossible, you know. Even if I were to be away for a time, after that, for you and me, it would not be impossible."

"Please, dear Ahmed—"

"It is not impossible! I know," he said bitterly, oblivious of the fact that they were standing in the middle of the road, "that Pakistan is a poor country. We do not have food to export, like you and the Americans, and we do not have oil like the Middle Eastern states and the English. So we join with the countries that are left."

"I respect Pakistan very much."

"You were a child when you were there," he said severely. "But all the same it is not impossible to be happy, even in the People Bloc."

A trolleybus was coming, three cars long and almost silent on its rubber-tired wheels. Nan tugged him out of the way, glad for the chance to change the subject.

The difficulty with international conferences, she

thought, was that you met political opponents, and sometimes they did not seem like opponents. She had not meant this involvement with someone from the other side. She certainly did not want its inconvenience and pain. She knew what the stakes were. As a translator with four fully mastered languages and half a dozen partials, she had been all over the world—largely within the Food Block, to be sure, but even so, that included Moscow and Kansas City and Rio and Ottawa. She had met defectors from the other sides. There had been a Welsh girl in Sydney; there were two or three Japanese on the faculty of the university, her own neighbors in Sofia. They always tried desperately to belong, but they were always different.

Both the morning and Ahmed were too beautiful for such unhappy thoughts. That part of her mind which daydreamed and worried went from worry to daydream; the other part of her mind, the perceiving and interpreting part, had been following some events across the boulevard and now commanded her attention.

"Look," she said, clutching at an excuse to divert Ahmed's attention, "what's going on over there?" It was on the Liberation Mall. The blond woman she had seen at one of the receptions was having an argument with two militiamen. One had her by the arm. The other was fingering his stun-stick and talking severely to a man, a youngish professorial type, also from the conference.

Ahmed said, uninterested, "Americans and Bulgarians. Let the Fats settle their problems between themselves."

"No, really!" Nan insisted. "I must see if I can help."

But in the long run all that Nan Dimitrova accomplished was to get herself arrested too.

It was the American woman's fault. Even an American should have known better than to make chauvinist-filth jokes about the Red Army within earshot of the police of the capital of the most Russophile of nations. If she hadn't known that much, at least she should have known better than to insist on her treaty right to have the American ambassador informed of the incident. Up to that point the militiamen were only looking for an opportunity to finish reprimanding the culprits and stroll away. Afterwards it was a matter with international repercussions.

The only good thing about it was that Ahmed didn't get involved. Nan sent him away. He left willingly enough, even amused. The rest of them, the two Americans and Nan herself, were taken to the People's Palace of Justice. Because it was a Sunday morning, they had to sit for hours on bare wood benches in an interrogation room until a magistrate could be found.

No one came near them. No one would have minded in the least, Nan was sure, if they had accepted the invitation of the open door and slipped silently away. But she did not want to do that by herself. The Americans were not willing to take the chance, the woman because she appeared to think some sort of principle was involved, the man evidently because the woman was involved. She eyed them with displeasure, especially the bleached blond, at least five kilos too well fed, even for the Food Bloc. You cannot choose your allies, she thought. The man seemed to be all right, if not too fastidious about whom he indulged his sexual pranks with. Still, as the time passed and the militiamen brought them croissants and strong tea, the confinement drew them together. They chattered cheerfully enough until the people's magistrate at last arrived, gruffly refused to hear any talk of treaties or ambassadors, instructed them in future to use the common sense God had given them and the good manners their mothers had no doubt taught them, and let them go.

By then they had completely missed the 10:00 A.M. session of the conference. Almost as bad, they had missed the special lunches arranged for the delegates. As it was a Sunday morning in spring; every restaurant in Sofia was booked full with private wedding parties, and none of them got any lunch at all.

That was the first time the three of them met.

The second was very much later, and very, very far away.

Danny Dalehouse found that a colleague had read his paper for him. So missing the morning session turned out not to have been an utter disaster, and in fact looked like producing a hell of a big plus. Margie was bright enough to realize she'd been dumb, and ego-strong enough to admit it. However serious Margie had been about the grant while strolling down the boulevard, full of wine, pot, and roses, now she was rueful enough to remember her promise.

All the way home from the conference in the clamjet, Dalehouse sat with his notebook on his knee, drawing up a proposal, until it was time to go to his bunk. By dawn they were over white-and-brown Labrador, the jet moving more slowly through the cold night air. Dalehouse ate his breakfast alone, except for a sleepy TWA stewardess to scramble his eggs and pour his coffee, and looked out at the clouds as the clamjet roller-coastered in and out of them, wondering what the planet of Kung's Star would be like.

THREE

●

THE DAY AFTER Marge Menninger got back to her Washington office, she received Dalehouse's draft proposal. But she had already begun the process of getting it granted.

She had left the conference early to catch a ride on a NASA hydrojet, a rough and expensive ride but a fast one, back to her apartment in Houston. From there she had called the deputy undersecretary of state for cultural affairs. It was after office hours, but she got through with no trouble. Marge was on easy terms with the deputy undersecretary. She was his daughter. Once she had told him she'd had a pleasant trip she came right to the point:

"Poppa, I need a grant for a manned interstellar flight."

There was a short silence. Then he said, "Why?"

Marge scratched under her navel, thinking of all the reasons she could have given. For the advancement of human knowledge? For the potential economic benefit of the United States and the rest of the food-producing world? For the sake of her promise to Danny Dalehouse? All of these were reasons which were important to someone or other, and some of them important to her; but to her father she gave only the one reason that would prevail: "Because if we don't do it the son-of-a-bitching Paks will."

"By themselves?" Even three thousand kilometers away, she heard the skepticism.

"The Chinese will put up the hard stuff. They're in it too."

"You know what it's going to cost." It wasn't a question; they both knew the answer. Even a tactran message capsule cost a couple million dollars to transport from one star system to another, and they weighed only a few kilos. What she had in mind was at least ten people with all their gear: she was asking for billions of dollars.

"A lot," she said, "but it's worth it."

Her father chuckled admiringly. "You've always been an expensive child, Margie. How are you going to get it past the joint committee?"

"I think I can. Let me worry about that, poppa."

"Um. Well, I'll help from this end. What do you want from me right now?"

Marge hesitated. It was an open phone connection, and so she chose her words carefully. "I asked that Pak for a copy of his full report. Of course, I'm a little handicapped until I get my hands on it."

"Of course," her father agreed. "Anything else?"

"There's not much I can do until I see the full report."

"I understand. Well. What else is new? How did you like our brave Bulgarian allies?"

She laughed. "I guess you know I got arrested."

"I only wonder it doesn't happen more often. You're a terrible person, love. You didn't get it from *my* side of the family."

"I'll tell mom you said that," she promised, and hung up; and so, by the time she was back in Washington, she had received by a private route a microfilmed copy of the Pakistani's entire report, already translated for her. She read it over diligently, making notes. Then she pushed them away and leaned back in her chair.

The son-of-a-bitching Pak had held back a *lot*. In his private report, three times as thick as the one he had read in Sofia, there was an inventory of major life forms. He hadn't mentioned that at all in Sofia. At least three species seemed to possess some sort of social organization: a kind of arthropod; a tunneling species, warm-blooded and soft-skinned; and an avian species—no, not avian, she corrected herself. They spent most of their time in the air, but without having developed wings. They were balloonists, not birds.

Three social species! At least one of them might well be intelligent enough to be civilized.

That brought her back to Danny Dalehouse, his paper on first contact with sentient life forms at the subtechnological level, and his draft proposal. She looked again at the bottom line of the proposal and grinned. Young Danny didn't have any hangups about asking for what he wanted. The bottom line was seventeen billion dollars.

Seventeen billion dollars, she reflected, was about the assessed valuation of Manhattan Island . . . the GNP of any of twenty-five or thirty of the world's nations . . . two months' worth of the United States fuel deficit in the balance of payments. It was a lot of money.

She put the papers and her notes in a bright red folder stamped MOST SECRET and locked them away. Then she began to get Danny Dalehouse what he wanted.

There was a lot to be said about Marge Menninger, and the most important thing was that she always knew what she wanted. She wanted a lot, and a lot of different things. Her motivations were clearly and hierarchically arranged in her mind. The third or fourth thing from the top was likely to be achieved. The second was a near certainty. But the one on top was ironbound.

A week later she had Dalehouse's final proposal and an appointment to testify before the House-Senate Joint Committee on Space Development. She used the week to good purpose, first to tell Dalehouse (on the phone, and spelled out by facsimile immediately afterwards) how to change his proposal to maximize its chances of approval, then to fill in the few gaps in her knowledge of what was required.

To throw a transmitter capsule or a shipload of human beings from one star to another, you first have to put them in orbit.

Tachyon transportation itself is a model of technological elegance. Once you have elevated your capsule to its proper charge state, it becomes obedient to techyónic laws. It moves easily at faster-than-light speeds, covering interstellar distances to any point in the galaxy in a matter of days. It uses surprisingly little energy in the process. The paradox of the tachyon is that it requires more energy to go slow than to go fast.

Getting the capsule to the charge state is the hardest part. For that you need a rather bulky launch platform. The platform is expensive. More than that, it is heavy.

Getting the platform into orbit is not elegant at all. It is brute force. A hundred kilograms of fuel have to burn for every gram launched in the tachyon state. Fuel is fuel. You can burn oil, or you can burn something you make by using oil to make it—say, liquid hydrogen and liquid oxygen. Either way, in excess of half a million metric tons of oil had to burn to get ten people and minimum equipment on their way to Kung's Star.

Half a million metric tons!

It wasn't just the dollar value. It was four supertankers

full of fuel, all of which had to come from one of the fuel-exporting nations, which were showing signs of throwing their weight around again. The QUIP-Three interbloc conferences (Quotas for Imports and Prices) were going badly for the food-exporting countries. If Marge didn't get the expedition well begun, with the necessary fuel tucked away in the big tank farms at Galveston or Bayonne, the increasing fuel prices would drive the costs well past even Danny Dalehouse's estimates.

When all the figures were safely transferred from paper to the inside of her head, Marge locked her desk in the Washington office. She headed for Hearing Room 201 in the old Rayburn Office Building with the knowledge that her work was cut out for her.

The obstacles might have deterred another person. Marge did not accept deterrence. Her disciplined mind dissected the immediate problem into its components, and she concentrated her attention on the attack for each. The problem with the joint committee separated easily into four parts: the chairman, the minority leader, the chief counsel for the committee, and Senator Lenz. She prepared her strategies for each.

The minority leader was her father's friend and could safely be left to him.

The chairman was ambitious to be president. He would be likely to make waves whenever he saw a chance for publicity. The way to deal with him was to keep a low profile and give him as little opportunity to take a campaign position as possible. After she was sworn in and read her prepared statement, he was the first to question her.

THE CHAIRMAN. Well, madam, I'm sure your motives are of the worthiest, but do you know how hard we're working here on the Hill to keep the deficit down?

CAPT. MENNINGER. I certainly do, Mr. Senator.

THE CHAIRMAN. And yet you expect us to give you God knows how many billion dollars for this project?

That was promising! He hadn't said "this hairbrained project" or "this preposterous extravagance."

CAPT. MENNINGER. I don't "expect" it, senator. I hope for it. I hope the committee will approve the proposal, because in my judgment it is an investment that will be returned manyfold for years and years to come.

THE CHAIRMAN. We can't spend the taxpayers' money on hopes.

CAPT. MENNINGER. I know that and appreciate it. It isn't hope I'm asking you to share. It's judgment. Not only mine, but the collective judgment of the best-informed experts in this area.

THE CHAIRMAN. Um. Well, there are many worthy claims based on very sound judgment. We can't grant all of them.

CAPT. MENNINGER. Of course, senator. I wouldn't be here if I wasn't confident of your fairness and competence.

THE CHAIRMAN. Well, do any of my distinguished colleagues have questions for this witness?

They did, but they were mostly perfunctory. The important people, like Senator Lenz and the minority leader, held back for another occasion; the minor members were principally concerned with getting their own positions on record.

The chief counsel was a trickier problem. He was smart. He was also wholly dedicated to making his bosses look good by keeping the joint committee out of trouble. Margie's hope was to make saying yes look less troublesome than saying no.

MR. GIANPAOLO. You spoke of returns on an investment. Do you mean actual cash or some abstract kind of knowledge or virtue?

CAPT. MENNINGER. Oh, both, Mr. Gianpaolo.

MR. GIANPAOLO. Really, Ms. Menninger? *Dollar* returns?

CAPT. MENNINGER. Based on prior experience and what is already known about this planet, yes. Definitely.

MR. GIANPAOLO. Can you give us an idea of what these dollar returns will be?

CAPT. MENNINGER. In broad terms, yes, Mr. Gianpaolo. The tactran reports indicate valuable raw materials and the presence of intelligent life—at least, a near certainty of the former and a strong possibility of the latter. Of course, these are only instrument reports.

MR. GIANPAOLO. Which, as I understand it, are subject to conflicting interpretations.

CAPT. MENNINGER. Exactly, Mr. Gianpaolo, and that is why it is necessary to send a manned expedition out. The whole reason for the expedition is to find out what we can't find out in any other way. If we knew what it would find, we wouldn't have to send it. But there is a a different kind of return that I think is even more important. I think of it as "leadership."

MR. GIANPAOLO. Leadership?

CAPT. MENNINGER. The whole free world of food-exporting nations looks to us for that leadership, Mr. Gianpaolo. I don't believe any of us wants to fail them. This is an opportunity that comes only once in a lifetime. I am here because I cannot in all conscience take the responsibility for losing it. It is, in the final analysis, this committee's burden to carry.

Since nothing would be decided in open session, Marge was confident there would be time to make the members understand that that "burden" could best be unloaded by voting her the money.

If Marge Menninger had had her druthers, the testifying would have stopped there. But Gianpaolo was orchestrating the event. He was too wise to end on the note she preferred. He blunted her dramatic impact by dragging a long series of technical data out of her—"Yes, Mr. Gianpaolo, I understand that the planet's surface gravity is point seven six that of Earth, and its atmospheric pressure about thirty percent higher. But the oxygen level is about the same." He read her quotes about the "semi-greenhouse effect" and asked her what was meant by someone's remarks about "the inexhaustible reserve of outgassing from the cold side, as interior heat boils out volatiles." He got her, and himself, into a long complication about whether the designation of the star they were talking about was really Bes-bes Geminorum 8326 or Bes-bes Geminorum 8426 according to the New OAO General Catalogue— apparently both were given, because some typist made a mistake—until the chairman got restive. Then, satisfied that the audience was more than half asleep, he called for a ten-minute recess and returned to the attack.

MR. GIANPAOLO. Captain Menninger, I'm sure you know what it costs to launch a tachyon-transmitted space vessel. First—

CAPT. MENNINGER. Yes, sir, I believe I do.

MR. GIANPAOLO. First there is the immense expense of the launching vehicle itself. The costs for that alone, I believe, are in the neighborhood of six billion dollars.

CAPT. MENNINGER. Yes, sir. But as the vice-president announced in his message to the Tenth General Assembly of the World Conference on Exobiology, we already have such a launch vehicle. It can be used for a large number of missions.

MR. GIANPAOLO. But as the vice-president also announced, the time of that vehicle is fully booked. Prelaunch aiming time is as much as thirty days.

CAPT. MENNINGER. Yes, sir.

MR. GIANPAOLO. But your schedule calls for a launch to this—what is the name of it?

CAPT. MENNINGER. It has been referred to as "Son of Kung," sir, but that name is not official.

MR. GIANPAOLO. I hope not. You want a launch every ten days.

CAPT. MENNINGER. Yes, sir. Essential backup.

MR. GIANPAOLO. Which means canceling the mining survey mission to Procyon IV. I am sure you know that this planet has been identified as having a very dense core, with therefore a good potential for supplies of uranium and other fissiles for our power plants.

The British had sent that probe out. Meticulously they had announced that under existing international agreements they were making the telemetry public. That was all public knowledge. Gianpaolo was just getting on the record.

CAPT. MENNINGER. Yes, sir. Of course, that works out as a very marginal operation, considering the investment necessary to mine and refine uranium and to ship it to us back here. The Bes-bes Geminorum planet has much more potential—as I have already testified.

MR. GIANPAOLO. Yes, Captain Menninger, you have made us aware of your opinions.

And that was all hogwash. What the British had *not* announced, but what both Marge and Gianpaolo knew from previous briefing, was that British scintillation counters had found no ionizing radiation to speak of in Procyon IV's rather unpleasant atmosphere. Uranium there might be, but if so, it was thousands of meters deep. Marge was getting on the record too, although this particular record was private.

By the time she was through testifying, she was satisfied that things were moving in the right direction.

There remained the problem of Senator Lenz. He had far more muscle in the committee, and in the Senate generally, than anyone else—even the chairman. He had to be dealt with individually and privately, and Marge had plans for that.

She booked her return to Houston the long way around, by way of Denver. Her father drove her to Dulles Airport in his own car. Well, actually it wasn't his own. It belonged to a government agency. So did Godfrey Menninger, when you came right down to it. The car was both a perquisite of rank and an indispensable necessity in what he did for the agency; twice a day, other employees of the agency went over it with electronic sniffers and radio probes to make sure it had been neither bombed nor bugged.

God Menninger told his daughter, "You did pretty well at the hearing."

"Thanks, poppa. And thanks for that Pak's report."

"Had what you wanted in it?"

"Yep. Will you talk to the minority leader for me?"

"Already have, honey."

"And?"

"Oh, he's all right. If you get past Gus Lenz, I think you've got the committee taken care of. He didn't say much at the hearing."

"I didn't expect him to."

Her father waited, but as Marge did not go on he did not pursue the question. He said, "There's a follow-up on your Pakistani friend. He's at some kind of a meeting at K'ushui, along with some pretty high-powered people."

"K'ushui? What the hell is a K'ushui?"

"Well," said her father, "I kind of wish I could give you a better answer than I know. It's a place in Sinkiang province. We haven't had, uh, very full reports yet. But it's not far from Lop Nor and not *too* far from the big radio dish, and Heir-of-Mao's been there five or six times in the past year."

"It sounds as though they're going to move."

"I would say so. I plugged in your estimates, and the best interpretation is that Heir-of-Mao's starting to do what you want us to do."

"Shit!"

"Not to worry," said her father. "I told that to the minority leader in strictest confidence. And I have no doubt he'll tell Gianpaolo. So it'll work for you, you know."

"I wanted to be first!"

"First doesn't always pick up the marbles, honey. How

many people discovered America before the English put it in their pocket? Anyway, tell me what's so interesting about this planet."

Margie looked out at the high-rise apartments in the Virginia suburbs, ziggurats climbing away from the south exposure with the black-on-black textured squares of their solar heating panels.

"It was all in Ahmed Dulla's report, poppa."

"I didn't read it."

"Pity. Well, there's a little star with a lot of crummy little planets and one big one about the size of Earth. Gravity's a little lighter. Air's a little denser. It's a lot of real estate, poppa. And it reeks of life."

"We've found life before."

"Mosses and jellyfish! Crystal things that you can *call* alive if you want to. This is different. This is a biota as varied as our own, maybe. Maybe even a civilization. The planet's interesting in another way, too. It doesn't rotate, I mean relative to its primary—like the moon doesn't rotate relative to Earth. So the lit side of it has a sun in the sky all the time."

Her father listened comfortably, scratching his abdomen just below the navel, while his daughter went on about the planet. When she paused for breath, he said, "Wait a minute, honey." He leaned forward to turn on the radio; even in a routinely debugged car God Menninger didn't take chances. Over the twang of synthetic guitars he said, "There's something else you ought to know. The fuel countries are talking among themselves about a sixty percent price rise."

"Jesus, poppa! I'll never drink another shot of Scotch!"

"No, it's not the British this time. It's the Chinese, funnily enough."

"But they're people exporters!"

"They're anything-they-like exporters," her father corrected. "The only reason they're in the People Bloc is that they can swing more weight there. Heir-of-Mao plays his own game. This time he slipped the word to the Greasies that China was going to raise its own prices unilaterally, whatever the bloc votes to do. So that was all the hardliners in Caracas and Edinburgh needed. The Saudis were for it, of course. They want to stretch out what oil they've got left. And the Indonesians and the rest of the little ones just have to go along with the big boys." He paused thoughtfully. "So your coming along with a chit for half a million tons of oil gets a little complicated right now."

"I see that, poppa. What are we going to do? I don't mean about my project, I mean the country."

"What we are not going to do," he said grimly, "is raise grain prices. We can't. Heir-of-Mao's joker is that the price rise is for export sales only. He considers any sales inside the People Bloc as domestic. So he's selling cheap to the Peeps, and that means they're getting what they need for irrigation and fertilizer at bargain-basement prices. If we raise the price we'll make it worth their while to stop importing in another three or four years. We could stand it in this country, maybe. But the Soviets, the Indochinese, the Bulgarians, the Brazilians, and the rest of the Latins—they couldn't handle it. Their economies would be wrecked. It would break up the bloc. No doubt that's what Heir-of-Mao has in mind."

He parked the car in the Dulles short-term lot. Before snapping off the radio he said, "It won't happen for a couple of months, I think. So you want to get your project on the way as fast as you can."

Marge slid out into the damp, hot evening air. The humped backs of boarding clamjets loomed over the parking lot hedge. They could hear the noise of two of them warming up and the gentler rush of another taking off.

Marge followed her father as he picked up her bag and started toward the terminal. "Poppa," she said, "can I tell the senator about, uh, that?"

"Christ, no! Not that he doesn't probably know it already. But you aren't supposed to know."

Surprisingly, she laughed. "Well, I was going to handle it a different way anyway. Hey, hold it, poppa. I'm not taking the Houston flight."

"You're not?"

"Uh-uh. I'm going home by a different route."

Menninger kissed his daughter good-bye at the check-in counter for the Denver clamjet. He watched her disappear into the gate tunnel with mingled admiration and rue. He had been thinking about asking just how she proposed to handle Senator Lenz, but he didn't have to. This was the flight Lenz would be on.

Because it was a night flight, the jet sat there for twenty minutes of preheating before it could take off. The passengers had to be aboard, and the stews scurried up and down with ear stoppers and sympathy. The best heat source there is is a jet turbine. The engines that would thrust the plane through the air in actual flight were now rotated inward, the shell-shaped baffles diverting the blast to pour countless thousands of BTUs into the clam-shaped lifting section.

Marge took advantage of the time to scrub her face, brush her hair, and change her makeup. She had seen the senator come aboard. She debated changing from her uniform into something more female and decided against it. Wasn't necessary. Wasn't advisable. It might look calculating, and Marge calculated carefully ways to avoid looking calculating.

The full-energy roar of the warm-up jets stopped, and everyone belted in for takeoff. That was a gentler sound. The clamjet bounced a few times and soared steeply up.

As soon as they were at cruising altitude Marge left her cubicle and ordered a drink in the forward first-class lounge. In a couple of minutes Senator Lenz was standing over her, smiling.

Adrian Lenz had two terms and two days seniority in the Senate; a friendly governor had appointed him to fill a forty-eight-hour vacancy just for the sake of the extra rank it would give him over other senators elected the same year. Even so, he was not much over forty. He looked younger than that. He had been divorced twice; the Colorado voters laughed about their swinging senator's bad luck but reelected him without much fuss. He could have been chairman of his own committee, but had chosen instead to serve on committees that were of more interest —and more visibility. One of these days "Gus" Lenz was going to be the President of the United States, and everyone knew it.

"Margie," he said, "I knew this was going to be a nice flight, but until now I didn't know why."

Margie patted the seat beside her. "You going to give me my seventeen billion?" she asked.

Lenz laughed. "You don't waste time, Margie."

"I don't have time to waste. The Peeps are going to go there if we don't. They're probably going to go anyhow. It's a race."

He frowned and nodded toward the stewardess; slight, dark, she wore her United Airlines uniform like a sari.

When the drinks were served he said, "I listened to your testimony, Margie. It sounded good. I don't know if it sounded seventeen billion dollars' worth of good."

"There was some material in the supplementary statement you might not have had a chance to read. Did you notice the part about the planet having its own sun?"

"I'm not sure."

"It's small but not very far away. The thing mostly radiates in the lower wavelengths. There's not too much visible light, but a hell of a lot of heat. And the planet doesn't turn in relation to it, so it's always hanging there."

"So?"

"So *energy*, senator. Solar power! Economical."

"I don't understand exactly what you're saying. You mean this substellar thing is hotter than our sun?"

"No, it's not nearly as hot. But it's a lot closer. The important thing is it doesn't move. What's the big problem with solar power here? The sun doesn't stay put. It wanders around all over the sky, and half the time it's not in the sky at all, because it's night here and so the sun's on the other side of the earth. I mean, look at our ship here. We had to preheat for nearly half an hour to get the gas light enough to lift, because it's after dark. On the side of the planet that faces its sun—the only side that interests me, Gus—it's never dark."

Lenz nodded and sipped his drink, waiting for more.

"It's never dark. It's never winter. The sun stays put, so you don't have to make your Fresnel lenses movable. And almost as important, the weather isn't a problem. You know what the score is on our own solar-power installations. Not counting clamjets in the daytime—because they're up over the clouds a lot of the time—we lose as much as twenty-five percent working time because the clouds cut out the sunlight."

Lenz looked puzzled. "This planet doesn't have any clouds?"

"Oh, sure. But they don't matter. The radiation is almost all heat, and it punches right through the clouds! Figure it out. Here we lose half the solar-generating time to night; another few percent to dawn and dusk, because the sun's so low it doesn't yield much power; as much as sixty percent additional for half the year because it's winter; and another twenty-five percent to cloud cover. Put them all together and we're lucky to get ten percent utilization. On this planet a cheaper installation can get damn near a hundred percent."

Lenz thought about that for a moment. "Sounds interesting," he said cautiously, and signaled for a refill.

Margie left him to sort things out in his own mind. Sooner or later it would occur to him to ask what good energy some hundred light-years away was going to do the voters in the state of Colorado on Earth. She had an answer for that, too, but she was content to wait until he asked for it.

But when he asked a question it caught her by surprise. "Margie? What've you got against the Paks?"

"Paks? Why—nothing, really."

"You seem to take this Ahmed's competition pretty seriously."

"Not on a personal level, Gus. I'm not *crazy* about Paks. But I've been on friendly terms with some. I had a Pak orderly when I was teaching at West Point. Nice kid. Kept my clothes ironed and never bothered me when I didn't want him around."

"That sounds like a nice appliance to own," Lenz observed.

"Yeah, yeah. I take your point." She stopped to think. "That's not where it's at, though. I'm not against Ahmed because he's a Pak. I'm against the Paks because they're the other side. I can't help it, senator. I root for my team."

"Which is who, Margie? Just the Food Bloc? Just the United States? Maybe just the female commissioned officers of the US Army?"

She giggled comfortably. "All of them, in that order," she agreed.

"Margie," he said seriously, "we're just shooting the bull here over a couple of drinks. I don't want to get too heavy."

"Why not, Gus? Order up a couple more drinks and let's get to it!"

He obeyed. While they were coming he said, "You're a nice girl, Margie, but a little too bloody-minded. Pity you went to West Point."

"Wrong, Gus. The pity is that so few young Americans have the chance now."

He shook his head. "I voted to phase down the service academies and cut the military budget."

"I know you did. Worst vote you ever cast."

"No. There was no choice. *We can't afford war, Margie.* Can't you understand that? Even Pakistan could blow us off the map! Not to mention the Chinese and the Turks and the Poles and the rest of the People Bloc. Not to mention the British, the Saudis, the Venezuelans. We can't afford to fight anybody, and nobody can afford to fight us. And everybody knows it. They're not our enemies—"

"But they're competing with us, senator," said Captain Menninger, suddenly sitting up straighter and speaking with more precision. "Economically. Politically. Every other way. Remember Clausewitz: war is the logical extension of politics. I grant," she said quickly, "that we can't go that far. We don't want to blow up the planet. I know what you're saying. It's like that famous saying of—what was his name, the Russian cosmonaut? Years and years ago. Sevastianov, I think: 'When I was in space I saw how tiny the world was, and realized how important it was for all of us to learn to live together on it.' Well, sure, Gus. But learning to live together doesn't mean that some people can't live a little better than others. It's a fact of life! The Fuel people keep jumping their prices. And the People people keep demanding more money for their export workers, or else they'll keep them home, and what will we do for orderlies and airline stewardesses? And we compete back. Well, Gus, when I compete, I compete hard. I play to win! This Kung's Star planet is something I want to win. I think there's goodies on this planet. I want them for *us*. Us being defined as the Food Bloc, the United States, the state of Texas, the city of Houston, and all the other subdivisions you named or want to name, including blond ex-professors from West Point, if you like, in descending order of size of community. Whichever community you want to talk about, if it's mine, I want it to be first, best, and most successful! I think that's what they call patriotism, senator. I really doubt that you want to knock it."

He looked at her thoughtfully over the new drinks, and raised his. "To you, Margie. You really are some kind of iron-pants."

She laughed. "All right," she said, softening. "I'll drink to that. Now, what about my bill?"

Lenz finished his drink and put it down. "For better or

worse we're part of an economic community, and that's a fact of life for *you*, Captain Margie Menninger. You can't sell this to me as a United States venture. You might as a cooperative deal for the Food Bloc."

"Cripes, Gus! We'd still be paying for the whole thing!"

"Maybe ninety percent of it, yes."

"Then why not do it all and take it all?"

"Because," he said patiently, "I won't vote for that. So?"

Margie was silent for a moment, considering her priorities. She shrugged. "So all right," she said. "I don't mind if we include a few token gooks. Maybe two or three Canadians. A Brazilian. Maybe even a Bulgarian. In fact, there was a Bulgarian at the convention—"

She stopped herself. In mid-sentence it had occurred to her that in some sense she owed that Nan Whatever-it-was-ova a sort of a favor; but it had occurred to her simultaneously that the Bulgarian girl had been excessively close to the very Pak she was most worried about.

"No," she said, "on second thought I'm not sure I want a Bulgarian. They're too tiny a power to worry about, frankly. But maybe one or two people from the Soviets. If we send ten, and if at least six are genuine made-in-America US citizens, I can see bringing along a few from the rest of the bloc."

"Um." Lenz looked thoughtfully at her for a moment, moving slightly in his seat to the gentle pitching of the clamjet as it rose and fell through the night sky. "Well," he said, "we'll see." He smiled at her. "What shall we do with this night God has given us, Margie? It's too late to think hard and too early to go to sleep. Want to watch the stars for awhile?"

"Exactly what I want," she said, finishing the last of her drink and standing up. They made their way through the nearly empty lounge to the forward observation section and leaned against the padded rail. The clamjet was swooping gently over the rolling hills of West Virginia. Ahead of them Venus followed a crescent of a moon toward the horizon. After a while Lenz put his arm around her.

"Just checking," he said. "Old Iron-Pants."

Margie leaned against him contentedly enough. Lenz wasn't a big man. He wasn't particularly handsome either, but he was warm and muscular, and his arm around her felt good. There were worse ways of lobbying for votes than this, she reflected as she turned her face to his.

He came through. The full committee reported the bill out, and on a hot Georgia afternoon two or three months later, Margie was called away from her company to take a high-priority phone call. She had not bathed for three days; summer field maneuvers were conducted as close to real war conditions as possible. She was sweating, filthy with both camouflage paint and Georgia clay, and she knew she smelled pretty high. Also, her company was just about to take a hill that she had personally spotted and attacked, so when she got to the phone she was in no good mood. "Captain Menninger," she snarled, "and this goddamn better be important!"

Her father's voice laughed in her ear. "You tell me," he said cheerfully. "The President signed your bill ten minutes ago."

Marge sank back onto the first sergeant's immaculate chair, heedless of his looks. "Jesus, poppa," she said, "that's great!" She stared out at the walls of the command trailer without seeing them, calculating whether it was more important to get back to taking that hill with the rest of the weekend soldiers or to get on the phone and start Danny Dalehouse in motion.

"—what?" She had become aware that her father was still talking.

"I said there was some other news too, not quite so good. Your Pak friend."

"What about him, poppa?"

"That, uh, vacation he was going to take? He took it last week."

FOUR

●

THE PILOT was Vissarion Ilyich Kappelyushnikov. He was short and dark in the standard cosmonaut tradition, with a lot more Tatar in his family tree than his name would suggest. The expedition's eco-engineer was also a Soviet national, but Cossack-tall and fair-haired; his name was Pete Krivitin. The nominal commander of the expedition was an American, Alex Woodring. And they were all going at it at once. Alex was trying to arbitrate between the two Russians, helped by Harriet Santori, the translator. She wasn't really helping, but then the commander wasn't really succeeding at arbitrating. Kappelyushnikov wanted to land and get it over with. Krivitin wanted one more look at the probe reports before he would certify the landing site. Harriet wanted them all to act like adults, for heaven's sake. Woodring's difficulty was that until they landed, Kappelyushnikov was the captain of the ship and Alex's authority was only potential. And it had been going on for more than an hour.

Danny Dalehouse swallowed the desire to intervene again. He loosened the straps of his deceleration couch and peered out the porthole. There was the planet, filling the window. From less than a hundred thousand kilometers, it no longer looked "away"; it was beginning to look "down." So let us the hell *get* there, he thought testily. These people didn't seem to realize they were screwing around with his personal expedition, which none of them would have been on if he hadn't persuaded that blond army female to authorize it.

A voice in his ear said, "Think we'll ever get there?"

Danny drew back. The woman beside him was Sparky Cerbo, as amiable a person as there was on the expedition; but after nineteen days of sharing less than twenty cubic

33

meters of space, they were all getting edgy. The ongoing spat an arm's length away didn't make it any better.

"It doesn't look like much, does it?" Sparky went on, determinedly making the effort.

Dalehouse forced himself to respond. It wasn't her fault that he was sick of the sound, the sight, and the smell of her—and besides, she was right. Son of Kung didn't look like a proper planet at all. Danny knew what planets were supposed to look like. Some of them were red and bleak, like Mars. More often they were white or mottled white, like everything else from Venus through the gas giants. This one wasn't even trying to look right.

It wasn't so much the planet's fault as Kung's itself; as a star, it was simply incompetent. If Son of Kung had been in orbit around Earth's Sol, it would have looked pretty fine. It had much the same makeup as Earth. What it didn't have was decent sunlight. Kung glowered, not much brighter than Earth's moon during a total lunar eclipse. The only light that fell on Son of Kung was bloody red, and what it looked like from orbit was an open wound.

It would have helped some if it had had a real terminator, but Kung's light was so dim that there was no clear division between "daylight" and "night" sides—only a blurry transition from dark to darkest. Krivitin had assured them that once they landed and their eyes dark-adjusted, they would be able to see reasonably well. But from space that seemed doubtful. And for this, thought Danny, I gave up a perfectly good job at Michigan State.

The Russian language yelling peaked to climax and abruptly stopped. Krivitin, smiling as composedly as though the screaming match had been no more than a friendly chat about the weather, pulled himself around the lashed-down and nested machinery in the center of the main cubicle and peered in at them. "Sara, dear," he said in his perfect English, "you're wanted up front. You better come too, Daniel."

"We're going to land?" Sparky demanded.

"Most certainly not! Cappy has finally understood the necessity for another orbit."

"Hell," said Sparky, even her indomitable desire to please crumbling at last. Dalehouse shared her feelings: another orbit was close enough to another day, with nothing for him to do except try to stay out of the way.

"Yes, I agree," said Krivitin, "but Alex wants you to try to tap the Peeps' signals again."

Harriet complained, but Dalehouse stopped listening. He shucked off his straps and reached wearily for the cassettes of data he had stored away for deceleration.

He plugged in, put the speaker in his ear, and touched the switch. There was a slight tape hiss, an occasional scratch or click, and a distant, somber wail. Those were the sounds from the wolftrap lander. Its primary mission was to secure biological samples and test them in its built-in laboratories; but its microphones had picked up sounds that did not come from itself. He had listened to them fifty times already. After a time he shrugged, stopped the tape, and put in a different cassette.

This time the sounds were louder and clearer, with far more definition. The lander in this case had been a neutral-buoyancy floater with a small reserve of thrusting power and a locater for carbon dioxide. Like a female mosquito seeking a blood meal to fertilize its eggs, it was meant to drift until it found a trail of CO_2, and follow it until it found prey. Then it simply floated nearby as long as there were sounds for it to hear and transmit. But what sounds! Sometimes they resembled a chorus of bagpipes, sometimes a gang of teenage boys in a crepitation contest. Dalehouse had graphed the frequencies—from well below human hearing range to higher than a bat's squeak—and identified at least twenty phonemes. These were no bird-calls; this was language, he was certain.

Heat smote his exposed skin, and he turned back to the port; Kung had drifted into view, looking like a thin-skinned Halloween pumpkin with the embers of Hades inside its mottled surface. He squinted and pulled a neutral-density blind over the porthole; it was not dangerous to glance at it, but there was the chance of burning out your cornea if you stared too long.

In the warmth he felt sleepy. Why not? he thought, snapping off the tape. He leaned back, closed his eyes, and was just drifting off when he heard his name called. "Dalehouse! Krivitin! DiPaolo! Front and center, everybody."

He shook himself awake, wished for a cup of coffee, and pulled himself toward the workspace. Alex Woodring said, "You'd better all see this. The Peeps have filed another report, and Harriet's taped it for us."

Dalehouse wriggled closer for a better view of the video screen just as it blinked and lighted up. There was a plant on the screen, rust-red and fernlike, with raspberrylike fruits hanging from its fronds. "Roll the tape, Harriet," Woodring said impatiently. The images on the screen leaped and flickered, then stopped.

At first Dalehouse thought the picture was of another Klingan flower, possibly some desert succulent: red and yellow blobs oozing what he supposed was some sort of sap— Then it moved.

"Dear God," whispered somebody. Dalehouse felt something rise in his throat.

"What is it?"

"I think it used to be a white mouse," said Morrissey, the biologist.

"What *happened?*"

"That," said the biologist grimly, but with a trace of professional satisfaction, "is what I don't know yet. The Peeps are transmitting their voice reports in code."

"They're supposed to share information!" snapped Dalehouse.

"Well, maybe they will. I assume Heir-of-Mao will have his UNESCO delegation deliver a report. And when it's released in New York, Houston will no doubt send us a copy. But not very soon, I think. The picture was clear. When you come right down to it, that's all we need to know: Klong is not as hospitable as we would like. I—" He hesitated, then went on. "I don't think it's an infectious disease. It looks more like an allergic reaction. I can't really imagine an alien microorganism adapting that quickly to our body chemistry, anyway. I suspect we're as poisonous to them as they are to us, so for openers, we don't eat anything, we don't drink anything but our own sealed supplies and distilled water."

"You mean we're landing anyhow?" the Canadian electronicist said incredulously.

Captain Kappelyushnikov snarled, *"Da!"* He nodded vigorously, then muttered to the translator, who said smoothly:

"He says that that is why we came here. He says we will take all precautions. He says on the next orbit, we go."

Dalehouse played the strange songs from the mosquito probe a few times, but the equipment he needed to do any

serious analysis had been stowed away and it made little
sense to set it up again. Time to kill. Drowsily he peered
out at the planet, and drifted off to sleep wondering what
to call it. Kungson, Child of Kung, Son of Kung—"Klong,
Son of Kung" was what one of the Americans had chris-
tened it—by any name, it was worrisome. When he woke
he was given a tube of thick petroleum jelly to smear on
himself—"Shuck your clothes and cover your whole body;
maybe it will protect you from some kind of poison ivy or
whatever that is until we get straightened out." Then he
dressed again and waited. The electronicist had patched
herself in to monitor any further ground transmissions and
was pinpointing sources on a likris map of the sunward
surface of Klong.

"There seem to be *two* stations broadcasting," Dalehouse commented.

"Yeah. Must be the base camp and, I suppose, somebody off on an expedition. There's the Peep base"—she
touched a dot on the purplish sea, on one side of a
hundred-kilometer bay—"and there's the other station."
That was across the bay. "We know that's their base; we
photographed it last time around. Nothing much. They
aren't really set up yet, I'd say. That signal's pulse-coded,
probably basic science data on its way to their orbiter for
tachyon transmission back home."

"What's over on the other side of the bay?"

"Nothing much. There's a sort of nest of some of the
arthropods there, but *they* don't have radio." She pulled
the earpiece away from her temple and handed it to
Dalehouse. "Listen to that signal."

Dalehouse put the phone in his ear. The sound was a
staccato two-tone beep, plaintively repeated over and over.

"Sounds sad," he said.

The woman nodded. "I think it's a distress signal," she
said, frowning. "Only they don't seem to be answering
it."

FIVE

•

WHAT CAN BE SAID about a being like Sharn-igon that will make him come clear and real? Perhaps it can be approached in a roundabout way. Like this.

Suppose there is a kind and jolly man, the sort of person who takes children fishing, dances the polka, reads Elizabethan verse, and knows why Tebaldi was the greatest Mimi who ever lived.

Is this Sharn-igon?

No. This is only an analogy. Suppose we then go on to ask you if you have ever met this man. You hesitate, riffling through the chance encounters of a life. No, you say, a finger against your nose, I don't think so. I never met anybody like that.

And suppose we then say to you, But you did! It was a week ago Thursday. He was driving the A-37 bus you took from the station to the Federal Building, and you were late for your appointment with the tax examiner because this man would not change a five-dollar bill.

What do you say then? Perhaps you say, Christ, fellow! I remember the incident well! But that was no amiable folk dancer. That was a bus driver!

That's how it would be with Sharn-igon. It's easy enough to imagine you meeting him (provided we don't worry about how you get there). Let's make the mind-experiment to see what would happen. Suppose you are standing outside of time and space somehow, like an H. G. Wells god looking down from a cloud. You poke your finger into the infinitesimal. You touch Sharn-igon's planet, and you uncover him. You look him over.

What do you see?

One might try to describe him to you by saying that Sharn-igon was politically conservative, deeply moral, and fundamentally honest. One might try to elicit your sympathy by saying that he (like who that you know?) was screaming inside with unhealed pain.

But would you see that?

Or would you glance and gasp and pull back your finger in loathing and say:

Christ, fellow! That's no person. It's an alien creature! It lives (lived? will live?) a thousand light-years away, on a planet that circles a star I have never even seen! And besides, it looks *creepy*. If I had to say what it looked like, giving it the best break I could, I would have to say that it looked like half of a partly squashed crab.

And, of course, you would be right. . . .

The way Sharn-igon looked to himself was something else again.

For one thing, he is not an instant invention for your eye to see. He is a person. He has relationships. He lives (will live?) in a society. He moves (moved?) around and through a dense web of laws and folkways. He wasn't like every other Krinpit (as his people called themselves), no matter how indistinguishable they might look to your eyes. He was Sharn-igon.

For example, although it was Ring-Greeting time, Sharn-igon hated Ring-Greeting. To him it was the loneliest and worst part of the cycle. He disliked the bustle, he resented the false and hypocritical sentiment. All the shops and brothels were busy as everyone tried to get gifts and to become pregnant, but it was an empty mockery in Sharn-igon's life, because he was alone.

If you had asked him, Sharn-igon would have told you that he had always hated Ring-Greeting, at least ever since his final molting. (When he was a young seed just beginning to wave on his male-mother's grate he loved it, naturally enough. All seeds did. Ring-Greeting was for kids.) That wasn't quite true. The cycle before, he and his he-wife, Cheee-pruitt, had had a very cheerful Greeting.

But Cheee-pruitt was gone. Sharn-igon signaled at his screen, almost stumbling over an Inedible Ghost that lay before it. There was no answer. He hesitated. Something—perhaps the ghost—seemed to be calling his name. But that was ridiculous. After a moment of indecision, he scuttled across the crowded run to the—call it a bar—to chew a couple of quick ones.

Look at Sharn-igon munching on strands of hallucino-

genic fern among a crowd squeezed two or three deep
around the Krinpit who was kneading and dispensing the
stuff. He was a fine figure of a person. He was masculinely
broad—easily two meters from rim to rim; and pleasingly
slim—not more than forty centimeters to the tip of his
carapace. In spite of his mood, unpaired males and females of all descriptions found him attractive. He was
young, healthy, sexually potent, and successful in his
chosen profession.

Well, that is not strictly true, because a paradox is
involved.

Sharn-igon's profession was a form of social work. The
more successful he was in terms of his own personal ego
needs, the worse his society was. It was only when Krinpit
were in trouble that they turned to persons like Sharn-
igon. The Krinpit were socially interdependent to a degree
not usually associated with a technological culture on
Earth. Maybe one could find that sort of close-knit clan
among the Eskimos or Bushmen, where every member of
the community had to be able to rely on every other or
they would all die. For that reason Sharn-igon was happiest when he was least wanted. Ring-Greeting was bringing
its usual crop of damaged egos born of loneliness amid the
holiday cheer. He was busier than he had ever been, and
so less happy.

Stand on your cloud and look down on Sharn-igon. To
you he surely looks strange, and maybe quite repulsive,
true. His crescent carapace is sprinkled with what look
like chitinous sails. Some are a few centimeters high, some
much smaller; and around them race, clicking and scrap-
ing, what look like lice. Actually, they aren't. They are not
even parasites, except in the sense that a fetus is a parasite
on its mother; they are the young. Sharn-igon is not the
only Krinpit in the bar carrying young. Of the hundred
individuals in the bar, eight or ten are in the brood-male
phase. Sometimes one of the scurrying little creatures drop
off or inadvertently gets carried off on the shell of another
Krinpit as they rub together. They are instantly aware of
what has happened and go wild in the attempt to get back.
If they fail, they die.

Each end of Sharn-igon's shell is pleated chitin jointed
with cartilage. That part is always in motion, expanding
with accordion folds, tilting, spreading like a fan. He slides
along the packed dirt floor or the bodies of Krinpit under

him (in the conviviality of the bar no one minds being crawled on) on a dozen double-boned legs.

After he had had three quick ones and was feeling better, he left the bar and sidled down the turfy run, not hurrying, with no particular destination in mind. On each side of the run are what you might think of as rather shabby Japanese screens. They are not decorated in any way, but they are jointed and folded, and they come in all sizes. They set off the homes and commercial places, some of which, like the bar, are filled with scores of Krinpit, some almost empty. The screens too are studded with the tiny saillike projections, but otherwise they are unadorned. What you would notice at once is that they are not colored. The Krinpit do not understand color, and in the light of Kung's Star, blood-red and dusky, you would not see much color at first either, even if it were there.

That is how it would look to you, with your human eyes. How would it look to Krinpit eyes? Immaterial; it is a senseless question, because the Krinpit have no eyes. They have photosensitive receptors on their carapaces, but there is no lens, no retina, no mosaic of sensitive cells to analyze an image and translate it into information.

But if the scene was dark, it was also noisy.

Every one of the Krinpit was constantly booming its name—well, not its "name" in the sense that the name of Franklin Roosevelt's wife was Eleanor. The name was not an arbitrary convention. It was the sound each Krinpit made. It was sound that guided them, that palped the world around them and returned information to their quite agile and competent brains. The sonar pulses they sent forth to read the echoes were their "names." Each was different, and every one always being produced while its owner lived. Their main auditory apparatus was the drum-tight undersurface of the belly. It possessed a vent like a dolphin's that could produce a remarkable range of vowel sounds. The "knees" of the double-boned legs could punctuate them with tympanous "consonants." They walked in music wherever they went. They could not move silently. The exact sounds they produced were controllable; in fact, they had an elaborate and sophisticated language. The sounds which became their recognition signals were probably the easiest for them, but they could produce almost any other sound in the frequency range of their hearing. In this their voices were quite like humans'.

So wherever Sharn-igon went he was surrounded by that sound: *Sharn,* a rising protracted noise like a musical saw, overlaid with white hiss; *igon,* a staccato double drumbeat dropping down to the tonic again. It was not just Sharn-igon. All the Krinpit were constantly making their basic name-sounds when they were not making others. It was not just the Krinpit. Their environment sang to them. Each of the enclosures was marked by wind-powered sound-making machines. Nearly all of them had ratchets or droning pipes or bull-roarers or circle-bowed strings clamóring out their own particular recognition signal.

So to a human eye Sharn-igon was a lopsided crab scuttling in a clattering mass of others, in hellish red gloom, with an inferno of raucous sound coming from every direction.

Sharn-igon perceived it quite differently. He was strolling aimlessly along a well-remembered street. The street had a name; it translates rather closely as "the Great White Way."

At the intersection of the Breeders' Wallow Sharn-igon fell into conversation with an acquaintance.

"Do you have knowledge of whereabouts of Cheee-pruitt?"

"Negative. Conjecture: statistically probable that he would be by lakeside of village."

"Why?"

"Some persons hurt or ill. Many onlookers. Several Anomalous Ghosts reported."

Sharn-igon acknowledged the statements and turned toward the lakefront. He recalled that there had seemed to be a ghost near Cheee-pruitt's residence some time before. And it was anomalous. Basically there were two kinds of ghosts. The Ghosts Above were common and easily "visible" (because they made so much noise) but returned no echo signal to speak of to a Krinpit's sonar. They were good eating when they could be caught. The Ghosts Below were almost invisible. They seldom made visible sounds and returned not much echo; they were mostly observed when their underground digging damaged a Krinpit structure or farm. They too were good eating and were systematically hunted for that purpose when the Krinpit were lucky enough to locate a nest of young.

But what were the anomalous ones, neither Ghosts Above nor Ghosts Below?

Sharn-igon scuttled through the Breeders' Wallow to the Place of Fish Vendors, and along the lakefront to the bright commotion at the Raft Mooring. There was something almost invisible bobbing in the gentle roll of the bay. Though the Krinpit used metal only very sparingly, Sharn-igon recognized the brightness of it; but the bright metal seemed to float over something so soft and immaterial that it returned no real reflection to his sounding. The bright part, though, not only reflected Sharn-igon's sounds almost blindingly, it generated sound of its own: a faint, high, steady whine, an irregular dry-sand rustle. Sharn-igon could not identify the sounds; but then, he had never seen a TV camera or a radio transponder.

He stopped one of the Krinpit moving irritably away from the group and asked what was happening.

"Some Krinpit attempted to eat the ghost. They are damaged."

"Did the ghost harm them?"

"Negative. After eating, they became damaged. One ghost is still there. Advise against eating."

Sharn-igon bounced sounds off the stranger more carefully.

"Have you too eaten of the ghost?"

"A very little, Sharn-igon. I too am damaged."

Sharn-igon touched mandibles and moved on, concerned about Cheee-pruitt. He didn't hear him anywhere in the crowd, but the din was blinding. At least two hundred Krinpit were scratching and sliding over each other's carapaces, milling around the bloody mass that had been one of the "ghosts." Sharn-igon halted and sounded the area irresolutely.

From behind him he thought he heard his own name, badly spoken but recognizable: *Sharn-igon*. When he turned, his highly directional sound sense identified the source. It was the ghost. The one that had seemed to speak his name. Sharn-igon approached it cautiously; he did not like its smell, didn't like its muffled, shadowy sound. But it was a curiosity. First his own name: Sharn-igon. And in between—what? Another name? It was certainly not a Krinpit name, but the ghost kept repeating it. It sounded like OCK med dool-LAH.

On the other shore of the Bay of the Cultural Revolution, fifty kilometers away, Feng Hua-tse rinsed the honey buckets in the purplish waters and carried them back toward the bubble cluster that was the People's Bloc headquarters. From the shore you couldn't see the landing craft itself at all. The extruded bubbles surrounded and hid it. Through the translucent walls of the nearest of them (they could have been made opaque, but the group decision had been that energy conservation was more important than privacy) he could see the vague shadows of the two women detailed as sick-bay orderlies. They had not been given the job because they were women. They had the job because they should have been in bed themselves. Barely able to stagger, they could more or less take care of themselves and the two bed cases. And there was no one to spare to do it for them.

Feng put the clean buckets inside the sick-bay bubble, resenting the waste of the precious nightsoil. But it was his own decision that the wastes from the casualties should be dumped in the bay rather than used to fertilize their tiny plot of garden. Until they were sure what had killed one member of the expedition and put four more on the sick list—nearly half their effectives wiped out at one stroke!— Feng would not risk contamination. It was a pity that their biologist was the sickest of the survivors; his wisdom was needed. But Feng had been a barefoot biologist himself in his youth, and he kept up the experiments with the animals, the tactran reports to Peking, and the four-times-daily examinations of the sick.

He paused in the radio room. The video screen that monitored the small party which had crossed the bay was still showing the same monotonous scene. Apparently the camera had been left on the raft, and apparently the raft had drifted in the slow, vagrant currents of the bay, so that the camera showed only an occasional thin slice of shoreline a quarter of a kilometer away. Once in awhile you could see one of the arthropods scuttling along, and now and again a glimpse of their low, flimsy buildings. But he had not yet seen either Ahmed Dulla or the Costa Rican who had gone with him.

Outside the bubble for the communications equipment the two West Indians were desultorily scooping dirt into woven baskets. Feng spoke sharply to them and achieved a momentary acceleration of pace. They were sick too, but it was not yet clear whether it was the same sickness as the others. They, he thought bitterly, should feel at home here. The heat and humidity were junglelike. What was worst was the lighting, always the same dusky red, never bright enough to see clearly, never dark. Feng had had a headache since they arrived, and it was his private opinion it was only from eyestrain. Feng, at least, had not eaten any of Son of Kung's food. In this he was luckier, or wiser, than the four in the sick bay and the one who had died, not to mention the dozen rats and guinea pigs they tested the stuff on. Feng swore. Why had he let that long-nosed hillman Dulla talk him into splitting their forces? To be sure, it had happened before the five became violently ill. Even so it had been a mistake. When he got back to Shensi, Feng admitted to himself, there would be a long day of self-criticism ahead.

If he got back.

He picked up two baskets of dirt in his shoulder yoke and carried them with him as he went to inspect the dam. That was his greatest hope. When it was completed, they would have electricity to spare—electricity to power the ultraviolet lamps, still stored in the landing craft's hold, that would turn the feeble, pale seedlings into sturdy crops. There was nothing wrong with this soil! No matter how many got sick, even if they died, it was not the soil's fault; Feng had rubbed it between finger and thumb, sniffed it, turned a spadeful over and gazed wonderingly at the crawling things that inhabited it. They were strange, but they meant the soil was fertile. What it did not have was proper sunlight. That they would have to make, as soon as the dam was built; and then, Feng swore, they would produce crops that any collective in Shensi province would envy.

It was raining as he started back, slow, fat, warm drops that ran down Feng's back under his cotton jacket. Another good thing: plenty of water. Not only was it good for the plants, but it kept the spores down, and Feng was highly suspicious of them as the source of the sickness. Even through the clouds he could feel the warmth of Kung Fu-tze. It was not visible, but it gave the clouds the angry, ruddy look of sky over a distant great city. It would stay that way until the air mass that carried the clouds moved away; then there would be that distant hot coal and the purple-black sky with its stars.

Feng took the forest path back to the headquarters, checking the traps. One held two multilegged creatures like land-going lobsters, one dead, the other eating it. Feng dumped them both and did not reset the trap. There was no point in it. They were too shorthanded to bother with more animal specimens than they had already. Three of the traps were sprung but empty, and one was simply missing. Feng muttered to himself irritably. There was a lot they didn't know about the fauna of this fern forest. For one thing, what had stolen the trap? Most of the creatures they had seen were arthropods, buglike or crustaceanlike, none of them bigger than a man's hand. Bigger ones existed. The sentients in the settlement across the bay were proof of that—they were the size of a man. But the wild ones, if they existed, stayed out of sight. And there was something that lived in the tall, woody ferns. One could hear them, even catch a glimpse of them from time to time, but no one in the expedition had yet caught or even photographed one. It stood to reason that if there were small creatures there would be bigger ones to eat them, but where were they? And what would they look like? Wolf teeth, cat talons, crab claws...? Feng abandoned that line of thought; it was not reassuring. To be sure, the local fauna would no doubt find humans as indigestible as the humans had found the local fauna.

But they might not realize that in time.

It began to look as though humans would not find anything at all to eat on Klong. The biologist had been reduced to taking samples of microorganisms from each member of the party and culturing them on plates of agar. It was no longer possible to use laboratory animals. They had all died. And one by one he tried every promising-looking bit of plant or animal they brought him, dropping a broth of it onto the agar, and one by one each of them destroyed the darkening circle of growing bacteria. They were perfect antibiotics, except for one thing: they would have killed the patient more quickly than any disease.

Nevertheless. Ring the trees. Let them die. Ditch those soggy pastures. . . . But the trees did not appear to have a proper bark. In fact they weren't really trees. Slash and burn might not work here. But something would! One way or another, the fields of Child of Kung would prosper!

Feng became aware that his name was being called.

He turned away from the place where the last trap had been, trotting back toward the settlement. As he approached the beach and the fronds thinned, he saw one of the walking casualties waving in excitement.

Feng arrived out of breath. "What, what?" he grumbled.

"A radio message from the long-nose! It is a distress signal, Hua-tse."

"Tchah! What did he say?"

"He said nothing, Hua-tse. It is the automatic distress call. I tried to raise him, but there was no response."

"Of course," snarled Feng, gripping his hands together in anger. Another thing to admit to before the commune. Two members of the party endangered, perhaps lost, because he had foolishly permitted the division of their forces. Two irreplaceable persons—a hillman and a Hispanic, to be sure; nevertheless, persons. Their absence would be serious. And not just the persons. One of their three television cameras. The radio transponder. The precious plastic that had gone into making the skin of the boat. There was just so much of that. They had squandered a great deal on the bubbles to house the sick, the equipment, all their sparse possessions. That was foolishness, too; the fern forest was a limitless supply of woody stems for frames, fronds for ceilings and walls. In this drenched warmth they needed no more than that, but he had weakly permitted the blowing of bubble huts instead of using what nature provided.

Could they build another boat? It was by no means sure that there was plastic enough even for the hull and the sails; and when it was gone, where would they get more? Who could he send? Of their original eleven, one was dead, two were missing, and four were sick. Was it not even more foolish to further divide their forces, to attempt to repair the damage the first foolishness had cost? And what could they do if they did in fact build another boat and sail across the bay? That which had happened to the hillman and the Hispanic could just as well happen to whoever went after them. They had very little in the way of weapons, no more to spare than Dulla and the other man had taken with them in the first place, and little enough good that had done them—

"Are we going, Hua-tse?"

His attention was jarred back. "What?"

"Are we going to try to help our comrades?"

Feng gripped his hands tighter. "With what?" he demanded.

SIX

●

ON A PLANET that has no night the days are endless, Danny Dalehouse reflected, a meter down into the Klongan soil and at least that much more to go. His muscles told him he had been digging this latrine for at least eight hours. The discouragingly tiny spoil heap beside him contradicted them, and the ruddy glow that backlighted the clouds overhead offered no help. Latrine digging was not what he had signed on for. But it was something that had to be done, and he was clearly the most superfluous member of the party in line to do it—only why did it have to take so long?

They had been on the planet only three days (not that there were any days, but the old habits died hard), and already the pleasure was wearing thin. The parts that weren't actively unpleasant like digging latrines were a bore. The parts that weren't already boring were scary, like the madly violent thunderstorm that had blown away their first tent only hours after landing, or irritatingly uncomfortable, like the itchy rashes they had all developed and the stomach troubles that had made the latrines so vital. And to make it worse, they seemed to have company. Kappelyushnikov had come swearing in Russian to report that a third tactran vessel had climbed down its charge state to orbit Klong. Greasies, no doubt. That meant everybody in the world was now represented on Klong. What price the solitary pioneer?

His spade struck air.

Danny lost his balance, spun, and came down in a fetal crouch into the pit, his face almost in the hole that had unexpectedly opened up. From it came a cool, musty smell. It made him think of unopened cellars and the cages of pet mice, and he heard quick, furtive movements.

Snakes? He rejected the thought as soon as he formed it. That was an earthly fear, not appropriate on Klong. But whatever it was could easily be even more deadly than a nest of rattlers. He leaped with prudent speed out of the trench and yelled, "Morrissey!"

The biologist was only a few meters away, sealing plant samples pickled in preservative into plastic baggies. "What's the matter?"

"I hit a hole, maybe a tunnel. You want to take a look?"

Morrissey looked down at the purplish seed pod in his forceps and back at Dalehouse's trench, torn. Then he said, "Sure, only I have to stow these away first. Don't dig any more till I finish."

That was a welcome order, and Dalehouse accepted it gratefully. He was getting used to taking orders. Even as a latrine digger he was subject to instant draft whenever some presently more valuable member of the expedition needed another pair of hands: Harriet to set up her radio, Morrissey to heat-seal his baggies, Sparky Cerbo to locate the canned tomatoes and the kitchen knives that had vanished during the thunderstorm—anyone. Twice already he had had to empty the landing vehicle's chemical toilet into a shallow pit and scrape the soil of Klong over it, because the rest of the crew couldn't wait for him to finish the job they were preventing him from finishing.

It was a drag. But he was on Son of Kung! He could smell the strange Klongan smells—cinnamon and mold and cut vegetation and something that was a little like mom's apple pie, but none of them really any of those things. He could see the Klongan landscape—he could see quite a lot of it, a shovelful at a time.

It was what he had expected in an expedition of specialists. Dalehouse was not a cook, not a farmer, not a doctor, not a radio surveyor. He had none of the hyper-trophied skills that all the others possessed. He was the expedition's only generalist and would stay that way until they made contact with the local sentients and he could employ the communications skills he was advertised to have. Meanwhile he was stoop labor.

The Russian pilot, Kappelyushnikov, was yelling his name. "You, Danny, you come have drink. Put back sweat!"

"Why not?" Danny was pleased to notice that Cappy was

holding aloft a glass containing a centimeter of water, grinning broadly. He had finally got the still to working. Dalehouse swallowed the few drops and wiped his lips appreciatively, then his slippery brow. Kappelyushnikov was right enough about that. In the dank, humid air they were both covered with sweat. The still was powered with a small oil-spray flame, which made it like burning hundred-dollar bills to operate. Later it would be moved to the lakeshore and driven by solar power, but right now they needed water they could drink.

"Very good, is it?" Kappelyushnikov demanded. "You don't feel faint, like is some poison? Okay. Then we go bring a drink to Gasha."

The translator had given herself command of the setting-up phase of the camp, and no one had resisted; she was spending hours over her radio trying to make sense of the communications, but she claimed the other half of her mind was able to keep track of everyone's duty assignments. She might have been right, Dalehouse thought. She was the least agreeable person on the expedition, and no one particularly wanted to disagree with her. She was also close to the least physically attractive, with stringy black hair and an expression of permanent disappointment. But she was grudgingly grateful for the water.

"Thank you for getting the still going. And the latrine, of course, Danny. Now, if the two of you—"

"I'm not finished," Danny corrected. "Jim wants to check out a hole first. Is there anything new on the radio?"

Harriet smiled with closed lips. "We have a message from the Peeps."

"About that guy who's stuck?"

"Oh, no. Take a look." She handed over a facsimile film that said:

The People's Republics extend the hand of friendship to the second expedition to arrive on Child of Kung. Through peaceful cooperation we will achieve a glorious triumph for all mankind. We invite you to join us for the celebration of the fifteen hundredth anniversary of the writings of Confucius, after whom our star was named.

Dalehouse was perplexed. "Isn't that some kind of a winter holiday?"

"You are very well informed today, Dalehouse. It is in December. Our instructor called it the Confucian answer to Hanukkah, which is of course the Jewish answer to Christmas."

He frowned, trying to remember—already, it was becoming hard. "But this isn't even October yet."

"You are very swift indeed, Danny. So translate that, won't you?" requested the translator.

"I don't know. Are they saying something like, 'Don't bother us for a couple of months'?"

"Is more like to drop dead," the pilot put in.

"I don't think so. They aren't being unfriendly," Harriet said, recapturing the fax and squinting at it. "Notice that they referred to Kung Fu-tze by the latinized form of the name. That's a pretty courteous thing for them to do. Still—" She frowned. At best Harriet's eyes were always faintly popped, like a rabbit's, because of the heavy contacts she wore. Now her lips were pursed like a rabbit's too. "On the other hand, they were careful to point out we're the *second* expedition."

"Meaning they're the first. But what's the difference? They can't make territorial claims because they got here ahead of us; that's all spelled out in the UN accords. Nobody gets to claim any more than a circle fifty kilometers around a self-sustaining base."

"But they're pointing out that they could have."

Cappy was bored with the protocol. "Any love letters from the Oilies, Gasha?"

"Just a received-and-acknowledged. And now, about that latrine—"

"In a minute, Harriet. What about the Pak who's stranded?"

"He's still stranded. You want to hear the latest tapes?" She didn't wait for an answer; she knew what it would be. She plugged in a coil of tape and played it for them. It was the Peeps' automatic distress signal: every thirty seconds a coded SOS, followed by a five-second beep for homing. Between signals the microphone stayed open, transmitting whatever sounds were coming in.

"I've cut out most of the deadwood. Here's the man's voice."

Neither Dalehouse nor Kappelyushnikov included Urdu among their skills. "What is he say?" asked the pilot.

"Just asking for help. But he's not in good shape. Most of the time he doesn't talk at all, and we get this stuff."

What came out of the tape player was a little like an impossibly huge cricket's chirp and quite a lot like a Chinese New Year festival in which Australian aborigines were playing their native instruments.

"What the hell is that?" Danny demanded.

"That," she said smugly, "is also language. I've been working on it, and I've sorted out a few key concepts. They are in some sort of trouble, I'm not sure what."

"Not as much as Pak is," grunted Kappelyushnikov. "Come, Danny, is time we go to work."

"Yes, that latrine is—"

"Not on latrine! Other things in life than shit, Gasha."

She paused, glowering at him. Kappelyushnikov was almost as dispensable as Danny Dalehouse. Maybe more so. After the expedition was well established, Dalehouse's skills would come into play, or so they all hoped, in making contact with sentient life. The pilot's main skill was piloting. A spacecraft by choice. If pressed, a clamjet, a racing vessel, or a canoe. None of those existed on Klong.

But what he had that was always useful was resourcefulness. "Gasha, dear," he coaxed, "is not possible. Your Morrissey still has his micetraps in the trench. And besides, now we have water, I have to make *wasserstoff*."

"Hydrogen," Harriet corrected automatically. "Hydrogen? What in the world do you want with hydrogen?"

"So I will have a job, dear Gasha. To fly."

"You're going to fly with hydrogen?"

"You understand me, Gasha," the Russian beamed. He pointed. "Like them."

Danny glanced up, then ran for the tent and the one remaining decent pair of binoculars—two pairs of them, too, had turned up missing after the thunderstorm.

There they were, the windblown flock of balloonists, high and near the clouds. They were at least two kilometers away, too far to hear the sounds of their song, but in the glasses Dalehouse could see them clearly enough. In the purplish sky they stood out in their bright greens and yellows. It was true, Dalehouse verified. Some of them were self-luminous, like fireflies! Traceries of veins stood out over the great five-meter gasbag of the largest and

nearest of them, flickering with racing sparks of biolumi-
nescence.

"Damn," he snarled. "What are you saying, Cappy? Do
you think you can fly up there?"

"With greatest of ease, Danny," the pilot said solemnly.
"Is only a matter of making bubbles and putting *wasserstoff* in them. Then we fly."

"You've got a deal," said Dalehouse firmly. "Tell me
what to do and I'll do it. I'll—wait a minute! What's
that?"

The balloon swarm was scattering, and behind it, coming through the place it was vacating, was something else,
something that beat with a rhythmic flash of light.

The sound reached him then. "It's a helicopter!" he cried
in astonishment.

The chopper pilot was short, dark, and Irish. Not only
Irish, but repatriated to the UK from eleven years in
Houston, Texas. He and Morrissey hit it off immediately.
"Remember Bismarck's?" "Ever been to La Carafe?"
"Been there? I lived there!" When they were all gathered
he said:

"Glad to meet you all. Name's Terry Boyne, and I bring
you official greetings from our expedition, that's the Organization of Fuel-Exporting Nations, to yours, that's you.
Nice place you've got here," he went on appreciatively,
glancing around. "We're down toward the Heat Pole—ask
my opinion, you folks picked a better spot. Where we are
it's wind you wouldn't believe and scorching hot besides, if
you please."

"So why'd you pick it?" asked Morrissey.

"Oh," said Boyne, "we do what our masters tell us. Isn't
it about the same with you? And what they told me to do
today was to come over and make a good-neighbor
call."

Harriet, of course, stepped right in. "On behalf of the
Food-Exporting States we accept your friendly greetings
and in return—"

"Please to stow, Harriet?" rumbled Kappelyushnikov.
"But we are not only other colony on Klong, Terry
Boyne."

"What's 'Klong'?"

"It's what we call this place," Dalehouse explained.

"Um. 'Klong.' We've been told to call it 'Jem'—short

for 'Geminorum,' you see. Heaven knows what the Peeps call it."

"Have you been to see them?"

Boyne coughed. "Well, actually that's more or less what it's about, if you see what I mean. Have you people been monitoring their broadcasts?"

"Sure we have. Yours too."

"Right, then you've heard their distress signals. Poor sod, stuck with those beasts that our translator says call themselves 'Krinpit.' The Peeps don't respond. We offered to help out, and they as much as told us to fuck off."

Morrissey glanced at Harriet. Their translator was doing better than she. He said, "We've had much the same experience, Terry. They indicated we weren't welcome in their part of the world. Of course, they have no right to take that kind of a stand—"

"—but you don't want to start any bloc-to-bloc trouble," finished Boyne, nodding. "Well, for humanitarian reasons—" He choked, and took a great swig of the drink Morrissey had handed him, before going on. "Hell, let's be frank. For curiosity's sake, and just to see what's going on over there—but also for humanitarian reasons—we want to go and fish the guy out of there. The Peeps obviously can't. We suppose the reason they shut you and us out is that they don't want us to see how bad off they are. You folks can't—" He hesitated delicately. "Well, obviously it would be easier for us to go in with a chopper than for you to send an expedition overland. We're willing to do that. But not alone, if you see what I mean."

"I think I do," Harriet sniffed. "You want somebody to share the blame."

"We want to make it a clearly interbloc errand of mercy," Boyne corrected. "So I'm all set to go over there and snatch him out this minute. But I'd like one of you to go along."

Eight out of the ten members of the expedition were speaking at once then, with Kappelyushnikov's shouted "I go!" drowning out the rest.

Harriet glared around at her crew and then said petulantly, "Go then, if you want to, although we're so short-handed here—"

Danny Dalehouse didn't wait for her to finish. "That's right, Harriet! And that's why it ought to be me. I can be spared, and besides—"

"No! I, *I* can be spared, Danny! And I am pilot—"

"Sorry, Cappy," said Danny confidently. "We already have a pilot—Mr. Boyne there—and besides, you have to make your *wasserstoff* so you can take me flying when I come back. And, two, making contact with alien sentients is my basic job, isn't it? And"—he didn't wait for an answer—"besides, I think I know the guy who's stuck there. Ahmed Dulla. We were both hassled by the cops in Bulgaria a couple of months ago."

Wook, wook, wook changed to *whickwhickwhickwhick* as the pilot increased the pitch of the rotors and the copter rocked off the ground and headed for a cloud. Danny clung to the seat, marveling at the profligacy with which the Fuel Bloc spent its treasure—four metric tons of helicopter alone, tachyon-transported from Earth orbit at what cost in resources he could not guess.

"You don't get airsick, do you?" shouted Boyne over the noise of the blades. Danny shook his head, and the pilot grinned and deflected the blade edges so that the chopper leaned toward and began to move after a bank of cumulus.

To Danny's disappointment, the flock of balloonists was out of sight, but there were still small and large creatures in the air, keeping their distance. Dalehouse couldn't see them very clearly and suspected they wanted it that way, staying at the limits of vision and disappearing into cloud as the copter came close. But below! That was laid out for him to enjoy as the chopper bounced along less than fifty meters over the tallest growth. Groves of trees like bamboo; clusters of thirty-meter ferns; tangles of things like mangroves, twenty or more trunks uniting to form a single cat's-cradle tangle of vegetation. He could see small things scuttling and leaping to hide as they twisted overhead, colors of all sorts. The unwinking red glower of the dwarf star toned down rock and water, but the brightest colors were not reflections. They were foxfire glow and lightning-bug tail, the lights of the plants themselves.

Of course Dalehouse had studied the maps of Klong, orbital photos supplemented by side-scatter radar. But this was different, seeing the landscape as they soared above it. Back along the shore was their own camp, on a narrow neck of land that locked off a bay from the wider ocean, or lake, a kilometer or two away. There was the lake (or ocean) itself, curving around like a bitten-into watermelon slice, and in the light from Kung almost the same color. Down the shore of it was the Peeps' encampment. Past that, off toward the part of Klong that lay just under the star, where the land was dryer and the temperatures even higher, was the Greasies' camp. Both of those were out of sight, of course. The copter swung out across the water. Boyne pointed, and Dalehouse nodded; he could see their destination just taking form through the gloomy haze, on the far shore.

Boyne had not been entirely frank, Dalehouse discovered. He had not mentioned that this was not his first flight to the Krinpit community. There had been at least two overflights before that, because there were photos of the layout. Boyne pulled a sheaf of them out of an elastic pocket in the door of the copter, sorted through them, and passed one over to Danny. "There, by the water's edge!" he bawled. His finger jabbed at a curled-up figure a few meters up the beach. Drawn up nearby was a plastic coracle, and there were sheds and more obscure structures all around. There were also some very unpleasant-looking creatures like square-ended crabs: Krinpit. Some of them were suspiciously close to the huddled figure.

"Is he still alive?" Danny shouted.

"Don't know. He was a day or two ago. He's probably okay for water, but he must be getting damned hungry by now. And probably sick."

From the air the Krinpit village looked like a stockyard, most of the structures comprising only unroofed walls, like cattle pens. The creatures were all around, Danny saw, moving astonishingly quickly, at least when matched against his image of Earthside crustaceans. And they were clearly aware the chopper was approaching. Some raised up to point their blind faces toward it, and an ominous number seemed to be converging on the waterside.

"Creepy looking things, ain't they?" Boyne shouted.

"Listen," said Danny, "how are we going to get Dulla away from them? They don't just look creepy. They look mean."

"Yeah." Boyne rolled down his window and leaned out, circling the helicopter around. He shook his head, then pointed. "That your buddy?"

The figure had moved since the photograph had been taken, was no longer in the shelter of one of the sheds but a few meters away and lying outstretched, face down. Dulla didn't look particularly alive, but he wasn't clearly dead either.

Boyne frowned thoughtfully, then turned to Dalehouse. "Open that case between your feet there, will you, and hand me a couple of those things."

The "things" were metal cylinders with wire loop at the end. Boyne took half a dozen, pulled the loops, and tossed them carefully toward the Krinpit. As they struck, yellow smoke came billowing out of them, forming a dense cloud. The Krinpit staggered out of the smoke as though disoriented.

"Just tear gas," Boyne grinned. "They hate it." He stared down. Nearly all the creatures that had been converging around the prostrate man were fleeing now ... all but one.

That one was obviously in distress, but it did not leave the vicinity of the prone human being. It seemed to be in pain. It moved dartingly back and forth as though torn between conflicting imperatives: to flee; to stay; perhaps even to fight.

"What are we going to do about that son of a bitch?" Boyne wondered out loud, hovering over the scene. But then the creature moved painfully away, and Boyne made his decision. He dropped to the ground between the Krinpit and the unconscious Pakistani. "Grab 'im, Danny!" he yelled.

Danny flung open his door and jumped out. He scooped up the Pakistani with more difficulty than he had expected. Dulla did not weigh much over fifty kilos here, but he was boneless as rubber, completely out of it. Danny got him under the arms and more dragged than carried him into the helicopter while Boyne swore worriedly. The rotors spun, and they started to lift off, and there was a rushing, clattering scramble from the other side. Two hundred kilograms of adult Krinpit launched itself onto the side-pallet. Boyne gibbered in rage and jockeyed the controls. The chopper staggered and seemed about to turn on its side; but he got it straight and it began to pull up and away.

"What are you going to do, Boyne?" yelled Danny, trying to pull Dulla's legs inside so he could close the door. "You can't just leave that thing there!"

"Hell I can't!" Boyne stared worriedly at the stiff-jointed legs that were trying to scrape through the plastic to get at him, then turned the copter up and over the water. "I've always wanted a pet. Let's see if I can get this bugger home!"

By the time he got back to his own camp, full of wonder and worries, Dalehouse was physically exhausted. He made a quick report to the rest of the expedition and then fell into a dreamless sleep.

"Night" was an arbitrary concept on Klong. When he woke, the sky was the same as it always was, clouds and the dull red cinder of Kung hanging far off center above. It was back to work as usual. Kappelyushnikov, or somebody, had done some digging for him. He had less than an hour's work, mostly neatening up the edges. He welcomed it, because he had more than an hour's pondering to do.

After rescuing the Pakistani, Boyne had laid a beeline course for his own home base. He had not even asked if Dulla was alive; his attention was taken up to saturation by the hideous and very active creature only centimeters from his left ear and by the demands of piloting. Warned by radio, the Greasies had nets prepared. They had the Krinpit lashed and stowed before the beast knew what was happening. Then a quick meal while Dulla got some sort of emergency medical treatment, mostly cleaning him up and flowing a little glucose into his bloodstream. Then over the barren, hot ground to the Peeps' camp, where they left the sick man, accepted some haughty thanks from the Chinese in charge of the place, and took Dalehouse home.

All in all, he had been gone five or six hours. And every second filled with some new input to worry over in his mind.

He really begrudged them the Krinpit. There was no doubt the creature was intelligent. If the buildings hadn't proved that by themselves, its methodical attempt to gouge its way into the helicopter, and its patient acceptance of failure when the plastic proved too tough, bespoke thought. It had struggled only briefly when the Greasies threw the nets over it, then allowed itself to be hauled into a steel-barred cage. Only after the cage door had slammed behind it did it systematically cut through the netting to free its limbs. Dalehouse had spent all the moments he could spare just watching it and trying to make sense of its sounds. If only he had taken the brain-split at some point in his studies! He knew that Harriet or even that Bulgarian girl, Ana, could have reasoned out some sort of linguistic pattern, but it was only noise to him.

Then there was the wonder of the Greasy camp itself. Steel bars! A helicopter! Bunks on legs, with metal springs! He could not begin to imagine what profligate burning of irreplaceable fuel had made it possible for them to hurl all that stuff at superlight speed to an orbit around Kung, and then to lower it safely to the surface of the planet. They even had air conditioning! True, they needed it; the surface temperature must have been well over forty so near to the Heat Pole. But no one forced them to settle where they would need the permanent drain of air conditioners to survive.

And by contrast, the Peeps. That was pathetic. Old What'sy had put the best face possible on it, but it was clear that the return of Dulla meant to him principally another casualty to try to take care of, with hardly anybody healthy enough to do the nursing—much less do anything else. He had proudly given the visitors to understand that another expedition was on the way, "nearly as big as our own." But how big was that?

Jim Morrissey interrupted his train of thought. The biologist had been out of the camp and had not heard the report; now he wanted it all over again, firsthand. Dalehouse obliged and then asked, "Did you catch anything in your micetraps?"

"Huh? Oh." Obviously that was long in Morrissey's past by now. "No. I ran a wire-tethered probe down the tunnel, but it kept hitting blind alleys. They're pretty smart, whoever they are. As soon as you broke into their tunnel they closed it off."

"So you don't have any animals to send back to Earth?"

"No animals? Never say it, never think it, Danny! I've got a whole menagerie. Crabrats and bugs, creepers and flyers. God knows what they all are. I think the crabrats are probably related to the Krinpit, but you can't really trace relationships until you do paleontology, and Christ, I haven't even made a beginning on the taxonomy yet. And plants—well, anyway, you might as well call them plants.

They don't have stomata or mesophyll cells. Would you believe that?"

"Sure I would, Jim."

"Where the photosynthetic process happens I don't know," Jim went on, marveling, "but it's the same good old thing. Starch production driven by sunlight, or what passes for sunlight—$6CO_2$ plus $6H_2O$ still yields $C_6H_{12}O_6$ and some spare oxygen, on Earth as it is in the heavens. Or the other way around."

"That's starch?" Dalehouse guessed.

"You bet. But don't eat any of it. And keep putting that jelly on your skin every time it rubs off. There're congeners in all that stuff that will do you in."

"Sure." Dalehouse's attention was wandering, and he hardly listened as Morrissey catalogued the vegetation he had so far identified on Klong: something like grasses that covered the plains; succulents like bamboo, with hollow stems that would make fine structural materials; forests of plants that looked like ferns but were fruiting and with woody stems. Some of them grew together from many trunks, like mangroves; others towered in solitary splendor, like redwoods. There were vines like grapes, spreading by transporting their hard-shelled seeds through the digestive tracts of animals. Some of them were luminous. Some were meat-eating, like the Venus flytrap. Some—

"That starch," Dalehouse interrupted, pursuing his train of thought. "Can't we eat it? I mean, sort of cook the poison out of it, like tapioca?"

"Danny, stick to what you know."

"No, really," Dalehouse persisted. "We're shipping a lot of mass in the form of food. Couldn't we?"

"No. Well, maybe. In a sense. It takes only a little bit of their proteins to kick off a reaction I can't handle, so don't experiment. Remember the Peeps' white mice."

"If they're plants, why aren't they green?"

"Well, they are, kind of. In this light they look purple because Kung's so red, but if you shine a flashlight on them they're kind of greenish yellow. But, you know," he went on earnestly, "it's not the usual chlorophyll. Not even a porphyrin derivative. They do seem to use a magnesium ion—"

"I better get this finished up," said Danny, patting the biologist on the shoulder.

It was almost done. He lugged the chemical toilet from the lander and balanced it over the slit trench, and then reported to Harriet.

"All done. First-class American crapper ready for use."

She came over to inspect and then pursed her tiny lips. "Dalehouse, do you think we're animals? Can't you at least put a tent over it? And before it rains again, would you mind? Look at those clouds. Damn it, Danny, why do I have to tell everybody what to do around here?"

He got the tent up. But the storm, when it came, was a rouser. Lightning scored the entire sky, cloud to ground and air to air. Kung was completely obscured, not even a dull glow to mark where it hung in the sky, and the only light was the lightning itself. The first casualty was the power system. The second was Danny's outhouse tent, torn flying away by the eighty-kilometer gusts. By the time it was over they were drenched and miserable, and all of them were busy trying to put the camp together again. East Lansing had had no storms like Klong's, and Danny viewed with dismal foreboding the next few years on this treacherous planet. When he realized he had been more than twenty hours without sleep, he tumbled into bed and dreamed of a warm morning in Bulgaria with a pretty blond woman.

When he woke, Jim Morrissey was poking him. "Out. I get the bed next."

It wasn't really even a bed—just a sleeping bag on an air mattress—but at least it was warm and dry. Dalehouse reluctantly yielded it to the biologist. "So the camp survived?"

"More or less. Don't go near Harriet, though. One of her radios is missing, and she thinks we're all to blame." As he climbed into the bed and stretched his legs down to the warm interior, he said, "Cappy wants to show you something."

Danny didn't rush to see the pilot; odds were, he considered, that it was just some other stoop-labor job that needed doing. It could wait until he had something to eat—although, he reflected, chewing doggedly through a guaranteed full daily requirement of essential vitamins and minerals (it looked like a dog biscuit), eating wasn't a hell of a lot more fun than digging latrines.

But that wasn't what Kappelyushnikov had in mind. "Is no more manual labor for you and me for awhile, Danny," he grinned. "Have now been honored by appointment as chief meteorologist. Must make more *wasserstoff* to check winds, and you help."

"Harriet was real shook up by the storm," Dalehouse guessed.

"Gasha? Yes, that is what she wants, better weather forecasting. But what I want is exotic travel to faraway places! You will see."

Kappelyushnikov's still had been converted to solar power, a trough of brackish water from the lake running between aluminum reflecting V's, and the vapor trapped on a plastic sheet overhead. The drops slipped down into a tank, and part of the fresh water was being electrolyzed into hydrogen and oxygen. From the hydrogen collector, a seamless plastic balloon, a small compressor whirred at regular intervals to pump the gas into a heavy metal cylinder.

Kappelyushnikov checked the pressure gauge and nodded gravely. "Is plenty. Now you go borrow theodolite from head boss, Gasha. Do not take no for answer; and then I will show you something that will truly amaze you."

Fortunately for Dalehouse, Harriet was somewhere else when he went for the theodolite, a small sighting telescope that looked like a surveyor's transit. By the time he got back with it Kappelyushnikov had filled a plastic balloon with hydrogen and was expertly balancing its lift against the weight of a silver ruble. "My good-luck piece," he said dreamily. "Yes, fine. You have pencil?"

"What's a pencil? I have a ballpoint."

"Don't make fun of old-fashioned Soviet values," Kappelyushnikov said severely. "When I let go of balloon, you keep eye on watch. Every twenty seconds you tell me, I call off readings, you write down. You understand? Okay, let go."

The little balloon did not leap out of Dalehouse's fingers; it only drifted upward, bobbing gently as vagrant zephyrs caught it. In the still after the storm there was no strongly prevailing wind that Dalehouse could feel, but he could see the balloon move erratically. At each time-hack Kappelyushnikov read off right ascension and declination bearings. After the seventh reading he began to swear, and after the ninth he straightened up, scowling.

"Is no good! Lousy Kungson light! I cannot see. Next time we will tie on candle."

"Fine, but would you mind telling me what we're doing?"

"Measuring winds aloft, dear Danny! See how balloon curved around, started back way it came? Winds at different levels blow various individual different directions. Balloon follows. We follow balloon. Now we reduce readings, and soon I will truly astonish you with more than you wish to know about Klongan wind patterns."

Dalehouse squinted thoughtfully at where the balloon had disappeared into the maroon murk. "How are we going to do that?"

"Oh, Danny, Danny. How ignorant you Americans are! Simple trigonometry. I have right ascension sighting of balloon after twenty seconds, correct? So I have one angle of right triangle. Second angle must be ninety degrees—you understand that this is so? Otherwise would not be right triangle. So simple subtraction from one hundred eighty gives me angle remaining, and I have thus described triangle perfectly, except for dimension of sides. Okay. I now feed in dimension of first side, and simple transformation—"

"Whoa! You didn't measure anything. Where did you get the dimension of one side?"

"Altitude of balloon after twenty seconds, of course."

"But how do you know—"

"Ah," said Kappelyushnikov smugly, "that is why care is so important in weighing of balloon. With fixed lift, balloon rises at fixed rate. Lift is equal to one silver ruble, and so in each twenty seconds rises nine point seven three meters. We now perform same arithmetic for declination and we have fixed position of balloon in three-dimensional space. Here, walk while we talk." He took the jotted readings from Danny and scanned them, frowning. "Such terrible writing," he complained. "Nevertheless, I can read them perhaps well enough to feed into computer. Is very easy computation."

"Then why do you need a computer?"

"Oh, I could easily perform operations myself. But computer needs practice. Wait one, Danny."

While the Russian was mumbling to himself over the keyboard, Harriet poked her head in the tent. "What are you doing?" she demanded sharply.

"Important scientific research," said Kappelyushnikov airily, without looking up. To Danny's surprise, the translator did not react. She looked sullen, confused, and unhappy—not conspicuously different from her normal look. But her normal behavior was a good deal more abrasive than her demeanor now. She came quietly into the tent and sat down, thumbing dispiritedly through her translation notes.

"Have it!" cried the pilot happily, and pressed a command button. The liquid crystal over the computer flashed colored darts of light, then revealed a plot of wind arrows. "Colors of spectrum," Kappelyushnikov explained. "Red is lowest, up to fresh grass green for highest. You see? At fifty meters, wind heading one forty-five degrees, eight kilometers per hour. At one hundred meters, backing to ninety-five degrees and now fifteen kilometers. And so on. Triumph of Soviet technology."

Dalehouse nodded appreciatively. "That's very nice, but what do we want to know that for?"

"Meteorology," Kappelyushnikov grinned, winking and moving his head toward Harriet.

The woman looked up and burst out, "Cut that out, Vissarion. I'm in no mood for you to make fun of me. Tell Dalehouse your real reason."

The Russian looked surprised, and a little thoughtful, but he shrugged. "All right. Poor American Danny, you are helpless without your machines. But not I. I am pilot! I do not wish to be earthworm like one of those things we shit on in your latrine, Danny. I want something to fly. They will not give me fuel. They will not let me have structural materials for glider—would be easy, except for launching; plenty of winds here, you see. But Gasha says no, so what can I do? I look up and see balloonists floating around sky, and I say I also will be balloonist!" He pounded his fist on the top of the computer. "Have gas. Have navigation information for winds aloft. Have Soviet know-how. Have also little extra bonus of low gravity and high pressure of air. So now I will make little balloon, big enough for me, and I will pilot again."

A surge of enthusiasm infected Dalehouse. "Hey, that's great. Would it work?"

"Of course would work!"

"We could use it to take after those balloonists, get close to them. Harriet, do you hear that? It would give us a chance to try to talk to them."

"That's fine," she said, and Dalehouse looked at her more closely. Even for Harriet she looked sullen.

"What's the matter?" he asked.

She said, "I located the radio."

"The one that blew away in the storm?"

She laughed, like a cartoon figure laughing: *heh, heh, heh.* "It takes a real idiot to believe that one. How could it blow away? Goddamn thing weighs twenty kilos. It occurred to me it might be transmitting, so I listened, and it was. I tried RDFing, and I got a fix right away. Straight down," she said, staring at them. "The damn thing is right down underneath us in the ground."

A minute was still a minute. Danny made sure of that, because he had begun to doubt. His pulse was still forty-two in sixty seconds by the clock. He could hold his breath for three of the minutes and maybe a bit more. The small coinage of time had not altered in value. But one thousand four hundred and forty minutes did not seem to make a day anymore. Sometimes it felt as though a whole day had passed, and the clock said only six or seven hours. Sometimes it would occur to him to be tired, and the clock would show as much as thirty hours since he slept last. Fretfully Harriet tried to keep them all on some regular schedule, not because it seemed necessary, but because it was orderly. She failed. Within—what? a week?—they were sleeping when they wanted to and eating when they felt hungry and marking the passage of time, if at all, by events. The first near-visit by balloonists was after the big storm and before the Peeps received their reinforcement of personnel. The time Kappelyushnikov triangulated the missing radio for Harriet and discovered it was at least twenty meters underground was just after they sent their first reports and shipment of specimens back to Earth. And the time balloonists came to visit—

That was a whole other thing, the kind of event that changes everything fore and aft.

Dalehouse woke up with his mind in the sky. He did his chores. He helped Morrissey check his traps, prepared a meal of desecrated stew, fixed a valve in the shower stall by the lake. But what he was thinking of was Kappelyush-nikov's balloons. Danny had talked him out of the big single hydrogen-filled bag: too big, too clumsy, too hard to manufacture, and above all too likely to kill its passenger if anything popped its skin. So they had painstakingly blown a hundred pibal-sized bags, and the Russian had knotted up a netting to contain them. The aggregate lift would be as much as you wanted. All it took was more balloons; you could multiply them to lift the entire camp if you liked. But if one or two popped, it did not mean a dead aeronaut. The passenger would descend reasonably slowly—to be more accurate, they were hopeful the passenger would descend slowly. He might damage himself, but at least he would not be spread flat across the Klongan landscape.

Kappelyushnikov would not allow Danny to do the final stages of filling and tying the balloons—"Is my neck, dear Danny, so is my job to make sure it stays okay."

"But you're taking so damn long. Let me help."

"*Nyet*. Is very clear," grinned the pilot, "that you think pretty soon you too will fly my balloons. Maybe so. But this time I am sole cargo. And besides, have still static lift tests to finish. Until then not even I fly."

Dalehouse moved impatiently away, disgruntled. He had been on Klong for—whatever length of time it was—a couple of weeks, at least. And the author of "Preliminary Studies toward a First Contact with Subtechnological Sentients" had yet to meet his first subtechnological sentient. Oh, he had seen them. There were burrowers under his feet, and he was sure he had caught a glimpse of something when Morrissey exploded a charge under a presumed tunnel. The Krinpit had been his fellow passenger for half an hour. And the balloonists were often in the sky, though seldom nearby. Three separate races to study and deal with! And the most productive thing he had done was dig a latrine.

He fidgeted his way into Harriet's tent, hoping to find that she had miraculously made some giant leap in translation of one of the languages—if they were languages. She wasn't there, but the tapes were. He played the best of them over and over until Kappelyushnikov came in, sweating and cheerful.

"Static test is good. Plenty lift. Now we let whole mishmash sit for a while, check for leaks. You are enjoying concert of airborne friends?"

"It isn't a concert, it's a language. I *think* it's a language. It's not random birdcalls. You can hear them singing in chords and harmonies. It's chromatic rather than—do you know anything about music theory?"

"Me? Please, Danny. I am pilot, not longhair fiddle player."

"Well, anyway, it's a chromatic rather than diatonic, but the harmonies are there, not too far off what you might hear in, say, Scriabin."

"Fine composer," the Russian beamed. "But tell me. Why do you listen to tapes when you have real thing right outside?"

Startled, Danny raised his head. It was true. Some of the sounds he was hearing came from somewhere outside the tent.

"Also," Kappelyushnikov went on severely, "you are breaking Gasha's rice bowl. She is translator, not you, and she is very difficult lady. So come now and listen to your pink and green friends."

The balloonists had never been so close, or so numerous. The whole camp was staring up at them, hundreds of them, so many that they obscured each other and blotted out part of the sky. The red glower of Kung shone through them dimly as they passed before its disk, but many of them were glowing with their own firefly light, mostly, as Kappelyushnikov had said, pink and pale green. Their song was loud and clear. Harriet was there already, microphone extended to catch every note, listening critically with an expression of distaste. That meant nothing. It was just the way she always looked.

"Why so close?" Dalehouse marveled.

"I do not wish to break your rice bowl either, dear Danny. You are expert. But I think is possible they like what we put up for chopper pilot." And Kappelyushnikov waved to the strobe beacon on the tower.

"Um." Danny considered a moment. "Let's see. Do me a favor and get one of the portable floodlights. We'll see them better, and maybe it'll bring them even closer."

"Why not?" The Russian disappeared inside the supply tent and came back with the portable in one hand and the batteries in the other, cursing as he tried to avoid stumbling over the wires. He fumbled with it, and its dense white beam abruptly extended itself toward the horizon, then danced up toward the balloonists. It seemed to excite them. Their chirps, squeals, flatulences, and cello drones multiplied themselves in a shower of grace notes, and they seemed to follow the beam.

"How do they do that?" Harriet demanded fretfully. "They've got no wings or anything that I can see."

"Same as I, dear Gasha," boomed the Russian. "Up and down, to find a truly sympathetic current of air. Here, you hold light. I must watch experts and learn!"

The balloonists were coming closer. Evidently the light attracted them. Now that there was enough brightness to make the colors plain, the variety of their patterns was striking. There were cloudlike whorls, solid bands, cross-hatchings, dazzle designs that resembled World War I camouflage.

"Funny," said Dalehouse, staring longingly at the swarm. "Why would they have all those colors when they can't see them most of the time?"

"Is your opinion they can't," said Kappelyushnikov. "Light like beet juice is strange to us; we see only the red. But for them perhaps is— Ho, Morrissey! Good shot!"

Dalehouse jumped a quarter of a meter as the camp's one and only shotgun went off behind him. Overhead, one of the balloonists was spiraling toward the ground.

"I get," yelled Kappelyushnikov, and sprinted off to intersect its fall.

"What the hell did you do?" blazed Dalehouse.

The biologist turned a startled and defensive face toward him. "I collected a specimen," he said.

Harriet laughed disagreeably. "Shame on you, Morrissey. You didn't get Dalehouse's permission to shoot one of his friends. That's the price you pay for being a specialist in sentients—you fall in love with your subjects."

"Don't be bitchy, Harriet. My job's hard enough. This'll make it impossible. Shooting at them is the surest way to drive them away."

"Oh, sure, Dalehouse. Anybody can see they're stampeding in terror, right?" She waved a casual hand at the flock, still milling through the light and singing as they soared delightedly overhead.

Kappelyushnikov came back with a rubbery sac draped over his shoulder. "Almost had to fight off one of your

Krinpit friends to get it," he growled. "Was big, ugly
mother. Don't know what I would have done if he had
truly contested ownership. But he scuttled away."

"There are no Krinpit around here," Harriet said sharply.

"Are now, Gasha. Never mind. See how pretty our new
pet is."

The creature was not dead. It did not seem even
wounded, or at least there was no blood. The shotgun
pellets had blown a hole in the gasbag and nothing else. Its
little face was working, looking like the countenance of an
engorged tick, with great eyes staring at them. It was
making the tiniest of sounds, almost like gasps.

"Disgusting," said Harriet, drawing back. "Why isn't it
screaming?"

"If I knew the answers to questions like that," said
Morrissey, dropping to one knee beside the creature to see
it better, "I wouldn't have to collect specimens, would I?
But at a guess, it would be if I hadn't shot the breath out
of it. I think it uses the hydrogen for vocalizing. God
knows what it breathes. Must be oxygen, of course, but—"
He shook his head and glanced up. "Maybe I ought to
collect a few more."

"No"

"Christ, Dalehouse! You know, Harriet's right about
you. Well—I know. At least let's see how phototropic they
are. Hand me those shells." Kappelyushnikov passed over
the plastic belt of ammunition, and Morrissey pawed
through it until he found a signal flare.

"You'll set fire to them, Morrissey! That's hydrogen in
those bags!"

"Oh, cripes." But the biologist aimed carefully to one
side of the flock. More and more of them were entering
into the beam, now steady, as Harriet had put it on the
ground pointing up; the whole diffuse swarm was con-
tracting into a knotted mass.

When the flare went off, the whole flock seemed to
twitch like a single organism. They didn't swarm toward it.
They stayed bunched in an ellipsoidal huddle along the
axis of the beam of light; but their song changed to a
frantic crescendo, and there seemed to be a systematic
rearranging of positions within the flock. The smaller and
less brightly colored individuals bobbed toward the lower
portions of the school, and the larger and gaudier ones

lifted toward the top. Dalehouse stared in fascination, so entranced that he did not realize his face was sticky and wet until Kappelyushnikov grunted in surprise.

"Hey! Is raining?"

But it wasn't rain. It was sweet and pungent on their lips, with an aftertaste that was animal and fetid; it fell like a gentle dew on their upturned faces and clung to their skins.

"Don't swallow any!" cried Morrissey in belated panic, but some of the people were already licking their lips. Not that it mattered, thought Dalehouse; the stuff was all over them. If it was poisonous, they were done for.

"You fools!" cried Harriet, stamping her foot. She had never been attractive, and now she looked like a witch, sallow face in a grimace, uneven teeth bared. "We've got to get this stuff off. Kappelyushnikov! You and Morrissey get buckets of water at once."

"*Da*, Gasha," said the pilot dreamily.

"*Now!*" she screamed.

"Oh, of course, now." He lumbered off a few steps, then paused and looked coquettishly back over his shoulder. "Alyusha, dear. You help me get important water right away?"

The navigator simpered. She answered him in Russian, something that made Kappelyushnikov grin and Harriet swear. "Don't you clods know we're all in *danger?*" she cried, catching at Dalehouse's hand imploringly. "You, Danny, you've always been nicer to me than those other bastards. Help me get water."

He returned the pressure of her hand and whispered, "Hell, yes, honey, let's get some water."

"Danny!" But she wasn't angry anymore. She was smiling, allowing him to tug her toward the lakefront.

He ran his tongue over his lips again. Whatever the dew was, the more he tasted it the better he liked it: not sweet, not tart, not like fruit or meat, not like flowers. It was not like anything he had ever tasted before, but it was a taste he wanted more of. He saw Harriet touching her pointed tongue to her own thin lips and was suddenly seized with the need to taste that Klongan mist from her mouth. He felt the damp heat rising inside him and caught her roughly around the waist.

They kissed desperately, their hands busy ripping each other's clothes off.

It never occurred to them to think of hiding themselves. They cared nothing for what the others in the expedition might think of them, and the others cared no more for Harriet and Dalehouse. In couples and clusters the entire expedition was down on the ground in a mass fury of copulation, while overhead the swooping balloonists sang and soared through the searchlight and their gentle mist rained down on the human beings below.

SEVEN

●

ANA DIMITROVA sat in a window table of a Greek tea shop in Glasgow, writing industriously on her daily letter to Ahmed. She did not send them all. That would be ruinously extravagant! But every week, at the end of Sunday, she spread them out on a table and copied out the best parts, enough to fill four dots in a microfiche. It was never enough. She leaned forward into the northern sunshine, left elbow on the table next to the cooling cup of strong, sweet tea, head resting on the hand, oblivious to the noise of the lorries and the double-decker yellow-and-green buses on the Gallowgate road outside, and wrote:

—it seems so long since last I kissed your lovely eyelids and wished you good-bye. I miss you, dear Ahmed. This place is terrible! Terrible and strange. It smells of petroleum and internal-combustion engines, the smell of wicked waste. Well. They have only another five or ten years and then their North Sea oil will be gone, and then we will see.

The headaches have been very bad, I think because these languages are so uncouth. It is actual pain to speak in them. It will be all right, though, dear Ahmed. The headaches pass. The ache in my heart lasts much longer—

"More tea, miss?"

The harsh English words crashed into Nan's ear. She winced and raised her head. "Thank you, no."

"We'll be serving lunch in just a bit, miss. The souvlaki's very tasty today, cook says."

"No, no. Thank you. I must be getting back to my hotel." She had dawdled longer over the letter than was right, she thought remorsefully, and now she had to hurry, and the headache was back. It was not just that the woman was speaking English. It was the way she spoke it, the rough Scottish consonants that buzzed and rattled in the ear. Although in truth it did not much matter what language, or at least what non-Slavic language, she was hearing. The headaches were more frequent and more severe. It was probably because she had become a diplomatic translator. The international vocabulary of science was easy enough to translate, since so many of the words had the same roots in all languages. In diplomacy the risks were greater, the nuances subtler and more threatening. The choice of an adjective meant nothing in translating a report on X-ray polarimetry, but in a speech about locating a drilling claim on the Mid-Atlantic Ridge it might mean the difference between peace and war.

Nan paid her check and dodged cautiously across Gallowgate among the towering buses that so mischievously raced along the wrong side of the street. The diesel stink made her cough, and coughing made her headache worse.

And she was late. She was to be picked up for the airport at one, and it was past noon already. She walked virtuously past the shops (so bright and gay!) without looking in a single window. There were styles here that Sofia would not see for another year. But why bother? It would have been nice to buy new clothes to wear for Ahmed. With him so many billions of kilometers away, Nan wore what was easiest to put on and least likely to attract attention. Evenings she spent alone when she could, listening to music and studying grammar. Her best treat was to reread the sparse letters he had returned for her prodigious outflow—although they were not stimulating. From what he said, Son of Kung sounded a grim and awful place.

She cut through a corner of the Green to walk along the riverside toward her hotel, hoping to avoid the noise and the invisible, but not unsmellable, exhaust from all the vehicles. No use. Lorries rumbled along the embankment, and the sludgy surface of the Clyde itself was pocked with oil tankers and barges and creased with the wakes of hydrofoils. How did one *live* in a place like this? And it all could have been avoided. A little forethought. A little planning. Why did they have to put oil refineries in the middle of a city? Why stain their river with waste and filth when it could have been a cool oasis? Why be in such a rush to pump the oil from the bottom of the sea when it could have provided energy, even food, for another hundred generations? Why use oil at all, for that matter —especially in these packs and swarms of cars and lories— when the city could have been built around public transportation, electrically powered, or powered with the hydrogen that Iceland, not so very far away, was so eager to sell.

But on Son of Kung . . .

On Son of Kung it could be all different. She wished she could be there. With Ahmed. Not just to be with Ahmed, she told herself stoutly, but to be part of a new world where things could be done properly. Where the mistakes of Earth could be avoided. Where one's children would have a future to look forward to.

Hers and Ahmed's children, of course. Nan smiled to herself. She was an honest person, and she admitted that Kungson seemed all the finer because Ahmed was there. If only she were not *here!* There were worrisome things between the lines of what he wrote. So many of his expedition had been sick. So many had died, just in the first days—and his only letters had been in those first days. Why, he himself could have—No. She would not countenance that thought. There was enough else to fret about. For example, the picture he had sent of himself. He had looked worrisomely thin, but what she had noticed most about the picture was the hand on his shoulder. The person who owned the hand was not visible, but Nan was almost sure it was a woman's hand. And that was even more worrisome.

"Miss Dimitrova! Hoy, there. Nan!"

All at once she perceived that her feet had carried her into the lobby of the hotel, and she was being greeted by a man she almost recognized. Dark, short, plump, a little past middle age, he had a diplomat's smile and wore clothes that, even across the immense old lobby, she was sure were real wool—if not cashmere.

He filled in the blank for her. "I'm Tam Gulsmit. Remember? We met at the FAO reception last month." He snapped his fingers for a forkboy. "Your bags are all ready—unless you care to freshen up? Have time for a drink?"

Now she recalled him well. He had been persistent in his attentions, even to the point of lying in wait for her as she came out of the powder room and drawing her into an offensively close conversation in the hall. She had explained to him that it was no use. It was not merely a question of being in love with someone else. That was not his concern; she did not have to tell him her reasons. It was a matter of socialist morality. V. I. Lenin had said it. Free love was all very well, but who would want to drink from a glass that every passerby had fouled with his lips? (And yet in Moscow, she remembered, the public drinking fountains had just such glasses chained to them, and each one surely smeared with a thousand lips.) Let the Fuel powers do what they liked—partner swapping, group orgies, whatever. She was not there to pass judgment, but a socialist girl from Sofia did not even smoke in the street, because she had been taught certain principles of behavior that did not leave her when she grew up.

"Sir Tam," she began—she remembered that he had one of those quaint British handles to his name—"it is a pleasure to see you again, but I must fly now to New York for the United Nations debate. I have no time—"

"All the time in the world, sweets, that's what I'm here for. Boy!"

Tardily the bellboy rolled up with his forklift, and that was scandalous, too: her one little zipper bag did not need a fuel-guzzling machine to carry it; she had toted it a kilometer at a time herself.

Sir Tam chuckled indulgently. "Aren't we quaint? This great, rambling old ruin—that's the Britishness of it, isn't it? We're great at backing a losing horse long past the point where anyone else would have chucked it in. Lucky for us we can afford it! Now, is there anything else you need to bring?"

"But truly, Sir Tam, a car is being sent to take me to the airport. It will be here any minute."

"Here already, sweetie. I'm it. Our Government have provided me with a Concorde Three, and I'd just rattle around in it by myself. When I heard that a friend of God Menninger's needed a lift I took the liberty of coming for you myself. You'll like it. There's plenty of room, and we'll make New York in ninety minutes."

Scandalous, scandalous! Of course the British could afford anything, ocean of oil under the North Sea, their octopus tendrils already grabbing at the Mid-Atlantic Ridge. But morally it was so wrong.

She had no chance to refuse. Sir Tam overcame all

objections, and before she knew what was happening she was lifted gently by cherry picker into—dear God!—a supersonic hydrojet.

As soon as they belted up, in deep, foam armchairs with a suction-bottomed decanter and glasses already on a little table between them, the aircraft hurled itself into the air. The acceleration was frightening. The way the ground dropped away beneath them was not to be believed. Strangely, there was less noise than she had expected, far less than the warm-up roar of a clamjet.

"How quiet," she said, leaning away from Sir Tam's casually chummy arm.

He chuckled. "That's five thousand kilometers an hour for you. We leave the sound far behind. Do you like it?"

"Oh, yes," said Nan, trying to prevent him from pouring her a drink. She failed.

"Your voice sounds more like 'oh, no.' "

"Well, yes, perhaps that is so. It is terribly wasteful of oil, Sir Tam."

"We don't burn oil, sweetie! Pure hydrogen and oxygen —have to carry them both, this far up. Not an ounce of pollution."

"But of course one burns oil, or some other fuel, to make the hydrogen." She wondered if she could keep the conversation on propellant chemistry all the way across the Atlantic, decided not, and took a new tack. "It is frightening. One can see nothing from these tiny windows."

"What is there to see? You get turned on by clouds, love?"

"I have flown the oceans many times, Sir Tam. There is always something. Sometimes icebergs. The sea itself. In a clamjet there is the excitement of the landfall as one approaches Newfoundland or Rio or the Irish Coast. But at twenty-five thousand meters there is nothing."

"I couldn't agree with you more," said Sir Tam, unstrapping and moving closer. "If I had my way there'd be no windows in the thing at all."

Nan moistened her lips with the whiskey and said brightly, "But it is all so exciting. Could you perhaps show me around this aircraft?"

"Show you around?"

"Yes, please. It is so new to me."

"What's to see, love?" Then he shrugged. "Matter of fact, yes, there are a few features I'd like to call to your attention."

She stood up gratefully, glad to get his hand off her knee. The headaches had lessened, perhaps because now they were breathing quite pure air instead of the Glaswegian smog, but she was annoyed. He had made it clear that they were the only passengers; that was not deceitful. But she had expected at least the chaperonage of the stewardesses, and they, all three of them, had retreated to their little cubbyholes in the aft of the aircraft. The little paneled lounge was far more intimate than she liked.

But worse was in store. What she had thought was a service cubicle turned out to be a tiny, complete bedroom suite. With—could one believe it?—a *waterbed*. Easily a metric ton of profligately wasted mass! For nothing, surely, but profligately immoral purposes!

"Now there," said Sir Tam over her shoulder, "is a feature worth studying. Go ahead, Nan. Let your impulses carry you. Try it out."

"Certainly not!" She moved away from his touching hand and added formally, "Sir Tam, I must tell you that I am an engaged person. It is not correct for me to allow myself to be in a situation of this kind."

"How quaint."

"Sir Tam!" She was almost shrieking now, and furiously angry, not only with him but with herself. If she had used a tiny bit of intelligence she would have known this was coming and could have avoided it. A delicate hint that this was the wrong time. A suggestion of—what? Of a social disease, if necessary. Anything. But she was trapped, the waterbed before her, this gland case behind, already with his lips against her ear, whispering buzzingly so that her headache exploded again. Desperately she caught at a straw.

"We—we were speaking of Godfrey Menninger?"

"What?"

"Godfrey Menninger. The father of my good friend, Captain Marge Menninger. You spoke of him in the hotel."

He was silent for a moment, neither releasing her nor trying to pull her closer. "Do you know God Menninger well?"

"Only through his daughter. I was able to keep her from going to jail once."

His arm was definitely less tight. After a moment he patted her gently and stepped away. "Let's have a drink," he said, ringing for the stewardesses. The satyr's smile had been replaced by the diplomat's.

The conversation was back on its tracks again, for which Ana was intensely grateful. She even managed to return to the little cubicle with the armchairs and to persuade the stewardess to bring her a nice cup of strong *chai* instead of the whiskey Gulsmit suggested. He seemed greatly interested in the story of Margie Menninger's little episode, in every detail. Had they been fingerprinted? Was the people's magistrate a court of record, whatever that was? Had Ana spoken to anyone in the militia about the incident later on, and if so what had they said?

Such trivial things seemed to interest him, but Nan was content to go on dredging up memories for him all the way across the Atlantic, as long as it meant his keeping his hands to himself. When she was wrung dry he leaned back, nursing the new drink the stewardess had poured for him and squinting out at the blue-black and cloudless sky.

"Very interesting," he said at last. "That poor little girl. Of course, I've known her since she was tiny." It had not occurred to Ana that Margie Menninger had ever been tiny. She let it pass, and Sir Tam added, "And dear old God. Have you known him long?"

"Not in a personal sense," she said, careful not to add lying to the fault of being untruthful. "Of course he is of great importance in cultural matters. I too am deeply concerned about culture."

"Culture," repeated Sir Tam meditatively. He seemed about to produce a real smile but managed to retain the diplomatic one instead. "You are a dear, Nan," he said, and shook his wristwatch to make the red numerals blink on. "Ah, almost there," he said regretfully. "But of course you must allow me to escort you to your hotel."

The morning session of the UN was exhausting. There was no time for a real lunch because she had to post-edit the computer translations of what she had already translated once that morning before they could be printed. And the afternoon session was one long catfight.

The debate was on fishing rights for Antarctic krill. Because it was food, tempers ran high. And because sea lore is almost as old an area of human interest as eating, the translation was demanding. There were no places where she could coast, no technical words that were new-coined and common to almost all languages. Every language had developed its own words for ships, seaman-ship, and above all, eating, at the dawn of language itself. Only three of Nan's languages were in use—Bulgarian, English, and Russian. The Pakistanis were not involved in the debate, and there were plenty of others proficient in the Romance languages. So there were long periods when she could listen without having to speak. But there was no rest even in those periods; she needed to remember every word she could. The UN delegates had the awful habit of quoting each other at length—sometimes with approval, sometimes with a sneer, always with the risk of some tiny hairsplit that she had to get just right. Her headaches were immense.

That was, of course, the price you paid for having the two hemispheres of your brain surgically sliced apart. Not to mention the stitching back of parts of them that kept you from stumbling into things or falling down, or the DNA injections that left your neck swollen and your eyes bulging for weeks at a time and sometimes caused seizures indistinguishable from epilepsy. That had been a surprise. They hadn't told her about those things when she signed up to become a split-brain translator—not really. You never did know what pain was going to be until you had it.

What made the whole day an order of magnitude worse was that she was starved for sleep. Sir Tam had followed her to her very door and then planted a foot inside it. His hands had been all over her in the limousine all the way in from the airport. The only way she could think to get rid of him was to pretend such exhaustion that she could not stay awake another second, even though it was just after lunch, New York time. And then she found she had talked herself into it.

So she did go to sleep. And woke up before midnight with the chance for any more sleep gone. And what was there to do with the eleven hours before the morning session would begin?

A letter to Ahmed, of course. A few hours with English

irregular verbs. Another hour or so listening to the tapes she had just made to check her accent. But then she was tired and fretful. What she needed most was a walk from her apartment past the university into the fresh morning air of the park, but that was ten thousand kilometers away in Sofia. In New York you did not go walking in the fresh morning air. And so she had turned up for duty in the translator's booth feeling as though a hard day's work was already behind her, and her head throbbing and pounding in two different rhythms, one in each temple. . . .

Her mind had wandered. She forced it back. It was Sir Tam asking for the floor now, and she had to put his words into Bulgarian.

His face was purple-red, and he was shouting. With one half of her brain Nan wondered at that while the other half was automatically processing his words. So much passion about such little fish! Not even fish. They were some sort of crustacean, weren't they? To Nan, "krill" was something that old-fashioned peasant grannies stirred into their stews to give them body. It came as a grayish-white powdery substance that you bought in jars labeled "fish protein concentrate." You knew that it was good for you, but you didn't like to think about what organs and oddities were ground up to make it. In food-rich Bulgaria, nobody grew excited about the stuff.

But Sir Tam was excited. The Fuel Bloc needed it desperately, he shouted. Had to have it! Was entitled to it, by all the laws of civilized humanity! The Fuel Bloc already possessed the fleets of long-range factory ships that could seine the cold Antarctic Ocean. He quoted *Pacem in Maris* and the British-Portuguese Treaty of A.D. 1242. The tiny bodies of the creatures that made up the krill, he declaimed, were absolutely essential to British agriculture, being the very best kind of fertilizer for their crops.

At which the Uruguayan delegate interrupted, snarling, "Agriculture! You are using this essential protein to feed to animals."

"Of course," Sir Tam replied stoutly. "We are not blessed with the advantages given your country, Señor Corrubias. We do not have immense plains on which our cattle can graze. In order to feed them properly, we must have imports—"

Someone in the American delegation laughed out loud, not a pleasant laugh, and the Uruguayan drummed on his desk derisively. "So it is cattle you feed, Sir Gulsmit? But we have it on the evidence of your own Ministry of Health that you give the krill to your cats and budgies! Do you then make minced kitten patties, perhaps? Or fresh chops of parrakeet?"

Sir Tam looked long-sufferingly at the president pro tem. "Sir, I must ask the courtesy of the floor."

The president was a spare Ghanaian who had not once glanced toward any speaker. He did not do so now. His eyes stayed on the letters he was signing one by one as his secretary put them before him. He said, "I would request of the delegate from Uruguay that he reserve his remarks until the delegate from the United Kingdom has concluded."

Sir Tam beamed graciously. "Thank you. In any case, I am almost finished. Of course, some part of our imports of krill does find its way into pet food, some part into protein additives for the justly famous British beef, some part into fertilizer to help us grow the vital foods that nature has otherwise denied us. Is that a matter for this body? I think not. What is of concern is the behavior of member states in their conduct of world affairs. We infringe no international treaty in continuing the long British tradition of the sea, in harvesting what is freely available to all in international waters, and of course in making suitable use of those pelagic areas which, by existing treaties freely arrived at by the member states, have long been reserved to us. But even this is not relevant to the motion before us today! That motion, I remind you, relates only to the proposal for a United Nations peacekeeping team to supervise the Antarctic fisheries. 'Peacekeeping,' my dear fellow delegates. A team to keep the peace. And therefore our position is clear. No such team is needed. The peace has been kept. There have been no incidents. There certainly will be none of our making. The United Nations has better things to do than to seek solutions for problems that do not exist."

And he sat down, managing to do so with a bow to the president pro tem, a sardonic grin for the Uruguayan, and yes, even a wink for Ana, up in the translator's booth! She shook her head in distress at this frivolous-minded person. But perhaps he was serious after all, for he was already writing something on a scrap of paper and beckoning a page, even as the Ghanaian finished signing his letters, slapped his portfolio shut, glanced at the clock, and managed not to catch the Uruguayan delegate's eye as he said, "I am informed that the address of the next delegate may occupy a substantial period of time. Since it is now four, I suggest we recess this debate until ten o'clock tomorrow morning."

A buzz rose up from the floor. Nan leaned back for a long moment, massaging her temples before she stood up and allowed herself to contemplate the next half hour: a quick meal, a bath, and then a lovely long sleep—

No. It was not to be. As she opened the door to the booth the page dashed up, out of breath, and handed her the note from Sir Tam. It said:

> Absolutely essential you attend the party in the DVL, and that I have the pleasure of escorting you.

So there was no rest, no rest. She might have refused the invitation. But Sir Tam had taken the precaution of telling the head of the Bulgarian mission to the United Nations about it, and she was no sooner in her room than he was on the phone insisting she go.

She bathed quickly and dressed in what she guessed might be appropriate, then trotted back across the street from her hotel to the great quaint oblong building, so unlike its newer and fortresslike neighbors. Her head was pounding all the way. Diffidently she whispered her name to the guard at the Distinguished Visitors Lounge. He consulted a list, smiled frostily, and let her in.

What a tumult! How much smoke, and what odors of food and drinks! And there was Sir Tam, to be sure, tiny bouquet of flowers in one hand, the other hand on the shoulder of a plump, dark, grinning man whom Nan did not at once recognize but who was the very Uruguayan with whom Sir Tam had been exchanging insults an hour before.

"Nan! Ho, Nan! Over here!" He was beckoning her to him. She could not think of a reason for refusing, and knew before it happened that Gulsmit would be *touching* her again. And it happened just that way. The flowers turned out to be a bouquet of Parma violets, outrageously out of season and, of course, for her. Gulsmit insisted on pinning the corsage on her demure bodice himself, taking much more time over it than was necessary while the others in his little conversational group jovially pretended not to notice.

It angered Nan that the Scot should put himself on such terms of evident intimacy, especially in this hyperactive atmosphere, where people who had been trading threats with each other all day were now laughing and mingling and drinking together. Not only that. Every person in this little group was from a rival bloc. What would the head of her delegation say? Sir Tam and the Saudi were Fuel. The Uruguayans were People. So were the two jolly Chinese women in their spike-heeled shoes and neo-Mao jackets of silk brocade and metal thread.

"You'll never guess, Nan," grinned Sir Tam after introducing her, "what our friends have up their sleeves for tomorrow. Tell her, Liao-tsen."

The older of the Chinese women laid her hand on Ana's arm, smiling. Clearly she had been drinking a great deal. Her consonants were fuzzy, but she said, comprehensibly enough, "The People's Republic of Bengal will put forward an emergency resolution. It is a very pretty resolution, Miss Dimitrova. All about 'the alleged multinational expedition of the Food-Exporting Powers' and their 'acts of violence against the natives of Son of Kung.' "

"Violence? What is this about violence?" demanded Nan, startled and suddenly fearful. If there was fighting on Kungson . . . if Ahmed found himself in the middle of a war . . .

"That's the funny part, dear girl," chuckled Sir Tam. "It seems your friend God's little junket has begun shooting down harmless balloonists. But not to worry. I don't think it's going to pass. It's not a party matter, is it, Señor Corrubias?"

The Uruguayan shrugged. "There has been no official consultation among the People's Republics, that is true."

"And unofficial?" Gulsmit probed.

Corrubias glanced at the elder Chinese woman, who nodded permission, and said, "I can tell you my personal opinion, and that is that the acts of violence we have heard described are not of much importance. Can one really get upset about rubber jack-o'-lanterns floating around in the sky?"

"There is also the matter of the underground race," said the Chinese woman. She took another sip of her drink, looking merrily mysterious over the top of it at Sir Tam, before going on comfortably, "But that too . . . well, a few burrows broken into, that's all. After all, how can we be sure that the creatures who inhabit them are indeed intelligent? We would not object to a Nebraska farmer, for example, opening a mole run as he plowed his corn paddies."

"One might also," said Ana boldly, surprising herself at the harshness of her voice, "speak of the crustacean race that has suffered some casualties." But Sir Tam stopped her by a gentle pressure on the shoulder. She did not protest. She had suddenly begun to fear that it was Ahmed's group that had caused those casualties, about which she knew so worryingly little.

"I would really enjoy watching you two fight it out," said Sir Tam, laughing to take the menace out of his words. But Nan wondered if he didn't really mean it. She also wondered why he was so carefully and publicly possessive of her, arm around her shoulder, hovering over her drink and refilling it from every passing tray. Surely all these foreign people would suppose they had been in bed together. She blushed at the thought. It would have been bad enough to be guilty of an immoral dalliance, like any common tart, and to have it known. But she was not even guilty! The name without the game—how awful! Why would Sir Tam go out of his way to create such an impression? Could it be that the lax morality of the Fuel people was such that he valued the appearance of sexual adventure as much as the relationship itself? Was he trying to show that he was still sexually potent? And what sort of people was she living among here?

"Please excuse me for a moment," she said, glancing about as though looking for a woman's w.c. But as soon as she was well away from Sir Tam, she circled around the white-paneled room to the buffet tables. At least she would bring up her blood sugar. Perhaps that would relieve the headaches and the exhaustion, and then she would think of a way to relieve the pressure from Sir Tam.

The table would have been lavish even in Sofia! But was it not the Tibetans who were giving this party? And why did they feel obliged to spread so wasteful a display of food? Caviar that certainly did not come from the Himalayas; delicate fruit ices that surely were unknown in their sparse, high valleys; pâtés in the original wooden boxes from France. And look what they had done! The centerpieces were carved replicas of the races of Kungson! A balloonist, half a meter thick, in butter! A crustacean carved from what looked like strawberry sherbet! A long, almost ratlike creature—was it a burrower?—made from foie gras! And there, standing next to her, was a distinguished-looking gray-haired man who was directing a pale-haired younger man to fill a plate from the display. A spoonful of the burrower, a few slices of some sort of meat, a croissant, a scoop from the balloonist to butter the roll. He caught her eye and smiled pleasantly without speaking.

It was all incredibly ostentatious. It quite took Ana's appetite away. She looked away from the food and saw Sir Tam across the room, eyes on her. Strangely, he nodded encouragement and pointed—to whom? To the graying, tall man next to her?

She looked more carefully. Had they ever met? No. But he had a face she seemed to know, from a photograph, she thought—but a photograph that had meant something to her.

She turned to speak to him, and the pale-haired man was suddenly between them, polite but at a state of readiness. For what? Did they think she was an assassin?

Then she remembered where she had seen the face. "You're Mr. Godfrey Menninger," she said.

His expression was inquiring. "Yes?"

"We've never met, but I've seen your picture in a newspaper. With your daughter. I'm Ana Dimitrova, and I met your daughter a few months ago in Sofia."

"Of course you did! The angel of rescue. It's all right, Teddy," he said to the younger man, who stepped back and began collecting silverware for Menninger's plate. "How nice to meet you at last, Ana. Margie's here somewhere. Not near the food, poor thing. She has her mother's metabolism. She can't even look at a layout like this without putting on a kilo. Let's go find her so you can say hello."

Captain Menninger was sipping her Perrier water and allowing a fifty-year-old Japanese attaché to think he was making headway against her defenses when she heard her father's voice behind her.

"Margie, dear, a surprise for you. You remember Ana Dimitrova?"

"No." Marge studied the woman carefully, not competitively but in the manner of someone trying to learn a terrain from a map. Then the card file in her head clicked over. "Yes," she corrected herself. "The Bulgarian woman. How nice to see you again."

It was not anything of the kind, and she intended the Bulgarian bint to understand that. On the other hand, Margie had no particular wish to make an enemy of her, either. There might be a time when her connection with that Pak she was screwing—Dulla? Yes. Ahmed Dulla, member of the first Peeps' expedition to Klong—could be a useful line to pursue. So she turned to the Japanese and said:

"Tetsu, I'd like you to meet Nan Dimitrova. She was such a help to me in Bulgaria. You know how foolish I am about making jokes—I just can't help this mouth of mine. It says things that get me into the most terrible trouble. And so, of course, I said something ridiculously awful. Political, you know. It could have had really sticky consequences. And along came Nan, total stranger, just a good person, and got me out of it. How is that nice young man you were with, Nan?"

"Ahmed is on Kungson," said Nan. She was unwilling to give offense, but she was not obliged to like this plump blond's nasty little put-down games.

"Is he! Why, that's a coincidence. You remember Dr. Dalehouse, of course? He's there too. Perhaps they'll meet." She saw that her father's aide had just signaled something to him and added, "Poppa, you're looking worried. Am I saying something awful again?"

Godfrey Menninger smiled. "What I'm worried about is that if I'm going to give you a lift to Boston, it's time we were on our way. You do remember you have a date at MIT tonight?"

"Oh, dear. I'd forgotten." Wholly untrue. Margie had not forgotten the time of her date, which was the following morning, and she had no doubt that her father had not either.

"Also," he went on, "you'll be sneezing and scratching if we stay here much longer. Or had you also forgotten that you are allergic to flowers?"

Margie had never in her life been allergic to anything, but she said, "You do take such good care of me, poppa. Nan, I'm sorry this was so short, but it's really nice seeing you again. And Tetsu, don't be a stranger next time you're in Houston. Stop by and say hello." The Japanese hissed and bowed. Of course, Margie reflected, she could be out of town if he ever did happen to show up in Houston. Not that it mattered. She had already accomplished her objective. Past a certain age, even going to bed with a man did not give you quite as firm a grip on his emotions as communicating the impression that you certainly would like to if you ever got the chance.

In her father's car, with the bodyguard-aide sitting in front, she said, "Now what was that all about, poppa?"

"Maybe your little Bulgarian friend isn't quite as much of a country girl as she seems. Teddy swept her as a matter of routine. There was a microphone in her corsage."

"Her? Bugged? That's a crock!"

"That's a fact," he corrected. "Maybe her delegation put it on her, who knows? That place was full of sharks. It could have been any one of them. And speaking of sharks—"

"You want to know what I picked up," she said, nodding, and told him what the Japanese had said about the Bengali resolution.

He leaned back in the seat. "Just the usual UN Mischief Night, I'd say. You turn over my garbage can, I throw a dead cat on your roof. Are they going to press it?"

"He didn't say, poppa. He didn't seem to take it very seriously."

Her father rubbed the spot below his navel thoughtfully. "Of course, with the Peeps you never know. Heir-of-Mao has an investment in Klong. The Bengalis wouldn't be starting anything they didn't clear with the Forbidden City."

Margie's hair prickled erect at the back of her neck. "Are you saying I should worry? I don't want my mission withdrawn!"

"Oh, no. No chance of that, honey. Relax, will you? You're too much like your old lady. She never did learn to swing with the action. When the PLO kidnapped you I thought she'd have a nervous breakdown."

"She was scared shitless, poppa. And you never turned a hair." Not even, she thought, when your own four-year-old daughter was bawling into the jetliner's radio.

"But I knew you were going to be all right, honey. I really did."

"Well, I'm not bringing that up again, ol' buddy."
Margie folded her hands in her lap and stared out the
window. Between the UN complex and the airport there
was no building, no street, that Margie had not seen a
dozen times before. She was not really seeing them now.
But they helped spur and clarify her thoughts, the long
tandem buses hobbling down the slow lanes, the apartment
dwellers walking their dogs, the school kids, stores, police
on their tricycles, sidewalk vendors with their handmade
jewelry and pocket computers. Thomas Jefferson, as he
returned to Monticello, might have looked out of his
stagecoach in just the same detached but proprietary way
at the slaves weeding his crops.

She said slowly, "Listen, poppa. I want to get our
mission reinforced. Now."

"What's the hurry?"

"I don't know, but there's a hurry. I want it done before
the Peeps and the Greasies cut us off at the roots or get
enough of their own people up there to own Kungson. I
want us there first and biggest, because I want it all."

"Shit, honey. Didn't they teach you about priorities at
the Point? There's the krill business and the Mid-Atlantic
Ridge and the Greasies threatening to raise their prices
again—do you have any idea how tough all this is? I've
only got one stack, and there's only room for one thing at
the top of it."

"No, poppa, I don't want to be told how hard it is.
Don't you understand this is a whole planet?"

"Of course I do, but—"

"No. No buts. I guess you don't really understand what
it means to have a whole planet to play with. For us,
poppa, all for us. To start from scratch with, to develop in
a systematic manner. Find all the fossil fuels, develop
them in a rational way. Locate the cities where they don't
destroy arable land. Plant crops where they won't damage
the soil. Develop industry where it's most convenient. Plan
the population. Let it grow as it is needed, but not to
where you have a surplus: good, strong, self-reliant people. American people, poppa. Maybe the place stinks now,
but give it a hundred years and you'd rather be there than
here, I promise. *And I want it.*"

Godfrey Menninger sighed, looking in love and some
awe at the oldest and most troublesome of his children.
"You're worse than your mother ever was," he said rueful-

ly. "Well, I hear what you say. The Poles owe us one. I'll
see what I can do."

TechTowTwo sprawled over the bank of the Charles
River, more than twice the cubage of all the old brick
buildings put together. There were no classrooms in Technology Tower Two. There was no administration, either. It
was all for research, from the computer storage in the
subbasements to the solar-radiation experiments that decorated the roof with saucers and bow ties.

The Massachusetts Institute of Technology had a long
tradition of involvement with space exploration, going
back even before there was any—or any that did not take
place on a printed page. As early as the 1950s there had
been a design class whose entire curriculum revolved
around the creation of products for export to the inhabit-
ants of the third planet of the star Arcturus. The fact that
there was no known planet of Arcturus, let alone inhabit-
ants of it, did not disturb either teacher or students.
Techpersons were used to unhinging their imaginations on
demand. In the Cambridge community that centered
around MIT, Harvard, the Garden Street observatories,
and all the wonderlands of Route 128 there had been
designers of interstellar spacecraft before the first Sputnik
went into orbit, anatomists of extraterrestrials when there
was no proof of life anywhere off the surface of Earth, and
specialists in interplanetary communications before anyone
was on the other end of the line. Margie Menninger had
taken six months of graduate studies there, dashing from
Tech to Harvard. She had been careful to keep her
contacts bright.

The woman Margie wanted to see was a former president of the MISFITS and thus would have been a power in
the Tech world even if she had not also held the title of
assistant dean of the college. She had arranged a breakfast
meeting at Margie's request and had turned out five
department heads on order.

The dean introduced them around the table and said,
"Make it good now, Margie. Department heads aren't
crazy about getting up so early in the morning."

Margie sampled her scrambled eggs. "For this kind of
food, I don't blame them," she said, putting down her
fork. "Let me get right to it. I have about ten minutes'

worth of holos of the autochthons of Son of Kung, alias Klong. No sound. Just visible." She leaned back to the sideboard and snapped a switch, and the first of the holographic pictures condensed out of a pinkish glow. "You've probably seen most of this stuff anyway," she said. "That's a Krinpit. They are one of the three intelligent, or anyway possibly intelligent, races on Klong, and the only one of the lot that is urban. In a moment you'll see some of their buildings. They're open at the top. Evidently the Krinpit don't worry much about weather. Why they have buildings at all is anyone's guess, but they do. They would seem much the easiest of the three races to conduct trade with, but unfortunately the Peeps have a head start with them. No doubt we'll catch up."

The head of the design staff was a lean young black woman who had limited her breakfast to orange juice and black coffee and was already through with it. "Catch up at what, Captain Menninger?" she asked.

Margie took her measure and refused combat. "For openers, Dr. Ravenel, I'd like to see your people create some trade goods. For all three races. They're all going to be our customers one of these days."

The economist took his eyes off the holo of a Krinpit coracle to challenge Margie. " 'Customers' implies two-way trade. What do you think these, ah, Klongans are going to have to sell us that's worth the trouble of shipping it all those light-years?"

Margie grinned. "I thought you'd never ask." She pulled an attaché case off the floor and opened it on the table in front of her, pushing the plate of eggs out of the way. "So far," she said, "we don't exactly have any *manufactured* objects. But take a look at this." She passed around several ten-centimeter squares of a filmy, resilient substance. "That's the stuff the balloonists' hydrogen sacs are made out of. It's really pretty special stuff—I mean, it holds gaseous H_2 with less than one percent leakage in a twenty-four-hour period. We could supply quite a lot of that if there was a specialty market for it."

"Don't you have to kill a balloonist to get it?"

"Good question." Margie nodded to the economist with a lying smile. "Actually, no. That is, there are other, nonsentient races with the same body structure, although this one is, I believe, from one of the sentients. How about a market? If I remember correctly, the Germans had to use the second stomach of the ox when they were building the *Hindenburg.*"

"I see," said the economist gravely. "All we need to do is contact a few Zeppelin manufacturers." There was a general titter.

"I'm sure," said Margie steadily, "that you will have some better idea than that. Oh, and I ought to mention one thing. I brought my checkbook. There's a National Science Foundation grant for research and development that's waiting for someone to apply for it." And for that gift too, I thank you, poppa, she thought.

The economist had not become the head of a major department of the faculty without learning when to retreat. "I didn't mean to brush you off, Captain Menninger. This is actually a pretty exciting challenge. What else have you got for us?"

"Well, we have a number of samples that haven't been studied very carefully. Frankly, they aren't really supposed to be here. Camp Detrick doesn't know they're gone yet."

The group stirred. The dean said quickly, "Margie, I think we all get the same picture when you mention Camp Detrick. Is there anything connected with biological warfare in this?"

"Certainly not! No, believe me, that doesn't come into it at all. I sometimes go out of channels, I admit, but what do you guess they'd do to me if I broke security on something like that?"

"Then why Camp Detrick?"

"Because these are alien organisms," Margie explained. "Except for the sample of balloonist tissue, you'll notice that every item I've got here is in a double-wrapped, heat-sealed container. The outside has been acid-washed and UV-sterilized. No, wait—" she added, grinning. Everybody at the table had begun looking at their fingertips, and there was a perceptible movement away from the samples of tissue on the table. "Those balloonist samples are okay. The rest, maybe not so okay. They've been pretty carefully gone over. There don't seem to be any pathogens or allergens. But naturally you'll want to use care in handling them."

"Thanks a lot, captain," said the designer stiffly. "How can you be so sure about the tissue?"

"I ate some three days ago," she said. She had their full attention now and swept on. "I should point out that the grant naturally includes whatever you need to insure safe handling. Now, this group contains plant samples. They're photosynthetic, and their principal response is in the infrared range. Interesting for you agronomists? Right. And these over here are supposed to be art objects. They come from the Krinpit, the ones that look like squashed cockroaches. The things are supposed to 'sing.' That is, if you're a Krinpit and you rub them on your shell, they make some interesting sounds. If you don't have a chitinous shell, you can use a credit card."

The woman from design picked up one of them gingerly, peering at it through the transparent plastic. "You said you wanted us to develop some kind of trading goods?"

"I sure do." The last thing Margie pulled out of her dispatch case was a red-covered mimeographed document. The words MOST SECRET were dazzle-printed on the jacket. "As you can see, this is classified, but that's just military hang-ups. It will be turned over to the UN in about ten days anyway, or most of it will. It's the most comprehensive report we've been able to prepare on the three principal races of Klong."

All six of the faculty members at the table reached for it at once, but the design woman was fastest. "Um," she said, flipping through it. "I've got a graduate student who would eat this up. Can I show it to him?"

"Better than that. Let's leave this copy and the samples with our friends, and let's you and I go talk to him."

Fifteen minutes later Margie had succeeded in getting rid of the department head, and she and a slim, excitable young man named Walter Pinson were head to head. "Think you can handle it?" asked Margie.

"Yes! I mean, well, it's a big job——"

Margie put her hand on his arm. "I'm sure you can. I'd really appreciate it if you'd tell me how you plan to go about it, though."

Pinson thought for a moment. "Well, the first thing is to figure out what their needs are," he offered.

"That's fascinating! It must be pretty difficult. I would hardly know where to start. Offhand, I'd say their biggest need, all of them, is just staying alive. As you'll see, everything on the planet spends a lot of its time trying to eat everything else, including the other intelligent races."

"Cannibalism?"

"Well, I don't think you can call it that. They're different species. And there are a lot of other species that are trying to eat the intelligent ones."

"Predators," said Pinson, nodding. "Well, there's a starting point right there. Let's see. For the predators like the balloonists, for instance, anything that would set them on fire would help protect the sentients. Of course," he added, frowning, "we'd have to make sure that these were used only to defend the sentients against lower forms of life."

"Of course!" said Margie, shocked. "We wouldn't want to give them weapons to start a war with!" She glanced at her watch. "I've got an idea, Walter. I didn't have much of a breakfast, and it's getting on toward lunch. Why don't you and I get something to eat? There's a place I used to know when I was a graduate student. In a pretty frowsty old motel, but the food was good—if you have the time, I mean?"

"Oh, I have the time," said Pinson, looking at her appreciatively.

"It's up past Harvard Square, but we ought to be able to get a cab. And please let me—I have an expense account, and it's all your tax money anyway." As they walked toward the elevator, a mob of undergraduates flocked toward a lecture hall. Looking toward them, Margie asked, "Do you by any chance know a student named Lloyd Wensley? I think he's a freshman."

"No, I don't think so. Friend of yours?"

"Not really—or anyway, not since he was a little kid. I used to know his family. Now, about these, ah, implements for self-protection—"

Several quite pleasant hours later, Margie got into a cab outside the old motel. If the food had not been really as good as she remembered it, the rooms still came up to standard. As they approached Harvard Square she had an impulse. "Go down Mass Ave," she ordered the driver. "I want to make a little detour." After a few blocks she directed him into a side street, and looked about.

She recognized the neighborhood. There was the supermarket. There was Giordan's Spa, and there, over the barbershop, only now it was over a hardware store, was the three-room corner apartment where she had lived with

Lloyd and Lloyd Junior through the ten months that measured both her graduate year and her marriage. It was the closest Marge had ever come to motherhood, fill-in to a six-year-old for the real mother who had died when he was three. It was the closest she had ever come to wifehood, too, and closer than she would ever come again. Old Lloyd! Thirty years old when she was nineteen, and so fucking *courtly* in the Officers' Club that you'd never guess what he was like in bed. Not even if you'd tried him out a time or two, as Margie had been careful to do. Just looking up at the window of their bedroom made Marge's neck ache with the memory of being head-jammed into a corner of the bed, half choked with pillows, so Lloyd could pump himself dry as quickly as convenient. As often as convenient. When he thought convenient. You didn't ask a cuspidor for permission to spit in it, or a wife for sex. The cuspidor couldn't struggle, not if you had it jammed into position just right, and it wouldn't cry out. Neither would the wife, especially with the six-year-old stepson only marginally asleep just outside the door.

It would have been nice to see Lloyd Junior, all grown up. But better not. Better the way it was. She hadn't seen either of the Lloyds since the annulment, and no use pressing your luck. It had been a pretty frightening, dehumanizing experience for a young girl; how lucky she was, thought Margie, that it hadn't scarred her forever!

When she got back to her hotel there was a taped message from her father: "To hear is to obey. Catch a news broadcast."

She turned on the bedside TV while she packed, hunting for an all-news station. She was rewarded with five minutes about the latest Boston political corruption scandals, and then an in-depth interview with the Red Sox's new designated hitter. But at last there was a recap of the top international story of the day.

"In a surprise move at the United Nations this morning, the top Polish delegate, Wladislas Prczensky, announced that his government has accepted the challenge presented by the Bengali resolution. The Food powers have agreed to send out an investigatory commission with broad powers to investigate the alleged cases of brutal treatment of native races on the planet whimsically called 'Klong' or 'Son of Kung.' There will be no representatives of major powers such as the United States or the Soviet Union on the commission, which will be made up of UN peacekeeping officers from Poland itself, Brazil, Canada, Argentina, and Bulgaria."

EIGHT

●

DANNY DALEHOUSE reached out to grab the theodolite as it tipped in the soft ground. Morrissey grinned and apologized. "Must've lost my balance."

"Or else you're stoned again," said Dalehouse. He was angry—not just at Morrissey. In the candor of his heart he knew that most of his anger was at the fact that Kappelyushnikov was flying and he was not. "Anyway," he went on, "you've knocked this run in the head. Next time why don't you just go sleep it off?"

They had all been freaked out by the stuff the balloonists had sprayed on them, and from time to time, for days afterward, all of them had recurring phases of lust and euphoria. Not only were Morrissey's more intense, but Dalehouse was pretty sure the biochemist was still exposing himself. He had discovered that something in the semen or sperm of the male balloonists was highly hallucinogenic—better than that, was the long-sought-after true aphrodisiac fabled in song and story. It wasn't Morrissey's fault that his researches put him clear out of it from time to time. But he shouldn't have insisted on helping with the theodolite readings.

Far overhead Kappelyushnikov's cluster of bright yellow balloons gyrated as the pilot experimented with controlling his altitude to take advantage of the winds at various levels. When he was finished tracking them they would have basic information that could allow them to cruise the skies. Then Dalehouse's turn would come. But he was tired of waiting.

"Cappy," he said into the radio, "we've lost the readings. Might as well come on down."

Harriet was walking toward them as Kappelyushnikov's answer came through. It was in Russian; Harriet heard, and flinched irritably. That was in character. She had been

97

a perfect bitch about the whole thing, Dalehouse thought. When they returned to normal after that first incredible trip, she had flamed at him, "Animal! Don't you know you could have got me pregnant?" It had never occurred to him to ask. Nor had it occurred to her, at the time. It was no use reminding her that she had been as eager as he. She had retreated into her hard defiant-spinster shell. And ever since, she had been ten times as upright as before and fifty times as nasty to anyone who made sexual remarks in her presence or even, as with Kappelyushnikov just now, used some perfectly justifiable bad language.

"I've got some new tapes for you," Harriet sniffed.

"Any progress?"

"Certainly there's progress, Dalehouse. There's a definite grammar. I'll brief the whole camp on it after the next meal." She glanced up at Cappy, having a last fling with his balloon as half a dozen of the Klongan gasbags soared around him, and retreated.

A definite grammar.

Well, there was no use trying to hurry Harriet. "Preliminary Studies toward a First Contact with Subtechnological Sentients" seemed very far away! Dalehouse counted up the score. It was not impressive. They had made no contact at all with the crablike things called Krinpit or with the burrowers. The gasbags had been hanging around quite a lot since the day they had showered the expedition with their milt. But they did not come close enough for the kind of contact Danny Dalehouse wanted. They bounced and swung hundreds of meters in the air most of the time, descending lower only when most of the camp was away or asleep. No doubt they had been trained to avoid ground-limited creatures through eons of predation. But it made it hard for Danny.

At least, with the gasbags in sight, rifle microphones had been able to capture quite a lot of their strident, singing dialogue—if dialogue was what it was. Harriet said she detected structure. Harriet said it was not birdsongs or cries of alarm. Harriet said she would teach him to speak to them. But what Harriet said was not always to be believed, Danny Dalehouse thought. The other thing he thought was that they needed a different translator. The split-brain operation facilitated language learning, but it had several drawbacks. It sometimes produced bad physical effects, including long-lasting pain. Once in a while it produced personality changes. And it didn't always work. A person who had no gift for languages to begin with came out of surgery still lacking the gift. In Harriet's case, Danny would have guessed all three were true.

They had transmitted all the tapes to Earth anyway. Sooner or later the big semantic computers at Johns Hopkins and Texas A&M would be checking in, and Harriet's skills, or lack of them, would stop mattering so much.

What Danny needed, or at least what Danny wanted, so badly he could taste it, was to be up there in the sky with one of the gasbags, one on one, learning a language in the good old-fashioned way. Anything else was a compromise. They'd tried everything within their resources. Free-floating instrumented balloons with sensors programmed to respond to the signatures of life; wolftraps for the Krinpit; buried microphones for the burrowers; the rifle mikes and the zoom-lens cameras for the gasbags. They had kilometers of tape, with pictures and sounds of all manner of jumping, crawling, wriggling things, and in all the endless hours hardly as much as ten minutes' worth that was any use to Danny Dalehouse.

Still, something had been accomplished. Enough for him to have composed a couple of reports to go back to Earth. Enough even for his jealous colleagues at MSU and the Double-A-L to pore over eagerly, even if not enough to satisfy Danny. It was still learning, even if much of it was negative.

The first thing to perish was the pretty fable of three independent intelligent races living in some sort of beneficent cooperation and harmony. There was no cooperation. At least, they had seen no signs of that, and many to the contrary. The burrowers seemed never to interact with the others at all. The gasbags and the Krinpit did, but not in any cooperative or harmonious way. The balloonists never touched ground, as far as Danny had seen, or at least not on purpose. There were at least a dozen species that enjoyed eating balloonists when they could catch them—sleek brown creatures that looked a little like stub-winged bats, froglike leapers, arthropods smaller than the Krinpit—not least of them, the Krinpit themselves. If a gasbag ever drifted low enough for one of them to reach it, it was dead. So the entire lives of the balloonists, from spawn to fodder, were spent in the air, and their ultimate burial was always in the digestive tract of some ground-bound race—so tawdry a fate for so pretty a species!

Kappelyushnikov was coming in low and fast, tossed by the low-level winds. He pulled the rip cord on his balloon at five meters and dropped like a stone, wriggling out of the harness to fall free. He tumbled over and over as he landed, then got up, rubbing himself, and ran to catch the deflated balloon cluster as it scudded before the breeze.

Danny winced, contemplating his own first flight. The last little bit of ballooning was going to be the hardest. He turned to help Cappy pick up the fabric, and a rifleshot next to his head made him duck and swear.

He spun around, furious. "What the hell are you up to, Morrissey?"

The biologist put the rifle at shoulder-arms and saluted the tumbling form of one of the hovering gasbags. "Just harvesting another specimen, Danny," he said cheerfully. He had judged height and wind drift with precision, and the collapsed bag was dropping almost at their feet. "Ah, shit," he said in disgust. "Another female."

"Really?" said Danny, staring at what looked like an immense erection. "Are you sure?"

"Fooled me too," Morrissey grinned. "No, the ones with the schlongs aren't the males. They aren't schlongs. I mean, they aren't penises. These folks don't make love like you and I, Danny. The females sort of squirt their eggs out to float around in the air, and then the boys come out and whack off onto them."

"When did you find all that out?" Dalehouse was annoyed; the rule of the expedition was that each of them shared discoveries as soon as made.

"When you were bugged at me for being stoned out of my mind," Morrissey said. "I think it has to do with the way they generate their hydrogen. Solar flares seem to be involved. So when they saw our lights they thought it was a flare—and that's when they spawned. Only we happened to be underneath, and so we got sprayed with, uh, with—"

"I know what we got sprayed with," Dalehouse said.

"Yeah! You know, Danny, when I took up this career they made dissecting specimens sound pretty tacky—but every time I go near one of the males' sex glands I get high. I'm beginning to like this line of work."

"Do you have to kill them all off to do it, though? You'll

chase the flock away. Then how am I going to make contact?"

Morrissey grinned. He didn't answer. He just pointed aloft. Dalehouse, in justice, had to concede the unspoken point. Whatever emotions the gasbags had, fear did not seem to be among them. Morrissey had shot down nearly a dozen of them, but ever since the first contact the swarm had almost always stayed within sight. Perhaps it was the lights that attracted them. In the permanent Klongan twilight, there was no such thing as "day." The camp had opted to create one, marked by turning on the whole bank of floodlights at an arbitrary "dawn" and turning them off again twelve clock hours later. One light always stayed on—to keep off predators, they told themselves, but in truth it was to keep out the primordially threatening dark.

Morrissey picked up the balloonist. It was still alive, its wrinkled features moving soundlessly. Once down, they never uttered a sound—because, Morrissey said, the hydrogen that gave them voice was lost when their bags were punctured. But they kept on *trying*. The first one they had shot down had lived for more than forty hours. It had crept all around the camp, dragging its gray and wrinkled bag, and it had seemed in pain all of that time. Dalehouse had been glad when it died at last, was glad now when Morrissey plunged the new one into a killer bag for return to Earth.

Kappelyushnikov limped up to them, rubbing his buttocks. "Is always a martyr, first pioneer of flight," he grumbled. "So, Danny Dalehouse. You want go up now?"

An electric shock hit Danny. "You mean *now?*"

"Sure, why not? Wind isn't bad. I go with, soon as two balloons fill."

It took longer than Dalehouse would have thought possible for the little pump to fill two batches of balloons big enough for human passengers—especially since the pump was a hastily rigged nonsparking compressor that leaked as much gas as it squeezed into the bags. Dalehouse tried to eat, tried to nap, tried to interest himself in other projects, and kept coming back to gaze at the tethered clusters of bags, quietly swelling with hydrogen, constrained by the cord netting that surrounded them.

The weather had taken a turn for the worse. Clouds

covered the sky from horizon to horizon, but Kappelyushnikov was stubbornly optimistic. "Clouds will blow away.
Is positive skies will be clear." When the first pinkening of
sky began to show, he said decisively, "Is okay now. Strap
in, Danny."

Mistrustfully, Dalehouse buckled himself into the harness. He was a taller but lighter man than the Russian, and
Kappelyushnikov grumbled to himself as he valved off
surplus hydrogen. "Otherwise," he explained, "you go back
to state of Michigan, East Lansing, *shwoosh!* But next
time, not so much wasting gas."

The harness had a quick-release latch at the shoulders,
and Dalehouse touched it experimentally.

"No, no!" screamed Kappelyushnikov. "You want to
pull when you are up two hundred meters, fine, pull! Is
your neck. But don't waste gas for nothing." He guided
Danny's hands to the two crucial cords. "Is not clamjet,
you understand? Is free balloon. Clamjet uses lift to save
fuel. Here is no fuel, only lift. Here you go where wind
goes. You don't like direction, you find different wind.
Spill water ballast, you go up. Spill *wasserstoff*, you go
down."

Dalehouse wriggled in the harness. It was not going to
be very much like sailplaning over the eastern shore of
Lake Michigan, where there was always a west wind to
bounce off the bluffs and keep a glider aloft for hours. But
if the Russian could do it, he could do it. I hope, he added
to himself, and said, "All right, I think I have the hang of
it."

"So let's go," cried the Russian, grinning as he slipped
into his own harness. He bent and picked up a fair-sized
rock, gesturing to Danny to do the same. The other
members of the expedition were standing back, but one of
them handed Danny a rock, and at Kappelyushnikov's
orders they untethered the balloons.

Kappelyushnikov danced over toward Danny like a
diver stilting across a sea bottom. He came as close as he
could under the bulk of their balloons, peering into his face.
"You are all right?" Danny nodded. "So drop the rock and
we go!" Kappelyushnikov cried. And he cast his own rock
away and began to float diagonally upward.

Dalehouse took a deep breath and followed his example,
watching the Russian move upward.

Nothing seemed to happen. Danny did not feel any

acceleration, only that his feet seemed to have gone abruptly numb and there was no sensation of pressure on their bottoms. Because his eyes were on Kappelyushnikov he neglected to look down until he was fifty meters in the air.

They were drifting south, along the coastline. Far above them and inland, over the purple hills that marked the edge of the fern forest, the extended swarm of balloonists was grazing on whatever tiny organisms they could find floating in the sky. Below and behind was the dwindling campsite. Danny was already higher than the nose of their return rocket, the tallest object in camp. Off to his left was the sea itself, and a couple of islands in the muddy waters, covered with many-trunked trees.

He wrenched his attention away from sight-seeing; Kappelyushnikov was shouting at him. "What?" Dalehouse bellowed. The gap had widened; Cappy was now forty meters above him and moving inland, evidently in a different air layer.

"Drop . . . little . . . water!" shouted the Russian.

Dalehouse nodded and reached tentatively for the valve cord. He pulled at it with a light touch.

Nothing happened.

He pulled again, harder. Half a liter of ballast sprayed out of the tank, drenching him. Danny had not realized that the passenger was directly under the ballast tank, and gasping, he vowed to change that element of design before he went up again.

But he was flying!

Not easily. Not with grace. Not even with the clumsy control that Kappelyushnikov had taught himself. He spent the first hour chasing Cappy across the sky. It was like one of the fun-house games where you and your girl are on different rotating circles of a ride, when neither of you can take a step except to change from one spinning disk to another. Though Kappelyushnikov did all he could to make capture easy, he never caught the Russian—not that first time.

But—flying! It was exactly the dream he had always had, the dream everyone has had. The total conquest of the air. No jets. No wings. No engines. Just gently swimming through the atmospheric ocean, with no more effort than floating in a saltwater bay.

He reveled in it, and as time went on—not in the first

flight or the tenth, but the supply of hydrogen was limitless, if slow in coming, and he made as many flights as he
could—he began to acquire some skill.

And the problem of reaching the gasbags turned out to
be no problem at all.

He didn't have to seek them out. They were far more
skilled at flying than he, and they came to him, bobbing
around like great jack-o'-lanterns with hideous ticklike
faces, peering inquisitively into his own face, and singing,
singing. Oh! how they sang.

For the next week, or what passed on Klong for a week,
Dalehouse spent every minute he could in the air. The life
of the camp went on almost without him. Even Kappelyushnikov was more earthbound than he. There was nothing to hold Dalehouse there, and he found himself almost
a stranger when he landed, slept, relieved bladder and
bowels, ate, filled his balloons, and soared again. Harriet
snapped at him for demanding more than she could handle
in translation. The camp commander complained bitterly
at the waste of power in generating hydrogen. Jim Morrissey pleaded for time and help in collecting and studying
the other species. Even Cappy was surly about the wear
and tear on his balloons. Danny didn't care. In the skies of
Klong he was alive. He progressed from feckless interloper
to skilled aeronaut; from stranger to, almost, one of the
great drifting swarm. He began to be able to exchange at
least rudimentary ideas with some of the gasbags, especially the biggest of them—two meters across, with a pattern
that looked almost like a tartan. Danny named him "Bon-
nie Prince Charlie," lacking any clue as to what the gasbag
called itself. Himself. Danny began to think of him as
almost a friend. If it had not been for his physical needs,
and one other thing, Dalehouse would hardly have bothered returning to the camp at all.

The one other thing was Harriet.

He could not do without her help in translation. It
wasn't enough. He was convinced a lot of it was wrong.
But it was all he had in the endeavor to communicate with
these beautiful and monstrous creatures of the air. He
raged to the rest of the encampment and insisted on his
complaints being relayed to Earth; he insulted her almost
to the point of tears—from eyes that he would have sworn
had never felt them before. It was not enough to suit him

. . . but voyage by voyage, hour by hour, some sort of communication began to build up.

You never knew what part of your learning was going to be useful. Those long sessions of Chomsky and transactional grammar, the critiques of Lorenz and Dart, the semesters on territoriality and mating rites—none of them seemed very helpful in the skies of Klong. But he blessed every hour of sailplaning and every evening with his local barbershop quartet. The language of the gasbags was music. Not even Mandarin made such demands on pitch and tonality as did their songs. Even before he knew any words, he found himself chiming in on their chorus, and they responded to it with, if not exactly welcome, at least curiosity. The big plaid one even learned to sing Danny Dalehouse's name—as well as he could with a sound-producing mechanism that was deficient in such basic phonemes as the fricative.

Danny learned that some of their songs were not unlike terrestrial birdcalls; there was one for food, and several for danger. There seemed to be three separate warning sounds, one for danger from the ground, and two for dangers, but evidently different kinds of dangers, from the air. One of the terms sounded almost Hawaiian, with its liquids and glottal stops; that seemed to belong to a kind of feral gasbag, a shark of the air that appeared to be their most dangerous natural enemy.

The other—Dalehouse could not be sure, and Harriet was not much help, but it appeared to relate to danger from *above* the air; and not just danger, but that kind of special macho risk-taking danger that involved mortal peril, even death, but was infinitely attractive for reasons he could not perceive. He puzzled over that for hours, making Harriet's life a living hell. On that point, no solution. But the tapes went back to Earth, and the computer matches began to come back, and Harriet was able to construct sentences for him to say. He sang, "I am friend," and, heart-stoppingly, the great crosshatched gasbag he called Charlie responded with a whole song.

"You are, you are, you are friend!" And the whole chorus joined in.

The fickle Klongan weather cooperated for eight calendar days, and then the winds began to rise and the clouds rolled in.

When the winds blew, even the gasbag swarm had

trouble keeping station with each other, and Danny Dalehouse was blown all over the sky. He tried to keep the camp in range; and because he did, so did the whole swarm. But in the effort they were widely separated. When he decided to give up at last, he called good-bye and heard in response the song that seemed to mean "sky danger." Dalehouse repeated it; it seemed appropriate enough, considering the weather. But then he became conscious of a deep fluttering sound behind the whine of the winds—the sound of a helicopter.

Dalehouse abandoned the flock, climbed high enough to find a return wind, then jockeyed himself expertly down through the cross-breezes toward the camp. There it was, dropping through the frayed bottom of a cloud: the Greasy copter, with a Union Jack on its tail strut. So profligate of energy! Not only did they ship that vast mass through tachyon transit at incredible cost, but they had also shipped enough fuel to allow the pilot to take joyrides. And what was it carrying slung between its skids? Some other kind of machine! Typical Greasy oil-hoggery!

Danny swore disgustedly at the wastefulness of the Greasies. With a fraction of the kilocalories they poured out in simple inefficiency and carelessness he could have had a decent computer, Kappelyushnikov could long since have had his glider, Morrissey could have had an outboard motor for his boat and thus a nearly complete selection of marine samples by now. There was something wrong in a world that let a handful of nations burn off energy so recklessly simply because they happened to be sitting on its sources. Sure, when it was gone, they would be as threadbare as the Peruvians or the Paks, but there was no comfort in that. Their downfall would be the world's downfall. . . .

Or at least *that* world's downfall. Maybe something could be worked out for *this* one. Planning. Thought. Preparation. Control of growth so that scarce resources would not be pissed away irrevocably on foolishness. A fair division of Klong's treasures so that no nation and no individual could profit by starving others. An attempt to insure equity to all—

Dalehouse's train of thought snapped as he realized that he had been daydreaming. The winds had carried him farther than he intended, almost out over the sea. He vented hydrogen frantically and came down almost in the water, falling fast. He picked himself up and watched the ripped cases of the balloons floating out of reach in the water. Cappy would be furious.

At least he wouldn't have to carry them on what looked like a long walk back up the shore to the camp, he thought. It was some consolation, but it didn't last long. Before he was halfway back it began to rain.

And it rained. *And* it rained. It was no such ferocious, wind-slamming storm as had hit them soon after the landing, but it lasted most tediously and maddeningly long, far past the point where it was an incident, or an annoyance, to the point, and past the point, where it seemed they were all sentenced to fat, oily drops turning the ground into mud and the camp into a steam bath for all the miserable rest of their lives. There was no chance of ballooning. There were no native balloonists in sight to follow anyway. Kappelyushnikov grumpily seamed and filled new balloons in the hope of better times to come. Harriet Santori tongue-lashed everyone who came near her. Morrissey packed samples in his tent and pored over mysterious pictures and charts, coming out only to stare furiously at the rain and shake his head. Danny composed long tactran messages to SERDCOM and the Double-A-L, demanding gifts for his gasbag friends. Krivitin and Sparky Cerbo concocted some kind of witches' brew from the native berries and got terribly drunk together, and then even more terribly sick as their bodies strove to defend themselves against the alien Klongan protein traces in the popskull. They very nearly died. They surely would have, exploded Alex Woodring, shaking with anger, if they had done any such moron's trick earlier; the first total vulnerability had dwindled to reactions that no longer brought death—only protracted misery. Danny inherited the job of tending them and, at Harriet's angry insistence, of packaging samples of their various untidy emissions for Jim Morrissey to analyze.

Morrissey was crouched over his pictures and diagrams when Danny came in, and when his duty was explained to him, he flatly refused it. "Cripes, Danny, I've got no equipment for that kind of thing. Throw those samples in the crapper. I don't want them."

"Harriet says we must know how serious the poisoning is."

"We already know that, man. They got real sick. But they didn't die."

"Harriet says you can at least analyze them."

"For what? I wouldn't know what to look for."

"Harriet says—"

"Oh, screw Harriet. 'Scuse me, Danny; I didn't mean to remind you of your, uh, indiscretions. Anyway, I've got something better for us to do now that the rain's stopping."

"It hasn't stopped, Jim."

"It's slowing down. When it does stop, Boyne's going to be coming around to collect the backhoe I borrowed from him. I want to use it first."

"For what?"

"For digging up some of our light-fingered friends." He pointed straight down at the floor of the tent. "The ones that swiped Harriet's radio."

"We already tried that."

"Yes, we did. We found out that the important thing is speed. They'll close up the tunnels faster than you'd believe, so we've got to get in, get moving, and get to where they are before they have a chance to react. We'll never have a clear field to pick them up otherwise—unless," he added offhandedly, "we flooded the tunnels with cyanide first. Then we could take our time."

"Is that all you think of—killing?" Dalehouse flared.

"No, no. I wasn't suggesting it. I was *excluding* it. I know you don't like killing off our alien brothers."

Dalehouse took a deep breath. He had seen enough of the balloonists to stop thinking of them as preparations and learn to consider them, almost, as people. The burrowers were still total unknowns to him, and probably rather distasteful—he thought of termites and maggots and all sorts of vile crawling things when he thought of them— but he wasn't ready for genocide.

"So what were you suggesting?" he asked.

"I borrowed a backhoe from Boyne. I want to use it before he takes it back. The thing is, I think I know where to dig."

He gathered up a clump of the papers on the upended footlocker he was using for a desk and handed them over. The sheets on top seemed to be a map, which meant nothing to Dalehouse, but underneath was a sheaf of photographs. He recognized them; they were aerial views of the area surrounding the camp. Some he had taken himself, others were undoubtedly Kappelyushnikov's.

"There's something wrong with them."

He said. "The colors look funny. Why is this part blue?"

"It's false-color photography, Danny. That batch is in the infrared; the bluer the picture, the warmer the ground. Here, see these sort of pale streaks? They're two or three degrees warmer than what's on either side of them."

Dalehouse turned the pictures about in his hands and then asked, "Why?"

"Well, see if you figure it out the same way I did. Look at the one under it, in orthodox color. You took that one. Turn it so it's oriented the same way as the false-color print—there. Do you see those clumps of orangey bushes? They seem to extend in almost straight lines. And those bright red one? They are extensions of the same lines. The bushes are all the same plant; the difference is that the bright red ones are dead. Well, doesn't it look to you like the pale lines in the false-color pictures match up with the lines of bushes in the ortho? And I've poked a probe down along some of those lines, and guess what I found."

"Burrows?" Dalehouse hazarded.

"You're so damn smart," grumbled Morrissey. "All right, show me some real smarts. *Why* are those plants and markings related to the burrows?"

Dalehouse put down the pictures patiently. "That I don't know. But I bet you're going to tell me."

"Well, no. Not for sure. But I can make a smart guess. I'd say digging out tunnels causes some sort of chemical change in the surface. Maybe it leaches out the nutrients selectively? And those plants happen to be the kind that survive best in that kind of soil? Or maybe the castings from the burrowers fertilize them, again selectively. Those are analogues from Earth: you can detect mole runs that way, and earthworms aerate the soil and make things grow better. This may be some wholly different process, but my bet is that that's the general idea."

He sat back on his folding campstool and regarded Danny anxiously.

Dalehouse thought for a second, listening to the dwindling plops of raindrops on the tent roof. "You tell me more than I want to know, Jim, but I think I get your drift. You want me to help you dig them up. How are we going to do that fast enough? Especially in the kind of mud there is out there?"

"That's why I borrowed Boyne's backhoe. It's been in position ever since the rain began. I think the burrowers sense ground vibrations; I wanted them to get used to its being there before we started."

"Did you tell him what you wanted it for? I got the impression they were digging burrows themselves."

"So did I, and that's why I didn't tell him. I said we needed new latrines, and by gosh, we do—sometime or other. Anyway, it's right over the best-looking patch of bushes right now, ready to go. Are you with me?"

Danny thought wistfully of his airborne friends, so much more inviting than these rats or worms. But they were out of reach for the time being . . .

"Sure," he said.

Morrissey grinned, relieved. "Well, that was the easy part. Now we come up against the tough bit: convincing Harriet to go along."

Harriet was every bit as tough as advertised. "You don't seriously *mean*," she began, "that you want to drag everybody out in a *downpour* just for the sake of digging a few *holes*?"

"Come on, Harriet," said Morrissey, trying not to explode. "The rain's almost stopped."

"And if it has, there are a *thousand* more important things to do!"

"Will be fun, Gasha," Kappelyusknikov chipped in. "Digging for foxholes like landed oil-rich English country gentlemen! Excellent sport."

"And it isn't just a few holes," Morrissey added. "Look at the seismology traces. There are big things down there, chambers twenty meters long and more. Not just tunnels. Maybe cities."

Harriet said cuttingly, "Morrissey, if you wonder why none of us have any confidence in you, that's just the reason. You'll say any stupid thing that comes into your head. Cities! There are some indications of shafts and chambers somewhat bigger than the tunnels directly under the surface, yes. But I would not call them—"

"All right, all right. They're not cities. Maybe they

aren't even villages, but they're something. At the least, they are something like breeding chambers where they keep their young. Or store their food. Or, Christ, I don't know, maybe it's where they have ballet performances or play bingo—what's the difference? Just because they're bigger, it follows that they're probably more important. It will be less likely, or at least harder, for them to seal them off."

He looked toward Alex Woodring, who coughed and said, "I think that's reasonable, Harriet. Don't you?"

She pursed her lips thoughtfully. "Reasonable? No, I certainly wouldn't call it *reasonable*. Of course, you're our leader, at least nominally, and if you think it wise for us to depart from the—"

"I do think it's a good idea, Harriet," Woodring said boldly.

"If you'll let me finish, please? I was saying, if you think we should depart from the agreement we all made that group decisions should be arrived at *unanimously*, not by a vote or some one person throwing his weight around, then I suppose I have nothing further to say."

"Gasha, dear," said Kappelyushnikov soothingly, "shut up, please? Tell us plan, Jim."

"You bet! First thing we do is open up as big a hole as we can with the backhoe. All of us are out there with shovels, and we jump in. What we want is specimens. We grab what we see. We should take them pretty much by surprise, and besides," he said, with some self-satisfaction, "two of us can carry these." He held up his camera. "They've got good bright strobes. I got that idea from Boyne when we were drinking together; I think that's what they do at the Greasies'. They go in with these things, partly to get pictures and mostly to dazzle them. While they're temporarily blinded we can grab them easily."

Dalehouse put in, "Temporarily, Jim?"

"Well," Morrissey said reluctantly, "no, I'm not real sure about that part. Their eyes are probably pretty delicate—but hell, Danny, we don't even know if they have any eyes in the first place!"

"Then how do they get dazzled?"

"All right. But still, that's the way I want to do it. And we'll take walkie-talkies. If anything, uh, goes wrong—" He hesitated and then started over. "If you should get disoriented or anything, you just dig *up*. You should be able to do that with your bare hands. If not, you just turn your walkie-talkie on. We might be unable to get voice communication from under the surface, but we know from the radio that was stolen that we can at least get carrier sound, so we'll RDF you and dig you out. That's if anything goes wrong."

Kappelyushnikov leaned forward and placed his hand on the biologist's mouth. "Dear Jim," he said, "please don't encourage us anymore, otherwise we all quit. Let's do this; no more talk."

Predictably, Harriet would have nothing to do with the venture, and she insisted that at least two of the men stay behind—"In case we have to dig you heroes out." But Sparky Cerbo volunteered to go in, and Alicia Dair claimed she could run the backhoe better than anyone else in the camp. So they had half a dozen in coveralls, head lamps, goggles, and gloves, ready to jump in when Morrissey signaled the digging to start.

He had been right about the mud; there wasn't any, except right around the main paths of the camp, where they had trodden the Klongan ground cover to death. But the soil was saturated, asd the backhoe threw as much moisture as it did dirt. In less than a minute it had broken through.

Morrissey swallowed, crossed himself, and jumped into the hole. Alex Woodring followed, then Danny, then Kappelyushnikov, di Paolo, and Sparky Cerbo.

The plan was to break up into pairs, each couple to follow one tunnel. The trouble with the plan was that it was predicated on there being more than two directions to take. There weren't. The pit they dropped into was not much more than a meter broad. It smelled damp and—and bad, Danny thought, like a stale cage of pet mice; and it was no more than a tunnel. Di Paolo jumped down onto Danny's ankle, and Sparky Cerbo followed, got him square in the middle of the back. They were all tangled together, cursing and grumbling, and if there was a burrower within a kilometer that didn't know they were coming, that burrower, Danny thought, would have to be dead.

"Quit screwing around!" yelled Morrissey over his shoulder. "Dalehouse! Sparky! You two follow me."

Dalehouse got himself turned around in time to see Morrissey's hips and knees, outlined against the glow from his head lamp, moving away. The cross-section of the tunnel was more oval than round, shallower than it was broad; they couldn't quite move on hands and knees, but they could scramble well enough on thighs and elbows.

"See anything?" he called ahead.

"No. Shut up. Listen." Morrissey's voice was muffled, but Dalehouse could hear it well enough. Past it and through it he thought he heard something else. What? It was faint and hard to identify—squirrel-like squeals and rustlings, perhaps, and larger, deeper sounds from farther away. His own breath, the rubbing of his gear, the sounds the others made all conspired to drown it out. But there was *something*.

A bright flare made him blink. It hurt his eyes. It came from Morrissey's strobe, up ahead. All Dalehouse got of it was what trickled back, impeded by the rough dirt walls almost without reflectance. In the other direction it must have been startling. Now he was sure he heard the squirrel squeals, and they sounded anguished. As well they should, Danny realized, with a moment's empathy for the burrowers. What could light have meant to them, ever, but some predator breaking in, and death and destruction following?

He bumped into Morrissey's feet and stopped. Over his shoulder, Morrissey snarled, "The fuckers! They've blocked it."

"The tunnel?"

"Christ, yes, the tunnel! It's packed tight, too. How the hell could they do that so fast?"

Dalehouse had a moment's atavistic fear. Blocked! And in the other direction? He rolled onto his side, extinguished his light, and peered back between his feet down the tunnel. Past Sparky's crouching form he could see—he was sure he could see—the reassuring dim red glow from the Klongan sky. Even so, he could feel the muscles at the back of his neck tensed and painful with the ancient human terror of being buried alive, and he suddenly remembered that the direction they had taken was the one that went under the backhoe. What if its weight crushed the roof through and pinned them? "Ah, Jim," he called. "What do you think? Should we get back to the barn?"

Pause. Then, angrily, "Might as well. We're not doing any good here. Maybe the guys had better luck the other way."

But Cappy and the others were already outside, helping them out as they emerged. They had got only eight or nine meters into their tunnel before it was blocked; Dalehouse's group had gone more than twice as far. It came out the same in the end, though, Dalehouse reflected. Incredible that their reactions could be so fast! No doubt they had been trained into them over endless Klongan millennia. Whatever the reason, it was not going to be easy to collect a specimen, much less try to make contact. Danny thought of his airborne friends longingly; how much nicer to fly to make contact than to wiggle through the mud like a snake!

Kappelyushnikov was brushing him off, and then, more lingeringly, doing the same for Sparky Cerbo. "Dearest girl," he said, "you are disgracefully filthy! Let us all go swim in lake, take our minds off troubles."

Good-naturedly the girl moved away from his hand. "Maybe we should see what Harriet wants first," she suggested. And, sure enough, Harriet was standing at the entrance to the headquarters tent, a hundred meters away, evidently waiting for them to come to her.

As they straggled in, she looked them up and down with distaste. "A total failure, I see," she said, nodding. "Of course, that was to be expected."

"Harriet," Jim Morrissey began dangerously.

She raised her hand. "It doesn't matter. Perhaps you'll be interested in what has happened while you were gone."

"Harriet, we were only gone twenty or thirty minutes!" Morrissey exploded.

"Nevertheless. First there was a tactran signal. We're being reinforced, and so are the Peeps. Second—" She stepped aside to let them pass through into the tent. The others who had stayed behind were clustered inside, looking, Dalehouse thought, curiously self-satisfied. "I believe you wanted a specimen of those underground creatures? We found one trying to steal some of our supplies. Of course, it would have been easier if so many of you hadn't been wasting your time on foolishness, so you could have helped when we needed you—"

Kappelyushnikov bellowed, "Gasha! Get to point, right now. You caught specimen for us?"

"Of course," she said. "We put him in one of Morrissey's cages. I was quite severely scratched doing it, but that's about what you can expect when—"

They didn't let her finish; they were all inside and staring.

The stale mouse-cage smell was a thousand times stronger, almost choking Danny Dalehouse, but there it was. It was nearly two meters long, tiny eyes set close together above its snout, squeezed tight in anguish. It was squealing softly—Danny would almost have said brokenheartedly— to itself. It was gnawing at the metal bars of the cage and simultaneously scrabbling at the plastic flooring with duck-foot-shaped claws. It was covered with a sort of dun-colored down or short fur; it seemed to have at least six pairs of limbs, all stubby, all clawed, and all incredibly strong.

Whatever its teeth were made of, they were *hard;* one of the bars of the cage was almost gnawed through. And its squeals of pain never stopped.

NINE

•

THE SWARM WAS half fledglings now, tiny balloonets that had just cast off their parachuting threads of silk and now struggled bravely to keep up with the great two-meter adult spheres. In the constant chorus of the swarm, the fledglings' voices were as tiny as their gasbags. Their shrill peepings used the least possible amount of hydrogen, to preserve their precarious lift balance against the few drops in their ballast bladders.

Charlie patrolled majestically through the swarm, driving the bulk of his body reprovingly against a cluster of infant balloonets who were singing against the swarm melody, rotating his eye patches to scan the skies for *ha'aye'i*, listening to the countersongs of praise and complaint from the other adults of the swarm, and always, always, leading them as they sang. There was much praise, and much complaint. The praise he took for granted. To the complaint he attended with more care, ready either to remedy or rebuke. Three females sang despairingly of little ones who dropped their flying tails too soon, or who could not hold their hydrogen and so drifted helplessly down to the voracious world below. Another pealed a dirge of anger and sorrow, blaming the deformed fledglings on the Persons of the Middle Sun.

This was just; and Charlie led the swarm in a concurrence of sympathy and advice. "Never"—(*Never, never, never,* sang the chorus)—"never again must we breed near the New Suns."

The females chorused agreement, but some of the males sang in counterpoint, "But how can we know which is real Heaven-Danger and which is not? And where may we breed at all? The Persons of the Three Suns are under all our air!"

Charlie's answering song was serene. "I will ask my

116

friend of the Middle Sun. He will know." (*He will know, he will know,* chorused the swarm.)

But a male sang a dire question. "And when the swarming rapture is on us, will we remember?"

"Yes," sang Charlie. "We will remember because we must." (*We must, we must.*)

That should have settled it. And yet, the song of the swarm was not at peace. Undertones buzzed and discorded against the dominant themes. Even Charlie's own song faltered now and then, and repeated itself when it should have burst into triumphant new themes. Currents were stirring under the surface of his mind. They never reached consciousness; if they had, no power could have kept him from expressing them in song. But they were there. Worries. Doubts. Puzzles. Who were these Persons of the Three Suns? Where had they come from? They seemed the same, as like as any swarms of balloonists. Yet Charlie's friend 'Anny 'Alehouse had explained that they were not the same.

First there had been the Persons of the Small Sun. They had seemed no more than another species of devouring Earth-Danger creatures in the beginning, although they had created a tiny sun almost at once. But their camp was almost at the limit of Charlie's range, and the swarm had not troubled themselves about those Persons.

Then there was the group of Charlie's friend; and almost at once, the third group, the Persons of the Big Sun. They were worrisome! Their sun was always shining brightly, brighter than the Heaven-Danger at its brightest. Since it was almost the deepest of Charlie's instincts to swarm in the direction of a bright light, it was actual pain to turn and swim away from the Big Sun. They had almost been trapped when the Persons first arrived—when all three of the parties of Persons of the Suns arrived— because each of them came roaring down through the air on a pillar of Sun-Flame. But none had been close enough to cause them to swarm. By the time the flock had maneuvered near, the flames were gone and the lights were darkened. Then the Persons of the Big Sun had sent one of themselves up into the air in the great queer thing that fluttered and rattled; it was harder than the *ha'aye'i* Sky-Danger, and even more deadly. Something about it drew balloonists into its swinging claws, and more than a dozen of Charlie's swarm had been ripped open and gone flutter-

ing down to the ground, helpless, despairing, and silent.
Now they avoided it in fear and sorrow. Two out of three
of the groups of New Persons, and both to be avoided! The
one because they killed, the other because they did not fly
at all, were no more than any other Ground-Danger, would
not have been thought to be Persons at all—

Except for 'Anny 'Alehouse.

Charlie sang of his friend, who redeemed his whole
race. 'Anny 'Alehouse and his sometimes companion,
'Appy—they were Persons! They flew as Persons flew, by
the majesty and the grace of the air itself. It was a sad
thing that even their Middle Sun had flared like a true
Heaven-Danger and caused the flock to breed poorly. But
it did not occur to Charlie to blame Morrissey's flare on
Dalehouse or Kappelyushnikov; it did not occur to him to
think of blame at all. When Kung flared, the balloonists
bred. They could not help it. They did not try. They had
never developed defenses against a false flare, one lacking
in the actinic radiation that helped them make their
hydrogen and triggered their fertility. They had never
needed any—until now. And they had no way to learn a
defense.

The swarm was drifting toward a swelling cumulus
cloud; Charlie swelled his singing sac and boomed out,
"Hive up, my brothers!" (*Hive up, hive up,* came the
answering chorus.) "Hive up, sisters and mates! Hive up,
young and old! Watch for *ha'aye'i* in the wet shadows!
Huddle the little ones close!"

Every member of the swarm was singing full-throatedly
now as the swarm compacted, swimming into the ruddy-
pink, cottony edges of the cloud. They could see each
other only as ghosts, except for the oldest and biggest
males, whose luminous markings gave them more visibility. But they could hear the songs, and Charlie and the
other senior males patrolled the periphery of the swarm. If
ha'aye'i were there, the males could not defend the
swarm—could not even defend themselves to any purpose.
But they could sing warning, and then the swarm would
scatter in all directions, so that only the slowest and
weakest would be caught.

Cumulus clouds formed at the top of updrafts of warm
air, and the *ha'aye'i* often sought them out to supplement
their comparatively weak lift. There was always a price;
what the *ha'aye'i* gained in speed and control, not to

mention claws and jaws, they paid for in smaller lifting bags, so that for them it was always an effort to stay in the air. The *ha'aye'i* were sharks of the air. They never slept, never stopped moving—and were always hungry.

But this time the swarm was lucky. There were no killer balloons in the cloud, and they emerged intact. Charlie trumpeted out a song of thanksgiving as the flock entered clear air again. All joined.

The swarm was drifting toward the Heat Pole. Charlie rotated his eye patches to catch clues of the movement of the air. He always knew in what direction the winds blew on each level; he was taught by the movement of cloudlets, by the fluttering of dropped fledgling silk, most of all by a lifetime of experience, so that he did not have to think of how to capture a favorable wind; he *knew*, as surely as any New Yorker hurrying down Fifth Avenue knows the number of the next cross street. He did not want to stray too far from his friend of the Middle Sun, whom he had not seen for some time. He trumpeted for the swarm to rise a hundred meters. The other males took up his song, and from all the gasbags, great and small, drops of water ballast fell. There would be no trouble replacing it for the adults, who were naturally and automatically catching and swallowing the tiny misting of dew during their passage through the clouds. The smaller ones made hard work of it. But they valiantly released swallowed gas into their bags, and the females watchfully butted the littlest ones higher. The swarm stayed together at the new level as its drift changed back in the direction of the camp of the Middle Sun.

No *ha'aye'i* in sight. Plenty of water on their skins to lick off and swallow, part to hold as ballast, part to dissociate into the oxygen they metabolized and the hydrogen that gave them lift. Charlie was well content. It was good to be a balloonist! He returned to the song of thanksgiving.

They were nearing the edges of their territory, and another swarm bobbed high above them a few kilometers away. Charlie observed them without concern. There was no rivalry between swarms. Sometimes two of them would float side by side for long periods, or even coalesce. Sometimes when two swarms were joined, individuals from one would adhere to another. No one thought anything of that. From that moment they were full members of their

new swarm and joined in its songs. But it was more
common that each should stay in its own unmarked but
known volume of air. They grazed the pollen fields of their
own home air without coveting those of their neighbors.
Though after half a dozen breedings there might be no
single individual still alive of the original swarm, the
swarm itself would still drift placidly over the same ten
thousand square kilometers of ground. One place was
almost like another. Over any one of those square kilometers the sustaining air was always around them. The pollen
clouds blew through them all.

Still, some parts of their range were more attractive
than others. The mesa where the Persons of the Big Sun
had built their shining shells and lit their blazing lamps
had been one of their favorites, pollen drifting down off
the hills in a pleasant stream, and few ha'aye'i. Charlie
sang sorrowfully of his regret as he thought of it, now that
they must avoid it for all time to come. The bay of the
ocean-lake where 'Anny 'Alehouse lived was, on the contrary, usually to be avoided. The water evaporating from
the sea meant columns of rising cloud, and killer balloons
no doubt in half the columns. If any member of the swarm
had chosen to question Charlie's decision to return there, it
would have been quite reasonable to do so, in practical
terms. But in terms of the lives of the balloonists themselves it was quite impossible. Their group decisions were
never questioned. If a senior adult sang, "Do thus," it was
done. Charlie was the most senior of adults, and so his
song usually prevailed. Not always. Now and then another
adult would sing a contrary proposal ten minutes later, but
if Charlie returned to his own ten minutes after that, there
was no complaint. Each of the other adults loyally picked
up his song, and the swarm complied.

There was also the consideration that Charlie had
brought to the swarm his friend of the Middle Sun, with
his astonishing and fascinating new sounds. This was a
Person! Puzzling, yes. But not like those earthbound grub-
bers of the Small Sun or the strange creatures of the Big
Sun who flew only with the help of killing machines. As
the swarm drew near the camp of the Middle Sun, all of
the adults rotated their bodies so that their tiny faces,
like the features of engorged ticks, looked downward,
anxious to spy 'Anny or 'Appy. Even the balloonets were

caught up in the happy fever of the search; and when the first of the swarm spotted Danny rising to meet them, the song of the flock became triumphant.

How strange 'Anny 'Alehouse looked this time! His lifting sac had always been disagreeably knobby and lacking in any decent coloration, but now it was swollen immensely and knobbier than ever. Charlie might not have recognized him if there had been more than one other like him in all the world to confuse him with. But it was 'Anny all the same. The swarm swallowed hydrogen and dropped to meet him, singing the song of welcome Charlie had invented for his friend.

Dalehouse was almost as overjoyed to see the swarm again as the swarm was to see Dalehouse. It had been a long time! After the storm there had been the time for cleaning up; and before they were through the second ship had dropped out of the tachyon charge state to bring them new people and a whole host of new equipment. That was fine enough, but to make them welcome and to integrate the new things into the old had taken time—more than time. Some of what they had brought had been gifts for the balloonists, and to deliver the gifts meant more load had to be lifted, which meant a bigger cluster of balloons, which meant making and filling new ones and redesigning the ballasting system to compensate. Danny was far from sure it had been worth it.

But there had also been half a kilo of microfiches from the Double-A-L, and those had been worth a lot. Professor D. Dalehouse was now a name to conjure with among xenobiologists. They had quoted his reports in every paper. And the papers themselves had given much to think of. Among the conferees at Michigan State a battle had raged. In the evolution of the balloonists, where was Darwin? When a female scattered her filamentary eggs into the air of Klong like the burst of a milkweed pod and all the males spewed sperm at once, where was the selection of the fittest? What kind of premium on strength, agility, intelligence, or sexual attraction would make each generation somehow infinitesimally more "fit" than the one before in an ontogeny where all the males spurted all their genes into a cloud of mixed female genetic material, with the wind for a mixer and random chance deciding who fathered which on whom? The balloonists kept no Leporello lists. Well any one of them might have fathered a *mille-tre;* but if so he never knew it.

Charlie could have settled the debate if asked. All the balloonists were sexually mature as soon as they were able to drop their spider-silk parachute threads and float free. But all balloonists were not equal in size.

The older, the bigger. The bigger, the more sperm or eggs they flung into the collective pool. Human beings, by contrast, cease to play a part in evolution before half their lives are over. Wisdom does not come at twenty-five. By the time there is a significant difference between a Da Vinci and a dolt the days of breeding are over. Selection plays no further part. Nor does it in resistance to the degenerative diseases of the old, which is why in two million years the human race has not selected against cancer, arthritis, or arteriosclerosis. Raunchy young cells have been disciplined by the stresses of fifty thousand generations. But past the breeding age the cell runs out of programming. It doesn't know what to do next. It begins to fall apart.

With the balloonists it was different. The Charlie-sized giants among them sprayed half a liter of mist-of-sperm into each receptive cloud of eggs, while the tiny first-swarm male balloonets squeezed out hardly a drop. The Charlies had proved their fitness to survive by the most conclusive of tests: they had survived.

Dalehouse was eager to try to settle questions like that as he called to Charlie and swung in to meet him, even more eager to try the new language elements the big computers on Earth had generated for him. What was occupying most of his attention, though, was his gift from Earth. Like the swarm's greeting song, it was an example of the thing his society did best. It was a weapon.

It was not entirely a free gift, Dalehouse reflected, but then there is nothing without a price. Charlie's song cost him some of his reserve of lifting gas, as the songs that were their life always cost the swarm. If they sang, they vented gas. If they vented gas, they lost lift. If they lost lift, sooner or later they drifted helplessly down to the eager mouths on the surface and were eaten. Or, almost as bad, had to live on there, helpless and voiceless, until they were able to accumulate and dissociate enough water molecules to recharge their stocks—quickly if Kung was kind enough to flare for them, painfully slowly otherwise. It was a price they paid gladly. To live was to sing; to be quiet was to be dead anyway. But in the end, for most of them, it was the price of their lives.

The price of the gift Danny Dalehouse brought was the lives of the five balloonists who had been sent back to Earth in the return capsule.

The designers at Camp Detrick had made good use of the samples. The two who were dead on arrival were dissected at once. Those were the lucky ones. The other three were studied *in vivo*. The biggest and strongest of them lasted two weeks.

The Camp Detrick experimenters also had a price to pay, because eight of them came down with the Klongan hives, and one had the severe misfortune to have his skull fill up with antigenic fluid, so that he would never again for the rest of his life stress an experimental subject. Or, indeed, hold a fork by himself. But probably the balloonists who had been his subjects would not have thought that price unfair.

Danny Dalehouse unslung the lightweight carbine from one shoulder and practiced aiming it. Its stock was metal shell, and sintered metal at that; it weighed hardly a kilogram, but half that weight was in high-velocity bullets. It was poor design. He felt sure the recoil would kick him halfway across the sky if he fired it, and anyway, what was the use of high-velocity bullets? what target was there in the Klongan air that needed that sort of impact to destroy it? But the word from Earth brought by the reinforcement party that had been labeled a UN peacekeeping committee was that it must be carried. So he carried it.

He put it back and, somewhat uncomfortably, took Charlie's gift off the other shoulder. Now, that was more like it. Somebody somewhere had understood what Charlie's people could do and what they needed in order to protect themselves against predators. It weighed even less than the carbine, and it contained no propellants at all. Its tiny winch could be operated by the claws of a Charlie to tighten a long-lasting elastic cord. Its trigger was sized to fit a balloonist, and what it fired was a cluster of minute needles or, alternatively, a capsule of some sort of fluid.

Needles were for airborne predators. The fluid, or so Danny was told, was against creatures like the crabrats, if a balloonist was forced down and needed defense; and it would only incapacitate them without killing.

It would tax all of Dalehouse's linguistics to convey any part of that to Charlie, but the way to get it done was to begin. He held the crossbow up and sang, carefully attending to the notes he had been taught by the computers at Texas A&M. "I have brought you a gift."

Charlie responded with a burst of song. Dalehouse could understand no more than a few phrases, but clearly it was a message of gratitude and polite inquiry; and anyway, the little tape recorder at his belt was getting it all down for later study.

Danny moved on to the next sentence he had been taught. "You must come with me to find a *ha'aye'i*." That was hard to sing; English does not come with glottal stops, and practicing it for an hour had left Dalehouse's throat sore. But Charlie seemed to understand, because the song of thanks changed to a thin melody of concern. Danny laughed. "Do not fear," he sang. "I will be a *ha'aye'i* to the *ha'aye'i*. We will destroy them with this gift, and the swarm will no more need to fear."

Song of confusion, with the words *the swarm* repeated over and over, not only by Charlie but by all his flock.

The hardest part of all was yet to come. "You must leave the swarm," sang Dalehouse. "They will be safe. We will return. But now just you and I must fly to seek a *ha'aye'i*."

It took time; but the message ultimately seemed to get across. It was a measure of the balloonist's trust in his friend from Earth that he was willing to embark on so fearful an adventure with him. The members of the flock *never* left it by choice. For more than an hour after they had droppped to a lower level and left the flock behind, Charlie's song was querulous and sad. And no *ha'aye'i* appeared. They left the Food Bloc camp far behind, drifting down the shore of the sea-lake and then across a neck of it to the vicinity of the Peeps' tattered colony. For some time Dalehouse had been wondering if the Texas computers had really given him the right words to sing. But then Charlie's song turned to active fear. They dipped low under a bank of clouds, warm-weather cumuli that looked like female balloonists turned upside down, and from one of them dropped the predatory form of a killer.

Danny was uneasily tempted to slay this first one with his own carbine. It was frightening to see the *ha'aye'i* stoop toward them. But he wanted to demonstrate his gift to Charlie.

"Watch!" he cried, clumsily grasping the grip that had been designed for balloonist claws. He circled the swelling form of the airshark in the cross-haired sight, designed for balloonist eye patches, feeling the low vibrations of Charlie's muttered song of terror. At twenty meters he squeezed the trigger.

A dozen tiny metal spikes lashed out at the *ha'aye'i*, spreading like the cone of fire of a shotgun shell. One was enough. The shark's bag ripped open with a puff of moisture. The creature screamed once in pain and surprise, and then had no more breath to scream with. It dropped past them, its horrid little face writhing, its claws clutching uselessly toward them, meters away.

A bright trill of surprise from Charlie, and then a roaring paean of triumph. "This is a great good thing, 'Anny 'Alehouse! Will you slay all the *ha'aye'i* for us?"

"No, not I, Charlie. You will do it for yourself!" And hanging in the air, Danny showed him the clever little crank that worked the elastic cord, the simple breech that the cluster of needles dropped into. For a creature who had never used tools before, Charlie was quick to grasp the operation. Dalehouse had him fire a practice round at a cloud and then watched patiently while the balloonist painfully wound the winch for himself and loaded again.

They were no longer quite alone. Unbidden, the swarm had drifted after them and was floating half a kilometer away, all their eye patches rotated toward them, their distant song sweet and plaintive, like a puppy's lonely begging to be let in. And down below, the Peeps' camp was near; Dalehouse could see one or two upturned faces curiously staring at them. Let them look, he thought virtuously; let them see how the Food-Exporting Powers were helping the native races of Klong, if they had so little to do with their time. There were only a handful of them left of the original expedition, and their much-boasted reinforcements showed no signs of arriving.

Reinforcements. Reminded, Dalehouse began the rest of his message for Charlie. "This gift," he sang, "is yours. But we would ask a gift of you, too."

"What gift?" sang Charlie politely.

"I do not know words," sang Danny, "but soon I will show you. My swarm-mates ask you to carry some small things to other places. Some you will drop to the ground. Some you will bring back." Teaching Charlie how to point the cameras and sound-recording instruments was going to take forever, Dalehouse thought glumly; and how were they ever going to tell him where to drop the clusters of wolftrap sensors and seismic mikes? What seemed so simple on Earth was something else entirely on Klong—

"Beware, beware!" sang the distant, frantic voices of the swarm.

Tardily Danny looked around. The ha'aye'i's rush caught them unaware. It came from behind and below, where Dalehouse had not thought to look. And Charlie, fondling his new toy and trying to understand what Dalehouse wanted of him, had been careless.

If it had not been for the distant shrieking of the swarm, the creature might have had them both. But Charlie spun faster than Dalehouse, and before Danny could unlimber his carbine the balloonist had shown how well he had learned his lesson by killing the killer. Either of them could have reached out and caught the long, wicked claws of the ha'aye'i as it fell past them; it was that close.

"Well done!" yelled Dalehouse, and Charlie pealed in rapture:

"Well, well done! How great a gift!" They rose to rejoin the swarm—

Lances of golden fire reached up faintly toward the flock from the Peeps' camp below.

"My God!" shouted Danny. "The fools are setting off fireworks!"

The rockets exploded into showers of sparks, and all through the swarm balloonists were bursting into bright hydrogen flame.

TEN

●

WHEN DULLA WAS AWAKE, which was not much of the time, he was only blurrily conscious of what was going on. At first there had been a recurrent *whick, whick* that he could not identify, and some person who seemed vaguely familiar manhandling him into whatever it was that was making the sounds. Then pain—a lot of pain. Then long periods when people were talking to him or around him. But he felt no impulse to answer. In his brief conscious times he discovered by and by that he was no longer in pain. The treatment the Greasies had given him had been unpleasant, but it seemed to have done the trick. He was alive. He was rehydrated. The swellings had gone down. He was no longer blind. He was only very weak.

When he woke up and realized that he was not only awake but actually seemed able to keep his eyes open for awhile, Feng Hua-tse was standing by his cot. The Chinaman was looking very stretched out, Dulla thought with some contempt; he looked even worse than Dulla himself felt.

"You are feeling better?" Feng asked sadly.

Dulla thought it over. "Yes. I think so. What has happened?"

"I am glad you are feeling better. The long-noses brought you here from the place of your beetle friends. They said you would live, but I didn't think so. It has been a long time. Do you want to eat?"

"Yes—no," Dulla corrected himself. "I do, but not at this moment. I want the w.c. first."

"Shall I help you?"

"No. I can do it myself."

"I am glad of that, too," said Feng, who had been functioning as bedpan orderly for all the days of Ahmed Dulla's recovery and longer before that than he cared to remember. The Pakistani raised himself painfully from the inflatable cot and moved slowly toward the slit-trench latrine.

He gazed disapprovingly around the camp. One of the noises he had been hearing identified itself for him: a slapping, rasping sound that turned out to be the water-wheel. So at least there should be power. But where were the promised floodlights, the growing crops, the comforts? Where were all the people?

Feng had followed him and stood gazing mournfully as Dulla relieved himself. "Why do you stand there?" snapped Dulla, tying up his pajama cord and making hard work of it. "What has happened? Why has so little been done?"

The leader spread his hands. "What can I say? There were ten of us. Two died with you in this venture you found so necessary. One other died here. Two were so ill they had to be returned to Earth—by courtesy of the Greasies. We had no one well enough to fly the return capsule. The Italian is asleep, and the two women are gathering fuel."

"Gathering fuel! Are we become peasants again, Feng?"

The leader sighed. "I have done my best," he said. It was a sentence he had been saying over and over to himself for a long time. "Help is coming. Heir-of-Mao himself has ordered it. Two great ships, material and persons, soon—"

"Soon! And until then, what? Do we do nothing?"

"Go back to bed," said Feng wearily. "You exhaust me, Dulla. Eat if you will. There is food. The Fats gave it to us; otherwise there would be none."

"And now we are beggars," sneered Dulla. He swayed and caught hold of Feng's shoulder. "For this I studied and came all these light-years! For this I almost died! How foolish we will all look when we return in disgrace to Earth!"

Feng shook his head heavily. He disengaged the Pakistani's hand from his shoulder and stepped downwind—the man was odorously unwashed. He did not need to hear any of this. He knew it for himself. He had accepted the charity of the Fats for the food without which they all would have starved; of the Greasies for the rescue of Dulla and for the return to Earth of the sick members of the expedition—who would no doubt even now be telling their debriefers how badly Feng Hua-tse had managed the expedition with which he had been entrusted. There would be large-character posters going up in K'ushui about that even now. They would be very critical of him. When they got back to Earth—*if* they got back—the best hope he had was to become a barefoot biochemist along the Yellow River again.

Of course, if somehow they mercifully spared him until the two great ships arrived—

Ah, then! He had pored over the tactran messages and pictures yearningly. The second ship would bring not ten, not fifteen, but a majestic thirty-four new persons. An agronomist! Someone to take up Feng's own pitiful beginnings, the mushrooms he had sown, the wheat seedlings he had coaxed to sprout—the fittest of them would survive, and the fittest of their descendants would flourish. There were two more translators, both split-brained, one of them a skilled littoral pisciculturist as well. The Great Water might yet yield food they could eat. A doctor—no, Feng corrected himself, a fully schooled surgeon with a world reputation in the treatment of traumatic injuries. True, he was nearly two meters tall and black as a boy-child's hair, by his photograph. But still. Three of the new additions had had limnology crash courses, and one of them, who had once been an officer in the Red Guards, had also had three years of experience as a scout in the Gobi, and later in the Himalayas.

And the worldly goods the other ship would carry! Photovoltaic generators, capable of pouring out 230-volt a.c. in really significant quantities. Plastic to spare. Pioneering tools—axes and machetes, and a few rifles for the collection of specimens as well as for "game." Folbots. Magnesium-frame bicycles. A doubly redundant computer with no fewer than six remote-access terminals. Radio equipment. Laser equipment. Food. More food; food enough for all of them for many months . . .

It seemed a dream!

But what was not a dream was that very surely, Feng knew, among those thirty-four persons would be one who would come over to him and quietly say, "Feng Hua-tse? I am directed by Heir-of-Mao to receive your report on why your custodianship of this project has not lived up to expectations." And then would come the sweating time. There would be no excuses accepted. He would not be interested in the mushrooms that were refusing to grow or the specimens that Feng himself had painfully kept alive. He would only be interested in why three had died and two had been sent home and ten had accomplished so very little.

All this was in Feng Hua-tse's mind, but all he said was, "Go back to sleep, Dulla. I am out of patience with you."

Dulla did not go back to sleep. Anger had given him strength. What he did was wake up the Italian.

"Oh, you are alive again?" Spadetti yawned and rubbed the blue-black stubble on his chin. "We thought you were going to die," he said cheerfully. "I almost bet a day's ration on it. I would have been very angry to lose."

"I have been talking to Feng, that bungler!"

"It is not all Uazzi's fault, Dulla. We were the first. We made the mistakes that must be made so others can learn."

"I did not want to be teacher to the Fats and the Greasies! I did not want them here at all. This can be our planet, to shape as we will!"

"Yes," admitted Spadetti, "I had some such thought myself. But, chi sa, what can you do? Each step seemed right at the time. Even yours, to make friends with the natives—"

"Those beasts! One cannot make friends with them."

"Oh, not true, Dulla. Our rivals have succeeded. The Fats have balloonists carrying their cameras all over the planet, or so they promise on the tactran. The Greasies are teaching their moles and earthworms how to burrow under our camp and listen to what we say. Perhaps they are listening now."

"Nonsense! How stupid you are!"

"Stupid, perhaps, but no, it is not entirely nonsense," smiled the Italian, unoffended. "Perhaps I have made it a little bit of a joke, but I am not sure that I am joking. And what have we accomplished? I will be more exact, Dulla. What did you yourself accomplish, except to get two people killed, when you visited our frutti-del-mare friends? We failed. It is as simple as that." He yawned and scratched. "Now, Dulla, per favore, let me wake up by myself a little, I am not so happy with this reality around me that I want to leave my dreams so rudely."

"Drink your wine and dream then," said Dulla coldly.

"Oh, Dulla! But that is not a bad idea. If one only had a true wine instead of this filth."

"Pig," said Dulla, but softly enough that Spadetti did not have to admit he had heard it. He returned to his cot and sat heavily on the edge of it, ignoring Spadetti's soft-voiced imprecations as he tasted the jungle juice he had made for himself. Perhaps it would kill him. Why not? The smell of it kept Dulla from wanting to eat, though he knew he should; he judged he had lost ten kilos at least since landing on Son of Kung, and he could not spare very many more. He sat breathing heavily, sucking through a straw at a flask of flat, tepid water from the still. By and by he noticed that there was a plastic pouch under his bed. He upended it and covered the cot with a drift of tiny white fiche prints.

"I see you have found your love letters," called the Italian from across the tent. "Unfortunately, I cannot read your language. But she is quite a pretty girl."

Dulla ignored him. He gathered them up and carried them to the radio shack, where the only working viewer was. Spadetti had been right; they were almost all from the Bulgarian girl, and they all said much the same thing. She missed him. She thought of him. She consoled her lonely sorrow with the memory of their days together in Sofia.

But in the photographs there was Ana in Paris, Ana in London, Ana in Cairo, Ana in New York. She seemed to be having an interesting time without him.

Rich countries! At bottom, were they not all the same, whether the wealth was in fuel or in food? Wealth was wealth! A greater distance separated him from the fat Bulgarians than from—from even the Krinpit, he thought, and then realized almost at once that he was being unjust. Nan was not like that. But then, she had had the advantage of spending much of her childhood in Hyderabad.

Away from the smell of the Italian's imitation wine, Dulla realized he was hungry. He found some cracked corn and ate it while he went through Ana's letters quick-ly, and then, more slowly, the synoptics from Earth. Much had happened while he was out of it. The Fats had been reinforced from Earth—it was called a UN peacekeeping team, but that deceived only the most naive. The Greasies had established a satellite astronomical observatory and were monitoring changes in the radiation of Kung. There were problems with the satellite, and the results were unclear. Even so, Dulla studied the reports with fascination and envy. That should have been his own project! It was what he had trained for, all those graduate years. What a waste this expedition was! He glanced distastefully at the gaping rents in the tent, at the instruments that were scattered out to rust because there was no one to use them. So much to be done. So much that he could not think where to begin and so could do nothing.

There was a racket outside which made Dulla glance up, frowning—Feng and the Italian quarreling about something, and behind them the distant squawking of a herd of balloonists. If Heir-of-Mao had been a little more openhanded, and if Feng had been a bit less of a fool . . . then they might have had a helicopter, like the Greasies, or the wit to make balloons, like the Fats, and he too might have had the chance to fly with the flocks. That chance was lost. Even the Krinpit, whom he himself, Ahmed Dulla, had resolved to make contact with, were as strange to him as ever. It was not fair! He had taken the risk. He remembered well how he had felt as he lay helpless among the curious, jostling masses of crablike creatures. If they hadn't tried to eat the other two first, he knew he would have wound up as a meal. And for nothing. The one Krinpit they had a chance to communicate with, to keep for a specimen, Feng had allowed to be stolen by the Greasies.

There were sudden new sounds from outside, hissing white sounds that made Dulla get up and peer out of the tent. He saw flames reaching toward the sky and Feng struggling with the Italian while one of the Jamaican women swore angrily at them both.

"What is happening here?" Dulla demanded.

The Italian pushed Feng away and turned toward Dulla, his expression repentant. "Uazzi wished to greet our friends," he said, peering aloft. The rockets had climbed up into the maroon murk and exploded, and there were smaller explosions all around them. Balloonists had caught fire from the shower of sparks. "I helped him aim, but perhaps—perhaps my aim was not good," he said.

"Foolish one!" cried Dulla, almost dancing with rage, "Do you see what you have done?"

"I have burned up a few gasbags. Why not?" grumbled Spadetti.

"Not just gasbags! Rub the wine out of your eyes and

look again. There! Is that a gasbag? Do you not see it is a
human being hanging there, wondering why we have tried
to kill him, anxious to return to his base with the Fats or
the Greasies and report that the People's Republics have
declared war? Another blunder! And one we may not
survive."

"Peace, Dulla," panted Feng. "It does not matter if the
Fats and the Greasies are angry at us now. Help is on the
way."

"You are as big a fool as he! Shooting off fireworks like
some farm brigade celebrating the overfulfillment of its
cabbage quota!"

"I wish," said Feng, "that you had not been rescued,
Dulla. There was less struggle here when you were with
the Krinpit."

"And I wish," said Dulla, "that the Krinpit who tried to
kill me was our leader here instead of you. He was less
ugly, and less of a fool."

That Krinpit was many kilometers away, and at that
moment almost as angry as Dulla. He had been driven to
the brink of insanity with the infuriating attempts of the
Poison Ghosts of the Fuel camp to converse with him,
with hunger, and above all with the continual blinding
uproar of the camp.

In the noisy, bright world of the Krinpit there was never
a time of silence. But the level of sound was always
manageable: sixty or seventy decibels most of the time,
except for the occasional thunderclap of a storm. It almost
never reached over seventy-five.

To Sharn-igon, the Fuel camp was torture. Sometimes it
was quiet and dim, sometimes blindingly loud. The Krinpit
had no internal-combustion engines to punish their auditory nerves. The Greasies had dozens of them. Sharn-igon
had no conception of how they worked or what they were
for, but he could recognize each of them when it was
operating: high clatter of the drilling machine, rubbery
roar of the helicopter, rattle and whine of the power saws,
steady chug of the water pump. He had arrived at the
camp almost blind, for the nearness of the helicopter's
turbojet had affected his hearing just as staring at the
uncaged sun would damage a human's eyes; the afterimage
lasted for days and was still maddeningly distorting to his
perceptions. He had been penned behind steel bars as soon

as he arrived. However hard he gnawed and sawed, the bars of the cage would not give. As soon as he made a little scratch in one it was replaced. The Poison Ghosts troubled him endlessly, echoing his name and his sounds in a weirdly frightening way. Sharn-igon knew nothing of tape recording, and to hear his own sounds played back to him was as shattering an experience as it would be for a human to see his own form suddenly appear before him. He had realized that the Poison Ghosts wanted to communicate with him and had understood a tiny portion of what they were trying to say. But he seldom replied. He had nothing to say to them.

And he was nearly starving. He survived, barely, on the little he would eat of what they put before him—mostly vegetation, of which he disdained the majority as a human being would spurn thistle and grass. His hunger was maddeningly stimulated because he could smell the tasty nearness of Ghosts Below penned near him, and even a Ghost Above now and then. But the Poison Ghosts never brought him any of these to eat. And always there was the blinding roar of noise, or the equally unpleasant silences when the camp slept and only the faint echo from tents and soft bodies kept him company. Human beings, scantily fed on bread and water in an isolation cell, with bright lights denying them sleep, go mad. Sharn-igon was not far from it.

But he clung to sanity, because he had a goal. The Poison Ghosts had killed Cheee-pruitt.

He had not learned to tell one from another in time to know which was the culprit, but that was a problem easily solved. They were all guilty. Even in his madness it was clear to him that it was proper for him to kill a great many of them to redress their guilt, but what had not become clear to him was how. The chitin of claw and shell-sword were rubbed flat and sore against the bars, and still the bars held.

When all the sounds were out he chatted with the Ghost Above, straining longingly against the bars. "Desire to eat you," he said. If it had not been for the bars, the Ghost Above would have been easy prey. It had lost most of its gas and was crawling about the floor of a cage like his own. Its song was no more than a pathetic whisper.

"You cannot reach me," it pointed out, "unless you molt. And then I would eat you." Each spoke in its own language, but over thousands of generations all the races of Klong knew a little of the language of the others. With the Ghosts Above you could not help being exposed to their constant singing, and even the Ghosts Below could be heard chattering and whistling in their tunnels. "I have eaten several of you hardshells," the Ghost Above wheezed faintly. "I particularly like the backlings and the first molt."

The creature was boasting, but Sharn-igon could believe the story easily enough. The balloonists fed mostly on airborne detritus, but to make their young healthy they needed more potent protein sources now and then. When the breeding time was on, the females would drop like locusts to scour the ground clean of everything they could find. Adult Krinpit in shell were too dangerous, but in molt they were fair game. Best of all was a clutch of Ghosts Below caught on their thieving raids to the surface—for Krinpit as well as balloonist. The thought made Sharn-igon's salivary glands flow.

"Hard-shell," whispered the Ghost Above, "I am dying, I think. You can eat me then if you like."

In all honesty, Sharn-igon was forced to admit, "You may be eating me before that." But then he perceived that something was strange. The Ghost Above was no longer in its cage. It was dragging slowly across the floor. "How escape?" he demanded.

"Perhaps because I am so close to death," sang the Ghost Above faintly. "The Killing Ones made a hole in my sac to let the life out of me and then closed it with a thing that stuck and clung and stung. But it has come loose, and almost all my life has spilled away, and so I was able to slide between the bars."

"Wish I could slide through bars!"

"Why do you not open the cage? You have hard things. The Killing Ones push a hard thing into a place in the cage when they want to, and it opens."

"What hard thing are you speaking of? I have worn my shell to pulp."

"No," sighed the balloonist. "Not like your shell. Wait, there is one by the door. I will show you."

Sharn-igon's conception of keys and locks was quite unlike a human's, but the Krinpit too had ways of securing one thing to another temporarily. He chattered and scratched in feverish impatience while the dying gasbag slowly dragged itself toward him, with something bright and hard in its shadowy mouth.

"Could push hard thing into place in my cage?" he wheedled.

The Ghost Above sang softly to itself for a moment. Then it pointed out, "You will eat me."

"Yes. Will. But you very close to dying anyway," Sharn-igon pointed out, and added shrewdly, "Sing very badly now."

The balloonist hissed sadly without forming words. It was true.

"If push thing in place in my cage so that I can go free," bargained Sharn-igon, "will kill some of the Poison Ghosts for you." He added honestly, "Intend to do that in any case, since they killed my wife."

"How many?" whispered the balloonist doubtfully.

"As many as I can," said Sharn-igon. "At least one. No, two. Two for you, and as many as I can for me."

"Three for me. The three who come to this place and cause me pain."

"All right, yes, three," cried Sharn-igon. "Anything you like! But do quickly, before Poison Ghosts come back!"

Hours later, at almost the last of his strength, Sharn-igon staggered into a Krinpit village. It was not his own. He had seen the sounds of it on the horizon for a long time, but he was so weak and filled with pain that it had taken him longer to crawl the distance than the tiniest backling. "Sharn-igon, Sharn-igon, Sharn-igon," he called as he approached the alien Krinpit. "Am not of your place. Sharn-igon, Sharn-igon!"

A gravid female scuttled past him. She moved slowly because she was near her time, but she ignored his presence.

That did not surprise Sharn-igon. It was what he had expected. Indeed, each lurching step into the alien village was harder for him than the one before, and he was a professional empathizer. "Sharn-igon," he called bravely. "I would speak to one among you, although I am not of this place."

There was no answer, of course. It would not be easy to make contact. Each village was culturally as well as geographically isolated from every other. They did not fight. But they did not interact. If a party of Krinpit from one village chanced upon an individual or a party from another, they depersonalized each other. One Krinpit might push another from a different village out of the way. Two alien Krinpit might each take an end of a many-tree trunk that was barring their mutual way. Both would lift. Neither would address the other.

Genetically the villages were not isolated. The seedlings dropped from their he-father's backs when they were ripe to do so, wherever they might be. If they chanced to be near an alien village when they did—and if they were lucky enough to make their way to it without becoming food for a Ghost Below or any other marauder—they were accepted there as readily as any autochthon. But adults never did such a thing.

On the other hand, an adult had never found himself in Sharn-igon's position—until now.

"Sharn-igon, Sharn-igon," he called over and over, and at last a he-mother crept toward him. It did not speak directly to him, but it did not retreat, either. As it moved, it softly made the sound of its name: Tsharr-p'fleng.

"Have had good Ring-Greeting, alien brother?" Sharn-igon asked politely.

No answer, except that the sound of the stranger's name grew a trifle louder and more assured.

"Am not of this place," Sharn-igon acknowledged. "Most unpleasant for me to be here. Am aware is unpleasant also for you. However, must speak with you."

Agitatedly the other Krinpit scratched and thumped its name for a moment and then managed to speak. "Why you here, Sharn-igon?"

He collapsed on the knees of his forelegs. "Must have food," he said. The balloonist had been so very thin and frail that he made only half a meal, and of course Sharn-igon had been careful not to eat any part of the Poison Ghosts. He was not sure he had succeeded in killing all three, but two at least were certain, and the other would be a long time recovering. That settled the score for the balloonist.

But not for Cheee-pruitt.

If Sharn-igon had not been a professional empathist he could not have broken through the barriers between villages. As it was, it took much time and all of his persuasion; but at the end of it Tsharr-p'fleng helped him to a dwelling pen and ministered to his needs.

Sharn-igon devoured the crabrat they brought him while Tsharr-p'fleng engaged in agitated conversation with others of the village just outside the wall. Then they came in and ranged themselves around Sharn-igon, listening to him eat. He ignored their polite scratches of curiosity and concern until every morsel was gone. Then he pushed away the splintered carapace and spoke.

"Poison Ghosts killed my he-wife and did not eat him."

A flickering sound of disgust.

"They captured me and held me in a place without doors. They removed my backlings and took them away. I do not think they were eaten, but I have not heard them since."

Brighter sounds—disgust mixed with sympathy and anger.

"Moreover, they have also captured Ghosts Above and Ghosts Below and many of the lesser living things, and have eaten none of them. I therefore killed three of the Poison Ghosts. Intend to kill more. Are you back-mates with the Poison Ghosts?"

The he-mother rustled and spoke with contempt. "Not those! Their back-mates are the Ghosts Below."

Another said, "But Poison Ghosts have ways of killing. They have spoken to us in our language and told us to beware of them, lest they kill us."

"Beware of what? What did they tell you to do?"

"Only to refrain from harming any of them, for then they will kill all in our village."

Sharn-igon said, "The Poison Ghosts do not speak truth. Listen! They say they come from another world, like stars in sky. What are these stars?"

"They say they are like heat from sky," muttered the other.

"Have felt heat from sky. Have felt no heat from these other stars. I hear nothing from them. No matter how loud I shout, hear no echo from any of them."

"We have said these things ourselves," said Tsharr-p'fleng slowly. "But we are afraid of the Poison Ghosts. They will kill us, without eating."

"They will; it is true," said Sharn-igon. He paused. Then he went on. "Unless we kill them first. Unless all of our villages together fall upon them and kill them, without eating."

ELEVEN

●

MARGE MENNINGER'S HAIR was no longer blond. The name on her passport was not Margie Menninger. According to her travel orders, she was now a major, en route to a new duty station; and although the orders authorized a delay en route, it was unlikely that the general who signed them had contemplated that it would be spent in Paris.

In the little room of her hotel she fidgeted over the so-called croissant and what passed for orange juice, and phoned down to the concierge to see if the message she was expecting had arrived.

"I regret it, Meez Bernardi, but there is nothing," sighed the concierge. Marge took another bite of the croissant and gave it up. France was nominally part of the Food Bloc—by the skin of its teeth, and by the relabeling of Algerian wine for export—but you couldn't prove it by what they gave you for breakfast.

She was tired of this room, with its leftover smells of *khef* and sexual athletics from its previous occupants. She wanted to move around and couldn't. And while she was fretting away time in this room, the Peep ships were going through pre-launch, the training of backup crews for the next Food Bloc mission was limping along without her, and God only knew what disasters were taking place in Washington and at the UN.

She abandoned the breakfast and dressed quickly. When she came downstairs, of course there was a message at the concierge's desk, on a flimsy blue slip of paper:

> Miss Hester Bernardi will be picked up at 1500 hours for her appointment.

It had obviously been there all along. Margie did not bother to reprimand the concierge; she would take care of

that at tipping time. She pushed her way out into the Rue
Caumartin, deciding what to do next. Six hours to kill!
And for the life of her she could not think of any
productive use to make of them.

It was a warm, drizzly day. The stink of gasoline
drenched the air over the Place de l'Opéra. Food Bloc or
not, France was cozy with the Ay-rabs, as well as with the
Peeps. That was another reason you could not trust the
frogs, Margie thought darkly. One of her grandfathers had
marched into this city in Wehrmacht gray, and the other,
in the opposite direction a few years later, in American
olive drab, and both of them had passed on to her their
feelings about the French. They were inconstant allies and
unreliable subjects, and the few who ever seemed to have
any sense of national purpose usually wound up having
their heads shaved or chopped by the many who did not.
In Margie's view, the French were not a bit better than the
English, the Spanish, the Italians, the Portuguese, the
Asians, the Africans, the Latins—and about ninety percent
of the Americans too, when you came right down to it.

But the immediate problem was not what was wrong
with humanity, but what she could do with this day. There
was only one answer. She could do the thing most American women came to Paris to do. She could shop.

She not only could shop, she must; it was the best way
of avoiding attention. She not only must, she wanted to.

It was one of Margie's most closely guarded secrets that
periodically she went on shopping binges, out of one store
and into another, pricing fabric, trying on dresses, matching shoes with gowns. In her little Houston apartment
there were two closets, plus half of what was meant to be a
guest room, filled with her purchases. They were thrown
jumbled onto shelves, pushed under a bed in their original
store bags: sweaters she would never wear, material half-
sewn into drapes that would never be hung. Her living
room was spartan, and her bedroom was always immaculate, because you never knew who might drop in. But the
secret rooms were part of the hidden personality of
Margie Menninger. None of what she bought was very
expensive. It was not because she was economical. She had
unaccounted funds at her disposal, and the prices never
mattered. But her taste was for quantity rather than
quality. Periodically she would wage war against the over-
flow, and then for awhile Goodwill and the Salvation

Army would fatten off her discards. But a week later the hoard would have grown again.

Margie did not bother with the tourist traps along the Champs Élysées or with the tucked-away boutiques. Her tastes were for stores like Printemps, Uniprix, and the Galeries Lafayette. The only fly in the ointment was that she could not buy anything. She could not carry it where she was going and did not want to attract attention by leaving it, so she tried on, and she priced, and for six hours she made the lives of a score of Parisian shopgirls a living hell. That didn't bother Margie Menninger at all. By the time the taxicab picked her up at her hotel, punctually on the tick of three o'clock, her good nature was restored. She leaned back against the hard plastic seat of the cab, ready for what was to come next.

The driver stopped at the Place Vendôme long enough for another passenger to jump in. Behind tourist shades was the face of her father, which was no surprise to Margie.

"Bonjour, honey," he said. "I brought you your toy."

She took the camera he offered her and hefted it critically. It was heavier than it looked; she would have to be careful not to let anyone else pick it up.

"Don't try to take pictures with it," he said, "because it won't. Just hang it around your neck on the strap. Then, when you get where you're going"—he pushed the shutter lever, and the casing opened to reveal a dull metal object inside—"this is what you give your contact. Along with a hundred thousand petrodollars. They're in the carrying case."

"Thank you, poppa."

He twisted in the seat to look at her. "You're not going to tell your mother that I let you do this, are you?"

"Christ, no. She'd have a shit hemorrhage."

"And don't get caught," he added as an afterthought. "Your contact was one of Tam Gulsmit's best people, and he is going to be really ticked off when he finds out we turned him. How are things going at Camp Detrick?"

"Good shape, poppa. You get me the transport, I'll send some good people."

He nodded. "We've had a little lucky break," he offered. "The Peeps fired on one of our guys. No harm done, but it makes a nice incident."

"Didn't he fire back, for Christ's sake?"

"Not him! It was your old jailhouse buddy, the one from Bulgaria. As near as I can tell, he doesn't believe in the use of force. Anyway, he did exactly what I would have told him to do. He got the hell out of there and reported back to the UN peacekeeping force, and he had tapes and pictures to prove what he said." He peered out the window. They had crossed the Seine. Now they were creeping through heavy traffic in a working-class neighborhood. "This is where I get out. See you in Washington, love. And take care of yourself."

Early the next morning Margie was in Trieste. She was not Hester Bernardi anymore, but she wasn't Marge Menninger either. She was a sleepy Swiss-Italian housewife in a sweaty pantsuit, driving to the Yugoslav border in a rented Fiat electrocar with a crowd of other Sunday-morning shoppers looking for cheap vegetables and bargains in Yugoslavian kitchenware. Unlike them, she drove straight through to Zagreb, parked the car and took a bus to the capital.

When she reached Belgrade, the object her father had given her was at the bottom of a plastic shopping bag with an old sweater and a shabby pocketbook on top of it. And she had had very little sleep.

Margie could not have grown up in the household of Godfrey Menninger without learning the easy dialogue of espionage. In all the world, she was the only person with whom her father had always been open. First because she was too little to understand, and so he could speak freely in her presence. Then because she had to understand. When the PLO kidnapped her she had been terrified past the point a four-year-old can survive, and her father's patient explanations had been the only thing that let her make sense of the terror. And finally, because he trusted her to understand, always, that the grotesque and lethal things he did had a purpose. He never questioned that she shared that purpose. So she had grown up in an atmosphere of drops and liquidations and couriers and double agents, at the center of a web that stretched all around the world.

But now she was not at the center of the web; she was out where the risks were immense and the penalties drastic. She walked quickly down the busy streets, avoiding eye contact. The closet-sized shops had their doors open, and confusing smells came out of them: a knifelike aroma of roasting meat from a dressmaker's (when had she eaten last?), the sting of unwashed armpits from what seemed to be a costume-jewelry boutique. She crossed, dodging a tram, and saw the office she was looking for. The sign said Electrotek München, and it was over a sweatshop where fat, huge men in T-shirts worked at belt-driven sewing machines.

She checked her watch. There was more than an hour before her first possible contact. The man she needed to meet was a short, slim Italian who would be wearing a football blazer with the name of the Skopje team. Of course, no one like that was in sight yet—even if he turned up for the first rendezvous, which her father had warned was unlikely.

Down the block there was a cluster of roofed sheds surrounding a gabled two-story building that looked like any American suburban town's leftover rainroad station. A farmers' market? It seemed to be something like that. Margie pushed her way through crowds of women in babushkas and women in minifrocks, men in blue smocks carrying crates of pink new potatoes on their shoulders, and men with a child on each hand, studying counters of chocolates and jellies. It was a satisfyingly busy mob. She was not conspicuous there.

She was, however, hungry.

Strawberries seemed to be in season. Margie bought half a kilo and a bottle of Pepsi and found a seat on a stone balustrade next to an open suitcase full of screwdrivers and cast-aluminum socket wrenches. What Margie wanted most was a hamburger, but no one seemed to be selling anything like that. But others were eating strawberries, and Margie was confident she looked like any one of them, or at least, if not like them, like some housewife who might have stopped en route to any ordinary destination to refresh herself.

At two punctually she was back in front of Electrotek München, studying a Belgrade bus guide as instructed. No short, slim Italian appeared. Twice she caught snatches of words that seemed to be in English, but when she looked up from her bus guide and glanced casually in that direction, she could not tell which of the passersby had spoken. She pitched the bus guide into a corner sewer and walked angrily away. The second appointment was not until ten o'clock at one of the big old luxury hotels, and what in God's name was she going to do until then?

She had to keep moving. It was very hard to stroll for more than seven hours, however many Camparis and soda you are willing to stop and drink. God bless, she passed something that called itself, in Cyrillic letters, an Expres-Restoran, and when she realized that it was a cafeteria, one problem at least was solved. She pointed at something that looked like roast chicken and probably was, and with the mashed potatoes and bread that went with it, at least she was full. Full of time. She emptied herself of as much of it as she could: a stroll through the botanical gardens, a long window-shopping stroll down the Boulevard Marshal Tito. And then it began to rain. She retreated into a *bioskop* and watched a Czech comedy with Serbo-Croatian subtitles until nine. The only problem was staying awake; but when she got to the hotel there was a real problem. Ghelizzi did not show up there either.

By now she was almost dizzy with fatigue, her clothes were sweaty and rain-stained, and she was sure she was beginning to smell. Poppa had not really thought these arrangements through, she thought with some bitterness. It should have occurred to him that the waiters at the hotel bar would not fail to notice a sweaty, dirty foreign woman among all their marble and their string trios. If she had been a man, it might not have mattered. A man could have been checking out the hotel whores—the skinny, dark-at-the-roots blond playing solitaire by the fireplace, the plump one with the bright red hair who had left the aperitif lounge twice in one hour, with different men, and was back again, ready for the next. Margie refused another Campari and sent the waiter for a Turkish coffee. The next appointment was not until the following afternoon, and where would she sleep?

The whores had rooms. If she had been one of them ...

The idea did not disturb Margie in any moral way, but it took only a second for her to discard it as impractical. Even if she had a room, the waiters would surely throw her out to protect the existing monopoly the first time she looked toward one of the solitary males. They were already looking at her with interest and beginning to take the cloths off some of the tables in the farther end of the room.

Margie picked up her coffee and moved to the table of the streaked blond. She spoke to her in English, confident that in a tourist hotel the girls would be fluent in the necessary words in any major language.

"How much for all night?" she asked.

The blond looked scandalized. "For yourself? How disgusting! I could not possibly do such a thing with a woman."

"Fifty dinars."

"One hundred."

"All right, one hundred. But I have very special tastes, and you must do exactly as I ask."

The blond looked skeptical, then shrugged and signaled the waiter. "First you must buy me a real Scotch whiskey while you explain what these tastes are. Then we will see."

In the morning Margie woke up refreshed. She used the whore's tiny shower to get clean, dressed quickly and paid the woman off with a smile.

"May I ask a question?" the whore offered, counting the money.

"I can't stop you from asking."

"This thing you had me do, simply rubbing your neck each time you woke until you fell asleep again? Is that truly satisfying to you?"

"You wouldn't believe how satisfying," smiled Margie. She strolled grandly out of the hotel, nodding politely to the local police in their baggy gray uniforms open at the neck, hands on the guns in the cardboard holsters. A few blocks down the boulevard took her to the London Cafe, and there, nursing a beer at one of the indoor tables, was the slim, short Italian wearing a Skopje football cap.

She sat down and ordered a coffee, then visited the women's w.c. When she came back the Italian was gone. The bag she had left on her chair did not appear to be disturbed, but her exploring fingers told her the camera was gone, and in its place was a guide folder about the hovercraft cruise to the Iron Gorge.

She made her way back across the border the same way she had come. By the time she was in Trieste again and able to resume the identity of the Swiss-Italian housewife, she was fully restored. On the clamjet to Paris she locked herself in the toilet and studied the contents of the travel folder.

How Ghelizzi had come to be a person of trust in Sir Tam's army of spies was beyond her; he had not impressed her as being the sort of man one would repose faith in. But he had delivered the goods this time. The little device was on its way, and the complete file of secret tactran messages between Earth and the Fuel Bloc camp on Klong was in her hands in microfiche. Her father would be very proud.

TWELVE

●

WHAT ANA DIMITROVA had seen of the United States was what she had seen of most of the world: airports, hotel rooms, meeting halls, city streets. So at first she looked around with lively interest as the electrobus whined along an eight-lane superhighway toward the place she had been ordered to report to. So much open space, not even farmed! And contrarily, so many places lined up one after another as they passed through communities—places to eat, places to sleep, places to drink, places to buy gas. What prodigious devourers these Americans must be to keep them all flourishing!

More than half of her companions in the bus were Americans, and they were busy devouring, too, several smoking in flagrant disregard of the signs, a couple chewing gum, three in the back seat passing around a bottle in a brown paper bag. The army sergeant who had offered her part of a chocolate bar was now offering the Canadian agronomist woman some round hard candies with holes in them. Nan was making an effort to like the others because she surely would be seeing a lot of them in training. It wasn't easy. One by one, each of the American men had made friendly overtures to her which turned in seconds into sexual ones. Even the Vietnamese colonel, so tiny and delicate that she had sat down next to him at first, thinking he was a woman, had begun to make personal remarks in his beautiful high-pitched English. She had changed seats six times so far and now resolutely sat staring out the window even though she was no longer seeing anything. Such compulsive consumers—she could not help feeling that they seemed obliged to consume her as well.

She touched the tiny microfiche from Ahmed at the bottom of her blouse pocket. She had no reader for it, but she needed none. As always it was formal, not very rewarding, and extremely short:

My dear Ana,
   I appreciate the letters you have been sending and think of you often.

> With great affection,
> Dulla

He could have spent a few P$ more, she thought resentfully, and then, as always, brought herself up sharply. Ahmed was from a poor country. Even fiched and faxed, the cost per square centimeter of a letter from Kungson to Earth was very high. (But in her own letters she had poured money out like water. (But she could not judge him; she had not had the life experience of measuring every penny. (But it was not just the economy of space and money—how much more he could have said if he had chosen, in even fewer words!—it was the economy of emotion that she begrudged.))) Three deep in parentheses, she took her mind off Dulla and resolved to think about more profitable subjects, and then realized the bus had stopped.

Three uniformed Americans had entered by the driver's seat. One of them gestured for silence and said to the bus at large, "You people are welcome, and let's see some ID."

Craning her neck, Nan could see a barricade with two other soldiers standing by it. They were not at attention, but they were watching the bus quite carefully, and she observed that what had looked like a well-clipped hedge stretching away on both sides of the barrier had barbed wire inside it. How curious. They were treating this place as though it were some sort of military installation rather than a center for preparing scientists and support personnel for a peaceful expedition to Kungson. Big-power customs were so strange to her. When the MPs came to her, she handed her passport over and smiled at the tall black one who was studying it. He returned her look impassively.

"Name?"

Of course, it was right there, next to his thumb. "Ana Elena Dimitrova."

"Place of birth?"

"My place of birth? It is Marek, Bulgaria. That is a city south of Sofia, not far from the Yugoslavian border."

"Put your thumb here, please." She pressed against the little pad he extended to her and then on a square white card, which he tucked into her passport. "Your papers will be returned to you later," he said, and then unbent. "You like to dance? There's a nice group at the club tonight. Ask for me if you don't see me. Name's Leroy."

"Thank you, Leroy."

"See you later, honey." He winked and moved along. Ana found a tissue and wiped the ink off her thumb wonderingly. These Americans were even worse than Sir Tam—not just the Americans, she corrected herself, thinking of the Vietnamese colonel and his agile, tiny hands. Would it be like this always? Would it not be even worse when she was part of the small colony on Kungson and they were all living in each other's pockets anyway?

But at least then Ahmed would be somewhere near! In the wrong encampment, yes. But she would find a way to see him. Let her just get on the same planet with him again, and they would be together! It made the whole ordeal seem worthwhile.

By the next day, not even that made it seem altogether attractive. She could not have attended Leroy's dance that night if she had wanted to. There was no time. Issue of new clothing: "You will wear these here fatigues at all times, except when instructed by your instructors." Assignment to quarters: "You will maintain cleanliness at all times. At all times all personal possessions are to be kept in your footlockers." Preliminary briefing: "You will fall out at oh six hundred hours for breakfast. From oh seven hundred to eleven hundred you will participate in your individual refresher courses of instruction in the application of your specialized skills on Klong. From twelve hundred to sixteen-thirty you will complete your survival course to teach you your survival skills for surviving in the environment of Klong. From eighteen hundred to lights out at twenty-two hundred you will conduct your personal affairs except when required to participate in additional refresher courses or survival instruction. Weekends? Who's the guy who wants to know about weekends? Oh, you. Well, there aren't any weekends here." By the time all that was finished it was nearly midnight, and then Ana dragged her suitcase to the tiny, bare room that had been assigned to her, coldly furnished like the showcase cell in a county jail, only to find out that her roommate was the Vietnamese colonel. Even here rank had its privilege. But Ana was having none of it, and so it was back to the billeting office and a good deal of argument, and by the time she was able to get to sleep in a new room with a female roommate it was nearly two.

Breakfast was discouragingly huge—eggs and sausage and cereal, and breads with jams and marmalades, and peanut butter in opened liter cans on every table—and for dessert they spent an hour receiving inoculations. None of them were painful, but from the grins and jokes of the medics Ana knew that they would be later on. And then she lined up with the other two dozen of her detachment in a wet, cold wind, and they were marched off to their various refresher courses in the application of their specialized skills. Ana's tiny group included the Canadian woman and two men unknown to her, and they wound through the camp streets, past a baseball field and a bowling alley, between barracks and anonymous buildings with armed guards patrolling before them, out into an open field half a kilometer square. In the center of it was a sort of tethered balloon shaped like a sausage, fifty meters long, with guards around the perimeter and three of them grouped before the entrance. There was a fence surrounding the whole thing, and more guards at the gate in the fence; and before any of them were permitted inside, they had to go through the same tedious business of checking IDs one more time.

Off to one side there was a tall chimney coupled to the main tent by a flexible plastic tube. The chimney roared. Though there was no smoke, the shimmering at the top showed that some very hot gases were boiling high into the air out of it. It did not seem to serve any function that Ana could guess. But then, neither did the weapons that all the permanent personnel carried. Who were they meant to be used against? What possible enemy threatened a training base for a scientific expedition which, after all, was in a sense the property of the entire world?

When she finally got through the gates and the guards, she found herself in a long, open shed covered with the opaque white plastic of the bubble. The atmosphere was damp and heavy, filled with strange smells, and the lighting was sultry red. At first she could see very little, but she was aware that people were moving about between rows of what seemed to be smaller, transparent bubbles. The lighting came from a bank of gas-glow tubes, all red, and there was not very much of it.

The guide who had brought her to this place was speaking to her. "Are you all right?"

"Yes, I think so. Why not?"

"Sometimes people can't stand the smell."

She sniffed gingerly: pepper and spice and jungle rot. "No, it is fine."

The Canadian woman said, "Everything sounds funny."

"There's positive pressure in the outer shell. Your ears probably popped a little. That's so that if there's any air leakage it will all be inward, not out, and of course the air from this chamber gets incinerated at fifteen hundred degrees as it is pumped out—maybe you saw the chimney."

"One has heard stories of dangerous diseases," Nan ventured.

"No. There aren't any. Oh, sure," the guide went on gloomily, "you can get killed around here. But that's allergies, not disease, and you've all had your shots for them. Dimitrova, you're for linguistics. You come with me; the rest of you stay right here till I get back."

He led her through the hothouselike room, past the rows of plastic bubbles. As her eyes became dark-adapted she could see that each of them contained some sort of specimen—mostly plants, and some of them were immense. One towered ten meters, nearly to the top of the shell. It looked like a giant cluster of ferns, and Ana marveled at the money that had been spent to transport that immense mass over the light-years. Apart from the outside roaring of the incinerator, the sounds of pumps, and the noises the people in the shell made, there were sounds she could not identify—a sort of faint, wailing, high-pitched song, and groaning, clattering noises. They came from where she was heading for. The guide said, "Welcome to our zoo."

And then she saw the balloonist.

She recognized it at once; there could not be another

creature as strange as that anywhere in the universe! But it looked . . . damaged. It was tethered inside a cage. Its great bubble was throbbing but almost limp, sagging against the ground. She stared, fascinated, and saw that a flexible plastic coupling had been taped neatly to a hole in the gasbag, and the plastic line went to a cylinder of gas. A woman with a tape recorder was crouched by the cylinder, adjusting the gas valve as she listened to the balloonist's plaintive song.

No wonder the voice sounded so faint! He was operating at a fraction of normal pressure, far too little to let him fly, only enough to let him gasp a sobbing sort of song. The woman looked up and said, "You're Dimitrova? I'm Julia Arden, and this"—pointing at the balloonist—"is Shirley. She's singing about her childhood right now."

Ana shook hands courteously, staring at the sad, wrinkled little creature. Those sounds did not seem like language! She could not imagine understanding them, much less translating them, no matter how many times they halved her brain! She said doubtfully, "I will do my best, Mis Arden, but do you think you can really teach me to talk to that?"

"Me? Maybe not. I'll help, and so will the computers, but the one who's going to teach you is Shirley herself. She loves to sing to us. Poor thing. She doesn't have much else to do with her time, does she?"

Nan looked at the creature for a moment and then burst out, "No, but what a shame, really! Can you not see she is in pain?"

The other woman shrugged. "What do you want me to do about it?" Her tone was less hostile than defensive. "I don't suppose Shirley volunteered for this duty, but then, neither did I. Your job is learning her language, Dimitrova, and let's get on with it."

"But to see a creature in pain—"

Julia Arden laughed and then shook her head. "Sweetie, you only got here last night. Wait a day or two. Then you can talk to me about pain."

From 0700 to 1100 Ana Dimitrova stretched the muscles of her mind until she thought she would die of it, and from 1200 to 1630 she balanced the diet by doing the same to her body. Julia Arden had been right. Within forty-eight hours Ana was an expert on pain. She woke up each morning with a hazy overcast of brightness that she knew was the foretaste of migraine. She went to bed each night with so many aches, throbs, and bruises that it took all the will she had to refrain from swallowing the pills they had given her. She could not afford pills. She needed her mind alert, even while she slept, because sleeping was only another kind of study for Ana, with the taped calls of the balloonists murmuring under her pillow all night long.

The headaches, all right—they were something she was used to. Worse than that, the shots were producing their effect. Her skin was covered with little blisters and bumps, some that itched, some that were tender, some downright painful every moment of time. Not just pain. She wheezed and coughed. Her eyes ran uninterruptedly, and so did her nose. She was not alone; everyone in her group was having the same reaction to the allergy shots. If this was the prophylaxis, what could the illness itself be like? And then she saw the holos of the unfortunate Peeps who had died of their reactions before the countermeasures had been developed, and they defined for her the difference between prophylaxis and reality. It was not comforting to her. It was terrifying! How had Ahmed fared in all this? He had said nothing in his letters, but perhaps he was only being brave.

And every afternoon—feel well, feel ill, no matter—there she was out on the exercise field. Push-ups and five-hundred-meter runs, obstacle courses and rope climbing. Her hands were raw, then blistered, then calloused. Even through the coveralls her knees were scraped bloody. Everywhere on arms and legs where there was not a pimple or a blister, there was a bruise.

To be sure, she scolded herself, for all of this there was a clear purpose! Kungson was no picnic dell; it was a place of strange and perhaps lethal dangers. These measures, however brutal, were only to help her meet those dangers and conquer them. If she had not volunteered for the job, she had also not refused it when offered.

And finally, the most potent argument of all. It was the way to Ahmed. So she did her best all the time and was secretly proud of the fact that some of the others were doing less well than she. The tiny Vietnamese colonel, Nguyen Dao Tree, fell in a heap from the knotted ropes one afternoon and was taken to hospital. (He was back the next day, limping but game.) One woman, an older one, perhaps almost forty, fell flat on her face halfway up a rocky hill; she was taken away too, and she did not return.

One made quick friendships in such a place. She learned to call the colonel "Guy" and to respect his quick mind and sense of humor. She learned, too, to avoid being alone with him or with the sergeant, Sweggert—or indeed with any of the men, all of whom seemed to possess special reserves of strength when in the presence of an attractive female. Or an unattractive one. Her roommate, Corporal Elena Kristianides, was certainly not pretty, but more than once Nan staggered back to find the door locked and sounds of faint moans and giggles inside. When at last admitted, she always said forgivingly, "Please, it is all right, Kris. Do not speak of it." But it was not all right. She needed her sleep! Why didn't they need it too?

As days became weeks the fatigue lessened, the bruises healed, the reactions to the antiallergens diminished. The headaches stayed the same, but Nan was used to them, and she learned to take part in the friendly chatter in the mess hall. Always there were such stories! They were going to Kungson on a one-way trip and were expected to breed there and raise a new race of humans. They were not going to Kungson at all, but to a new planet, not yet announced or even named. They were not going into space at all. They were going to be parachuted onto the Scottish coast to commandeer the oil refineries. They were going to Antarctica, which was going to become a new Food Bloc colony, since a process had been discovered for melting the ice cap. At first Ana was frightened by such stories, then amused, then bored. She began making up stories of her own and found them as quickly passed along as any other. But some of the stories seemed true. Even some terrible ones: an unexplained accident in space that had destroyed the Peeps' resupply ships and even their tachyon-transit satellite itself. She let herself be late for dinner that night to listen to the evening news; sure enough, it was official. How terrifying! What would it mean to Ahmed? But then the news went on to say that the expeditions of the Fuel and Food blocs had offered help to the expedition of the People's Republics, and with her heart full, Ana hurried to the dining room, demanded attention, and proposed that they all sign a letter of sympathy and good wishes to their colleagues of the People's Bloc. The faces all turned to her, then whispered among themselves, half-embarrassed, but in the long run they let her write the letter, and they all signed. The next afternoon her training supervisor even excused her early to carry the document to the office of the camp commandant. He listened to her blankly, read the document three times, and then promised to send it through channels. At dinner that night she reported glowingly what had happened, but her news was drowned in other news. There were three new stories. First, that they were to receive a large shipment of new trainees the next day. Second, that a date had been set for their flight to Kungson, less than three weeks in the future. And third, contradictorily, that the whole project was about to be canceled.

Such stories! Nan stood up angrily, rapping her fork against her thick chinaware cup. "How can you all believe this nonsense?" she demanded. "How can all of these be true at once?" But not many of the others were paying attention, and she felt a tug at her elbow.

It was the colonel, who had, as he often did, squeezed in between Ana and her roommate at the table in order to try his fortunes one more time. "Sweet, beautiful Ana," he said, "don't make a fool of yourself. I know something of these stories, and they are all true."

That one of them was true was proved the next morning. Sixty-five more persons arrived at the base, and Ana knew one of them! It was the blond woman who was Godfrey Menninger's daughter.

Of course, everything was turned topsy-turvy. All of the billeting accommodations were changed to make room for the new arrivals—no, not for that reason alone, Ana realized, because most of the new ones, and quite a few of the old ones, were housed in another barracks half a kilometer away. Nan lost her WAC corporal roommate and feared at once that she would get Colonel Guy back again. But that did not happen. He went to the other barracks, and Nan was moved in with the Canadian woman, whose specialty seemed to be growing food crops in unusual circumstances. Marge Menninger caught sight of Nan in the crowd and waved to her. But they had no chance to speak—not that Ana had any particular reason to want to speak to the American, anyway—and in all the confusion, she was nearly an hour late for her morning session with the female balloonist.

The creature was no longer a specimen to Ana. She was a friend. Into the cognitive half of Ana's brain the songs of the balloonists had poured. In the first day she had learned to understand a few simple phrases, in a week to communicate abstract thoughts; now she was almost fluent. Ana had never thought of herself as having any kind of a singing voice, but the balloonist was not critical. They sang to each other for hours on end, and more and more Shirley's songs were sad and despairing, and sometimes even disconnected. She was, she told Ana, the last survivor of the dozen or more of her species who had been wrenched from Kungson and hurled to this inhospitable place. She did not expect to live much longer. She sang to Ana of the sweetness of warm pollen in a damp cloud, of the hot, stinging sadness of egg-spraying, of the communal joy of the flock in chorus. She told Ana that she would never sing in the flock again. She was thrice right. She would not have dared sing with her voice so pitifully harsh and weak because the gas pump gave her only faltering tones. She had no chance of being returned to Kungson. And she knew death was near.

Two days later she was dead. Ana arrived at the zoo to find her cage empty and Julia Arden supervising the sterilization of its parts.

"Don't take on," she advised gruffly. "You've learned all you need to know."

"It is not for the learning that I weep. It is because I have lost someone dear."

"Christ. Get out of here, Dimitrova. How did they let a jerk like you into this project in the first place? Crying over a dead fartbag and sending love letters to the Peeps—you're really out of it!"

Ana marched back to the barracks, threw herself down on her cot, and allowed herself to weep as she had not done in months—for Shirley, for Ahmed, for the world, and for herself. "Out of it" described her feelings exactly. How had everything become so hideous and complex?

That afternoon in the exercise field was an ordeal. The physical strain was no longer a real problem, but for some days now the "exercises" had taken a new turn. All of them, her own original detachment as well as the new arrivals, had been working less to strengthen their muscles and reflexes than to learn to handle unfamiliar equipment —unfamiliar to Ana, at least. She observed that all of the new people, and some of the old, had obviously had experience with it already. Such equipment! Heavy hoses like water cannon, backpack tanks and nozzles like flamethrowers, laser, even grenade launchers. For what grotesque purpose was all this intended? Tight-lipped, Ana did as she was told. Repeatedly she found herself in difficulties and had to be bailed out by one of the others. The colonel saved her from incinerating herself with a flamethrower, and Sergeant Sweggert had to rescue her when the recoil of her water cannon knocked her off her feet.

"Please do not concern yourself" she gasped furiously, pulling herself erect and reaching once more for the hose. "I am quite all right."

"Hell you are," he said amiably. "Lean into it more, honey, you hear? It doesn't take muscle, just a little brains."

"I do not agree."

He shook his head. "Why do you get so uptight, Annie?"

"I do not like being trained in the use of weapons!"

"What weapons?" He grinned at her. "Don't you know this stuff is only to use against vermin? Colonel Menninger spelled it all out for us. We don't want to kill any sentients; that's against the law, and besides, we'll all get our asses in a crack. But all the intelligent ones got little cousins, crabrats and airsharks and things that dig around in the dirt and come out and chew your ass off. *Those* are what we're going to use this stuff for."

"In any event," said Ana, "I do not require assistance from you, sergeant—even if I believe you, or your Colonel Menninger, which I do not."

Sweggert looked past her and pursed his lips. "Hello, there, colonel," he said. "We was just talking about you."

"So I noticed," said Margie Menninger's voice. Ana turned slowly, and there she was. Looking, Ana observed without regret, quite poorly. The shots were having their way with her; her face was broken out in cerise blotches, her eyes were red and running, and her hair showed dark roots. "Get on with it, sergeant," she said. "Dimitrova, see me in my room after chow."

She turned away and raised her voice. "All right, all of

you," she cried. "Get your asses down! Let's see how you crawl!"

Rebelliously Ana dropped to the ground and practiced the way of worming herself across an open field that she had learned the day before. These were infantry tactics! What nonsense for a scientific expedition! She conserved her anger carefully, and it lasted her the rest of the afternoon, through dinner, and right up to the moment she knocked on Menninger's door in that other barracks halfway across the base.

"Come in." Lt. Col. Menninger was sitting at a desk in a white, fluffy dressing gown, rimless granny glasses on her nose, a half-eaten dinner tray pushed to one side. She looked up from some papers and said, "Take a seat, Ana. Do you smoke? Would you like a drink?"

The angry fires inside Ana banked themselves. But they were still ready to blaze out. "No, thank you," she said, in general, to all.

Margie stood up and poured herself a scant shot of whiskey. She would have preferred marijuana, but she did not care to share a joint with this Bulgarian. She sipped a centimeter off the top of the drink and said, "Personal question. What have you got against Sweggert?"

"I have nothing against Sergeant Sweggert. I simply do not care to make love with him."

"What are you, Dimitrova, some maximum women's libber? You don't have to ball him on the parade ground. Just let him give you a hand when he wants to."

"Colonel Menninger," Ana said precisely, "are you ordering me to encourage his sexual overtures so that I can complete the obstacle course more readily?"

"I am not ordering you to do diddly-shit, Dimitrova. What is it with you? Sweggert comes on to everything with a hole in it. It's his nature. He comes on to me, too. I could put the son of a bitch in Leavenworth for the places his hands have been on the drill field. But I won't, because he's a good sol— Because he's essentially a good person. He'll help you if you let him. You can always tell him to fuck off later on."

"This I consider immoral, Colonel Menninger."

Margie finished her drink and poured half of another. "You're not too happy here, are you, Ana?"

"That is correct, Mis Menninger. I did not ask for this assignment."

"I did."

"Yes, no doubt, perhaps you did, but I—"

"No, that's not what I mean. I asked for it for myself, but I also asked for it for you. I picked you out by name, Ana, and it took hell's own conniving to make the Bulgarians turn you loose. They think you're pretty great at translating." She tossed down the rest of the drink and took off her glasses. "Look, Ana, I need you. This project is important to me. It should be important to you, too, if you have a spark of patriotism in your body."

"*Patriotism?*"

"Loyalty, then," said Margie impatiently. "Loyalty to our bloc. I know we come from different countries, but we stand for the same thing."

Ana found herself more puzzled than angered by this strange American. She tried to sort her feelings out and express them exactly. "Bulgaria is my home," she began. "I love my home. The Food Bloc—that is a much more abstract thing, Mis Menninger. I understand that in a world of two hundred nations there must be alliances and that one owes one's allies some sort of allegiance, or at least courtesy. But I cannot say I feel loyalty. Not to the Food Bloc."

"To the whole human race then, honey," said Margie. "Don't you see it? You just said it for yourself—a world of two hundred nations. But Klong can be a world of *one* nation! No fighting. No spies. No cloak-and-dagger shit. Who colonized America?"

"What?" It took Ana a moment to realize she was supposed to answer the question. "Why—the English? Before them, the Dutch."

"And before them maybe the Italians and Spaniards, with Columbus, and maybe, for Christ's sake, anybody you like—the Vikings, the Polynesians, the Chinese. Who knows? But the people who live in America now are the *Americans*. And that's who's going to live on Klong in another generation or two. The Klongans. Or whatever they call themselves. A single race of human beings. Never mind where they come from here! They'll be all the same, all part of the same wonderful ... well, dream. I don't mind calling it a dream. But you and I can make it come true, Ana. We can learn how to live on Klong. We can build a world without national barriers and without the kind of senseless competition and rapacity that have ruined this one. Do you know what it means to have a whole new world to start over on?"

Ana was silent. "I—I have had some thoughts of that sort myself," she admitted.

"Of course you have. *And I want to make it happen*. I want to lay the foundations for a world society that understands planning and conservation and cooperation. Do you know how much we're putting into this? *Four ships*. Nearly ninety people. Thirty-five tons of equipment. The invasion of Europe cost less than this one launch, and believe me, everybody involved is screaming. It costs too much. It upsets the Peeps. The Greasies will raise their prices. We need the resources to solve the problems of the cities. Half the Congress would like to call it off tomorrow—"

"One has heard rumors," Ana said cautiously, "that the launch may be canceled."

Margie hesitated, and a shadow crossed her face. "No," she corrected. "That will not happen, because it is too important. But that is why I asked for you, Ana. If we can send ninety people, they must be the best ninety people there are. And you are the best translator I could find." She reached out and touched Ana's sleeve. "Do you understand?"

Ana drew away as soon as she could without giving offense, her thoughts uncertain. "Y-yes," she said unwillingly, and then, "but, on the other hand, no. What you say is most persuasive, Mis Menninger, but what has it to do with the use of flamethrowers and other weapons? Are we to build this fine monolithic world by destroying everyone else?"

"Of course not, Ana!" cried Margie, with as much shock and revulsion in her voice as she knew how to put there. "I give you my word!"

There was a silence. "I see," said Ana at last. "You give me your word."

"What else would you have me do?"

Ana said thoughtfully, "One has so little contact with the rest of the world here. I would like very much an opportunity to discuss this with others. Perhaps with my own delegation at the United Nations?"

"Why not?" exclaimed Margie. She looked thoughtful for a moment and then nodded. "I'll tell you what. As soon as training's over we're all going to get three days off. I'm going to New York myself. Come with me. We'll eat some decent food, go to a few parties. And you can talk it over with anyone you like. Agreed?"

Ana hesitated. At last, unwillingly, she said, "All right, Mis Menninger. That sounds attractive." It did not, for many reasons, but as a just person Ana had to concede that it sounded at least fair.

"Fine, honey. Now, if you don't mind, I'm overdue for a long, hot bath."

Margie locked the door behind the Bulgarian woman and ran herself a tub with some satisfaction. What the stupid prunt didn't know was that she was leaving Camp Detrick direct from the launch pad. The next chance she would have to talk anything over with anybody would be on Klong, and there let her say whatever she liked.

But Ana Dimitrova was only one problem, and maybe the easiest to solve. "One has heard rumors that the launch may be canceled" indeed! If Dimitrova had heard them, then everybody had heard them, and maybe the rumors were close to being true.

Margie allowed herself five minutes of luxurious soaking in the tub. When she got out she draped a towel around her body, not from modesty but from distaste; the shots had raised angry red welts all over her skin, and even with the ointment and the pills they itched. She did not want to be seen like that. Certainly not by the senator. It was bad advertising for the merchandise.

As she was dialing Adrian Lenz's private number she looked at herself in the mirror, frowned, and switched to voice only. "Hello, honey," she said as soon as he was on the line. "I'm sorry there's no picture, but this place doesn't have all mod. cons., and anyway"—she giggled—"I don't have any clothes on."

"Hello, Margie." Senator Lenz's voice was neutral. It was the sort of tone one uses to a brother-in-law or an airport security guard; it said, I acknowledge there is a relationship between us, but don't push it. "I assume you're calling me about your proposed new launch."

"Just 'proposed,' Adrian? You voted for it three weeks ago."

"I know my own voting record, Margie."

"Of course you do, Adrian. Listen, I didn't call you up to quarrel with you."

"No, you didn't," said the senator. "You called me up to try to keep me in line. I was pretty sure you'd call. I'm even pretty sure of what you're going to say. You're going to tell me that we've got a hell of a big investment in Klong now and if we don't nourish it the whole thing might go down the tube."

"Something like that, senator," Marge Menninger said reluctantly.

"I was sure of it. You know, we've heard those arguments before. Every time the DoD wants something outrageous they start by asking some piss-ant amount as a 'study grant.' Then a little more because the study showed some really promising idea. Then some more because, gosh, senator, we've gone this far, let's not waste it. And then, the next thing you know, we've got some stupid new missile or antiballistic defense system or nuclear bomber. Not because any sensible person wants it, but because there was no place to stop. Well, Margie, maybe this is the place to stop Klong. Three days from now there's a committee meeting. I don't know which way I'm going to vote, because I don't have all the information yet. But I'm not making any promises."

Margie kept the disappointment out of her voice, but she was less successful with the anger. "This project means a hell of a lot to me, Adrian."

"Don't you think I know it? Listen, Margie, this is an open line, but I thought you might be interested in something. I've got tomorrow's early edition of the *Herald* here, and there's a story from Peiping. 'Authoritative souces' say that repair crews at their tactran satellite have definite evidence that the explosion which destroyed the satellite and two transport ships was of suspicious origin."

"I watch the news, Adrian. I saw that. And there was another story, too, that said that dissident elements within the People's Republics were thought to be responsible."

The senator was silent. Margie would have given a lot to have seen the expression on his face just then, even at the cost of revealing the sorry condition of her own, and her hand reached out to restore the vision circuit to the call. But then the senator said, "I guess that's all we should say under the circumstances, Margie. I agree with you about one thing. You've gotten us into this pretty deep." And he broke the connection.

Margie sat thoughtfully blow-drying her hair for the

next ten minutes, while her mind raced. Then she picked up
the phone and dialed the orderly room. "Colonel Menninger," she said. "Notify the training officer that I will not
be present for tomorrow's formations, and have transportation ready for me at oh eight hundred. I need to go to
New York."

"Yes, ma'am," said the OD. He was not surprised. All
members of the project were restricted to the base, and the
orders said there were no exceptions. But he knew who
had written the orders.

Margie sat impatiently in the audience section of the
Security Council chamber, waiting to be called. The
delegation from Peru was explaining its recent vote at
considerable length while the other nine members of the
council waited in varying degrees of fury to explain each
other's. The question seemed to have something to do with
the territorial limits for fishing fleets. Normally Margie
would have paid close attention, but her mind was a good
many light-years away, on Klong. When the young black
woman came to fetch her for her appointment she forgot
about Peru before she had left the auditorium.

The woman conducted her to an inconspicuous room
marked Authorized Personnel Only and held the door
open for her without going, or looking, inside.

"Hello, poppa," said Margie as soon as the door was
closed, turning her cheek to be kissed.

Her father did not kiss her. "You look like hell," he
said, his voice flat and without affection. "What the fuck
have you been teaching these 'colonists' of yours?"

Margie was caught off guard; it was not any of the
questions she had expected from him, and certainly not
what she had come to discuss. But she responded at once.
"I've been teaching them survival tactics. Exactly what I
said I was going to teach them."

"Take a look at these," he said, spreading a sheaf of
holoflat pictures before her. "Art exhibits from Heir-of-
Mao's private collection. Cost me quite a lot to get them."

Margie held one up, wiggling it slightly to get the effect
of three-dimensional motion. "Makes me look fat," she
said critically.

"These came out of the pouch of a courier in Ottawa.
You recognize them, I guess. There's one of your boys
throwing a grenade. And a nice shot of a flamethrower

drill. And another one of a girl, I won't say who, stabbing what looks a hell of a lot like a Krinpit with what looks a hell of a lot like a sword."

"Oh, hell, poppa, that's no sword. It's just a flat, sharp knife. I got the idea from watching the stew chef opening up oysters at the Grand Central Clam Bar. And that Krinpit's only a dummy."

"Hell's shitfire, Margie! That's combat technique!"

"It's survival, dear," she corrected. "What do you think? The biggest and ugliest dangers our boys and girls are going to face are the Krinpit and the burrowers and the balloonists and, oh, yes, not to forget the Greasies and the Peeps. I'm not advocating killing, poppa, I'm just teaching them how to handle themselves if killing is going on." Her face clouded. "All the same, I wish I knew who took those pictures."

"You will," he said grimly. "But it doesn't matter; those are just copies. The Peeps have the originals, and Tam Gulsmit's probably got a set of his own by now, and the Peeps and the Greasies on Klong are going to hear about it by next week at the latest, and interexpedition friendship is over. Did you listen to the debate in the council?"

"What? Oh, sure—a little."

"You should have listened a lot. Peru has just extended its ocean borders to a thousand kilometers."

Margie squinted, perplexed. "What does that have to do with maybe some fighting on Klong?"

"Peru wouldn't do that without a lot of backing from somebody. They're nominally Food, sure, because of the anchovy catch. But they don't have a pot to piss in when the fish go deep, so they try to keep friendly with the other blocs."

"Which one?"

Her father pushed the corners of his eyes up. He did not do it because there was any risk of this supersensitive room being bugged; it was only a reflex not to speak the name of Heir-of-Mao unnecessarily.

Margie was silent for a moment while the card sorter in her brain ordered her hierarchy of priorities. She came back to Number One. "Poppa," she said, "Peru can stick their anchovies in their ear, and I'm not going to lose sleep about which one of my people is a spy, and if we get a little scandal about combat training we'll survive it. None of it's going to matter in two or three weeks, because we'll be there, and that's what I came to see you about. Adrian Lenz is crawfishing. I need help, poppa. Don't let him cancel us out."

Her father leaned back in his chair. Margie was not used to seeing Godfrey Menninger looking old and tired, but that was how he looked now.

"Sweetie," he said heavily, "do you have any idea how much trouble we're in?"

"Of course, I do, poppa, but—"

"No, listen. I don't think you do. There's a tanker aground on Catalina Island today, with six hundred thousand tons of oil that isn't going to get to Long Beach. Wouldn't matter, normally. Southern California keeps plenty of reserves. But their reserves got diverted to your project, so they're low now. Unless they get that tanker afloat in forty-eight hours, Los Angeles is going to spend the weekend in a brownout. What do you think is going to be the public reaction to that?"

"Well, sure, a certain amount of shit is going to—"

He raised his hand. "And you saw the story in this morning's papers. The Peeps know their tactran satellite was deliberately destroyed."

"No, it wasn't! That was an accident. The bomb was just supposed to knock out the supply ship!"

"An accident in the commission of a crime becomes part of the crime, Margie."

"But they can't prove—I mean, there's no way in the world that they can pin it on me unless—"

She looked at her father. He shook his head. "The Italian isn't going to tell them anything. He's already been taken out."

So poor Guido was not going to live to spend his hundred thousand petrodollars. "He gave good value," she said. "Look what you got out of his microfiches. You have proof that the Greasies set up their base where they did because they had seismic scans to show oil under it. That's against treaty right there."

"Don't be a child, Margie. What does 'proof' have to do with it? Sir Tam and the Slopies can't prove you handed Ghelizzi the bomb, but they don't have to prove, they only have to know. And they do. Peru proves it. Not to mention a few other little news items you may not have heard about yet, like the American embassy in Buenos Aires being firebombed this morning. That's a little message from Sir Tam or Heir-of-Mao, I would judge. What do you suppose the next message is going to be?"

Margie realized she had been scratching her blisters and made herself take her hand away. "Oh, shit," she said glumly, and thought hard while her father waited.

But really, she reflected, the basic rules were unchanged. The equation of power was utterly clear. No nation could afford to fight any other nation in the whole world anymore. Food, Fuel, and People each owned enough muscle to smash both the others flat, and all of them knew it. Worse than that. Even the tiniest nation had a minute sliver of muscle of its own, gift of the breeder reactors and the waste reclaimers. Not enough to matter in a global sense, no. But Peru could enforce its decisions if driven to. Ecuador could kill Washington or Miami, Denmark could destroy Glasgow, Indonesia could obliterate Melbourne. Fire-bombings and riots—well, what did they matter? There was a permanent simmer of border incidents and small-scale violence. Each year, a few thousand injured, a few score or hundreds dead. But the lid never blew off, because everybody knew what would happen.

"Poppa," she said, "you know nobody can do anything *really* serious. The balance of power prohibits it."

"Wrong! The balance of power breaks down as soon as somebody makes a mistake. The Peeps made one when they fired rockets at our gasbags on Klong. *I* made one when I let you carry that bomb to Belgrade. It's time to pull the fuses, honey."

For the first time in her adult life, Margie Menninger felt real fear. "Poppa! Are you saying you're not going to help me with Lenz?"

"I'm saying more than that, Margie. I agree with him. I'm seeing the President tomorrow, and I'm going to tell him to scrap the launch."

"Poppa!"

He hesitated. "Honey, maybe later. After things quiet down—"

"Later's no good! You think the Peeps aren't going to reinforce as soon as they can get another satellite up there? And the Greasies? And—"

"It's settled, Margie."

She looked at him, appalled. This was the God Menninger that his whole agency knew and she had rarely seen. It wasn't her father she was looking at. It was a human being as implacable and determined as she herself had ever been, and with the accustomed support of a great deal of power to back his decisions up.

She said, "I can't change your mind." It wasn't a question, and he didn't give it an answer.

"Well," she said, "there's no reason for me to hang around here then, is there? Good-bye, poppa. Take care of yourself. I'll see you another time."

She did not look at him again as she got up, collected her brown leather officer's bag and her uniform cap, and let herself out.

If her father was as determined as she, the other side of the coin was that she was no less determined than he. She stopped in the visitors' lounge and entered a public phone booth to dial a local number.

The woman on the other end was a strikingly handsome human being, not a sex symbol but a work of art. "Why, Marjorie," she said. "I thought you were off doing spy stuff for your father or something—Marjorie! What's the matter with your face?"

Marge felt her blotched chin. "Oh, that. That's just a reaction to some shots. Can I come over to see you?"

"Of course, lover. Right now?"

"Right this second, mom." Margie hung up the phone and hurried toward the elevators. But before she entered them she stopped in a ladies' room to check her make-up.

Marge Menninger's mother lived, among other places, in the residential tower section of one of New York City's tallest and most expensive skyscrapers. It was an old-fashioned place, built when energy was cheap, so that it made economic sense at that time to economize on insulation and rely on huge inputs of BTUs all winter long and continuous air conditioning all summer. It was one of the few that had not been at least partly rebuilt when oil reached P\$300 a barrel, and it would have been ruinously expensive for most tenants—even most well-to-do tenants. The condominium apartments were no more expensive to buy than any others in a good neighborhood. But if you had to ask what the maintenance costs would be, you couldn't afford them. Alicia Howe and her present husband didn't have to ask.

The butler welcomed Margie. "How nice to see you, Miss Menninger! Will you be using your room this time?"

"Afraid not, Harvey. I just want to talk to mom."

"Yes, Miss Margie. She's expecting you."

As Alicia Howe rose to be kissed, she made a quick, all-seeing inventory of her daughter. Those awful splotches on her complexion! The clothes were passable enough, as army uniforms went, and thank heaven the child had been born with her father's smiling good looks. "You could lose a couple of kilos, lover," she said.

"I will, I promise. Mom, I want you to do me a favor."

"Of course, hon."

"Poppa's being a little difficult about something, and I need to go public. I want to hold a news conference."

Alicia Howe's husband owned a lot of televison: three major-city outlets and large interests in a dozen satellite networks. "I'm sure one of Harold's people can help you out," she said slowly. "Should I ask what the problem is?"

"Mom, you shouldn't even know there's a problem."

Her mother sighed. She had learned to live with God Menninger's off-the-record life while they were married, but since the divorce she had hoped to be free of it. She never talked to her ex-husband. It wasn't that she disliked him—in her heart, she still thought him the most interesting, and by a long way the sexiest, of her men. But she could not cope with the knowledge that any little slip of the tongue from him to her, and from her to anyone, might bring catastrophic consequences to the world.

"Honey, I do have to tell Harold something."

"Oh, sure, mom. But not as a problem. What I want to talk about is Kl—Jem. The planet Jem. I'm going there, mom."

"Yes, of course, you told me that. In a year or two, maybe, when things settle down—"

"I want to settle them down, mom. I want the United States to send enough muscle up there to make it fit to live in. Fit for you to visit someday, if you want to. And I want to do it now. I'm supposed to leave in eighteen days."

"Margie! Really, Margie!"

"Don't take on, will you? It's what I want."

Alicia Howe had not been able to prevail against that argument in more than a dozen years. She had no hope of prevailing against it now. The thought of her daughter flinging herself through space to some terrible place where people died disgustingly was frightening. But Margie had demonstrated a capacity for taking care of herself.

"Well," she said, "I guess I can't send you to your room. All right. You haven't told me what you want me to do."

"Ask Harold to get me onto one of his newsmaker programs. He'll know how to do it better than I can tell him. They're backing away from my planet, mom, cutting the funding, complaining about the problems. I want the public to know how important it is, and I want to be the one to tell them." She added strategically, "Poppa was right behind me on this at first, but now he's changed his mind. He wants to call the whole thing off."

"You mean you want to put the squeeze on your own father?"

"Exactly right."

Alicia Howe smiled. That part was sure to appeal to her current husband. She spread her hands resignedly and moved toward the phone. "I'll tell Harold what you want," she said.

Ana Dimitrova sat with her eyes closed in a broad, low room, elbows on a ring-shaped table, head in her hands, earphones on her head. Her lips were moving. Her head twitched from side to side as she tried to match the rhythms of the taped balloonist song that was coming over the headset. It was very difficult, in large part because it was not a balloonist's voice making the sounds. It was a Krinpit's. The tape had been made several weeks before, when Detrick's last surviving Krinpit had had no one left to talk to but Shirley, the one surviving balloonist.

But her name had not been Shirley. Her name, rather beautiful, had been *Mo'ahi'i Ba'alu'i*, which meant something like Sweetly Golden Cloud-Bearer. Krinpit rasps and tympani did not easily form the balloonist sounds. But Shirley had understood him—no, Ana corrected herself, Mo'ahi'i Ba'alu'i had understood him. Ana was determined to do the same, and so she played and replayed sections of the tape:

Ma'iya'a hi'i (these creatures unlike us) *hu'u ha'iye'i* (are vicious animals).

And Cloud-Bearer's response:

Ni'u'a mali'i na'a hu'iha. (They have killed my song).

Ana pushed the headphones off her ears and allowed herself to rub her eyes. The headaches were very bad tonight. And this awful room! Twenty headsets and tape-control panels before twenty identical hard-backed chairs, all around the ring. So bleak! So unsympathetic!

Unsympathetic? Ana clucked her lips at herself. That was one of the English language's booby-trap words: sympathetic, *simpatico*. They sounded so much alike. But they did not mean the same thing, and it was embarrassing to a translator of Ana's skills to fall into the blunder of confusing them. It proved she was too tired to work anymore this night, and so she switched off the tape decisively, hung the earphones on their hook, and stood up to go. She intended to wish a courteous good night to those few other eager project personnel who had shared her desire to put in overtime at the tape ring. But there weren't any. They had all left while she was concentrating.

It was nearly eleven o'clock! In six hours she would have to be getting out of bed!

Hurrying down the empty company street toward her room, Ana paused halfway, changed course, and entered the dayroom. Really, these headaches were too bad! But there was a dispensing machine in the dayroom, and sometimes one of the American soft drinks containing caffeine would constrict the blood vessels and reduce the thumping, thumping throb long enough for her to get to sleep.

But as she dropped a dollar into the machine and waited for the cup to fill, it seemed to her that coming here had been a mistake, after all. Such an ear-drubbing of noise! A dozen couples were dancing frenziedly to a stereo at one end of the room. At the other a young Oriental man had a guitar, and a group was singing with him, quite at cross-purposes to the music on the stereo. Quite uncaring. And even more noise came from the television alcove: a babble of excited voices, laughter. What could they be watching? She drifted closer to peer at the screen. Someone was lifting a pillowcase out of a sonic washer and exclaiming rapturously over its pristine shine. Were these people excited over a commercial?

"Oh, Nan," cried her roommate, elbowing toward her. "You missed it. She was *wonderful.*"

"What? What did I miss? Who was wonderful?"

"Lieutenant Colonel Menninger. It was really super. You know," confided the woman, "I never really liked her. But tonight she was just beautiful. She was on the six o'clock news. It was just a little person-to-person interview, like a follow-up to a story about Jem. I don't know why they picked her, but I'm glad they did! She said such wonderful things! She said Jem gave hope to all the unhappy people of the world. She said it was a planet where all the old hatreds could be forgotten. A place where—what did she say?—yes, a place where each child could elect a morality and an idea, and have the space and the freedom to live his life by it!"

Ana coughed Coca-Cola in a fine spray into her cupped hand. "Colonel Menninger said that?" she gasped.

"Yes, yes, Nan, and she said it beautifully. We were all touched. Even people like Stud Sweggert and Nguyen the Tryin' were *really* moved. I mean, they even kept their hands to themselves. And the newscaster said something about sending troops to Jem, and Colonel Menninger said, 'I'm a soldier myself. Every country has soldiers like me, and every one of us prays we'll never have anything to do. But on Jem we can do something useful! Something for peace, not for destruction. Please let us do it.'—What?"

Nan had been marveling to herself in Bulgarian. "No, no, please go on," she said.

"Well. And just now they repeated parts of it on the late report, and they said the public response has been incredible. Telegrams, phone calls. To the White House and the UN and the networks—I don't know where all."

Ana forgot her headache. "Perhaps I have been doing Colonel Menninger an injustice. Truly, I am amazed."

"Well, I am too! But she made me feel really good about what we're doing, and everyone's talking about it!"

And they were. Not only in the barracks dayroom. Senator Lenz's phones were ringing, and it was constituents urging him to make sure the heroes on Jem got support. Newsrooms around the country were watching the electronic tally of calls from the public: Jem, Jem! Spot pollsters were reporting great and growing public concern. God Menninger's phone rang only once, but the person on the other end was the President of the United

States. When he hung up, Menninger's face was tense and stern, but then it relaxed and he broke into a smile. "Honey," he said to empty space, "damn your black heart, you do your old man proud."

THIRTEEN

●

FOR TWENTY KILOMETERS Charlie and his flock tried to follow the little biplane as it chugged and bounced through the sky of Jem. No use. The balloonists soared high, swooped low, found winds that carried them toward the heat pole, but never fast enough to keep up. Charlie sang a mournful farewell song into his radio as they turned away, and the sound penetrated even the noisy rattle of the little engine inside the plane. "Too much noise," shouted Kappelyushnikov cheerfully into Danny Dalehouse's ear. "Turn off, please?"

"Let me say good-bye first." Dalehouse sang into the tiny radio, then switched it off. Far behind and half a kilometer overhead, the flock boobed acknowledgment. Dalehouse craned his neck to see forward, but the camp of the Greasies was of course nowhere yet in sight. They were flying almost directly toward the Heat Pole—"southeast" by the convention of considering the poles of rotation as north and south, however irrelevant that was to compasses and sextants—and it was uphill almost all the way. How foolish of the Greasies to locate their camp in the least hospitable part of the planet! But who could figure why the Greasies did things?

Kappelyushnikov leaned over and slapped him on the shoulder. "You wish to puke?" he called encouragingly, pointing over the side of the cockpit. Dalehouse shook his head. "Is all right, you know," Cappy went on. "Is little rough, yes. We are fighting winds, not making love to them like in balloon. But you have truly outstanding aircraft technician in charge!"

"I'm not complaining."

And in fact, he had no reason to complain. The biplane was a technological marvel on Klong—on Jem, as they were supposed to call it now, he reminded himself. At least they were flying! The Greasy camp was hard to reach any other way. There were no cars on Jem, because no roads. Only a tracked vehicle could go very far, and even the Greasies did not have them to spare. Because, in their pigheaded way, the Greasies had camped ten kilometers from the nearest usable water, boats were out. You could fly there for this semi-summit meeting that was supposed to make everyone on Jem friends again. Or you could walk. And Dalehouse spared a thought of compassion for the poor, proud, pedestrian Peeps, who were no doubt doing just that somewhere below.

So just to be flying was a triumph, although he wished Cappy had not brought up the subject of airsickness. It was not so much the motion that was bothering him as the food they had been eating. With twenty-two more mouths to feed, the old catch-as-catch-can meal style was down the drain. Unfortunately, the new people had brought their appetites, but they had forgotten to pack a chef to satisfy them. The food was unbearable. No one dared complain. The person who bitched would be the next cook.

Still, the community was growing. The third resupply ship had brought a great deal! This sputtering little two-winged airplane, folded and stacked and foolish-looking, but demonstrably workable, because it was working. The little plutonium-powered machines and instruments that had given Morrissey sensors to study the Creepies in their tunnels under the ground and Dalehouse himself radios to pass on to Charlie. A new Argus orbiter to photograph clouds and help them predict the weather. Or at least to guess at it a little more accurately.

It had even helped them in their attempts to make contact with sentients. Sort of. Charlie was delighted with his crossbow and his radio. Jim Morrissey had taken another tack. He had used the new power auger to make three widely spaced holes along a Creepy burrow. The end holes held soft charges of explosives, the center one a hose connected to the exhaust of the auger's little gasoline putt-putt. When Morrissey blew the charges he sealed both ends of that section of the tunnel, and the carbon monoxide caught four burrowers before they could dig away. By then they were no good for Dalehouse's purposes, of course, but they were a joy to Morrissey.

Even further marvels were on their way. The third

resupply had brought eight metric tons of equipment, but according to the tactran messages the next would bring nearly fifty, plus maybe a hundred additional personnel. It would be a city! The summons to the meeting at the Fuel camp had not only been a welcome tour of Jem, it had been a reprieve from the tedium of erecting tents to receive the reinforcements.

What the tactran had failed to say was just what the reinforcements would be used for. They certainly needed any number of specialists they didn't have. A *real* cook. A dentist. Some better-looking women. A better translator . . . reminded, Dalehouse leaned back to see how Harriet was faring behind him.

The translator was most uncomfortably curled up in a space no more than a meter square, and studded, at that, with bolts and levers that must have been tattooing Harriet's hips and ribs indelibly. If she had been anyone else Dalehouse would have thought of some friendly, commiserating remark. For Harriet he could find none. Her eyes were closed. Her expression registered resignation to the palpable injustice of being the smallest of the three of them, and thus the one to be squeezed into the tiny rear compartment.

"Getting close," Kappelyusknikov bawled in his ear.

Dalehouse leaned forward, rubbing at the glass as though the Jemman murk were on the inside rather than all around. There was nothing but maroon cloud—

Then the stark white rim of the Heat Pole glittered through a break. And something else. The clouds themselves were clearly bright. As the biplane tunneled out of the last of the cloud bank they were leaving, Dalehouse saw the cause before him.

"Jesu Crist!" cried Kappelyusknikov. "Have they no shame?"

The light was the Oily camp. It stood out on the horizon like a bonfire, penetrating Jem's dour maroon murk with beacons, lighted windows—my God, Dalehouse marveled, even streetlamps! It was no longer an expeditionary camp. It looked like a small town.

The vertical beacon dipped and swept across the biplane to acknowledge their approach, then courteously away so that they were not dazzled. Kappelyushnikov muttered inaudibly into his radio mouthpiece, listened for a moment, and then began to circle.

"What's the matter?" Dalehouse demanded.

"Is nothing the matter, only we are no longer in hurry," said the pilot. "Peeps will be unavoidably one hour detained, so let us study this miracle before landing on it."

A miracle it very nearly was. There were only about forty people in the Greasy camp, but they seemed to have almost that many buildings. *Buildings,* not tents or plastic huts. What had they made them out of? And what buildings! Some were barracks, some seemed individual bungalows. One looked more like a tenth-size copy of the Eiffel Tower than like a structure one could live or work in. Another was a good twenty-five meters in length. And— what was that curious shallow, round-petaled cone on the far side of the camp? It seemed to be constructed of bent strips of shiny metal arrayed around a central black cylinder. Could it be a solar generator? If so, it was almost megawatt size! And—that stubby tower with the horizontally rotating fan. Wasn't that the exhaust from an *air conditioner?*

Harriet had roused herself and was leaning forward over Dalehouse's shoulder to see. Her breath buzzed annoyingly in his ear as she said sternly, "That is a ... *lascivious* waste!"

"Oh, yes, dear Gasha!" cried the pilot. "How wonderful would be if we, too, could afford one!"

Over the rattles and groans that came from his Krinpit escort, Ahmed Dulla heard a sputtering distant sound. "Put me down. Wait. Try to be quiet," he called peevishly in the mixture of Urdu and their own language that made communication possible between them. Or sometimes did. He lowered himself from the litter in which they had been carrying him and climbed onto a knee of a many-tree, pushing aside the pinkly glowing fronds to stare around the sky. A tiny two-winged aircraft was chuttering along just below cloud level. "So. Another triumph of technology arrives," he said.

The Krinpit, Jorrn-fteet, reared back to study him more carefully, its stubby claws waving. "Your meaning is not loud," it rattled.

"No matter. Let us move on." Dulla was in no mood for a nice chat with these grossly hypertrophied bugs, however useful they were to him. "Go carry the litter and my bag; I will walk," he ordered. "It is too steep here for riding."

They were climbing from the shallow valley of the river now, up through the last of the forested slopes onto the dry highlands. The vegetation began to change from many-trees and ferns to things like succulents, stubby barrels with glowing, bright red, luminous buttons. Dulla looked at them all with distaste. Study the plants, find new products; it is in this way that my fathers became independent of the machines of the outside world. So Feng Hua-tse had advised before he left; but Dulla was an astrophysicist, not an herbal healer, and he had no intention of following the fool's instructions.

There was no overhang between him and the sky now, and he could see the little biplane circling, far off toward the bright white line of the Heat Pole. So. The Greasies had their helicopter, the Fats now had a plane, and what did the representative of the People's Republics have to take him to this meeting? A litter carried by animals that looked like squashed crustaceans. Dulla fumed. If Feng had listened to him, they would have insisted that the three-party meeting be held at their own camp. So they would have been spared this humiliation of arriving on a plastic frame carried by creatures out of some children's nonsense fable—if not the humiliation of exposing to the Fats and the Oilies the meanness of their encampment. What a disaster! And all Feng's fault, or Heir-of-Mao's. The expedition should have been properly supplied and reinforced in the first place, but leave it to the Chinamen to hoard coppers to the ruination of the project.

Without warning the Krinpit stopped, and Dulla, lost in his thoughts, almost tripped over them. "What, what?" he complained. "Why are you standing here?"

"A very loud thing moves quickly," rattled Jorrn-fteet.

"I do not hear anything." But now that he was awakened from his reverie he did see something, a swell of dust behind the hills. As he watched, a machine topped the rise, coming toward him. It was still a kilometer away, but it looked like a half-track.

"Another triumph of conspicuous waste," sneered Dulla. "How dare they come for me, as though I could not make the journey by myself?" The Krinpit rattled inquiringly, and he added, "Never mind. Put down the litter; I will carry my knapsack myself now. Hide yourselves. I do not want the Greasies to see you."

But the words conveyed no meaning to the Krinpit. A Krinpit could never hide from another Krinpit as long as they were close enough to hear each other. Dulla struggled to explain. "Go back to the place behind the hill. The Greasies will not hear you there. I will return in the space it took us to come up from the river." He was not sure they understood that, either. The Krinpit had a clear sense of time, but the vocabulary of terms to mark its units did not map well from one language based on a diurnal cycle to another which had evolved on a planet without easy temporal reference points. But they lurched away obediently, and Dulla walked steadily toward the approaching half-track.

The driver was a Kuwaiti, apparently a translator, because he greeted Dulla in flawless Urdu. "Would you like a lift?" he called. "Jump in!"

"You are very courteous," smiled Dulla. "Indeed, it·is a little warm for strolling today." But it was not courtesy at all, he fumed internally, it was only more of their damnable arrogance! Ahmed Dulla was quite sure that he was the only person on Jem whose native language was Urdu, and here the Greasies had made sure they had someone who could speak to him! As though he himself were not already proficient in four other languages!

The time would come, he promised himself, when he would humble the ostentatious swine. So he rode up over the gullied hills toward the Greasy camp, chatting amiably with the Kuwaiti, remarking politely on the fine appearance of their camp, his face smiling and his heart swelling with rage.

The official host for the meeting was named Chesley Pontrefact, London-born but not of native roots that went many generations back. His skin was purplish brown and his hair white wool. Coded tactran messages had given Dulla a good deal of background on every member of the Greasy expeditions, as well as the Fats, and he knew that Pontrefact was an air vice-marshal and nominal commander of the Greasy expedition. But he also knew that real power belonged to one of the civilians from Saudi Arabia.

Pontrefact bustled about the long conference table (wood! shipped all the way from Earth!) offering drinks and smokes. "Brandy do you, Dr. Dalehouse?" he inquired solicitously. "And perhaps a Coca-Cola for you, sir? I'm afraid we don't have orange juice, but at least there's ice."

"Nothing, please," said Dulla, seething. Ice! "I suggest we begin our meeting, if that is convenient."

"Certainly, Dr. Dulla." Pontrefact sat down heavily at the head of the table and glanced inquiringly around. "Mind if I take the chair, just for form's sake?"

Dulla watched to see if any of the Fats were going to object and spoke a split second before they did. "Not at all, Marshal Pontrefact," he said warmly. "We are your guests." But one should show courtesy to guests, and what was this seating arrangement but a deliberate insult? Pontrefact at the head, two of his associates at the foot—the Kuwaiti translator and a woman who could be no one but the Saudi civilian who was the Greasies' decision maker. On one side of the table were all three of the Fats— Dalehouse, their Russian pilot, and their own translator; and on the other—only himself. How much more deliberately could they point out that he was alone and insignificant? He added diffidently, "Since we are all conversant, I believe, with English, perhaps we can dispense with the translators. It is an old saying of my people that the success of a conference is inversely proportional to the square of the number of participants."

Quickly, "I shall stay," said the Fats translator. Pontrefact raised his white-caterpillar eyebrows but said nothing; Dulla shrugged politely and gazed toward the chair, waiting for the proceedings to begin.

The Saudi whispered to the interpreter at some length. Across the table, Dalehouse hesitated, then got up to extend his hand to Dulla. "Good to see you looking fit, Ahmed," he said.

Dulla touched his hand minimally. "Thank you." He added grudgingly, "And thank you for assisting in returning me to my own camp. I have not had a chance to express my gratitude since."

"Glad to help. Anyway, it's good to see someone from your expedition—we don't see many of you, you know."

Dulla glared. Then, stiffly, "I have come a long way for this meeting. Can we not begin?"

"Oh, hell," said Pontrefact from the head of the table.

"Look, mates, the whole reason for this meeting is to try to work together better. We know what a balls-up our masters have made at home. Shall we see if we can do a bit better here?"

Dulla said happily, "Please limit your observations to your own people." It was as he had suspected; the Greasies were going to insult everyone but themselves. Let this West Indian whose grandfather was a ticket collector on the London Underground make a fool of himself if he chose. Not of the People's Republics.

"But I'm in dead earnest, Dr. Dulla. We invited you here because it's clear we are all working at cross-purposes. Your own camp is in serious trouble, and we all know it. The Food people and our own lot are a bit better off, yes. But you don't have a proper doctor, do you, Dr. Dalehouse? Not to mention a few other things. And we can't be expected—that is, we don't have limitless resources either. Under the UN resolution we are all supposed to cooperate and divide the responsibilities. Particularly the science. We undertook the geology, and you can't say we haven't played fair about that. We've done a great deal."

"Indeed so," put in Kappelyushnikov blandly. "Is pure coincidence that most is in personal vicinity and relates primarily to fissionables and to salt domes."

"That is, to petroleum," Dulla agreed. "Yes, I think we are all aware of that, Marshal Pontrefact." How thoughtful of the Fats and the Greasies to begin quarreling among themselves so soon!

"Be that as it may," the chairman went on doggedly, "there's a hell of a lot to be done here, and we can't do it all. Astronomy, for instance. We did orbit a satellite observatory, but—as I am sure you know—it ran into malfunctions. Let me show you something." He got up and moved to a likris screen on the wall. When he had fiddled with it for a moment the crystals sprang into varicolored light, showing some sort of graph. "You've seen our solar generator. This shows the solar input for our power plant. As you see, there are spikes in the curve. This may not seem important to you, but our generator is a precision instrument. It isn't going to do its job properly if the solar constant isn't, well, constant."

Dulla stared in black envy at the graph. That was what he was here for, after all—because he was a specialist in stellar studies! He hardly noticed when Dalehouse put in, "If Kung is acting up, it may mean more to us than a few wiggles in your power supply."

Pontrefact nodded. "Of course it may. We notified this to Herstmonceux-Greenwich with a copy of the tape. They're quite upset about it. Kung may be a variable star."

"Hardly," sneered Dulla. "It is known that a few flares are possible."

"But it is not known how many, or how big; and that's exactly what we need to know. What, if I may say, we confidently expected to know from the astronomical researches that were meant to be conducted by your expedition, Dr. Dulla."

Dulla exploded. "But this is too much! How can one practice astrophysics when one is hungry? And whose fault is that?"

"Certainly not ours, old chap," Pontrefact said indignantly.

"But someone blew up our ships, *old chap*. Someone killed thirty-four citizens of the People's Republics, old chap!"

"But that was—" Pontrefact stopped the sentence in mid-syllable. He made a visible effort to control his temper. "Be that as it may," he got out again, "the plain fact is the work's got to be done, and someone's got to do it. You have the instruments and we don't, at least not until proper telescopes arrive from Earth. We have the manpower, and you evidently don't."

"I beg your pardon. Allow me to inform you of my academic standing. I am director of the Planetology Institute at Zulfikar Ali Bhutto University and have graduate degrees in astrophysics from—"

"But no one's disputing your degrees, dear man, only your fitness to function. Let us send our own astronomer over. Better still, let Boyne airlift your equipment here, where there's better seeing—"

"Certainly not! Not either!"

"I really don't think that's quite fair, do you? We've certainly cooperated in providing food, for instance—"

"Such food! For your people, not for ours: all flour, hardly any rice."

Dalehouse said placatingly, "We'll turn up some rice for you if that's what you like."

"How gracious of you!" Dulla sneered.

"Now, wait a minute, Dulla. We've done our best for you—and we have a couple of complaints of our own, if you want to know. Like shooting at me!"

Dulla grimaced. "That was only Hua-tse's foolishness with fireworks. The People's Republics have already expressed their regrets."

"To whom? The dead balloonists?"

"Yes," sneered Dulla with exaggerated humility, "of course, it is so; we do apologize to your close friends, the comic gasbags. And to yours too, sir, the vermin who dig in the earth and whom you find so useful!"

"If you mean the Creeps," said Pontrefact, his control of his temper wearing thin, "at least we don't use them as litter bearers."

"No! You use them to help you exploit the mineral riches! Is it not true that there has been radiation disease among them?"

"No, it isn't! At least, not here. We did use a few to dig samples for us in other areas, and yes, they did encounter some radiation, but I must say that I resent the imputation that we are exploiting the natives."

"Oh, I am sure you would not do that, Marshal Pontrefact, especially as your own ancestors must have experienced so much of that from the other side, as it were."

"Now, look here, Dulla!"

But Pontrefact was interrupted by the Saudi woman, who said: "I think we should recess for lunch. We have much to discuss, and shouting at each other will not help. Let's resolve to try to do better in the afternoon."

But the afternoon session, if quieter, did not seem very productive to Danny Dalehouse. "At least we got a decent meal out of it," he said to Kappelyushnikov outside the longhouse where they had met.

"Is as ashes in my mouth," growled the Russian. "Oh, how many nice things they have here. Not just food."

That was not to be argued. Across from the meeting-house a new building was going up. A tracked dumpster deposited a scoop of earth into a hopper; the man running it shoved a lever forward, there was a high-pitched whine, and moments later, the sides fell away and the operator lifted out a finished panel of hard brick. The trick was in adding something to the compacted earth as a stabilizer.

"And have you seen what's up on the hill?" asked Harriet with jealousy in her tone. On the slopes above the colony there were terraced rows of green seedlings. *Green!* The Greasies were using banks of incandescent plant lights to grow Terrestrial food!

"Feel like time when I was seventeen years," said Kappelyushnikov. "Kid sailplane pilot, winner of All-Region Height and Endurance Contest, fresh from Nizhniy Tagil, walking down Kalinin-Prospekt first time in life, and oh, my God, how overwhelming was Moscow! Trams, skyscrapers, bookstores, restaurants." He pointed to the plasma column of the solar generator, with its rosette of reflectors around it. "Is daunting, dear friends. No wonder Greasies call us here to issue orders of day. They have muscle to enforce!" He shrugged, then grinned as they rounded the last barracks and saw the little landing field. "Hoy! Boyne!" he shouted. "Come say good-bye to country cousins!"

The Irish pilot hesitated, then came toward them. "Hello," he said noncommittally. "I've just been putting our friend Dulla on a jeep on his way home."

"He didn't seem in a very good mood," Dalehouse observed.

The pilot grinned. "His feelings were hurt, I'd say. He didn't want us to see that he was using Krinpit transportation to get here. You didn't know that? They came up the river by boat, and then the Krips carried him up eight or ten kilometers until we picked him up."

Harriet said spitefully, "He might have been in a better mood if you hadn't gone out of your way to insult him, Dalehouse."

"Me? How?"

"He thought you were making a joke about the fact that so few of the Peeps have survived. His face went all tight."

Dalehouse protested. "I didn't mean anything like that. He's such a thorny son of a bitch."

"Forget," advised Kappelyushnikov. "He is such close friend of cockroaches, let them worry about his feelings."

"Well, I don't understand that either, Cappy. The Krinpit almost killed him."

"Then how is possible they become native bearers for fine Pakistani sahib as he daringly marches through jungle?"

"I can explain that," Boyne said gloomily, "although I can't say I like it. That first Krinpit you and I carried here, Dalehouse, the one that calls itself Sharn-igon? It's mad at all human beings. Apparently its girlfriend, or actually I think it was a boyfriend, died from the first contact with the Peeps, and it just wants to get even. Only its idea of getting even seems to be to make as much trouble for as many human beings as it can. It's raised a hell of a fuss with the Krips near here; we can't make any contact with them at all. I guess it thinks the Peeps are pretty well screwed, so it's willing to help them screw the rest of us. Looks damn bad for the future, if you ask me."

He was walking along with them toward the airstrip, but his manner seemed reserved; he made no eye contact with any of them, and what he said was more of a monologue than a conversation.

Kappelyushnikov said placatingly, "Hey, Boyne, you pissed about something?"

"Me? Why should I be?" But Boyne still did not look at him.

Kappelyushnikov glanced at the others, then back to the pilot. "Hey, Boyne," he wheedled. "We two are members of great interstellar brotherhood of pilotry, should not be pissed at each other."

"Look, it's not you personally," said Boyne angrily. "I got my ass eaten out for lending you chaps the backhoe, not to mention talking a little more openly than I was supposed to about what we were doing here."

"But we're all in this together," Dalehouse put in. "It's like Pontrefact said at the meeting. We're supposed to share information."

"Oh, Ponty's got the right idea, but that's supposed to go both ways. You didn't see fit to mention some of your own little deeds, did you? Like arming the balloonists against the Krinpit?"

"We didn't! I mean, that's my own department, Boyne. We've given them a few simple weapons to protect themselves against the *ha'aye'i*, that's all."

"Well, they've been using them against everything they can catch. Not to mention that business with the Peeps' supply ship."

"That was an accident!" Dalehouse said.

"Sure it was. Same as it's an accident that your plane—" He hesitated, then closed his mouth.

"Come on, Boyne, what are you trying to say?" Dalehouse demanded.

"Nothing. Forget it." Boyne glanced back toward the camp, then said rapidly, "Look, this peace conference was a bust, right? Nothing got settled. And the way things are going—well, I've got a bad feeling. The local Krips are gassing our Creepies in their burrows every once in awhile—that's Peeps' doing, I suppose. The Peep ship gets blown up; you say it's an accident, but the gen says CIA. You're giving the Loonies weapons. And your plane—well, shit, man," he said, glaring at Kappelyushnikov. "I've got eyes. So right now I don't feel like having a heart-to-heart, all right? Maybe some other time. So, so long, and have a nice flight home." He nodded briskly and turned back to the Greasy base.

Kappelyushnikov broodingly watched him go. "I too have bad feeling," he said. "About dear friend and fellow pilot Boyne, too. Questions I would like to ask, but this is not good time."

"I'd like to know more about what they're using the Creepies for," Dalehouse agreed. "And frankly, that bit about our being responsible for the Peeps' accident is beginning to get under my skin. Do you think there's any possibility it could be true?"

Cappy regarded him thoughtfully. "You are very nice person, Danny," he said sadly. "Perhaps you do not wonder enough. Like, do you wonder why Greasies have landing strip when gillicopter lands anywhere?"

"That hadn't occurred to me," Dalehouse admitted.

"Occurred to me," said the Russian. "Just like occurred to Boyne to wonder why strange little hatch dear Gasha rode on is in our plane. You and Gasha look at it, you say, 'Oh, what a nuisance. Cannot understand purpose.' But when pilot looks at it, Boyne or me, we say at once, 'Oh, how strange that aircraft designed for peaceful exploration has built-in bomb bay.' "

Thirty meters below the airstrip, Mother dr'Shee woke with the smell of cyanide in her splayed nose, too faint to be dangerous, too strong to ignore. The Shelled Devils were at it again.

She yipped peremptorily for the brood-member on duty. It turned out to be t'Weechr, the runt of the litter and the one the others saddled with the least attractive jobs—including, she realized justly, attending to the wants of the Mother when she first woke up. There were only seven in this present brood of hers, and all of them male, and none of them the size or the strength or the wit of their father. It was a loose and unsettling time, and it spoiled her temper.

"Food," she ordered harshly. "And drink. And someone to groom me while I am waiting."

T'Weechr said humbly, "There is no one but me, Brood Mother. I will be quick with the food and groom you while you eat."

"And why is there no one?"

"The New Devils are teaching, Brood Mother. All are commanded to be present."

"Tssheee." If dr'Shee had been a human, the sound would have been a grunt, written "Humph" for convenience's sake. But she was not actually displeased, merely fretful; and when t'Weechr returned it was not only with tubers and a shell of water, but there were even some fresh leaves and fruits from Above.

"Taken or given?" she demanded, sniffing them suspiciously.

"These were gifts of the New Devils, Brood Mother," the youth apologized.

"Tssheee." They were, however, tasty, and she was hungry. She defecated neatly into the shell when she was finished, and t'Weechr folded it closed.

"Is there any other service, Brood Mother?" he asked, licking a final strand of her fur into neatness.

"No. Be gone." He touched noses and wriggled away to deliver the package to the rotting rooms. The next brood would mix it with the planting mud and plaster it into the ceilings of the farm tunnels when they prepared the next crops. By then it would be well aged, and of great value in growing the tubers.

Runt or not, t'Weechr was a good child. She would miss him when the litter matured and scattered. And that time was not far off. At every awakening now, her dugs had been smaller and harder. The breeding males knew it, and every time she left her nest they wriggled close to touch her, nose to anus, testing to see how near she was to courtship. Only yesterday the male with the scarred leg had said, half-jesting, "What would you like next time, dr'Shee? Krinpit shell? A live Flying Devil? The head of a New Devil?"

"Your own head," she had said, half-irritated, half-flirtatious. He had snorted laughter through the spreading folds of his nose and crept away, but he would be back. It was not an unpleasing thought. Dr'Shee's brood-sister had mated with that one, two litters ago. A fine brood, three females! And the sister had said he was indefatigable at rut. Well. A proper courtship was a proper courtship, but she could not help hoping that he might turn out to be the male with the finest gift to lay before her.

Faint and distant vibrations in the earth set her whiskers to quivering. That was the New Devils, too. Time was when such tremors had meant only a particularly violent thunderstorm Above, or perhaps the crash of a falling many-tree. Now the New Devils scraped and shoved hillocks and boulders around at will, and the earth was no longer easy to her senses. As she moved around her chamber, sniffing and touching to make sure everything was in its place, it was touch and smell and taste that principally guided her. Sometimes her males had plastered bits of fungus and vegetation into the walls along with the secretions that made their tunnels hard and waterproof, and from the plant decay there was some faint glow. Dr'Shee appreciated the light but did not need it. For her people, eyes were almost a handicap, especially on their infrequent dashes to the Surface, when only the densest of clouds and worst of storms dimmed Kung's radiance enough for them to bear.

"Greeting, dr'Shee."

She sniffed in startlement and then recognized the female at the entrance to her chamber. "How are you, qr'Tshew? Come in, come in."

The other female entered, and dr'Shee said at once, "I will send for food."

"I have eaten," said qr'Tshew politely. "What lovely courtship gifts." She fondled dr'Shee's collection. Six breedings, six fine gifts: a hard thing stolen from the New Devils that no one understood; the leg of a crabrat—that had been her first gift, and the least worthy, but in some ways the most satisfying of her courtship gifts; even the claws of a balloonist. Every one had been stolen from the Surface itself, at great risk, and delivered to her at a cost.

Few males survived more than two or three mad, half-blind dashes to the Surface to steal courtship gifts. The enemies were everywhere.

Manners satisfied, qr'Tshew came to the point. "The father of my last brood has died of a bad breathing," she said. "Also three young of other mothers."

"What a pity," said dr'Shee. She was not referring to the male, of course; once a male had achieved breeding he was done, for that female. But to have young die of the cyanide gas!

"I fear for our way of life," said qr'Tshew primly. "Since the New Devils came, our litters have not been the same."

"I have had the same thought," dr'Shee admitted. "I have spoken of it to my sisters."

"And I to mine. I and my sisters have thought something we wish to share. Our young are being taught things by the New Devils. Dr'Shee, shouldn't we mothers learn what the litters are learning?"

"But they are learning ways of bringing death! You and I are mothers, qr'Tshew!" Dr'Shee was shocked.

"The Krinpit bring death to us, do they not? The broods in the upper galleries have blocked off the tunnels where the bad air came from, but is it not certain that the Shelled Devils will break through again and more bad air will come?"

"I cannot bring death, except of course for food."

"Then let us eat them, shells and all," said qr'Tshew grimly. "Touch closely, dr'Shee. There is a story—" She hesitated. "I do not know how true it is. It came from a Krinpit and might as well have come from a Flying Devil." That was an old saying to indicate dubiousness, but in this case, dr'Shee realized, it was actually true. "This Shelled Devil taunted one of my sister's brood by saying that New Devils had destroyed an entire city of our race. He said the New Devils thought of us as vermin and would not rest until we were all gone. That is why they have given the Krinpit the bad air."

"But the New Devils are teaching our litters how to destroy Krinpit."

"The next part of the story is puzzling, but I think it is so. The Shelled Devil says that there are three kinds of New Devils. One kind destroyed the city. Another kind gave them the bad air with which they harm us here. And the kind that teaches our litters is a third kind. They have destroyed Flying Devils and Krinpit, as well as persons of the two other kinds of their own race. But they do not destroy us."

Dr'Shee thrashed her long, supple body in agitation. "But that is not true!" she cried. "They have taken several litters from their classes to some other place, and only a few have returned. And they have been weak and slow, and speak of their brood-mates dying!"

"My sisters and I have heard this also," agreed qr'Tshew.

"Tssheee!" The petaled folds of dr'Shee's nose were rippling furiously. "It feels," she said at length, "as though the teaching of bringing death is not a bad thing. If we bring death to the Krinpit, then they will not be able to bring more bad air to us. If we help our New Devils to bring death to the others, then they will not be able to aid the Krinpit or the Flying Devils against us."

"I have had this same thought, dr'Shee."

"I have a further thought, qr'Tshew. Once we have brought death to these others, perhaps we can then bring death to our own New Devils."

"And then our litters will be ours again, dr'Shee!"

"And our burrows will be safe and dark. Yes! Do not go away, qr'Tshew. I will summon t'Weechr and he will begin to teach us these lessons!"

FOURTEEN

●

EVEN IN JEM's favorable conditions—air denser, gravity less than Earth—there was a peremptory equation of lift. Danny Dalehouse could carry whatever he liked simply by adding balloons to his cluster. Charlie had no such power. He could carry what he could carry, and there was an end to it. To carry any of Dalehouse's gifts meant sacrificing ballast and therefore mobility. To carry them all was impossible. When Dalehouse scolded him for giving the crossbow to a flock-mate—at a time when the *ha'aye'i* seemed everywhere!—Charlie sang placatingly, "But I must keep the speaker-to-air! I cannot have both, cannot have both."

"And if you are killed by a *ha'aye'i*, what good will the radio do you?" But Charlie didn't even seem to understand the question. He and the flock were singing a sort of rhapsody about the speaker-to-air and how it enriched their chorus; and Dalehouse abandoned the effort.

Charlie's possession of the radio wasn't all good. It meant that Dalehouse could really keep in contact with the flock from the ground as long as they stayed in line of sight or somewhere near it, and that fact had not escaped Major Santangelo, the new camp commandant. It was getting less easy to escape into the air. At the same time, it was getting less attractive to stay in the camp. Santangelo had established command at once. He had proved it by sending Harriet and Alex Woodring off to try to make contact with a distant tribe of burrowers, hopefully uncontaminated by contact with the Greasies. And the camp was being run along increasingly strict military lines.

Dalehouse broke through the flock's song. "I must return. Four more flocks of our people are joining us, and I wish to be there when they arrive."

"We will come with you, we will come with you—"

"No, you won't," he contradicted. "Too many *ha'aye'i* near the camp." That was the truth, and that, too, was a consequence of the "gifts" he had given them. Since the Oilies had found out that Santangelo's "scientific instruments" were being used by the balloonists to keep tabs on what was going on in their camp they had taken to shooting down every balloonist that came within a kilometer of them. So balloonists were growing locally scarce, and the predators hungry.

"Fly by the Wet Valleys," he commanded. "Learn if our people are well there."

"No need," sang Charlie. "See the wings of your friend 'Appy coming from there even now!" And back behind the shoreline, there it was, Cappy's little biplane coming back from visiting the outpost, circling in for a landing.

"Then good-bye," sang Dalehouse, and expertly vented hydrogen until he came down to the level of the onshore winds that carried him back to the camp.

He was getting really good at ballooning, and he was smiling as he drifted down over the commandant's pet project, the little mud fort on the shore, and dropped to earth on the first bluff. He gathered up the deflated balloons, slung their loose-netted bulk over his shoulder, and walked happily enough up to the hydrogen shed.

That was the end of happiness. Half the camp was gathered around Kappelyushnikov and Santangelo, farther up the hill. Jim Morrissey and half a dozen others were coming toward him, their faces grim. Dalehouse caught Morrissey's arm as he passed. "What's the matter?" he demanded.

Morrissey paused. "Trouble, Danny. Something's happened to the outcamp. Harriet, Woodring, Dugachenko—they're missing. Cappy says the camp's been ripped apart, and they're gone."

"Harriet?"

"All of them, damn it! And there's blood and Krinpit tracks all over the place. Let go, we've got to get down to Castle Santangelo—in case they invade by sea, I guess. Anyway, you'd better get up there and see what your orders are."

Orders! How like an army officer to overreact and start issuing orders in all directions! Dalehouse let them go past and walked belligerently up to the group around Santangelo and the pilot. Someone was saying, "—I didn't know there were any Krinpit in the Wet Valleys."

"If you were in Beverly Hills you wouldn't know there were any rattlesnakes in California, either, but if you wandered around Hollywood Hills they'd bite your ass off. That's enough for arguing," the major said. "Those of you with assigned defense posts, get to them. We've got four ships coming in in the next twenty hours. It'd be a good time for anybody to catch us off guard, and we're not going to be caught. Move it!"

Dalehouse, who had been given no assigned defense post, was not anxious to get one. He moved away briskly with the others as the group broke up, circling around the outskirts to approach the communications shack.

Inside, the comm team on duty was watching a continually shifting display of moving symbols against a green grid of coordinate lines: the four resupply ships, already in orbit around Jem, making their final course corrections before dropping down to the surface. Dalehouse had expected Kappelyushnikov to show up there, and he did, moments after Dalehouse himself.

"Ah, Danny," he said dismally, "you have good taste for finding nice place to fuck off. Wait one while I see if asshole traffic controller has accidentally got ships in right orbit." He peered into the screen, grumbled at the crew on duty, then shrugged and returned to Dalehouse. "Is on course," he reported. "Now question is, is course right? We find out. Poor Gasha!"

"Are you sure she's dead?"

"Have not seen corpus delicti, no. But Danny, there was very much blood, two liters at least."

"But you didn't see the bodies."

"No, Danny, did not. Saw blood. Saw tents chopped up to fine Venetian lace, clothes all over, food, radio smashed, little scratchy bug-tracks everywhere. I looked. No bodies. So I yelled some, listened, poked into bushes. Then came home. So poor Gasha, not to mention poor Alexei and poor Gregor."

Danny shook his head wonderingly. "The Krinpit are damn noisy beasts. I don't see how they could catch the camp by surprise, and if they weren't surprised they should've been able to take care of themselves. Santangelo made them carry guns."

Kappelyushnikov shrugged. "You want to, I fly you there and you study scene of crime for yourself. Right now, excuse. First ship is about to come out of orbit, and I must keep controller up to personal high standard of accuracy."

Half the personnel in the first ship were a combat team—a fact which would have come as a distinctly unpleasant shock to Dalehouse at one time but now seemed less so. While they were still in orbit, the Vietnamese colonel commanding them had been briefed by radio, and the squad formed up outside the ship as they debarked, and immediately drew weapons and trotted to reinforce the perimeter guards. The second ship was also mostly military, but among the faces was one Dalehouse recognized. It took him a moment to make the connection, but then it was clear: the Bulgarian girl who had interceded for him and Marge Menninger in Sofia. He called to her and waved; she looked startled, then smiled—rather attractively, he thought—and called a greeting.

That was as far as it went just then, for by that time the new colonel had conferred with Major Santangelo, and the whole camp was mobilized. The Vietnamese—his name was Tree—commandeered Kappelyushnikov and the airplane, and they were gone for more than two hours, orbiting the camp in widening circles, first at high altitude, then nearly brushing the tops of the trees. All the tents had to come down. By the time the third rocket landed the tents were up again, now lined up six to a row, four rows paralleling each other, in what had become a company street. At each corner of the encampment pits were dug, and out of the third ship came machine guns and flame-throwers to go into them, while the few rankless nonspecialists who had not been tapped for unloading, tent detail, or pit digging had been set to pounding steel stakes into the ground ten meters outside the limits of the camp. Among the third ship's cargo were two huge reels of barbed wire, and by the time the last ship began its drop they had been strung along the stakes.

For once the Jemman skies were almost clear as the fourth ship came into sight high over the far horizon of the ocean-lake. First there was a broad, bright, meteoritic splash of light as the ablative entry shields soaked up the worst of the excess energy and spilled it away in incandescent shards. Then the ship itself was in naked-eye range, falling free for a moment. A quick blue-white jet flare made a course correction. Then the trigger parachute came free, pulling the three main chutes after it. The ship seemed to hang almost motionless in the ruddy air; but slowly, slowly it grew larger until it was almost overhead, two hundred meters up. Then the chutes were jettisoned and the ship lowered itself, on its blinding, ear-destroying rockets, to the beach.

Dalehouse had seen, he counted, five of those landings now, not including the one he himself had been in. They were all almost miraculous to watch. And they were all different. The ships themselves were different. Of the new four, only one was the tall, silver shape of his own ship. The other three were squat double cones, ten meters from rounded top to rounded bottom as they crouched on their landing struts, nearly twenty meters across at their widest.

The first person out of the ship was Marge Menninger.

It was not a surprise. The surprising part was that she hadn't come earlier. Dalehouse realized he had been half-expecting her on every ship that landed. She looked tired, disheveled, and harried, and obviously she had been sleeping in her olive-drab fatigues for all of the transit-time week. But she also looked pretty good to Dalehouse. The female members of the Food Bloc party had not been chosen for their sexuality. Apart from a rare occasional grapple with someone he didn't really like very much—sometimes impelled by tickling one of the balloonists into parting with a few sprays of joy-juice, sometimes by nothing more than boredom—Dalehouse's sex life had been sparse, joyless, and dull. Margie reminded him of better times.

Margie had also come up in the world since Sofia; the insignia on her collar tabs were no longer captain's bars but full colonel's eagles, and as she moved aside to let the rest of the troops debark, Colonel Tree and Major Santangelo were already beginning to report to her. She listened attentively while her eyes were taking inventory of the camp, the defense perimeter, and the progress of the debarkation. Then she began speaking in short, quick sentences. Dalehouse was not close enough to hear the words, but there was no doubt that the sentences were orders. Tree argued about something. Good-humoredly, Margie slipped her arm around his shoulder while she answered, then patted his bottom as he moved off, scowling, to do as he was told. She and Santangelo moved up toward the command center, still talking; and Dalehouse began to revise his notions of what to expect from seeing Margie Menninger again.

But as they approached where he was standing, she caught sight of him and threw out her arms. "Hey, Dan! Beautiful to see you!" She kissed him enthusiastically. "You're looking real fine, you know? Or as close to fine as you can in this light."

"You, too," he said. "And congratulations."

"On what, being here? Oh, you mean the eagles. Well, they had to give me that to handle Guy Tree. Dimitrova ought to be around somewhere. Have you seen her? Now if we could only get the Pak to come for a visit, we could all have a nice time talking over good old days in the Bulgarian slammer."

"Colonel Menninger—"

"All right, major, I'm coming. Stay loose, Dan. We've got catching up to do."

He stared after her. In the old Rotsy days in college, before he had dropped out as it became clear that nobody would ever need to fight wars anymore, colonels had seemed quite different. It wasn't just that she was female. And pretty, and young. Colonels had seemed to have more on their minds than Margie Menninger did—especially colonels coming into a situation where the panic button had been so recently pressed.

A husky man in a sergeant's uniform was speaking to him. "You Dr. Dalehouse? There's mail for you at the library."

"Oh, sure. Thanks." Dalehouse took note of the fact that the sergeant's expression was both surprised and a little amused, but he understood both reactions. "Nice kid, the colonel," he said benevolently. He didn't wait for an answer.

Most of the "mail" was from Michigan State and the Double-A-L, but one of the letters was a surprise. It was from Polly! So long ago, so far away, Dalehouse had almost forgotten he had ever had a wife. He could think of no reason why she would be writing him. Nearly everyone in the first two parties had also received mail, and the lines at the viewers were discouraging. Dalehouse put the collection of fiches in his pocket and headed for Kappelyushnikov's private store of goodies in the hydrogen shed. The pilot had long since scrounged the things he deemed essential to the good life on Jem, and among them was his own microfiche viewer. With considerable curiosity, Dalehouse slid his ex-wife's letter into position.

Dear Daniel:

I don't know if you knew that Grandfather Medway died last summer. When his will was probated it turned out he left the Grand Haven house to us. I guess he just never got around to changing the will after our divorce.

It isn't worth a whole lot, but of course it's worth something—the lawyer says its assessed value is $43,500. I'm a little embarrassed about this. I have this strong feeling that says you're going to say you'll waive your share. Well, if that's really what you want I'd appreciate it if you'd sign a release for me and have it notarized—is there anybody there who's a notary? Otherwise, will you tell me what you'd like to do?

We are all well, Daniel, in spite of everything. Detroit had another blackout last week, and the rioting and looting were pretty bad, the new emergency surtaxes are going to be hard to handle. Not to mention the heatless days and the moratorium on daytime TV and the scary news about international politics. Most people seem to think it's because of what's going on up where you are—but that's not your fault, is it? I remember you with a lot of affection, Daniel, and hope you do me.

                                                        Pauline

Sitting on the edge of Kappelyushnikov's personal cot, Dalehouse put the viewer down thoughtfully. The Grand Haven house. It was really only a bungalow, at least fifty years old and only sketchily modernized. But he and Polly had spent their honeymoon in it, in a snowy January with the wind whipping up over the bluff from Lake Michigan all day and all night. Of course she could have the house. Somebody in the camp could probably notarize a quitclaim, at least legally enough to satisfy some up-country surrogate court.

He stretched out on the cot, thinking about his ex-wife and her letter. News from Earth had not seemed either very interesting or very relevant, and Dalehouse had spent a lot more time thinking about the balloonists and the complications of life on Jem than about the brief paragraphs on the camp wall newspaper. But Polly made it sound serious. Riots, looting, blackouts, heatless days! He decided he would have to talk to some of the new people as soon as they quit bustling around and getting settled. That Bulgarian girl, for instance. She could fill him in on what was really happening back home, and, besides, she was a pretty nice person. He lay drowsily trying to decide whether it was better to do that now or to keep on enjoying the private space to think his own thoughts.

The decision was taken out of his hands. "Hello, Dr. Dalehouse," came Ana Dimitrova's voice. "Mr. Kappelyushnikov said you'd be here. But I must confess I was not sure he was in earnest."

Dalehouse opened his eyes and sat up as Cappy and the girl stooped through the entrance to the shed. The pilot's expression made it clear that, whatever he had told the girl, he had hoped there would be no one there, but he rallied and said, "Ah, Anyushka, you must learn to trust me. Here is old friend to see you, Danny."

Dalehouse accepted the formal handshake she offered. She had a nice smile, he observed. In fact, if she had not chosen to wear her hair pulled severely back and avoid the use of makeup, she could have been quite attractive.

"I was hoping to get a chance to talk to you, Miss Dimitrova."

"Heavens, Ana, please. Old cellmates must not be formal with each other."

"But on other hand," said the pilot, "must not impose on dear Danny, who is no doubt hungry and must get to mess hall at once or risk missing excellent dog-meat-and-slime meal."

"Nice try, Cappy," Dalehouse acknowledged. "No, I'm not hungry. How are things on Earth, Ana? I've just been hearing some bad stories."

Her expression clouded. "If the stories you have heard have been of violence and disaster, then, yes, that is how things are. Just before we left the television news spoke of martial law in the city of Los Angeles, and also in several cities of Europe. And there was some sinking of an Australian naval vessel off the coast of Peru."

"Dear God."

"Oh, there is much more than that, Dr. Dalehouse— Dan. But we have brought all the recent newspapers, as well as tapes of television programs—it is really quite an extensive library, I understand. I believe there are more than twenty thousand books in microfiche, at Colonel Menninger's express orders."

"Twenty thousand books?" Dalehouse shook his head. "You know, I never thought of her as a reader."

Ana smiled and sat cross-legged on the floor before him. "Please, let us be comfortable. I too am sometimes astonished at Colonel Menninger." She hesitated, then said, "She is not, however, always to be relied on. I had expected some time to consult with my government before coming here, on her promise. But it did not happen. None of us were allowed to leave the camp until we were flown to the launching point. Perhaps it was because she did not want to risk exposing us to the unstable conditions we might have found."

"As bad as that?"

"Worse," growled Kappelyushnikov. "You see, Danny? We should be grateful to be here on safe tropical-paradise planet like Jem, where only once in awhile isolated party gets wiped out by giant cockroaches."

"That's another thing," said Danny. "Marge Menninger doesn't seem particularly worried, after the flap yesterday."

"No reason to worry, dear Danny. I and little Vietnamese colonel have scoured every centimeter from ten klicks in all directions, using magnetometer, IR scanners, and good piloting eyes. Is no metal thing bigger than breadbasket anywhere around, I promise, and not more than three, maybe six, creatures larger than crabrat. So sleep safely tonight, Danny. In own bed," he added pointedly, and did not need to add "soon."

Nan was quicker than he. "That is good advice, Cappy," she said, standing up. "I think I will take it for myself."

"I will escort you," rumbled Kappelyushnikov. "No, do not disturb self, Danny. I see you are quite tired."

Ana sighed. "Gospodin Kappelyushnikov," she scolded, "apart from the fact that I am tired and quite disoriented from all these new experiences, you and I have barely met. I do hope that we will be friends. Please don't make that difficult by behaving like some Cossack with a peasant maid."

Cappy looked abashed, then angry. Then he grinned. "Anyushka, you are fine Slavic girl. Yes, we will be friends at once. Later on, perhaps more—but," he added hastily, "only in proper Soviet style, no premature touching, all right? Now let us all three stroll through pleasant Jemman murk to your tent."

Ana laughed and slapped him on the shoulder. "Russian bear! Come, then." She led the way outside and stood for a moment, glancing around at the quieting camp. The floodlights that marked official "day" were out, but Kung was clear and ruddy in the sky overhead. "I do not know if I can get used to a world where it is never night," she complained.

"Is severe handicap for certain purposes, yes," Kappelyushnikov agreed. They climbed the bluff and walked along it toward the female tent area. At the very edge, surrounded by a border of rounded stones in lieu of a lawn, was a tent larger than the others. It already had a flat rock before it stenciled *Col. M. Menninger, Commanding.*

"Margie's doing herself well," Dalehouse commented.

"Is privilege of rank," said Kappelyushnikov, but he was staring down the beach at the four new ships, one tall and slim, three squat, resting on their landing struts.

"That's strange, isn't it?" Dalehouse said. "Those three are quite unlike the others."

Cappy glanced at him. "You are truly observant, Danny." But his tone was strange.

"All right, Cappy. What's the secret?"

"Secret? Simple pilot is not told secrets. But I have eyes, and I can make conjectures."

"Come on, Cappy. You're going to tell us your conjecture sooner or later. Why not do it now?"

"Two conjectures," he corrected. "First, observe shape of three new spacecraft. Imagine sliced in half, forming two little cones each. Then imagine all six cones set on base around perimeter of camp, and the glass removed from those long, narrow ports that are so unnecessary for navigation of space. What have we then?"

"Upside-down cones with unglazed long, narrow ports," Dalehouse guessed.

"Yes, exactly. Only when installed on defense perimeter we have other name for them. We call them 'machine-gun emplacements.' " He sighed. "I think is triumph of two-faced engineering design, not accident, that this is so."

"But one can scarcely believe that," objected Ana. "This is, after all, a peaceable exploration party, not an invading army!"

"Yes, also exactly. Is only coincidence that so many members of peaceable exploration party are also soldiers."

Both Dalehouse and the girl were silent, studying the landed spaceships. "I would like not to believe you," said Ana at last. "But perhaps—"

"Wait a minute!" Dalehouse interrupted. "Those three ships—they don't have any return stage! That's why they're so short!"

Kappelyushnikov nodded. "And that is second conjecture," he added heavily. "Only is not really conjecture. Library of twenty thousand books is not light reading for weekend. Spacecraft that come apart to make forts are not for round trip. Vessels without return-capsule capability are not accident. Total of sum is clear. For many of us, is not intended we ever go back to dear old planet Earth."

Getting into the Jemman sky again the next day was a victory for Dalehouse, and he did not know how many more of those victories he would have. The day had begun unpromisingly. As soon as the "morning" lights were on he had found a mini-memo on the bench inside his tent door to let him know that, as from 0800 hours that standard day, he was to consider himself under military discipline with the assimilated rank of captain. On the way to breakfast he had passed an orderly carrying two covered trays into Margie's tent. An orderly! Not even the late Harriet Santori had gone that far. And on the way back past the tent, the Vietnamese colonel had been coming out.

Who Marge Menninger kept in her bed was no concern of his, and all this other military Mickey Mouse was irrelevant to his purpose on Jem. All the same, Dalehouse was not enjoying his flight as much as usual that day.

For one thing, Charlie and his flock were nowhere around—partly because Major Santangelo had insisted they overfly some of the other parts of Jem to bring back intelligence. Mostly because Dalehouse himself was reluctant to have them there, with so many *ha'aye'i* waiting in the clouds to prey on them. At least he had insisted they stay a full two kilometers away from the Greasy camp;

maybe that was enough for safety. Meanwhile, Dalehouse had his lightweight carbine with him, and he was hoping to take out at least a couple of the *ha'aye'i* before Charlie drifted back. There was already one balloonist in the camp as a sort of combination convalescent and pet, waiting for his *ha'aye'i*-ripped gasbag to mend enough for flight. Dalehouse didn't want Charlie to join him.

Trying to look appetizing, he drifted under the base of a low cumulus humilis. It was exactly the sort of place the air-sharks chose for hiding. But if there was one in the cloud it wasn't hungry just then.

He vented gas and dropped away from the cloud as the updraft began to suck him toward it; if there were *ha'aye'i*, he wanted to meet them in clear air, not where they could be upon him before he could shoot. A return flow carried him back toward the camp, and he looked down from half a kilometer on a busy scene. About twenty people were still unloading the new ships. Others were clearing brush and forest to widen the perimeter around the camp, and up past the camp toward the hills, in a natural meadow of thorn-bearing ground vines, a tiny tractor was plowing furrows. That was new! The tractor must have come out of one of the ships, and the furrows looked exactly as though someone was planning to farm.

That was reasonable enough, and even good news—certainly they could use fresh vegetables, and if the Greasies could grow them so could the Fats. But something about it troubled Dalehouse. He couldn't put his finger on it; something about using soldiers to farm? Forced labor on land?

He dismissed the thought; he was getting too low.

He vented some ballast, and the water sluiced down on the newly plowed land like a toy-scale rain shower. The thing that was tickling his memory was beginning to be annoying. For some reason, it reminded him of his undergraduate anthropology professor, a gentle and undemanding man a lot like Alex Woodring—

Like Alex Woodring, who was dead. Along with Gasha and the Bulgarian corporal he had never really come to know.

He was having none but depressing thoughts. His reserves of hydrogen and ballast were getting a little low, and evidently the *ha'aye'i* had learned to distinguish between a balloonist and a human being swinging from a netted cluster of bags. They were not to be tricked this day. Reluctantly he swung back over the beach, vented gas, and dropped to the pebbly sand.

By the time he had picked up and stowed the deflated balloons Margie Menninger was approaching, along with the woman sergeant who was her orderly. "Nice flying, Danny," she said. "Looks like fun. Will you take me up with you sometime?"

He stood regarding her for a moment. She really looked very pretty, even in the maroon Kung-light that darkened her lips and hid the gold of her hair. Her fatigues were new and sharply pressed, and her short hairdo flopped becomingly as she moved. "Any time you say, Marge. Or is it 'colonel'?"

She laughed. "All you brand-new officers are the same, very rank conscious. We're off duty right now, Danny, so it's Marge. You'll learn."

"I'm not sure I want to learn how to be a soldier."

"Oh, you'll catch on," she promised. "Tinka, take the point. Let's go for a walk, shall we?"

The sergeant moved out ahead of them, trotting to the barbed-wire enclosure. The troops in the pit at the corner lifted a section of the wire aside so the three of them could pass through; the sergeant in charge gave Margie a soft salute, and she nodded pleasantly back.

"If a person went swimming in this water," she said, "would she find herself being eaten up by something?"

"Not so far. We do it all the time."

"Looks pretty tempting. Care to join me?"

Dalehouse shook his head, not in negation but in wonder. "Margie, you're something. I thought colonels had to keep busy, especially when they think their troops need armed guards and barbed-wire fences day and night."

"Dear Danny," she said good-naturedly, "I haven't been a colonel very long, but I taught the theory of it to a couple thousand plebes at the Point. I think I have a pretty good grasp of the basic principles. A colonel doesn't have to do much; she just has to see that everybody else gets everything done. I already put in four hours of pretty solid work this morning."

"Yes, I saw Colonel Tree coming out of your tent."

She looked at him thoughtfully. She didn't comment but

went on, "As to your other point, the perimeter watch is SOP from now on, but there are patrols in the woods and aerial reconnaissance every hour, and besides, Tinka's a qualified expert with all hand weapons. I think you'll be all right."

"I wasn't worried about my personal safety."

"No, you weren't. You were worried about the troops under my command, and on their behalf I thank you for your concern." She grinned and patted his arm. "Hold on a minute." She fished a cigarette case out of her pocket, ducked behind him to get out of the wind, and expertly lit up. She inhaled deeply and held it, passing him the joint. When she exhaled, she called to the sergeant, "Tinka!"

"Yes'm."

"Next batch of dope you clean for us, save the seeds. Let's see if we can grow the little buggers here."

"Yes'm."

Danny took a long hit, beginning to relax. Being with Margie Menninger was never dull, at least. As he slowly exhaled he looked her over in some admiration. She had adjusted at once to the heat, the disconcertingly low gravity, the thick air that had troubled them all for weeks. She was some kind of woman.

By the time they had finished passing the joint back and forth they were out of sight of the perimeter guard where the beach widened under a high, bare bluff. Margie stopped, looking around. "Seems as good as any," she commented. "Tinka, take your position."

"Yes'm." The sergeant scrambled agilely up the side of the bluff to the top, and Margie shucked her fatigues. She wore nothing underneath. "If you're coming, come. If not, stay and help Tinka keep watch." And she splashed into the water.

Dope, company, or whatever, Dalehouse was feeling better than he had all day. He laughed out loud, then skinned out of his own clothes and joined her.

Ten minutes later they were both back on the beach, lying not very comfortably on their clothes, waiting to dry.

"Ouch," said Margie. "If I ever get any extra people for punishment detail, I think I'll see if they can get the rocks out of this sand."

"You get used to it."

"Only if I have to, Danny. I'm going to make this a nice

camp if I can—good duty. For instance, you know what we're going to have tonight?"

He rolled his head to look at her. "What?"

"The first official Jemman Food-Exporting Bloc encampment dance."

"A *dance?*"

She grinned. "See what I mean? Those turkeys who were running this place never thought of that. But there's nothing to it: spread out some flats on the dirt, put a few tapes in the machine, and there you are. Saturday night special. Best thing in the world for morale."

"You are probably about the US Army's best colonel for having fun," Dalehouse said.

"For all the rest of being a colonel, too, Danny. Don't you forget it."

"Well, I won't, Margie. I believe it. Only it's kind of hard to remember under the, ah, present circumstances."

"Well, I'll put my clothes back on if it'll help you concentrate. This isn't just fun and games. I wanted to talk to you."

"About what?"

"Whatever you want to tell me. How you think things are going. What isn't being done that ought to be. What you've learned being here that I haven't found out yet."

He propped himself up on an elbow to look at her. She returned his gaze serenely, scratching her bare abdomen just above the pubic hair. "Well," he said, "I guess you've seen all the reports about making contact with the sentients."

"Memorized them, Danny. I even saw some of the sentients at Detrick, but they weren't in very good condition. Especially the Creepy."

"The burrower? We haven't had very good luck with them."

"Piss-poor, I'd say."

"Well—yes, that's fair. But we did get about ten specimens, two of them alive. And Morrissey has a whole report on them not transmitted yet. He says they're farmers—from underneath, which is kind of an interesting idea. They plant some kind of tubers in the roofs of their tunnels. He was planning to talk to that expert you were supposed to bring—I don't know her name."

"Sondra Leckler? She didn't come, Danny. I had her scratched."

"Why?"

"Political. She's Canadian." She looked at him thoughtfully. "Does that fact mean anything to you?"

"Not a thing."

"No, I didn't think so. Canada voted for Peru's thousand-mile limit in the UN. That's cozying with the Peeps, right there. And everybody knows Canada's got the hots for the Greasies because of their goddam Athabasca tar sands. They're politically unreliable right now, Danny. There were four Canadians scheduled for this shipment, and I scratched all their asses right off."

"That sounds pretty paranoid," he commented.

"No, realistic. I've got no time to teach you the facts of life, Danny. What else? I don't mean about the burrowers."

He regarded her thoughtfully. She lay on her back, hands behind her head, comfortable in her nudity as she squinted toward the glowing red Kung. For a slightly plump girl her waist curved beautifully into her hips, and her breasts were rounded even while she lay flat on her back. But under that blond hair was a brain Dalehouse did not fully understand.

He dropped back and said, "Well, there's the balloonists. I know the most about them. Our regular flock is off toward the Heat Pole, but there's another one out over the water. They're basically territorial, but—"

"You were at the Greasy camp awhile ago, weren't you?"

"Yeah. When we were still on visiting terms. Is that what you want me to tell you about?"

"Among other things."

"All right. They've got a hell of a lot of stuff we don't, Margie." He described the machine that molded building blocks, the plasma generator, the farm, the air conditioning, the *ice*.

"Sounds pretty nice," she commented. "We'll have all that stuff too, Danny, I promise you. Did you see a plane and four gliders?"

"No. There was an airstrip—Cappy commented on it; it didn't make sense, with just a helicopter. But they didn't have a plane then."

"They do now. I thought they'd sneaked a reinforcement in that you didn't catch. Did you know about the base on Farside?"

"*Farside?* You mean the dark half of Jem? What the hell would anyone want there?"

"That's what I need to find out. But they've got it. Why do you think I stayed four extra orbits before I came down? I made damn sure I photomapped and radar-surveyed everything I could; I know every satellite around Jem, I know every spot on the surface that's using energy, and I don't like all of what I know. The Farside base was a real shock. Did you see any children in the Greasy camp?"

"Children? Hell, no! Why would—"

"Well, I think they're moving whole families in, Danny, which seems to indicate they've got more than an exploring expedition in mind."

"How could you tell whether they had children from space?"

"No way, Danny. I didn't say the orbital reconnaissance was the *only* way I knew what was going on with the Greasies. One other thing. No, two. Have they got a baseball field?"

"Baseball?" He was sitting up now, staring at her. "What the hell would they do with a baseball field? Cricket, maybe, and no doubt football, but—"

"That's a break," she said, without explaining. "Last question. Did you happen to run into a fellow named Tamil?"

"I don't think so." Dalehouse thought hard. "Wait a minute. Short fellow with a shaved head? Chess player?"

"I don't know. He's an Indonesian."

"Well, I'm not sure, but I think there was a petrochemist with a name like that. I didn't talk to him. I don't think he spoke English."

"Pity." Margie ruminated for a moment, then sat up, shading her eyes. "Are those your balloonists out there?"

As Dalehouse turned to look, Margie was standing, taking a few steps toward the shore, and what he looked at was not the sky but her. The artist Hogarth had said that the most beautiful line in nature was the curve of a woman's back, and Margie, silhouetted against the ruddy sky, was a fine figure of a woman. Half-amused, Dalehouse realized by the stirrings in his groin that he was beginning to display interest. But only beginning. The stimulus was that beautiful and remembered butt; the suppressant was the things she said. He would be some little while figuring out just how it was he did feel about Margie Menninger.

Then he got his eyes past her and forgot the stirrings. "There are *ha'aye'i* out there!" he said furiously.

"What'ys?"

"They're predators. That's not our regular flock; they just drifted in, because of the lights, most likely. And those clouds are full of *ha'aye'i!*" The flock was close enough to be heard now, singing loudly, only a few hundred meters away. And far beyond and above them three slimmer shapes were swooping toward them.

"That's a what-you-call-it there? Jesus! Look at that mother," she cried, as the first of the airsharks expertly ripped at the bag of a huge female, slipped past, turned end-for-end, and reversed itself. It came back ten meters lower to catch the deflated balloonist as it fell, braying its death song. "That's a fucking *Immelmann* that thing just did! Nobody's done that since World War One!"

"This isn't a performance, damn it! They're dying!" Two more of the predators had struck, and two more balloonists were caught farther down the shore. But at least it was not Charlie's flock. None of those victims were friends. "See that stuff coming out of the female?" he asked. "Those are her eggs. They're long spider-silk kind of things. They'll float around forever, but they won't be fertilized because none of the males have—"

"Fuck her eggs, little buddy. I'm rooting for the shark! What a killing machine! Shit, Danny, I can see why things are going badly here. You people picked the wrong allies. We ought to team up with the sharks!"

Dalehouse was scandalized. "They're animals! They're not even intelligent!"

"Show me a professor," she said, "and I'll show you a fart-brain. How intelligent do you have to be to fight?"

"Christ. The balloonists are our friends. We've got them doing surveillance for us. The *ha'aye'i* would never do that. Now you want us to line up with their natural enemies?"

"Well, I can see there might be problems." She stared wistfully at the *ha'aye'i*, which had ripped away the inedible bag and was now feasting on the soft parts of its still-living prey. "Too bad," she said philosophically. She stepped back toward Danny, still watching the spectacle, and took his hand. "You're really sure about this? There's no way to persuade our gooks to get along with the sharks?"

"No way at all! Even if you could somehow reach the *ha'aye'i* to explain what you wanted. The *ha'aye'i* don't even sing. That's the whole meaning of life to balloonists. They could never deal with creatures that didn't sing."

"Oh?" Margie looked at him thoughtfully. Then she released his hand and sat down again, leaning back on her arms and looking up at him. "Tell me, Danny, would you like to make me sing?"

He stared at her. Why, she was sexually excited by watching the slaughter!

He glanced at the top of the bluff, where the back of the head of the orderly was motionless in sight. "Maybe we'd better be getting back," he said.

"What's the matter, sweetie? Don't like having an audience? Tinka won't bother us."

"I don't care about her."

"Then what?" she asked cheerfully. "Hey, I bet I can guess. You're hassled about the colonel."

"Tree? He's got nothing to do with me."

"Aw, come off it, sweets." She patted the ground beside her. After a moment, he sat down, not very close. "You think I've been getting it on with old Nguyen the Tryin'."

"No. I don't think it, I know it."

"And suppose I have?"

"Your business," he said promptly. "I'm not saying it isn't. Maybe I've got some sexist-pig notions, but—"

"But no maybe. You fucking well do, Danny-boy." She was smiling without softness now.

He shrugged. "Let's go back, colonel."

"Let's stay here. And," she said, "I've got the rank on you, and when a colonel says 'let's' to a captain, what it means is *do it*."

There was no more stirring in Dalehouse's groin; he was both angry and amused at his own anger. He said, "Let's get this straight. Are you ordering me to fuck you?"

"No. Not at the moment, dear boy." She grinned. "I hardly ever order officers to fuck me. Only enlisted men, and very seldom them, because it's bad for discipline."

"Are you saying the colonel ordered you to fuck him?"

"Danny dear," she said patiently, "first, he couldn't— I've got the rank. Second, he wouldn't have had to. I'd fuck Guy any time. For any reason. Because he's technically my superior officer and I don't want to rub in the fact that I'm the one who's commanding. Because it'd make things go smoother on the mission. Because it's interesting to get it on with somebody half my size. I'd fuck a Krinpit if it would help the war effort, only I don't know how we'd bring up the kids. But," she said, "a girl's entitled to a certain amount of non-goal-oriented recreation, too, and Danny, I really have the fondest memories of you from last year in Bulgaria."

Fully relaxed, she rummaged under her for her clothes and pulled out another joint.

Dalehouse watched her lighting it. Her body was tanned over every inch—no bikini marks—and looking a lot better than the fishbelly white that came after a while on Jem. She scratched between the crease that hid her navel and her pale pubic hair, exhaled peacefully, and passed him the joint. The thing was, Dalehouse conceded to himself, that he really had the fondest memories of her last year in Bulgaria, too, and it did not seem to matter that he also had some bad memories.

"You know the thing that gets me about you?" he asked. "You make me laugh about a hundred different ways. Lean over this way, will you?"

When they had used each other up, they rested for a moment. Then Margie jumped up and dashed into the water again. Dalehouse followed; they splashed and roared; and as they came out he was astonished to discover that suddenly he didn't feel quite used up anymore. But Margie was calling up the bluff. "Tinka! Time hack!"

"Thirteen twenty hours, ma'am!"

Margie slipped into her fatigues quickly and leaned over to kiss Dalehouse as he was standing with one leg in his pants. "Time to get back. I've got a busy afternoon before the dance, and Danny, I'd appreciate it if you'd do something for me."

"What's that?"

"Teach Tinka how to do that balloon thing this afternoon."

"Why?"

"I want you to run an errand for me. It's important."

He considered. "I can get her started, anyway. But I don't know if she can learn it all in a few hours."

"She learns fast, I promise. Come on—I'll race you back!"

They ran the hundred meters. Marge got off first, but by the time the outpost was in sight Dalehouse had caught up with her. As he passed she reached out and took his hand and pulled him back to a walk. "Thanks for the exercise," she panted.

"Which exercise—swimming, running, or fucking?"

"All of them, dear Danny." She breathed hard, and then, just before they got within earshot of the perimeter guards she halted him. "One thing I ought to mention to you," she said.

"What's that?"

"I just want to set the record straight. With Nguyen Tree I'm fucking. With you I was making love."

Twelve on perimeter guard, two in sick bay, three in the comm shack, and eight more on the other twenty-four-hour details that always had to be manned: that left over a hundred and twenty people in the Food camp, and nearly every one of them was at the dance. Marge congratulated herself as she flung through a hora. It was a big success. When the dance ended and the rhythm changed to something Latin, she shook off the three men who came toward her. "I've got to sit this one out and catch my breath," she said. "After the next number I make my little speech. Then you're all on."

She retreated behind the little stand and sat cross-legged on the ground, breathing deeply. Marge Menninger's parents had endowed her with good genes, and she had taken care of the equipment; after a long day and a solid hour's dancing she was not tired and her wits were all about her. And the day had been not only long but good. She had got the camp over their scare about the loss of the three people by treating it as if it didn't matter. She had brought them all together in the dance. She had laid the groundwork for Tinka's little mission, organized an effective perimeter guard, broken the back of the job of unloading and stowing cargo, and begun six other tasks equally important. And she had got it on with Dan Dalehouse, on terms of her own making but obviously acceptable to him. That was a personal matter, but not unimportant. Marge was careful to keep an eye on long-range prospects. And as a possible permanent future pair, if permanent pairing turned out to be the way things were going to go on Jem, Dalehouse was the best bet she had yet identified.

It was Marge Menninger's conviction, recent but certain, that this job was what she had been born for. The important thing was to do it the right way, which was her own way, which had to be laid out from day one. No false starts. A happy camp—plenty of work to keep them busy and plenty of time to enjoy themselves. And a productive camp. Jem belonged to her and hers, and now they had it.

While she was waiting for the cha-cha to end she considered the next day. Ship One would be empty, and a team could be started on separating the two halves and moving them into position in the perimeter. Dalehouse or Kappelyusknikov—which? the Russian, she decided—Kappelyushnikov could be briefed on Tinka's mission, or at least enough of it so that he could escort her partway to the Greasy camp. A work team could be organized to start putting up poles for the farm plot. She would meet and learn to know at least six of the advance party; in two weeks, she should know everything she had to know about everyone in the camp. Orders would be cut naming Guy Tree as her G-1 and Santangelo as G-2. The others she would wait on; there might be people she hadn't met yet who should have the jobs. And, if things went well, during the three hours she allowed herself for a midday break, she would go for a walk in the woods. If you could call them woods. They needed to be dealt with too: Knock down some of those skungy ferns, scoop out some farm ponds to drain that soggy swamp. It would work—all they needed was a couple of bulldozers. Which reminded her that she needed at least to make a first approximation of a requisition list for the next shipment from Earth. That couldn't wait. With all the fuss the civilians were kicking up, Marge Menninger wasn't sure how many more shipments there would be. She already knew a number of goodies she wanted, but the old-timers would probably think of more. So she would need to talk to some of the old-timers. Morrissey, Krivitin, Kappelyushnikov—she would fill in the others later.

The smell of pot from beyond the stand pleased her. She thought of lighting up before getting up to make her speech—it was another way of showing her personal style. But it had been less than half an hour since the last one, and Marge knew her tolerances exactly; it might make her fuzzy.

The cha-cha ended, and the girl at the tape machine, looking toward Margie, switched it off. Marge nodded and climbed the stand.

The laughter and buzz dwindled as the hundred-odd people turned to face her. She smiled out at them for a moment, waiting for silence. They looked exactly like the plebes at West Point had looked, exactly like the audience in the Senate hearing room, like every audience she had ever faced. Marge was in touch with her audiences; she could always make them like her, and for that reason she liked them.

"Welcome to the first weekly Food Bloc Expedition Saturday Night Dance. I'm Colonel Marjorie Menninger, USA, and I'm your camp commander. Some of us already know each other pretty well by now. The rest of us are going to get to know each other very well very soon, because when you come right down to it we don't have much choice, do we? I'm not worried about that, and I hope you're not. We are a pretty select bunch." She allowed her gaze to drift past the audience to the edge of the lighted area, where two of her grunts were holding another while he vomited, and added, "Although you might not know that at first." A small laugh, but genuine. "So let's start getting to know each other. Guy? Saint? Where are you?" She introduced Tree and Santangelo as they stood forth. "Now Vince Cudahy—are you there? Vince is a mathematician, but he's also our chaplain. He used to teach at Fordham, but he's agreed to be nondenominational for the purposes of this mission. So if any of you want to get married, Vince is authorized to do it." Small chuckle. "He's a little old-fashioned, so he'd prefer it if you're of different sexes." Somewhat larger laugh, but a little questioning note in it. "And in case you do," she went on, "or even if you don't, you ought to meet Chiche Arkashvili. Cheech? There she is, our medical officer. Try not to get sick over the next twenty-four hours, because she's still setting up. But then she'll be ready for business, and back home in Ordzhonikidze her specialty was obstetrics." No laugh at all this time. She hadn't expected one. She gave them a moment to draw the logical conclusion and then pressed it home. "As you can see, we're planning a permanent base, and I'm planning to make this the best duty any of you have ever had so that a lot of you will want to re-up and stay here. And if you do—and if any of you take seriously what I've just been talking about and decide to settle down and have a family on Jem, I'm offering a special prize. A thousand petrobucks for the first baby born in our camp—provided you name it Marjorie, after me." She waited a beat and added, "Two thousand if it's a boy." She got the laugh she wanted and closed it out. "Now on with the dance." And as the music started she jumped off the platform, grabbed the first man in reach, and started them all going.

For the next half-hour Marge Menninger played hostess, at which she was very, very good. She danced with the men who didn't much dance, kept the music going, made sure the drinks kept coming. What she wanted was for everybody to have a good time. The next day was time enough for them to start thinking about permanent colonies and how much choice they would be likely to have about extending their stay. When chance permitted she got a word in with the people who had known what she was going to say, asking how they thought it had gone. It had seemed to go well. It made her feel good, and she found she was really enjoying the party. She drank with the drinkers, smoked with the dopers, and danced with everyone. It was safe enough now. When the time came to shut the dance down Tinka would let her know, and meanwhile Tinka would keep an eye on her colonel.

Coming back from the brand-new latrine, Marge paused to enjoy the sight of her people having fun. It was going to be all right! They really were a good bunch, hand-selected, fit, well trained. Whatever she had said to anyone else, in a secret, inside part of her heart Marge had felt a small but unsettling fear that her first really independent command might take qualities she hadn't known she would need. So far, not. So far, everything was going precisely as she had planned, according to the priorities she had laid out in her own mind. Priority 1, safeguard the integrity of the unit. And it was safeguarded; she could see the perimeter guards in regular patrol, a little disgruntled at missing the dance but carrying out their orders meticulously. Priority 2, accomplish the mission assigned. And that was well on the way. Priority 3, subject to accomplishing 1 and 2, make it a busy and happy camp. And that looked good, too.

She walked around the outskirts of the dance, nodding and smiling, not quite ready to get back on the floor. Tinka appeared beside her, one hand on her government-issue pouch, looking questioningly at her. Marge shook her head. She didn't need another joint just then. She was feeling happy and relaxed, but just the littlest bit light-headed. Part of it was the smarmy heat and the peculiar instability that came from weighing only about three-quarters what she had been used to for ten years. But she was feeling a little edgy, too, and checking dates in her mind, she thought she knew why. When she came near the medical officer she said in her ear, "Got your freezers going for the sperm and ovum bank yet, doc? Because I think I'm getting ready to make a donation."

"Noon tomorrow we'll be ready," Chiche Arkashvili promised. "But the way the boys and girls have been disappearing into the bushes, I don't know if we'll need it."

"Better to have it and not need it than need it and not have it. If I could, I'd—"

She stopped. "What would you do, colonel?"

"Forget it. Don't let me keep you from urgent business," said Marge amiably, and watched the doctor go on toward the latrine. If she could, she'd get a whole stock of frozen sperm and ova from Earth, because the bigger the gene pool you started with, the better the chances you'd have a healthy, stable population in another two or three generations. But she was not quite ready to put that request in her next letter to Santa Claus. She would have quite enough trouble with the items she was already determined to requisition, and from Christ's own number of light-years away her powers of argument were limited.

A few meters away the Bulgarian girl was in some sort of altercation with Stud Sweggert, the sergeant Marge had put onto the first of her ships. Normally she wouldn't have interfered, but there was something she wanted from Dimitrova.

"Tinka," she said softly over her shoulder.

"Yes'm."

"Stay with." Marge went up to the arguing couple, who stopped as she came close. "Sorry to break this up," she said.

Dimitrova glared at her. Feisty little prunt; it crossed

Marge's mind that her first impulses about Ana Dimitrova might have been best, but it was not a useful thought anymore. She discarded it.

"There is nothing to break up, colonel," the girl said. "The sergeant wished to show me something I did not want to see."

"I bet he did, honey," Marge smiled. "Will you excuse us a second, sergeant?" And, when he was out of earshot, she asked, "How is your Indonesian, Dimitrova?"

"Indonesian? It is not one of my four-oh languages, but I believe I could translate a document satisfactorily."

"I don't want a document translated. I want to know how to say, 'Good morning. Where is the baseball park?' "

"What?"

"Shit, lady! Just tell us how to say it."

Ana hesitated and then, with some disdain, said, *"Selamat pagi, dimana lapangan baseball?"*

"Um." Marge rehearsed it to herself for a moment, glancing at Tinka. The orderly shrugged. "Well, write it down for me. Now, how do you say, 'Have you a map?' "

"Saudara punja peta?"

"Got that?" asked Marge, looking at the orderly. "Not sure? All right, Dimitrova, take Tinka to my office and write it out for her. Make sure she gets it right." For a moment she thought the Bulgarian might object, but then she nodded and the two of them started away.

Sergeant Sweggert was still standing there, three meters away, watching her with calm interest. Margie laughed. "What are you doing, sergeant—waiting to ask me for a dance? Or do you want to show me that little thing you were so anxious to drag out for Dimitrova?"

"Hell, colonel. You've got me all wrong."

"I bet I do, Sweggert," she said good-naturedly, "you're not a bad guy, but it's against my policy to, ah, fraternize with enlisted men. Except in an emergency, of course. And what you've got to show has been widely seen already, I guarantee you."

"Ah, no, colonel! It was educational. They got a tame gasbag here, and it's real interesting."

"Yeah?" She looked at him more closely, and from the way he stood, the way his head sank into his shoulders, she realized that the man was pretty full of something. But he was also RA, and whether they chose to call the present time night or day, as a practical matter Kung made it pretty close to broad daylight. "I'll take a look," she decided. She followed him behind the cook-tent, and there was one of the balloonists, clinging to a rope and singing softly and mournfully to itself. It was much bigger than the female she had seen at Camp Detrick, but obviously in some sort of trouble.

"What's it saying?" she demanded.

The sergeant said with a straight face, "I really don't know, ma'am. You want to hold him a minute? Just pull down on the rope."

Margie looked at him thoughtfully for a moment, but he was right—it was interesting. She pulled on the rope. "Damn thing's strong," she complained. "Hey, Sweggert! What are you doing?"

He had leaned down and pulled something out from under a tarpaulin. "Just a strobe light, ma'am."

"And what are you going to do with it?"

"Well," he said, cunningly, "I haven't never seen it, but the guys say if you give one of these things a flash it's real interesting."

She looked from him to the sad, wrinkled face of the balloonist, and back. "Sergeant," she said grimly, "it damn well better be or I'll have your ass on toast. Flash your fucking strobe."

"Is that an order, ma'am?"

"Flash it!" she snarled. "Or—"

And then he did.

FIFTEEN

●

AFTER FOUR DAYS of trying, Ana was finally granted permission to use the radio for a call to the People's camp. When the communications clerk signaled *go*, she leaned forward and spoke in Urdu into the microphone. "This is Ana Dimitrova calling from the camp of the Food-Exporting Bloc. I wish to speak to Ahmed Dulla, please."

The comm clerk switched off the microphone and said, "Now you wait. It usually takes about ten minutes for a return message."

"Message? Can I not speak directly to Dr. Dulla?"

"Not with the Peeps, honey. We transmit a message, they transmit an answer. If they feel like it."

"How very queer. Well, thank you, I will wait outside." As she left she added, "Please call me when the answer comes."

"Count on it, sweets."

What a nuisance, she thought crossly, sitting lotus-legged in the warm electric-heater glow from Kung overhead. Still—ten minutes! She had waited much longer than ten minutes to hear Ahmed's voice. And at least his plight could no longer be as serious as she had feared at first. The word was out in the camp that the People's Republics, through what superhuman exertions one could hardly imagine, had succeeded in reestablishing communication with their outpost on Jem. A ship had landed—a small one, to be sure, but at least they were no longer helplessly dependent on the other colonies for the means to survive. How that must have angered Dulla!

Around her the camp was very busy. Nearly a hectare had been cleared and seeded on the slopes above, and the stanchions were in place for the lights that would make the seeds grow. Power would be next, and that was already being attended to. The Food Bloc at last had its own solar-power plant in process of assembly, and meanwhile there was a nuclear-fueled steam plant already in operation—small, expensive, but reliable.

Ana was the best of the three translators in the camp and, since the disappearance of Harriet Santori, the only one who seemed capable of picking up the fine structure of an only partly understood language. Her Krinpit was quite imperfect, and there seemed little chance to practice it. For the burrowers she had spent much time with this James Morrissey, who seemed to have taken them as his personal reason for existence; but none of it had come to much. The microphones he insinuated so gently into the tunnels sometimes picked up a scrap or two of squealing, chittering, half-muffled sounds; but evidently the burrowers detected them at once and avoided them—when they didn't steal them. More than once Morrissey had pulled out a probe and found the working head neatly disconnected.

But with the balloonists she had become almost fluent. She had worked closely with Professor Dalehouse, so far only by radio; the intriguing but frightening prospect of soaring with him under a cluster of bags of hydrogen was for some indeterminate time in the future. Then the Russian pilot, Kappelyushnikov, had taken off with Colonel Menninger's orderly and a cluster of hydrogen tanks on some foolish, secretive errand, and she had been ordered off the radio until further notice. Instead she was assigned to clerical work in the tiny hospital, where there was no clerical work to speak of, since it had as yet no real patients.

But. Regardless. No matter what the small frustrations and annoyances, was she not on Jem, only a matter of a few score kilometers at most from Ahmed? Not to mention the dizzying excitement of being on Jem at all. Another planet! Circling another star! So far from home that not even the sun itself could be found in the ruddy Jemman sky! She had not yet dared to go out into the jungle (though others had, and returned safe and excited at the strangenesses they had seen). She had not even swum in that great lake, or sea, so temptingly near; she had not thought to bring a bathing suit, had not yet found time to make one, and certainly would not follow the custom of those others who frolicked in nothing at all along the beach. Just now she could see a batch of them splashing and shouting. They were supposed to be working on the hydroplanes that were being assembled at the water's edge, but their thoughts, she would warrant, were far less on transportation than on the animal joy of the beach.

Not, she thought justly, that that in itself was wrong; why should they not? It was not Ana's concern if other persons had moral standards different from her own, so long as they did not try to inflict them on her. And splashing would in fact be great fun in this muggy heat—

"Dimitrova!" She jumped up and ran inside the tent for her answer, but it was only:

"Ahmed Dulla is not available at present. The message will be given to him."

In English. And English with a very bad accent, at that; whatever Heir-of-Mao had sent, it was not good translators. She thanked the comm clerk, concealing her disappointment, and strolled toward the perimeter. Off duty, not time to eat, too early to sleep; what should she do since she could not do the thing she wanted most?

Really, it was too disappointing! Where could he be?

She was annoyed to discover that she was beginning another headache. How infuriating! For some reason she had not had very many in her first days on Jem—perhaps because everything was so intensely exciting that she had no time to think of headaches. She did not want one now. Ana was an industrious person by nature, and it occurred to her that idleness was not likely to prevent the headache, but only to make it worse. What to do? If she only had a proper costume, how agreeable it would be to help the boatbuilders on the beach. Or to climb the slope and assist in planting—but no, at the moment they were only plowing, and she did not know how to run the tractor. The power plant? She knew nothing of it, of course, but she had sturdy limbs and a willingness to use her muscles. Why not?

Unfortunately, as she approached she discovered that one of the noncoms working on the project was Sergeant Sweggert.

She changed course and walked briskly away.

She had avoided Sweggert since the night she had come back with the colonel's orderly and found the two of them in rut, out in the open for all to see! Of course, no other had seen. Nan had turned away at once, sweating with embarrassment, and there had been no one else, or all the camp would have been talking of it. Tinka would not speak, Sweggert would perhaps not dare to, and the colonel—well, Ana did not have the delusion that she understood the colonel. But Colonel Marge Menninger she had not been able to avoid, and the woman had said nothing of the incident, had in fact showed no signs that it had ever taken place. That bleached American, copulating with a man whose name she perhaps did not even know! No, that was unfair; they knew each other. But certainly not socially. Oh, yes, to be sure, she would blame it on the aphrodisiac effect of the—the mist, she put it to herself, that the wounded balloonist emitted. One had heard all about that by now. Still, how appallingly lewd! Not to say—what was the word?—"tacky."

Ana found herself at a guard post in the perimeter fence, and at once it became clear what she wished to do. "I am going for a walk," she told the corporal in charge, who shrugged and watched impassively as Ana squeezed between the strands of the barbed wire.

In a few steps she was out of sight of the camp.

If she could not see Ahmed, at least she could see Jem. She pushed through the violet-oily growth, here all flickering with blue-green lights, and paused to listen: tiny skittering sounds from the underbrush, the rustle of the plants in the wind. There was no wildlife here that would harm her, she had been assured. Because of the presence of the camp, there were not many animals at all. Some had been frightened away, some poisoned away; where the garbage details had brought a day's collection of slops into the woods and buried them, you could see the ferns withered, the crabgrass ground cover dry. Terrestrial biochemistry was as hostile to Jemman as the other way around, but the Jemmans had not had a Camp Detrick to make them salves and injections against the rot.

But what was left—how fascinating and how strange! Forests of plants like ferns, but fruiting and with woody stems; succulents almost like bamboo (the hollow stems would make good structural materials, and Ana's thrifty soul instructed her to tell the colonel not to waste precious iron on tent stakes anymore); vines like grapes, with hard seeds no doubt meant to be spread in the excrement of small animals (if any survived in this part of the forest);

and the mangrovelike giants called "many-trees," a dozen or more trunks linking together at the crown, which made a canopy over her.

She stopped and looked around. There was no question of getting lost, she reassured herself, as long as she kept the red-glinting water in sight on her left. At any time she could simply climb down to it and return along the beach.

And there was no question of being tired here, either, when one climbed so lightly over fallen logs and rocks. It was an excellent time for taking a nature stroll, she thought, squirming between the trunks of a many-tree that glittered blue-green in firefly beads—if only her head did not hurt so.

In front of her was a lump of fungus, gray-pink and without lights of its own. It looked quite like a brain, she thought. In fact, rather like her own. Since the brain splitting had been done under local anesthesia she had seen every step, sometimes in the mirror overhead, sometimes in the closed-circuit likris screen. That was how her brain had seemed to her, quite remote and unfeeling. Even when the sharp hooked blade had halved it in one smooth motion, it had been hard to connect that sight with the insistent dragging pressure that was all she felt. . . . Later, when they were reconnecting some of the necessary nerves, she suddenly felt the reality of it. She would have been ill except for the surgeons's motherly scorn. "A great strong girl like you!" she had laughed. "No. Nonsense! You will not vomit." And Nan had not. . . .

What was that noise?

It sounded like distant sticks rattling against hollow logs and someone moaning. It was the sort of sound she had heard before, on tapes at Camp Detrick. The crustaceans, yes! But perhaps not the social race. Perhaps those wild and surely dangerous ones that had been only rumored—

The human voice that came from behind her was severe.

"Is it sensible for you to be alone here, Ana?"

In Urdu! With that stern compassion she had heard so often! She knew before she turned that it was Ahmed.

An hour later, a kilometer away, she lay in his arms, unwilling to move lest she wake him. The Krinpit's sound was always audible, sometimes near, sometimes moving farther away; she smiled to herself as she thought that the creature had surely been near while they were making love. No matter. It was not a matter for shame, what she would proclaim anywhere. It was not at all like that American bleached blond, because—well, of course, because it was with Ahmed.

He twitched, snorted, and woke up. "Ah, Ana! Then I did not dream this!"

"No, Ahmed." She hesitated and then said in a softer voice, "But I have had that dream many times. . . . No! Not so quickly again, please, dear Ahmed—or yes, whenever you like; but first let me look at you." She shook her head and scolded, "You are so thin! Have you been ill?"

The black-bead eyes were opaque. "Ill? Yes, sometimes. Also sometimes starving."

"Starving! How terrible! But—but—"

"But why starve? That is simple to answer. Because your people shot down our transports."

"But that is quite impossible!"

"It is not impossible," he contradicted, "because it happened. Food for many days, scientific instruments, two ships—and thirty-four human beings, Ana."

"It must have been an accident."

"You are naive." He got up angrily, pulling his clothes together. "I do not blame you, Ana. But those crimes are a fact, and I must blame someone." He disappeared behind a many-tree, and after a moment she could hear the splashing of his urine against the bole.

And also another sound: the Krinpit's rattle and moan, growing close again. If only she had had more time with the tapes at Detrick! But even so, she could distinguish a pattern that was repeated over and over. *Sssharrn—*, and then two quick notes: *eye-gone*.

She called weakly, "Ahmed?" and heard his laugh.

"Ah, Ana, does my friend frighten you? He will not harm us. We are not good for him to eat."

"I did not know you had such friends."

"Well, perhaps I have not. No. We are not friends. But as I am the enemy of his enemies, we are allies at least. Come along, Sharn-igon," he said, like a householder strolling a puppy, and came back into view.

Scuttling lopsidedly behind him was a great nightmare creature, rattling and moaning. Ana had never been so close to an adult, live Krinpit, had never quite realized their size and the loudness of their sounds. It did not have a crab's claws. It had jointed limbs that waved above it, two that tapered to curved points like a cat's claw, two that ended in fistlike masses of shell.

It paused, seeming to regard Nan, although as far as she could tell it had no eyes. And among the sounds, she recognized words in Urdu! Syllable by syllable, it scratched and grumbled out a sentence.

"Is this one to die?"

"No, no!" said Ahmed quickly. "She is—" He hesitated, then emitted sounds in the Krinpit language. Perhaps it was his accent, but Ana could not understand a word. "I have told him you are my he-wife," he explained.

"He-wife?"

"They have a very rich sexual life," he said.

"Please, Ahmed. I am not ready for a joking little chat. The Krinpit said 'to die,' and what does it mean?"

"Naive Ana," he said again, looking at her thoughtfully. Then he shrugged. He did not reply, but he unwrapped a ruddy-brown leaf from an object he had been carrying. It was a flat metal blade, broader at the end, the edge razor-sharp. The hilt was sized to fit a man's hand, and the whole thing half a meter long.

"Ahmed! Is that a sword?"

"A machete. But you are right; it is a sword also now."

"Ahmed," she said, her heart pounding harder than the throbbing in her head, "some days ago three persons from the Food camp were killed. I have thought it was an accident, but now I am not sure. Shall I ask you if you know anything of this?"

"Ask what you like, woman."

"Tell me!"

He thrust the machete into the loamy ground. "All right, if you will have it so, I will tell you. No. I did not kill those Fats. But yes, I know of their death. I do not mourn them, I hope many more will die. And if it is necessary for me to kill a few, I shall not shrink from it!"

"But—but— But Ahmed," she babbled, "dear, gentle Ahmed, this is murder! Worse than murder, it is an act of war! Suppose the Food Bloc retaliates? Suppose our home-lands do not accept this as a mere struggle far away, but themselves retaliate on each other? Suppose—"

"Have done with your supposing!" he shouted. "What can they do to retaliate? Bomb Pakistan? Let them! Let them destroy Hyderabad and Multan, let them bomb Karachi, let them wipe out all the cities and burn the whole coast. You have been there, Ana. How much of Pakistan can be destroyed? What bombs can blast through mountains? The people will survive. The leeches that flock to the cities to beg, the government parasites—yes, the intellectuals, the proud bloodsuckers like you and me—what do I care if they all die? The people in the valleys will live!"

She was silent, frightened, searching for words that might sway him and finding none. "Ah," he said in disgust, "what is the sense of this? But do not be angry with me."

"Angry? That is not what I feel," she said miserably.

"Then what? Hatred? Fear? Ana, what are we to do? Let them starve us? We have one small ship to save us, and what have the Fats and the Greasies? Navies! And if the fighting spreads—" He hesitated and then burst out, "Let it! Let all the rich ones kill each other. What do we care? Remember, six out of ten human beings on Earth are ours! If there is war on Earth—if only a million survive, then six hundred thousand of them will be citizens of the People's Republics. And here—"

She shook her head, almost weeping. "And here? Sixty percent too?"

"No. More. On Son of Kung—if anyone survives—one hundred percent ours."

SIXTEEN

•

THE RAINS were all around, squall clouds driving toward them, squall clouds already past them, up toward the Heat Pole, where the raindrops fell a kilometer or two and then evaporated, never striking the hot, salt ground. The flock was spread out over a kilometer of sky, and grumbling in dissonant chords.

"Have patience," Charlie scolded them. "We must stay, must stay."

And they echoed, "We must stay," but it was poorly sung.

No matter. Charlie had promised his two-legged friend that they would stay on station, waiting to observe certain strange and incomprehensible events, and the flock would do as he vowed.

Still, it was uncomfortable to him, like an itch or a sunburn to a human being, to have the swarm in such disarray. The place he had promised to watch was upwind of the camp of the Big Sun. It did not do to come too close to that. Many of his flock, and even more of other flocks, had been punctured or burned by the far-striking missiles of that camp, and so he had to try to keep the flock from drifting toward it, seeking every counterflowing gust, and still avoid the squalls as much as possible. Dalehouse had told him that it would be difficult. But he had also said it was important.

Charlie rotated his eye patches over the entire horizon. No sign of the aircraft he had been told to expect. But he did see a vagrant drift of thistledown and spinner silk moving across the hills below. A crosscurrent! He sang his flock together and vented gas.

The swarm followed, dropping into a level where the wind took them away from the rain to a likely-looking area of updraft. They followed well, everything considered. Expertly he guided them under the base of a fair-weather cumulus, and they rose with the drift.

The song of the swarm became contented. It was at the top of these invisible pillars of rising air that the best feeding was found: pollen and butterfly-seed capsules, the small, soft creatures that filled the same ecological niche that insects did on Earth, dried salt particles from the wavelets of landlocked seas, and even tinier things. A flock at feed was queer-looking, with every fin and frill extended to trap whatever touched it. It was also at risk, or once would have been. It was a favorite time for the *ha'aye'i* to knife in, slashing every bag they passed and tearing the life out of the victims before the helpless gaze of their flock-mates. Helpless no more! Charlie sang a boastful song of his great friend Danny Dalehouse, who had given them the far-striking weapons that drove the *ha'aye'i* a hundred clouds away. Or sometimes did. Now each male and some of the females in his own flock had the weapons, and the *ha'aye'i* had come to recognize Charlie's swarm and avoid it.

Although, in truth, it was no longer as tempting to the predators as it had once been. So few were left! Once there had been hundreds, now fewer than a score.

There was still no aircraft on the horizon, nothing happening on the mesa upwind of the camp of the Big Sun. Charlie relaxed and fed with his swarm, and as he ate he became more mellow. He led the flock in gentle songs of childhood and joy.

There had been a time when Charlie was a tiny pip-sized pod, pumping mightily to bulge the creases out of his little gasbag but still tied to the ragged end of his sailing ribbon and to the winds that bore it where they liked. Gusts blew. Air-to-air lightning spat all around him. Because he had no real control over his altitude he was sometimes tossed up through the tops of towering convection clouds, with the dull red sun hot on his tiny balloon and actual stars shining through the murky sky; other times he was so low that he brushed hills and fern trees, and shelled or furred creatures clutched after him as he spun by. Eighty out of a hundred of his brood-mates died then, in one of those ways or in some other. Ten more died almost as soon as their drift-ribbons fell away, when they were tasty hors d'oeuvres for the *ha'aye'i*, or sometimes for the protein-hungry adults of another chance-met flock. Or even of their own. Only a few out of each hundred survived to reproduce. And then there were still the *ha'aye'i*. And the storms. And the clutching beasts from below.

But still—to be a balloonist! To soar and to sing! Above all, to share the chorused flocklore that united them every one, from the tiniest pod to the leaky, old, slow giants that even the *ha'aye'i* scorned. Charlie's song was triumphant, and all the flock around him stopped their greedy gobbling to join the harmony.

Still his eye patches rotated watchfully toward the mesa; but still there was no sign of the airplane or of the New Friend he had been told would rise from the spot. And they were drifting with the cloud, away from the camp of the Big Sun.

Many of the flock were sated now, softly singing their private courtesy songs of thanksgiving. They were a fine flock, although, Charlie admitted, very few in number.

He sang to them, "Stop feeding, stop feeding! We must go!"

"Go where, go where?" grumbled a chorus of the slower and hungrier ones, and an individual song sounded above the choir.

Faintly: "I must eat more. I die." That was the old female, Blue-Rose Glow. Her bag had been meanly seared when half the flock was set aflame.

"Not now, not now," sang Charlie commandingly. "Follow!" And he sang the new song, the duty song he had learned from his friend Danny Dalehouse. It was no longer enough to float and sing and replenish hydrogen and breed. Not anymore. Station must be kept and the mesa observed. And the camp of the Big Sun must be avoided, and the *ha'aye'i* guarded against, and the swarm kept together; so many imperatives, both the new and the old! And so he led them through their slow, bobbing dance, crisscross with the winds.

For a long time he led them, watching ceaselessly as he had promised. Even so, it was not he who first saw the thing. From far behind, old Blue-Rose Glow sang feebly, "There is a new Sky-Danger."

"Catch up, catch up!" he commanded. "You sing poorly." It was not sung in unkindness but only because it was true.

"I leak," she apologized. "Nevertheless it is there, almost in reach of the Earth-Dangers, far away."

He rotated his eye patches and rose to another air current. There it was. "I see the Sky-Danger," he sang, and the rest of the flock confirmed. It was not a *ha'aye'i*. It was the hard mechanical thing from the camp of the Middle Sun, as he had been told. In it, he knew, was the Other Friend who had sometimes soared with Danny Dalehouse, and also the New Friend he had not yet seen.

It was all as had been said by Danny Dalehouse. The biplane slunk in at treetop level and set itself down on the dry mesa a dozen kilometers upwind of the Greasy camp. While the swarm watched, Kappelyushnikov and a female person emerged and began to fill a net of balloons out of tiny tanks.

When the New Friend's cluster began to swell and she rose gently from the ground, the aircraft took off again, turned quickly, and slipped back down the slope toward the distant ocean-lake. The New Friend rose into the prevailing poleward wind and drifted directly toward the camp of the Big Sun.

Charlie dared come no closer, but he saw her venting gas as she approached the camp. She tumbled into the underbrush somewhere nearby; and it was all as had been foretold.

"The thing is done," Charlie caroled triumphantly.

"And what now?" asked the swarm, milling around him, staring after the New Friend as she fell.

"I will ask the air," he sang. His little insect legs fumbled at the switch of the hard, shiny speaker-to-air Danny Dalehouse had given him. He sang a questioning greeting to his friend.

He tried twice, listening between times as Dalehouse had taught him. There was no answer, only an unpleasant hissing song of static and distant storms.

"We must go near to the camp of the Middle Sun," he announced. "The speaker-to-air cannot sing so far." His skilled eyes read the signs of the clouds and the fern tops far below, seeking the currents he wanted. It was too bad that Dalehouse could so seldom soar with the flock these days because of the hated *ha'aye'i* of his own kind, but Charlie knew that once they were in line of sight the speaker-to-air would bring his song.

"Follow!" he sang. He swarmed the flock around him. They dropped, all fourteen of them, through a fast-moving layer of stratus cloud into the backflow near the surface.

When they emerged, old Blue-Rose Glow was gone, the leaks in her bag finally too great to allow her to remain air-borne. So was the young female called Shrill-Squeal, nowhere in sight, even her songs no longer audible.

By the time they approached the camp of the Middle Sun and Charlie began to sing through the radio to Dalehouse, there were only twelve left in the flock.

Marge Menninger looked up as Kappelyushnikov came in from the orderly room, closing the flap to her private office behind him. "Any word?" she asked.

"Danny has had radio from gasbag, yes. Your friend was seen to descend near Greasies, all in order."

"How long ago?"

"With gasbags, who can say? Perhaps some hours. Not long after I departed spy-drop scene."

"All right. Thanks." After he left, Marge started to call the communications tent, then decided against it. If the Greasies radioed that they had rescued Tinks, blown helplessly off course, the communications clerk would let her know. And he hadn't. So the Greasies were playing it covert and slick, and what was Tinka up against in their camp? Had they figured out that she really wasn't there by accident? Could she . . . ? Were they . . . ? Wasn't it . . . ? Questions multiplied themselves in Marge's mind endlessly, and there was no straightforward way of getting answers. You could get your ass lost in those swamps of contingencies and subjunctives.

That was not the way Marge Menninger ran her life. She made a decision. In one hour exactly she would have the comm clerk radio a query to the Greasies, and until then she would put it out of her mind. Meanwhile, lunch was fifty minutes away, and what to use that time for?

The fifteen notes she had made to herself on this morning's calendar had all been checked off. All current projects were on schedule, or close enough. Everyone had been assigned tasks. The first hectare of wheat was in the ground, sixteen different strains competing to see which would thrive best. The perimeter defenses were in order. Three turrets still sat on the beach, ready to be put where needed when she wanted to expand the perimeter or establish another post. She looked at the 1:1000 map, two meters long and a meter high, that covered almost all of

one wall of her office. That was something! It showed
every feature within a kilometer of where she sat—seven
creeks or rivers, a dozen hills, two capes, several bays.
Grid references were not enough, they needed names.
What better way to name them than to let individual
members of the camp pick them? She would organize a
drawing; each winner could name something, and that
would give them something to do. She called in her
temporary orderly and dictated a short memo for the
bulletin board. "Check it with the communications section," she finished. "Make sure we list all the features
worth naming."

"Yes'm. Colonel? Sergeant Sweggert wants to see you.
Says it's not urgent."

Margie wrote *Sweggert* on her calendar. "I'll let you
know." Then she put Sweggert out of her mind, too. She
had not yet decided what to do about Sweggert. She had a
wide variety of options, from laughing it off to court-
martialing him for rape. Which she elected would depend
a lot on how Sweggert conducted himself. So far he had
had the smarts to keep a low profile around her.

On the other hand, she thought, her authority to
court-martial anybody for anything rested on the military
chain of command, which extended up from her through
the tactran link to higher authority on Earth. And who
was to say how long Earth would give a shit about backing
her up? Or about whether the colony lived or died? The
news from home was bad, so bad that she had not passed
all of it on to the camp. The tactran message acknowledg-
ing her shopping list had advised that it was touch and go
whether she would get everything she had asked for. And
requests for further supplies after that shipment were,
quote, to be evaluated in terms of conditions at the time of
receipt of requisition, unquote.

It was what she had expected. But it was sobering.

On her pad for the afternoon she made two notes:
*Medic. —bank okay? Food— 6 mos. estimate firm? Stretch
1 yr w rationing?*

It was a damn nuisance that the agronomists all seemed
to be Canadian! Margie needed some smart and private
help—smart, because how they managed their crops was
quite likely to be life-and-death for the colony; private,
because she didn't want the colony to know that just yet. If

she got everything on her shopping list she would have plenty of seed stock. But who knew whether she had the ones that would grow best?

Dismiss that thought, too.

Forty minutes left.

She unlocked the private drawer of her desk and lit a joint. Assume the shopping list all gets delivered. There was enough on it for pretty fair margin against most kinds of disasters, she thought, and there was no sense worrying until she had to.

The requisition list included a good chunk of personal things for Margie herself: clothes, cosmetics, microfiche sewing patterns. With the patterns there would be enough variety in styles to suit everyone in the camp, male or female, for a good long time, assuming they found some way of producing fabrics to make the patterns on. It would be nice to have some pretty clothes. She was already beginning to feel the absence of Sakowitz, Marks and Sparks, Sears, and Two Guys. One day, maybe, she thought, drawing a deep hit. Not Sakowitz, no. But maybe a few boutiques. Maybe some of the people in the camp had sewing or tailoring skills, and maybe it was about time she started locating them. She flipped the calendar ahead a few pages and made a note on a virgin page. That Bulgarian prunt was the kind of girly-girl who would like to sew, possibly even as much as Margie did herself; she had been pretty morose after her long walk in the country-side, but she did her work and might need something to occupy her mind. It didn't seem that she wanted a man for that purpose; at least, she had thoroughly discouraged Guy Tree and Cappy and Sweggert . . .

Sweggert.

"Jack, send the sergeant in," she called.

"Yes'm. He's gone back to the perimeter, but I'll get him."

As she leaned back, marshalling her thoughts about Sweggert, the handset buzzed; it was the communications clerk. "Colonel? I was just talking to the Greasies about Sergeant Pellatinka."

"I didn't tell you to ask them."

"No'm. But I kept sending on her frequency like you ordered, and their radioman cut in to ask if we had lost her. So I said she didn't answer. So they said they'd send out a party to look for her."

Margie sat back and took a thoughtful drag on the joint. According to the balloonists, there was no way the Greasies couldn't have seen her come down. So now they were overtly lying.

Sergeant Sweggert shared a number of traits with Marge Menninger. One of them was that he was willing to go to a lot of trouble to get things right, and then if he saw a chance for improvement he was willing to do whatever it took to make them righter. When he perceived that moving the Number Three machine-gun emplacement two meters toward the lake would improve the field of fire, he moved it. Or his squad did. The fact that it took five hours of backbreaking work did not affect his decision. He lent a hand to put the HMG on its tripod and swung it to check the field. "Fucking lousy," he told the crew, "but we'll leave it for now. Get that ammo restowed."

He crouched behind the gun, swiveling it through full traverse. It was an act that gave him pleasure. As far as the shore of the lake on the extreme left and the beginning of the fern forest on the right, there was no way that any sizable creature could approach without being a clear target for the gunner. The claymores and smoke bombs were emplaced and fused, and his command-post detonating radio was keyed to each of them. The floodlights were in position, with quadruple redundancy. At any given moment only a quarter of them were lit, searching the entire area around the perimeter. Every hour that quarter went off and the next quarter came on so that any burned-out bulbs or wiring deficiencies would distribute themselves equally and could be fixed in the down-time. In actual combat, of course, they would all be on. Most would be shot out, but not in time to let anyone cross that perimeter. Not alive.

Although, he admitted to himself as he climbed out of the dome, the chances that anyone would try a straight-forward frontal attack were very small. Maybe an attack from the sky. Maybe by long-range rocket fire. Maybe not at all. This whole fucking shoot-up was crazy, if you asked Sergeant Sweggert. What the fuck was there to fight about in this asshole place without a bar or a town or even, for God's sake, a decent tree or field? If you had asked him, that was what he would have said, in total sincerity, but it would not have stopped him from fighting for it.

And inside he was swearing. The colonel wouldn't have kept him waiting like this a week ago. If she was going to shaft him, what was she waiting for? . . . "Sarge." He looked up. "They're calling you from the orderly room." He turned idly and saw the corporal waving.

"Aggie, take over," he ordered. "If I come back and that ammo isn't restowed, it's all your asses."

He strolled back toward the HO tent and walked in. Marge Menninger was eating out of a mess kit, reading from a small-screen viewer. She didn't look up. "The perimeter's looking good, Sweggert," she said. "Got that machine gun back in place?"

"Yes'm. Colonel? There's a bunch of gasbags around, and that one we been using is about used up. We'll be relieved in a couple of minutes. Can we get a fix from the new ones?"

She put down her spoon and looked at him. After a moment, she said, "Just who do you mean by 'we,' soldier?"

"Oh, no, ma'am!" Jesus, she was touchy! He knew he was close to trouble. "I don't mean nothing, ma'am, just that the detail's been working hard and they need a little break. We'll—they'll come out of it in an hour, and the relief'll be there anyway."

She studied him for a moment. "That's four-oh, Sweggert, but only half the detail. Keep the rest sober."

"Sure thing, colonel. Thank you, colonel." He got out of there as fast as he could. Shit, he should've been more careful, knowing how she felt and all. Not that she was all wrong. If he hadn't been drunk he wouldn't have done it. But, shit! It was worth it. Remembering the way she had been with a skin full of the balloonist mist, his groin grew heavy.

When he got back to the detail he looked at them with some disapproval. Corporal Kristianides was skinny and had sideburns all down her cheeks, but she was the best he had to pick from. "Aggie, take Peterson and four others; you're on duty till the relief shows up. Kris, you and the rest come along with me. We're gonna take ourselves a jizzum break. Anybody don't want to come, switch with somebody don't want to stay. Let's move it."

The balloonists were out over the ocean-lake now, half a kilometer away and low. Sweggert marched his dozen troops across the camp to the empty tents at the end of the company street; he would do it in the open if he had to, but damned if he wouldn't take a little privacy when he could get it. The tethered balloonist, further than ever from recuperating, had been moved there days since, along with the strobe light.

Sweggert stopped, swearing. Nan Dimitrova and Dalehouse were talking to the balloonist, and only a few meters away the Russian pilot, Kappelyushnikov, was complaining about something to Colonel Tree. Privacy, *shit*. But it didn't matter; he had Colonel Menninger's permission, and she was the one who counted. He retrieved the strobe and pointed it toward the hovering swarm.

Predictably, Dalehouse butted in. "What do you think you're doing, Sweggert?"

Sweggert took time to aim the strobe and flash it to bring them in before he answered. "Gonna have a little fun. The colonel said it was okay."

"Hell she did! Anyway—"

"Anyway," Sweggert interrupted, "why don't you go check with her if you don't believe me? Would you move a little, sir? You're getting between them and the light."

Ana Dimitrova laid her hand on Dalehouse's arm to keep him from replying. "It is not fun for the balloonists, Sergeant Sweggert. To experience sexual climax is very painful and debilitating. As you can see, this one is seriously affected. It may die."

"What a way to go, hey, Ana?" Sweggert grinned. "Take it up with the colonel—hey, Dalehouse! What are you doing?"

Dalehouse had switched on his radio and was singing softly into it. Colonel Tree, beginning to pay attention, walked toward them, and Sweggert turned to him. "Colonel! We have Colonel Menninger's permission to get the Loonies in for a fix, and this guy's telling them to screw off!"

Tree stopped with his hands clasped behind his back and nodded gravely. "A dilemma," he said in his soft child's voice. "It will be quite interesting to see what they do."

What they were doing was spreading themselves all over the sky, some dropping lower to catch the onshore breeze, others hesitating. They were singing loudly and discordantly, and the sounds came distantly from the sky and tinnily from the radio in Dalehouse's hand. Sweggert stood rock-still, controlling the rage that was building up in him. Fucking Cong! When you had the CO's permission, that was all you were supposed to need! Why wouldn't Tree back him up?

"Gimme that," he growled, reaching out for Dalehouse's radio.

But Dalehouse's expression had changed. "Hold it," he snapped, and sang a quick phrase into the radio. The answer came back as a cascade of musical phrases; Dalehouse looked startled and Ana Dimitrova gasped, her hand to her lips. "Tree," he said, "according to Charlie, there's some Krinpit down the beach, and they're eating a couple of people."

"But Krinpit do not eat human beings," objected Colonel Tree, and Sweggert chimed in:

"There's nobody down there. Nobody's gone through the perimeter all day."

Dalehouse repeated his question into the radio and shrugged. "That's what he says. He could be wrong about the eating part, I guess—he doesn't have a very clear concept of killing, except to eat."

Sweggert put down the strobe. "We better tell the colonel," he said.

Colonel Tree said, "That's correct. You do so, Dalehouse. Sergeant, form your squad on the beach in thirty seconds, full combat gear. We're going to see what's happening."

Half an hour later Marge Menninger herself, with thirty armed grunts behind her, met the first party coming back along the beach. There were no casualties, or at least none from the Food Bloc, but they were carrying two people. One was in a sort of sling made from two jackets knotted together, the other on Sergeant Sweggert's shoulder, fireman-carry. They were both dead. When Sweggert put his burden down it was obvious why he had been easy to carry. Both legs were missing, and so was part of his head.

The other body was less mutilated, so that Marge Menninger recognized her at once.

It was Tinka.

Marge stood numbly while Sweggert made his report. No Krinpit in sight; they had got away, so far that they couldn't even be heard. Both people were dead when they got there, but recently; the bodies were still warm. For that matter, they were still warm now. And the man had had a packet in a waterproof wrapping inside his shirt. Margie accepted it and tore it open. Microfiches—scores of them. The man's ID card, which showed that he was the Indonesian Tinka had gone to contact. A pair of child-sized spectacles—flat glass, not optically ground. Why glasses? For that matter, how had the two got here? Had they been caught as spies and then somehow escaped? And how had they come the long distance from the Greasy camp to the beach where they died?

By the time they got back to the base, she had an answer to at least part of the question, because Dalehouse reported that the balloonists had spotted something farther down the beach that looked like the remains of a deflated rubber boat. She swung the tiny glasses from their elastic band as she listened, nodding, taking in all of it as information to process, not quite ready to take in the information of Tinka's death as a pain to feel.

She looked down at the glasses. They were now almost opaque.

"That's interesting," she said in a voice that was very nearly normal. "They must be photosensitive glass. Like indoor-outdoor sunglasses." She glanced up at the sullen red coal of Kung overhead. "Only what in the world would anybody want with them on Jem?"

SEVENTEEN

•

SIX KILOMETERS down the shoreline from where he had slain the Poison Ghosts, Sharn-igon paused in his flight to scratch out a shallow pit under a bluff. He needed to hide because he needed to rest.

Digging was always dangerous for a Krinpit because of the Ghosts Below. But here it was unlikely they would be near—too close to the water. They did not like to risk their tunnels flooding. And the many-tree on the bluff above him was a good sign. The roots of the many-tree were distasteful to them.

As he settled himself in, Sharn-igon wondered briefly what had become of his cobelligerent, the Poison Ghost Dulla. He did not feel concern, as one might for a fellow being. He did not think of Dulla in that way. Dulla was a weapon, a tool, without "being-ness." After they had slain the Poison Ghosts Dulla called "Greasies," they had both fled, and of course Dulla had fled faster and farther. Sharn-igon did not think of that as a betrayal. If he had been the nimble one and Dulla the slow-moving, he would certainly have done the same. Dulla's utility as a tool lay in his speed and in the way he was able to speak words to other Poison Ghosts that caused them to hesitate, to be uncertain, while Sharn-igon had time to come in upon them and kill. It was so very easy to kill Poison Ghosts! A few slashes, a blow with the club-claw—it took no more than that. Sometimes they had weapons, and Sharn-igon had learned to respect some of those weapons. But the two on the beach had had so little—a bright-sounding popgun whose tiny bullets bounced off his shell, a thing that squirted some sort of foul, stinging smell that made him feel queer and unpleasant for a moment but did not slow him in the kill. Such as they he could kill with or without his tool, the Poison Ghost Dulla.

He switched his carapace back and forth to wedge himself deeper in his pit and rested, his hearing receptors watchful toward the water, his feelers drilled deep into the soil to listen for fibrations from any approaching Ghosts Below. It was the burrows he feared, more than any danger from the water or the beach.

Of course, in normal circumstances an adult Krinpit in shell was a match for a dozen of the Ghosts Below—as long as he could stay on the surface, or at least in sound of it. In the open, Ghosts Below seemed deaf, running almost at random. But these were not normal circumstances. Sharn-igon was not only weary; he felt sick. He felt irritable, tense, bloated—ready, he would have said to his he-wife (but Cheee-pruitt was months dead, his carapace dry), to stridulate and jump out of his shell. But it was not the right time for that. He was not due for many months yet, so it couldn't be normal pre-molt tension.

Abruptly his sphincter loosened. He regurgitated everything he had eaten in a great flood—meat of deafworm, scraps of chitin of crabrat, half-digested fruits and fungi and leaves.

Vomiting left him weak but calm. After resting for a moment, he covered the mess over and then methodically began to clean his shell. No doubt the Poison Ghosts were taking revenge for being killed on the beach. It had to be their scraps of flesh still caught in Sharn-igon's chelae that were making him ill. That—and the inner sickness that had claimed him when the Poison Ghosts first came to his city and began the remorseless chain of circumstance that had taken all joy from his life.

Krinpit did not cry. They had no tear ducts; they had no eyes to have tear ducts in. They did have the emotion of sorrow, and no culture-driven taboos against expressing it in their own way. That way was stillness. A quiet Krinpit —or as close to quiet as a Krinpit could get—was a weeping Krinpit.

For most of an hour, once he had polished the last dried particle of alien blood off his tympanum, Sharn-igon was nearly soundless: a rasp of claw against carapace, an occasional respiring moan, little else.

Unbidden, sounds of happier times echoed in his mind. He heard Cheee-pruitt again, and the little female—what was her name?—whom they had impregnated and who bore their young. She had been a dulcet creature. She had

had almost a personality of her own, along with the bittersweet appeal of any mated female, her young growing and eating inside her until too much was destroyed and she died, and the brood polished her carapace clean and emerged to the loud, exciting world of their wife-father's back.

But everything was changed now.

It was all the fault of the Poison Ghosts! Ever since the first of them had arrived and Cheee-pruitt—dear, lost Cheee-pruitt—had had the unwisdom to try to eat it, Sharn-igon's world had fallen apart. Not just Cheee-pruitt, all of it. The Krinpit he had mobilized against the Poison Ghosts Dulla called Greasies had been punished severely. His own village-mates had been attacked from the air in reprisal, and so many of them were dead. And how many had he succeeded in killing in return? A few. Hardly any. The two on the beach, the handful that he and Dulla had surprised at the outpost—not enough! And all of Dulla's plans had come to little: the Krinpit village nearest to the Fats had wavered and wobbled, promised to join in an attack and withdrawn the promise; and meanwhile all he and Dulla could do was skulk around like crabrats, looking for strays to attack and finding none. Until the two came out of their sinking vessel—

There was a sound from the water.

Sharn-igon froze. It was not possible for him to be wholly silent while he breathed at all, but he did his best.

He listened out of his shallow cave and heard a small, almost inaudible, blurred echo from the water. A coracle. And in it what seemed to be a Poison Ghost.

Another to kill? It was approaching. Sharn-igon thrust himself out of the cave and reared up to defend himself; and then he heard his own name shouted across the beach: "Sharn-igon!" And then those barbarous sounds that were the name of his mistrusted ally, or his truced foe: "OCK-med doo-LAH."

He scuttled across the sand, half to greet Dulla, half still ready to kill, as Dulla yelled and pleaded. "Hurry! The Fats will be searching this whole coast. We must get out!"

With Sharn-igon aboard, the coracle rode very low in the water. It could not easily sink. Its cellular shell entrapped too much air for that. But it could swamp.

Crossing Broad Water it often did, and then both of them splashed and bailed and kept a watchful eye or ear for Ghosts Above until they could get under weigh again. The little sail helped them when the wind blew fair, but there was no keel. When the wind shifted, the sail had to come down and they had to paddle. It seemed to take forever; and Sharn-igon felt increasingly ill; and at every stroke or splash the grim recriminations continued.

"But for you, my he-wife would still be alive."

"You are foolish, Sharn-igon. He tried to kill us; it is not our fault he died of it."

"And my village was attacked, and another village destroyed entirely, and I myself am ill."

"Speak of something else, Sharn-igon. Speak of the promises your Krinpit made to join in the attack on the Fats and how they broke them."

"I will speak of my sorrow and my anger, Ahmed Dulla."

"Then speak also of mine! We too have suffered in fighting with you against the common enemy."

"Suffered?"

"Yes, suffered! Before my radio was destroyed—by you, Sharn-igon, by your clumsiness!—I could hear no voice from my camp. They may be dead, all of them!"

"How many, Ahmed Dulla?"

"A dozen or more!"

"A dozen or more of you have then died. Of us, how many? Of persons, two hundred. Of females, forty. Of backlings and infants—"

But it was not until they had crossed Broad Water and Sharn-igon heard the silence from his city that he perceived the immensity of the tragedy. There was no originated sound! There were only echoes—and what echoes!

Always before, when he crossed Broad Water, the city had presented a bustling, beautiful sound. Not this time. He heard nothing. Nothing! No drone of immature males at the waterfront shredding the fish catch. No songs from the mold-eaters on the Great White Way. No hammering of stakes to build new palisades on the made land on the point. He heard the echo of his own sounds faintly returning to him and recognized the shadowy outline of the mooring rocks, a few sheds, one or two boats, some structures half destroyed, a litter of empty carapaces. Nothing else.

The city was dead.

The Poison Ghost Dulla chattered worriedly to him, and Sharn-igon made out the words. "Another attack! The place is empty. The Greasies must have come back to finish the job."

He could not reply. Stillness overcame him, a great, mourning silence so deep that even the Poison Ghost turned toward him in wonder. "Are you ill? What is happening?"

With great effort Sharn-igon scratched the words out on his tympanum. "You have killed my city and all my back-mates."

"We? Certainly not! It could not have been the People's Republics; we have not the strength anymore. It must have been the Greasies."

"Against whom you vowed to protect us!" roared Sharn-igon. He rose on hind legs to tower over Dulla, and the Poison Ghost cringed in fear. But Sharn-igon did not attack. He threw himself forward, out of the coracle, with a broad *splat* that sent the waves dancing. The water was shallow here. Sharn-igon managed to keep some of his hind feet on the oozy bottom, while enough of his breathing pores were above the surface to keep him from drowning. He charged up the shoreline, scattering the littered water in a V of foam.

The tragedy made him still again, at every step and at each fresh echo. Dead! All dead. The streets empty except for abandoned carapaces, already dry. The shops untended. The homes deserted. Not a living male, not a female, not even any scrambling, chittering young.

Dulla waded through the stink of dead and floating marine animals, towing the coracle and staring about. "What a horror!" he exclaimed. "We are brothers now more than ever, Sharn-igon."

"All of my brothers are dead."

"What? Well, yes. But we must be as brothers, to take revenge! We must be allies against the Greasies and the Fats."

Sharn-igon reared up, trapping him against the wall of a ruined shed. "I now need new allies, Ahmed Dulla," he ground out, falling upon him. In the last moment Dulla saw what was to happen and tried to escape. But it was too late; his quickness was not enough when he dodged from the snatching claws only to take the full force of the murderous club of chitin that stove his head in.

When he was quite sure Dulla was dead, Sharn-igon staggered away, blundering through the dried shells that had once been friends, to rest creakily against the wall of a shop he had once known.

He took little satisfaction in the death of one more Poison Ghost. He did not even mourn any longer for the death of his city. A nearer pain touched him. His joints were aching, his body felt bloated, his carapace seemed to be sundering at the seams. It was not his time. But there was no doubt about it. Alone in the open tomb that had once been his home, with no one to care for him while he was helpless, he was beginning to molt.

EIGHTEEN

•

AT 0130 HOURS, Major Santangelo, along with the pilot-engineer who had brought in the third ship, reported in.

"Some good news, Margie. There's a coal outcropping in the Bad Hills, two kilometers up. Plus we can burn wood and biomass, and Richy here says we can make a steam boiler with plates from one of the landing craft. If your turbine arrives, that means we can drive the generator up to full capacity, fifty kilowatts, without using up our fuel reserves."

"When?"

Santangelo looked at the engineer. "Ten days? Call it two weeks."

"Call it one week," Margie snapped. "What about alcohol?"

"Well, Morrissey's got a kind of a yeast—something like a yeast—anyway, he's getting fermentation. Should be putting the first batch through the solar still tomorrow. You can probably smell it."

"Saint, I can *taste* it. I need that alcohol to stretch out the airplane fuel!"

"I'll goose him along," Santangelo promised.

"Do it," said Margie. When they were gone she picked up the handset and called the radio shack. "Any ETA yet?"

"No, ma'am. They're still in orbit, figuring a minimum-energy descent." She hung up. At least the resupply ship was in orbit around Jem, not light-years away. But that last little step was a killer. The captain had radioed that his maneuvering reserve was low and he was waiting for the most favorable approach. That might be days! Worse than that. If the Cape had launched them without plenty of reserve, that meant things were seriously wrong at the

Cape. Even wronger than the coded tactrans from Earth had indicated, and that was wrong enough.

She looked at her watch: 0145. "Send in Dr. Arkashvili," she called, and the medic came in on cue, bearing a cup of steaming black coffee.

"Medical supplies, Margie. But a little sleep would do you more good."

Marge sniffed the aluminum cup rapturously and took a scalding sip. "I wish they'd land," she said fretfully. Among the goodies on her shopping list were coffee beans, or seeds, or whatever it took to try to grow coffee for themselves. Otherwise the next couple of years, anyway, might be coffee-free. Of course, the Greasies probably had some growing already, to make that vile stuff they handed out in the little brass pots, but they weren't likely to give any away. They weren't giving anything away now, not even information over the radio; and the Peeps simply were not answering at all.

At least the camp was gratifyingly healthy, according to the medic's report. The antiallergens were standing up well, and there was nothing else in the Jemman environment to make a human being sick. A few headaches, probably from the climate and from the switch to a twenty-four-hour day; some dentistry; an appendix that needed watching; a request for a vasectomy—

"No," said Margie sharply. "Don't do any vasectomies. Or laparoscopies, either."

The doctor looked thoughtful. "You're going to have some knocked-up personnel."

"You're supposed to be able to handle that, right? Anyway, give them the pill, diaphragms, condoms— anything reversible or temporary. I get along fine with an IUD, and I can always take it out if I want to have a baby."

"Which you might?"

"Which all of us females may damn well have to, Cheech. That's an order: everybody capable of breeding *stays* capable. How's the baby bank?"

"Coming along fine. I've got twenty-eight ova in cryonic hold, and about a hundred sperm samples."

"Good, Cheech, but not good enough. I want a hundred percent compliance with that. If anything happens to anybody, I don't want his genes lost. Or hers. They don't take up much space, do they? Then I want, let's say, four samples from each, and—what are you grinning about?"

The medic said, "Well, it's just that a couple of the ova turned out to be prefertilized. They're fine. They'll keep in the deep-freeze indefinitely, but whenever you want them reimplanted we won't have to go to the bother of getting them started."

"Hum." Margie scratched thoughtfully. "I'm almost sorry you took the sample; we could start having kids any time now. Who were they? Come on, Cheech, none of this medical confidentiality; I'm your commanding officer."

"Well, one was Ana Dimitrova."

"No shit! Whose kid?"

"You can ask her if you want to. I didn't."

Marge shook her head wonderingly. "I would have guessed her about last," she said. "And the other one? Now, wait a minute! It couldn't be me! The IUD—"

"The IUD doesn't keep an ovum from getting fertilized; it only prevents it taking root and developing."

Margie sat back and stared at the doctor. "I'll be damned," she said.

Nguyen Dao Tree was ten minutes late for his 0200 appointment, and he arrived sleepy-eyed and irritable. "This twenty-four hour day of yours is not comfortable, Margie," he complained.

"You're not the one to bitch, Guy. I took the midnight-to-eight myself. If you'd spend your sleeping time sleeping instead of tomcatting around with every woman in the camp—"

"As to that, Marjorie," he said, "I much preferred when you and I slept on the same schedule."

"Yeah. Well. Maybe we'll have to do something about that, Guy, but right now we're late for inspection." She swallowed the last of her coffee, now cold but still delicious, and led the way.

Complaints aside, the three-shift day was working well. On the plus side, the perimeter was well guarded, the hectarage under cultivation was growing by nearly two thousand square meters every day, the each-one-teach-one training schedule Santangelo had set up so that the skills of the community were shared among several persons (what if Chiche Arkashvili died? or their one and only surviving agronomist?) was on track. On the minus, aerial surveillance showed large numbers of Krinpit roaming around the woods, coffee was not the only food item to be running low, and the resupply ship still could not give a firm landing time.

Margie allowed one hour of each day for her inspection, and she used every minute of it. No white-glove chicken-shit. The inspection was rough and dirty; if everybody was doing their job and the jobs were being done, that was it. Her Bastogne grandfather had not cared if the troops were shaved, only if they could fight. And Margie had learned the skills appropriate to a fortress under siege.

That was what they were. No one had attacked the perimeter, not even a wandering Krinpit. But they were isolated in a world of enemies. From spy satellites and balloonists, from the breaking of codes and from what little could be gleaned from their infrequent radio contacts, above all from the contents of the Indonesian's pouch, Margie had formed a pretty good idea of what the Greasies were up to. Or had been up to a few weeks earlier. They had occupied the Peeps' camp; they had requisitioned quantities and varieties of personnel and equipment that made her drool. Even her letter to Santa Claus (who might or might not be hanging in orbit, waiting to come down her chimney) had not been so greedy. They had subdued the local autochthons, apparently by killing off all the nearby Krinpit and shooting down any balloonist who came near. Their burrowers they seemed to have tamed. And they were using them for minerals exploration, because it seemed the Greasies had perched themselves on a Kuwait of oil and a Scranton of other fossil fuels. They had devised an enzyme, or possibly it was a hormone—the information had been unclear—which took Krinpit out of action as effectively as 2, 4-D had dried up the jungles of Vietnam, by causing them to molt. They had acquired something from their Creepies that let them make building materials out of dirt, as the burrowers themselves hardened the interior surfaces of their tunnels. They had—Christ, what had they not done! If only her father had listened to her and given her the support she demanded, how gladly and competently she could have done the same!

Not that she had done badly. But for Marge Menninger there was no such thing as second best, and the Greasies at that moment controlled the entire planet. Barring the dozen hectares her colony sat on, it was all theirs. Their aircraft roamed it at will, so the spy satellites said. They had three separate colonies now, counting the one that had once belonged to the probably no longer surviving Peeps. And apart from the rare occasions when she dared send Kappelyushnikov on a quick survey flight (what would she do if there were some unexplained "accident" to her one and only aircraft?), she was blind except for what the satellites and the few living balloonists could tell. She had even grounded Danny Dalehouse. Not only because of the risk to him—but that was a reason in itself, she admitted privately; she did not want him killed—but because the electricity that made his hydrogen was better used for floodlights to protect the camp and make the crops grow. Also she had apprenticed him to the agronomist, along with Morrissey and the Bulgarian girl—wait a minute, she thought to herself; Dalehouse and Dimitrova? Maybe so. Probably not. They had been friendly, but not *that* friendly. But then who?

For that matter, she thought, looking at Guy Tree as he chattered away about contingency plans in the event of a major Krinpit attack, who was the father of her own sort-of-child? Dalehouse? Tree? That son of a bitch Sweggert, with his cute little tricks? They were the most likely candidates, but which?

In other times, one part of Marge Menninger would have contemplated with sardonic amusement that other part of Marge Menninger which really, dammit!, wanted to *know*. At present she had no room for that sort of amusement in her mind. The thought of mentioning to Nguyen Tree that the two of them might be in the process of becoming somewhat delayed parents crossed her mind just long enough for her to dismiss it. It promised some good comedy, but it also promised complications she did not want to handle. First things first.

"Are there any archers in the camp?" she asked.

Tree stopped in the middle of explaining his proposal for arming a couple of canoes. "What?"

"People who know how to shoot a bow and arrow, dammit. We must have some. I'd like to organize a contest, part of the sports program."

"Very likely so, Marjorie. I don't believe there are any bows and arrows, however."

"If they know how to shoot them, they know how to

make them, don't they? Or anyway, it'll be in the microfiches. Get started on that, please, Guy. We'll give prizes. Coffee, cigarettes. I'll donate a bottle of Scotch." The thought that had crossed her mind as he spoke of how he planned to mount a light machine gun in a canoe was that the supplies of ammunition for the guns would not last forever, either, but she wasn't ready to say that even to her second in command.

Tree looked puzzled, but paused to make a note in his book. "It would be a useful skill for hunting, I suppose."

Margie nodded without replying. Hunting what? Every animal they had seen on the surface of the planet was well enough armored to laugh off any homemade bow—a conspicuous blunder on the part of evolution in this place, she was convinced. But she let it go.

As they were inspecting the power plant a messenger from the communications shack trotted up. "Ship's on its way in, colonel," she reported, panting. "They've already retrofired. We ought to see them in a couple of minutes."

"Thank God," said Margie. "Put it on the PA. Guy, get twenty grunts for unloading. Tell Major Arkashvili to stand by in case they land rough."

They didn't land rough. But they didn't land right, either. The drogue chute deployed handsomely, the craft came swinging down on its cluster of three big chutes they jettisoned on schedule, and it came in on its rockets. But it never made it to the beach where the others had landed. It came in almost a kilometer short and dropped into the jungle and out of sight.

The good part was that no one was hurt. The fifteen persons on board all came into the camp on their own power; and twelve of them were both young and female. God had answered Margie's prayer that far, at least. The bad part was that everything on the ship had to be manhandled over eight hundred meters of bad terrain, through jungle and over half a dozen ravines. No matter. They were there. And as Margie scanned the bill of lading she began to relax. It was all there, every last thing she had asked for, and more besides. Seeds and hand tools, weapons and training manuals. It was not enough—there was no such thing as enough—but it was all she had hoped.

First priority was to get everything movable inside the

perimeter of the camp. That meant organizing working parties and armed guards to go with them. No Krinpit had been spotted near the landing site, but the woods were full of them. It wasn't until the first detachments began straggling back with cases of food and boxes of microfiches, folded bicycles and crates of electronic parts, that Margie relaxed long enough to greet the new arrivals. She shook each hand, spoke each name, and turned them over to Santangelo for assignment to quarters. A short black major hung behind. "I've got something for you, colonel," he said, patting a dispatch case. "In private, if you please, ma'am."

"Come ahead. Vandemeer, is it?" He nodded politely and followed her into her office, where he placed his dispatch case on her desk.

"This is it, ma'am," he said, unsnapping the case.

It was not a dispatch case. When he had undone the snaps the side peeled back and revealed a microprocessor with a liquid-crystal panel. He touched one of the buttons and it sprang into light, displaying a row of close-typed symbols.

"There's your guidance, ma'am. There are twelve satellite busters in orbit, and these are the controls."

Margie touched it. A warm feeling grew in the pit of her stomach and spread, an almost sexual excitement. "You're checked out on this, Vandemeer? Can you locate the Greasies' satellites?"

"Yes, ma'am. We've got acquisition and lock on four of theirs, including their main tactran receiver. Also the Peeps; they have two, but they don't seem to be active." He expertly punched a combination into the processor, and the colors of the symbols changed. "Green lights are ours. Red are Peeps. Yellow are Oilies. The lines that are still white are standby. If anything else comes within two million klicks the guidance system will track and identify it, and one of the spare birds will lock on."

The warmth was spreading. That had been the biggest and most important item on Margie's Christmas list, and the one she had been least sure of getting. Now the sons of bitches survived at her pleasure!

"Thanks, major," she said. "I want you to show me how to work this thing, and from then on I want it in your possession or mine, twelve hours a day each, until further notice."

"Yes, ma'am," he said unemotionally. "And I have something your father asked me to hand to you personally."

It was a letter, not a microfiche. A paper letter, in an envelope with her name on it in Godfrey Menninger's own handwriting. "Thanks, major," she said again. "Go get settled in, and take the controller with you." As he turned, she added, "Major? Are things pretty bad at home?"

He paused, looking at her. "Pretty bad," he said. "Yes, I would say that, colonel. They're pretty bad."

Margie stood holding the letter for a moment. Then she jammed it in her pocket and went out to see how the unloading was coming along, because she wasn't quite ready to get the uncensored word on how bad "pretty bad" was.

Putting it away did not let her forget it was there. While she was chewing Sergeant Sweggert out for talking up two of the new girls when he should have been shifting cargo, she was fingering it. When she was breaking up an argument over what had become of a case of flashlights—"Jesus, colonel, I just put them down for a second; I thought one of the other guys took them!"—her hand returned to it. When the mess tent called a halt for breakfast, she could resist no longer, and she took her tray and her letter back into her office and ate while she read.

Marge, honey,

You've got it all, everything on the list. But there's no more where that came from. The Greasies have ordered our rigs off the Mid-Atlantic Ridge. It's a bluff. We're calling it. But every drop of booster fuel is now sequestered for missiles until they back down—and then there's Peru. The Peeps have flanged up a phoney "election," and we're not going to sit still for it. So we'll be at full military alert for months to come, maybe longer than that.

You're on your own, honey. Figure at least a year. And it may be more than that, because of the president's being threatened with impeachment, maybe worse—there was an assassination attempt with two National Guard tanks last week. I told him what to do. Declare martial law. Send Congress home. Crack down all around. But he's a politician. He thinks he can ride it out. If he does, that means the rest of his term he'll be trying to score brownie points with the voters, and that means cutting back a lot of important programs.

And one of them might be you, honey.

I wouldn't be telling you this if I didn't think you could handle it. But it looks as if you'll have to.

That was all, not even a signature. Margie sat with the letter in her hands and minutes later noticed that she had forgotten to finish her breakfast.

She no longer wanted it, but neither would she waste food—especially not now. She forced herself to eat it all, and it wasn't until she had swallowed every scrap that she realized the sound of the camp had changed. Something was wrong.

While Sergeant Sweggert was eating he heard two sounds, not very near and not very loud. They sounded like shots. No one else in the mess tent seemed to have heard anything. He scraped the plate of its canned ham and dehydrated eggs, picked up the big chunk of bread, and strolled toward the entrance, still chewing.

There was a third shot.

This time there was no mistake. Some dumb son of a bitch was playing with his piece. You couldn't blame him—if Sweggert got a Krinpit in his sights he would have been tempted to blow it away, too. But three shots was wasting ammunition. He speeded up and headed toward the perimeter. As he rounded the cook tent he saw a dozen people standing around the uphill emplacement peering up the trail toward the spot where the resupply ship had landed. Others were converging on the post, and by the time he reached it there were twenty, all talking at once.

The shots had come from the trail. "Who's out there?" he demanded, grabbing Corporal Kristianides by the shoulder.

"Aggie and two grunts. They decided to get another load in before they bucked the chow line. Lieutenant Macklin just took a patrol up after them."

"So sit down and shut up till they get back," Sweggert ordered; but it was an order he didn't want to follow himself. It wasn't like Aggie to shoot up the jungle. The crowd was getting bigger; Colonel Tree came trotting up, looking like a little China doll, then half a dozen from the mess tent, then the colonel herself. Ten people were talking at once, until the colonel snarled, "All of you, at ease! Here comes Macklin. Let's see what he has to say."

But Macklin didn't have to say a word. He came stepping along the worn place that had become their path, carbine at port arms, looking both ways into the jungle. As he got closer they could see that the two men behind him were carrying someone, and the last soldier was backing toward them, carrying her weapon as Macklin carried his.

What they were bringing in was a body. It was female, and that was all you could say. The face was unrecognizable. When they dropped her down, it was plain that not only the face had been attacked. One arm was shredded up to the shoulder, and there was a bullet hole between her breasts.

"Krinpit," snapped Major Santangelo.

"Krinpit don't have guns," said Colonel Menninger, tight-lipped. "Maybe Krinpit, but they had company. Tree! Check the perimeter. I want every weapon manned and a reserve at every point. Santangelo, fall the off-duty troops in. Give Sweggert and me two hundred meters, then follow us. Sweggert, take three people, and you and I are going to take the point."

"Yes'm." He spun around, took Corporal Kristianides's gas-operated recoilless away from her, and picked three from his squad at random while Colonel Menninger was listening to Lieutenant Macklin's report. He had got only about halfway up the trail, where he found the casualty and a couple of spilled and ransacked cases of supplies. Where the other two were he didn't know. He had come back for reinforcements. Marge Menninger listened to no more. She turned him over to Major Santangelo and signaled Sweggert to move in.

At twenty-second intervals, they dogged it across the open space that was the field of fire, reforming under the arch of a many-tree. As Sweggert waited for the others, he could hear the rattle and moan of some shelled creatures, but not very near. The next man in heard it too and turned a questioning face to Sweggert, mouthing the word *Krinpit*. Sweggert nodded savagely and motioned silence. When Colonel Menninger crossed the field of fire, she trotted ten meters past them, then dropped to a knee and looked around warily before raising a hand and ordering them in.

Fucking hairy, thought Sweggert. It was like that bitch to pick him for something like this! She'd had it in for him ever since he had it in her. He hand-signaled the rest of the patrol to move up one at a time, two on one side of the trail and the other with him and the colonel on the other, and when they had made their run he waited ten seconds and then sprinted to drop down beside the colonel. "That's where they got her," he breathed, pointing ahead on the trail, where half a case of fluorescent tubes lay crunched and scattered on the ground.

"I see that, sergeant! Keep moving, I don't want Santangelo running up my ass."

"Yes'm." He stooped low, dodging through the underbrush, and flopped down. The distant Krinpit rattle was still audible, but not closer. The patrol leapfrogged through the jungle until the bulk of the resupply ship loomed ahead, with its tramped-down clearing before it. He waved to catch Colonel Menninger's eye, then pointed to the top of a many-tree. She nodded, and when his turn came again he raced for the nearest of its trunks, slung his GORR over his shoulder, and started up the clump of growth. It was not much like climbing a real tree; it was easier. The flat, arched branches were like a series of steps, and the stalactitic growths that hung down between them made good handholds. The problem was that it was hard to see. Sweggert had to change position twice before he could get a clear view of the rocket.

What he saw was the base of the ship, and right in front of it the bodies of the other two grunts. They had been savagely mutilated. There was no sign of Krinpit, and the sounds he had heard seemed to have gone farther away.

Sergeant Sweggert began to feel a little better. Why the fuck should he worry about Krinpit? They were noisy bastards; there was no way one of them could get within twenty meters with him hearing it. And then the GORR would take care of it. Of course, he speculated, maybe they weren't alone. Maybe there were a couple of Greasies with them. But what did that matter? Greasies were Greasies—they were spics, Ay-rabs, or limeys—and the day hadn't come when he worried about meeting one of them in the woods. He pushed his cap back and settled down. If anything showed up in that clearing he would blow its ass off, and meanwhile he had the entertaining spectacle of Margie Menninger silently worming her way forward on the ground, almost right under him. Off to the other side of the trail somebody else was moving, equally silently; he swiveled the GORR to sight in on it, but as the figure slid between bushes he saw that it was one of his own patrol. He returned the gun and slowly centered it on Marge Menninger, moving the cross hairs in the reticle down from the base of her skull to her hips. Wouldn't it be nice, he speculated, if he could give her one she'd never forget, right up the old—

The faintest of sounds behind him made him freeze.

A little too late, he comprehended a mistake in his thinking. Krinpit and human beings were not the only creatures on Jem. As he started to turn he saw a skinny, stretched-out creature, longer than he was tall, climbing toward him with at least half a dozen legs, while others held what looked like some kind of a gun. The damn thing was wearing sunglasses, he thought with surprise, trying to bring the GORR around. He was too slow. He never heard the shot that went through his head.

Marge Menninger was the first one back into the camp. She didn't wait for the cleanup; once they knew what they were looking for, the forty armed troops scoured the area. All they got was three of the burrowers, but one of them was the one who had killed Sergeant Sweggert. You were always a lucky son of a bitch, she thought; now you don't have to worry about a court-martial for rape anymore. She collared a passing man and sent him running toward the communications tent, and before she was in her office she heard the announcement coming over the PA: "Major Vandemeer! Report to the colonel on the double!"

She met him at the door. Good man, he was trotting over half-dressed, but he had the case with him. "Open it up," she snarled. "They're arming the Creepies against us, guns and glasses. That's what Tinka was trying to get back to tell me. Move it, man!"

"Yes'm." But even the stolid Major Vandemeer fumbled as he undid the snaps. "Ready, ma'am," he reported, fingers poised.

The red fury in her mind was balanced by the warmth spreading at the base of her belly. She scratched vigorously and snapped, "Take 'em out!"

"Who, ma'am?"

"The Greasies! Bust their birds, all of them!" She watched the complicated ritual and then frowned. "While you're at it, take the Peeps' out too."

NINETEEN

●

GODFREY MENNINGER woke up wondering who was shaking the foot of his bed.

No one was. He was alone in his room, exactly like a hundred thousand Holiday Inn or Howard Johnson's Motor Lodge rooms all over the world. There was the phone on a nightstand beside the bed, the TV set staring grayly across at him from the long desk-plus-chest-plus-luggage-rack that stood against the wall. The phone was almost the only visible element that made it different, for it was a push-button jobber with colored lights flickering across its face. The other element of strangeness was harder to see. The drapes over one wall covered an immense likris display panel, not a window. There was no point in having a window He was two hundred meters under the earth.

It was 6:22 on the clock.

Menninger had left orders to be awakened at seven. Therefore it was not a call that had awakened him. Therefore there were only a couple of other possibilities, and none of them were attractive. God Menninger considered picking up the phone or switching on the TV or pulling back the drapes over the likris situation screen, any of which would have told him at once what was happening. He decided against doing so. If it had posed an immediate threat he would have been notified at once. Margie's disciplined and hierarchical approach to problem solving had not been taught at West Point; it had come to her on her father's knee. If she was good at putting unwanted thoughts out of her mind, he was superb. He dismissed the question, slipped into his brocaded robe, went into the bathroom, and made himself a cup of instant coffee with tap water.

God Menninger's waking-up minutes were precious to him. He was of the opinion that both his marriages had failed because he had been unable to make either wife understand that he was never, not ever, to be spoken to for at least half an hour after waking. That was coffee time and summoning-up-strength time and remembering-what-he-had-to-do time. Conversation destroyed it. A weakness of Godfrey Menninger's character was that he was apt to destroy anyone who infringed on it.

The coffee was at just the right temperature, and he drank it like medicine, swallow by swallow, until it was down. Then he threw off the robe, sat cross-legged on the bed in the half-lotus position, let his body go calm, and began to say his mantra.

Godfrey Menninger had never really understood what happened among his neurons and synapses when he practiced transcendental meditation, nor had he ever really tried. It did not seem to do any harm of any kind, except to cost him some twenty-four hundred seconds out of every twenty-four hours. He seldom discussed it with anyone else and therefore did not have to defend it. And it seemed to work. Work how? Do what? He could not exactly have said. When he did it he felt more confident and more relaxed about his confidence. That was not a bad return on the investment of less than three percent of his time. As he sat, his body withdrawing from him, the reiterated *ta-lenn, ta-lenn* of the mantra becoming a sort of drapery of sound that surrounded him without being present, his whole brain became a receptor. It contributed nothing. It only perceived. On the inside of his eyelids he saw faces and shapes that melted into each other. Some were beautiful and some gargoyles. Some were etched in the sharpest of drypoint lines. Some seemed to be beaten out of gold. They held no emotional content for him. The demon snarls did not frighten. The loveliness did not attract. They were only there. Wispy chains of words floated past his consciousness like snatches of conversation from the next table at a restaurant. They spoke of ultimata and megatonnages and a remembered caress and the need for a haircut, but there were no imperatives in them anywhere. The circulating memory that pumped them past his mind sucked them away again without residue.

More than two thousand kilometers away and half a kilometer down, inside a submarine belonging to the Fuel Bloc, a vice admiral in the Libyan navy was programming The One That Had His Name on It. Menninger did not know it. His thoughts floated free into infinity in all directions, but all directions lay within that inner space of his mind. He could not have done anything useful about it if he had known.

The bed moved again.

It was not an earthquake. There were no earthquakes in West Virginia, he thought, bringing himself up out of reverie, getting ready to open his eyes. It was sharper than an earthquake would have been, more quick and trivial than the slow battering of a crustal slip. It was not particularly strong, and if he had still been asleep it might not even have awakened him. But it was something. And then the lights flickered.

Two hundred meters down in the side of a West Virginia mountain, the lights were not meant to flicker. A ^{239}Pu megawatt generating plant, vented through a kilometer of piping to emerge on the other side of the hill, was immune to most external events. Lightning bolts did not strike transformers underground. Winds could not tear loose a line, since there were no lines in the open air. And then, tardily, the flickering colors on the base of the telephone all went out. A single red light flared, and the buzzer sounded. He picked up the phone and said, "Menninger."

"Three missiles came in, sir—near misses. There's no structural damage. Point of origin backtracks probably to near Sinkiang province. The city of Wheeling is out."

"I'll be there in a minute," he said. He was still coming up from his meditation, and so he did not look at his own situation panel, but he also did not stop to shower or shave. He rubbed deodorant on his armpits—French whore's bath, but good enough—ran a brush over his hair, pulled on his coveralls and shoes, and walked briskly down the placid, beige-carpeted corridor to his command room.

The situation map was alight from end to end.

"Here's your coffee," said General Weinenstat. That was all she said. She knew his ways. He took the cup without looking at her, because his eyes were on the board. It displayed a Mercator projection of the earth in outline. Within it, bright red stars were targets taken out. Bright blue stars were also targets taken out, but on the wrong side: that was Washington and Leningrad and Buenos Aires and Hanoi and Chicago and San Francisco. Broken red profiles in the ocean areas of the map were enemy missile-launching vessels destroyed. There were more than a hundred of them. But there were also nearly sixty broken blue ones. Pulsating targets, red and blue, were major concentrations not yet destroyed. There were relatively few of them. The number decreased as he watched. Kansas City, Tientsin, Cairo, and the whole urban complex around Frankfurt ceased to exist.

The second cup of coffee was not medicine but comfort. He took a sip of it and then asked, "What's their remaining second-strike capability?"

"Marginal, Godfrey. Maybe one hundred missiles operational within the next twenty-four hours, but we're cutting that down all the time. We have almost eighty. And only two of our hardened installations are scratched."

"Local damage?"

"Well—there are a lot of casualties. Otherwise, not bad. Surface contamination is within acceptable limits—inside shielded vehicles, anyway." She signaled an orderly for a coffee refill and added, "Too early to tell about long-lived isotope capture, but most of the Corn Belt looks okay. So's Mexico and the Pacific Northwest. We did lose the Imperial Valley."

"So we're not bad for now."

"I would say so, yes, God."

"For the next twenty-four hours. Then they can start to redeploy." She nodded. It was a known fact that every major country had squirreled away missiles and components. They were not at ten-minute command like the ones in the silos or on the subs. They could not be launched by pushing a button. But they could not be taken out at long range, either, since you didn't know where they were hidden. He added, "And we can't look for them, because the satellite busters have half-blinded us."

"We've all-blinded them, Godfrey. They don't have an eye in orbit."

"Yes, yes, I understand," he said testily. "We've won the exchange. The damn fools. Well, let's get to work."

Menninger's "work" was not directly related to the exchange of missiles that was remodeling the surface of the earth to a facsimile of hell. That was not his responsibility. It was only a precursor, like a friend's retiring to the bathroom to fit in her diaphragm while he slouched, waiting, on the edge of the bed. She would not need his advice or his help at that stage, and neither would the

Chiefs of Staff while the actual fire fight was going on. His involvement would be central immediately thereafter.

Meanwhile, one of the damn fools had finished the programming and was trying to round up enough of a crew for the launch. It wasn't easy. The neutron bomb had done just what ERW weapons were supposed to do—penetrated the carelessly scant meters of water and the steel tube of his submarine and knocked out most of the crew. The Libyan vice admiral himself had taken nearly five thousand rads. He knew he had only hours to live, but with any luck his target would have less than that.

Three hours' sleep was not enough. Menninger knew that he was quick-tempered and a little fuzzy, but he had trained his people to know that too, and they made allowances.

At five-minute intervals the map disappeared and the likris screen sequenced itself through a round of ten-second displays: profiles of industrial capacity destroyed and remaining, curves of casualties, histograms of combat-effectiveness estimates. In the Ops Room next to God Menninger's command post, more than fifty persons were working on overdrive to correct and update those figures. Menninger hardly glanced at them. His concerns were political and organizational. Rose Weinenstat was on the scrambler to the Combined Chiefs every few minutes, not so much to give information or to get it as to keep them aware, every minute, that the most powerful unofficial figure in government had his eye on them all the time. His three chief civilian liaisons were in touch with state governments and government agencies, and Menninger himself spoke, one after another, with cabinet officers, key senators, and a few governors—when they could be found. It was all US, not Fats; the rest of the Food Bloc was in touch through the filter of the Alliance Room, and when one of them demanded his personal attention it was an intrusion.

"He isn't satisfied with me," General Weinenstat reported. "Maybe you should give him a minute, Godfrey."

"Shit." Menninger put down his pen at the exact place on a remobilization order where he stopped reading and nodded for her to switch over.

The face on his phone screen was that of Marshal Bressarion of the Red Army, but the voice was his translator's. "The marshal," she said, sounding tinny through the scrambler, "does not question that you and the Combined Chiefs are acting under the President's orders, but he wishes to know just who the President is. We are aware that Washington is no more, and that Strongboxes One and Two have been penetrated."

"The present President," said Menninger, patiently restraining his irritation, "is Henry Moncas, who was Speaker of the House of Representatives. The succession is as provided in our basic law, the Constitution of the United States."

"Yes, of course," said the translator after Bressarion had listened and then barked something in Russian, "but the marshal has been unable to reach him for confirmation."

"There have been communications problems," Menninger agreed. He looked past the phone, where Rose Weinenstat was shaping the words "in transit" with her lips. "Also," he added, "I am informed the President is in the process of moving to a fully secure location. As the marshal will realize, that requires a communications lid."

The marshal listened impatiently and then spoke for some seconds in rapid-fire Russian. The translator sounded a good deal more uptight as she said, "We quite understand, but there is some question of lines of authority, and the marshal would appreciate hearing from him directly as soon—hello? Hello?"

His image faded. General Weinenstat said apologetically, "I thought it was a good time to develop transmission difficulties."

"Good thinking. Where is the son of a bitch, by the way?"

"Henry? Oh, he's safe and sound, Godfrey. He's been ordering you to report to him for the last hour or so."

"Um." Menninger thought for a moment. "Tell you what. Send out a radiation-safe team to escort him here so I can report. Don't take no for an answer. Tell him he'll be safer here than in his own hole." He picked up the pencil, scratching the pit of his stomach. Which was complaining. He wanted orange juice to build up his blood sugar, a stack of flapjacks to give a foundation for the next cup of coffee, and that cup of coffee. He wanted his breakfast, and he was aware that he was cranky because he was hungry. "Then we'll see who's President," he added, to the air.

On the edge of the Bahía de Campeche the Libyan vice admiral had got his crew together and his submarine up to two hundred meters, running straight and level. None of them were functioning well, with prodromal diarrhea and vomiting often enough so that the whole ship smelled like a latrine, but they could serve. For awhile, at least. They did. Libya's naval doctrine called for one big missile instead of a few dozen little ones. As this one big one broke the surface of the gulf it was immediately captured by a dozen radars. The scared but as yet untouched tourists on their lanais in Mérida saw bright, bad flashes out west, over the water, as a Cuban cruiser locked in and fired ABMs. None of them caught it. It was a cruise missile, not ballistic, easy to identify but hard to predict as it drove itself north-northwest toward the Florida panhandle. A dozen times defensive weapons clawed at it as it crossed the coast, and then it was lost to view. There were plenty of installations along the way charged with the duty of detecting and destroying just such a weapon, but none that were functioning anymore.

The latest picture from Margie showed her with one foot on the shell of a dead Krinpit, looking tired and flushed and happy. It was as good a picture of his daughter as God had had since her bearskin-rug days, and he had it blown into a hard print for his wallet. General Weinenstat looked at it carefully and passed it back to him. "She's a credit to you, God," she said.

He looked at it for a moment and put it away. "Yeah. I hope she got her stuff. Can you imagine her mother? I told her Margie wanted some dress patterns, and she wanted me to put in about a thousand meters of fabric."

"Well, if you'd left her raising to her mother she wouldn't be getting the kind of efficiency ratings you've been showing me."

"I suppose not." The latest one had been nothing but praise, or at least up to the psychologist's report:

Latent hostility toward men due to early marital trauma and mild inverse-Oedipal effect. Well compensated. Does not affect performance of duties.

I really hope that's so, thought Godfrey Menninger. Rose Weinenstat looked at him carefully. "You're not worrying about her, are you? Because there's no need—wait a minute." General Weinenstat touched the thing in her ear that looked like, but wasn't, a hearing aid. Her expression turned somber.

"What is it?"

She turned off the communicator. "Henry Moncas. His shelter took a direct hit. They're trying to find out who's President now."

"Shit!" Godfrey Menninger stared at the remains of his breakfast for a moment and saw none of it. "Oh, shit," he said again. "It looks bad, Rosie. The worst part is we never had a choice!"

General Weinenstat started to speak, then changed her mind.

"What? What were you going to say, Rosie?"

She shrugged. "No good second-guessing, is it?"

He pounced on her words. "About what? Come on, Rosie!"

"Well—maybe moving into Canada—"

"Yeah. That was a mistake, all right. I'll give you that. But not ours! The Greasies knew we couldn't let them move troops into Manitoba. That was Tam Gulsmit's mistake! Same with the Peeps. Once we were engaged we had to take Lop Nor out—quick, clean, minimum casualties. They should've accepted it instead of retaliating—"

But he could hear voices within him denying it, speaking in the tones of Tam Gulsmit and Heir-of-Mao. "We were safe moving troops in to protect the tar sands, because we knew you couldn't afford to invade." "You shouldn't have bombed Lop Nor. You should have known we would have to retaliate." The voices within God Menninger's mind were the only voices they would ever have again. Heir-of-Mao lay with eyes bulging and tongue protruding from his lips, dead in the deep shelter under Peking, and the atoms that had once been Gulsmit's body were falling out from the column of fire over Clydeside.

The Libyan missile had bypassed Atlanta and Asheville and Johnson City, matching their terrains against the profiles imprinted in its memory. The safety interlocks on its thermonuclear charge were falling away one by one as its tiny, paranoid brain began to recognize its nearness to the thing it was unleashed to destroy.

"It's bad, Rosie," said Godfrey Menninger at last, rising to return to his desk. Maybe he should have let Margie's mother have the raising of her. Then Margie would probably have had a husband and a couple of kids by now. And perhaps—perhaps the world would have been a different place. He wondered if he would ever hear from her again. "Rosie," he said, "check Houston. See if the communication links with Jem are holding up. With the other colonies, too, of course."

"Right now, Godfrey? Give me ten minutes; I've got a call coming in from the DoD."

"Ten minutes is fine," he said; but before the ten minutes was up he was dead.

TWENTY

•

THE CORACLE first appeared between showers, far out over the water. In the pit beside Ana Dimitrova, Corporal Kristianides—no, Lieutenant Kristianides now, she corrected herself—stood up and turned the field glasses on it.

"Krinpit," she said. "Son of a bitch. Lay your gun on it, Nan, but don't fire unless I tell you to."

Unnecessary order! Not for worlds would she have fired. Not until she saw for herself that there were only Krinpit in the boat, and not Ahmed Dulla. Perhaps not even then, for this insanity of guns and shooting was awful even to play at. She had not yet had to fire at a living being, was far from sure that she could, and had said as much; but no one wanted to hear. But the good thing about her machine gun was that it had a telescopic sight, and she was glad enough to aim it.

The coracle disappeared into a squall, but not before she had seen that there was no human being in it, though it was large enough for several.

When it appeared again it was larger and nearer, and she could see that the single Krinpit was working furiously to keep it bailed and the trapezoidal sail intact, and paddling to bring it straight into the camp. By then everyone had seen, and at least a dozen weapons were pointed at it. Over the PA system Guy Tree's voice shrilled an order to hold fire. Down on the beach Marge Menninger stood, a GORR under her arm, oblivious of the rain that soaked her. Ana wiped the wet off her sight as carefully as she had been taught and looked again. She had no skill at recognizing individual Krinpit by sight, but this one did not look familiar.

Disappointment of a hope. But what a foolish hope, she scolded herself. How improbable that Ahmed would once

266

again miraculously appear. And even if he had, who was this Ahmed who had taken her and used her and left her again? He was not the person of Sofia, she thought gloomily, and roused herself and tried to think more constructively.

It was a failure. There was so little to think constructively about! The world she had left was blowing itself up, and the world she had come to seemed determined to do the same. What went on in the secret conferences among Marge Menninger and her warrior knights in the headquarters shed she did not know, nor wish to. But it might well be the death of all of them.

The Krinpit was in the shallows now. It raised itself and splashed over the side, and the coracle bobbed away as it lurched ashore. It seemed to be in bad shape. It staggered in a half-circle on the shore and then fell to the ground with a painful crash as Colonel Menninger and half a dozen of her warriors formed a wary perimeter around it.

Perhaps they would kill it, she thought. Well, let them. Everyone else was standing and staring, but Ana's attention wandered—until one of the riflemen came running toward her.

"Dimitrova, front and center!" he was calling. "It's the one that speaks Pak! Colonel wants you to come translate!"

When Ana Dimitrova was nineteen years old, precocious senior at the University of Sofia, candidate for the callosectomy that would forever sunder the two halves of her brain and lead to a distinguished career in translation, she had watched a film on the subject. It was not her choice. They would not accept her application without it. The first part was quite tedious, though instructive, as it described the anatomy of that senseless and defenseless kilogram of pinky-gray jelly that mediated and transformed and commanded all the senses and defenses of the body. Before her very eyes a surgeon took a human brain in his hands and peeled away tissue to expose that great suety bridge that connected the two halves and that, in her, she would ask someone to sever. There was a long explanation, quite hard to follow, of how nerves crossed, so that the right half of the brain seemed to take responsibility for the left half of the body, and vice versa: strange quirk of anatomy! She saw how the nerves carrying visual impressions intersected at the optic chiasma, but not completely—as though prankish evolution had tired of the joke and decided not to finish it. All that part of the film was difficult to absorb, as well as unsettling to look at. But then there were some comic parts. Each half of the brain commanded its own network of afferent and efferent nerves. The efferent nerves, the ones that directed action, were spared in the resection or reconnected afterwards, which was why the split-brain people were able to walk without stumbling. Most of the time. The afferent nerves, the ones that accepted sensory impressions from the world, were kept apart. So each half of the brain could receive and process and store its own information, not shared with the other. That was why translation became easy.

But.

But some kinds of afferent input were not value-free. They produced glandular responses. They caused emotions. This was where the comic part came in. The film showed a woman, one of the earliest volunteers for the surgery. She had an earplug in one ear and was reading from a prepared text. The voice-over narration explained what she was doing: delivering a translated talk to a mathematical congress. But while one half of her brain was reading and translating and speaking, the other half was listening to the words coming in over the earplug; and those words were the filthiest of scatological jokes. The woman began to stammer and falter, and over her face spread the rosiest of blushes, though the operating half of her brain had not an idea in the world why. Blushes. Stammers. Headaches. Depression. They were the symptoms of leakage from one half to the other. The scar tissue that blocked the flow of impulses through the corpus callosum let each half of the brain work efficiently on its own. But feelings seeped through. All the time Ana Dimitrova was translating for Colonel Menninger she could feel them pounding at her—

"He says that as the People's Republics are no longer a force, he wishes to help us against the Fuel Bloc."

"Fucking great. What's he going to do, scratch them to death with his sharp little feet?"

—and the headache was the worst she had ever had: sickening, sandbag blows at the base of her skull. She felt nauseated and was not helped by the Krinpit.

Sharn-igon was repulsively ill. Even the dull, recurrent rasp of his name—Sharn-igon, Sharn-igon—was badly played, like a defective radio. His carapace was a sickly yellow instead of the rich mahogany it had been. It was cracked and seamed. At the edges of it, where undershell joined the massive armor of the top, seams did not quite join, and a thin, foul liquid oozed out.

"He has molted," she explained to the colonel, "and feels he is about to molt again. Perhaps it is because of the chemicals the Fuel people used against them."

"You don't look so fucking great yourself, Dimitrova."

"I am quite capable of continuing, Colonel Menninger." All the same, she moved away from the Krinpit. The exudations of his shell had darkened the sand around him, and the smell was like rancid fat. Moving did not help. The headache, and the pain behind it, grew with every moment.

Marge Menninger ran her hands through her wet hair, pulling it back so that her ears were exposed. She looked almost like a little girl as she said, "What do you think, Guy? Have we got ourselves a real blood-hungry tiger?"

Coloriel Tree said, "One does not refuse an ally, Marge. But the Greasies would eat these jokers up."

"So what is he saying exactly, Dimitrova? That he'll tell all his Crawly friends to attack the Greasy camp if we want them to?"

"Something like that, yes. What he says," she added, "is not always easy to understand, Colonel Menninger. He speaks a little Urdu, but not much, and he speaks it *very* badly. Besides, his mind wanders. It is a personal matter with him, to kill. He does not care who. Sometimes he says he wants to kill *me*."

Menninger looked appraisingly at the Krinpit. "I don't think he's in shape to do much killing."

"Must one be well for that?" Ana flared. "I am sick in my heart from talking of killing, and from killing itself! It is a wicked insanity to kill when so few persons are still alive."

"As to that," said Margie mildly, raising her hand to stop Guy Tree from exploding, "we'll talk another time. You look like shit, Dimitrova. Go get some sleep."

"Thank you, Colonel Menninger," Ana said stiffly, hating her, perhaps hating even more the look of compassion in Margie's eyes. How dare the bloody trollop feel pity!

Ana stalked off to her tent. It was raining hard again, and lightning lashed over the water. She hardly felt it. At every step the throbbing in her head punished her, and she knew that behind the headache a greater pain was scratching to come out. Pity was the solvent that would melt the dam and let it through, and she wanted to be by herself when that happened. She stooped into the tent without a word to the woman who shared it with her, removed only her shoes and slacks, and buried herself under the covers.

Almost at once she began to weep.

Ana made no sound, did not shake, did not thrash about. It was only the ragged unevenness of her breathing that made the black girl in the other cot rise up on one elbow to look toward her; but Ana did not speak, and after a moment her roommate went back to sleep. Ana did not. Not for an hour and more. She wept silently for a long time, helpless to contain the pain any longer. Hopes gone, pleasures denied, dreams melted away. She had held off accepting the thing that the Krinpit had said almost in his first sentence, but now it could not be denied. There was no longer a reason for her to be on Jem. There was hardly even a reason to live. Ahmed was dead.

She woke to the loud, incongruous sound of dance music.

The storm of silent weeping had cleared her mind, and the deep and dreamless sleep that followed had begun the healing. Ana was quite composed as she bathed sparingly in the shower at the end of the tent line, brushed her hair dry, and dressed. The music was, of course, that other of Marge Menninger's eccentricities, the Saturday night dance. How very strange she was! But her strangeness was not all unwelcome. One of the fruits of it had been the patterns and fabric that had come in the last ship. Ana chose to put on a simple blouse and skirt, not elaborate, but not purely utilitarian either. She was a very long way from dancing. But she would not spoil the pleasure of those who enjoyed it.

She cut past the generator, where the Krinpit was rumbling hollowly as it scratched through the clumps of burnable vegetation for something to eat, a guard with a GORR trailing its every step, and visited the fringe of the dance area long enough to get something to eat from the buffet. (Of course, she had slept through two meals.) When men asked her to dance she smiled and thanked them as she shook her head. The rain had stopped, and sullen Kung glowed redly overhead. She took a plate of cheese and biscuits and slipped away. Not that there was far to go. No one walked in the woods anymore these days. They lived and ate and slept in a space one could run across in three minutes. But all who could be there were at the dance, and down by the beach were only the perimeter guards. She sat down with her back against one of the machine-gun turrets and finished her meal. Then she put her plate down beside her, pulled her knees up to her chin, and sat staring at the purple-red waves.

Ahmed was dead.

It was not much comfort to tell herself that her dreams had been foolish to begin with, that Ahmed had never taken her as seriously as she had taken him. Nevertheless, it was true, and Ana Dimitrova was a practical person. She had learned the trick of dissecting pain into its parts. That she would never see him again, touch his strong and supple body, lie beside him while he slept—that was purest pain, and there was no help for it. But that she would never marry him and bear his children and grow old by his side—that was only a spoiled fantasy. It had never been real. That loss could not hurt her now, because it was of something she had never owned; and so her pain was diminished by half.

(But, oh, how that half still ached!)

She wept gently and openly for a moment, then sighed and rubbed the tears away. What she had lost, she told herself, she had lost long ago. From the moment Ahmed came to Jem, he had become a different person. In any event, it was over. She had a life to make for herself, and the materials to make it from were all in this camp; there was nothing else anywhere. You should dance, she scolded herself. You should go up where they are laughing and singing and drinking.

Plainly and simply, she did not want to. It was not merely that she didn't want to dance, not yet. It was more deep and damaging than that. Ana, translating for the Krinpit, had heard enough of what was going on in the minds of Marge Menninger and Nguyen Tree and the other hawks who directed the fate of the camp. So much madness in so few minds! They were determined to carry on a war, even here, even after Earth had blown itself into misery! And yet there they all were, smiling and bobbing around the floor. Her own brain had been divided by a surgeon's knife. What had divided theirs, so that they could plot genocide in an afternoon and drink and cavort and play their sexual games at night? How Ahmed would scowl at them!

But Ahmed was dead.

She took a deep breath and decided not to cry again.

She stood up and stretched her cramped limbs. The Krinpit was lurching slowly down toward the water for a drink after his unappetizing meal, the soldier wandering after. She did not particularly want to be near him, but she needed to rinse her plate—either that or carry it back to the cook tent, which was too near the dance floor. She kept her distance, paralleling his scuttling path, and then she heard someone call her name.

It was the Russian pilot, Kappelyushnikov, sitting cross-legged at a gun pit and talking to Danny Dalehouse, on duty inside it. Why not? Ana changed course to approach them and wished them a good evening.

"Is truly good, Anyushka? But Danny Dalehouse has told me of death of Ahmed Dulla. I am deeply sympathetic for you."

There it was, the first time someone had spoken of it to her. She discovered that it was not impossible for her to respond.

"Thank you, Visha," she said steadily. "What, have you become a monk that you do not dance tonight?"

"Is no one I care to dance with," he said gloomily. "Also have been having most interesting discussion with Danny on subject of slavery."

"And what have you concluded, then, Danny?" she asked brightly. "Are we all slaves to your mistress, the beautiful blond colonel?"

He did not answer directly, but chose to be placating. "I know you're upset, Ana. I'm sorry, too."

"Upset?" She nodded judiciously, looking down into the pit at him. "Yes, perhaps. I must assume that my home has been destroyed—yours, too, I suppose. But you are braver than I. I am not brave; I become upset. It upsets me that what has happened on Earth is now to happen again, here. It upsets me that my—that my friend is dead. It upsets me that the colonel intends to kill a great many more persons. Can you imagine? She proposes to tunnel under the Fuel camp and explode a nuclear bomb, and that upsets me."

Why are you doing this? she asked herself; but she knew

that she could not accept more sympathy without crying, and she was not ready to cry before these men. At least she had diverted them. Dalehouse was frowning.

"We don't have any nuclear weapons," he objected.

"Softheaded person!" she scoffed. "Your mistress has what she wants to have. I should not be astonished if she had a fleet of submarines or a division of tanks. She wears weapons as she wears that cheap perfume. The smell of them is always around her."

"No," he said doggedly, peering up at her, "you're wrong about the nuclear weapons. She couldn't conceal that from us. And she's not my mistress."

"Do not flatter yourself that I care. She may have her sexual excesses with whomever she likes, and so may you."

Kappelyushnikov coughed. "I think," he said, "dance has suddenly become more attractive."

As he stood up, Ana put her hand on his arm. "I am driving you away. Please forgive me."

"No, no, Anyushka. Are difficult times for all, nothing to forgive." He patted her hand, then grinned and kissed it. "As to myself," he said, "I see beautiful blond colonel roaming about alone, and perhaps she wishes to dance or otherwise relate to some new person, such as I. Also do not care for cheap perfume worn by big cockroach. You do not yourself desire to dance? Or otherwise relate? No. Then stay with friend Danny."

They watched him walk steadily toward Marge Menninger, strolling past her checkpoints. They heard her laugh as Cappy spoke to her; then he shrugged and moved on toward the dance floor.

The Krinpit, in his random stagger around the beach, was coming closer. It was true that the stench of his exudations was strong. So was the sighing, droning sound of his presence. Ana listened, then said gloomily, "This one is muttering about his love now," she said. "It was killed somehow, I cannot tell how. I think Ahmed had something to do with it, and it is for that that it is determined to kill human beings. But it had become Ahmed's ally! Dan, is not that lunacy? It is as though killing has become an end in itself. It no longer matters who is killed or for what possible gain the killing is done. Only the killing itself matters."

Dalehouse stood up in his shallow rifle pit, looking up

the hill toward the dancers. "She's coming this way," he said. "Listen, before she gets here. About her being my mistress—"

"Please, Danny. I spoke without thinking and because I am, yes, upset. It is not a time to worry about personal matters."

Clearly he was not satisfied and would have pursued the subject, but Margie was now too close. She paused to light a cigarette, studying the Krinpit and its guard, now a model of military deportment, his recoilless at port arms as the colonel approached. Then she came smiling over to Danny and Nan. "Getting it on, are you?" she said amiably. "When was the last time you checked your earphones, Danny?"

Guiltily Dalehouse clapped the phone to one ear. He had been neglecting the buried microphone probes, which were supposed to warn of burrowers digging toward him under the ground. There was no sound. "Sorry, Margie," he said.

She shook her head. "When you're on duty, that's *colonel*. And when I say frog, you hop. Now that that's understood," she said, smiling sunnily, "would either of you folks like a hit before we talk some business?"

"I am not in the habit of using narcotics," Ana said.

"Pity. Danny?" She watched while Dalehouse filled his lungs, and as she took the stick back from him, she said, "I want you to draft your gasbag friend. One hundred and—" She glanced at the wristwatch. "One hundred and eight hours from now, give or take a little, we're going to hit the Greasy camp, and he's going to be our air arm."

Dalehouse coughed and spluttered. "He—he can't—"

"Take your time, Danny," she encouraged. "While you're getting your breath, just listen for a moment. Storm's over. Looks like we've got maybe five or six good days. I'm taking fifteen front-line effectives, plus you, Danny. We'll mop up that camp without breathing hard. Only I don't want to take a plane, and I don't want you or Cappy floating around up there where they can see you, and that leaves Charlie."

"Charlie can't fight!"

"Well," she said reasonably, "come to that, I don't figure you for your real Geronimo trained killer, either. But I don't expect it of you. You communicate. Charlie observes. The Greasies won't pay any attention to one more fartbag hanging around—"

"Bullshit they won't! They've been shooting balloonists down all along."

"Danny," she said, "I'm not asking your advice. I'm giving you an order." She dragged on the joint, down to the last centimeter, and then carefully rubbed it out and pocketed it before exhaling. "You see," she said, "the Greasies are going to come to the same conclusions I did, only it'll take them a little longer. One of us has to run things. The only way to do that is to knock the other out. All Charlie has to do is hang in there with his radio and keep us posted if they send up a plane or put some people out in the woods. I'll bring the company up overland. But we're naked without air cover. We need to know when to get out of sight. That's easy enough for him, right?"

"Well, sure. But—shit, Margie. He's almost the last survivor. It's a lot to ask—"

"But I'm not asking, Danny. You keep making that same mistake. I'm ordering. If he doesn't, he'll make a nice flame." She scratched under her belt, regarding him amiably. "So after the dance I break the news to the camp, and tomorrow this time we're on our way."

"To atom-bomb the Fuel Bloc," said Ana bitterly.

Marge Menninger's face froze. After a moment she said, "I guess I'll let that pass, Dimitrova. I didn't specifically order you to keep your mouth shut. But I won't let it pass again. What you hear when you're translating is *classified*."

"Holy Christ," Dalehouse said. "You really have a nuclear bomb?"

"Bet your ass, Danny. You've got a piece of it right there in your ground mikes."

"Where? You mean the plutonium power-packs? That's no good, Margie—colonel, I mean. There's not enough of them. Even if there were, you couldn't flange them together to make a bomb."

"Wrong and wrong, Danny. Takes eighteen hundred grams and a bit to fission. I have a little over six thousand grams, all tidied away in the stores marked 'fuel replacements.' All this was planned a long time ago, and they'll fit together because some pretty high-powered weapons people designed them to do that before the first ship took off. Oh, it's not one of your hundred-megaton jobs. Maybe not even a kiloton, because I don't have containment to keep the parts together very long. But I don't want a big one. I don't want to wipe out the Greasy camps, I want to own them. I want to take out their ammunition and their food stores, and I know just the place to put baby for that. Then they can beg."

She looked serene and innocent as she said it, and Dalehouse responded with shocked disbelief. "That's— that's unprovoked aggression! A stab in the back!"

"Wrong, Dalehouse. That's preemption. The Greasies don't have a choice, either. They just haven't figured it out yet."

"Bullshit! It's what the Japanese did at Pearl Harbor all over again!"

She opened her eyes wide. "Sure, why not? There was nothing wrong with Pearl Harbor, except they fucked it up. If they'd gone on to take out the carrier fleet and follow up with a landing, history would be a lot different. You'd be saying 'Pearl Harbor' the way you say 'Normandy' now, only you'd be saying it in Japanese."

She seemed quite pleased with herself, but then she hesitated. She sought a dry place on the ground and sat down before adding, "But I will admit to you two dear old friends from Bulgaria that right now I'm scared and tired and not what you'd call real happy with the way things are going. I—what's the matter with that thing?"

The Krinpit was staggering closer to them, moaning and stridulating. Ana listened. "He is quite hard to follow. He is speaking of Poison Ghosts and Ghosts Above—that is, of ourselves and of balloonists. He seems to have us confused in his mind."

"All enemies look alike after awhile, I guess. Tell him to back away. I don't like the way he smells."

"Yes, Colonel Menninger." But before Ana could summon up the commands in Krinpit-Urdu, Margie stopped her again.

"Wait a minute. What was that?" There had been a voice on the PA system along with the blare of dance music.

"I couldn't make it out," said Dalehouse, "but I do hear something. Out in the woods. Or in the air—"

Then the dance music abruptly died, and a scared voice replaced it. "Colonel Menninger! All personnel! Aircraft approaching!"

The sounds were clear now, two sets of them: the whickering putt-putt of a helicopter, and a quicker, higher sound. The dancers scattered.

Over the trees two shapes appeared. Neither was moving very fast, but they came without warning: the Fuel helicopter and a stub-winged STOL plane, one they had not seen in the air before. They did not come in peace. Soldiers strapped to the pods of the helicopter were firing incendiary rockets while wing-mounted machine guns on the STOL strafed the camp. The fixed-wing plane made a roaring run that took it out over the water; then it rose, turned, and dived in again. On its second pass the guns did not fire, but four tiny rockets leaped out from under the wing, streaked into the store shed, and set fire to a row of tents.

The Greasies had not been so slow after all.

Here and there, around the camp and inside it, perimeter guards and the more quick-witted of the dancers were beginning to return the fire. Margie jumped to her feet and began to run toward the nearest rocket launcher, and then, on its third pass, the stub-winged plane swerved toward her. It was using both machine guns and a flamethrower now. As the bullets stitched toward her, Margie dodged and fell, almost beside the Krinpit; and the creature rose up high above her. It launched itself, two hundred kilograms of half-molted body, on top of Marge Menninger.

Sharn-igon knew that this would be his last molt, terribly premature, agonizing, fruitless. He would never experience the satisfying itch of his new carapace as it hardened and stretched over the soft inner pulp, never feel the sexual stirring of the newly shelled and embark on the quick conquest of a female with a he-mate. As the Poison Ghosts Above zoomed in toward the camp, he tried to warn these new allies. But they were deaf to the brilliant sounds from over the trees, deaf to his warnings.

The pain was too much.

It had been his intention to assist them in killing each other to the maximum extent possible, and then to kill the survivors himself. But perhaps he had done all the assisting he would ever do. The agony of his new shell, already beginning to crack again, tormented his thoughts. The blinding sounds of the aircraft and the explosions dazed him.

There was only one Poison Ghost left that he could kill. It would have to be enough. He raised himself on his pitifully soft-shelled limbs, leaned forward, and crashed down on top of her just as the soft, deadly tongue of the flamethrower licked at them both.

By then the whole camp was firing at the aircraft—or that much of it that was still able to fire. But the planes were out of reach. They hung out over the water, a kilometer and more away, the helicopter dancing lightly, the STOL turning in small circles, and did not return to the attack.

The next assault came from another place.

A scream from one of the machine-gun pits, and the two soldiers in it were down, ripped to shreds. Out of the pit came a long, limber, black shape wearing tiny goggles and racing on its dozen limbs to the nearest knot of humans; and another behind him, and another.

The burrowers managed to kill more than ten of the survivors. But that was all. Even with the sunglasses they were no match for trained human soldiers on the surface of the planet. If the planes had continued their attack— but they didn't. The human defenders quickly rallied, and at the end there were fifty burrowers stretched out on the ground, soiling the sand with their watery black blood. No more came because there were no more in the nest to come. That burrow had been wiped out.

Dan Dalehouse stood peering out over the sea while one of Cheech Arkashvili's assistants bandaged a deep gash on his arm. The planes were gone. In the middle of everything, they had quietly flown down the coastline and away.

"And why didn't they finish us off?" he asked.

There was no answer.

TWENTY-ONE

●

BY THE TIME they found Margie Menninger, still alive, the fight was long over and the camp was almost functioning again.

She had lain under the dead and stinking Krinpit for more than two hours, stunned, half-suffocated, unable to shift the gross dead weight on top of her, her limbs twisted painfully but unhurt. Like the djinn in the bottle, at first she would have given a king's ransom to her rescuer. When they finally heard her sand-gagged attempts at a bellow and dug her out, what she wanted to give was death.

They helped her a few steps away, with their heads averted from the stink. She gagged and swore at them, and when they tried to help her stand she collapsed and vomited into the sand again. The doctor came running, but a doctor wasn't what Marge needed. What she needed was to get the cesspool stench of the Krinpit off her and out of her nostrils. She let Cheech strip off her coveralls and assist her to the edge of the water, and then she splashed around until the smell was gone and she could walk again. Limpingly, yes. But under her own power. Wearing a bra and bikini panties, with her gun belt over her shoulder, she walked up the shore past the dead Krinpit, seared into a sort of omelette of meat and shell, until someone came up with a terrycloth robe. She was giving orders as she walked.

Why had they stopped?

The camp had been at their mercy. With great precision they had knocked out the heavy weapons on the first pass. There was not a rocket launcher or a machine gun untouched—nothing but hand weapons. Of the hundred eight persons in the Food camp, twenty-two were dead, nearly fifty were wounded or burned. The planes had been

279

unscathed. The burrowers had been wiped out entirely, but if the planes had finished their work first, the burrowers would have had an easy time with the survivors. Why? The timing had been exact. As soon as the planes had stopped shooting, the burrowers came out. That could not have been a coincidence, and the goggles the burrowers wore were proof that the Greasies had prepared them for the job. But then they hadn't followed through.

Why not?

But thank God for poppa and his parting gift! A metric ton of ammunition had been blown up, but there were metric tons left untouched by virtue of the spare supplies in the final ship. Tents burned and food was destroyed. But there was more. If Cappy's airplane had been stitched across by machine-gun fire, there were spare parts to fix it. And that greatest of gifts, the six kilograms of ^{239}Pu in its carefully crafted sheaths—that was still intact. The dead were irreplaceable, of course. Worse still were the casualties, because some of them were not merely a loss but a debit. Nguyen Dao Tree, who had lost a leg and a lot of blood to go with it; six persons badly burned, two others with serious abdominal wounds—a whole cluster of damages for Cheech Arkashvili to try to repair. For each one of the worst off, there was the cost of an able-bodied person to tend him. There was no tent still standing big enough to hold them all, and so Cheech had put them onto cots dragged out of the damaged tents, out in the open. Some of the bedding was scorched, and if it began to rain again they would be in trouble. But for now they were as well off as they were likely to be, Margie thought as she moved among them.

One of them got up as Margie approached: Lieutenant Kristianides, one whole side of her body in gauze and antiburn dressing. But functioning. "Colonel," she said. "I had to leave the radio—"

Marge glanced at the doctor, who shook her head. "Get back in bed, Kris. Tell me about it later."

"No, I'm all right. When they shot the tent up I ran out. But I left the tape going. I was getting their chatter, only it was in all different languages."

"Thanks. Now get back in bed," Marge ordered, and looked around. "Dalehouse, front and center!" she called. "Check the radio shack. If the tape's still working, give me a yell."

He didn't look too good himself, she thought as he put down the tray of dressings and headed up the hill without a word—but then, none of them did. Especially herself. Margie's own tent had been totaled, and she was wearing fatigues belonging to a woman who would never again need them—not unfair, but she had been a taller and fatter woman than Marge Menninger.

When Dalehouse called her, she had forgotten about the tapes. But she went up to the shack, which was unburned and not really harmed except for bullet holes, commandeering Ana Dimitrova on the way. The tape was voice-actuated, and Dalehouse had already found the right place to begin. Ana put on the earphones and began to translate.

"First one of the pilots says, 'On target,' and the base acknowledges. Then there are some carrier noises, as though they were going to transmit and changed their minds, and then the base says, 'Suspend operations at once. Do not attack.' And one of the pilots, I think it is the Egyptian, says in a different Arab dialect, 'Strike already in progress. We have taken out their weapons dump. Body count around twenty-five.' Then there is some mumbling that I cannot make out, as though they are talking at the base with the transmitter on but not close enough to pick it up. And then the base says, 'Urgent. Suspend operations immediately.' And then the other pilot, the Irishman, says they are observing from over the water, waiting for instructions, and then the base orders them to return without further attack. That is all there is on the tape until they get landing instructions later on."

"That's it?" Margie asked.

"As I have said, colonel, yes. There is nothing else."

"Now, why would they change their minds in the middle?" Margie asked. Neither Dalehouse nor Dimitrova offered an answer. She hadn't expected one. It didn't matter. The Greasies had declared war, and if they backed out in the middle of it that was their problem, not hers. She would not back out. To Marge Menninger, the attack on her base—*her* base!—answered all questions right there. *Why* didn't really matter. The only question was *how*—how to carry the fight to them, and win it.

"Can you dig with that shoulder?" she asked Dalehouse.

"I guess so. It's not bleeding."

"Then go help Kappelyushnikov dig graves. Dimitrova,

you're a radio operator now. No transmissions. Just listen. If the Greasies say anything, I want to hear about it right away."

She left them and headed for the surviving latrine. She didn't particularly need to go to the bathroom; she just wanted to be alone for a moment to clarify her thoughts. She ranked her way to the head of the line, closed the door, and sat there smoking a cigarette and staring into space.

There was no question in her mind that she could win this war, because she had some powerful cards to play. The plutonium store was one of them. The other was Major Vandemeer's little dispatch case. There were still four birds in orbit; one could hit the Greasy main camp, and another their Farside base, anytime she gave the order—and that would be that.

The trouble was, she didn't want to destroy the Greasy facilities. She wanted to acquire them. The birds and the bomb were overkill, like trying to take care of a mosquito with a mortar.

No. It would have to be a straight overland operation. Maybe the plutonium, if it could be placed exactly right. Not the missiles. It was a pity the Greasies had launched their preemptive strike before she was quite ready to launch hers. But not a disaster. The worst thing about the raid was that her cadre of effectives had been seriously reduced. How was she going to mount her retaliatory strike without grunts?

Marge Menninger had just taken the only decision that gave the human race a future on Jem, even though she didn't know it.

"The only good thing about all this," Dalehouse said to Kappelyushnikov, "is that most of the casualties were military. At least now we can get on with the real business of the expedition."

Kappelyushnikov grunted and threw a few more spadefuls of dirt before he answered. "Of course, is so," he said, pausing and wiping sweat off his face. "Only one question. What is real business of expedition?"

"To survive! And to preserve. God knows what's happening on Earth. We may be all that's left of the human race, and if anything's going to be left of, what, maybe five thousand years of science and literature and music and art, it's here."

"Very discouraging amount of responsibility for two gravediggers," Kappelyushnikov commented. "You are of course right, Danny. We have saying in Soviet Union: longest journey begins with single step. What step do we take now?"

"Well—"

"No, wait, was rhetorical question. First step is apparent. Have finished covering up graves of now absent friends, so you, Danny, please step up to colonel's headquarters and report burial services can begin."

He jammed his spade into the dirt and sat down, looking more despondent than Dalehouse had ever seen him.

Dalehouse said, "All right. We're all pretty tired and shook up, I guess."

The pilot shook his head, then looked up and grinned. "Am not only tired, dear Danny, am also very Russian. Heavy load to carry. We have other saying in Soviet Union: in thousand years, what difference will it make? But now I tell you the truth, Danny. All sayings are bullshit. I know what we do, you and I and all of us. We do the best we can. Is not much, but is all there is."

Dalehouse laid down his spade and trudged up the hill to the headquarters shack, thinking hard. A heavy responsibility! When you looked at it carefully, there was no way to preserve everything; so much that was irreplaceable would inevitably be lost—probably already was lost. There was not much chance that the Arc de Triomphe and the British Museum and the Parthenon had all survived, not to mention some billions of fairly irreplaceable human beings. It was hard for Danny to accept that he would never again see a ballet or listen to a concert. Or fly in a clamjet or drink in a revolving restaurant on top of a skyscraper. So much was gone forever! And so much more would inevitably vanish as they tried to rebuild. . . .

Yet there was one great asset not yet destroyed: hope. They could survive. They could rebuild. They could even rebuild in a better way, learning from the mistakes of the past, on this virgin planet—

There was a knot of people gathering around the headquarters shack, and Marge Menninger, with a couple of her aides, was trotting up to join them. Dalehouse hurried his pace and arrived in time to hear Ana saying, "This message just came in, Colonel Menninger. I will play the tape for you."

"Do it," snapped Marge, out of breath and exhausted. Dalehouse moved closer to her. She seemed near to collapse. But as the tape player hummed and scratched, she pulled herself together and stood listening intently.

Danny recognized the voice. It was the black air vice-marshal, Pontrefact; and what he said did not take very long.

"This is an official message on behalf of the Fuel Exporting Powers to the Food camp. We offer an immediate and permanent armistice. We propose that you remain within twenty kilometers of your camp, in the direction toward ours, and we will observe the same limits from ours. We request an answer within one hour."

There was a pause, as though he was shuffling papers in his hand, and then the rich Jamaican tones began again.

"As you are aware, our air strike against your camp was provoked by your destruction of our satellites. It was ordered only after full exploration of all alternatives. Our intention was to wipe your base out completely. However, as you are also aware, we terminated the strike after inflicting relatively minor damage on your base. The reason for this decision is the reason for this offer of armistice now.

"Our star, Kung, is unstable. It is about to flare.

"We have been aware for some time that its radiation level has been fluctuating. Within the past twenty-four hours it has become more extreme. While the air strike was in progress we received information from our astrophysicists that a major flare will occur in the near future. We do not have an exact time. Our understanding is that it may occur as early as forty-eight hours from now, and almost surely within the next two weeks. If you accept our offer of armistice, we will transmit all technical data at once, and your people can make their own judgments."

The voice hesitated, then resumed in a less formal way. "We have no knowledge of conditions on Earth at present and suppose you have none as well. But it is clear that for all practical purposes we on Jem are alone in the universe at this time. We think we will need all the resources we have to prepare our camp for this flare. If we continue to fight, we suppose we will all die. I do not propose that we work together. But I propose that we stop fighting, at least until this crisis is past." Another pause. Then: "Please respond within an hour. God help us all."

Margie closed her eyes for a moment while everyone waited. Then she opened them again and said, "Call them back, Dimitrova. Tell them we accept their offer, ask for their technical data at once, and say we will be in contact again when we have something to say. Folks, the war is over."

Ten minutes later, the whole camp knew it. Margie had gone on the public-address system, played the tape from Marshal Pontrefact, and broken the news of the disaster and the truce. She had called a general meeting for 0300 hours, about ninety minutes from then, and ordered Alexis Harcourt, the nearest thing they had left to an astronomer, to go over the data from the Greasies and report before that time. Then she turned to Danny Dalehouse and said, "I don't have a bed anymore, but I need about an hour's sleep real bad."

"There's a spare in my tent."

"I was hoping you'd ask." She peered up toward the sullen glow in the clouds where Kung was hiding and shook her head. "It's been a son of a bitch of a day," she said as they picked their way toward the tent row. "And it's not over yet. Know what I'm going to do at the meeting?"

"Am I supposed to guess?"

"No way, Danny. You'd never make it. I'm going to announce the impending retirement of Colonel Marjorie Menninger from active service."

"What?"

"Pick your teeth up, Danny, and don't just stand there," she advised, tugging him along. "We're going to convert this place to civilian government, effective as soon as the emergency is over. Or maybe before. I don't care. Maybe all you guys who're bitching about the army way of doing things are right. I have to say that my way hasn't been working out too well, everything considered. So I think we're going to need elections for a new government, and if you want my advice you'll run."

"For what? Why me? Margie, you get me all mixed up!"

"Why you? Because you're practically the only original settler left, you know that? Just you and Cappy. Because nobody hates your guts. Because you're the only person in the camp who has the age and experience to handle the job of running things and who isn't a soldier. Don't let me pressure you. It's your decision. But you've got my vote. If," she added in a different tone, "anything we decide makes any difference at all now."

They were at his tent, and Marge paused at the flap, staring up at the sky. "Oh, shit," she said, "it's beginning to rain." It was—big drops, with promise of more behind them.

"The casualties!" he said.

"Yeah. We're going to have to get them under cover. And that's a pity, Danny, because I was kind of hoping we could catch us a little R and R before the meeting."

In spite of everything, Danny could not help himself. He laughed out loud. "Marjorie Menninger, you are some kind of strange. Get in there and get some sleep." But before she turned, he put his arms around her for a moment. "I never would have thought it of you," he said. "What converted you to civilian values?"

"Who's converted?" Then she said, "Well, maybe it was that fucking Krinpit. If it hadn't been for him, you'd've been burying me a little while ago, too. I didn't trust him, either, but he gave his silly life to save me."

With so few of them left, they didn't really need the PA system to cope with the fifty-five or sixty persons listening, but they hooked in one speaker for the benefit of the casualties who were well enough to hear, in their tents down the hill. The rest sat or stood on the wet planks of the dance floor in the sullen, steady rain while Marge Menninger spoke to them from the little dais. She turned the stage over to Harcourt.

He said, "A lot of the data from the Greasies isn't astronomy, it's geology. They've done a lot of digging. They say there seem to be flare episodes every twenty or thirty years. There's no set pattern, but by the amount of ash and char, they think your average flare involves about a seventy-five percent increase in radiation spread out over a period of a week or more. That's enough to kill us. Partly heat. Mostly ionizing radiation.

"Now, when does it happen? Their best guess is ten

days—give or take ten days." There was a murmur from the audience, and he nodded. "Sorry about that, but I don't have the training to make it any closer than they do; in fact, I'm only taking their word. The picture I get is of slowly increasing heat over a period of a couple of weeks. I think we've been having that, and maybe it's why the weather has been so lousy. Then the flare. Surface temperature goes up to maybe three-fifty degrees. That's Kelvin —say, somewhere between where we are now and the boiling point of water. I don't *think* it goes over that, for not very long, anyway. But there are peak flares, and they're like striking a match. If anything can burn, it will. Apparently the forests burn, but maybe not right away— they'd probably have to dry out first. Then the flare recedes, the temperature comes down, the air drops out moisture, and you get rain to put out the fires. Probably a hell of a lot of rain, over a period of weeks or months. Then you're back to normal."

"Only dead," somebody called out from the audience. Harcourt spread his hands defensively.

"Maybe not. If you're in shelter, you might survive." He started to continue, then stopped himself. Margie came up beside him.

"You don't sound too confident."

"I'm not. The—ah, the geological record doesn't inspire much confidence. The Greasies took cores from more than a hundred different sites, and they all showed the same pattern—recurring char and soil, back thousands of years."

Dalehouse stood up. "Alex," he called, "why hasn't it killed off everything on the surface of Jem long ago?"

"You're asking for a guess? I guess it has. At least all the vegetation. It burns off, then regrows from roots, most likely. Seeds probably would survive, though. And those drenching rains after each flare would give the new growth a good start in fertile soil—the char's great fertilizer; primitive man used to slash and burn to get his farms started, back on Earth. I don't know about the animals. I'd guess the Creepies would be all right in their tunnels if they didn't starve to death waiting for new growth to live on. Probably a lot of them do. Maybe the same for the Krinpit, because it would take a lot to kill them off. They don't have to worry about being blinded by the radiation, because they don't have any eyes to begin with. And those shells are pretty good armor for their vital organs. Probably get a lot of mutations, but in the long run that's as much good as it is bad for the race."

"What about Charlie?"

"I don't know. That's harder. I guess a really good flare might wipe out damn near all the adults. But that's when they spawn, and the spawn might survive—also, no doubt, with a lot of mutations. I'd say evolution moves pretty fast here."

"Well, look," Margie cut in, "if all these things can survive, why can't we?"

Harcourt shrugged. "They're adapted, we're not. Besides, I'm talking about *races* surviving, not individuals. Maybe as few as one percent live through it. Maybe less." He looked around the audience. "One percent of us leaves how many?" he asked.

"Yeah," Margie said slowly. "Well, I think we get the picture. We need to get under something big enough to stop both heat and radiation, and we need to do it in a hurry. Got any ideas on what we can make a roof out of?"

Harcourt hesitated. "Not a clue," he confessed. "Certainly the tents won't do it. Oh, and I should mention the winds. They probably get pretty fierce, with all that insolation. So anything we did build would have to stand up to maybe two-hundred-kilometer-an-hour hurricanes. Maybe more. I, uh, I thought for a minute of using the Creepies' tunnels, and that might work—for some of us, anyway. But I doubt more than ten percent of us would live through maybe two or three weeks underground without very good ventilation and certainly without air conditioning—and that air down there is going to get *hot*."

There was a silence while everyone considered possibilities. Then Kappelyushnikov came forward. "Is one thing we can do," he announced. "Not many of us. Maybe fifteen, twenty. Can get in return capsule and go into orbit."

"It's just as hot there," Marge Menninger protested.

Cappy shook his head. "Is only radiation. Steel hull reflects ninety-nine percent, maybe. Anyway, plenty. Only problem—who decides which twenty lucky people go up?"

Marge Menninger thought for a moment, then said, "No, that's a last ditch, Cappy. There's another problem with it: what do those lucky fellows do when they come down again? There aren't enough of us left now. I don't think twenty would be enough to survive. If we went up—strike that; I'm not saying I would be one of the 'we.' If anyone went up, it'd be just as smart to keep on going. Try to get back to Earth. Maybe go to one of the other colonies. The chances would be as good as coming back here when the whole planet's fried."

Harcourt nodded but corrected her automatically. "Not the whole planet."

"What?"

"Well, only half the planet. Our half. The part that faces Kung. The far side probably wouldn't even notice there was a flare going on. That's no good for us," he went on quickly, "because we can't live there; we don't have time to build an airtight heated dome and move everything— What's the matter?"

Margie had burst out laughing. "Son of a bitch," she said. "Shows how wrong you can be when you start trying to trust people. Those bastard Greasies aren't giving us a square count! They didn't stop fighting because they wanted to make peace. They stopped because we were as good as dead anyway!"

"But—but so are they—"

"Wrong! Because they *have* a Farside base!" She shook her head ruefully. "Folks," she said, "I was going to make a real magnolious announcement about turning the reins over to civilian government, only now I think that's going to have to wait. We've got a military job to do first. When this side of the planet goes, they've got that snug little nest on the side that never gets radiation from Kung anyway, and they couldn't care less if the son of a bitch blows up. That's going to be a nice place to be. And we're going to take it away from them."

TWENTY-TWO

•

THESE WERE THE mesas and canyons of the high desert. Danny Dalehouse had flown over them in less than an hour and seen them only as quaint patterns in an unimportant carpet beneath. Marching over them was something else. Kappelyushnikov ferried them in as close as he dared, there at a time, once four, with the little biplane desperately slow to wallow off the ground. He made more than a dozen round trips and saved them a hundred kilometers of cutting through jungle. Even so, it was a three-day march, and every step hard work.

Nevertheless, Dalehouse had not felt as well in weeks. In spite of bone-bruising fatigue. In spite of the star that might explode at any moment. In spite of the fact that Marge Menninger's shopping list had overlooked a supply of spare hiking boots, and so he limped on a right foot that was a mass of blisters. He was not the unluckiest. Three of the effectives had been unable to go on at all. "We'll come back for you," Margie had promised; but Dalehouse thought she lied, and he could see in the eyes of the casualties that they were certain of it.

And still he would have sung as he marched, if he'd had breath enough for it.

It had been raining on and off for nearly forty hours—mean, wind-driven rain that kept them sodden in the steamy heat even when it let up, and chilled when it drenched them. That didn't matter, either. It was regrettable, because it meant that Charlie and the two remaining members of his flock could not keep in touch with them visually. (He had had to take the radio away from the balloonist before they left—far too easy for the Greasies to intercept.) Whenever the clouds lightened, Dalehouse searched the sky for his friend. He never saw him, never heard his song, but he knew he was up there somewhere. It wasn't serious. The weather that kept Charlie from scouting danger for them kept the Greasies from providing it.

There were twelve of them still toiling toward the Greasy camp. They had left the rest of the survivors—the highly impermanent survivors, if this expedition didn't do what it was supposed to—back at the base with orders to look as though they were twice as numerous as they were. Margie herself had transmitted the last message to the Greasies: "We are beginning construction of underground shelters. When the flare is over we can discuss a permanent peace. Meanwhile, if you approach we will shoot on sight." Then she pulled the plug on the radio and crawled into Cappy's plane for the last ferry trip.

They had less than ten kilometers to go—a three hour stroll under good conditions, but it would take them all of a day. It was scramble down one side of a ravine and crawl up the other, peer over the top of a crest and scuttle down its other face. And it was not just the terrain. They were all heavily loaded. Food, water, weapons, equipment. Everything they would need they had to carry on their backs.

The red cylinders marked "Fuel Elements—Replacement" were the worst. Each cylinder contained hundreds of the tiny clad needles and weighed more than a kilogram. Twelve of them made a heavy load.

At first they took turns carrying the puzzle pieces that would unite to form a nuclear bomb. One of the tricks was to make sure they didn't unite prematurely, and at every stop Leiutenant Kristianides supervised the stacking of knapsacks so that no two bomb loads were within a meter of each other. The chance was very small that they could in fact be dropped, kicked, or jostled into a configuration of critical mass. Making that happen on purpose when desired had been a serious challenge for some of the best munitions experts on Earth; for that purpose they carried another twenty kilos of highly sophisticated casing and trigger. Without that there was no real danger—or so Marge assured them all. But they were careful anyway, because in their guts none of them believed the assurance. Perhaps not even Marge.

At the end of the first march Margie had gone through the party, checking loads. When she came to Ana Dimitrova, sitting hugging her knees next to Danny Dalehouse, she said softly, "Are you sterile?"

"What? Really! What a question!" But then Margie shook her head.

"Sorry, I'm just tired. I should have remembered you aren't." And she grinned and winked at both Dalehouse and Ana; but when they picked up packs again Nan's load was changed to water flasks, and limping old Marguerite Moseler was carrying the fuel rods.

Margie looked terrible, and at every stop she seemed to look worse. Her plumpness was long gone. The bone structure of her face showed for the first time in years, and her voice was a rasp. More than that, her complexion was awful. When the Krinpit had buried her for two hours, its molting juices overrode her defenses. A day later she had broken out in great purplish blotches and a skin discoloration like sunburn. She said it did not hurt; there, too, Dalehouse thought she lied.

But he thought she was telling the truth about one very important thing, and perhaps that was the reason he could not repress a feeling of cheer. The bomb they were carrying would not be used.

He had been the one to propose it, and she had accepted the idea at once. "Of course," she said. "I don't want to destroy their camp. I want it, all of it—not only for us, but for the future of the human race on Jem. The bomb's best use is as a threat, and that's what we'll use it for."

He said as much to Ana at their last halt before coming in sight of the Greasy base. "She's planning for future generations. At least she thinks it's worth keeping your chromosomes intact."

"Of course," said Ana, surprised. "I have that confidence too." And so, Danny Dalehouse was discovering, did he. Bad as things were, he had hope. It carried him through that last belly-crawl, three hundred meters in the drenching rain, into the muddy cave that was their point of entrance for the burrower tunnels under the Greasy base. It sustained him while Major Vandemeer and Kris Kristianides painfully and gingerly assembled the parts of the detonator and fitted the fuel rods into it. It survived after Margie and Vandemeer and two others wriggled their way into the abandoned courses and disappeared from sight. The part of his life, of all their lives, that they were living through at that moment was misery and fear. Maybe worse than that, it was self-reproach; they were doing something that Dalehouse could not think of as noble or even tolerable. It was a holdup. Armed robbery. No better than a mugging. But it would be *over*. And a better time would come! And that hope kept him going for two full hours after Margie and the others had crawled away. Until Kris Kristianides, looking scared and harried, checked her watch and said, "That's it. From now on, everybody stay inside. Face the wall. Hands over your eyes. When the fireball comes, *don't look up*. Wait ten minutes at least. I've got goggles. I'll tell you when you—"

Then they drowned her out, Dalehouse first and loudest. "She's going to do it! But she promised—"

"Shit, Dalehouse, she couldn't keep that promise! The Greasies would think it was a bluff. She's going to take out their arms and food just like we planned, and then we'll move in and wipe them up."

"What insanity!" cried Ana. "There'll be nothing there! The fallout will kill us if we go into the camp."

"Maybe. I've got a counter; we'll check everything out. The important thing's the planes. If we get them we can get to their base on Farside." She hesitated. She had been carefully rehearsed in all this and had carried the secret with her for more than a day. But she had dreaded this moment. If it had not been for her burns, she would have been in the warrens with the colonel and the major, and a lot happier there than she was here. "Anyway," she finished, "there's nothing we can do about it now. She'll blow the bomb in the next ten minutes. Get your faces down!"

And then, at last, hope was dead.

For the Brood Mother, too, all hope was gone. Blind and alone she moved slowly down through the tunnels to the only place left for her to be.

The thirty-meter level was for pups and outcasts. It was a place to play growing-up games or, at the end of all games, a place to die. Mother dr'Shee had never been there before. She had been a biddable pup, trained early to responsibility. As a tiny thing she had found it tingly-thrilling to listen to the stories of the half-growns, shivering in delight as she groped for the teat in her nurse's sheltering silk. But she had never explored the adventurous levels for herself. Not once. She had known that the time would come soon enough when, at the end of her life, she would drag herself down to see those old, unvisited levels and die.

In that she had been partly wrong. It was time to die, and she was there. But she could not see.

With dignity the Brood Mother raised her forebody to its fullest stretch and called, "Is anyone near?"

There was no reply. No sound. No scent except the stale, spoiled smell of elders long dead. She tried again, not because she had any hope of being answered, but for the sake of being methodical. "Person or pup, can anyone hear my voice?"

Nothing. If there had been an answer, it could only have been one of the wild young males who roamed the upper corridors, seeking only to kill. But there was not even that.

So another of her senses had become useless to her. Hearing meant nothing when there was nothing to hear.

It was a pity she was blind, but she bore no malice toward the Two-Legs who had burned out her eyes with their stroboscopic lights. She had in any case revenged herself upon a number of them in advance—for poisoning her tunnels, for abducting her young, for perverting the brood into new and vile practices. Most of all for coming to disturb her life in the first place. She had fought against it all, against the Two-Legs and sometimes against members of her own brood turned against her by the new ways of the Two-Legs. And now the tunnels were empty, and she was blind. *Tssheee!* It would have been less—less *final* to be here and alone if she could have seen at least an occasional phosphorescent glimmer of fungus or decay. What was left of her senses? Taste no longer mattered. There was little to eat. Smell was unrewarding, with neither males nor pups to nuzzle. She could still feel the powdery dust floor beneath her, the curving wall at her side. Dr'Shee took comfort from being tightly enclosed, as she had been through all the happiest parts of her life . . .

Which was now over.

She stretched and sighed a feline, purring sound of despair. She was beginning to be very hungry. The Two-Legs had ruined most of the food stores when they poisoned the tunnels to get at her and her few surviving allies. But the tunnels stretched ten kilometers in all directions. Somewhere there would be something, in this immense engineered warren that had been her world. She did not seriously think of seeking it. A Brood Mother did not debase herself to prolong a life that was over.

Woomp—

The tunnel around her moved. It was not a shake or a tremor, but a deliberate and almost peristaltic movement. Mother dr'Shee had never before experienced such a thing. Burrows sometimes crumbled, Krinpit invaded them, the rains might wash through a roof. But for all the earth to move? Such a thing could not happen! For the Brood Mother such an event was exactly as disquieting as it would have been for a fish to scull its tail and yet not move, or for a human being to feel the air about him turn glassy and shatter.

And then, from thirty meters above and more than a kilometer away, she heard the sound that followed. It was more than a sound; it was a pressure in the air that stung her ears and left them filled with a distant, discordant chatter, like the peeping of a hungry litter. But there were no pups to cry for her, ever again.

For some reason Margie's right knee was only scraped and sore, while the left one was bloodily gouged, the leg of the coverall worn through, the skin itself long since rubbed away. It was harder and harder for her to keep up with the two ahead of her. God had not intended her to crawl through tunnels ninety centimeters high for hours on end. . . . Which God she meant was not quite clear. To spare her knee she tried for awhile a three-legged gait, putting a little weight on her left toes, the rest on right leg and hands. That was a bummer. She wound up with the worst cramp she had ever had in the calf of her leg. She had to stop and press it out while Vandemeer behind her almost caught up and the two ahead kept on going. So then she speeded her pace and ripped the knee still more.

She paused and glanced at her watch. Still more than a quarter of an hour before the device would go off. Before that the two grenades they had left at bends in the tunnels would bring down enough dirt to tamp the explosion; and they were a good kilometer away by now. Probably far enough for survival, if not comfort. "Take ten," she shouted. She rolled over and rested her limbs, breathing hard of the stale and tainted air. Funnily, it was not really dark in the tunnels. That she had not expected. Once her eyes had adjusted, she could see little will-o'-the-wisp lights, so faint and pale that they hardly had color at all. Swamp gas, foxfire, Wilis—whatever they were, they were welcome.

She heard a quick, quiet scuffle down the tunnel behind her, then a *thwuck*.

Then silence again.

"Van?" she called. "Major Vandemeer?"

The dirt walls swallowed her words, and there was no reply. Painfully she rolled herself over, turned herself around, and crawled back.

The mouse-droppings odor was very strong. She touched the switch of her little helmet light and saw that the major was dead. One of the burrowers had been here, and the dart that protruded from Vandemeer's face proved it.

"Shit," whispered Margie, and then belatedly lifted her head and drew her pistol. The light showed nothing for sure down the crooked, uneven tunnel—was that a glint of something? a reflection from an eye? She fired twice.

When she looked again there was nothing there. But every few meters there were little side passages and bays, and a dozen creepies could be waiting there for her to turn her head.

She almost raised her voice to call the others back but stopped herself as she was opening her mouth. For what? They could not bring the major's body back. Doubled over as it was—he seemed to have been turning when he was shot—he almost blocked the tunnel. Maybe that was the last service he could render his cause—to slow down pursuit.

There was a better way. She had two grenades left. She pulled one off her belt, set it to ten clicks, turned around, and scuttled as rapidly as she could after the others. When she had counted a hundred seconds, she dropped, locked her hands over the back of her neck, and waited for the distant, muffled thud that told her she had dropped a part of the tunnel roof down to bury the major.

When the grenade went off, it occurred to her that it was strange she had not caught up with the others. "Sam! Chotnik! Sound off!" she cried. They didn't answer; they hadn't heard her order to stop. She left the helmet light on and hurried after them, the pain in her knee no longer signifying. When the red numerals on her watch told her it was time for the nuclear blast, she still had not caught up.

She rolled over on her back again. For this blast it did not matter whether she protected her neck. She would be killed or she would not, and the only factor that mattered was whether there was enough earth between her and the explosion. There should be. When the impellers drove the sets of plutonium needles in to mesh with each other, there would be a nuclear blast. But not a big one. They would not stay in contact more than a few microseconds. If she had placed them right, they would expend their force up through the roof of the tunnel, carrying the Greasies' arms stores with them, and not much else. If she had placed them right. She was far less sure of that than she had pretended to Vandemeer and the others. The maps that Tinka and the Indonesian had given their lives to get to her were extremely complete and clear. But reading them in the open air was one thing; trying to follow them as you crawled from level to level underground was something quite different. She was not even sure that they had followed the same route on the way out as going in. They should have drawn a silken cord after them or broken off bits of gigerbread cookies for a trace—

At that moment the explosion occurred. Right on time. And she was still alive.

It was not even frightening. It was, she thought, as it would have been in her mother's womb if her mother had fallen. Some external event had taken place. But here in the tunnel she moved with the ground, and even the sound of the explosion was too huge and slow to be frightening.

So that part of the plan, at least, had worked. Now, if Kris could rally the patrol to the attack—If they remembered their radiation ponchos and the wind was not too unfavorable—If the Greasies did not pull themselves together fast enough to resist—If the bomb had been in the right place after all—There were too many ifs. Her place was with her troops, not here.

A sighing, slithering sound a few meters behind her caught her attention. She turned the headlamp toward it and saw that a section of the roof had collapsed into the tunnel.

Shaken loose by the nuclear blast? Maybe. More likely not. Creepies had been known to try to trap a foe by plugging tunnels before. She was terribly easy to find and follow, with the trail of blood from her knee.

It was time to get out of there. Doggedly detaching herself from the pain and from the fear that one of them was silently creeping up behind her, she resumed her crawl.

In ten meters her head struck dirt.

She turned on the light again. It was fresh dirt. The burrowers had closed both ends of the tunnel. She whirled quickly. Nothing moved behind her. She was alone.

Margie Menninger said to the wall, "The most basic human fear is of being buried alive." She waited for a moment, as though hoping someone would answer. Then she pulled out her pistol with one hand and reached for her entrenching tool with the other. It wasn't there. Then she remembered she had left it where they assembled the bomb.

Fingers then.

She dropped the pistol and tore at the dirt plug with her bare hands. Furiously. Then in terror. At last because there was nothing else for her to do.

From horizon to horizon, as far as Charlie could see, there was a solid undercast of clouds, and taller ones poked up all around. The storm was weakening off toward the ocean, but here, somewhere above the Greasy camp, it had been hours since he had seen the ground at all, days since he had last seen the little party of his friend 'Anny. And it was impossible to stay on station! At all levels up to ten thousand meters and more the wind was strong and solidly toward the Heat Pole, and it dragged him remorselessly away. Charlie could read the fraying of the anvil-shaped tops of the cumulonimbus; it showed that at fifteen thousand meters there was a return flow. But he and the two females of his flock who survived were worn and tired. They had lost much lift. It took them forever to reach those lofty levels.

As they labored upward a new flock came sailing down from the Pole, and Charlie led his tiny fragment to join it, eager for a new audience for his songs about the new friends from Earth, hungry to hear songs he had not heard before. It had been long and long since he had joined in a proper eisteddfod, and his soul ached for it. The new flock was small, fewer than sixty adults, but there were voices in it he had never heard, and he sang greeting toward them with joy.

White light lashed across them.

The flare caught them all by surprise. Charlie was one of the fortunate ones. He was facing away from the blast, and so he was not blinded at once. He saw the high cirrus starkly outlined, blue-white against the sullen, crimson Jemman sky, saw the shapes of the new flock picked out in brighter, sharper colors than he had ever seen. Minutes later he heard the sound, and behind him and below a new thundercloud boiled up out of the undercast.

Chorus of welcome became a dirge of pain and fear. Charlie could only reply with a lifting song. The seniors of the new flock took it up, and the swarm dropped ballast, belched swallowed hydrogen into their sacs, and rose. A few did not. They were not merely blind; they were in too great pain to respond.

Although they were far from the blast, when the winds struck, the swarm was thrown helter-skelter across the sky. Charlie had never felt such gusts before. Always in other storms there had been warning—gathering clouds and the deadly play of lightning to tell them it was time to swallow hydrogen and ride out the storm, or soar to escape above it. This time there was no warning and no escape. His feeding flaps and winglets felt as though they were being torn out at the roots. Captive of the huge sail of his surface, he was thrown through the new flock, caroming off their seniors, cannoning balloonets out of the way.

And then, without warning, he felt the familiar creeping tension of the surface of his gas sac and recognized the sweet, stinging odor of the females. Estrus, swarming time, time to breed!

The spinnerets of the females were working furiously now, spraying threadlike ova and pheronomes into the air. All around the swarm, the air was fragrant with the demand to breed. For Charlie, and for all the males, there was no question about what to do next: hive up, spray milt, soar back and forth through the stinging mist while their teats elongated, convulsed, spread their seed. The skins of their air sacs tightened, drawing the features of their tiny faces into caricatures. Behind the expressions that looked like pain was pain. The overtures to sex were no joy to Charlie. They were like being locked in an Iron Maiden with acid-tipped spikes. Only the relief that came when the semen squirted out made the pain end.

But it was wrong, wrong!

Charlie sang out his question and his fear, and the new flock sang with him. What breeding was this, with the flare coming from the enemy ground and not the sky? What was this heat that smote them like a fist, following on the thunder and the wild gales? Charlie could see that in the turbulence most of the silklings had been missed by the milt. They were all over the sky. Within his own body he could feel it was wrong. Where was the bubbling of hydrogen to replenish his sac, radiation-stung out of his body fluids? And what—what was this monstrous, bubbling cloud that was growing so fast it was drawing them all toward it?

And that was the question that answered all the others and put an end to questions forever for Charlie as the searing heat of the nuclear cloud burned out his eye patches, cracked his gas sac, touched off the hydrogen that spilled out, and ended his songs for always.

TWENTY-THREE

●

As NUCLEAR EXPLOSIONS went, it was inconsiderable. Less than a kiloton, it would hardly have been noticed in the multimegaton blasts that had scoured the surface of Earth. When the imploding grenades forced the bright plutonium needles out of their sheaths to mate, they were in contact for only a few microseconds before their own immense reaction drove them apart.

But by then the explosion had occurred. The needles, the shell, the walls of the tunnel around them had been vaporized to a hot gas, billions of atmospheres of pressure, irresistibly determined to escape. It escaped. Within a few thousandths of a second it had formed its pipsqueak fireball, fifty meters across, racing upward at five hundred kilometers an hour, brighter than Kung, brighter than Earth's sun, brighter than hundreds of them put together. The fireball grew and soared, first bright red with its burden of nitric acid, then whitening and losing its brightness as it began to cool.

Even through closed eyes that stark flare was visible to the people huddled in the cave, and the shock front that swept over them shook the cave and their bodies. The noise was immense. After it, over the echoes, Kris Kristianides was shouting, "Stay down! Don't open your eyes! Wait!" For nearly ten minutes she kept them there, and then, slowly, she peered through half-closed lids and the dark goggles and announced they could get up.

Tentatively they poked their heads over the ridge. Squinting, they saw what Marge Menninger had done.

The nuclear cloud boiled tall through the layers of stratus. It had punched its own hole in the rain clouds, but its mushroom top was out of sight. Nearer, the Greasy camp seemed hardly touched: a shed blown over, a couple of tents burning, people moving dazedly around.

301

"She—she missed the base!" cried Kris, and Danny Dalehouse could not tell whether her tone was angry or glad. But what she said was true. The bottom of the blast was half a kilometer away from the camp toward the Heat Pole. Marge had got herself lost. The half of the blast that went into explosive pressure had wasted itself on the sand and succulents of the steppe.

But the third that went into heat had done better. The nearest persons in the Greasy camp were staggering around, blind and in agony. No one had given them goggles. No one had warned them not to look toward the blast.

"Check your pieces," Kristianides ordered. She had taken the goggles off, and under them her eyes were red. But her voice was determined. "Put on your cloaks. Let's go. We're moving in."

Dalehouse stood up and pulled the plastic poncho over his head like an automaton. (Would that really protect against any fallout at all?) He picked up his recoilless and slapped a cartridge into the breech. (Why am I doing this?) He started off with the others in a ragged line of skirmish, all nine of them walking slowly toward the Fuel base.

At every step he was telling himself that it was wrong. Wrong tactically: the nuclear blast had knocked out no more than a few unfortunates, and they were likely to get their heads blown off by the survivors. Wrong strategically: they should never have allowed themselves to get into this position. And wrong, most wrong of all, morally. What kind of world were they fighting for when they killed people without warning?

Dalehouse looked uneasily back and forth at the others in the line. All were staring straight ahead at the Fuel camp. Didn't any of them feel the way he did?

He stopped in his tracks. "Kris," he said, "I don't want to do this."

She turned slowly so that the muzzle of her gun covered him. "Move your ass, Dalehouse."

"No, wait, Kris. Let's—"

She said tightly, "I was expecting that from you. We're going in there. All of us. Colonel Menninger set this up, and I'm not going to let it go to waste. Now move it."

The others had stopped to look at them. None of them

spoke; they only waited while Dalehouse watched the barrel of the GORR come into line with the bridge of his nose. He sighed deeply and said, "No, Kris." And then he stood there as her expression changed and hardened and he realized that, yes, she was going to pull the trigger—

"Put down your rifle, lieutenant," Ana called.

She was behind Kris and a little to one side, and she had her own gun pointed firmly at the lieutenant's back. "I do not wish to kill," she said, "but I, too, do not want to attack this camp."

Dalehouse didn't wait to see what would happen. He stepped forward and took the GORR from Kristianides's hands. He threw it back over the crest of the hill they had just crossed and then followed it with his own. After a second Ana did the same, and so, one by one, did the others.

"You fucking fools!" Kris raged. "They'll shoot you down like rats!"

Dalehouse did not answer. He stared toward the Greasy camp, where a few persons who were not blind or incapacitated had begun to appear. They had weapons, and they were gazing at the drama on the hill.

Dalehouse raised his hands over his head and began to walk steadily toward them. Out of the corner of his eye he saw Ana doing the same thing. Maybe Kris was right. Maybe one of those armed people kneeling in the shelter of a smoldering tent would begin to shoot. But it was out of his hands. Whatever guilt there was, it would not anymore belong to him; and for the first time in months he felt at peace.

TWENTY-FOUR

●

AND SO, AT THE LAST, what can one say of them? What is to be said of Marjorie Menninger and Danny Dalehouse and Ana Dimitrova—and of Charlie and Ahmed Dulla, or of Sharn-igon and Mother dr'Shee? They did what they could. More often than not, they did what they thought they should. And what can be said of them is what can be said of all persons, human and otherwise, at the end: they died. Some survived the fighting. Some survived the flare. But in the long run there are no survivors.

There are only replacements. And time passes, and generations come and go.

And then, what can one say of that beautiful and powerful woman named Muskrat Greencloud An-Guyen?

One can say that she bears the traces of Margie and Nan and some of the others. Some through the passage of chains of DNA, some only because of what they did or who they were. She never knew any of them, of course, because they are all six generations dead; she is a replacement.

Like all of us, she is not a single person. She wears three personas, or six, or a hundred if you count the subjective memories and stereotypes other persons carry around that bear the label "Muskie An-Guyen." To a former lover, she is the sweetly sweaty companion of a weekend at Lake Hell. To her grandchildren, she is the docent who leads them through the museums and the zoo. To your average registered Republicate lot-caster of the Boyne-Feng Metropolitan Area, she is the selection judge who supervises the machineries of government. Or, actually, of nongovernment. Muskie is one hundred percent solidly behind the

Six Precepts of the Jemman Republics, and *No strong central government* is the last and maybe most important of them. "Government" is a dead wickedness to Muskie, burned out in the Blast and starved in the Desperation. It has been gone from Jem this century and a half. No one wants to see that pawkish horror back, least of all Muskie. It is as obsolete as armies and indolence and waste. Muskie will keep it so, if it demands her last drop of blood as well as the utmost sacrifices by her militia volunteers and gift acceptors.

But to see who Muskie is, let us look at the three principal faces she wears to show the sultry and satisfied world of Jem.

The first of these is Muskie the nurturer. She provides more than a tenth of the food for Boyne-Feng, and nearly all of it that comes from underground. She does not do it by herself, of course. See her as she stands in the gallery gate. The morning shift is coming on duty. The bad old days of "owners" died when government did Muskie is not an owner. She is only one among equals. But she is a special one.

You might think she looks like a Virginia planter overseeing slaves, or perhaps like a Shensi landlord accepting squeeze from the tenant farmers in her paddies. This would be deceiving. There is no ownership. There is not even any compulsion. The tokens the Krinpit laborers give her one by one as they scuttle past to the underground farms are not extorted. They are gifts. They are freely given. If Muskie is not pleased with the gift of one of them, she does not reproach him or order him to give more. She simply refuses it. Then the Krinpit chooses to go back to his village, where he may freely starve. A meter or two past Muskie's station the Creepie overseers spray the Krinpit with anti-allergen lacquer. No force is employed here, either. If the Krinpit do not choose to make gifts to the overseers, they need not turn back. The overseers will then choose not to spray them. The Krinpit will then itch or molt or die as a consequence of exposure to the terraborn crops they handle. It is the Krinpit's right to choose this if they wish. There is absolutely no compulsion, by anyone, of anyone, at any time. That is part of the Six Precepts.

The Krinpit know this and rejoice in their freedom—not to mention rejoicing in the radios, the gaily raucous drums and zithers, the chemical intoxicants, beads and metal tools that they prize. These are freely given to them when they freely give up the tokens that Muskie has freely given to them at the end of each voluntary work shift. The Creepies also know that this is true. They are also grateful, especially for the Two-Legs' improvements on their savage old burrows, and they freely assist the stronger, bigger Krinpit laborers by instructing them in where to plant the floor crops of mushrooms and the roof crops of potato and yam. They too now rejoice in the possession of beads, devices, and intoxicants their rude progenitors never knew. The balloonists know it—what fun they have with their taped music and their repeated orgasms! And, of course, Muskrat Greencloud An-Guyen knows it really well. She has everything she wants. Perhaps the best part of what she has is the certain knowledge that the Six Precepts are always followed, and so justice is always served, and everybody else on Jem—and that means everybody, Krip or balloonist, stranger or son—has everything, too. Though not usually as much of everything as she.

Then there is Muskie the civil volunteer. Not merely a discussant or a participator, like everyone else. She is a selection judge who gives freely of her time to serve the whole community, even at holidays.

She leaves the agricultural galleries and goes aboveground into the warm, bright dome of Fat City. Muskie is still a sturdily beautiful woman. She is tanned by the ultraviolet lights of the pool-grotto, tall, solid rather than plump; she weighs sixty standard kilos, but she has a fifty-centimeter waist, and her lovers prefer her to partners half her age. Eyes follow her as she comes smiling into Remembrance Hall, removes her slacks and slicks for comfort, gives Ring-Greeting to all, and reclines on a foam couch. "I would like to begin," she says sunnily. The other six volunteer selection judges agree that they, too, would like to discuss the issues of the day.

Most of the issues are routine, and consensus appears at once. (They are all saving themselves for the big one.) From his place under the bust of Mother Kristianides, wide-browed and serene as she looks down on them, Roanoke t'Schreiber describes the progress in cleaning up

Lake Hell. All the city's sewage is being pumped there. The native aquatic life is being satisfactorily killed off, since *Escherichia coli* is antibiotic against most forms of Jemman life. "Another two million bowel movements and we'll have it sparkly clean," he comments. Sod House Flareborn looks up from inspecting her ten-centimeter fingernails to wonder if the militia should be freely given extra tokens, since so many of them have unfortunately (though voluntarily) given up their lives in the exploration of additional Creepy burrows and the liberation of distant camps of Krinpit. All agree that this seems desirable. The woman in militia fatigues who has been hovering by the door leaves with a smile of satisfaction.

Then Muskie's face clouds and she observes, "I have heard that there has been another tactran from Alphabase."

There is silence in the chamber. This is the issue that holds the seeds of dissent, and even change. No one really wants to get into it. All the judges stir uncomfortably on the couches under the busts of the ancestors, each waiting for the others to speak.

At last t'Schreiber offers an opinion. "I, for one, think it was unwise of our predecessors to attempt to resume space exploration. They freely gave much value to put new tactran satellites in orbit. What have we gained? Sorrow and confusion." He lists the contacts made: a garble that *might* have been from the Martian colony; pitiful pleas for help from old Earth itself; a dozen cocky messages from the base at Alpha Centauri suggesting an attempt at an actual flight to and from Jem. From the rest of the universe, nothing.

Muskie waits uncomfortably, shifting position and scratching just above the plaque of her string bikini. Then she says, "I wonder if we should answer messsages from Alphabase anymore."

No one responds.

Therefore it is agreed; and the judges turn to speaking of the gratifying growth in human population—from one hundred eighty survivors to eighteen hundred in the third generation, and now nearly a quarter of a million in the sixth. There is no longer a fear that humanity might not survive. On Jem Man flourishes.

This reminds Muskie that her newest baby is about

ready to be born. She speaks softly into her telephone to the hospital. The mare is in the delivery room even at that moment. But the news is bad. The baby was born dead.

"I blame myself," says Muskie to the doctor remorsefully. "Sarah Glowbag—was that her name?"

"Mary Glowbag," the doctor corrects her.

"Yes, Mary. She was nearly sixty years old. I should have invited a younger mare to brood my baby."

"Don't let it spoil your day," consoles the doctor. "One must expect a failure now and then. Nearly all of your children have lived, and remember, you have three others in the oven right now."

"You're very kind." Muskie hangs up with a smile. But the news has upset her—and just at Christmas, too. "I would like to leave now," she tells the other judges, and of course they also wish to close the discussion and return to their homes.

And then there is Muskrat the mother, the honored one at the head of her family.

This is no small part of her. Her family is huge. Forty-four living children, the dozen oldest long since having made her a multiple grandmother, the three youngest still unborn in the borrowed wombs of other women. (She reminds herself to make a voluntary gift to Sarah, or Mary, Glowbag for her kindness in carrying her most recent implanted ovum to term. Not as large as usual, of course; after all, the child had been born dead.) At Christmas all of them will come to give her Ring-Greeting, and she looks forward to the day with pleasure.

But not all of a family's concerns are pleasurable. As she walks across the pleasant gardens toward the place where she sleeps and keeps her belongings, a short, pale youth pushes toward her through the shrubs. He is d'Dalehouse Dolphin An-Guyen, and he is one of her sons. He has been running. He is breathing hard. Muskie sighs and says, "How nice of you to hurry to give me Ring-Greeting, Dolph."

He stops and blinks at the pretty Christmas many-tree in the center of the garden, with its ring-shaped lights and yellow Star of Earth at the top. Obviously he has forgotten about the holiday. Muskie sighs again. "Merry Christmas anyway, Dolph. I know you're going to reproach me some more. Sit down and catch your breath first."

They sit on a pressed creepystone bench under a grape arbor. (A few raisins had survived the flare-storm under a bunk in that Outpost of the People. From the six germinable seeds that were found in them had come all the wine on Jem, and this arbor.)

Muskie does not look at her son. She knows that in spite of his faults, he is too well brought up to begin before she has given him encouragement, and she wants him to feel the peace of this place. All around the garden are the statues of the First Generation, the eighteen Mothers in gold, the fifty-two Mares in crystal, the eighty-nine Fathers in granite quarried from the cliffs under the Heat Pole. (The twenty-one survivors who contributed no genes to the pool, even by cloning, have statues too, but they are ranged outside the park. None of them were even mares.) There are further distinctions in the statues. The eighty-one survivors who returned from Farside have their names picked out in frost-etched silver. The thirty-two who survived in the burrows under the Outpost of Food when the flare caught them before the ferrying to Farside was complete are marked in ruby. And the sixty-seven others —few of them viable—who survived the flare in caves, under machines, inside space capsules, or wherever they could hide from the rage of the star are marked in orange chrysolite, the color of flame. That was six generations back. Muskie could have been descended from 2^6 of them, more than a third, but actually only eleven are truly her ancestors, with considerable overlap. (For instance, she is quintuply each descended from Marjorie Menninger, Ana Dimitrova, Nguyen Tree, and Firstborn McKenzie, the tiny phocomelic child born to the one woman who survived both the nuclear bombing of the Outpost of Fuel and the flare. She lived only long enough to bear her damaged child, but the child was marvelously fertile.)

When Muskie feels that this holy place has done all it can for her son, she scratches below the waistband of her slacks and says, "All right, Dolph, you may as well say it."

He cannot wait to get the words out, he is so impatient. "All right, I'll say it! You've made a mistake, Mother Muskie. We can't say no to Alphabase!"

" 'Can't'?"

He is doggedly stubborn. Even ferocious. "Yes, that's what I said, *can't*. It's a crime against the human race!

Jem's rotting away before your eyes, Mother Muskie. This is the best chance we've ever had to get things going again. They've got high-energy technology on Alphabase! Do you know what it means, what they're suggesting? They're able to put ten tons standard into the tachyon charge state—we couldn't do that to save our lives."

"Dear Dolph," she begins, sweetly reasonable, "we have more pressing problems right here on Jem. Do you know how many wild flocks of Loons there are? Krips who still wallow in savagery? Creepies unreached and unbenefited. We have a duty—"

"We have a duty to humanity!" he cries.

"Yes. Certainly! And we are carrying it out. Our ancestors gave their lives to save us, and we are true to the Six Precepts. There is no tyrannical government, no coercion, no contending nationalities here. We haven't raped Jem, we've wooed it. We live off renewable resources, while the Alphs are back to industry and all the evils of technology."

"Dear God," he shouts, "resources? The quarter-million of us don't begin to scratch the surface of them! Do you know that fossil fuel is forming faster than we use it?"

"Good! Proper! That makes it renewable. But be reasonable, Dolph dear. Why spoil everyone's happiness by striving for something foolish? Suppose everyone wanted to do what you say. Who would mine these fossil fuels?"

"Krips. Creeps. People. Machines! I don't care. If they don't want to, they should be ordered to!"

Muskrat is shaken. "You have spoiled my Christmas," she says sorrowfully, and walks away. What a shame! A foolishly stubborn boy and an incompetent mare, and her whole holiday was ruined before it had rightly begun. Dolph is her favorite son, or often is. She admires his tiny, quick body and his bright mind. But what rot, really! What a bore! Why can't he accept paradise like everyone else and be happy in it?

Dolph's holiday is spoiled, too, and he sits on the creepy-stone bench so angry and frustrated that he does not even hear the carols beginning.

> A'es 'e fi'eles,
> lae'i 'riumphan'es.

If only she could be made to understand! The winning of Jem had cost so much in blood and pain. Not just in that first terrible year. Over and over again, every time Kung had flared in those first decades. There had been eight flares since the days of the ancestors, and only the last two or three had been fairly painless. Plenty of warning. A frenzied rush to ionproof the domes and hustle essential perishables inside. A week of confinement while the star raged, a year or so of one or another kind of scarcity until the planet replenished itself. But that left half a dozen sieges of misery, the first worst, but all of them catastrophic. Was all that to go for nothing?

> *Veni'e a'oremus,*
> *'Ominum.*

A Creepie overseer darts whickering past him toward the many-tree, followed by four noisy Krinpit gardeners in their bright red and green Ring-Greeting coats of lacquer. He becomes aware of the choir belatedly.

> *—save us all from Sa'an's power*
> *When we were gone as'ray—*

Hell of a season of joy this is, he thinks to himself. Season of suicide! Time of deciding to die on the vine while all the rest of the galaxy goes on to who knows what triumphs of technology and adventure! Glumness battles Christmas inside him. Gradually glumness loses. He remembers what the Creepie had been carrying—palely glowing ultraviolet strobes—and decides to stroll over to the Christmas many-tree.

The Krinpit are pushing away benches and picnic tables to make room, moaning and clattering to themselves; they finish and scuttle away. The Creepie positions his strobes and waits for orders. On the tree itself, the tethered balloonists are singing their little hearts out.

> *Schlaf im heilige ruhe,*
> *Schlaf im heilige ruh'.*

All around the tree young people like him are removing their clothes and slipping in between the gaily decorated trunks. "Time to start!" they cry; and the Loons begin the jolly, lively "Good King Wenceslas." Obediently the Creepie touches off the strobes. The Loons gasp and continue to sing and begin to emit their milt, and all under the lovely tree the couples link in the traditional Rings.

And Dolph can stand it no longer. Gloom loses. Christmas wins. He flings off his clothing and plunges into the trunks of the many-tree. Why fight Utopia? he thinks to himself. And so in that moment he completes the process of growing up. And begins the process of dying. Which is much the same thing.

ABOUT THE AUTHOR

FREDERIK POHL is a double-threat science fictioneer, being the only person to have won this field's top award, the Hugo, as both a writer and an editor. As a writer, he's published more than 30 novels and short story collections; as an editor, he published the first series of anthologies of original stories in the field of science fiction, *Star Science Fiction*. He was, for a number of years, the editor of two leading magazines, *Galaxy* and *If*. His awards include four Hugos and the Edward E. Smith Award. His interests extend to politics, history (he's the *Encyclopaedia Britannica's* authority on the Roman Emperor Tiberius) and almost the entire range of human affairs.

OUT OF THIS WORLD!

That's the only way to describe Bantam's great series of science fiction classics. These space-age thrillers are filled with terror, fancy and adventure and written by America's most renowned writers of science fiction. Welcome to outer space and have a good trip!

FANTASY AND SCIENCE FICTION FAVORITES

Bantam brings you the recognized classics as well as the current favorites in fantasy and science fiction. Here you will find the beloved Conan books along with recent titles by the most respected authors in the genre.

☐	20281	WAR OF OMISSION Kevin O'Donnell	$2.50
☐	20488	THE HEROES OF ZARA	$2.50
		Guy Gregory	
☐	14428	LORD VALENTINE'S CASTLE	$2.95
		Robert Silverberg	
☐	01166	URSHURAK	$8.95
		Bros. Hildebrandt & Nichols	
☐	20156	BABEL-17 Samuel R. Delany	$2.50
☐	20063	GATES OF HEAVEN Paul Preuss	$2.25
☐	22562	NOVA Samuel R. Delany	$2.75
☐	20987	TRITON Samuel R. Delany	$2.95
☐	14861	DHALGREN Samuel R. Delany	$3.95
☐	20870	JEM Frederik Pohl	$2.95
☐	13837	CONAN & THE SPIDER GOD #5	$2.25
		de Camp & Pratt	
☐	13831	CONAN THE REBEL #6	$2.25
		Paul Anderson	
☐	14532	HIGH COUCH OF SILISTRA	$2.50
		Janet Morris	
☐	20722	DRAGONDRUMS Anne McCaffrey	$2.50
☐	22556	DRAGONSINGER Anne McCaffrey	$2.75
☐	22557	DRAGONSONG Anne McCaffrey	$2.75
☐	20914	MAN PLUS Frederik Pohl	$2.75
☐	14846	THE GOLDEN SWORD Janet Morris	$2.50
☐	20592	TIME STORM Gordon R. Dickson	$2.95

Buy them at your local bookstore or use this handy coupon for ordering:

PACT WITH THE DEVIL

"To achieve the best magic possible, the practitioner should perform this and all rites in the nude."

Nicole stepped out of the circle, careful not to smudge the powder lines. Quickly undressing, she re-entered the circle, holding the book. She strained her eyes to read the small print in the flickering candle light.

"O Emperor Lucifer," she began in a soft whisper, "Chief of all the spirits which rebelled, I beg Thee to favor me in this conjuration, which I am about to perform to Thee and Thy Ministers. . . ."

She waited. It was now that the book indicated that the summoned one should appear. She continued waiting. Where was he? Had she done something incorrectly in performing the rite?

Glancing at the book, she saw that one more sentence remained.

"I promise Thee, O great and mighty Lucifer, to reward Thee in whatever way Thou see fit, if my request for the love of Myles Lawrence is granted and given unto me this night."

The clock on the shelf above the TV set struck three times. . . .

HANDS OF LUCIFER

JOHN TIGGES

LEISURE BOOKS   NEW YORK CITY

For Reiko and Carey
The two neatest "outlaw" in-laws in the world.

A LEISURE BOOK

Published by

Dorchester Publishing Co., Inc.
6 East 39th Street
New York, NY 10016

Copyright©1987 by John Tigges

Printed in the United States of America

PART ONE
"I Conjure Thee . . ."

Thursday, September 4, 1986
to
Friday, September 19, 1986

"The sleep of reason produces monsters."

Goya

1

Thursday, September 4, 1986 12:58 A.M.

Nicole Kilton reached out, turning on the lamp next to her bed. Although the light had been out for only a few minutes, she neverthess blinked, quickly readjusting her eyes to the brightness. Myles Lawrence remained sitting on the edge of the bed, his shirt off. Nothing else had changed since she had undressed, gotten into bed and turned out the lights.

"Myles?" she asked quietly. Something was wrong. She had sensed it ever since he had arrived around midnight. She felt his preoccupation while they watched part of the late movie on television. Now that she thought about it, he also had seemed tense during the late newscast, on which he served as anchorman. His normal, relaxed air had been missing during his portion of the program but she had not thought anything of it at the time.

But now his peculiar way of acting seemed to bring everything into focus. She and Myles had dated long enough to enable her to read his emotions, his feelings, his reactions—without him uttering a word.

There had been times when she wondered if it were because she was so astute at that sort of thing or if Myles were that transparent. She doubted the latter and questioned the former. If she was ever to get her Masters degree in psychology and be of any worth as a psychiatrist's assistant, she would need the ability to evaluate people's states of mind and help them to a clearer understanding of their problems. But that wouldn't happen for a while—not until she had enough money saved to return to graduate school. The money from her parents' estate had supported her and paid for her college education. With that money gone, she was on her own and was scared to take out a sizable loan for further tuition. Her advanced education would have to wait a while longer, at least until she saved the necessary funds.

Where Myles and she were concerned, she only hoped she wasn't practicing on him, trying to understand his motivations without allowing him to explain. That would hardly be fair to either of them.

Myles acknowledged her with a grunt but said nothing.

"That's hardly the response I would expect from a TV news anchorman," she said lightly, inching her way toward him. When her bare breasts touched his arm, he stood, moving away from the bed as if repelled by her nearness. He walked to the window and peeped through the Venetian blinds at the dark outside.

Something indeed was bothering him. Nicole quickly replayed the evening. They had kissed when he arrived shortly before midnight, then had eaten a sandwich that Nicole usually had prepared for his arrival after the eleven o'clock news. They had begun watching the late movie on KSLL-TV, Myles' station, but he had fidgeted and she had picked up on his sense of uneasiness. She should have realized then that something was wrong.

"You'd feel better if you talked about it, Myles." She worked her way to the edge of the bed, reaching for her robe. After she had slipped into it, she turned to the mirrored wall behind her bed, fluffing her hair. She had been ready for sex when they prepared to retire. Once she had gone to bed, she had expected him to join her within seconds. Now the mood had evaporated, destroyed by his refusal to talk.

He turned to face her, a look of relief crossing his face when he saw her tying the sash of her nylon robe. "I don't know where to begin," he said softly. When she took a step toward him, he retreated to the window until his back rattled the blind.

Nicole felt as if she had the plague or some

horrible disfigurement that suddenly drove him from her. "Talk to me, Myles. Please?"

"I don't want to hurt you," he whispered.

"Hurt me?" She almost swallowed the words. How could he hurt her? "I don't understand."

"I . . . I want to break up. I . . ." He stopped, unable to continue—or perhaps playing the moment for all it was worth to see how she would react.

"Break . . . break up? Why? I thought we had something good going. Something that . . ."

"That's just it. I don't want anything 'good going' right now, to use your words. I'm only twenty-seven. I want to get out and live—a lot. I didn't really mean for the two of us to get so deeply involved. But . . ." His voice faded.

"But we did," she completed softly. She studied him for a long moment. Myles was handsome in a broad sense of the word. He could easily have been a male model or done major commercials for national television or, had he so desired, become an actor, who in time would have had teenage girls wild about him. His square jaw, at first glance, seemed almost too wide for the rest of his face but it instantly conformed, complimenting the steady blue eyes and black hair that bordered his face. His long, thin nose was virtually unnoticeable despite the tip, which he maintained was too long. There was absolutely nothing about him that didn't fit.

No matter how he tried to cover his

emotions, his feelings were advertised by his eyes. No matter what he felt, his eyes told the truth, and Nicole could see he truly did feel bad.

"You feel rotten, and yet you're willing to put yourself and me through something like this?" She turned, walking back to the bed, catching her reflection in the mirror again. Scowling, she dropped onto the chest that sat at the foot of the bed and faced him. "Is there someone else?"

The words rung hollowly in her ears. Where had that thought come from? Why would she suspect something like that? A question like that went along with insecurity and jealousy. Was she either? Could she be both?

Myles took several steps toward her but stopped. He shook his head. "It . . . it's nothing like that. It's just that I've practically moved in here with you. We see each other every day. Every night. It's as if we were married, and I don't want to be a husband—not yet, at least. Not for a long while. I wouldn't be doing you any favors if we did get married."

Nicole frowned. "I don't understand."

"I haven't done everything that I want to do yet. As a single person."

Was that it? She quickly regained her composure. Perhaps he *was* doing her a favor if that were the case. Why run the risk of marriage only to have him get a bad case of marital wanderlust and then—what? Divorce? "I suppose you mean . . . other women?" She swallowed, waiting for his answer.

He looked up. "That's part of it, I guess. I want to travel around and see the country. I've been working for three years since I got out of school, and I sure hope that the end of the road for me isn't here in a college town, reporting the news at a small, second-rate UHF station. I've got more ambition than that."

Nicole struggled with a tear tickling the corner of her eye, fighting for a life of its own. She had felt her face flush the instant she had heard the words "break up" but had managed to control her emotions thus far. Wasn't that part of being a psychologist? She would have to learn that type of control. Control her emotions. Be in control of everything. Be calculating. Make the right decisions—not only for herself but for anyone who came to her for help. Would that much power—power over herself and others—make for happiness? Perhaps it would, in her chosen line of work if she ever attained that goal. But she doubted that it would where her personal life was concerned. She had thought of applying for graduate work last spring but had held off for financial reasons. She knew for the most part that people in the field of psychology and psychiatry were able to keep other people's problems from bothering them. At least, they weren't supposed to be affected.

But *damnit*! This was *her* problem. She was the one being handed a platter of crap from the guy she loved. At twenty-four, she had thought well enough of herself and Myles as a couple to believe that their relationship would blossom into full-blown love and eventually culminate in marriage. She snorted a derisive laugh and broke into tears.

Myles looked up, startled. "Are you all right?" He took another step toward her.

"No, damnit! No, I'm not all right," she cried, standing and grasping for support at the dresser, on top of which her collection of dolls wiggled and danced about, threatening to spill to the floor. But she caught herself and the impromptu dance by the toys stopped as suddenly as it had started. An antique Little Orphan Annie doll's head bobbed back and forth in diminishing gestures. "Myles, I love you. I thought you loved me. It's . . . it's just . . . just so damned shocking. So unexpected. I . . . I never once . . ." She felt her body trembling and roughly shook her head. Her soft, wavy brown hair flew outward, falling back in place when she stopped.

"I . . . I think I understand," he said lamely. "You're a super person. Sweet. Kind. Intelligent. Lov . . ."

"Oh, can it, Myles." She sobbed, fighting desperately to control the tears but nothing worked. "I . . . I don't need a letter of recommendation to survive this."

He dropped his head, moving toward the foot of the bed where his shirt lay draped over the edge, half on the floor. He slipped into it and awkwardly fumbled with the buttons.

Nicole watched him through her tears, his figure slithering in the watery view. When he finished, he stood there, watching her for a full minute in silence.

His nostrils flared before he spoke. "Will you be all right?"

"Of course not. I'll probably cry the whole night. What do you care?" She wiped her face with both hands. "I love you, Myles Lawrence. I want you . . . I want you to be with me forever. As my husband. One day, we will be together."

"You're making that sound almost like a threat," he said quietly.

"It's no threat. It's a . . . a statement of fact. You can rest assured that no matter what you do, you'll always be in my thoughts. I won't give up."

"I think you might be saying things you don't mean."

"Go on, Myles. Get out of here. But go with the thought you can come back any time you want. I'll be waiting for you."

He moved toward her. She didn't back away when he gently grasped her by the arms. "If we're meant to be together, we'll one day be husband and wife. I don't want you doing anything foolish."

"*Foolish?*" She almost screamed the word, wrenching from his hands. "I hope you don't think that I'd hurt myself in some way over this. That's the farthest thing from my mind. In fact, the sooner you get out of here, the quicker I . . . I can get to planning on how to

get you back. I . . . I will get you back, you
know?" She clenched her fists, her nails
digging into the palms, doing everything
possible to maintain some degree of calmness.

"Look here, Nicole, the last thing I need at
this point in my life is someone chasing after
me, making life miserable by always being
wherever I happen to be. I mean . . ."

"You're flattering yourself, Myles. I'll get
you back but I won't embarrass you . . . or me.
I promise you that." She looked at him, just as
his expression of apprehension was replaced by
a look of relief. His eyes softened, a relaxing
coolness taking over.

"I believe you. I should go. I . . . I'll see you
around . . . sometime."

He turned, leaving the bedroom. She
watched him go down the short hallway past
the living room to the front door. Opening it,
he hesitated for an instant and then left
without looking back.

Rooted to the spot. Nicole felt the wave of
nausea come like a splash of hot water. She ran
to the bathroom, falling to her knees just in
time, the stream of vomit choking her in its
intense desire to quit her body. Coughing and
spitting, she managed to bring herself under
control. Wiping her face on a washcloth, she
relished in its relief. Then, she returned to the
bedroom.

For a split second she felt tempted to dress
and run after him, but quickly decided that
that was the wrong tack at this time. She
would win Myles back, but not that way. She

only hoped her absence in his life would prove to be as devastating to him as his would be to her.

She sat down on the bed, slipping the robe from her shoulders. She caught the reflection of her body's profile in the mirrors that formed the headboard for her bed. Her large breasts proudly jutted out, denying her own sinking sense of defeat. Turning to face her image, she managed a wry smile. Her tear-reddened eyes matched her flushed complexion. She looked a mess but didn't care. Lying back across the bed, she wiped her face with both hands. There had to be something she could do—but what? How did one go about winning back a reluctant love?

But was Myles actually reluctant? Or was he giving her a routine to simply be rid of her? She doubted that very much. Myles and she had had a good relationship—at least *she* had thought it had been good. No matter what it had been before, she would make certain that the relationship—a quality relationship— would come about again. She and Myles Lawrence would be together again—soon!

Sitting up, she saw herself in the mirrors again, and an ironic smile crossed her round face. She stood, moving to the dressing table. When she had seated herself, she peered into its mirror, staring deeply into her own eyes.

"So," she said aloud, addressing the tear-streaked face staring back at her, "how do I go about getting him back? What do I do?"

She sat for a long while, studying herself, and then slowly stood. Picking up her brush, she vigorously ran it through her hair. Satisfied the tangles had been taken out and that her hair could be cared for in a quick manner the next morning, she slipped between the cool sheets.

How much time had elapsed since she had gotten into bed earlier? Glancing at the alarm clock, she winced. It was a little after two. They had turned off the TV set before the movie ended and had gone to the bedroom. Then Myles had dropped his bomb. It seemed like a lifetime had passed since he first broached the subject of breaking up, and here it was still early enough for her to get a good night's sleep.

She turned off the light after making certain the alarm clock was set and lay on her back, staring into the inky blackness that embraced her and the room. There had to be a way. There simply had to be a way to win back Myles. The last thing in the world she ever thought she would have to do was plot to win back a lost love. But what was she to do? She loved Myles —more than anything or anyone in her entire life.

Nicole turned over on her side and closed her eyes. Sleep did not come easily, and the last time she looked it was almost four in the morning before she managed to drop off.

She opened her eyes. Where was she? It was

dark. Black. She couldn't see anything. How long had she slept? It seemed like hours had passed since . . . What had happened? Something that had been almost traumatic. . . .

Myles? Where was Myles? She groped next to her. Sitting up, Nicole fumbled for the bedside lamp switch. Plunging the room into light, she blinked. What time was it? How long had she been asleep? She focused on the digital numbers until the blue blurs became hard, fast lines. *Four forty-five.* It had to be later than that. It just had to be. If time were going to pass that slowly for her, it would take a millenium for her to age a year.

She had dreamt. About Myles. Myles running away from her on a desert plain of some sort. There was nothing else. Nothing as far as she could see—except the diminishing figure of Myles Lawrence as he moved quickly away from her toward the distant horizon.

Nicole found herself crying when she recalled the dream. Crying—for no reason at all. No reason? There certainly was a reason. *Myles!* Myles had walked out last night—away from her and out of her life. He said he didn't want to be committed to anything permanent at the present time. She now wondered why he hadn't said "at this point in time," like he would have on one of his television newscasts. She hated that expression—useless words that said practically nothing.

What time had she fallen asleep? She remembered looking at the alarm in the dark when it was three fifty-one. Now it was four fifty-six. Had she slept less than an hour? *Less than one hour?* If she averaged that much, she could devote over twenty-three hours a day to reclaiming Myles' love and affection.

She lay back on the bed. Why had he left? He had started to say something about how great she was—what a nice person or some such drivel. Way down, deep inside, she felt there was someone else. There simply had to be. The two of them had gotten along too well together for him to simply break up without an adequate reason, hurting her and just walking away.

Hurting? Was she hurting? She felt numb. Her emotions, once under control, had sufficiently anesthetized her, enabling her to look at the problem from a detached viewpoint.

Then the tears came again—almost violently. She felt as if she might cleanse her soul if she cried long enough. Sobs, deeper than any she had ever experienced, unmercifully racked her, bringing loud gasps of air bursting from her throat. Struggling to get off the bed, she continued sobbing, crying as if there would be no sunrise today. Doomsday had just arrived. The judgment would begin promptly at nine and she would have to make an accounting of her life. No time to make amends or changes or smooth things out between her and anyone she might have offended at one time or another in her life. All her sins, all her wrongdoings, all her transgressions would be laid out for the whole world to see.

She stumbled into the bathroom and turned on the faucet. The splashing in the basin sounded too loud, too exaggerated. Cupping her hands, she caught some of the cold water and splashed her face.

What was wrong with her? She was thinking like a mad woman. The end of the world? Doomsday? Just how devastated was she that Myles had elected to call it quits? She must have deeper feelings for him than she had ever imagined. Her instinctive reflex to sob eased, and she looked up in the mirror at the wet face, puffy eyes and flushed cheeks.

"What a disaster," she mumbled. For the first time since she had awakened, she felt almost normal. The effect of Myles' announcement was still fresh, but the initial shock of its impact on her had waned somewhat—enough for her to look at the situation a bit more objectively. She would win him back no matter what the price might be.

Turning out the bathroom light, she returned to her bedroom. It seemed empty without him. He should be lying on his back, the gentle snore she had grown used to rippling through the quiet. But the quiet itself now was the only sound she heard.

Moving toward the living room door, she stopped for a second. She needed her rest. What about her work at Overstreet's art supply store? Would her boss, Phil Overstreet, be angry if she called in sick? If she did go into work, she'd collapse from lack of sleep by nine thirty—ten, tops. She'd fib to Phil and tell him she had a bug of some sort and wouldn't be any good in the store today. He'd have to buy it. It was all she could think of at the moment. She turned on the table lamp next to the couch and went to the stereo. Spinning the dial, she found a station and turned the volume as low as she could without completely losing the signal. No need to tell her neighbors that she couldn't sleep. Bruce Springsteen belted out "Pink Cadillac" in a total whisper that seemed foreign and unfamiliar to his style of singing. A cynical smile crossed Nicole's lips.

What would her first step be in winning back Myles? What would someone else do in a case like this? Go talk to her mother? Nicole had no mother. Nancy Kilton had died with her husband in a plane crash in Canada when Nicole was eighteen years old, halfway through her senior year in high school. She really had no one to whom she could turn. Before, she might have confided in Myles, but now he was the cause of her unrest.

She lay her head back on the couch, closing her eyes. What should her first move be? She yawned. It would have to be right, absolutely correct, if she were to win Myles back.

She stifled another yawn. Somehow Bruce Springsteen had changed into Pat Benatar and she wondered when he had added voice impressions to his repertoire as sleep again overtook her and she settled into its comforting arms.

2

Thursday, September 4, 1986 5:55 A.M.

The grayness, peculiar to that half-light,
half-dark of predawn, filled the bedroom and
Myles shifted from one spot to another, searching for a cool place on the sheets. Stretching
his muscular frame, he yawned. His wiggling
brought a sigh from Eunice Brooks, in whose
bed he lay. He froze to keep from awakening
her. Right now, he didn't want to talk with
anyone—especially Eunice.

After leaving Nicole's apartment, he had
come to Eunice. Eunice. She was the chief
reason he had sought to call an end—at least a
temporary end—to his involvement with
Nicole. Now, after pondering the question over
and over in his mind during the night, he still
wasn't certain he had done the right thing. It
had been difficult for him to simply walk out
on Nicole that way. He knew that she had pro-

bably spent the night crying, but she'd get over it. People usually got over their anxieties —no matter what they might say at the time. Still, he was concerned. Could she take the emotional beating? Would she be all right?

Nicole and he had not had any fixed arrangement and for that he had been thankful. It had made it easier—easier on him, easier on his conscience. But what about Nicole? How would she fare? She was probably devastated. The only reason he felt any guilt at all was the fact that he truly liked her. Or was it love? No, he didn't love her. Of that, he felt almost one hundred percent sure. He could not or would not allow himself to love her. Not now. Maybe one day. There had been many times when he found himself daydreaming about the two of them being married—with a mortgage, with children, with all the problems that go hand in hand with marriage.

When Eunice Brooks had come on to him, he quickly had evaluated his own circumstances. If he had turned his back on Eunice, he might have gone through life wondering if he had made a mistake. Then, too, how many more women like Eunice would he encounter in the future? Without satisfying his animal instincts at least once before settling down, he would have no way to guarantee that he would be able to control them the rest of the time. Did that make sense? At the time, he thought it to be absolutely perfect and logical reasoning.

Now, in the quiet and grayness of dawn, he

wondered. He had hurt Nicole. Of that he was positive. But, he had to think of himself, too. If he didn't, he might wind up hurting Nicole or someone like her in the future even more.

When Eunice snorted softly in her sleep, Myles turned to face her. Eunice was a beautiful woman. A perfect body. Lovely features. Long flowing, strawberry blond hair —just a shade or two lighter than Nicole's. Physically, the two women were similar but Eunice's tastes in bed games varied much more than did Nicole's. If for no other reason, Myles convinced himself that he should be thankful to Eunice for the sexual experience he found in her. Perhaps he might draw on what she had shown him, sometime in the future.

Beyond her sensual abilities, Eunice would have lost in any honest comparison between the two women. Where Nicole could carry on an intelligent conversation about a variety of subjects, Eunice felt pressed for a topic once the weather, television soap operas and the current Stephen King best seller had been exhausted. Eunice worked as a secretary for a department store manager and seemed content with her lot in life. On the other hand, Nicole was career oriented and not merely in a selfish way. She truly believed she could help people and wanted to obtain her Masters in psychology before feeling ready to really face the work-a-day world. Her job in the art store was only in passing, and Myles knew one day she would attain every goal she had set for herself. A serious thought struck him. Would she also gain her goal of winning him back as she had promised?

Myles pictured Nicole in his mind, then looked at Eunice lying next to him. She was beautiful but it was a surface beauty. Standing next to Nicole, Eunice might very easily win a beauty comparison, but it would be Nicole who would be the winner when personality was allowed to shine through.

Had he done the right thing? Time would tell. But how much time should he allow? He wondered if Nicole would wait until he had his fill of Eunice.

Myles shook his head in a disparaging way. He knew he had made a mistake but it was a mistake that he would soon rectify and then . . . He'd have to wait to find what the future would hold for Nicole and him.

"Are you awake, lover-boy?" Eunice said, her throaty whisper full of desire.

"Uh-huh!" He rolled on his side to face her.

"I'm glad," she said, snaking one finger along his chest, down his belly to toy at the root of his manhood. His penis jumped as if it had a mind and life of its own.

Thursday, September 4, 1986 9:07 A.M.

When she opened her eyes, Nicole jerked awake with a start. Where was she? What time was it? Bright sunlight flooded her living room. How and when had she come into this part of her apartment? Why wasn't she in bed?

The time question banged at her mind again. What *was* the time? It seemed too bright to be seven o'clock, her usual rising time. Off in the sleep-filled distance of her mind, she could hear a man's voice giving a monologue. *What the hell was that?* Then she saw the red light on her stereo tuner. She had turned on the radio last night. She remembered thinking about Bruce Springsteen imitating someone and smiled at the silliness of her thoughts. She stood, stretching away the aches of having slept in an upright position on the couch, and turned up the volume.

"And that's the nine o'clock news. Now, at eight minutes past the hour here's a golden oldie. Elvis Presley singing 'Love Me Tender.'"

She turned off the set. *Nine oh eight?* She was late for work. Why hadn't she. . . .

Myles! The whole night came back to her in a crashing swirl. Why had he done what he'd done?

She sat down heavily on the couch. Myles had denied it, but it had to have been another woman. But hadn't she vowed she'd get him back? The words of her oath-like statements replayed in her head like a tape recording. *"One day, we'll be together. It's no threat. I won't give up."* But what could she do? There had to be a way. But right now, she had no idea as to what that way might be.

She had to get her priorities in line. The first

thing she had to do was call Phil. Phil Overstreet was not the type to gripe if an employee was ill, but what bothered her was calling in late. The art store opened at nine. Usually, the first customers were students who would be on the way to their art class, stopping by to get just enough supplies to last them through whatever they might be studying.

Fumbling for the telephone, she dialed the number and, with the long cord trailed out behind her, walked into the bedroom. Phil's voice seemed normal when he answered.

"Overstreet's Art Store."

"Phil? This is Nicole. I'm sorry for calling in late but I had an awful night."

"Awful?"

"Horrible. I didn't get to sleep until around four. I vomited. And I . . ."

"Say no more, Nicole. I understand. You wouldn't be worth anything to me as an employee and I sure as hell don't want to catch whatever it is that you've got. Take care of yourself and come in when you're able. All right?"

"Thanks, Phil. I really appreciate it."

She hung up, a forlorn smile trying to curve her lips. If Phil knew the real reason, he'd probably be angry for a few minutes and then be over it. She hadn't lied. That part was important to her. She placed a high priority on her personal integrity and she would have felt guilty if she had lied to Phil.

After putting on a pot of coffee, she went to

the bathroom. Once she was in the shower, she felt more secure in her thinking. It felt as if she were in a wet, little world all her own. She was the boss, the queen, the ruler of it. What she said was law. The one thing she found impossible to leave outside, though, was her sense of confusion about Myles.

The water beat upon her body, smashing into her large breasts, cascading over her erect nipples, down her flat stomach to the triangle of hair, where it wended its way through until rivulets snaked down both legs to the floor of the shower stall. It felt good, cleansing, purifying. She reflected on the times Myles had kissed her breasts and mouthed her nipples. The water made her remember the exquisite thrill his lips had brought her. She found herself wishing that somehow, the water could wipe away the shock of the previous night. If that could happen, Myles would be in her bed when she stepped out to towel off her body.

In time, as the water continued battering at her, she found it difficult to recall Myles' face. How tall was he? What did he look like? How could she love him if she couldn't even remember what he looked like? Still, she remembered having read someplace that the word "love," as it applied to man/woman relationships, was the most difficult thing to define. And maybe that was the reason she was becoming confused. She was trying to define the indefinable.

She turned off the shower, and stepping out, grabbed the huge towel, wrapping it about herself. Maybe all of it had been a bad dream and Myles would really be in bed. Fearfully peeking around the corner of the door, she peered into the bedroom. No one was there.

Later that day.

For what seemed the thousandth time, she muttered to herself, "It's not fair. He shouldn't treat me like this. Not after all I've done for him!" But now, she was used to it. Words of reasoning placated her for a millisecond before reality fell back into place. Of course, the way he had gone about it had not been fair. He should *NOT* have treated her this way. And, yes, she had done a lot for him. Granted, he had done just as much for her but that wasn't the issue.

She knew she had tried to be all things to Myles. It was one thing she had learned from her mother before her death. *"Be compatible. Be flexible in your thinking. Listen to everyone else's opinion—most especially that of the man in your life. You'll find that people will be more willing to listen to you, if you listen to them."*

The one thing she had to acknowledge was the fact that her mother and father had enjoyed a rich, rewarding and fulfilling life together. Her father, as a Sergeant Major in the United States Army, had brought a great degree of discipline into his home, and she had experienced that strict behavior peculiar to one of his rank. But he had tempered it with love, kindness and understanding.

What would her father have done if he hadn't died on a mountainside in Canada? He had been protective of her as a child, but what would his reaction have been to a man who had rejected his adult daughter? She doubted if he would have resorted to any kind of violence, not that he was incapable of punching another man out. Instead, he would have talked with her, reasoning out that something positive was hidden within all the hurt pouring down on her head.

Suddenly, Nicole grew aware of her surroundings. She was sitting on a bench in a small park downtown with the September sun, bright and warm, flooding over her. She recalled having left her apartment about eleven o'clock and going for a walk. Where had she gone? Had she been contemplating her problems so intensely that she had walked into a park and sat down on a bench without being aware of it? Maybe *she* needed help.

She leaned against the green backrest. The one thing she had going for her was the fact she knew her strengths and weaknesses, though her worst fault was indecisiveness. Her greatest strength was her tenacity to hang in when the going got tough—once she had reached a decision. Now, she had to make that strength pay off. She would get Myles back even if it meant . . .

She winced, tears streaming down her face. What was she about to think? Even if it meant *—murder?—selling her soul?—stopping at nothing?* What did *nothing* entail? How about selling her soul? Did she even have one? She had been in and out of so many schools, public, private and parochial, that she found herself hardly accepting those tenets taught by the different religious institutions. While she was growing up, the sermons and homilies she had heard in different churches had not made much sense to her. What the hell was a *soul*?

Murder? No, that was one act she knew she certainly was incapable of performing.

Right now, she did not have any idea as to how to go about winning Myles back. But she *would* have him back or know the reason why.

A couple, college students, stopped in her line of vision, and she looked away when they kissed. *They* were together. *They* had each other. Who did she have? No one! Just unremitting loneliness. The mere idea of loneliness overwhelmed her. That was the one thing she felt she could not bear. *Loneliness.* She remembered when her parents had died and the awful sense of isolation that had engulfed her then. It had been the school psychologist who had brought Nicole to face reality and the eventual conclusion that she might be able to help people who had problems that were too much for any one person to handle by themselves. But that awful sense of loneliness had taught her never to be caught alone in any situation. The people at the double funeral had tried to be helpful, but she had managed to read a double meaning into everything that had been said to her. They were only trying to be nice to her and comfort her in her hour of need, but she had sensed only the awful aloneness. Her parents—her world—had died when she was only eighteen.

To ensure her own popularity at school once she had returned to classes, she had been easily available for dates with anyone who asked. Because she wasn't trying to prove something, she had not fallen into every bed that had been offered to her. The thing she needed more than anything else had been companionship. She had needed it then. She needed it now.

Where had the buildings come from? Shaking her head, Nicole looked about. *She was downtown. In the mall—downtown. Across from the building where Myles worked.*

She couldn't believe this. She was going mad. How could she walk from that park to here and not be aware of it? Was she that wrapped up in her thoughts? Or was the havoc of what Myles had wrought last night stringing her out so completely that she didn't know what she was doing?

Rooted to the spot, she played for an instant with the idea of going up to Myles' office on the top floor of the building and telling him what she thought of him. But she knew she couldn't. She loved him, truly loved him, and there was no way she could run the risk of hurting him. There was simply no way she could treat him in the same manner he had treated her.

Myles formed in her vision and she smiled. She panicked when she realized it really *was* Myles and not her imagination. He was coming out of the main entrance of the office building with another man—Scott McReady, the sports announcer at the TV station. They were probably going to lunch. She looked at her watch. Two o'clock. A late lunch?

She stepped behind a hot dog vendor's cart, ducking out of sight, pretending to have lost something. Keeping her eye on Myles and his friend, she stood when they rounded the corner and were gone from sight.

"D'you find it?" a voice said.

"What?" she mumbled, perplexed that someone was talking to her.

"D'you find whatever it was you dropped?" the vendor asked.

"Huh? Oh, sure. Sure. Thanks." She turned, hurrying away. Just what would a competent psychologist or psychiatrist have to say about her single-mindedness? She smiled inwardly. They'd think she was tenacious to the point of being mentally ill—but she knew better. She knew if she concentrated and worked at something—anything—long enough, she'd be able to master it. And this situation with Myles was certainly no different from anything else that had eluded her in the past.

She remembered the old alarm clock her

mother had given her to play with when she
was about ten or eleven. She had managed to
take it apart and, after much experimenting,
made the alarm work again. Her parents had
been amazed, her father decrying the fact that
his one and only daughter would more than
likely grow up to be a chief mechanic in some
factory. Then, too, there had been the time in
high school when she was a senior and a
transfer student. She had tried out for the
school play, knowing full well that if she got a
part, it would be a minor one at best. Still, she
had made up her mind to win the lead role, and
with one of the best acting jobs the drama
coach had said she'd ever seen, Nicole had
come through. The girl who had been slated for
the lead had been furious, but Nicole didn't
care about that. She had hung in there and won
and that was the most important part of anything. Winning. Succeeding. Getting what she
wanted. And the thing she wanted more than
anything else in life right now was Myles.

What were books doing in front of her? She
looked to the right, to the left, directly in front
of her. Books were everywhere. Then she
realized she was staring through the window of
a book shop—a secondhand book shop. She had
been there before with Myles. Books of every
description seemed to be lined up on the
shelves and laid out on the tables. Inside, she
could see a handful of people perusing while
the owner, a wizened old lady, sat behind a
table peering over her pince-nez glasses, keep-

ing an eye on any indigent who might try to
convert her shop into a public lending library.

For no reason that she could think of, Nicole
found herself entering the musty shop. It had
been at least six months since she had been in
there, and she wondered how quickly the merchandise turned over. On the table nearest the
door, various best sellers of recent vintage,
bright book jackets still intact for the most
part, sat upright, attractively displayed.
Nicole walked by them. Along one wall, she
found hardcover romance stories, but romance
—the literary type—was not appealing to her
mental palate. She wanted the real thing, that
which she had lost.

She found history books, then books concerning hobbies, woodworking, hunting,
fishing, collecting, economics, geography and
social studies.

Then, she saw it. A little red antique book
nestled in among bigger ones, whose titles had
been worn smooth over the years. But the red
book, its gold lettering faded but still readable,
caught her attention. Reaching out with a tentative finger, she pulled it from its place and
held it up for examination. The title: *A Worthwhile Examination of Fpellf and Confultation
Manual for Demoniftf.*

Just what she needed, she thought, flipping
through the stiff, yellowed pages. She stopped
at one page to read an incantation for ensuring
the love of a good woman.

If there was one concerning the reclamation

of a wandering lover, she'd buy it. That she found on the next page—how to regain the love of a lost mate. Suppressing a grin, Nicole slapped the book shut and walked to the front. She laid it on the table in front of the woman and said, "How much?"

Without looking up from her book, other than to catch a glimpse of the article to be purchased, the old lady said, "Four dollars, sixty-nine cents plus tax."

"I'll take it," Nicole said softly, wondering how the old woman knew such an odd amount without looking at anything other than the book cover itself.

She paid the money and accepted the bag containing the book. Walking to the door, she smiled. She must really be desperate to even consider such a thing. But then, she hadn't really considered it. She had merely bought it on a whim, when she saw that there was indeed an incantation for regaining lost love.

The door closed behind her, and as she started for home, she thought the paper bag holding the book gave a little jump.

3

Thursday, September 4, 1986 3:50 P.M.

Nicole ignored the other pedestrians on their
way to or from work or shopping or home. She
too wanted to get home—to be by herself, to
commune with herself and no one else. The
events of the previous night and her gyrating
emotions had worked a peculiar effect on her,
and she wanted to get away from people as
much as possible. She had to sort out her
thoughts, make her plans, and prepare to ex-
ecute them.

The sea of people coming toward her parted,
and one face in particular, framed with frizzy
blond hair and a green beret perched at a cocky
angle on one side of the head, arrested her
attention. As the woman neared her, the
featureless face assumed eyes, a nose and a
mouth—and Nicole suddenly felt trapped.
Stacey Ford. Perhaps, if she kept her head

45

down or turned away, Stacey wouldn't see her. She doubted if she could handle Stacey at the moment.

While in college, Nicole had had no problem dealing with her. Stacey had decided that since her freshman year represented the first time she was completely on her own, she wanted to live life to the very fullest—experiencing everything as much as possible. By year's end, she had burned herself out. Lighting up at every opportunity, she had added cocaine to her repertoire of fun things along with beer and whiskey. The men in her life came and went, and Nicole remembered teasing her about putting a revolving door in her dorm room.

Shortly before the end of their second semester as freshmen, Stacey had disappeared and no one had seen her for the next four years. When she came back into Nicole's life, Stacey told of her experiences with a Far Eastern religious group, the Sun Children, and how she had found their tenets to be just what she was looking for at the time, or so she thought. By the end of six months, she had been completely disillusioned and ready to leave, but they had held her a virtual prisoner. It had only been through the efforts of her parents, a private detective and a Reverend Eddie John Stangood, that she had been spirited away and eventually brainwashed back to some semblance of normalcy.

Nicole remembered her own personal reaction when Stacey told her of Reverend

Eddie John—how good a man he was, how
close he was to the real Jesus, how the evil in
the world soon would be overcome and men
like the Reverend Eddie John would ascend to
a position of power in a righteous world and
govern everything in the name of Jesus. Nicole
had shuddered at the almost frenzied manner
in which Stacey had spoken. She recalled
having thought that perhaps Stacey had
jumped from the frying pan right into the fire
of another charlatan's salvation. But then,
Stacey was not the most intelligent person to
come into Nicole's life and she hoped now that
Stacey would not see her. All she wanted to do
was get home.

"Nicole!" Stacey's voice cut through
Nicole's revery.

"Hi, Stacey," Nicole managed weakly. If she
were lucky, it would not go much beyond the
stage of greeting one another.

"What's the matter, hon?" Stacey cocked
her head as if to get a better, more intimate
look at Nicole.

Nicole felt like recoiling but fought the urge
when Stacey put a damp, cold hand on hers.
"What do you mean?" Nicole asked as indif-
ferently as possible.

"You look like you haven't a friend in the
world. Let me tell you about Jesus!"

"Golly, Stacey, I don't have time. Besides,
there's really nothing wrong."

"I don't believe you. You're hiding something. I just know you are. When one gets as

close to the Saviour as I have, one picks up on many nuances and hints that most others miss."

Nicole swallowed her anger. The pomposity of such a viewpoint made her blood boil. "Hey, Stacey, would I lie to you?" she asked, shrugging and holding her one free hand out, palm up.

Stacey narrowed her blue eyes until she was peering at Nicole through slits. "Yes. Yes, I think you would. Just to keep from hearing about Jesus. Why don't you wake up and see Him as the Light, like I have? If you knew how happy I am, you wouldn't . . ."

"Stacey, listen to me," Nicole said sharply. "I don't want to hear about Jesus right now. Not today. Not tomorrow. Maybe never. Do you understand?"

As if someone had struck her across her face, Stacey stared for a full minute at Nicole. Then she said in a tiny voice, "I know you don't mean that. I'll be patient. You'll want to hear about Him before long. Jesus has told me to be patient with people like you. In time everyone will come around to him."

Nicole felt an unfamiliar pang of regret sweeping through her. She had purposely hurt Stacey and that was not at all like her. She believed in God and Jesus to a certain extent, perhaps not to the enthusiastic extremes that Stacey and the followers of evangelists like Reverend Eddie John did. It simply was not like her to be spiteful to anyone—especially over a person's beliefs in religion.

"I . . . I'm sorry, Stacey," Nicole managed. "I didn't mean that. I'm upset over something, and I shouldn't be talking to anyone for fear of lashing out like I just did to you."

"I knew it," Stacey chirped, a benevolent expression lighting her face along with the look of having just been proven right. "Jesus told me that something was bothering you. What is it?"

"I . . . I'd just as soon not say. It's something that I can work out by myself. Don't worry about it. All right?"

"I think you should meet Reverend Eddie John. I really do. Jesus and I . . ."

"Maybe sometime, but not right now," Nicole said, breaking in. The last thing she needed was a bible-thumping, bellowing preacher like the Reverend Eddie John Stangood harping at her. She'd seen him on one of the local television stations, threatening the nonbelievers with hell's fire and damnation. Anyone not in complete agreement with his interpretation of the bible was a nonbeliever in the Reverend Eddie John's eyes, and he had gone so far as to scream at the top of his voice that the pope, every minister, every priest and every evangelist in the world would go straight to hell unless they swore allegiance to Jesus, Reverend Eddie John Stangood and the Stangood Foundation of Goodwill.

Nicole pulled away from Stacey's hand that still held hers. "I really must go, Stacey. I'll see you around sometime. 'Bye."

"I'll pray for you, Nicole," she said loudly as Nicole moved away from her. The people passing by on either side ignored the wide-eyed blonde waving at the woman half-running, half-walking away.

Friday, September 5, 1986 to Friday,
September 19, 1986

During the next two weeks, Nicole didn't think about the book she had purchased on a whim but found herself luxuriating in self-pity, mindless of almost everything around her. Other than going to work, where she waited on customers more like an automaton than a warm-blooded human being, she spent most of her time at home, sipping white wine and staring at her television set whether it was on or not. She faithfully watched the news programs, her eyes welling up with tears whenever Myles appeared on the TV screen.

As the days grew into weeks, a black uneveness began filling her world, managing to keep her daily existence out of balance. While walking home, she would make resolutions to clean her apartment, or to work on a piece of needlepoint she had started weeks before, or do her nails, or maybe wash her hair. The promises to herself were endless until she opened the door to her other world. Then, she elected to spend another evening doing nothing.

Her work had not suffered much, and Phil had even promised a raise in the middle of September. Then, one Friday, she hurried toward her apartment, intent on spending another solitary weekend without interruption. She could not imagine herself being sociable with anyone, opting instead to seal herself off. Once inside her domain, she relaxed, reveling in the silence.

She downed more wine than usual before eating half a sandwich and hurrying to turn on the TV set at eleven when she could spend time with Myles' electronic image. The wine bottle, almost empty, leaned against the couch, and her eyes, heavy with fatigue and the effects of the Chablis, drooped until they closed in sleep.

Images as black as the inside of a darkened theater flitted through her sleeping mind, assuming an almost recognizable shape only to wither and merge into another. She awoke with a start. Befuddled, she tried to put together what time it was and why the TV set was displaying an old Humphrey Bogart movie. The first thing she resolved was the time. Eleven forty-nine. She had missed the news. Oh, God! She had missed the news and Myles. Now she wouldn't be able to see him until Monday evening when he returned to the news cast.

She stood, chastising herself over and over. Nothing was fair anymore. Myles certainly wasn't fair. And she wasn't being fair to herself either by falling asleep. She shouldn't have had so much wine. She'd have to cut down on it.

Rubbing her eyes, the dim light seemed brighter than usual and something caught her attention. Something red. Something red with pale gold markings on it. *The book!* The antique book she had bought impulsively several weeks before was sitting on the shelf behind the TV set, where she had thrust it when she had arrived home after her confrontation with Stacey Ford. Nicole had not thought of it once since then, but now it seemed to beckon to her.

Reaching over the set, she pulled it from its resting place, studying it for a long minute before lifting the cover. When she did, it fell open to the place where she had read the incantation for reclaiming a lost love or gaining a man's love. It seemed as though that had happened eons ago, but when she concentrated, she realized that only a mere two weeks had passed.

Moving back to the couch, she sat down, leaning toward the lamp. "I am possessed by burning love for this man," she read half aloud. "This love for *N* comes to me from Apsaras, who is ever victorious in everything. Let this man, *N*, yearn for me, desire me, let *N*'s desire burn for me. Let this love come forth from the spirit of the love-god and enter him.

"By the power and laws of Varuna, I invoke the burning force of love for me in *N*. This desire, the potent love-spirit created by the love-god which is present in everything, waiting to be recognized, I invoke the use thereof to secure *N*'s love for me.

"I invoke the magetnized waters of the love-force. Let *N* desire me as nothing has been desired before. I love him. I want him. He in turn must love me. He in turn must want me. And it is his love for me, by Varuna's Laws, that I cause to burn. *N*, thou wilt love me, with a burning desire.

"Oh, Maruts, let him become filled with love for me. Oh, Spirit of the Air, fill him with love for me. Oh, Agni, let him burn with love for me as I burn for him."

Nicole looked up not quite knowing what she might see. Nothing. A sly grin broke on her mouth. Did she think Myles would magically appear, burning with lust and love for her? She laughed aloud at her own foolishness.

How strange though that the incantation mirrored so many of her own burning feelings for Myles. She held the book up and examined it. It held a certain fascination now that she had rediscovered it on the shelf. The incantation seemed to ring in her head. Its words were her words. The meaning of it was her meaning —her purpose. Opening it, she thumbed through, stopping at a page displaying crude sketches of two stars. The caption below the drawings explained the difference in the two objects:

"Stars with five points are traditionally weapons of power in the practice of magic. The pentagram with one point projecting upward can be imagined as a man's body with arms and legs thrust out. When the point is upward, the symbol is one of dominance of the divine spirit (the upward pointing one) over matter (the other four points). An inverted pentagram, with two points extending upward, symbolizes the horns of the goat while the downward point is the face of the goat and the other two the animal's ears. The inverted pentagram is a sign of the devil and care should be practiced whenever drawing the pentagram to ensure that the upward point is drawn first. Otherwise the symbol of good becomes the symbol of evil, and demons with power unimaginable can be conjured up."

Nicole flipped the pages until the back cover closed with a soft smack against the last page. Did people really believe in such stuff? Believe enough to practice such nonsense? She nodded. Ever since Myles had left, she had been wondering how she could get him back. Nothing had occurred to her. Nothing until now. She looked at the small book resting in her lap and slowly reopened it.

For the next two hours, Nicole read the thin volume. It seemed to her that it was a calculated risk to go with the spirits of good since they may or may not grant the practitioner's wish or desire. The darker side, on the other hand, seemed more ready and willing to listen and to help. What would happen if she did try one of the spells? It was only so much foolishness. Wasn't it? But it was something to do. Maybe the powers of right would see how desperate she really was to have Myles back and would take pity on her and see to it that he did return.

She reread one pact that had caught her attention. It seemed safe enough since it invoked God, his Son and the Holy Spirit to help bring the demon or Lucifer, the fallen angel, to the practitioner in case the demon was reluctant. There was no mention of the demons helping God or the angels or whoever was conjured up in the "good" incantations.

Pursing her lips, Niclole nodded. It seemed she would have the elements of both sides working for her if she followed the treatise's directions and drew an inverted pentagram and summoned God to force Lucifer to do her bidding.

How would she make a pentagram? Where should she make it? She looked at the beige carpeting in the living room. That room was the largest in her apartment. It would have to be there, but how could she make a symbol? Her face brightening, she hurried to her bedroom, returning with a box of body powder. She began trailing a thin line of the white, perfumed dust, making a circle in the middle of the room after moving the coffee table to one side.

When the line closed on itself, she began tracing the outline of the inverted pentagram, starting with the horns of the goat. When it was finished, she picked up the book again and studied the words that were to be written in the points of the star and around the circumference of the circle. When they were finished, she drew another circle and enclosed the words, creating a border. Rummaging about the apartment, she found four candles and placed them at the proper locations.

After lighting the wicks, and with the book in hand, she stepped inside the double circle, turning to the page with the pact written on it. "Pact with Emperor Lucifer" was written across the middle of the page and something above it caught her attention. More instructions:

"To achieve the best magic possible, the practitioner should perform this and all rites in the nude."

Nicole stepped out of the circle, careful not to smudge the powder lines. Quickly undressing, she re-entered the circle, holding the book. She strained her eyes to read the small print in the flickering candle light.

"O Emperor Lucifer," she began in a soft whisper, "Chief of all the spirits which rebelled, I beg Thee to favor me in this conjuration, which I am about to perform to Thee and

Thy Ministers. O Prince Beelzebub, I adjure thee to protect me in this work. O Earl Astorath, favor me, and permit me tonight to obtain the appearance of the Great One, Lucifer, in human shape and without any evil effluvium. And that he may allow me, in return for the pact which I will make with him, to achieve the desire I have and the wish I make in this circle."

She repeated the incantation she had read earlier, inserting Myles' name at the appropriate places. When she finished, she felt a wave of relief wash over her. It might work. It just might work.

"O, Great Lucifer," she continued, her voice shaking just a bit, "I beg Thee to leave Thy throne, wherever it may be, and come to this place to speak with me. I have great need of Thy counsel. If Thou doest not do this, I will constrain Thee to appear, by the force of the Great Living God, His Son and His Spirit. Do my bidding at once, or Thou shalt be tormented forever by the force of the words of Power and the Great Wisdom of Solomon, which he used to compel revolted spirits to obey him and accept his contract.

"Appear, then, immediately, or I shall torture Thee with the force of these Words of Power from Solomon's Key!

"Aglon. Tetragram. Vaycheon. Stimulamatron. Exphares. Olyaram. Retragrammaton. Irion. Existion. Esytion. Eryona. Onera. Orasym. Mozm. Messias. Soter. Emanuel.

Sabaoth. Adonay. Te adoro. Et te invoco. Amen."

Nicole stopped for an instant, glancing about the room, her eyes widening. Nothing. Nothing had happened. But then, she wasn't finished.

"I conjure Thee, O Spirit. I summon Thee, O Lucifer, to appear within a minute by the power of the Great Adonai, by Elohim, by Ariel, Johavam, Agla, Membrot, Varvis, Pithona, Magots, Silphae, Rabost, Salamandrae, Tabost, Gnomus, Terrae, Coelis, Godens, Aqua, Gingua, Janua, Etituamus, Zariatnotmik.

"Palas aron azinomas. Bagahi Iaca Bacabe.

"Eheieh. Iod. Tetragrammaton Elohim. El. Elohim Gibor. Eloah Va-Daath. El Adonai Tzabaoth. Elohim Tzabaoth. Shaddai."

She stopped.

What was that? That noise? That pounding? She held her breath. The apartment was quiet. No sound. Nothing at all.

But what was that pounding?

She could distinctly hear it. When she released her breath, she controlled the urge to laugh. It was the sound of her own pulse in her temples. Her own blood, crashing through her veins, reverberated in a rhythmic cadence that sounded not unlike a pounding surf on some desolate shore.

She waited. It was now that the book indicated that the summoned one should appear. She continued waiting. Where was he? Had she done something incorrectly in performing the rite?

Glancing at the book, she saw that one more sentence remained after the point where the demon should have appeared. She waited four long breaths before raising the book enough to allow her to finish the rite.

"I promise Thee, O great and mighty Lucifer, to reward Thee in whatever way Thou see fit, if my request for the love of Myles Lawrence is granted and given unto me this night."

The clock on the shelf above the TV set struck three times. She waited.

Nothing.

It was all foolishness. It had to be. Why had she done it? She wondered about her own mental stability. Was the breakup with Myles affecting her to the point that she would try almost anything to win him back? Even black magic? Or making a pact with hell? She stepped out of the circle, kicking at the lines, spreading the dusty powder around before blowing out the candles.

After taking her discarded clothing to her bedroom, she slipped into a robe and brought a small vacuum cleaner to the living room. In seconds, the quiet machine sucked up the telltale body powder, and all signs of her bizarre ritual were gone. At least it was Friday and she wouldn't have to go to work the next day. What time? Friday? The small chiming clock indicated three ten. It was actually Saturday and she could sleep until she awoke.

She picked up the book that had fascinated her for the last several hours and chuckled. Returning it to the shelf, she made one last, quick visual check of the living room and turned out the light.

Seconds later, she collapsed on the bed, the sheet half-covering her nakedness. Her breasts rose and fell in an even rhythm. Sound asleep, she failed to notice the drop in the room temperature and little jets of steam puffed from her nostrils. The only sound in the room was her steady, even breathing—and the sound of scratching in the ceiling over her bed.

PART TWO

The Gifts

Tuesday, September 23, 1986
to
Friday, November 7, 1986

4

Tuesday, September 23, 1986 10:33 A.M.

Nicole stared through the plate glass window at the people hurrying past the art store. Aware of the fact that she had been preoccupied most of the time while at work, she accepted her mental wanderings as an opiate for her troubled mind. Myles had left several weeks before, and ever since, she had found a foreign sense of melancholy invading her waking moments more and more as each day passed.

Sighing heavily, she turned away, aware that she had to do something, and do something soon, or she'd wither up and simply blow away with the next breeze. She felt lonely—as if she were the last human on earth. All those bodies walking by the shop were figments of her imagination—memories of when she had been a live, contributing member of society. But people simply did not count for anything anymore. The only person she had communicated with to any degree over the last few weeks had been Phil Overstreet. And most of those conversations had been about business and buying additional stock and supplies. Nothing related to her as a person, as a human being, as a wounded entity.

Someplace, far off in the distance, she heard a bell ring and felt a wash of cool September air flow over her. Snapping out of her revery, she focused her attention on the front of the store to see a man entering. A customer. She'd have to wait on him since Phil had left to go for coffee.

"May I help you, sir?" she asked absently, approaching him.

"I need some wide-tipped felt markers," he said.

She looked up to find him studying her. Somehow, he looked familiar.

"Didn't you attend college here?" he asked.

She nodded. "I graduated in '84."

"So did I," he said, snapping his fingers. "Nicole Kilton? Right?"

Scrutinizing her customer, Nicole seemed to place him, but only as a face in a classroom somewhere in her past. Had he been one of her teachers? He appeared too young. "I'm sorry," she said lamely. "You have me at a disadvantage."

The man, not much taller than she, wore glasses that seemed to dominate his face, emphasizing his narrowly set eyes. She looked away while he stared at her, his face imprinted on her memory. If she had attended class with him, she had made no conscious or unconscious effort to remember him. He reminded her of a little animal, one that might drop to all fours and scurry away from her at any moment.

"Rob Lanstrom." He smiled kindly. "Psychology one and two. You sat in front of me."

She forced a smile, faking a look of recognition. "Of course. Doctor Hammerand's classes. That brings back a lot of memories."

"What are you doing, working here?" he asked, gesturing around the art shop. "Or do you own it?"

"Hardly," she said, relaxing just a bit. What did one say next? She felt at a loss when it came to carrying on a conversation. Had it been that long?

"Didn't you major in psych?" He studied her in an intense way that made Nicole feel not unlike a laboratory specimen being examined under a microscope.

"As a matter of fact, I did. How come you remember so much about me?"

He smiled shyly. "Back then, I had a crush on you like you wouldn't believe. I really did."

Nicole smiled graciously. "Out of curiosity, why didn't you ever speak to me? If you did, I'm sorry, but I don't remember."

"Are you kidding?" he said, laughing. "I would have been scared to death."

Nicole snickered. "What brought about the big change? How come you can talk about it now?''

"I guess that's what married life does to a person.''

Nicole nodded. "How long have you been married, Rob?'' It seemed to Nicole as though everyone except her had someone—even this mousy guy.

"Six months now. But tell me, Nicole, what are you doing working in here? This doesn't seem conducive to exploiting a college education.''

She looked away. "I'm saving money so I can go back to school and get my Masters in psychology. I'd like to be an assistant to a psychiatrist.''

"How long before you go back to school?''

Suddenly, Nicole wondered about this man confronting her. Why was he so nosy? Why had he remembered her out of all the people who had been in his classes? What business was it of his to know about her plans? The next thing he might suggest a liaison of some sort to satisfy his suppressed longing from college. She shook her head. If he was married for only six months, he probably wouldn't try something like that.

She shrugged. "At this point, I don't really know. Why?''

"Because I might be able to help you,'' he said, pausing dramatically for effect.

"I . . . I don't understand.''

"I'm employed at the Cascade Psychiatric Clinic. I'm assistant to the chief psychologist and have several other assistants more or less under my direction. At any rate, have you ever done any publicity or public relations work?"

Nicole shook her head. "Not really, why?"

"If you can stand Rose Tunic, you could probably qualify. They're looking for someone to train on the job. It's a nonexistant position right now because there hasn't been anyone doing the work. But things being what they are, the board of directors wants to acquire a higher profile for the clinic and has decided to hire someone for P.R. work."

"Who's this Rose Tunic?" she asked tentatively. The way he had said her name sounded almost ominous, as though he might be warning her of something.

"Oh, Rose is an old bitch who thinks she's running the place. She doesn't have anything other than her job to occupy her mind, and she can be pretty obnoxious at times."

"Why do you keep her on, then?"

"I don't think the doctors are aware of what it is she's doing. If they are, they're probably trying to ignore the fact."

"And if they're not," Nicole broke in, "it might prove to be difficult to sell to the public, psychiatrists who don't recognize a problem in their own office."

"*Touché,*" Rob said laughingly. "Seriously, why don't you consider trying. You've got nothing to lose."

Her brow puckered up in thought for a split second. At least, if she did get the job, she'd be more closely associated with her chosen field than here in the art store. "I think I will."

Rob dug in his jacket pocket and produced a card. "This is the address. Why don't you stop in anytime today or tomorrow. The employment agencies aren't going to be notified until next week. Tell them I suggested that you stop in."

Taking the card, she said, "Thanks a bunch, Rob. It really helps. I've been sort of down recently but I won't burden you with my problems. Just know that I owe you. All right?"

"Right," he said, reaching out to grab her shoulder when she turned away. "My marker pens. I still need them."

"I'm sorry," she said, motioning for him to follow her to the counter along the far wall.

Saturday, September 27, 1986   9:45 A.M.

Nicole blinked, then blinked again. She couldn't believe her eyes. There was her name in the newspaper. Nicole Kilton. And behind her name, the amount of eleven hundred dollars. She had won! She had actually won a prize in the state lottery. She had been buying several tickets each week for the last two years but never had even won so much as five dollars in the instant lottery portion of the contest. The amount dazzled her. Eleven hundred dollars! She wasn't alone in her good fortune. There were forty-one other winners, each winning various amounts. Her portion was one thousand, one hundred dollars.

Maybe things were beginning to turn her way again. Rob Lanstrom had offered her a job in public relations four days ago, and after having been interviewed the past Thursday, she had given Phil her two weeks' notice. Now, with this windfall of money, she'd feel a step closer to going back to school. She hadn't felt this good since before Myles had left, and now she was more determined than ever to make her life successful and win back his love. Could it have been her working at a nothing job, such as the art store, that had been an influence on Myles? No matter. She was on her way.

Dropping the paper on the table, she picked up her coffee cup to drain it. Then she heard the noise—the scratching sound from the walls. Mice? That was it. She didn't have to live in a rodent infested apartment. She could move out and get a better place to live. She had been hearing the sounds for the past few days, doing her best to ignore them. But her new turn of luck gave her confidence. She'd complain to the manager and insist that something be done. Wondering if anyone else in the building might be suffering from the same problem, she went to the telephone and dialed the manager's number.

"Hello," the manager's wife whined into the phone.

"Is your husband there, Mrs. Astin? This is Nicole Kilton in apartment 3-49C. I've got to talk to him. I've got a bit of a problem."

"He's out working in the complex someplace. In fact, I think he said something about going to your building. I'll tell him you called."

Before Nicole could say anything else, the dial tone buzzed in her ear. "Damn!" she said aloud, biting her lip.

When the phone had been replaced in the cradle, she could hear the sounds from the wall once more. She'd have to find the manager and bring him up here to listen.

Slipping into her coat, she strode to the front door. She opened it, barely able to keep from gasping in surprise. The manager stood outside her door, ready to knock.

"You're just the man I'm looking for," she said quickly, reaching out to grab his arm.

"Hey, wait a minute," he said. "What's up?"

Nicole stopped when he withdrew from her grasp, mentally scolding herself for having acted so hastily. She didn't even like Fred Astin. In fact, he gave her the creeps. Shortly after she had moved in, he had made some suggestive statement that indicated he'd give her special attention or anything she needed, if she reciprocated and gave him special attention in another way. She had given him no encouragement whatsoever, and soon the relationship was nothing more than that of manager/tenant. Now, she actually had tried to drag him into her apartment.

"I've got mice," she said loudly.

"Sh-h-h," he hissed. "Christ! Don't tell the other neighbors. Where? Where have you got mice?''

"In my walls. In the ceiling, I think. Probably all over the place," she said, motioning for him to come inside.

He stepped in, closing the hallway door. "Show me," he said simply.

A confident smile on her face, Nicole went into the kitchen, pointing to the wall where she had just heard mice scampering about.

Astin stood next to the wall, pressing his ear against it. After a few minutes, during which time the only sound was the hum of the electric kitchen clock and the purring of the refrigerator, he said, "I don't hear nothing."

"But . . . but I just heard them . . . just seconds ago. Tap on the wall. Maybe they're sleeping or something," she said.

Pulling a screw driver from his tool belt, Astin tapped on the wall with the handle, first in one spot, then in another. But no sounds new or different to the kitchen could be heard.

"Maybe you imagined it," he said. "Living alone can do strange things to a person. Pretty soon you start hearing things. Then it's somebody talking to you. 'Fore you know it, you're answering them and they come haul you off to the puzzle factory."

"I'm not hearing things," Nicole snapped.

"Neither am I," he said, snorting a guffaw.

"I'm serious, Mr. Astin," she said curtly.

"I . . . I'm sorry." His voice puled when he apologized. "I just enjoy a good joke every once in a while. If you want, I can tell the exterminator the next time he comes. It'll cost you but you'll get rid of the rats."

"Rats? I don't think they're rats."

"Rats. Mice. What difference? He'll get rid of them if you got them."

"Don't bother. If I hear them again, I'll let you know. Then, the exterminator can try."

"Okay by me, lady," Astin said, moving to the door. "You . . . ah . . . you ain't got anything else that needs ah . . . attention, do you?"

"Thank you," Nicole said icily, "but no."

Fifteen minutes after Fred Astin left, the scratching sounds began again and Nicole turned on the stereo to drown them out.

Monday, September 29, 1986 12:49 A.M.

Nicole rolled and tossed in bed. Her nude body, swathed in sweat, reacted to the chilled night air as she threw the covers off. Flat on her back, her eyes undulated rapidly as scenes played before her sleeping consciousness. Facial muscles worked jerkily as she fought to cry out. After several long minutes, her mouth opened and she began mumbling one word, over and over. Slowly gaining in strength and volume, her voice rose higher until she screamed out, *"Yes! Yes! Yes!"*

The sound of her own voice awakened her, bringing her out of the dream-like state. Shivering from the cool air on her damp nakedness, she fumbled with the covers for a moment before pulling them up around her.

What was wrong? What had she been dreaming? What had she been yelling when she awoke? Something. . . . The word *yes* had been screaming in her head. Had she been shouting it or dreaming that she had been yelling? Whichever, what did it mean? To what was she agreeing? She felt she was agreeing with someone about something or giving someone permission to do something.

What *had* she been dreaming? Why couldn't she recall it now that she was awake? Most of the time, she could. But this time, she found she couldn't get a thread of a notion as to what she had been experiencing while asleep.

She shuddered again and reached for her robe. Slipping into it, she tied it tightly around her small waist, accentuating her large breasts at the same time. Once she was on her feet, she paused. What time was it? How long had she slept? Turning, she found the digital clock displaying one oh one. Good God! Had she slept only an hour? But she felt as if she had slept for ages. Would she be able to get back to sleep? Maybe a glass of wine would help.

Padding to the kitchen in her bare feet, she pulled down a bottle of Rhine wine and poured a tumbler half full. She replaced the bottle in the cupboard and dropped an ice cube into the clear liquid before going to the living room. Sipping from her glass, she turned on the TV set and found a late night horror movie and a religious talk show after flipping the dial. Nothing else caught her attention and she switched it off. She downed the remaining wine and went back to the kitchen where she filled the glass this time.

Time swept by as Nicole drank several more glasses of wine before finally surrendering her exhausted body and slightly drunken spirit to bed. When she lay on her back and her breathing slowed to a steady, even rhythm, the scratching began. The room grew chilly. And the stereo in the living room turned on, filling the quiet void with soft music.

While Nicole served out her remaining time at the art store training the new salesperson, the same dream began frequenting her sleep every night. Little by little, she accepted the phenomenon and was able to roll over and return to sleep, not worrying or wondering too much as to what, *"Yes! Yes! Yes!"* meant.

Monday, October 13, 1986   9:30 A.M.

Rose Tunic, whom Nicole had met the day of her interview, stared at her through thick lenses. Nicole had thought nothing about the woman at all, even after Rob Lanstrom had given such a pointed description. Overweight by at least forty pounds, Rose was not the type to be too concerned how her dresses appeared, preferring to believe that each one, although two sizes too small, fit her as if it had been tailor-made. Rose had been friendly enough the first time Nicole had talked with her, but now for some reason, the office manager was sending out signals that warned the newcomer to stand clear.

"I just want to say one thing, Nicole," Rose said sharply from the doorway of Nicole's office. "There are those who work here who think that I should have been given this job. After all, I've worked here for six and a half years. I know everyone. I know what the aims of the clinic are. I know just exactly what this job entails, even though it has just been created. Just watch your step or . . ."

"I'm really happy to know that, Rose," Nicole said, her voice purring, " 'cause if I ever need any help, I'll know exactly who to ask. Thank you so much for telling me."

Her face flushing a deep crimson, Rose glared at Nicole for a long minute before turning to leave. When she reached the door, she said, "That's not what I meant. I'll just as soon . . ." Without finishing, she left, slamming the door.

Nicole had everything she could do to control a loud laugh but couldn't suppress a smile. Standing, she moved around her desk and went to the closet where a full length mirror hung, concealed on the inside facing of the door. She opened the dark compartment and checked her appearance. Picturing Rose Tunic in her mind, she nodded. The woman was frustrated with life, her appearance, her personality, her apparent failure in society. But was someone like that even aware of herself? She remem-

bered what Rob had said about Rose coming to
the clinic on weekends, poking through files
and keeping a finger on everything that trans-
pired within the confines of each office. Mentally noting to lock her desk and anything else
that might hold something she wouldn't want
the nosy office manager to find, she returned to
her desk. She had a meeting with Doctor
Claypool in half an hour to discuss the first
steps in building the clinic's image.

10:45 P.M.

That evening, Nicole drank more wine than
usual and ate little. The whole time was spent
reading several books that Doctor Claypool
had given her, sipping wine and making notes.
By eleven, she closed the last book and turned
on the television set. It was time for Myles to
give the news. That was something she hadn't
missed too many times since he had left. Each
night she sat opposite the set, drinking in his
electronic image—remembering, reliving, rejoicing in the more vivid memories of their
time together.

She fixed her attention on his mouth. That
mouth had given her so much pleasure with his
witty sayings and his tender caressing love-
making. That mouth hid his tongue, the tongue
that had explored every square inch of her
body, sending delicious shivers down her spine.

An uncontrollable sob broke through her
composure and she murmured, "Why, Myles?
Why?"

During a commercial, she hurried to the kitchen to refill her glass, returning to curse the weatherman for taking over with his portion of the news broadcast. Myles would be back, but for only an instant before the idiot sportscaster showed up to rave about the latest football poll or the Sunday games in the NFL. At least Myles would have the tube to himself during the last news story, usually a short, upbeat item about something that might make the viewer forget the awful items he had reported on earlier.

Then, the late movie was beginning. She turned off the set, saying goodnight to Myles who was no longer visible anywhere except in her mind and in the small portrait photo on the shelf above the TV. Making her way to the bedroom she put the empty glass on the dresser and slipped from her clothes. Her body ached. She was more than ready for bed and slid between the cool sheets and beneath the light blanket.

Her wine-drenched mind quickly succumbed and in seconds she was sleeping.

In an instant, the dream began and Nicole found herself in a large ballroom filled with people dressed in the most outlandish costumes. If had to be a masquerade ball. Angels and pirates danced together. Knights in shining armor whisked scantily clad nymphets across the floor. Off in the distance, she could hear the strains of a dance band playing some slow, seductive love ballad, and she felt herself swept away by the scene—

swept away by powerful arms that lifted her until her feet barely touched the floor.

Opening her eyes, she looked up at her partner, into the face of what appeared to be an animal. She was dancing with a goat of all things. Fighting to keep from smiling or laughing, she soared across the floor. She inhaled deeply, catching the smoky essence of after-shave lotion. Who wore cologne like that? Someone who . . .

MYLES!

She was dancing with Myles Lawrence and everything was fine. She felt fantastic. The way he held her—so intimate, so suggestive, so arousing. She could feel one hand slipping beneath her arm from the back to teasingly caress her breast. On one turn of the dance, he released his tight hold and she floated away from him to arm's length and she looked down to see how she was dressed. The urge to scream rose within her, accompanying the rushing flush of embarrassment. She was nude. She had nothing on but shoes. Embarrassing—and yet, she didn't really care.

Her goat-faced partner pulled her back, and just as the music stopped, a clock began tolling the hour. Purposefully counting the gongs, Nicole counted three and the clock stopped. Three o'clock.

"It's time to unmask," her partner said.

"I know," she said, anticipating the appearance of Myles' longed-for countenance.

"Shall we unmask, then?" he asked.

"Yes."

She reached up to find she had no mask on either. Accepting the fact, she watched her partner take his off, only to reveal another, identical mask.

"Shall we unmask, then?" he asked again.

"Yes." And the process was repeated.

"Shall we unmask, then?"

"Yes," she answered, more than a note of irritation rising in her voice.

"Shall we unmask, then?"

"Yes! Yes! YES!" she screamed at each question.

Nicole bolted upright in bed, her body dripping wet. What did that dream mean? Would she wind up confiding in Doctor Claypool or one of his associates about it? Why did Myles have a series of goat masks on? That made no sense whatsoever. None of it made sense. Was it even Myles with whom she had been dancing?

She lay back on the bed, falling asleep in minutes.

On the dresser, the Little Orphan Annie doll turned to face a Shirley Temple doll and one that Nicole had gotten for Christmas when she had been nine years old—her very own high fashion miniature mannikin. The Little Orphan Annie doll nodded solemnly and a smile crossed her painted face. The Shirley Temple doll returned the acknowledgment, nodding herself and smiling with her molded lips. The high fashion mannikin bowed from the waist and the rest of the collection turned to watch Nicole sleep.

And the scratching came louder in the walls.

5

Tuesday, October 14, 1986 7:00 P.M.

Myles stared at the ceiling of Eunice Brooks'
bedroom. Unconcerned by what his bed-
partner was doing to his lower body, he tried
concentrating on the evening's upcoming activities. He'd leave soon for the station to present the late news. Because Eunice was more
interested in anything other than coherent conversation, Myles had found himself staying at
the television station after his duties there had
been finished. At least there he had his fellow
newscasters, the weatherman and the sports
director, all who could carry on ideas beyond
their own domain, although the latter, Scott
McReady, usually worked the conversation
around to the latest deal in athletic trades or
the most recent football game.

If he faced the truth, Myles had to admit
that he did not relish the idea of coming back

to Eunice's apartment for anything other than sex—and he was slowly becoming bored even with that. He tilted his head, surveying the bobbing head of Eunice Brooks—sex machine. The one thing he could not deny was the fact that she was terrific in bed—but that did not a marriage make and he knew it.

Marriage?

Why had that idea entered his head? The reason he had walked out on Nicole had been his failure to make a commitment—or the desire to make one at this stage in his life. Sure, he had wanted to have a little more freedom than he felt he had with Nicole, but why would the idea of marriage suddenly invade his thoughts while Eunice was attempting to withdraw every drop of bodily juices he possessed?

He looked down again. No way could he ever envision being married to someone of Eunice's ilk. She was nice enough, pleasant enough. She certainly was interested enough in sex to satisfy even the most lust-filled person. It seemed to Myles that the woman even bordered on the perverted side of sex—not that there was anything wrong with that between two consenting adults. He had learned much from her that he would retain for the rest of his life. Whether or not he would be able to convince someone—like Nicole—to partake in these practices was another question.

Gasping at the amount of pressure she exerted on his throbbing penis, he closed his eyes while she drained him. The sensation of his legs turning to jelly increased until he felt that he would collapse if required to stand anytime in the next five or ten minutes. This weakened sensation crept up his legs, to his spasmodically jerking member, past it to his flat stomach, to his hairy chest, to his arms and head. He closed his eyes, feeling as if he would sink into the mattress, filtering through it until he came out beneath the bed.

Eunice stayed in place, her head resting on his lower abdomen. Her own afterglow remained constant as she traced esoteric lines along his legs, inner thighs and up to his crotch. He didn't care. He felt exhausted. She could do anything she wanted. Right now he would not argue the issue. But soon, very soon, he would walk out of her life and be done with her.

"Are you sleeping?" she asked, breaking the silence to invade his thoughts.

"No." How could she think that someone could sleep through one of her performances?

She sat up, bouncing to his side before lying down next to him. Resting her head on his chest, she said, "You know, Myles, I've been thinking."

Myles restrained himself from commenting on her mental capabilities and remained silent.

"Aren't you curious?" she asked.

"About what?"

"About what I've been thinking."

"No."

"Oh." She fell silent.

Myles waited. Was she thinking about what she was going to say or was she thinking about his own statement? In either case, he'd wait, since he felt he wouldn't be able to get up and leave even if he wanted.

"Why don't you and I get married?" she said suddenly, as if the idea had just formulated, taking root in her mind.

"What?" Myles cried, sitting up and dumping her to the side.

"Get married. You know. You 'n' me."

Myles struggled to get off the bed. That fried it. Now, she was broaching the subject of marriage. Next thing, she'd formally propose. He couldn't have that. He couldn't even entertain the thought for more than a split second. Married to Eunice Brooks? The fuck machine?

"What brought this on?" he asked, biding for time.

"Well, we've been dating for several weeks now and I don't know about you but I really dig the sex we have together. Don't you?"

Myles shrugged. "It's been fine," he managed weakly. Dating? She considered his sleeping over as dating? They had gone out to dinner twice, since he had left Nicole.

Nicole. Her face materialized in his mind. Why had he left her? She was a nice person to be with. She never pushed. She never suggested outlandish things. She was so level headed, so pure in her logical reasoning. Why *had* he left her?

"Fine?" Eunice blurted. "Fine? Is that all you can say? Fine?"

"All right, then," he countered. "It's been great. You are really something else when it comes to performing in bed."

A self-satisfied smile crossed her heart-shaped face. "So why don't we get married and make it all legal?" She snickered at the suggestion.

"A lot of reasons."

"Name some."

All of a sudden, Eunice Brooks was becoming a debater. A philosophical debater. A pushing, argumentative, philosophical debater. He didn't need that. None of it.

"First of all," he began, "I'm not ready to settle down and get married. If you were aware of what's going on in the world like I am, you wouldn't even consider an idea that might result in children."

Eunice stared at Myles, her face blank, devoid of any understanding. "What . . . what do you mean?" she asked, her lower lip pouting.

"Watch the news. Read the newspapers. Listen to the radio. Would you want to bring a child into this rotten world? I wouldn't. I'm not certain I'll ever get married. And if I do, there'll be a firm agreement that we will not have children."

Eunice's face brightened. "I agree. No children. Is that all that's bothering you? I don't think I could handle snotty-nosed kids who crap in their pants. Do you know what I mean?"

Myles turned away. Christ! She thought he was laying out conditions. Now what? Now what could he do? "I . . . I . . ." he began lamely, "I don't want to hurt anyone."

But he had, hadn't he? He had hurt Nicole who had not asked for anything other than his love and his presence. No strings. All she had wanted to give him was her love and her presence in return. He had been a fool.

"Who are you going to hurt?" she asked, a whimpering defeat in her voice.

Myles shook his head. "Look, Eunice, you're a nice enough person, but I did not come into this arrangement with the idea of getting married. I . . . "

"All right, already. So we won't get married," she said, sharply. "I was merely thinking out loud. If you don't want to get married, we won't."

"I . . . I hope you understand," he said.

He made a mental note to call Nicole the next day. Considering the close call he'd just had with Eunice, he was convinced that Nicole was better suited to him and that he had made a gigantic mistake by walking out on her.

He felt Eunice's hands kneading his shoulder muscles and turned slightly to see her head close to his. Her tongue flicked out along the back of his ear before jabbing him above the lobe. He felt his resolve withering again as his passions reawakened. Leaning back, he gave himself to Eunice Brooks.

Tomorrow, he'd call Nicole. Tomorrow—or the next day.

11:10 P.M.

The music heralding the imminent return of the eleven o'clock news filled Nicole's living room and she refocused her attention on the TV set. She looked forward to the half hour broadcasts each night, thinking of them as a late rendezvous with Myles. And that was exactly what they were for her. She had hoped she might detect a change in his appearance— one that might indicate a loss of weight or sleep or something showing that he had made a mistake leaving her, that he missed her, that he was miserable without her. But there was nothing. No sign of any kind. He looked as fit and healthy as ever, without that haunted look around his eyes that Nicole had thought she had found around her own. Perhaps he didn't care.

A commercial from a supermarket chain came on, showing Halloween candies and treats for sale. The scene cut to a front door opening and little masked ghosts and goblins screaming, "Trick or treat."

Nicole thanked heaven for one of the advantages of living in this adults-only complex. Such invasions of privacy were nonexistent, excluding the possibility of that scene taking place at her front door. Halloween at best was a stupid, dumb event whose only purpose seemed to be to sell candy and make merchants rich. She hated the thought of the approaching holidays beyond. What would Thanksgiving be like without Myles if Halloween was going to prove to be a problem for her? She didn't even want to think of Christmas.

She'd have to find some way to occupy her thoughts for the next few months until the holidays were over. Thank goodness she had her new job and the publicity campaign to keep her busy. She would simply work that much more diligently and not even think about Myles or what they had meant to each other.

A slapping sound from behind brought her out of the chair. Turning, she saw nothing. Then she heard the scratching again. And the sound of slapping once more, this time from the direction of the TV set. Spinning around, she found nothing out of place, until she looked at the floor. Beneath the TV table, almost out of sight, lay the red book she had used in that stupid ritual. And Myles' picture was on top of the TV set. When had she moved it there?

The scratching grew louder.

Nothing had happened to make her believe the rite or the book or anything else she had done that night would ever bring about the change she so desperately wanted. She had felt sick with desire for Myles, but he was a washout. She didn't want him anymore.

The room seemed chillier and the scratching continued, spreading to all four walls and to the ceiling. The book skittered across the rug until it lay at her feet.

Nicole felt the hackles on her neck move. What was happening? Was she dreaming? Things like a book moving across a carpet by itself simply didn't happen. Bending down, she picked up the small volume and concentrated on Myles, who was about to give the last news story before the end of the telecast. The book could wait.

She tried analyzing what he was saying but found she could not.

"At any rate," he said, flashing his toothy grin, "the dog is back with his owners after following his family from Dubuque, Iowa, to their new home in Augusta, Maine. Until tomorrow night, this is Myles Lawrence. Have a good night and a better tomorrow."

The book quivered of its own accord in her hand, and Nicole stared at it. It was her imagination. It had to be. Things like this couldn't happen. Incantations and mystical ceremonies were for stupid people hundreds of years ago. Not today. Not today's people. Smiling to herself, she stood. She returned the book to its shelf above the TV, before reaching down for Myles' picture. After replacing it on the shelf she turned off the set. The sudden quiet emphasized the fact that the scratching sound had disappeared as well. It was all her imagination. She wanted to get to bed so she could spend the next day finalizing her basic publicity campaign before presenting it to

Doctor Claypool and his associates the day after next. The last thing Nicole thought of was Rose Tunic trying to interfere with the publicity proposal. Then she thought of Myles returning to her again. She closed her eyes, falling asleep immediately.

The scratching inched close to her head, coming from behind the mirrors, and a coldness filled the bedroom. Both went unnoticed by Nicole. Then, the scratching and cold were gone.

11:27 P.M.

Eunice smiled vacantly at the television set and Myles' image, periodically blowing kisses to him. She looked foward to weekends when he'd be off work all day Saturday and Sunday. Those two days they didn't have to get up to do anything. He had said something about going out to dinner Saturday but she thought that would be a waste of time. If they got hungry between bouts of sex, they could grab a sandwich or something to sustain themselves.

During the commercial break after the sports report and before Myles' last story, she stood, stretching to her full five foot seven inch height. She stifled a yawn when Myles reappeared, listening intently as he told of a dog following its family from someplace in Iowa to Maine. When he finished, she clapped. She liked happy endings to stories like that.

Then the set went out of its own accord.

Startled, she stared at it for a long moment. A power failure? No, the lights were still on in the room. Did the set simply blow a tube or something? She stepped toward it and the lights dimmed until she could barely see anything in the room, heavy shadows clinging to the furniture and walls. Something had to be wrong with the electricity—someplace. She just knew that. Then, she thought she saw something move off to one side of her. Spinning in that direction she could see nothing. Something else moved in the other direction. Again, she turned, trying to see whatever it was.

A raspy, whispering laugh filled the room and she froze, unable to move. What was going on? What was happening? She felt cold and gasped when she saw clouds of steam jettisoning from her nose as her breath increased in short, sporadic puffs. The laugh died down and came back again, only much louder this time. And she thought she saw something else, something about four feet tall, dart from one side of the gloomy room to the other, ducking out of sight behind a chair.

"Who . . . who's there?" she demanded weakly.

Her only response was the dry chuckling. And scratching sounds that grew in volume with each ticking second. The noises seemed to fill the room, coming at her from all directions.

Someone—someone she could not see— slapped her hard across the face. Slipping backward, trying to regain her balance, Eunice fell to the floor. What was that? What had happened? Who had slapped her? Straining her eyes, she peered into the gloom but could see nothing—no one. Her face stung from the blow. It had felt as if a hard, roughened hand, heavily calloused from manual labor, had struck her full force across the mouth. She struggled to her feet, tears pouring from her eyes while sobs tore at her body.

"Come on! Stop it!" she wailed. "Who's there?"

Again the hand struck her. This time another hand, unseen, completely invisible, clutched her right arm while she was beaten unmercifully. Her head popped back and forth from the blows, tearing at her smooth complexion until blood mixed with her tears and vicious cuts spread open to the bone of her cheeks.

She sensed herself screaming even though she doubted that she made any sound, when the hand holding her right arm began squeezing, tightening until she thought she would go mad from pain. Her eyes widening, she watched as her upper arm caved in where she felt the grip of the unbelievably strong hand closing on it. Why couldn't she see anything—her assailant or whoever or whatever was attacking her? When blood erupted from her arm, the pressure continued until she heard a crunching sound and she passed out as her right arm was torn apart.

Invisible blows rained down on the unconscious form of Eunice Brooks as a rage vented itself on the girl's limp body. Little by little, her pummeled flesh fell from her bones. In turn they were pulverized into a yellow, soupy liquid, mixing with the bloody tissue that had, a few seconds before, been a living, breathing human being.

Wednesday, October 15, 1986 12:01 A.M.

Nicole slept soundly, unaware of the drop in temperature in her bedroom, oblivious of the scratching and the quiet, evil laugh that rippled through the air. She did not awaken when an unseen hand caressed her cheek, working its way toward her breasts where it touched her, fondling her. Then, quite un-noticed by the sleeping woman, the stereo and the television set in the living room turned on, filling the apartment with quiet, muffled sounds.

The dolls collectively nodded their heads in approval from their vantage point on the dresser.

6

Myles locked his car and looked up at the
apartment building. Inside Eunice waited for
him. Maybe he should just go home to his own
apartment. He hadn't spent a night there since
leaving Nicole. What was there about Eunice
and her insatiability where sex was concerned?
If he ever told anyone about it, he'd be called a
liar. He'd try to convince his listener that she
truly did indulge herself in every which way,
but it would be for nothing. No one would
believe him. And what if she ever tired of him?
Would she simply throw him out? He had to
get his priorities in order.

Slowly mounting each step leading to her
fourth floor apartment, he wanted to spend an
eternity on each riser. He could have taken the
elevator but that would have been too quick.
This way, he could take his time, and if he were

lucky, the whole night would be gone by the time he reached her door. When he reached the fourth floor, he looked at his watch. Two thirty in the morning.

Pausing before the door to Eunice's apartment, he hesitated for an instant before easing the key into the lock. When he turned it, he didn't make a sound.

The hiss of the television set subtly filled the apartment, and he found the blank eye of the set lighting the living room and part of the entry way with its bluish light. Damn! Did that mean she had fallen asleep in the easy chair? If so, could he get away with leaving her there and going to bed by himself? He could tell her he tried to awaken her but she hadn't responded.

Slipping off his top coat, he dropped it across a chair and stepped to the doorway of the living room. His eyes widened at the bizarre sight, at first thinking it to be some sort of awful joke. But the look of absolute horror etched into the slashed face of Eunice Brooks told him otherwise. Only her head rested in the middle of the room, surrounded by a bloody, pink mess that must have been the rest of her at one time. The pulp spread out in a puddle that embraced the whole of the open space between the furniture. Chunks of her face had been torn away, and the flesh that remained was puffed, blackened with bruises. Her dead eyes held his, riveting his attention.

"My God!" he managed hoarsely. It couldn't

be—couldn't be Eunice. It had to be some sort of sick prank. It simply had to be.

For the first time he noticed the bitter cold, shuddering involuntarily. It seemed to be freezing in the room. A small Boston fern, its leaves wilted and whitening, convinced him that the room was actually that cold. But it was nowhere near freezing outside. Still, he could see his breath puffing from his nose. How could it be that cold in the apartment?

Forcing himself with a herculean effort, he turned away, reentering the hallway. The thermostat was set on sixty-eight degrees and the thermometer indicated that the temperature in the hall was sixty-six. Impossible!

Picking up the phone, he instantly dropped it. Had he destroyed evidence? Fingerprints? If he had, it was too late. He'd have to call the police and tell them about Eunice. He'd also have to tell them that he had acted out of instinct to call for help, probably ruining any fingerprints that might have been on the phone.

Carefully dialing the emergency number, he waited, and when the voice answered on the other end, Myles reported the death of Eunice Brooks.

3:00 A.M.

Nicole smiled in the embrace of Myles. Tipping her head back, he kissed her, not roughly but tenderly and gently. She wanted to

*scream because of the pleasure this simple
show of love created within her. They had been
apart too long and . . .*

A chuckle snapped her attention away from
Myles. A deep throated, resonant chuckle.

Who was laughing? She opened her eyes to
the darkness of her own bedroom. Alone.
Totally alone. It had been a dream. Turning
over, she caught herself, ready to cry. That
would solve nothing. It had been only a dream.
She'd survive. She had to survive. She could
not allow the thought of Myles kissing her turn
her into an emotional wreck. She'd win him
back. Snuggling down beneath the covers, she
nodded and closed her eyes. She would win.
She knew that.

When her breathing steadied into sleep, she
did not consciously notice the drop in room
temperature again but instinctively pulled the
covers up tighter around her neck.

6:45 A.M.

"Just make certain you keep us apprised of
your wherebouts, Mr. Lawrence," Lieutenant
Sandy Michaelson said. He had come to the
apartment when the "black and white" had
reported the murder after answering the
summons put out by Myles Lawrence.

Michaelson watched Myles. He didn't
believe for an instant that the TV news
reporter could have been responsible for the
gruesome sight that had met him when he

entered the apartment. The investigating officers had tried to remain as quiet as possible to avoid awakening the entire building of sleeping tenants. Still, there were those who had peeked into the hall and had been, in time, questioned. No one had seen anything. No one had heard anything. The lack of eye witnesses was not surprising to Michaelson, but the fact that no one had heard anything puzzled him at best. How could a human being be demolished in the manner in which Eunice Brooks had died and not utter a sound? The lab man had said that the best he could do under the circumstances was to estimate the time of death somewhere in the last three to five hours. There was no body as such for an autopsy and the head would barely serve when it came to identifying the dead woman.

Michaelson had been on the force for twelve years but had never seen anything remotely resembling this murder scene. Myles Lawrence's reaction had been genuine. Of that, Michaelson felt one hundred percent positive. The fact that he had an air tight alibi from eight o'clock the previous evening until two that morning did the most to eliminate the anchorman from suspicion.

Now Michaelson had no idea where he could start. Glancing at his watch, he winced. It was almost seven in the morning. When the examination of the apartment was finished and their primary investigation completed, he'd take the information and sift through it, chart it, file it, study it, investigate each and every facet of each and every detail—no matter how small. And somewhere deep inside him, Lieutenant Sandy Michaelson felt that he would find nothing. Absolutely nothing.

11:00 P.M.

Nicole took took her seat opposite the TV set, humming along with the heralding fanfare that announced the late night news. When Barth Galloway appeared on the screen, sitting behind the desk, she listened intently.

"Myles Lawrence is off tonight," Galloway began simply without further explanation.

Nicole got to her feet, crossed over and flicked off the set just as Galloway said, "Police are investigating a murder which was reported by . . ."

The screen went blank. So Myles had a night off. Big deal. She'd be able to go to bed half an hour earlier and get that much more sleep. It was probably better that he wasn't on, since she had to put the finishing touches on her publicity campaign the next day. Then, she'd be able to hit the streets, with the news releases that Doctor Claypool and his advisors had approved. She decided to call on the television station where Myles worked sometime after the campaign began. By waiting awhile, she felt she'd be much more knowledgeable and able to answer any questions the news media might pose. If she did see Myles, she wanted to be in complete control.

She had no trouble falling asleep and did not awaken when what appeared to be the indentation of fingers suddenly pressed into the covers alongside her. In the living room, the television set came on and the late night news show continued without an audience in Nicole's apartment.

Thursday, October 16, 1986 7:03 A.M.

The next morning she found the local early morning talk show in full swing when she entered the living room. Pouting, she angrily crossed the room, reaching out to turn off the TV set.

"Ladies and gentlemen, the Reverend Eddie John Stangood," the host said, graciously standing to welcome his next guest.

Nicole stopped for a moment, stepping back. Stacey Ford's hero, the wonderful Reverend Eddie John Stangood, strode across the room, swaggering self-assuredly. Dark rimmed glasses gave the white-suited man a scholarly appearance.

"*We-yell*, it certainly is a pleasure to be *he-yere* this morning with you," Stangood said.

Nicole half-expected him to launch into a sermon such as the type he delivered on Sunday mornings on one of the local stations. What did Stacey believe? Couldn't she see that this man had to be a charlatan of sorts?

"The Reverend Stangood has taken the position that unless one is reborn and brought into his church, there is no chance for salvation for anyone. Is that correct, Reverend?'' the host asked.

"Yeh-yes. *Gee*-zus has told me directly that . . ."

Nicole turned off the set. She couldn't take this hogwash at any time, much less this early in the day.

The thought that the set had been on when she got up bothered her. She had to be losing her mind. That was the second or third time that she had found the television set on upon arising. What was making her do such absent-minded things?

Recalling the previous evening, she remembered that Myles had not been on the late news. She had turned the set off when she realized she wouldn't see him. In fact, when she thought about it for a few minutes, she even recalled what the substitute newsman was saying. Something about a murder. She remembered because his voice had withered and died as the set went off. Maybe her set needed attention. The switch might not be going off all the way and some vibration or something might be jostling the TV just enough to put it back on.

She couldn't waste her time this morning worrying about something like that. Work had to take precedence today. She had enjoyed a great night's sleep and would be able to leave for work a few minutes early. Relegating the troublesome TV set to the back of her mind,

she thought about the stereo going on in the
same manner before filing it in her memory
bank next to the television problem.

When she reached the office, she found most
of the secretaries talking about the peculiar
murder that had taken place.

"What do you think happened?" Julie Lewis
asked, turning to Nicole when she saw the
public relations director enter.

"Think? Happened?" Nicole asked. "What
are you talking about?"

"Didn't you see the paper last night or watch
the news?"

Nicole shook her head.

"A woman was murdered."

"So?" Nicole asked, shrugging. "Murders
happen all of the time."

"But most of the time the news media are
right there with all the sordid details. This
time there weren't any. Details, that is," Julie
said.

Nicole waited. There had to be more to what
the girl was saying.

"You don't believe me, do you?" Julie asked,
turning to the other girls. "Am I lying?"

They all shook their heads.

"I . . . I don't understand," Nicole said when
she saw the curious expressions on the girls'
faces.

"It said in the paper that the body was found
by some reporter or something. Last night on
the newscasts, they hardly referred to it other

than to say that the woman was found by a reporter. No details. Nothing about how she died or the weapon or anything. We think it's peculiar."

"That's all?" Nicole asked bluntly.

Julia nodded. "We think it's out of the ordinary. We were . . ."

"All right! All right! All right!" Rose Tunic cried, bursting from her office. "What's going on here?" Her nostrils flaring, the overweight woman's eyes shrunk as her cheeks puffed out.

"Nothing, Miss Tunic," Julie said, turning back to her typewriter.

The other secretaries fled the scene, making their way to their own desks. Nicole stood there for a moment.

"Don't you have an office?" Rose demanded, blocking Nicole's passage.

"You know I do, Miss Tunic," Nicole said quietly, "but you're standing in my way."

For a moment, Rose stood her ground before stepping aside. Nicole had all she could do to keep from laughing. The woman thought of herself as the one and only force in the office. She might have the other girls fooled but Nicole would have none of the woman's browbeating. Doctor Claypool was her immediate supervisor and main concern—the man to whom she reported and had to keep happy with her ideas and work. He had been more than helpful in getting her started in the right direction, and when her own ideas took over, he had seemed more than pleased. Rose Tunic could go jump in the lake as far as Nicole was concerned.

Friday, October 17, 1986   8:30 A.M.

Myles lay on his back, staring at the ceiling. He hadn't slept since finding Eunice's remains. Whenever he thought of that pool of pinkish jelly surrounding her severed head, he shuddered, fighting the awful urge to throw up. But since he hadn't eaten, there was nothing in him to vomit. When had he found her? After concentrating, he concluded only that he had found her the morning before yesterday. After the police dismissed him, advising him to stay in close contact, he had returned to his apartment, shutting the awful world out. Then, today had to be Friday.

He wished somehow that he could cry. Maybe that would help. But his feelings for Eunice finally clarified, once he realized that the woman was dead. He had cared for her only physically—not in the way he had found himself feeling about Nicole. Perhaps that was what had scared him and forced him to run from Nicole. He had been frightened by the growing swell of emotion he felt within himself for her. Now he realized definitely that he had made a mistake, that he had given up something precious.

If only Nicole hadn't gotten involved with someone else—if she still felt anything for him —if he could gather together the necessary emotional strength to face her again, he would do everything in his power to win her back.

He leaped off the bed, hurrying to the window. Why did he feel like this now? It was hypocritical of him, to say the least. There would be no funeral for Eunice, and for that he was thankful. He had learned from the police that her remains were to be shipped to her room in Sioux Falls, South Dakota. At first he had felt a moral obligation to offer to make the necessary arrangements. He couldn't recall if Eunice had ever said anything other than in passing about a family or relatives someplace. She had never gone into much detail.

If Nicole and he got back together, he'd benefit. But what if he and Nicole weren't meant for each other?

A piercing jab beneath his left ear brought a cry to his lips. What the hell was that awful pain? He rubbed his ear for a moment, easing the pain. Hopefully that would be the end of that.

Nicole. He had been thinking about Nicole. Nicole and he getting back together again. It would be more than nice if they did. If they didn't, he'd survive somehow and so would she.

The pain struck again. Whatever it was, it left when he rubbed his afflicted ear again. Enough of that. He stormed into the bathroom and quickly swallowed three aspirin tablets. When he turned to leave, the shower passively beckoned to him. He hadn't done much of anything the last forty-eight hours or so, and a hot shower would get him back on track. Slipping from his robe, Myles turned on the hot water and stepped in when clouds of steam billowed through the bathroom.

Monday, October 20, 1986   1:00 P.M.

Nicole could not have been more pleased with the manner in which the campaign initially had been received. The few people she had spoken with on Friday had been more than willing to cooperate, agreeing to do a story or grant her an interview.

But she had resisted going first to Myles' station. Was she afraid? Afraid of what? A confrontation wherein she would learn that he had fallen in love with someone else? Perhaps he was living with someone. Had he given up his apartment? Worse still, might he be engaged to marry? Whenever those awful thoughts bombarded her, she choked back her urge to cry, to scream, to give vent to her frustrated emotions. He had to be waiting for her. He simply had to be!

Today, she could not give herself logical reasons why she should not call on KSLL-TV. She had three other offices to call on, all of which were in the same building. If she ran into Myles while at KSLL-TV, she'd merely tough it out.

To ward off the possible meeting, she called on her other contacts first and at three o'clock pushed open the glass doors of KSLL-TV.

2:55 P.M.

~~Myles stood behind his desk. Coming back to~~ work had not been as traumatic as he had anticipated. He would be forever thankful that there had been no funeral for him to attend, but at least she would have mourners when her remains reached South Dakota.

Tonight, he would return to his job as anchorman and things would return to normal. Bending down, he jotted Nicole's name on a list of people he wanted to contact within the next day or two. What would he say to her? He had no idea and would not make any overture until he had rehearsed something. What he would do beyond that initial call was equally mystifying, but he knew he had to speak to her —and that he would do so before the end of the week. He needed that much time to pull himself and his thoughts together. Glancing at his watch, he decided he'd get a cup of coffee before the three-thirty meeting he had with the station manager. That would give him just half an hour. Picking up his coffee mug, he went to the office door and stepped into the hall.

3:00 P.M.

Nicole froze. No sooner had she entered the lobby of KSLL-TV than Myles stepped from his office into the hallway, walking directly toward her. When he looked up, their eyes met and locked. He looked terrible—as if he had had no sleep or certainly wasn't getting an adequate amount. Dark circles below his eyes added to his overall appearance of exhaustion.

She watched him come toward her. Why hadn't he stopped? Why hadn't he turned around when he saw her, retreating to the sanctity of his private office? Why was he walking directly toward her? Surely he had seen her. She tried remembering if he had looked so haggard the last time she'd seen him on TV. Something must have happened while he was off from work. Perhaps he'd been ill.

"Nicole," he said simply, his voice catching on the single word.

"Hello, Myles. How are you?" She felt surprise at the confidence in her voice.

"I could lie and tell you fine but actually the last few days have been pretty awful."

"Really? Why?" She hoped her voice didn't sound as cold or as calculating as the two simple words could have implied.

He studied her for a moment, seemingly to drink in her features like a man dying of thirst would do to a glass of water before consuming it. Coughing to clear his throat, he forced a smile.

"You heard about it, didn't you?"

"It? About what?"

"The murder of Eunice Brooks."

"Who?"

"The murdered girl I found."

"You found?" Her face flushed. Myles had been the reporter who had found the murdered woman? She had not read about the incident in the paper and didn't know if his name had been mentioned. If it had, the people at the clinic could not have associated her with Myles because she had never mentioned him to anyone. And as far as TV news was concerned, she had turned off the set each time she saw Barth Galloway preparing to broadcast in Myles' absence.

Myles gave her a sterile version of what he had found without going into all the gory details, relaxing visibly when she comforted him as much as she could in a public lobby. She could tell that he hadn't told her everything and wished he would open up. If he had been involved with the dead woman, it would do him more good to talk it out of his system than keep it bottled up inside.

"Can we talk in your office for a moment, Myles?"

"Sure," he said, taking her arm to guide her toward it.

When they were seated inside with the door closed, she said, "I know you well enough to realize that you weren't telling me everything out there. Why don't you dump on me? I can handle it."

An ironic smile crossed his face. "I rather doubt that, Nicole. Really. It was awful. The reason the news media has not gone into much detail is that the scene *was* so awful, so hideous that it couldn't be described in an acceptable way."

"I don't understand."

"And I hope you never have to, Nicole." He looked away, a haunted expression replacing the sad one on his face. He looked as if he were reliving the scene again.

"Myles, don't," she said, standing to cross the short distance to him. Reaching out she gently touched his hand, smiling when he looked up.

"I think that scene will stay with me as long as I live," he whispered. "It was Eunice who drew me away from you, you know."

She waited. Talking would do him good. What matter if what he said would hurt her? She wanted to know why he had left, what his reasoning had been. If she knew, she would be better able to fight the ghost of Eunice Brooks.

Little by little, Myles explained why he had left, how stupid his reasons seemed now.

"You know," he said, after pausing for a while, "you were on my mind a lot of the time. In fact, I was considering leaving Eunice and coming back to you, begging for another chance. She wasn't the brightest person around, and . . ."

"Myles," Nicole said, breaking in, "I'm still here. Waiting. I did nothing while you were gone. Somehow I knew we'd wind up together again. You know . . ."

"No," Myles said, pulling away from her and standing. "It's all over. The memory of Eunice would always be there between us. There's no way I could ever consider being with you again after the way I treated you. I was such a fool. Fools should not be given a second chance.''

"I don't believe that, Myles," she said quietly. "I don't think you do either. Time will heal . . .''

"Time will not heal anything. There's only one thing I can do. Leave . . . leave the area and . . .''

Before he could continue, he grabbed his left ear, sucking in his breath as the pain hammered at him.

"What is it, Myles?" Nicole moved toward him. Something was drastically wrong. His face contorted painfully as he rubbed his ear.

"It . . . it's nothing," he mumbled. "It . . . it'll pass. It always does."

"How long has that been going on?"

"It's happened only once or twice. If it continues, I'll go see a doctor."

"Promise?"

"I promise."

"I have to go, Myles. I have a meeting with the station manager at three thirty and it's a minute past that now. Will you call me?"

"I've got a meeting with him, too. Come on. I'll escort you," he said, taking her arm once more.

"Are you all right?" she asked, her concern for his apparent earache more evident than his.

"All right? Oh, you mean the ear. Yeah. The pain is gone now. Come on or we'll be late. I don't want him to think I waylaid you on purpose."

Allowing him to guide her by her arm as they walked down the hallway, she watched him out of the corner of her eye. She fervently hoped that he would change his mind about leaving. The way he had said it seemed to be almost spontaneous. Now that she had seen him again up close, she knew more than before that she wanted him. She felt she truly loved Myles. She'd do whatever it took to get him to stay.

7

Monday, October 20, 1986   11:12 P.M.

Nicole watched Myles that night while he
gave the late news. Marveling at his composure on camera, she compared the cool, articu-
late news reporter with the disturbed, upset
and almost distraught man she had encountered earlier that day. Myles' horror over
Eunice Brooks' death had shown her a whole
new aspect to his personality—one that
seemed to complete him as a person. She
always had known him to be a serious, concerned person who was completely aware of all
the troubles and ills of the world. That was
something he had gained from his chosen field
of work. There also had been the happy-go-
lucky side of him, the humor, the devil-may-
care attitude of his light moments. She had
liked all of that. His tenderness when it came
to making love had been the mortar that had

held the bricks of his personality together for Nicole. Now this new facet completed the man and she wanted him even more than she had in the past.

When the news program finished, she hurried to bed, and once beneath the covers, almost immediately fell asleep. After several hours had passed, the turntable in the other room began spinning slowly until it gained its proper speed, and the arm moved obediently from its resting place, stopping when it reached what should have been the edge of a record. Then the arm dropped, and although there was no disc on the turntable, the soft strains of a Strauss waltz began filtering through the apartment. The volume grew, infiltrating the bedroom, and Nichole's lips curved into a scinitar smile.

She bowed her head, holding out her arms to her dream-companion. Accepting his invitation to dance, she joined him and they spun about the floor, their feet barely touching the cold, black marble beneath them. The hands of the huge clock in the ballroom moved inexorably toward twelve, then one, then two, and as they hovered at right angles between twelve and three, the music changed into an abandoned dervish-like melody—wild and fast tempoed. The couple spun faster and faster until the room blurred into a haze of colors and streaks.

In the living room of Nicole's apartment, the small chiming clock wiggled as if being jostled by unseen hands until it slid to the edge of the shelf on which it rested. Floating in midair, it circled the room three times before sailing through the doorway, down the short hall toward the open bedroom. After three circuits of that room it slowed, hovering over Nicole's head. The three soft notes sounding the hour brought rapid eye movement to Nicole's undulating lids. The small clock circled the bed before retracing its route to the living room shelf.

"Shall we unmask?" her partner asked, reaching for his goat's mask.

"Yes," she said, removing her non-existent face covering.

When she saw he still had a mask identical to the one he had removed still covering his face, she felt her face redden.

"Shall we unmask?" he asked again, removing the mask only to reveal another.

"Yes." Her voice rose to an irritated level.

"Shall we unmask?" he asked her the third time, pulling the goat's face away again. He stared at her, his yellow eyes drilling into hers, ripping away any shield of secrecy that covered her soul, tearing down any resistance she might have mustered.*

"Yes! Yes! Yes!" she screamed, sitting up in bed.

Breathing heavily as though she had been running for hours, Nicole stared into the darkness. What was wrong? Had she been dreaming? What? What had she been dreaming? Dancing? She had been dancing.

Frowning, she concentrated but could not catch the main theme of the nightmare. It had to be a nightmare if she awoke terrified, sweating and breathing rapidly. What had she dreamt? Why couldn't she remember? Usually she could recall her dreams in great detail. Now, she could not recall anything other than the fact that she had been dancing. But with whom? Where? Why? How? The questions banged at her until her head finally thumped with a dull ache.

Fine. Now she needed an aspirin or two. Throwing back the covers, Nicole slipped from the bed, hurrying to the bathroom. Placing two of the white tablets on her tongue, she washed them down with half a glass of water and returned to bed.

After she turned out the light, she lay there for several minutes, her eyes searching the darkness for some thread of the dream. Nothing materialized and she turned to one side. Perhaps in the morning she'd recall the details. Then she'd not be concerned. Concern? Why should she feel concern over a dream? A silly dream?

She closed her eyes.

In the bathroom, the faucet began turning by itself, breaking the seal from the pipe extending through the sink. Soundlessly moving, the mouth of the faucet pointed to one side, then straight up, to the other side, down at the wash bowl, to one side, straight up and then—the curved piece of chrome floated away to settle on a shelf while the heavy stream of water shot straight out, past the bowl, curving within a foot or two of the basin to the floor. Striking the rug, the water made no sound at first, and as it soaked the pink floor covering, the noise of splashing grew. The door moved gently shut. The water continued flowing.

Tuesday, October 21, 1986   7:00 A.M.

Nicole opened her eyes at the first sound of her alarm's gentle ringing. Stretching, she sat up. She wanted to keep extra busy today and not even think of the day's significance—her birthday. God, how awful to be alone! At least she had her new job to lose herself in, directing all of her energy toward the success of the public relations campaign. Slipping from bed, she screamed when her feet touched the icy water covering her bedroom floor.

7:15 A.M.

"I'm telling you I have no idea what happened," she said nastily into the phone.

"Things like that simply don't happen, Miss Kilton." The manager's voice snapped sarcastically in her ear.

How did he know? He wasn't there. He hadn't seen anything of the damage to her apartment or furniture. "Will you have someone come over and take care of it? Today?"

"Of course I will. That's my job, isn't it? I'll

have a plumber there by nine at the latest. Do you have insurance?"

"Yes, I have insurance. Don't you remember it's stipulated in my lease that I have it."

"Just checking. At any rate, you'd best call your agent. They should be willing to stand for the damages."

Fuming at the delay in leaving for work, Nicole then dialed her insurance agent, who assured her that her possessions were insured, but that the building's owner was responsible for protection to the building itself. After receiving instructions to stay at a motel until the apartment was dried out and her damaged items replaced, she hung up and left for work.

During the next four nights, she stayed at a nearby motel, and once she had received the check to replace her damaged furniture, she shopped for a new bedroom set. The kitchen had had water but nothing there had been damaged, while the rug in the living room had absorbed most of the water that had been on the floor there, leaving the furniture barely wet.

Her first day back in her apartment, a Saturday, seemed endless as she looked forward to retiring for the night in her new water bed. She had thought of the irony of buying such a piece of furniture when it had been water damage that had led to her being able to purchase it in the first place. That night and the next she slept without apparently dreaming anything, something she had not anticipated. While at the motel, she had had dreams but not the strange one. Now that she had returned to her apartment she wondered if it would resume.

Monday, October 27, 1986

Completely refreshed on Monday morning, she showered and was on her way to work by eight fifteen. While waiting for the bus, she thought of Myles. She had hoped she would have heard from him by now. Certainly he should be sufficiently recovered from the trauma of Eunice's death by this time. Perhaps he never would call. Maybe she should call him.

Shaking her head, she stepped onto the bus when it pulled up. No. If he elected not to call her, then it was finished. Maybe she'd never see him again. Biting her tongue, she looked out the bus window at the flow of traffic, doing her best to dismiss Myles from her mind.

8:30 A.M.

A low growl rumbled through Nicole's apartment, while the small red book bounced about on the shelf. Simultaneously, as though perpetrated by one unseen entity, one set of many hands, the drawers to her dresser flew open, while the closet door tore from its hinges and Nicole's wardrobe floated about the bedroom, landing everywhere. The cabinets in the kitchen wrenched open, and the cans, cups, saucers, plates and everything else contained therein sailed about the kitchen, breaking as they hit the floor. Canned foods piled up in the sink, one on top of the next until a shaky thin tower reached the ceiling. The living room furniture ripped open, its cotton stuffing filling the air. All of the books on the shelf above the TV set fell to the floor—all except the red book. It stayed in its place. The chiming clock rocked in place, bobbing back and forth, until it took off, hurtling across the living room with a terrific velocity straight at the television set. The loud pop as the vacuum of the picture tube was broken filled the room and, as if punctuating the havoc wrought, the apartment fell silence except for the sound of heavy panting.

3:00 P.M.

Myles sat at his desk, fingering the key he had found in his desk drawer—Eunice's key, the key to her apartment. Somehow he had forgotten about it and had not returned it to the apartment manager after Eunice's death. He had thrown himself into work since returning to the station office the previous Monday and had not allowed himself much time to think about Eunice or Nicole or anything. Now, as if someone had opened a floodgate, the thoughts came pouring out. Eunice was gone. There was nothing he could do about that.

On the other hand, Nicole had seemed genuinely interested in his welfare when she had come into the office the week before. At first he had found it difficult to face her. He had hurt her. He felt he knew her well enough to read her emotions, even though she had almost successfully hidden them behind her display of self-confidence. Had that been the reason he had taken on the role of martyr, saying that he was going to leave?

Leave? Perhaps that wasn't such a bad idea after all. He could . . .

The pain struck instantly behind his ear. What was wrong with his ear? Or was there something wrong inside his head? What could be causing it?

He leaned back in his chair, staring at the ceiling while he massaged his ear. Little by little, the pain subsided. When had that happened last? He searched his memory. When Nicole had been here in his office. Last Monday. It probably wasn't too serious if it came that infrequently.

What had he been thinking about when the pain struck? Leaving?

The pain came again and Myles froze, staring at the ceiling for a long minute before rubbing the affected ear again.

6:00 P.M.

"Is this just the way you found it, Miss Kilton?" the uniformed policeman asked.

Nicole, her eyes reddened from crying, looked up at the young officer. "Yes."

"And you say the door was locked?"

"That's the strange part about it," she said, dabbing at the corner of one eye. "The key worked normally. I couldn't believe my eyes when I saw the damage."

"You got any enemies? Anybody who might want to get even with you for something?"

Nicole quickly shook her head. There was no one. There weren't enough people in her life to include someone who could be so vindictive. The only person in her life who didn't meet her personal criteria as a friend was Rose Tunic. But Rose was simply an unlikeable person. Nicole and she hardly had any dealings at work, and there was absolutely no reason why the office manager would want to destroy Nicole's apartment. "There's no one I can think of, Officer."

"Well, you'd best make certain that nothing is missing. You know—money, jewelry, other valuables."

Nicole shook her head. "There's nothing. I never leave money in the apartment and my jewelry is pretty pedestrian when it comes to value. In fact, there's nothing of value in the apartment other than the TV, stereo and books. They're all here. Or what's left of them."

"I guess we'll probably write it off to vandalism then. There's no telling what some people will do today."

Nicole looked at him, her puzzled expression bringing a half smile to his face.

"They probably broke in here," he said, "looking for money or stuff they could hock. When they found nothing other than the TV and stereo, they probably went a little nuts and destroyed the place. Beats me why they didn't take the boob tube and stereo and convert them into cash."

"Well, either way, I'm the loser, right?"

He nodded, closing his notebook. "I guess so. You got insurance?"

Nicole swallowed. "I hope so. I just turned in a sizable claim within the last week or so. My bedroom was flooded and the furniture ruined. I just moved back in yesterday."

"I'm sure you have, then," he said kindly.

"They're not going to be too happy with this little turn of events, are they?" she asked, forcing a wry smile.

"Hell, that's what they're in business for, Miss Kilton."

6:30 P.M.

"That may be the reason we're in business, Miss Kilton, but we would like to make a profit as well."

Nicole bit her lip. He was angry. The insurance agent might refuse to help her now that she had made him upset. At first he had thought she was being funny—playing a practical joke. Then, realizing that she was telling the truth, he began asking her pointed questions. When she thought that he was trying to renege on the claim, she had asked him what the purpose of his company was if not to make certain that she and people like her had insurance coverage on their possessions.

"Look, Miss Kilton, I'm sorry. I've had a bad month, and another claim from someone, especially one who just had a sizable check handed to them, is not my idea of ending the day in a very good way."

"Just assure me that I am covered, Mr. Davis," Nicole said.

"Oh, you're covered all right. Right down to your pajamas and the cat's as well. You did call the police?"

"Yes. They said you'd need the case number since there was a crime committed."

"That's right. May I come over and look the damage over? I'm not that far away. I could be there within twenty minutes or so."

"Please, come ahead. The sooner this thing is settled, the quicker I can get on with it."

"No idea who might have done it?" Davis asked.

"None. You sound like the police."

"I'll probably be asking you a lot of the same questions, Miss Kilton."

Niclole hung up and waited for the insurance agent to arrive.

Friday, October 31, 1986 7:00 P.M.

Myles locked his car, walking around it toward the entrance of his apartment building.

"Trick or treat," a rough, little voice demanded.

Myles stopped when the costumed child jumped out in front of him, blocking the way. "Well, now," he said, "what do we have here?"

The child, its features effectively hidden by the withered countenance of an old witch or troll, said nothing.

"I don't have any candy for you."

The child remained silent, holding out one hand, palm up.

"Will you be satisfied with money?"

Still, no response.

Myles reached into his pants pocket, withdrawing a handful of change. Dropping a quarter into the small hand, he moved to step around the Halloween beggar. When he reached the doorway to the main entrance, he stopped before inserting his key and turned to look back at the child. There was no one in sight. Had he imagined it? He knew he was tired but . . . What he needed was a vacation. A rest. Get away from the station for a while. Maybe cast about for a new job.

He turned the key and doubled over at the same time when the pain hit him. His ear again. Nothing had happened in the last four days. Now, all of a sudden, he was being afflicted again. At least Nicole had been sympathetic about it that day in his office.

The pain eased, disappearing in a few moments.

Riding up to his floor, Myles entertained the

mental image of Nicole, smiling as he stepped off the elevator.

Monday, November 3, 1986   6:30 P.M.

Seven days after her apartment had been destroyed, Nicole, who had moved back into the same motel though a different room, hurried home to her newly redecorated rooms, anticipating a restful evening. After admiring her new furniture, she prepared a simple supper. When she finished her evening meal, she sat back on the kitchen chair and thought of Myles. She had not watched him on the late night news while staying at the motel, but tonight she would remedy that. She wondered if he still looked the same. . . .

She stopped. Taking a deep breath, she gagged. What in the world was that terrible stench? She hurried to the sink, first thinking that the odor was not unlike sewer gas, but sniffing around the drain, she found nothing out of the ordinary. Opening the doors below, she inhaled deeply but smelled nothing different. When she stood, the fetid stink still lingered in the air.

Terrible. It was positively awful. Where could it be coming from? The bathroom? Hurrying there, she found nothing that indicated the strange smell emanated from that room.

Could it be coming from her new furniture? She went to the living room. She found the rancid smell was there as well, just as strong as it had been in the kitchen and the bathroom.

Bending down, she sniffed at the couch and the two small occasional chairs. Though they smelled normal, the stench hung in the air. The bedroom? She hurried there and found nothing.

After opening the windows, she got out a can of air freshener, spraying each room. Nothing helped.

Then, it was gone. One second she could smell it and the next it was gone. Well, whatever it was, she would not miss it. Putting the spray can away, she went to the living room, freezing in the doorway.

The stereo was playing, classical music softly filling the air in competition with the TV set, which also was on. She hadn't turned them on when she was in the living room checking the furniture. She had been too upset to have done that. Nor had she done it when she returned to open the windows.

"What's going on?" she asked aloud. "Come on. What's happening? Why are all these things happening to me? Well, there's one way to fix that." She crossed the room and pulled each plug out of its socket. "Let's see you work now!"

As if to mock her, the television set stared at her blankly with its blinded eye while the stereo sat mute.

Later that night, she plugged in the TV set to watch Myles, and when he signed off, she undid the electrical connection once more.

After she had retired for the night, she lay on her back staring into the void. She wanted Myles. She needed him. Tomorrow, she'd call him. Rolling over on her side, she prepared to go to sleep but suddenly sat up.

Through the bedroom door, she could see the glow of the TV set and hear the muted voices of a late night talk show. When she hurried to the living room, she found the stereo playing soft, dreamy music as well.

Biting her knuckle she turned all the lights on in the apartment and pulled the plugs again. Something weird—something out of the ordinary—was going on. But what? Or had she only thought that she had pulled the plugs?

For the next three hours she lay on her back, the lights in the apartment blazing brightly. Finally she dropped off to sleep.

Tuesday, November 4, 1986 8:00 A.M.

Several days after his encounter with the Halloween witch, Myles had decided to take things a bit more easy due to his recuring earache. Instead of leaping from bed and jumping into the shower first thing in the morning, he elected to take it slower. Getting up in a leisurely manner, he enjoyed a long, hot shower before indulging himself in several cups of coffee and the morning newspaper once he was dressed. The first few mornings totally agreed with him, and the last time he had had the pain became a dim memory.

The hot water flowed over him, washing away the night's sleep, invigorating his body as he soaped all over. One thing he definitely knew. If slowing down this way made him feel that much better, what would a full blown vacation feel like? He'd have to discuss the possibilities with the station manager and find out if he could take a week off. Perhaps he'd apply for a few positions he knew were about to be available.

Instantly, the pain pierced his mastoid area and he grabbed at his ear. What the hell? Rubbing vigorously, the discomfort diminished, leaving in a few seconds.

If he did go, he might entertain the thought of taking Nicole with him, if she would consider it.

The sound of the water rose until it sounded like a self-satisfied sigh.

10:00 A.M.

When Nicole called KSLL-TV the next morning, Myles wasn't in yet and she had no another opportunity to try the remainder of the day. After her luncheon break, she sat behind her desk, staring into space. The loss of sleep the night before had done nothing to enhance her daytime energy, and she felt sluggish and sleepy.

"You'd best try going to bed at night and you won't be falling asleep on the job," Rose Tunic said, standing framed in the doorway to

Nicole's office.

Nicole snapped out of her funk, staring at the overweight woman. "I wasn't sleeping," she lied. But had she been sleeping? Actually sleeping on the job? No. She had just reacted slowly when Rose looked in and stopped to drop her nasty little jibe. "If you must know, I didn't get much sleep last night but I wasn't trying to make up for it on company time, if that's what you were hinting at."

"I wasn't hinting at anything. If the shoe fits, wear it," Rose said, a smug look of self-satisfaction crossing her corpulent features. Without another word, she turned and left.

Nicole smiled. How like Rose to use a timeworn cliché to make her point. She wondered when the office manager had had her last original thought. From what she had seen, the woman acted almost entirely on instinct and not intellect. How could someone exist like that? Well, Nicole would be damned if someone like Rose Tunic could get her upset.

Upset. She thought back to the previous night and how jangled her own nerves had been by the strange occurrences. How could the TV and stereo plug themselves into the outlets and turn themselves on? That simply wasn't possible. Still, it had happened somehow. If nothing else she'd get a good night's sleep tonight. She felt dead on her feet and wished for five o'clock to arrive as soon as possible.

Thursday, November 6, 1986   7:30 P.M.

Myles sat behind his desk, fingering the stack of news stories he would report on the eleven o'clock news. He was positive that he'd have no problem with any of the stories. Something else was bothering him.

For the last three days, ever since he had the pain in the shower Tuesday morning, he had put two and two together, arriving at the same answer each time. Whenever he thought of leaving or quitting his job or moving away, the pain struck. When he thought of Nicole, the pain left. How could the two be related? Could medicine explain it? Pain didn't work that way. Love and its relative consequences didn't work that way. Or did it? Several times during the day, he had resolutely made an effort to write a letter of resignation only to be struck with the pain. He immediately thought of Nicole and the pain receded. Each time he tried, the results were the same. It seemed as if his pain were psychosomatic and directly related to his leaving or not leaving Nicole.

Checking his watch, he decided to stop by Nicole's after the eleven o'clock newscast and visit with her. If he felt all right when he was with her, he'd give every consideration to going back into her life. After all, he did feel strongly about her. And that probably meant he was one step removed from loving her—if he didn't already.

The telephone rang and he picked it up.

"Myles Lawrence here."

There was no response other than an agreeable "Um-hmmmmmmm," before the line went dead.

8:45 P.M.

Immediately after eating, Nicole washed her few dishes and put them away. Somehow she had managed to get through the afternoon and now that she was home felt that the only place for her was bed. It wasn't even nine o'clock yet but that didn't matter. She had to get to bed, to sleep.

"Perchance to dream?" she said aloud. She hadn't thought much about her peculiar recuring dream. Whatever was causing it probably would pass in time.

If she went to bed now, she'd miss Myles, but she could do without him for one night. She had done without him for quite a few nights while she stayed in the motel the second time. Of all things to have a motel room that had a TV set that would not bring in KSLL-TV. She remembered how angry she had been but then thought of it as a test to see if she could get by without Myles' electronic visit every night. She had survived nicely and tonight would not be traumatic without him. She was positive of that.

She bathed instead of showering, soaking for almost thirty minutes in lightly scented bath oil, washing away the fatigue of lost sleep and a hard day's work. When she turned out the light next to her pillow, the last thing she looked at was the digital clock and thought that it was the first time in ages that she had gotten to bed before ten o'clock.

Closing her eyes, she teetered on the brink of sleep for perhaps three seconds before plunging headlong into the abyss of slumber. The blackness embraced her, caressing her tiredness and she settled in, comfortable and warm.

At eleven o'clock, the TV set came on, Myles' voice blaring loudly above the blustery march of Tchaikovsky's Sixth Symphony, which poured from the stereo speakers. Bleary-eyed, she sat up, not quite certain where she was or what was happening. That noise? That voice? Myles? Was Myles here? Had he come back to her? Then the words began penetrating her foggy mind.

Something about Libya. The PLO. Something. Why was he saying that if he had come back to her?

THE TELEVISION SET WAS ON!

Leaping from the bed, she froze when a heavy knock came at the door. Who was knocking? Had someone called the police? No, there hadn't been enough time to do that. It had to be an irate neighbor.

Dashing to the front room, she turned off the television set and the stereo. The ensuing silence crushed in on the room.

"Yes? Who's there?"

"Little Bo Peep, you stupid broad," a heavy male voice growled. "What the hell's wrong with you, playing that crap so loud?"

"I'm sorry," she said through the door, not opening it for fear the man would physically attack her in his angry mood.

"Once more and I call the cops or the landlord. It's up to you whether I do or don't. Knock that shit off! Y' hear?"

"It won't happen again. I promise."

"It better not," he said, his voice softening as he walked down the hall to his own apartment.

Nicole leaned against the door. Things like this weren't possible. They simply were NOT . . .

The telephone rang. Now who or what? She lifted the receiver. "Hello?"

"Miss Kilton? This is Fred Astin. I've just received a phone call from one of your neighbors. Why are you playing your TV set so loud?"

"I . . . I . . ."

"Just a word of warning. If I get one more complaint or there's one more incident involving you or your apartment, I'll have to evict you. I have the right. It's in the lease you signed. It's under the nuisance clause in case you'd like to check it. Do I make myself understood?"

"Ye . . . yes, Mr. Astin. It's perfectly clear. Good night."

Astin slammed the receiver down on his end

before Nicole could hang up.

Tears of frustration rolled down Nicole's cheeks. Why couldn't she handle any of this? What in God's name was going on?

She sniffed, choking back a cry. The musty stink enveloped her. What was causing *that*? If someone caught a whiff of it and reported it to the manager, she'd be out. Anger slowly built within her, crowding out her frustration, pushing aside her feelings of desperation. Storming across the living room, she yanked out the television set plug and then did the same to the stereo components. Tying all of them together, she threw them down on the floor. She felt like stamping on them to vent her rage.

A soft knock at the door brought her around. Now who? What now? Just as angry as she had been when she attacked the stereo and TV set, she hurried to the door, throwing it open.

"You having a party?" a quiet voice asked.

She looked up into the eyes of two uniformed policemen. Her anger disappeared. Her neighbors were more than efficient. One had attacked her personally while someone else called the landlord and another the police. She'd have to bluff her way through it. "Not really, Officer," she said, forcing an air of indifferent surprise.

"The precinct got three calls within forty-five seconds, complaining of loud music and noise coming from your apartment. What's your story?"

"I don't really know," she said, hoping her lie would not be too obvious. "The manager called, too, saying the same thing. In fact, a man from down the hall was here before you, threatening to knock the door down or something if I didn't keep quiet."

"Well, what's your story?" the policeman persisted, leaning into the apartment, his eyes darting from left to right. "May we come in?"

"I'm here alone," Nicole said, stepping aside. "For some reason, my TV set and stereo decided to turn themselves on. It . . ."

"*They* decided?" the spokesman for the police team asked, cocking an eyebrow.

"I just said that, Officer. I think there might be something wrong with the switches or something. A little vibration from passing traffic and they go on. It's all I can think of. But I've remedied it for tonight. I've pulled the plugs and tied them together."

"Tied them together?" he echoed.

"I . . ."

Before Nicole could explain, both appliances went on again, this time louder than ever before. It simply wasn't possible. They couldn't be playing. She had pulled the plugs, tied them together and thrown them away from the wall toward the center of the room. Whirling about and stepping aside to allow the policemen entry to the living room, she gasped. Both plugs were in the wall while the knot she had tied had vanished.

"How the hell did you do that? I didn't see

you do anything. You're sure you're here alone?" He nodded at his partner who moved to the kitchen doorway, peering in.

"I told you I'm alone. If you don't believe me, look around. Make yourselves at home. I'm as much at a loss as you are. I don't understand any of it." Her voice took on a hysterical edge, one that she struggled to control. But how was any of this possible?

The officer moved to the TV set and stereo components, pulling both cords out of the wall. The sound stopped. "There now, we won't have to shout, will we?"

He seemed pleasant enough to Nicole. It probably was an act, and she backed away from him. Did they think her crazy?

"Look, Miss, no more of this. I don't know how you did that," he said, looking to his partner who nodded, then shrugged, confirming Nicole's story that she was alone. "But no more. It isn't fair to the other tenants. Do you understand? I don't want to book you for disturbing the peace."

Nicole looked away. It was best if she didn't argue anymore. They couldn't help her. Help her? Why did she suddenly need help? That wasn't the problem. She had to think of something—fast. "Don't worry, Officer," she began. "I intend on calling a repairman first thing in the morning. I'm sure that it's nothing more than a bad switch."

"That's probably a good idea," he said.

"Will you do me a favor before you leave?"

"If I can. What?"

"Tie the plugs together. Do it in such a way that I won't be tempted to watch TV or play a record anymore tonight. They might go loud again and I wouldn't want to disturb anyone."

He tried concealing his smile but failed and quickly tied the cords together, winding them around one leg of the TV stand. "There," he said, standing. "Let the repairman remove them in the morning. G'night, Miss."

She followed them to the door and said, "Thank you for being understanding, Officers."

She closed the door, securing the latch before they could say anything. Hurrying to the window of the living room, that overlooked the front of the building, she could see the police squad car parked at an angle in the drive. In a few minutes, the uniformed men strode out of the front entrance and got into their car. Slowly pulling away from the curb, it glided onto the street and was gone from sight in seconds.

Exhaling a sigh of relief, she wiped a hand over her face. She'd slept about an hour or so and would probably have no trouble getting back to sleep. Turning off the lights in the living room, she entered the hall that led to her bedroom but stopped, unable to move. She heard what sounded like a deep chuckle and then the television set and stereo began playing again. Or had the laugh come from the TV set? Racing back to the living room, she turned on the lights and stifled a scream. The new clock caught her attention. It had been almost midnight when the police left but now the hands were spinning wildly in opposite directions. The noise grew louder until it was unbearable. It wasn't possible for her small stereo to produce that much volume or for the television set to sound as if its audio were being amplified twenty or thirty times beyond its normal peak.

She thought she heard a tapping but could not locate its source. *What could that be?* At least she knew *where* the ruckus was coming from but had no idea *how.* Suddenly, the noise stopped. For only a split second. Just long enough for her to hear the gentle rapping at her front door. It didn't sound like her angry neighbor's knock. That would be a pounding that would threaten to knock the door off its moorings. The noise began again, and she went to the door, confident that she was unable to stop the electronic monsters' din.

Unlocking the door, she opened it, her jaw dropping agape when she saw Myles. He had come back.

Then, the awful, piercing sound stopped.

PART THREE

He Is Come!

Friday, November 7, 1986
to
Saturday, December 6, 1986

8

Friday, November 7, 1986   6:25 A.M.

Nicole felt a gentle pressure on her right
breast and snuggled in closer to Myles. Half
awake, she smiled, recalling the sense of ela-
tion she had felt when she realized that it had
been Myles knocking on the door to her apartment. As consciousness overtook her,
crowding out that delicious half sleep, half
awake sensation, she thought momentarily
about the cacaphony that had raged in her
apartment prior to his appearance at the door.
The stereo, the turntable without a record on
it, the television set—all had been operating at
full volume, producing a level of sound she
didn't think they were capable of emitting. The
hands of the clock had spun wildly in different
directions. And now that she thought about it,
she thought that the furniture might have been
moving of its own accord—bouncing, as if

someone were manipulating the chair and couch. But that was crazy—totally impossible. Wasn't it?

An involuntary moan escaped her lips when Myles began rubbing her nipple with his thumb and forefinger. God, it felt so good. How long had it been? Weeks! Over two months, in fact, but all that was over. Myles had declared his love for her last night in such a way that she felt the two of them would be together forever. Nothing would ever come between them again.

What had he said? She replayed the scene in her mind once more. He had stood there, his face appearing as if a smile would break out any minute, but he had remained somber—at least, for that long moment.

"Hi," he managed after they looked at each other for what seemed hours.

"Hi," she said, fighting to maintain some sort of control. She wanted to scream. *"You're back! You're back! You're back!"* But somehow, she stepped aside, gesturing for him to enter. When he did, they faced each other again. She closed the door, then stepped closer to him.

He backed away and said, "Give me a minute. I've got to say something first."

She waited.

"What I did," he began, his voice soft, almost muffled, "was inexcusably stupid. I didn't think of you once when I decided to take off without warning, and that was wrong.

When two people think a lot of each other and are in love—I guess we are in love, aren't we?—the desires of one should be the desires of the other. I didn't do that, and for that I'm sorry. I hope you forgive me."

Nicole stepped closer until their hands touched. She looked into his eyes.

"Myles," she said, "oh, Myles. You'll never know how I wanted you to come back, but I guess my pride prevented me from coming to you at any one time. I should have done something but . . ."

"As long as we both feel this way, why don't we put it out of our minds and get on with it? Talking about it will only keep the wounds open, and I don't want to hurt you anymore, ever again."

She threw her arms around his neck. "I love you, Myles Lawrence."

"And I love you, Nicole."

Their lips had touched, barely brushing before they firmly joined, their kisses saying more eloquently anything their minds could have verbalized.

Nicole moved even closer to Myles, feeling the warmth of his body. She had missed that. She had missed him. All that would be different now. She knew that. Their love-making had been fantastic, and both had dropped off to sleep, holding each other.

Her eyes searched the half dark of her bedroom. It would be time to get up soon but she'd wait for the alarm to do its job.

One thought invaded her euphoria—what had brought him back? Totally unannounced. Completely surprised by his sudden appearance, she had wanted to ask him but had resisted, and when they had kissed, the thought evaporated for the time being. Now it was back. Why had he indeed come back so . . . so . . . almost mysteriously? And what had caused the chaos in her apartment? For that matter, what had caused any of the peculiar things that had taken place in the last few weeks? The burst pipes. The vandalism of her clothing and apartment. The rank smell that came and went like a breath of something dead or dying or . . .

She stopped. Stop thinking of things like that, she ordered herself. Myles was back. That's all that mattered. They were together, and together, they could face anything. Perhaps she'd ask him what he thought about all the weird things that had happened. And everything had stopped when Myles arrived. Could the two be connected? The noise stopping when Myles showed up at her door? That was crazy! Impossible!

She screwed her face up in thought. The cords to the TV and stereo had been tied around the legs of the TV stand by one of the policemen. Had they still been there when the music and late night movie were blasting so loudly? She couldn't recall. Removing Myles' hand from her breast, she slipped from the bed, putting on her robe.

She tiptoed to the living room and turned on the lights. She gasped. The cords were knotted together, wound around the leg of the TV stand.

8:15 A.M.

"What noise?" Myles asked, sipping his coffee.

"Last night. When you were knocking. Didn't you hear a lot of racket coming from in here?" Nicole stared at him. Surely he had heard the stereo and TV. He would have to have been deaf not to have heard the noise. Earlier, the neighbors had heard it. It had been loud enough for them to complain to both the manager and the police. Why hadn't Myles heard it? Before she had opened the door, the noise had been deafening.

"I didn't hear anything, Nicole. Really, I didn't."

Could she be going crazy? Losing her mind? She had heard the sounds—hadn't she? Now she wasn't sure of anything. The cords were still wound around the table leg this morning, tied together at the end. There was no logical, rational way any of this could be explained. She felt sorry that she had said anything to Myles. What if he thought she were losing her mind?

"I guess I . . . I imagined it," she said softly.

"Imagined what? What kind of noise are you talking about?"

"It . . . it must have been something outside. I just thought I heard a noise before you knocked. That's all. Haven't you ever imagined something that turned out to be nothing?"

He grinned. "You bet. In fact, you witnessed it in my office the day you met with the station manager. The pain behind my ear?"

Nicole wrinkled her face in thought. Pain? What pain? Then, she recalled the intense discomfort Myles had suffered shortly after they had gone to his office before her appointment. It had only been for a minute or so. "What about it?" she asked.

"Remember how I had said I might leave town or look for another job someplace else?"

She nodded.

"That's when the pain struck me. I massaged it and said I probably would stay around, and it left."

"So? I don't understand."

"Everytime it seems that I thought of leaving or looking for work someplace else ever since Eunice died, the pain would attack me right behind my ear. When I thought of you and staying, it would leave."

"What? Are you joking?"

Myles shook his head. "It didn't make sense until last night. I was finishing the news stories I was going to report last night and kicked around the thought of a vacation or leaving. Wham! The pain hit home. I thought about you and the last time we had seen each other and the pain left. Just like that!'' He snapped his fingers. "At any rate, I recalled the other instances when the pain struck and the situation was just about the same each time.''

"That's unbelievable.'' Nicole stared at him. It seemed as if the pain had driven him back to her.

"Not really,'' Myles said quietly. "Not when one takes psychosomatic pain and experiences into account. I suppose it was my conscience kicking me in the mental ass for having walked out on you. At any rate, I'm back. And, that's the most important thing.''

"I guess you're right,'' she said softly. More than likely, he was right. But when she took everything into account that had happened in the past weeks, she wondered.

"Are you ready?'' he asked. "I'll drop you at the clinic. Tonight, I want to hear how you got that job. I was really surprised when you told me why you were at the station. Your work sounds interesting.''

"It is,'' she said, feigning excitement. She'd have to do more than fake enthusiasm when she reached the office. There was a meeting scheduled with Doctor Claypool shortly after nine and she would have to make her report about the results of her media contacts.

At least, Myles was interested, and that was more than she had hoped for at this juncture. He seemed changed somehow. When he said something, she felt that it was said with complete honesty and interest and concern. And it was all aimed at her and for that she was grateful. His sincerity and attention thrilled her. "What do you have planned for today?"

"Well, I'm going to do something I should have done long ago. Move in. At least, I will if it's all right with you. Is it?"

Hugging him with all her strength, she said, "Of course, it is. How many times did I ask you in the past?"

He held her at arm's length and said, "I thought we agreed that we wouldn't mention the past."

"I know, darling. But your moving in is predicated on our having been together so much in the past. It's not as if we first met last night and are doing something we both might regret in a day or two."

He kissed her in response and smiled. "Right you are. Where should I put my things?"

"Shove my stuff to one side of the bedroom closet and take whatever space you need."

By eight fifty-five, he dropped her off at the Cascade Psychiatric Clinic and left. Nicole watched him drive away. She felt so warm, so happy, so fulfilled. After entering the building, she smiled fondly at Rose Tunic who frowned back.

Saturday, November 15, 1986   10:20 P.M.

When they had begun their second week to-

gether, Nicole could not help but note how
smoothly things had gone since Myles' return
—no unusual incidents. While she sat in the
living room, watching a commercial for the
new 1987 Fords, she could hear Myles rustling
about in the kitchen, making popcorn.

"You'd better hurry. The movie's about
ready to come back on," she called.

"It won't be a minute. You want butter?"

"Yes . . . but hurry."

The sound of the commercial died and the
picture tube darkened for the movie to resume.
The picture stayed black for several long
seconds—and then she heard the scratching. It
was in the wall, directly behind her head. She
should have told the manager to call the
exterminator. Perhaps if she called him tomorrow and asked nicely he would agree.

The movie came back on, drowning out the
irritating noise from the wall, only in turn to be
overpowered by a loud crashing followed by
cursing coming from the kitchen.

Leaping to her feet, she raced to the small
kitchenette to find Myles sitting in the middle
of the floor, a look of exasperation on his face.

"What's wrong?" she asked, failing to
smother a laugh.

"The refrigerator door's stuck. I was trying
to get the butter out to melt for the popcorn. It
wouldn't come open and my hand slipped. I
guess I was pulling harder than I realized and
lost my balance." He struggled to his feet.

"Are you all right?" she asked, moving to

the refrigerator. The door opened easily when she tried.

"Oh, for . . ." Myles' face flushed, embarrassed by the ease with which Nicole had opened the door. "What do you suppose . . ."

"Don't be concerned," she said, forcing an air of light-heartedness. "It does that from time to time. Come on. Forget the butter or we'll miss the rest of the movie." She picked up the bowl of popcorn, hoping her lie would not be discovered. She had no idea what had happened to the door, hoping that whatever it was wouldn't fall into the same category of the other strange occurrences that had taken place during Myles' absence.

A quick-silver thought shot through her head. Did Myles' absence have anything to do with the water incident or the destruction of her apartment? Or the peculiar smell? She shook her head. That was all silly. Stupid! Turning out the kitchenette light, she joined Myles in the front room.

When the movie finished, they went to bed. Myles did not like the idea of going out every Saturday night when he didn't have to give the late news, preferring to enjoy an occasional quiet evening with Nicole. They had talked and eaten a sumptuous dinner, then watched a movie on the ARTS channel. As long as Myles was with her, she could not have wished for anything else.

After they fell asleep, the quiet sound of music filtered through the apartment, accompanied by a soft laugh that hovered over the bed. The sliding door to the closet wiggled for a second and then remained motionless.

Sunday, November 16, 1986   7:45 A.M.

The next morning, Nicole got up first, and after showering, dressed quickly. When Myles awakened, he smelled the coffee brewing and could hear bacon frying, its woody aroma filling the apartment. After stretching and doing a few push-ups, he showered and went to the closet to get a pair of slacks.

Sliding open the door, he stared wide-eyed before crying out, "Jesus Christ! What the hell's going on?"

The tone of his voice brought Nicole running to the bedroom. "What is it, darling?" she asked, jerking to a stop, frozen in her tracks.

Most of his clothing—the suits, sports jackets, slacks and shirts—were hanging from the bar, ripped into fine threads of fabric, shredded as if by a razor blade.

"What . . . ?" she asked, approaching him in a deliberate way. He stared at her, frightening Nicole. "What's the matter?"

He continued glaring, as if he were trying to bore a hole through her with his eyes. "You ask, 'What's the matter?' How can you ask that, Nicole? Why the hell did you . . . ?" He stopped, shaking his head. "You didn't. You couldn't. You wouldn't!"

"Wouldn't what? Do that? Rip your clothing

to shreds?'' she asked, incapable of believing that Myles would have even entertained such a thought for even an instant.

"I'm sorry, Nicole. I really am. You've got to admit that it's a bit of a shock, opening the closet to see all your clothing shredded like that."

She embraced him for a second before pulling away. "What happened? Was it all right last night?"

He nodded. "When I got my robe out, I didn't look. Why should I? How could someone have gotten in here during the night without waking one of us up? That doesn't seem possible, does it?"

She shook her head, agreeing with him. What could she say to him? *I forgot to tell you, but this place is haunted now. Maybe we should have gone to your apartment instead.* He wouldn't buy that. It was too simple. Myles had a penchant for being overly pragmatic at the wrong time. This was bound to be one of them. Should she tell him of the strange things that had happened? If for no other reason than to determine whose insurance company would be on the line for the risk involved. She'd have to tell him about the water incident and how vandals had sacked her home and how her insurance company had paid off both claims.

"I think I should tell you something," she said by way of broaching the subject to him.

After she finished, he nodded thoughtfully. "I wondered about the new furniture. In time, you would have told me. I guess I'd better tell my company and let them pay off. If yours becomes involved again, they might cancel your coverage."

When Myles' insurance agent was told of the previous claims, he agreed to do all he could to help them. The two suits that weren't torn apart were moved to the front hall closet, and Myles at least had something to go to work in the next day.

Monday, November 17, 1986 8:57 A.M.

When Nicole entered her office building that next morning, the first person she saw was Rose Tunic.

"Well, you certainly must have been partying all weekend," Rose said, staring at Nicole's weary face.

She had not slept most of Sunday night, wondering what indeed was going on in her home. Myles had had some difficulty in falling asleep but dropped off around one thirty. But she had lain awake all night, more or less keeping guard for the two of them. Now this fat, frustrated old maid was going to give her a hard time?

"Don't concern yourself, *Chunky*!" Nicole snapped, slamming the door to her office behind her as if punctuating the insult.

11:52 P.M.

That night, Myles returned home shortly before midnight to find Nicole sleeping in the easy chair, KSLL-TV still on, showing a late movie. He turned off the set before gently awakening her.

"I . . . I must have fallen asleep," she said groggily.

"Did you sleep much last night?" he asked.

"Not as much as I should have. I'll be all right."

The telephone rang and Myles quickly answered it. Nicole stretched, wishing for more sleep, and moved toward the short hall leading to the bedroom.

"I've gotta go," Myles said, coming up behind her. "There's an out-of-control fire at the Riverside Home for the Aged. I guess it's pretty bad. The camera truck is on its way there now and I'm to meet them. Don't wait up for me."

"Don't worry," Nicole said, yawning, "I won't."

Myles closed the door quietly behind him and she was alone. When the phone rang again, she jumped. It had to be for Myles. They must have forgotten to tell him something. Retracing her steps to the living room, she picked up the receiver on the fourth ring and said, "Hello?"'

"Nicole? Is that you?"

"Uh-huh!" she yawned. "Who's this?"

"Stacey. Stacey Ford. You sound like I woke you up. Did I?"

"Not really, Stacey. I was just going to bed though. What's up?" She hoped Stacey did not want to talk about something in particular or that she wasn't out rounding up recruits for the Reverend Eddie John What's-his-name. When she looked at the time, Nicole silently cursed.

"Nothing much. I was just curious as to how you were doing. I told the Reverend Eddie John about you. He suggested I give you a call."

Nicole wanted to scream or curse or do something that would give full vent to her feelings. The Reverend Son-of-a-bitch wanted his lady flunky to give her a call? At this hour? Why? To convert her over the phone? Biting her tongue for a moment, she said, "Now why would he have done that?"

"It's just the way he is. Really, Nicole. He thought I should give you a call and sort of touch bases with you."

"That's real nice, Stacey. But not tonight. I'm beat. I really am. I didn't get much sleep last night and I've got to get some sleep now or I'll have had it with my job."

"What about coffee tomorrow morning?"

"What time?" She'd agree to almost anything if she would be allowed to go to bed.

"Is ten all right?"

"That's fine. By then, I'll be ready for a cup of coffee. By the way, I'm not at the art store anymore."

"Oh, really? Where are you working now?"

Nicole gave her the address and they said
goodbye. When she dropped the phone in its
cradle, she sighed heavily. Reaching her
bedroom, she dropped her robe to the floor and
fell into bed. In seconds, she slipped off to a
sound sleep, unmindful of the vacant spot next
to her. Her last thought was of Myles and a
fervent wish that he get home as soon as
possible.

Her mind swirled, spiraling into the depths
of sleep, pulling her down to a deep level from
where she would not awaken easily.

*She stood before huge golden doors with red
handles. Stepping forward, she placed a tentative hand on one, pulling gently. The door
swung open without making a sound. Inside,
candles flared from behind red shades bathing
the ballroom in a crimson wash. Around the
floor, people stood as if chatting, but there was
no sound she could make out. They seemed
frozen in position—almost like statuary.*

*She walked to the center of the floor, turning
completely around as she did. The fine silk
dress she wore flared out as she pirouetted.
Elegant! She felt absolutely magnificent. But
where was her partner? She could not recall
ever having been in this place before. And she
was alone. She felt so alone—as if there were no
one else in the world. But there was. There
were people standing around the periphery of
the dance floor—and they all seemed to be*

staring at her. Music began playing somewhere in the distance. Then a gentle buzzing of voices, locked in earnest conversation, fingered its way toward her. The music grew louder and the people began dancing. She felt foolish. All alone in the middle of the floor and without a partner.

"May I have this dance?" a deep, resonant voice asked from behind her.

She whirled about to face a man wearing a goat mask. Without saying a word, she held out her hand, which he took in one of his, the other snaking around her waist.

In the living room, the red light of the stereo glowed evenly as the soft strains of *Roses From The South* wafted through the apartment.

9

Tuesday, November 18, 1986   2:45 A.M.

Nicole felt as if she were flying. Whoever it was she danced with—Myles?—twirled her across the wide open expanse, her feet barely touching the floor. The room seemed to expand whenever they neared one of the walls. Forcing her eyes open, she found that she and her masked partner were the only dancers on the floor. When she looked, she found the people who had been facing the dancing area had turned away, their backs squarely to her now. How strange. How—how peculiar. But she couldn't let something that bizarre interfere with her enjoyment of the dance. The man with whom she glided across the floor seemed to be most adept at moving to music. The music sounded like a waltz but it was distant and soft and she could not really make out what sort of rhythm was being played. Nevertheless, she and her partner moved in three-quarter time. What difference? The mood, the atmosphere, everything exhilarated Nicole until she felt an electric-like charge flowing across the surface of her skin.

A gonging sound pealed twelve times, echoing through the wide expanse of the hall. She looked up into the immobile, impassive face of her partner's mask. What did he look like? Handsome? Dark complected? Or light? What sort of nose? Smile? What color eyes? Did she care? She wanted to ask him his name and she tried to form the question in her mind, which didn't seem to respond. What was wrong? Why couldn't she get her brain to order her vocal chords and mouth to ask the simple question? The first word. What would be the first word of the sentence? What! Of course. The next would be—is. Then—your. And finally—name?

She opened her mouth. The gong sounded once. One o'clock. Not hardly. It had just tolled the hour of midnight. It couldn't possibly be one in the morning. It was too soon. Forcing her mouth open, she said, "What is . . ."

The gong sounded twice. Impossible. Time didn't pass that quickly. It couldn't. Time was inexorable. It did its own thing its own way. Nothing anyone ever did could alter that fact. Concentrating on the man with his face concealed who held her, she tried again. "What is your . . ."

Three resounding gongs brought the music

to a stop, and her partner stopped dancing, still holding her tightly.

"What is your . . ." she tried again. He stopped her with a finger to her lips. The digit felt rough, calloused, not at all like the finger of a man who could dance so smoothly. He pulled it away and she flicked her tongue out, over her lips. A peculiar taste invaded her mouth when she drew her tongue back. Something tasted awful. Strong. Flavored like—she couldn't quite place the unpleasant tang.

"Shall we unmask?" he asked quietly.

"Yes," she said automatically.

Reaching up he took off his mask, only to reveal the second visage of a goat.

Nicole touched her face, surprised to find that she, too, wore a facial covering. It was nothing but an eyemask and she removed it without difficulty.

"Shall we unmask?" he asked again.

"Yes," she said, reaching up to find her face bare.

He removed his goat mask, revealing a third.

"Shall we unmask?" he repeated for the third time.

"Yes!" she screamed and turned away, wrenching free of his grasp. Realizing that she was loose, she raced away from her masked dancing partner. She dashed toward the people lining the walls, their backs still to her. She stopped behind one.

"Help me! Please? Help me!" she cried plaintively.

The man to whom she addressed her plea turned to face her, but displayed another back to her. The man had no front. Forcing herself not to scream, she turned to the woman standing next to the man she had first addressed.

"Will you help me? I need help. Please? Help me! Please?" *she said, noting the strange begging nuance in her voice. Why was she asking for help? Why did she need assistance from these people? Turning away from the man, she touched the woman's shoulder.* Please?" *she repeated.*

The woman turned, to show that she, like the man, had no front side, only two backs. Why couldn't she find one normal person here? What was going on?

Footsteps from behind brought her about. The man with whom she had been dancing was approaching her. He still wore a mask and held out his hands to her.

Rooted in place, she stared. What did he want? Why didn't he unmask? Who was he, this man who wore a goat's visage over his own?

"Who ... who are you?" *she finally managed. She no longer cared what his name might be, but cared so much who he was, that now she had managed to complete a question to him.*

"Come," *he said simply, taking her hand in one of his. The calloused palm felt strange, rough, intimidating.*

"Where are we going?"

"You'll see," he said, leading her toward the middle of the dance floor.

As they approached, part of the floor began rising until a rectangular portion was waist high to her. When they reached the table-like dais, they stopped and she sensed people standing close by. Turning, she found the people who had been standing around the floor, their front sides restored, facing her and the strange man. Shuffling about, they formed lines that led out, away from the table. Two files of people would move together until they touched in the distance, forming a sort of "V," and when she turned, she found that there were four more such sets of lines. It somehow seemed familiar. Where had she seen such a diagram or layout before? Was it a diagram she had seen? From the distance more and more people came, joining hands around the five points formed by the lines of people flowing out and away from the table-like dais. When a double circle of people on the outside was complete, the man looked down at her.

"Are you ready?" he asked solemnly.

"Ready? For what?"

"You invoked the love-force. The love-force has been invoked and has served you. Maruts has obeyed your command. Agni fired the man's love for you and the man has returned to you." His voice rang hollowly.

"I . . . I invoked? What are you talking about?"

"You begged me to favor you. I answered.

*You sought the help of my ministers. Of Prince
Beelzebub. Of Earl Astorath. All of us have
favored you and granted your wish. You had
great need of my counsel. You even threatened
me with the great living God, His Son and His
Spirit, with the words of power and great
wisdom of Solomon. You invoked me. I served
you. Now, I want my just due." The words
echoed through the hall.*

*Nicole violently shook her head. "No. You
didn't come when I ordered you."*

*"I did. You weren't aware of me but I have
been with you ever since."*

"No! No! No!" Nicole screamed. "Never!"

*He reached out, touching her bare arms, and
lifted her effortlessly to the table.*

*"On this altar, you will pay your first install-
ment. You are mine now, as I was yours, to
command. You will do for me that which I
order."*

*Nicole wanted to fight, to resist, but found
she could not move. Nothing responded to her
futile mental commands. She was helpless. Defenseless. The cold of the altar on which she lay
didn't bother her, and she found her senses
reeling from the situation in which she found
herself.*

*A murmuring around her grew as the crowd
of people pressed in closer to the table.
"Lucifuge. Satanachia. Agaliarept. Fleuretty.
Sargatanas. Nebiros. Bael. Agares. Marbas.
Pruslas. Aamon. Barbatos. Buer. Gusoyn.
Botis. And all the demons. Come, join us.*

Watch our Emperor, Lucifer, have this slut.
Come, oh, Bathim. Pursan. Abigar. Loray.
Valefar. Foranii. Ayperos. Nuberus.
Glasyabolas. Come. Now!"

Nicole struggled to concentrate on the names
that were being intoned. Who were the people
they were calling, if indeed the strange words
were names? For some reason she knew they
were names—but names of whom? Or what?

A slow dawning brought her to her senses.
The dream! This was her dream. The one that
she had been having over and over again. She
had only remembered bits and pieces of it, but
now the whole of it was laid out before her—
and she would remember. She would finally re-
member. Or would she? It seemed to her that
she had had the same thought before whenever
experiencing it, but when she awoke, the entire
dream always eluded her, escaping into the
deepest recesses of her mind. No matter how
hard she tried, she could never dredge up more
than a thread or two of it. She'd try this time to
retain the experience.

The people crowding in around her continued
chanting one name over and over. "Lucifer!
Lucifer! Lucifer!"

Looking down the length of her body she saw
her partner standing near her feet. He reached
up grasping the goat's mask to remove it.
Would he have another under it? Pulling it
away with a sweep, he lay bare his face and she
shrieked at the visage before her. Almost
triangular in shape, the face held slanted eyes

that paralleled his "v" shaped mouth which in turn complimented the angular lines of his chin.

"Lucifer! The kiss! Lucifer! The kiss! Lucifer! The kiss! Make her yours! Make her yours! Make her yours!" *The cries grew louder and sharper in their fanaticism as the people bowed to the grim personage at her feet. Leaping to the table, he straddled her legs, before dropping to his knees. Ripping off the dancer's costume he had worn, he reached out tearing away her silk dress, exposing her nakedness.*

His glowing amber eyes swept over the damned congregation crying out to him. "Kiss!" *he boomed and leaned down, closer to Nicole's face.*

Closing her eyes tight, she turned her head away. She didn't want him to kiss her. Nothing happened. After several long minutes dragged by, during which she sensed the demon's nearness more than felt it, she tentatively opened one eye to find him still kneeling in the same position. Was he waiting for her to offer her lips to him? Then she saw a blur of motion behind him and opened her other eye. The people were passing by, kissing him on the hind side, extolling him in loud voices: "Hail Emperor Lucifer! Hail to Thee, Our Lord and Master!"

Great God! What had she gotten involved in? This dream in all its symbolism and weirdness had to mean something. But what? Why didn't she simply wake up? Could she wake up? Or—might she be dead? Gone to Hell? Paying for her sins. What sins? She had never done anything terribly wrong that she felt she would wind up in the netherworld like this.

The last of the creatures kissed the thing above her and he smiled at her. Kneeling erect, he threw his arms out, and at the same time, a blood engorged penis, as large in diameter as her arm and as long, sprang out in front of him.

Nicole screamed, trying to move away, but heavy hands reached out, grasping her and holding her in place. More hands pulled on her ankles, spreading her legs.

"No! No, dear God, no!" she screamed but was answered by the coterie pushing in closer and closer.

"Yes! Yes, dear Lucifer! Yes!" they cried, mimicking her.

The demon came closer, his gigantic member moving of its own accord, angled toward her crotch. When he touched her with it, she gasped at its fiery temperature. Then, he drove it home and she screamed—long and loud. The cry hung in the air, lingering, as the beast pumped at her fragile human body. The semen exploded inside her, icy cold, gushing out of her past his ramming organ, down the inside of her thighs. A hue and cry went up and the people again clamored loudly.

"The Kiss! She must give the Kiss! The Kiss! The Kiss! The Kiss!"

Nicole tried moving, tried thinking, tried

reasoning. Nothing worked. She was doomed. She was in Hell. She was dead. She had to be. This was no dream. She should have awakened long before this if it were truly a dream.

The demon withdrew his still rigid member, which quickly withered and shrank until it dangled spent and lifeless along his own thigh, its head bouncing between his knees. Standing, he turned his backside to her and knelt once more. He waited.

Nicole sat up, powerless to do anything but comply with the order she felt drumming in her head.

"Kiss! Kiss him! Kiss Lucifer! Kiss! Kiss! Kiss!"

When she neared him, he bent down, his buttocks spreading apart. Where did she kiss him? There? There in the middle of the cheeks? She shuddered, leaning foward. Puckering her lips, she felt her breath gasping spasmodically. She touched him—for the briefest of seconds— and withdrew.

Then she felt herself floating lightly through the air. Somewhere a maniacal laugh rang through the darkness and she was being hurled down, down, down. At last, she landed on something soft.

6:19 A.M.

Terrified, Nicole opened her eyes to the familiar darkness of her room. Her body, drenched in sweat, trembled uncontrollably.

The dream. She had experienced her dream, and this time she remembered everything. A sick feeling grew from a tiny pinpoint in her stomach, spiraling outward until her whole being vibrated with a nausea she had never felt before. The dream. What did it mean? She remembered thinking she might be dead and almost wished for it as her stomach heaved and jerked.

She sat up. And screamed.

There at the foot of her bed, she saw the same being with the triangular visage, who had violated her in the nightmare. Her strength, her will to live, all human desire wilted—and she fainted, sprawling back on the bed.

The demon lingered for a moment and then disappeared. The same evil smile that had graced his countenance while preparing to rape Nicole, played on his thin, wrinkled lips.

Nicole's faint became a dreamless sleep, and when hands again grasped her, she sat up, screaming at the top of her voice.

"Hey," Myles cried, surprised by her reaction, "take it easy. You having a bad dream?"

Nicole stared at him, failing to understand that Myles actually stood there, a foolish little grin on his face. Dreaming? Yes. That was it. She had been dreaming. Her dream. But now, for some unfathomable reason, she could recall everything in the minutest of details. The dance, the frontless people, the demon, his raping her, kissing him on the . . . She gagged, jumping from the bed and dashing headlong toward the bathroom.

THE DEMON! She had seen him standing at the foot of her bed. Or had that been part of her dream as well? In the bathroom, she knelt by the toilet, her head hovering over the water. She felt like vomiting but knew she couldn't. There was nothing in her stomach.

"Are you all right?" Myles asked from the doorway of the bathroom.

Assured that she wouldn't throw up, Nicole stood, forcing a smile. "I might be coming down with the flu or something."

"Sleeping bare-assed naked won't help if you're getting sick, you know," he said, motioning to her nudity.

She looked down. Where was her nightgown? She had put it on. She distinctly remembered having done so. Myles stared at her while she reconstructed her dressing for bed. She shrugged. "I guess you're right."

"Bad dream?"

"Uh-huh."

"Do you want to get up or go back to sleep? You could call in sick if you don't feel one hundred percent."

"What time is it?"

He looked at his watch. "Six thirty."

"I'd better think about getting up. How bad was the fire?"

"Very bad. Quite a few died in it. A real mess."

"Will you make coffee?"

"Sure," he said, leaving the bathroom.

When he was gone, Nicole ran to the bed and threw back the covers. She swallowed the scream that almost erupted. There, in the middle of the bed was her silk nightgown, shredded into threads. Something else held her attention for a long minute. The spot. She reached out to touch it. Cold. It was freezing cold and damp. Again, she desperately struggled not to scream. Without looking, one hand moved toward her lower abdomen. It felt normal. The fingertips trailed down, through her pubic hair and on to the insides of her thighs. Wet. Damp. Cold. That dream was too damned realistic.

She heard Myles making coffee, and when the cupboard doors slammed, she knew he'd be with her in seconds. Throwing her destroyed nightgown into the hamper, she was almost ready to throw the covers over the spot. What would Myles say? He'd be in bed shortly. How would she explain it?

"Hey, Nicole. Come here," he called from the kitchen.

"In a sec." She slipped into her dressing gown and, tying it about her middle, went to the kitchen only to meet Myles coming toward her. "What's the matter?"

"What's all over the kitchen table?"

"All over the table? I don't know."

"Well, take a look at it and tell me," he said, guiding her by one arm.

When they entered the small room, she

looked at the table, barely big enough to hold the dishes for two people's meals. It was clean. Spotlessly clean.

"Look at what?" she asked, turning to face him.

Stepping around her, he stopped short. "It was there a second ago. Really."

"What was there?"

"I don't know but it was sort of a whiteish-gray goop of some kind. No. More like uncooked egg white. Yeah. Uncooked egg white. That's it." He stared at her, waiting for an explanation.

"Well, whatever was there is gone now, isn't it?" she said, trying to sound undisturbed.

"For a minute, I thought it looked like . . ." Myles stopped.

She waited, but when he didn't continue, she asked, "What?" Holding her breath, she wondered what he would compare it to now.

"Like semen, damnit!" he said gruffly. "But it would have had to have come from a horse or a bull, there was so much of it."

"Tired, darling?"

"Goddamnit, don't patronize me, Nicole. I know I saw it. At least I think I did. Ah, crap. Let me go to bed. I'm exhausted." He pushed around her and went to the bedroom.

Following closely, Nicole practically tripped over his heels. When he looked at the bed and continued around it, she stopped in the doorway. The spot that had been there a moment before was gone.

HANDS OF LUCIFER

The only sound in the apartment—other than Nicole's quick breathing—was the bubbling of the coffee maker in the kitchen.

10

Tuesday, November 18, 1986   7:30 A.M.

Nicole studied Myles over the rim of her cup
as she sipped her coffee. He sat at the opposite
end of the couch, doing the same thing. "Are
you certain the coffee won't keep you awake
when you do go to bed?" she asked, placing her
own cup on the low table in front of the couch.

He smiled grimly. "I'm so beat a herd of ele-
phants charging through the apartment
wouldn't faze me."

He had told her some of the incidents about
the fire he had covered after they mutually and
silently agreed not to mention whatever it was
he had seen on the kitchen table. Nicole
wondered about it. She had seen the wet spot
on the sheets and mattress. Yet, when they had
returned to the bedroom, it, like Myles' discovery, had vanished as well. Perhaps it had
come from her and was ready to evaporate

anyway.

The dream in its entirety had been more than arousing. She had actually climaxed sometime during the night. All of the aftereffects had been there—the absolute feeling of total weakness, almost an inability to move, the glowing that traversed her entire body, right down to the sensation of euphoria—all of them had been there. She had climaxed during the night and had left some of her own bodily fluids staining the sheets. Fortunately, they had dried.

"What time do you think you'll get up?" she asked.

"Probably around three or so. I still have to report the news, you know." His voice quaked in its tired state. "What about you? Are you all right?"

She looked up, startled. "Wha . . . what do you mean?"

"Your dream. The one that made you scream when I awakened you. Remember?"

"Oh, that," she said, trying her best to sound nonchalant. When she looked at him, she realized she had failed.

"Don't try to down-play it, girl," he said gently. "If you had a bad one, tell me about it. It'll probably help you get over any fear it might have caused you."

How could she tell him? The whole thing was weird. But maybe if she talked about it with someone, it would go away and never bother her again. She'd simply have to trust her instincts concerning Myles.

"It all started with me standing outside this ballroom with golden doors trimmed in red," she began slowly.

When she finished, Myles stared at her. The fatigue lining his face still clung there but his eyes betrayed the curiosity of the newsman. "Wow," he managed. "That's about the sexiest thing I've ever heard."

"Myles!" she said. "That's about the last thing . . ."

"Hey, wait a minute. Don't go off half-cocked. Did you listen to everything you just told me? That was some pretty steamy stuff. As a budding psychologist, you should know that one is not responsible for the dreams one experiences. Am I right?"

She nodded slowly.

"Then I rest my case in that particular area. It *is* sexy. Have you ever had anything like this happen before?"

She turned away.

"I don't mean for real. I mean, have you had any dreams like that before last night?"

Without facing him, she said, "Yes."

Myles didn't respond immediately. When several minutes had passed, she turned to face him.

"Just like it? The same dream? Or were they different?" He smiled reassuringly.

"Yes," she managed, before coughing to clear her voice. "I've had the same dream before, I think."

"You think?"

"I mean, I remember bits and pieces of it. I guess it must have been the same one. It certainly stuck with me this time."

Nodding, an ironic smile crossed his face. "I don't think I'd worry about it, if I were you. Maybe you could talk to Doctor Claypool at the clinic. He'd probably set you straight in a minute or two. Don't dreams symbolize certain things?"

She nodded. "I don't think I'll say anything to him. At least, not right now. I don't want them to think they hired a 'case' who wants free treatment. I've only been there a short while. I'll wait. If it happens again and it bothers me, I'll think about talking to him. He's a nice man but I don't want to run the risk of having him change his opinion of me." A frown crossed her face when she recalled the last thing that had happened right after she awoke from the dream.

"What's the matter?" he asked.

"Huh?" Looking up, she found him closely watching her.

"You're frowning. Why?"

"I just thought of something else."

"What?"

She pondered the wisdom of telling Myles about the apparition she had seen—or thought she had seen—when she awakened from the dream. When she had told him of the dream itself, he had been supportive and she had found that most refreshing. If she and Myles were to have any type of lasting relationship, she would have to learn to place her trust in him. In turn, she'd have to learn to accept his trust.

"When I awoke right after having . . . having kissed his . . . his rear," she began, "I felt like I was floating or being carried. Off in the distance, I could hear this high pitched laugh. All around me, there was nothing but darkness. Then, I felt as if I had been thrown down. I know it felt like I was falling and falling and falling. Then, I landed on something soft and I opened my eyes."

"You already told me that part," Myles said, a hint of irritation in his tired voice.

"But then," she continued, choosing to ignore his complaint, "I opened my eyes and was in the bedroom. I was wringing wet with sweat and I felt sick to my stomach. I thought I was going to vomit and sat up. That's when I saw it."

Myles' eyes widened, a curious expectation replacing the exhaustion on his face. "Saw it? Saw what?"

Nicole swallowed. "I thought I saw the man or demon or thing or whatever it was, standing at the foot of the bed, staring at me. His eyes were sort of amber-like and his 'v' shaped mouth grinned at me. I . . . I felt like someone pulled my plug."

"Pulled your plug?" he repeated.

"Whatever strength I had left drained out of me, and I just fell back. I guess I fainted. The next thing I knew you were waking me up."

"Well, when you have a dream, you really conjure up a production number, don't you?"

Screwing up her face in thought, she looked past Myles, to the far end of the living room. "I . . . I'm . . . I'm not . . ."

He waited and when she didn't continue, he said, "You're not what?"

How could she tell him she thought she actually saw the demon standing at the foot of her bed? It sounded preposterous. Things like that didn't happen.

"Come on," he insisted. "Tell me. You've told me everything so far. At least I think you did. Don't hold back on me now."

"I really think I saw the demon or something standing at the foot of the bed. I actually saw it. It was standing there."

"Well, where did he go? He's not around now, is he?"

"Don't do that. You're making fun of me."

"I'm sorry. I really am. I didn't mean for it to sound like that. If you think you saw it, I'm sure it was real for you."

"Now that I've said it aloud, I know I don't merely think I saw it. I actually, really, truly did see it. I know that."

"Wait a minute. Tell me something. Why would something like a demon come around here? This is 1986. Demons don't go around scaring people any more. At least not that I know of."

Tears filled Nicole's eyes. Tears of frustration. Tears of concern for something she did not dare admit to anyone—most especially to herself.

"I'm sorry," he said lamely, realizing that she was weeping. "You have to admit the whole dream thing is pretty far out. What would have prompted a dream like that? Any idea?"

She shook her head.

"Have you watched any scary movies or read any scary books lately?"

Fighting her sobs, she managed, "No movies. But I did read *Kiss Not The Child* a while back."

"What was that about?"

"Demon worshippers and . . . and the son of Lucifer or Satan or someone. I . . . I don't remember much about it."

"Well, there you are. There's your reason for the dream. Didn't you say that you've been having the dream for some time?"

She nodded.

"Probably the book started the idea fermenting, and the dream grew until it manifested last night."

"You make it sound so simple."

"Hey, look, these authors dream up all this junk about demons and things that go bump in the night and do it in just the right way to blow the mind of the reader. That's all that happened. You didn't meet any new people, who might have affected you?"

Shaking her head, she hoped he was right.

"You don't think it had anything to do with the ritual I performed?" She bit her tongue. Why had she asked him that? She had never intended to tell anyone—much less Myles. She had thought of that night just seconds before when she first started crying. At first, she had concluded the dream and the rite were related somehow. But she couldn't admit that to anyone—not even herself. Now she had tipped her hand and asked him about it.

His newsman instincts aroused by the strange question, he homed in. "Ritual? What ritual?"

"Oh, Myles," she began, knowing full well she would have to tell him. "You'll think I'm crazy or something."

"No, I won't. Tell me. How can I help if you don't tell me everything?"

"Help? Help me how? What are you talking about?"

"Obviously you have something bothering you and want to tell me to get it off your chest. If it involves me or you or us—our lives together—you've got to tell me."

He was right. She knew that. She had no other choice but to tell him. Would he think her mad? Would he even entertain the idea of staying around any longer than it took to put his things together and run out of her life? Did she have to risk that now of all times? When she looked up, she found him staring at her, waiting for her to answer. "Do you love me?"

"Of course I do. You know that."

"Will you promise to hear everything I have to say? Promise you won't jump to conclusions about anything I'm going to tell you?"

"If it will make you happy, yes. I'm not the type to jump to wrong conclusions about anything. Even right conclusions. I usually reserve judgment until all the facts are in. You know that."

For the second time since awakening, Nicole was going to confess a deep dark secret to the man she loved. This one might drive him away from her forever. She had no way of knowing until she laid the awful truth out for him to examine. But it was something she had to do. She knew that.

"Right after you walked out on me, I went into a depression and mental funk like you wouldn't believe," she began.

When she finished, Myles whistled softly. "I had no idea that my leaving would affect you so badly. My God. I *am* sorry, Nicole. *Jesus!* To think my leaving made you go out and . . . Look, let's not talk about this anymore. It's over. It's in the past. Ancient history. Never happened. All right?"

"But Myles," she protested lamely. "Everything seems to fall into place. This is the first time I even admitted to myself that I had performed that silly thing. I was desperate and I guess a little drunk that night. I don't really remember all of it that clearly. But look at the strange things that have happened."

"Such as?"

She ran down the list of peculiar events that had taken place since she had performed the bizarre, bargaining supplication. The water in her apartment. The apparent act of vandalism. The awful smells. Her stereo and TV turning on by themselves. His wardrobe's destruction. Her dream. Seeing the demon. Even Myles' return, so sudden and unexpected.

"But that was my idea," he said, breaking into her discourse.

"Why did you decide to come back when you did?" she asked pointedly.

"I thought everything through and returning here was the answer. It's as simple as that."

"What about the pains you were suffering?"

"Psychosomatic!"

"How about the noise I heard and you didn't?"

Myles looked at her. "What noise?"

"Don't you remember? The night you came back. I asked you the next morning if you hadn't heard a racket in here while you were knocking. You said no."

"So?"

"So, earlier, the neighbors had complained to the manager, who called and chewed me out. Some of them went over his head and called the cops. They came and warned me. While they were here, the sets turned on by themselves."

"Oh, come on, Nicole."

"I'm not lying. I'm sure they have the incident on record at the police station if you'd like to check my story," she said coldly, almost dispassionately.

The icy bitterness in her voice brought an immediate reaction from him. "I'm sorry for doubting you. But you have to admit it sounds pretty far-fetched."

"Try this one for size, then," she said, softening the edge of her voice. "The morning after you came back, I recalled that one of the policemen had pulled the plugs and tied them together around the leg of the TV stand. When I thought of that, I got up and went to the living room. They were still tied together around the leg."

"What does that prove?" Myles asked incredulously.

"I asked you if you had heard any noise the night before when you were knocking. Well, the TV set and the stereo were playing at full blast. Why you didn't hear it, is beyond me."

"Me and everybody else," Myles said quietly.

"What do you mean?"

"If the neighbors had complained before, how come they didn't then?"

Nicole paled. "I'm . . . I'm scared, Myles."

"Of what?"

"I . . . I think I might be going crazy." She dropped her head, weeping quietly.

He moved toward her, embracing her when he sat next to her. "Hey, look, anyone can become upset about something if they worry about it long enough and hard enough. It's getting late. You have to go to work, and I have to get some sleep. Let's not think about it anymore today. Not until we see each other tonight. Is that a deal?"

She looked up. He seemed to be minimizing her fears. Is that all that was bothering her? A few silly fears and worries? "I . . . I guess you're right."

"Of course I'm right. Listen, nobody but nobody conjures up demons today. Hell, this is the twentieth century. The late twentieth century, I might add. Things like witches and spells and demons belong in the dark ages." He laughed tiredly.

Standing, Nicole said, "I guess you *are* right. When I started thinking of everything that's happened and tied it in to that silly thing I did, it became all messed up and twisted out of proportion."

"Look," he said, standing up next to her. "Let me make a suggestion. Suppose I visit a priest or minister today before I go to the station? I can tell him about everything that happened and see what he has to say."

"I don't think that'll be necessary. Besides, if I want to get some expert advice on any of this, I'll just ask Doctor Claypool."

"Well, to be honest, Nicole, I thought maybe we might have need for a priest or minister down the road before not too long. You do know what I mean?"

She managed a weak smile before nodding. "If you want to, there's nothing I can do to prevent it. Just don't make it sound like I'm ready to blow my top any second. Make it as . . . as . . ."

"Offhanded as possible?" he asked, finishing the sentence for her.

"Right. Offhanded. Casual. You know," she said, moving toward the hallway and the bathroom.

A shower would make her feel like a new person. At least, she hoped it would. When she finished dressing, twenty minutes later, Myles was already sleeping, his gentle snore bubbling through the quiet of the apartment.

She tiptoed out, ready to face another day, feeling a bit more comfortable with herself for having told Myles everything about the ceremony.

Closing the door with an inaudible click, her footsteps receded down the hall. When the apartment was quiet, the stereo turned on, playing an old Mantovani recording.

10:21 A.M.

"You really look bushed," Stacey Ford said, shaking a spoonful of sugar into her second cup of coffee. They had talked of college days and touched briefly on Stacey's life in the religious commune.

"Bad night," Nicole said, sipping her coffee. She felt Stacey had not wanted to see her merely to reminisce.

"What happened?"

"I had a dream that woke me up, and I didn't sleep very well because of it, I guess."

Stacey nodded in an assured, all-knowing way. "Do you know what I think your trouble is?"

Nicole jerked her attention from the counter where a girl had just spilled a decanter of coffee back to Stacey. "What?"

"I think you're looking for Jesus and aren't really sure of the fact."

"Look, Stacey, I didn't agree to coffee just to get a sermon on Jesus and my sinful way of life."

"I didn't say anything at all about your way of life, Nicole."

"I thought I'd save you the time."

"Don't get huffy, dear. Besides, you're the one who said it was sinful. Why, even people who lead relatively good lives can be upset because something is missing from their day to day existence. Jesus! That is the one and only answer to most—no—every problem today. If one puts their lives and futures in the hands of Jesus, everything will turn around for them. Believe me, I know of what I speak."

"And I suppose," Nicole said sarcastically, "that your Reverend Whatever-his-name-is is the man to put me in touch with Jesus?"

"Don't be cynical, Nicole."

"I . . . I'm sorry, Stacey. I've been working hard lately, getting this publicity campaign underway. When I don't get a good night's sleep, everything goes haywire."

"I understand, Nicole. I really do."

"Then, if you understand, lay off the religious hype and your Reverend . . ."

"Reverend Eddie John Stangood."

"Whatever," Nicole said, throwing the word away under her breath.

"He's really quite nice."

"Who? Jesus?"

"No. Yes! Jesus is wonderful, but I was referring to Reverend Eddie John. He's phenomenal. He really is. He does so many good things. And when he's in control . . ."

"Control? Control of what?"

"Jesus has told him in a vision that only those evangelists who preach the word of Christ on TV, and those who carry out His ministry on earth, will be among the chosen on earth when the Apocalypse takes place."

Nicole restrained herself. What a laugh! And Stacey was gullible enough to believe that her Reverend Eddie John Stangood was in direct contact with Jesus Christ? Nicole looked at her watch. "Good Lord, I've got to get going. I didn't realize it was so late."

They stood, dropping some change on the table for the waitress. Nicole turned, hurrying toward the door, with Stacey right behind her.

"Give Jesus a chance," she said, half running to keep up with Nicole.

"I'll think about it, Stacey. I really have to run. I'm late."

Stacey watched her dash up the steps of the clinic, which stood next door to the coffee shop they had just left. At the top of the steps she saw Nicole hesitate before forcing herself past the heavyset woman blocking the front entrance.

2:00 P.M.

Myles squirmed in the straight-back chair to which the lady, who answered the door, had escorted him. When she indicated he should sit down and had pointed directly at the chair on which he now sat, he felt obligated to obey. Her hawk-like nose and sharp piercing stare had squelched any desire on his part to pass the time of day with her. She left immediately to summon Father DuWayne Gorkland, the pastor of Saint Timothy's Church.

Myles had called him shortly after getting out of the shower and had made a two o'clock appointment with the priest for that afternoon. Before going to work and getting involved in the troubles of the city, state, country and world, he wanted to be free of the thoughts worrying him since he had awakened.

Standing when Gorkland entered, Myles smiled inwardly. The man stood about five feet six inches tall and probably weighed no more than one hundred forty pounds. His coal black hair, combed straight back, did nothing but call attention to his boyish face. Myles wondered how old he might be. Involuntarily pulling back from the man's wet palm, when they shook hands, Myles sat down in the chair, wiping his own palm dry.

"What can I do for you, Mr. Lawrence?" Gorkland asked, studying Myles' face closely. "Are you on television, by any chance?"

Myles smiled blandly. "Yes. Yes, I am, Father. Have you seen me before?"

"On the few occasions that I watch the thing. It's rather boring, don't you think?"

Myles shrugged. "I don't feel I'm at liberty to air my views concerning television's worth, considering my position with KSLL-TV."

Gorkland remained aloof and said, "I *am* rather busy, Mr. Lawrence. What do you need?"

"A friend of mine has been suffering from a dream—a recurring dream—and it seems to be about a demon or possibly the devil. She's had some rather weird things happen to her recently and . . ."

"This friend of yours . . . this lady friend . . . how close is she to you?"

"We're intimate friends. I believe that someday we'll probably marry. Why do you ask? Is that important?"

Gorkland shrugged. "Continue."

Myles outlined the out-of-the-ordinary things that had happened since Nicole had performed the rite. Pondering for a long minute as to whether he should tell the priest about Nicole having performed the paganistic ritual, he hesitated.

"Are the two of you living together?" Gorkland asked.

Myles blinked at the suddenness and direct-
ness of the question. "As a matter of fact, we
are."

"It never ceases to amaze me," the priest
snapped. "People think they can go around
sinning and doing whatever they want and
then when they think they have a problem,
they come running to the Church—to a priest.
Well, let me tell you one thing, young man,"
Gorkland said, standing, to pull himself to his
full height, "it won't work here. Go to con-
fession. Clean up your act. Get right with God
before you come around here trying to waste
my time. I have more than enough to keep me
busy with those good, God-fearing people who
belong to my parish. You don't belong to it, do
you? I thought not." He smiled grimly,
smugly.

"I don't suppose it ever occurred to you that
I might not *be* a Catholic," Myles said, cursing
his luck for having had the bad fortune of
calling on a hard-nosed throwback. Why did
the priest worry about his God-fearing parish-
ioners if they weren't in trouble? Or did he
merely want the time to himself and not have
to worry about making waves where others
were concerned? Why worry about the ones he
felt he had apparently saved already?

Gorkland finally looked up at Myles, his face
pale. "I . . . I apologize, Mr. Lawrence," he
offered lamely. "You have no idea the amount
of stress that I've been under lately. This so-
called 'new morality' is a tough pill for anyone

in my position to swallow. From what you've told me, I don't see how I could do any good for your friend. Perhaps a competent psychiatrist or psychologist might be better."

"Well, thank you for your time, Father," Myles said coldly. Standing, he moved out of the office. Would he meet with this type of lethargy wherever he went if he and Nicole thought that a clergyman was their only answer? At least Gorkland had apologized, which at the moment seemed like a lot more than Myles had expected.

Gorkland continued sitting at his desk, watching the newsman leave his office, an air of indifference hanging on his face.

Wednesday, November 19, 1986   12:22 A.M.

"Good night, darling," Myles said, leaning over to kiss Nicole on the lips. During the day she had fared better than either had expected. Except for her story about Stacey and the coffee break and the unpleasant moment with Rose Tunic when she returned fifteen minutes late, the day had gone quite smoothly for Nicole.

He had refrained from telling her of his encounter with Gorkland, other than to tell her that he had called on a priest and that the clergyman had suggested the science of psychiatry as a possible way out.

"Nice," had been her reply, and they had not talked of her dream or the disturbances of the last few weeks. Instead, they had opted to go to bed at once, hoping to collect some overdue sleep.

In minutes after kissing, Nicole lay on her back, her breasts rising and falling steadily in an evenly orchestrated sleep. Myles turned on one side and in seconds had drifted off.

He awoke immediately when he heard the ripping sound. He sat up in the dark, unable to see the blanket that had covered them sailing to the ceiling. The sheet beneath it was being torn full length from bottom to top, as if someone invisible grasped it at the foot of the bed and tore it in two.

"What the . . . ?" he mumbled sleepily, struggling to understand what was happening.

Before he could utter a sound or reach out to touch Nicole to awaken her, he felt her move next to him. Then, in the darkness, he could no longer feel her weight. He reached out, fumbling for the lamp switch on his side of the bed.

The only sound escaping his lips was a short, hoarse scream when he saw Nicole floating in midair, four feet above the bed.

11

Wednesday, November 19, 1986   1:45 A.M.

Myles leaped to his feet. What he saw had to be a dream. Nicole could not be floating above the bed. That was simply impossible. He hurried around to her side of the bed, gingerly reaching out to touch her. Would her skin feel any different? Was this all an hallucination? Why did he feel as if he didn't want to touch her?

Forcing himself, he stretched out his hand farther until he brushed the flesh of her left arm. She felt absolutely normal. Warm. Had he anticipated a cold sensation?

The door to the hallway slammed behind him. He jumped, turning in midair himself. Landing on both feet, he clenched his fists, not knowing what he expected to find facing him. Nothing. There was nothing. No one. Who had slammed the door? He tiptoed toward it. Just as he was about to turn the knob, the bathroom door opened and closed with a bang, only to open again. Then the hall door did the same, and the two began opening and closing alternately, banging shut only to slam against the wall the next instant. The medicine cabinet joined in the commotion as did the drawers of the bureaus. As the sliding doors of the closet began opening and closing, Myles turned his attention back to Nicole who still hovered over the bed.

When he stood next to her, she gently moved back and forth in line with his face. Grabbing her, he tried to force her back to the bed and was met with a hoarse chuckle that seemed to fill the room and his head.

Throwing his hands over his ears, he searched the room with widening eyes. Who was laughing? Who was making the ruckus with the doors? How and why and who was making Nicole hang in midair?

"Jesus Christ!" he mumbled under his breath, unable to comprehend.

Nicole immediately dropped to the bed and awakened. Sitting up, she looked at Myles, standing next to her, his hands over his ears, his eyes bulging out. The doors closed quietly and the drawers of the bureau remained shut the next time they were in that position.

When he realized that she was back on the bed and awake, he glanced at the doors and found them closed. Slowly removing his hands from his ears, he forced a smile and said, "Are you all right?"

Nicole shook her head. "Are *you* all right, Myles? Do you realize what you were doing?"

He thought for a moment and shook his own head.

She cupped her hands over her ears and bulged eyes out. "If you had puffed up your cheeks and stuck your tongue out, I would have thought you were doing a Harpo Marx impression. What was going on that made you do that?"

"Why do you ask what was going on?"

She peered at him, not sure of what he meant by repeating her question. "I . . . I don't understand."

"You have to believe what I'm going to tell you." He sat down on the bed next to her, grasping one of her hands in his. "You were floating over the bed."

She felt her skin go clammy. "Floating?" she managed after a short pause.

Nodding, he said, "I guess I believed some of the different things that you said happened. But I didn't buy everything. At least now I've seen some of the weird things myself."

"Weird things? What do you mean?"

He described the doors opening and closing, making all kinds of racket when they slammed shut or against the walls. "Even the medicine cabinet door was swinging back and forth," he finished.

Reaching out, she hugged him tight around the neck. "I'm scared, Myles. What are we going to do? Was the priest serious when he said we should consult a psychiatrist?''

Myles thought of Gorkland. No wonder the priest had been reluctant to offer any help. He had not expressed the case with any degree of conviction. All Myles had done was tell him, quite second-handedly, about Nicole's experiences. He had not been able to communicate the horror of an unseen presence in the apartment. And Nicole had had to face it alone before his return. When he felt Nicole tightening her hold around his neck and heard the gentle sobs coming from her, he knew he had to do something and do something soon.

"He said we should consult a doctor but I think I probably goofed when I told him about everything."

"Goofed?" she said, drawing back to look at him. "I . . . I don't understand."

"I didn't present everything as strongly as I should have. I had no idea that these things were so . . . so . . .''

"Real?" she finished for him.

He nodded. "And frightening."

"Your ruined clothing was real, wasn't it? Didn't you explain to him that that happened while we were in bed, asleep, not over four feet away from the closet?''

"Yeah. But I didn't do it in a convincing way. I'll go back to him tomorrow. I have to. My God, Nicole, we can't go on like this. We both need our sleep and look at us. Wide awake and going on . . .'' he turned to look at the digital alarm clock, ". . . three in the morning."

"Let's get up and make some coffee," she said, swinging her legs over the edge of the bed.

"Look at this," he said, holding up the torn sheet. "That's what woke me up. The sound of it ripping—or being ripped. It must have been torn from the bottom since it's still joined at the top by a few threads." He pointed to the end of the sheet that had been closest to their faces.

After looking at the cover, Nicole slipped into her dressing gown and went to the kitchen. Myles followed, tying the sash of his robe.

While she made coffee, he wondered about the priest, Father Gorkland. Why had he been so indifferent? Was it before he had told him that he might not even be a Catholic? Or that the man had berated him for living with Nicole without the benefit of marriage? What difference? Gorkland had apologized and Myles felt that it would be within the realms of propriety if he returned and restructured his way of telling of the events. When he thought of Nicole hovering in midair, he shuddered, forcing a smile when she sat down opposite him. For the rest of the night, they talked of their predicament and what the final outcome might be.

1:30 P.M.

Nicole's head jerked as she caught herself sleeping at her desk. That was pretty bad. It wasn't like her to do something like that—not even if she were exhausted to the point of collapsing. But her body had just tried to force her into a sleep. Wasn't that the point of collapse? Sitting up most of the night with Myles had not helped her tired state previously instigated by the dream of the night before. Although she had been asleep during it, the aftereffects had been draining. She had barely managed to get through the day after meeting with Stacey and her little run-in with Rose Tunic. But at least she had made it. The sleep and rest she was supposed to have gotten last night had been her incentive to get through that day. And it had been denied her. How would she survive today?

"Very nice."

The words, icy cold, rankled Nicole. Rose Tunic. Looking up, Nicole saw the overweight woman filling her doorway. Why Doctor Claypool and the others kept Rose around escaped her. She seemed to be more of a troublemaking, incompetent and unattractive liability as opposed to the general, stereotyped business asset that Claypool had spoken of when he had interviewed Nicole. She made a mental note to ask Rob Lanstrom about her.

"Yes, Miss Tunic?" she asked, demanding from her tired facial muscle a smile of some sort.

"I've been watching you."

"Really."

"Yes, and I must say you really aren't interested too much in your welfare or your job security here, are you?"

"I don't understand."

"Fifteen minutes late from your coffee break yesterday and today . . . well, let me say that sleeping at one's desk is highly improper at any place of business. But most especially here at the clinic."

Nicole waited. What was this overdressed walrus going to do? Blackmail her? Expose her to Doctor Claypool? In a way, Nicole almost wished that she would tell the doctor. If that happened, she could explain to him what had been going on in her apartment over the last weeks.

"If I see one more infraction of proper etiquette or business decorum on your part around this office—or any place else for that matter—I'll report you at once with a recommendation of instant dismissal. Do I make myself clear?" She peered over the teardrop-shaped horn-rimmed glasses, hanging precariously on the tip of her nose.

"Certainly. Now get out of my office so I can do some work . . . *Miss* Tunic!"

Without a word, the woman turned, waddling from the small room. Nicole picked up the phone and dialed Rob's number after looking it up. "Rob? Nicole. Have you got a minute? I want to ask you something."

2:00 P.M.

Rob lighted a cigarette after Nicole had settled opposite him. "What's up?" he asked, smiling.

"Rose Tunic."

"Oh-oh. Has the baby blimp been up to her old tricks again?"

"Old tricks?"

He adjusted the oversized glasses and drew on his cigarette. "Throwing her weight around. And I mean that figuratively not literally because if she ever did that, the seismographs would go crazy all over the country."

Nicole snickered.

"Did I say that?" Rob asked, feigning shock. "She likes to make her job of office manager much more important than it really is. Ignore her. You answer to Doctor Claypool and no one else. He passes on your ideas and work suggestions. No one else."

"Why is she like that?"

"Put yourself in her shoes for a second. You might have a tough time imagining this, but if you were about one hundred forty pounds over-weight and tried to wear dresses that were five sizes too small for you and looked like Rose Tunic, you wouldn't be much of a fun person either, would you?"

Nicole smiled wanly. "I guess not. Why doesn't she clean her act up, then?"

"I don't think she knows how. Either that or she's not aware what she actually looks like. I sure don't want to be the one to tell her. Do you?"

"I guess not," Nicole said, reluctantly agreeing. She had enough of her own problems. The last thing she needed was a person like Rose hanging onto her like a pet dog because she paid a bit of kind attention to her. Maybe down the road, once she and Myles solved the dilemma facing them at home, she might make an overture to Rose—but it would be a brief encounter at most.

Standing to leave, she stopped at the door. "Is Doctor Claypool ever negative on hearing about one of his employee's problems?"

Rob stood in a form of goodbye to his friend. "Rose? I don't know. I suppose he might. I guess it would come under the heading of a job benefit if that ever happened."

"Thanks, Rob," she said, swinging out the door. She felt better now that she had talked with him. Rose would no longer be a threat to her. And it certainly worked out well when he thought she was referring to Rose when she asked about Doctor Claypool being consulted by one of the clinic employees. She'd file that away for future use and talk it over with Myles if they decided they should consult with the doctor.

Walking back to her office, the slogan she had created for part of the publicity campaign for the clinic suddenly sprang into her mind.

"No matter what the problem is—we can help!" But would her problem qualify within the framework of that statement? What would Doctor Claypool say if she approached him and said something like: *"Say, Doctor, I've got this strange thing hanging around my apartment and I don't mean Myles. This peculiar son-of-a-gun just about drives the two of us nuts. It does all these weird things, like stinking up the place and flooding the bedroom and bathroom. He even made me float in midair once. What do you say about something like that, Doc?"*

She had studied enough about psychology to know that at best it was an empirical science, and items and instances for which there might be no definite proof could never be confronted as being real. Doctor Claypool would simply explain each one as best he could and not face the possibility that Nicole Kilton and her lover, Myles Lawrence, were being affected by a series of strange and unexplainable happenings—happenings caused by some unseen party.

3:37 P.M.

"I'm surprised to see you back here so soon, Mr. Lawrence," Father Gorkland said evenly.

"I'm happy that you consented to see me, Father. I think I might have done both of us a disservice yesterday."

"A disservice? I'm afraid I don't understand."

"I didn't tell you in a convincingly enough way about the things that have been going on. I merely related to you what Nicole had told me."

"Sort of like heresay testimony at a trial, eh?" the priest asked, without changing his facial expression.

Myles wondered where he had come up with that particular expression. Recalling how the priest had said he thought of television programing as being boring, he wondered what Gorkland did for relaxation. "I guess you might say that, Father."

"So what do you have to tell me? My time is just as tight today as it was yesterday, you know."

"Last night . . . no, make that this morning . . . I awoke to find Nicole hovering in midair. She . . ."

"Levitating?" he asked, his interest piqued ever so slightly.

"Yes . . . levitating. The sheets had been ripped in two and the doors in the apartment began opening and slamming shut by themselves. The . . ."

"By themselves, Mr. Lawrence?" he asked, failing to conceal his own particular brand of skepticism. "Really!"

Myles stared at him for a moment. The man seemed hopeless. "Yes. By themselves."

"You expect me to believe this, of course?"

"Look, Father Gorkland, I know it sounds unbelievable but it *did* happen. I saw it."

"Have you ever thought that it might be God trying to tell you that you and this Nicole person are living in sin? That he wants you to quit? The devil isn't running around opening and closing doors and making naked women float in the air. You do think it's caused by the devil, don't you?"

Myles stared at him, ignoring the priest's questions. "What makes you think Nicole wasn't clothed?"

Gorkland stopped short, looking up at him. "I naturally assumed that since the two of you were living in sin that . . ."

"I think you'd better get your head straightened out, Father. Look. I demand that you come and visit with her. See the apartment and find out firsthand what's going on. That's all I'm asking. You certainly are making it difficult for me to respect your position. Try to be a little more compatible. Aren't you supposed to win converts for the Church? Aren't you supposed to help people?"

"All right. All right. I'll come and visit with her. I hope you realize the terrific imposition, but I will come. Give me the address."

Myles jotted the apartment address and number down on a tablet the priest offered him. "What time shall I tell her you'll arrive?"

"Between eight and eight forty-five this evening. Will you be there?"

"I'm afraid I can't be. I'll be at the station preparing for the late newscast. I'll tell Nicole that you're coming over this evening." Myles stood, offering his hand to the priest.

After they had said goodbye and Myles had left the rectory, Gorkland picked up the telephone and dialed seven numbers.

"Chancery office," rang in his ear.

"Father Pins?"

"Yes?"

"Father Gorkland here. I just wanted to apprise the chancery office of my activities. I've been approached by a man who claims that the apartment in which he and his mistress live, or whatever the terminology is for sinful women, is being plagued by spirits of some sort."

"I see. Would you like to speak to the bishop?"

"No. I don't think that'll be necessary. I'm sure it's nothing. I'll check it out and if there is anything worth reporting, I'll get back to you."

"Very well, Father," Father Pins said.

Gorkland hung up, smiling benignly. He was positive it would be all for nothing.

12

DuWayne Gorkland ran a finger inside the Roman collar surrounding his neck. Right now, he wished he was someplace else, anyplace but outside the door that led to the apartment of a woman with problems. Of course, it was part of his job to do things like this. Unpleasant things. Why weren't there more happy duties connected with the priesthood? Why did people have to make life so complicated? Why couldn't they just live and let live? Did it always have to be the ultra-dramatic whenever someone needed him?

Possessed! That would be the first thing this woman—what was her name? He pulled out the slip of paper bearing the name of Nicole Kilton and the address Myles Lawrence had given him. Myles Lawrence was an enigma, too. Why couldn't he put a finger on

Lawrence's religious state? Was the man Catholic or not? At first, he had assumed that he wasn't, but then, the newscaster had said some glib thing about Gorkland's having assumed immediately that he was. What kind of talk was that? Was he or wasn't he a Roman Catholic? More than likely, if he were, he probably was not one who practiced his religion. Heathen!

He wondered what would happen when he met the woman. He'd have to be tough and make certain that he remained in control of the ideas generated by this woman—this sinner. But possession?

He'd nip that flower in the bud before it had half a chance at blooming into a full-fledged idea. Stuff like that just simply did not exist. He remembered everything he had ever learned on the subject in seminary. Then, he had been ready to believe—anything and everything. But the year before he was to be ordained, the Vatican had decreed that certain changes would be made concerning the sacrament of Holy Orders. The one that shook his faith most had been the removal of exorcism from the ranks of the minor orders that every priest had taken for the last—how many hundreds of years? If they could remove it just like that, like snapping one's fingers, it made the whole idea seem a bit superfluous at best. Surely the devil still existed. If he existed, didn't the possibility of demonic possession also exist? If both were possible, why was the minor order of exorcism—this privilege of doing battle with Satan—done away with and given to only a few chosen priests? The whole idea had bothered him then and had continually pestered him through his whole career as a priest. Never—not once in all the years that he had been a priest of God and Jesus—had the idea of possession ever been mentioned to him by anyone outside ordinary conversation. He had even read the more lurid novels concerning the subject. *The Exorcist* had caused quite a flap when it was published, but the one he had enjoyed the most had been *Garden of the Incubus,* which seemed the more accurate and better researched of the two.

What difference? he thought, slipping out of his overcoat. Draping it across his arm, he tentatively reached out with his forefinger to ring the bell. How difficult would this interview be? Would the woman become hysterical? He hoped not. He recalled the one time he had slipped in his career as a priest. Answering a parishioner's cry for help, he had called on her, a young housewife whose husband had beaten her. She had become frightened, then hysterical, and in an attempt to calm her, he had embraced her. Before he knew what happened, they had wound up in bed. Shortly thereafter, the woman had committed suicide and he had been transferred. The guilt of the sin had been removed in the confessional, but the memory had remained with him over the years. Now, he would have to face another woman on a one-to-one basis. Of course, he had done that over the years but not with the possibility that the woman could become hysterical. He'd control the situation if that happened. He'd have to.

He heard the bell ring and footsteps approaching the door. When it opened, he forced a smile. "I'm Father Gorkland. We have an appointment."

"Yes, Father," Nicole said, stepping back and gesturing at the same time that he should enter. "Please, come in."

Entering, he smelled her perfume. Was she trying to seduce him? A quivering shudder ran down his spine. The *jezebel*! He'd have to be on his guard. "Is Mr. Lawrence going to be here?"

"Myles is at the station, Father. Give me your coat and I'll hang it up."

"If it's the same to you, I'll just throw it over this hall chair." He dropped the coat before turning to face her. At least he'd be able to get away in a hurry if escape became necessary.

"Why don't we sit in the living room," Nicole said, moving toward the arched entryway.

The priest followed, selecting an overstuffed easy chair opposite the couch where Nicole sat down.

She hesitated. Who should speak first? Should they have some idle talk first? Or should she simply throw herself on his mercy and tell him everything? Even about the ritual?

She studied Gorkland. Small. In fact, Myles'
description had not done justice to the man. At
best, he barely came up to the level of her face.
But was size important when confronted with
demons and the devil? Faith—that invisible,
unmeasurable quality that men and women
were supposed to possess in unknown quantities—was the main ingredient when it came to
fighting unseen beings.

But her beings weren't all unseen. She had
seen one—the horrible thing standing at the
foot of her bed. Should she tell Gorkland about
that? The dream? Maybe. But she'd reserve
judgment on telling him about the apparition
she had seen. It had to have been a figment of
her imagination.

Then, too, there was the question of the
ceremony she had performed. Should she tell
this man, this priest of God, about that as
well? Trying to conjure up the devil in the form
of Lucifer hardly seemed the right thing to tell
a priest who was here to help her. He'd
probably rant and rave at her and call her a
heathen or a witch or something equally bad.
He'd condemn her. Considering the tirade he'd
unleashed at Myles about the two of them
living together in sin, she decided to relegate
the rite to the farthest recesses of her mind,
along with the thing she had seen at the foot of
her bed.

"Why don't you begin by telling me everything that has happened that you consider to

be out of the ordinary, Miss Kilton." Gorkland paused after having taken the initiative.

Coughing to clear her throat, Nicole said, "Myles and I had a breakup this past September and I was upset and frustrated because of it."

She went on to tell him of the depression into which she sank and how her only thoughts had been of Myles. Skipping over the book she had bought on impulse and the rite she had performed that one Friday night, she told of the water incident, the apparent vandalism, the smells, and most everything else that had happened.

When she finished, he brought his fingertips together, staring at her. "The water," he began. "That in itself is pretty much ordinary. I could hardly consider that something unusual. Probably faulty workmanship in the plumbing. As far as someone else breaking into your apartment and vandalizing your possessions, I could hardly take the suggestion that that is uncommon in this day and age. It happens all the time. Do I make myself clear?"

Nicole chewed on her lip for a moment before answering. It was slowly becoming apparent to her that the man was going to explain everything in a rational manner. Probably, he would even suggest that she seek help of some type. Hadn't he already done that with Myles? "I understand what it is you're saying, Father. It's just that all of it seems so blasted unreal."

"I don't see why it should seem unusual, my

dear. Vandals do break into homes and apartments every day and night of the year."

"But," she said, holding her hands up, "they usually have a reason. They're looking for something to steal. Nothing was taken from my apartment. If it's as you say, just ordinary circumstances, explain that if you would."

"Perhaps they found nothing worth taking." He smiled, a condescending look holding his face.

Standing, Nicole crossed the room to the stereo and TV set. "What about these? This is high quality equipment. If they were looking for something to steal and turn into cash, both of these things should have brought a good price at any pawn shop."

Gorkland shrugged, his smile intact.

"What about the smell?" Nicole wrinkled her nose when she thought of the vile, repulsive stink.

"What about it? That could be sewer gas backing up through your kitchen sink or through the shower or bathtub. Good heavens, Miss Kilton, you can't expect something like the things you've told me about to be coming from the devil or hell. Why think that?"

"What about the fact that the police were not able to find any evidence of someone breaking in when they investigated the vandalism incident?"

"Someone is very clever. That's all I can say."

"Then, Father, say something placating

about my TV set and stereo equipment turning themselves on." She was growing irritated with the man's offhanded way of trying to logically explain everything. She had to control her temper or run the risk of embarrassing herself as well as the priest.

Gorkland stood, brushing past Nicole, and went to the window overlooking the street below. "Vibrations. Vibrations from traffic. I'm positive. It's not really anything out of the ordinary after all, Miss Kilton." He turned to face her.

"Then, tell me how they suddenly came on when the police were here, answering the call of my neighbor's complaint? They were standing at the door and I was three or four feet away and just like that," she snapped her fingers, "they went on. Loudly. Very loudly."

"Because you didn't feel the vibrations doesn't mean they weren't there." He stopped smiling and a sober, self-confident expression crossed his face. Obviously, he was pleased in the manner with which he was fielding her questions and objections. He sincerely hoped she would forget about the incident that followed the police investigation. When he saw her eyes light up, he knew she was about to mention it.

"When the cops left," she said, slowly, evenly, "and right before Myles returned, they went back on again but they weren't plugged in. The police had pulled them out and tied the cords together. Explain that, Father

Gorkland." Her voice had grown bitter and an icy sarcasm hung on each word.

"Now you have one piece of unexplained evidence. Not too much when one considers that everything else has a ready explanation."

Before she pursued that one piece of evidence and before she brought up anything else, she bowed her head, biting her lip for a second. "Could I offer you a cup of coffee, Father? I'm afraid I haven't been a very good hostess."

"That would be nice," he said, returning to his chair.

"We can still talk while I make it," she said, entering the kitchen. "The apartment isn't that big."

"You're sure," he said, raising his voice just a bit to make certain she'd hear him, "that you haven't made any wishes or done anything that might be considered . . . well, contrary to God's law?"

"I'm not certain what you mean, Father," she said, measuring the ground coffee into the basket. She certainly was not going to tell him about the Satanic ritual she had performed. If he had proven to be somewhat different from Myles' interpretation of his prim character, she might have considered but not with the man sitting in her living room. To her, it was too apparent the priest had a few problems of his own.

"An idle promise in the form of a deal with . . . say, the devil."

"Such as?" She entered the living room, the

sound of water heating and perking through the coffee coming from behind her.

"Suppose you were in line for a promotion at work or for a raise. It wouldn't be uncommon to say to one's self something like: 'If I get that job or that raise, I'll do this or that or the other thing.' Sort of a bargain, if you will."

Nicole puckered her lips in feigned thought. "No. Nothing like that. Tell me, Father," she said quickly, "how do you explain what happened last night? Myles swears I was floating in midair. Is something like that possible?"

"You know it's not. In the old days, the Church demanded, among other things, that phenomena contrary to the certain laws of nature be evident before someone could be declared as being possessed. But today, we have psychiatry and psychology, and most of the clues from the past that were part and parcel of possession are no longer relevant."

"But the cover sheet ripping and me floating . . . good God, Father, can't you say something that will help me understand?"

"Don't be so quick to call on God in circumstances such as this." His voice snapped the words. His pragmatism was getting to Nicole, eating at her like a cancerous growth. Thankful for the quiet coming from the kitchen, she stood, excusing herself to go for the coffee.

"I think that the fact that you're living in sin with this man might be affecting you more than you realize." Gorkland stood, his attention caught by something over the TV set. Crossing the room, he reached out, pulling from its place on the shelf the antique red book trimmed in gold.

Nicole came back into the living room, carrying two cups of coffee.

"What is this?" he asked, his voice oily with righteousness.

After she placed the coffee cups on the table, she hurried to the priest. Reaching out, she grabbed the book away from him. "That's mine. It's none of your business."

"None of my business, eh? Well, let me tell you one thing, Miss Kilton. I know what's in that book. I held it long enough to see that it contains chants and curses and such from witchcraft and what have you. Shame on you. Shame on you, you harlot! You whore! You live with a man and cannot face the responsibility that a lifelong commitment entails. You then develop a mental problem because of it and try to get me to soothe your guilt-ridden conscience! Shame, indeed. I wouldn't help you now for anything. You've lied to me. You are lying to yourself and to God—if you believe in Him and ever pray to Him. But it is all for naught. You, my dear, are going to hell. Straight to hell. Then, you'll meet, face to face, the unholy force with which you have been flirting."

Nicole fought to restrain her temper. The sonofabitch was chastising her for a mistake. Whatever happened to common decency—and

John Tigges

yes, forgiveness? Wasn't that the priest's main
role? To represent God, offering forgiveness
for sins and transgressions? But not this one.
He was judging her and Myles, condemning
them to everlasting hell's fire. She didn't need
that type of guilt thrown on her.

"I think you'd better go, Father," she said
very quietly, in contrast to the rage fomenting
within her.

"I certainly am not needed here, witch! You
and your partner in sin will burn forever in hell.
You and . . ."

Nicole stormed to the door, throwing it open.
Tapping her foot, her irritation with the priest
ready to boil over, she waited. He could pick up
his own coat and get the hell out of her apartment and her life! Forever!

"The both of you are beyond hope," he said
flatly, slipping into his coat while standing in
the doorway to the hall.

Unable to close it because of where he stood,
Nicole waited for him to finish his verbal
onslaught. Defiantly returning his glare when
he stared at her for a long minute before
leaving, she slammed the door after he turned
to walk down the hall.

The sonofabitch! That bastard! That worthless piece of scum! She stood, feet apart, facing
the doorway where the priest had been
standing seconds before. She felt relieved,
peculiarly safe, now that he had left and she
was alone. Why had she thought that anything
would come of this meeting? Myles had

insisted on it, having told the priest everything that had happened. Convincing him to visit with her had been one colossal mistake. Perhaps another priest might have reacted differently, but this one had something bothering him. That was painfully obvious. Perhaps he wasn't as sure of himself when it came to a pecking order with Divine Providence. Maybe he had only given vent to his own insecurities and convictions when the opportunity had presented itself to do so with one he felt was worse off and more vulnerable than he.

Well, it was over.

The smack of something falling to the floor brought her around to find a picture, framed and covered with glass laying on the floor behind her. Somehow it had fallen from its place on the shelf in the entryway. It lay on its back, the glass covering the enlarged photo of her dead parents, intact. Not broken. Not even cracked. Without thinking, she picked it up, replacing it on the shelf. How could it have fallen over four feet onto the tile floor in the entryway and not shattered? She didn't care. At least it was all right and not broken. That was the important thing.

The clock in the living room chimed the three-quarter hour. She checked the time. Almost eleven? Impossible. How had time slipped away from her so quickly with the priest here? Almost two hours had passed. Myles would be on the air soon and she wanted to watch his newscast. A quick shower and she'd curl up with her favorite newscaster and then wait for him to get home.

Hurrying to the bedroom, she undressed and, after pulling a fresh towel from the small linen closet, adjusted the shower's temperature. Once she stood under the spraying water, she felt her taut muscles slowly relax. How could a shower undo so fast the physical discomfort which racked her body after the priest had left?

Nicole enjoyed showers and turned the hot water up just a bit. The steam billowed up, swathing her in foggy clouds. It felt so good, so relaxing. The jets of hot water whipped her arms, caressing her, touching her in such a way that inevitably her emotions awakened, thriving on the sensual beating her skin was receiving.

Opening her eyes with a startled cry, she looked about in the shower. The water felt as if it were actually fondling her nakedness. Her nipples stood out firm, but the strangest feeling was in her arms. The water felt like hands—hands that were slightly rough with callouses—the hands of a worker. Not like Myles' hands. His were soft, gentle hands. The water gently kneaded her skin and muscles, working its way toward her shoulders, her back. Her legs felt as if they might buckle from the state of euphoria in which she found herself. The manipulating sensation moved from her shoulders, down her back and around under her arms toward her breasts. Never before in her life had she experienced anything so relaxing, and at the same time, so arousing.

A scream escaped her lips when she felt the nipples of her breasts react as if they had been pulled—pulled hard. Opening her eyes, she found the water still gushing over her, the steam enveloping her as it had been. Why had her nipples felt like that? The massaging effect of the water continued to increase her pleasure and she heard a moan flowing from her. *God, it felt so good.*

Again her nipples were tweaked viciously.

This time she didn't open her eyes, leaning instead against the hot tile wall of the shower. She wanted to scream with delight. Only when she was about to climax with Myles had she ever experienced this feeling. The massaging went instantly to her hairy triangle, the calloused touch manipulating her clitoris in a savage, frenzied way.

What was happening to her? Why did she feel this way? How could water do what she was feeling? It didn't make sense.

Her breasts ached with the pain of being pinched again, and she opened her eyes to see her breasts jerking up and down as if someone were pulling on them.

"Wha . . . Ho . . . God help me!" she screamed and the pain stopped.

The shower door flew open and Myles, naked, stepped in.

"What are you doing here?" she asked, once she realized who it was. "What about the newscast?''

"I finished it thirty-five minutes ago. Why?"

Nicole stared at him through the steam. How could she have been in the shower for over an hour? That didn't make sense. She had just gotten in a few minutes ago. "What time is it?"

"A little after midnight. Why? You in a hurry to go someplace?"

She shook her head.

"How did it go with the priest?"

"Later," she said, encircling his neck with her arms. Their tongues met in quick jabs as each explored the other's mouth in turn. She wanted him—wanted him in a desperate way that she had not known since he had returned.

Reaching out, Myles turned off the water, and the sudden quiet of the apartment filtered into the shower as they continued kissing and fondling each other's wet body. Nicole locked one leg around behind Myles' backside, offering herself to him in the tiled cubicle. Without hesitating, he plunged into her, and locked together, they rocked back and forth as their animal instincts took control. When they climaxed, it was as if the hot water had been turned on once more and both felt their strength ebb away.

Thursday, November 20, 1986   1:00 A.M.

Later in bed, Myles lay on his back. Nicole had just finished telling him of her appointment with Gorkland.

"Damn," he muttered. "I was hoping that he'd come up with an idea or solution that would solve everything for us."

"I don't think I helped," she said lamely.

"I don't understand."

"I didn't cooperate with him very well. I didn't want to tell him about the ritual but I think he guessed everything when he found the book."

"Oh, oh!" Myles said.

"You didn't mention it to him, did you?"

Myles shook his head, half-raising himself to look at Nicole. "What did he say?"

"He called me a witch and you my partner-in-sin. He said we both were beyond hope. That we're going straight to hell."

"Not tonight," he said quietly. "I'm too tired. G'night."

Propping herself up on one elbow, Nicole kissed him on the mouth. "Goodnight, you sexy sinner, you." She turned on one side and in minutes, her steady breathing joined his in a duet of sleep.

Myles rolled over, facing Nicole's backside, and instinctively slipped his hand across to fall onto her breast. She in turn, snuggled in closer, their breathing the only sound in the room.

Then the duet was joined by a third breath, heavy and labored, that came from nowhere and yet filled the room. Myles' hand raised, as if someone lifted it from Nicole's breast, laying it on his hip. The covers worked their way back and down until her upper body lay exposed to the night air. Indentations, where unseen fingers and palms grasped her by one shoulder and hip, appeared and her body was gently rolled onto its back. Impressions on her stomach worked their way downward, past her naval, across the tiny mound toward her hairy nest.

She moaned without awakening, and a dry chuckle broke the quiet of the room.

13

Monday, November 24, 1986   5:30 P.M.

When nothing happened during the four
days following Father Gorkland's visit with
Nicole, both she and Myles relaxed, hoping
that the strange occurrences were over.

Considering that the holidays were fast
approaching, Nicole looked forward to Thanksgiving, which was the following Thursday. It
would be fun sharing Thanksgiving, Christmas
and New Year's with Myles. Then, too, his
birthday was coming up shortly after Thanksgiving. When she thought of that, a tear
formed when she recalled her own birthday's
uneventful passing in October. How could she
possibly have been happy with another
anniversary of her own birth date? The man
who had sired her and the woman who had
borne her and given birth to her were both
dead. The one man in her life, to whom she

would have given her all, had walked out on her and she had been miserable. But now, Myles and she were together and for that she was happy.

The Monday before Thanksgiving went smoothly. Rose Tunic had not been much of a factor in Nicole's mind since she and Rob had talked. More than likely it had been her own change of attitude toward the woman that had prompted a difference in the relationship. While walking from the bus stop toward the apartment complex, she reflected momentarily on her own sense of inadequacy the first few weeks on the public relations job. She had probably allowed the overweight, almost anti-social woman to dominate her. That was over—finished. If Rose Tunic wanted to play mind games, it would have to be with someone other than Nicole Kilton.

Although it was Monday and Myles should be working, he had arranged to take the night off and she had readied a meal that should have been cooking since three that afternoon, when the automatic timer activated the oven. She anticipated an extra night, other than Saturday or Sunday, when the two of them could enjoy a meal and generally loaf around the apartment if that was what they chose to do. Maybe they'd go to a movie. Or walk through some of the shopping malls, avoiding the onslaught of shoppers after Thanksgiving, getting early ideas for Christmas gifts. Of all the holidays, Christmas was the one she feared the most since the death of her parents. The first such holidays had been most traumatic, and it had only been her sociology teacher, Emma Foxworthy, who had prevented her from bottoming out that first Christmas when she was a senior in high school. The Foxworthy family had been more than gracious, sharing their holiday with her, and for the first time in several months, she had actually laughed and enjoyed herself.

Unlocking the door to her apartment, she stopped and froze. Something was wrong. She smelled something burning. What had she done wrong while preparing the meal that morning before leaving for work? Rushing to the kitchen, she expected to see clouds of smoke billowing from the oven, but the room was clear. She threw open the oven door and gasped. The meal, a pot roast with potatoes, carrots and onions around it, sat in the middle of the cubicle. totally unrecognizable. The meat was cinder black, the potatoes and other vegetables, charred to various shades of deep umber.

Shakily standing, she looked at the controls she had set that morning. They were still in the same position as she had set them. The oven had *not* gone on. The air inside was cool. The stove's top, which should have been warm to the touch, was cold. How had the meal burned?

Slipping out of her coat, she turned to hang it over a chair and jumped when the door opened.

"Hi," Myles called. "I'm home."

"Wonderful," Nicole muttered when he entered the kitchen.

"That's a nice way to greet the man you love. What's the matter?"

Stepping aside, she gestured toward the open oven. Myles bent down, looking inside.

"I thought I smelled something when I entered the apartment. What happened? Were the controls set incorrectly?"

"I wish it were that simple. Look," she said pointing to the dials at the back of the stove. "They're still set the same way. They didn't activate when they should have."

"Then how did the stuff burn?" Myles asked, not catching the hint of concerned fear in her voice.

"I . . . I don't know," she said, stepping closer to him. They embraced and Nicole felt more at ease.

Catching her slight trembling, he said, "You don't mean that . . . that . . . whatever has been . . . has been . . ."

"Causing all the grief and trouble around here is back at it again?" she said finishing for him. "I think so."

They looked at each other. Why hadn't the priest been of more help? Why had they not been able to convince him that something totally uncommon was taking place?

"What do you want to do?" he asked, tipping her chin until their eyes locked.

Shrugging, she said, "Let's get out of here

and go eat someplace. I'm starved, no matter what happened here. We can talk over dinner.''

"Okay." He picked up her coat, holding it for her. "Are you all right?"

"I'm upset. Damn! I was looking forward to tonight."

"It's not a total loss. We can still come back here and enjoy the evening."

"I hope you're right."

Without another word, they left the apartment. Just as they left, and before Myles locked the door, he wrinkled his nose. The fetid smell. It was back. After closing the door, he turned to Nicole. From her expression, he knew she hadn't detected the odor. For now, he wouldn't mention it. The last thing he wanted to do was ruin her dinner. She was disturbed enough, and because she was, he felt the same degree of discomfort. First dinner, then they'd have an after dinner drink and talk. Maybe then, if she seemed all right, he would decide if he should tell her.

Taking her arm in his, they walked down the corridor.

8:41 P.M.

Their appetite for food satisfied, Nicole and Myles had chatted about the approaching holidays, agreeing to go to a Thanksgiving buffet that Thursday. When Myles mentioned the burnt dinner, she shook her head, almost violently, saying she didn't want to talk of it.

After a second drink, they paid their bill and left. Neither talked as they drove back to the apartment. Once they were on the third floor, walking toward their apartment door, Nicole hung back, tugging on Myles' coat sleeve.

"What is it?" he asked, stopping to face her.

"What if . . ."

"What if what? Something else is wrong? Something else has gone haywire?"

She nodded.

"Maybe we should think about moving."

She giggled nervously. "Why haven't we talked about that before? It's so simple . . . so damned simple!"

"Simple and inconvenient," Myles said, taking her hand in his and starting down the hallway.

"What do you mean, inconvenient?"

"This apartment complex is the closest one to both the clinic and the station."

She looked at him. "Let's not let a matter of convenience stand in the way of our peace of mind."

"What about your lease?"

"I'll break it."

"Can you?"

She shrugged. "I don't see why not."

"Let's take a look at it," he said, thrusting the key into the lock. With one motion, he turned the knob and sent the door swinging in on its hinges. "Oh boy!" he muttered when he flooded the entryway with light.

"What's the matter?" she said, looking

around him. She sucked in her breath.

The furniture stood gathered together, piled in an inverted pyramid in the middle of the living room—not just the furniture from the front of the apartment but from the bedroom and kitchen as well. Everything except the water bed.

"How's that possible?" Nicole squealed, pointing to the pile. A small footstool was at the bottom. On it, the stereo tuner rested, holding the TV on top of it. The speakers from the stereo balancing outward from the television set were held in place by an inverted occasional chair. Sitting on the legs of that chair was the overstuffed chair that was part of the new living room set. It, in turn, held the couch, tipped at an angle. The kitchen table appeared to be wedged tightly between it and the ceiling. Kitchen chairs hung from protruding chair legs and table legs that had been forced into position here and there.

Myles slowly shook his head. The pile seemed to be defying gravity. How would they get the furniture down without being caught in an avalanche of chairs and tables? "Where's your copy of the lease?" he asked, stepping inside, closing the door once Nicole followed him.

"In a bureau drawer. The middle one. Where's the bureau? I don't see it."

Shrugging, he took her hand and went to the bedroom. Nothing was there other than the bed. Hurrying to the kitchen, they stopped short once they entered. The heavy chest of drawers stood balanced on one corner of the stove top, slowly spinning on its axis.

"Help me," Myles said, gingerly reaching out to stop the piece of furniture. Not knowing what to expect, he relaxed, relieved when it stopped. Gently tipping it toward him, he motioned for Nicole to step around and steady the base of it as he lowered it to the floor. Once it sat on its four legs, he slipped off his overcoat. "That's unbelievable."

"At least everything looks as if it weren't damaged in any way. Not like the last time."

"Find the lease."

Without a word, she went to the drawer and opened it. Pulling out the brown envelope, she handed it to Myles.

"Now let's see what we're up against here, legally speaking." He opened the envelope and spread the paper out on the kitchen counter before him. His eyes widened, and looking up, he found Nicole studying him.

"What's the matter?" she asked, moving closer.

He pointed at the paper and the strange wiggly lines covering it. "Are you sure this is it?"

She nodded and stared. "What is that?"

"I have no idea. It almost looks like Chinese or Japanese or some such foreign language. But as to what language, I have no idea."

Grabbing the envelope, Nicole glanced at the upper left-hand corner and read the return address of the firm that owned the complex. Her name was handwritten across the front in the same smooth flowing style that had been there all the time. "It's the right envelope, and look," she said, pointing to the letterhead of the top page, "there's the symbol of the company and the address and . . . Myles, I can't stand much more of this."

Embracing her, he said, "Take it easy. We'll figure this thing out sooner or later, with or without the help of some clergyman. Do you think you could get a copy of the lease if you called them in the morning?"

"That should be no problem. I can tell them I spilled something on my copy. What language do you think that is, assuming it is a language and not just a bunch of squiggly lines?"

Picking up the paper, he studied it for a moment. "It looks like a herd of worms with a problem crossed the paper. From what little I've seen of script from Iran and Iraq, it looks like it could be either or neither of them. I don't know. Are you that interested?"

"Not really. All I'm interested in is knowing what I have to do to get out of this agreement."

"Well, right now, we've got our work cut out for us. We'll have to move all of the furniture into place before we can go to sleep. At least, we got some decent rest over the weekend."

As they worked, Nicole fell silent, barely answering his questions or commenting on his statements.

Rewiring the stereo, he said, "I think we should have called the cops. This should have gone on record."

Nicole stared at him. "That happened the last time. I don't want the police involved anymore. After all, when someone begins imagining things it's a little difficult to make others believe in something one thinks one has seen. Besides . . ."

"Thinks one has seen? Are you serious?" He stood, spinning about to look at her.

"I've been thinking about what Father Gorkland said. He seems to feel that I've imagined a lot of the stuff that went on around here. The smells. Contributing normal things such as the water pipes breaking and things like that to some devious entity or person."

"I don't believe you're saying what you're saying. Remember, I've seen some of these things as well. How do you get off trying to explain furniture piled in the middle of the living room as a figment of our imagination? I saw it. You saw it. How could both of us . . ."

"Perhaps we both imagined it. Really. When you stop to think of it, what's so unusual about a pile of furniture? Some vandals broke in and played a practical joke on us. That's all."

"Vandals don't break in to play practical jokes and you know it. They didn't take anything. They didn't take anything the other time. Burglars or vandals just don't work that way. I'm sorry. You can't pass this off as products of your imagination."

"I really think Father Gorkland was right," she persisted. "We're both overworked and overwrought about all of this. We're merely trying to explain everything as something from hell or whatever. Do demons from hell—the devils—work like this?"

He shrugged. "The one thing I know is this. We've got to stick together on this thing. You can't believe one thing and me another. We have to find another minister or priest and tell him what's going on."

"No way. I don't want any more people like Gorkland around. I really don't, Myles."

"I'm not going to argue about something like that right now," he said, turning on the stereo. Soft music oozed from the speakers. He smiled when he saw her mood change from one of being argumentative to a more placid one when she heard the music. "We've got to get to bed or we'll both fall asleep standing up." He glanced at his wristwatch. "It's going on three. We've been jacking around all night with the furniture."

He bent down to move the footstool into position in the front of the overstuffed easy chair and froze. Beneath the stool lay the antique red book trimmed in gold. Neither had noticed that it wasn't on the shelf over the TV.

Nicole stood to pick it up. Without a word, she placed it on the shelf. Turning to Myles, she said, "Come on, let's get to bed."

Puzzled at best, he followed her to the bedroom after turning off the stereo. When he turned out the lights, the stereo went back on, its red light the only visible thing in the room.

Friday, December 5, 1986   6:59 P.M.

Seven days later, the incidents of the previous weekend had been relegated to the backs of both Nicole's and Myles' minds, minimized by the passage of time. Thanksgiving had come and gone uneventfully, and they were thankful for that if nothing else. Neither spoke of the happenings, and because nothing else went awry, both relaxed, mutually agreeing not to mention the subject again.

Christmas was a week closer and Nicole convinced Myles that they should go shopping for each other that Friday night before he had to go to work. He readily agreed to meet her immediately after she got off work and they would swing through several malls. Because of the time limit imposed by his job, they agreed to merely look but not purchase anything right then, opting to do so when they were alone. This trip might tip one or the other's hand at something that would appeal as a gift. In addition, Nicole wanted to buy Myles a gift for his birthday, which was the next day.

By seven that evening, they headed toward the apartment, where they picked up the mail and climbed the steps to the third floor. There, they would say their goodbyes until Myles came home close to midnight.

"After I see you inside, safe and sound," he said, "I've got to take off. I've a lot of work to do before the telecast."

Hesitating for a split second before jamming the key into the lock, he sniffed. "What's that?" he asked, inhaling short breaths, trying to identify the strange odor.

"What's what?" she asked. "I don't . . ."

Unlocking the door, he opened it and fell back. The stench, like a warm sea of putrescence, flooded out of the entryway, engulfing them.

"Great God!" he cried, gagging and holding his hand over his mouth.

"Oh, Lord," she said, falling back, her stomach pumping as it tried desperately to vomit its contents. Instead of diminishing as it swept into the hall, the malodorous rot grew in strength.

"Quick," Myles said, "inside." He pushed Nicole into the stink, slamming the door behind him.

"Why did you do that?" she demanded, running to the window to open it.

Rushing to the bedroom he threw open the window, then went to the kitchen were he turned on the exhaust fan. He did the same in the bathroom before returning to the living room. "I didn't want the smell to spread too much. Right now, until we know where we stand on the question of the lease, we shouldn't make waves."

"Oh," she said, nodding when she realized

why he had acted so quickly.

Within minutes the stink dissipated and they closed the windows.

"Will you be all right?" he asked.

"Of course I will. All that was was the sewer backing up."

"*Nicole!*" he snapped angrily. "You know better than that. It was the same stink you've described to me. Remember, I've smelled it before. It *wasn't* the sewer backing up."

"Then it's our imagination," she said, thumbing through the mail. Before Myles could say anything in rebuttal, she held up a brown envelope and said, "Here it is. This must be the lease." Dropping the rest of the mail, she slit it open, pulling out the stapled sheets.

"I won't have time to go over it now," he said. "I'm stopping by to see Gorkland."

"Why, for heaven's sake? We don't need him. He doesn't like either one of us very much. Why hang around him?"

"Because whether you want to admit it or not, we've got one helluva problem here. I don't think it has anything to do with the apartment although a change of scenery might do both of us a world of good."

"Well, what do you think it is?"

Her voice clipped off the words in an angry way, but the concerned, worried look on her face told him that she was trying to maintain an indifferent, unconcerned front. "I don't know. I don't know what could be causing these things, but somehow I think they're related to that book and the ritual you performed."

Tears welled in her eyes, and before she could say anything, sobs shook her body. He stepped closer, embracing her in a gentle hug. The last thing he needed right now was Nicole falling to pieces when he had to leave. Instead of abating, the crying grew until hysterical cries intermingled with deep-rooted sobs.

"Hey, you can't carry on like this for over another thirty seconds," he said, trying to sound light-hearted but failing miserably.

"I . . . I . . ." she stuttered, "it's . . . it's . . . all . . . all my fault!"

"It's no one's fault. If anything, it's mine for having walked out on you when I did. The way I did. That's what prompted you to try that rite. But I can't leave you now . . . not in the state you're in. We've got to call someone. What about a neighbor?"

She shook her head. "No . . . no way. I don't know any of them . . . other than to say . . . hello in the hallway. There . . . there isn't . . . isn't anyone. Just . . . just you!"

"Why don't you come along to the studio with me?"

"No. What . . . what would you say to someone about my red eyes? Once . . . once I start crying, I . . . I sob for hours. You've . . . you've never . . . never seen me cry before."

"We've got to do something. I won't leave you this way."

"Go ahead. I'll . . . I'll be all . . . right," she said, attempting a grin and laughing along with the sobbing when she realized how silly she sounded.

"No. I refuse. There must be . . . what about your friend from college?"

She stared at him. Who? Who did he mean? "Wh . . . who . . . do you mean?" she asked. "Not Rob . . . Rob from . . . work?"

"No. Not him. The girl you told me about."

"Sta . . . Stacey?" she managed and hiccupped.

"Yes."

"That might . . . might be dangerous."

"Why? Because she's a Jesus freak?"

She nodded.

"Tell her you don't want to talk about religion when she gets here. Tell her we had a fight. Anything. But let's get her over here. Now."

"What . . . what'll I . . . tell her?"

"The way you're sobbing, you can tell her we had a few words or something. She'll believe you. I know I would if I heard you sobbing like that. I'm going to stop by Gorkland's, regardless of what you say."

"Will . . . will you . . . have time?"

He nodded. "Call what's-her-name."

Nicole went to the phone in the hall and picked up the directory. After several minutes of hunting, she found Stacey's number and carefully dialed it.

Myles watched her closely, barely hearing

the one-sided conversation. When she hung up, she turned and said, "She'll be over in twenty minutes and . . . you . . . don't have to wait."

"I'll wait. I'm concerned about you. I love you. I couldn't just walk out like that and not be worried sick until I knew you were all right and with someone. Someone you can trust."

She shrugged, not really certain if she could trust Stacey when she thought of the zeal she possessed when it came to matters of religion.

"Why . . . why are . . . you . . . you going to Gorkland?"

"He already knows about everything for the most part. It won't be that difficult to talk to him about it. Maybe this time I'll get through to him."

"He . . . he knows too much . . . much about the two of us . . . us already," she said, blowing her nose in a tissue she pulled from her handbag. She went to the bathroom where she flushed her face with cold water. When she came out a few minutes later, her eyes, although still red from crying, did not appear too much out of the ordinary. When she talked, her sobs had slowed to only occasional ones.

Myles waited patiently, and twenty minutes after Nicole had hung up the phone, the door bell buzzed. "I'm going to duck out the back door," he said. "I don't want to confront her right now. She might take it on herself to start preaching to me about making you cry or fighting with you. If I'm going to have time to see Gorkland and get to the station before nine, I've got to go now. 'Bye, Nicole. I love you." Hurrying to the kitchen, he waited by the back door until he was positive that it was Stacey Ford who had rung the doorbell.

When he heard Nicole greet her friend, he stepped into the back hallway and closed the door quietly after hearing Nicole's opening sentence: "Come in Stacey . . . but remember . . . no talk about reli . . . religion."

8:33 P.M.

Father Gorkland eyed Myles suspiciously. "What is it this time, Mr. Lawrence?"

"I know you don't especially care for Nicole and me, Father, but we do need your help," Myles began.

"Forgive me for that slip of humanity, Mr. Lawrence. I should not have been so judgmental of you and Miss Kilton. Please sit down and tell me what's troubling you." He gestured to Myles to take a chair and did so himself when his guest was seated.

Myles quickly brought the priest up to date and finished with, "I think she might be slipping away from me. The way she's changed, citing your arguments about the phenomena being products of our imagination and so on, really bothered me. If you had seen the manner in which the furniture had been piled, you'd agree, Father."

Gorkland shook his head. "That's just it, Mr. Lawrence. I *didn't* see it . . . or anything else that you and Miss Kilton have told me. How could I go to the chancery office, seeking permission to confront something that at best would be the product of an overwrought imagination? It would be my overworked imagination if I were to do something like that."

"Do you mean you won't or can't?" Myles asked, narrowing his eyes.

"Both, I guess. I won't because there isn't enough proof—the kind of proof that is required by the Church today. Even if there were, a competent psychiatrist would still have to be consulted and those findings taken into consideration before any further discussion could take place. And I can't because . . ." His voice trailed off.

"Why can't you?" Myles demanded.

"I can't because I think both of you are completely wrong. Wrong in the way you live. Wrong in the way you interpret things around you. Wrong about your attitude toward religion. Wrong . . ."

Myles held up his hand for the priest to stop. "Forget that. Those are your particular prejudices. What about the Church? Can't the Church help us in some way?"

"Such as?" Gorkland asked, shrugging. "I've told you what the Church demands in cases such as you're hoping you have."

"Hoping? Hoping to have?" Myles said, gagging on the words. Did he think they were hoping for something evil? How could this man of God allow personal feelings to affect his decision when it came to helping someone?

"Aren't you hoping that these things that are happening are in reality caused by some dark force? Perhaps you hope to capitalize on the situation. People today are weird, strange at best."

"Look here, Father Gorkland, I don't have time to be arguing moot points of theology or about mankind's behavior today. Nicole and I have a real problem. Can't you leave the Church or the chancery that you mentioned, out of it and just come back? If you witness something like we have, you can do whatever it is one like yourself is supposed to do, and everyone will be the better off because of it."

"You're suggesting too many liberties for me to take. The chancery is my boss, so to speak. My hands are tied in situations like this. I must have the permission of the bishop if I am to proceed with anything out of the ordinary. Don't you understand?"

Myles, feeling defeat imminent, nodded.

"There's only one way a priest can proceed with an exorcism without getting the permission of the bishop. If the priest's life is endangered by an unseen entity, he may invoke the prayers of the rite of exorcism. But that is the only set of circumstances. Now, don't try to tell me that my life would be threatened if I were to come back to that apartment. I . . ."

"I understand, Father," Myles said, getting

out of his chair. "I'll be on my way, and I promise I won't be back to bother you any more." Turning, he left the priest's office.

He could feel the baleful stare of the man on his back until he turned at the door and hurried toward the entryway that led outside. Now what would they do? If this priest didn't believe them, what chance did they have with other men of the cloth? Probably slim to none. Outside, he went to his car and stared through the windshield for several minutes when he sat behind the wheel.

All he knew was that he loved Nicole and he would do anything to protect her from whatever evil force she had conjured up that night. The demon or devil or whatever was harassing them had better be on guard.

He turned the key in the ignition switch and the motor roared to life. Checking his rearview mirror, he eased the car away from the curb. He'd best seek out a minister or another priest. He simply had to. There was no way he felt confident enough to face this thing alone. Sure he'd lay his life down for Nicole, but why do it foolishly if there were another way to fight? He'd have to find another priest or minister as soon as possible. For some reason that escaped him, he felt they were running out of time.

11:11 P.M.

Nicole turned the sound of the television set down and watched Myles' image, his words choked off by the volume control. "There," she said, "at least we'll be able to watch him and continue our talk."

She turned to Stacey. The evening had been more successful than she had dared hope. The subject of religion had not been brought up, and for the most part the evening had been spent reminiscing about their days in college. Their talk had brought them around to the subject of different boys and men they had known during school, when the time for the newscast came around.

Stacey, who had been one year behind Nicole, said, "Why did you date your first year?"

Nicole pursed her lips in retrospect. There had been several but Jimmy Allen had been special to her. It had been Jimmy who had seduced her and taken her virginity. "Did you know Jimmy Allen?" she asked.

Stacey shook her head, waiting for Nicole to tell her about him.

"Well, Jimmy got me. Do you know what I mean?"

Stacey stared at her, a bewildered look crossing her face. "I . . . I don't understand."

"We went to bed. He was my first. I was a virgin and . . ."

Stacey's face grayed. "My good God, Nicole. You sound so callous, so hard, so . . . I don't know what! You actually went to bed with him and gave yourself to him? Just like that?"

Nicole's head swam, her stomach churning. Why had she said that? Now, the evening would be ruined. Stacey would start spouting religion, but wait! What about her college sexual escapades? "Do you mean to tell me, Stacey, that you're still a virgin?"

"Nothing of the kind. When I was going to college here I sinned and lost my virginity but now in retrospect, I can say that it was the devil at work. I did not want it to happen. But the way of the flesh won and I enjoyed sinning as if I had been drugged with lust. I was a sinner and then the Children of the Sun found me. But now, I have my sweet Jesus. He watches over me. He protects me. He helps me whenever I am placed in a position of temptation. You simply have to meet Reverend Eddie John. He'll help you out of this morass of sin that you've allowed yourself to get drawn into."

Stacey kept talking, rambling on about Jesus, her Saviour, and her own personal direct contact, the Reverend Eddie John Stangood. But Nicole heard nothing else, entwining with the words of the girl seated opposite her. It sounded more like a far off, distant siren, moaning and groaning as it built in intensity. The volume grew as the sound neared. But what was it? What could that sound be? She strained her ears desperately trying to distinguish it but failed the harder she tried.

Stacey continued prattling.

Nicole heard bits and pieces of the rhetoric Stacey spouted. Jesus was coming. Stacey wasn't exactly sure when, but come He would. And it would be right after Armageddon had been fought. Or was it before? Nothing was making sense to Nicole. The wailing cry continued growing and Nicole tried desperately to place its origin. It seemed to be coming from someplace in the room. Forcing herself to turn, she watched Stacey. The woman kept talking, completely unmindful of the piercing wail that mounted in growing decibles until Nicole thought her head would shatter. The room spun crazily about in her line of vision. The TV screen was showing a movie. Where had Myles gone? What time was it? Was he on his way home? Please! Please, dear God, let Myles hurry home. Let him get here now.

Jesus is coming!

Armageddon is closer than you think! One final battle and Reverend Eddie John's prediction will come true. He will be directly in contact with Almighty Jesus and the world will be Reverend Eddie John's.

The piercing cry burrowed into Nicole's brain. Why didn't she just fall over and die? It would be so much more simple. So much more painless. No more Stacey to preach to her. No more siren wail. No more—Myles?

She threw her hands over her ears, rocking back and forth.

"Well, if you don't want to hear the truth, I won't try to force it on you," Stacey said, standing.

The door to the hall opened and Myles peered in. "How are you two getting along?" he asked, forcing a note of cheer into his voice.

Instantly, the sound stopped and Nicole fainted.

14

Saturday, December 6, 1986   12:07 A.M.

"I think your cab is here," Myles said, dropping the curtains and turning back to face Stacey.

"I'm not sure if I should leave. I'm worried about Nicole." Reluctantly slipping into her coat, Stacey turned to Nicole, who sat on the couch staring into space.

Snapping out of her daze, she said, "Don't worry, Stacey. I'm fine. I really am. I guess I was just too tired or something. I should have gone to bed hours ago."

"If you're certain," Stacey said, confronting Myles with a quizzical expression.

"I'm sure she'll be fine . . . or is fine, right now. Nicole?" He waited for Nicole to confirm his diagnosis. When she nodded, he smiled broadly, crossing the room to Stacey's side. Taking her arm, he escorted her to the door and opened it.

"Cab's waiting," he said lightly.

"I'll call later in the morning. All right?" she asked, stopping in the hall for another endless second of waiting.

"Do that, Stacey," Myles said, closing the door. When he heard the sound of her footsteps diminishing down the hall, he slipped the chain lock in place and turned to face Nicole. "What really happened?"

By now he had accepted the idea, as preposterous as it sounded, that something unusual—something strange and eerie—had entered their lives. Not for a moment had he bought the story Nicole had mumbled about not having eaten and merely fainting from lack of food. Positive she had made that up for Stacey's benefit, he waited for her to say something.

"It was weird. I goofed when it came to subject matter for our conversation and accidentally set Stacey off on a tirade about Jesus and such. Then I heard it."

"It?" He looked at her, cocking an eyebrow.

"A peculiar sound."

He waited, studying Nicole's face as it screwed up in consternation.

"It sounded at first like a . . . a . . . siren of some sort. But the pitch was lower, not quite so shrill. At least it wasn't shrill at first. That came later. And it grew in volume. It was so God-awful loud. Why Stacey didn't react is beyond me." She looked up into his face, thankful to find concern instead of disbelief, worry instead of ridicule.

"Maybe," he said slowly, softly, "just maybe, Stacey didn't hear it."

Nicole stood. Walking to the window overlooking the front of the building, she peered out. The cab was gone and she could see no one three stories below. "Why wouldn't she have heard it? That's a little silly, Myles. My God, the noise was frightful. I think it was getting loud enough to make me pass out."

"What do you mean?"

"I'm not a fainter. I didn't feel dizzy until I heard that noise. I wasn't upset in my stomach nor did I feel the least bit sick."

"The noise made you pass out? Is that what you're saying?"

She nodded.

"Well," he said quietly after several seconds, "that might explain why Stacey *didn't* react. If it *was* in your head she probably didn't hear it. She probably couldn't hear it. I know I didn't hear anything. But then, I was only here for a moment before you passed out." When he looked at her, he found Nicole glaring at him. "What's the matter?"

"Are you saying that all of this was in my head? That I imagined it?"

Myles waited before answering. At first he had doubted some of the things she had told him. Then little by little, as he experienced some of the phenomena himself, he began accepting her story. But then, she began echoing Father Gorkland's explanation that all of it was the product of hers and then Myles' and her combined imaginations. Now she was back to wanting him to believe, reacting strongly to the suggestion that it had been in her head. He hadn't meant that at all.

"Look, Nicole," he said, moving across the room to her, "what I meant by that was you were the only one to hear it. I'm not implying that you're imagining it."

Tempering her attitude, she said, "How could that be possible?"

He shrugged. "There have been some pretty strange things that have happened here recently. Who's to say that something like that couldn't happen?"

"What are we going to do, Myles? We've talked to a priest who won't believe anything we say, and we've seen some pretty peculiar things. How do we adjust to something like this? Are we supposed to go through the rest of our lives, being tormented and teased like this?"

"You've just hit on something. We've never been actually threatened, have we? Neither one of us."

Puckering her forehead in thought, Nicole slowly shook her head. "What do you mean by threatened?"

"I don't think we've actually been in danger. Do you?" He looked at her but continued without giving her a chance to respond. "What I mean is this. It's as though there's a shield around you and me. Maybe whatever it is isn't able to touch us."

"Wrong," Nicole said, throwing her one hand up like a traffic cop. "Remember when you came home and found me in the shower? You got in with me?" She waited for him to recall. When he did with a nod, she continued. "I didn't tell you but the shower and I were getting pretty friendly."

"What?" Both eyebrows shot up in surprise and he stared at her.

"First of all, I lost all track of time. I thought I had only been in for a few minutes. In fact, I went in right after Gorkland left. I wanted to shower and be able to watch you on TV. It was about ten forty-five. Before I knew it, you were opening the door, standing there naked as a jaybird and wanting a little R and R yourself."

"I don't understand. Are you saying that because you lost track of time while enjoying a hot shower that that in itself is significant?"

Shaking her head, she said, "No. The water. The water felt different somehow."

"How do you mean 'different'?"

"Don't think I'm going crazy, but it felt as if hands were pawing me."

An ominous silence filled the room for several seconds before Myles coughed and said hoarsely, "Pawing you?"

She nodded but said nothing.

"I didn't feel anything."

"Maybe you weren't supposed to."

"Meaning?"

"Meaning I was the one who performed the ritual. I'm the one who conjured up a spirit or demon or whatever it is that's been hanging around here."

"Are you saying that it's got something going for you? Sexually?"

She forced a short, bitter laugh. "What else?"

"I think you're jumping to conclusions. One incident does not make an affair of the heart."

"Funny, Myles. That's not what I mean. Suppose that whatever is bothering us really came about because of the thing I did. Wouldn't that mean it was really unholy. Maybe Father Gorkland didn't catch the full significance of what we're telling him."

"Maybe we didn't either, if what you say is true. But why now? Why so long after the fact? You performed the rite quite a while ago. Right?"

She nodded. "It's well over two months ago. In September."

"Why did it wait so long to make a move on you?"

She shrugged.

"I can't believe we're saying some of the things we're saying, Nicole. Do you realize what you're suggesting is that an unseen thing, or whatever you want to call it, made a pass at you . . . and I'm going along with it as though some guy got fresh with you at a party? The whole thing is crazy beyond belief."

"You're probably right," she said. "None of it makes too much logical sense, does it?"

Myles crossed the room to the television set and reached up, taking down the small book. "Show me. Show me where the ritual is that you performed. I'm assuming it's in this book."

Nodding, she went to his side, taking the book from him. "Promise you won't laugh or poke fun at me?" Flipping through the pages, she looked up once she found the correct page, waiting for his answer.

"I'm not about to make fun of anything or anybody," he said, taking the book when she offered it to him.

Nicole sat back on the couch while he read. When he looked up, she said, "Why didn't you ask to see it sooner?"

A puzzled expression froze on his face. "I ... I don't know. It never occurred to me. I guess I thought, because I was back, that it didn't make much difference what the circumstances were that brought us together or what you might have done to help things along."

"You do believe me, then, don't you?"

"I guess so. But the point now is, are you in danger? This thing that I just read sounds like so much double-talk. I don't see much significance in anything that's included, but that doesn't mean that it might not work."

"What are we going to do? I'm frightened."

"Let's not panic. Tomorrow, we'll begin a search for another priest or minister. This time, we'll go in without hesitating about any of the facts."

"And in the meantime, what do we do?"

"Go to bed. We can't afford to lose a night's sleep. We'll have to be sharp if we're going to be talking to a lot of religious people tomorrow."

"A lot?" she echoed. "What about your birthday? That's an awful way to celebrate."

"We can celebrate another time. This is more important. I don't think we'll be so lucky as to find a priest who'll believe our story the first time we try. Do you?" He returned the book to the shelf over the television set.

"You're probably right." The shower incident came back to mind, bringing with it the sensation of the rough, calloused hands that had fondled her breasts and genitals. "Myles," she cried, running to him from the couch, "hold me."

"Hey, take it easy. We'll be all right. Nothing has happened yet. I doubt if it will. And if it does . . . well, whatever it is had better damned well watch out." He held her tight to his body, realizing how upset she really was by the way she trembled. "Come on, let's hit the hay. We'll probably laugh at it in the morning."

"But we are going to find another minister, aren't we?"

"You bet we are," he said, leading her to the bedroom.

As they undressed, he watched her. Why her

beauty, her nudity, her movements would arouse him now, considering the circumstances, escaped him. But when his penis jerked to life, he stepped closer to her.

Enfolding her in his arms, he kissed her, relieved to find her open to his unspoken suggestion. He lowered her to the bed, holding her close, their nakedness joining as one. He propped himself up on one elbow, continuing to kiss her mouth at the same time. His tongue darted in and out, being welcomed by hers. Both slipped in and out of each other's mouth, caressing, exploring, arousing.

He trailed one hand down her side then back up to her breasts. Fondling them in a gentle, soothing way, he felt her fingertips run across his own back and shoulders. Her touch, exquisitely sexual, continued its restrained massage. His free hand roamed over her body, exciting her to a fevered pitch when it rested on her hairy triangle. Reacting instantly, she thrust her hips upward, in an offering, giving gesture. When he felt her hot fingers touching his pulsating erection, he raised himself over her.

Nicole spread her legs, waiting for him to enter her, and gasped with pleasure when he took her. His thrusts were gentle at first, matching her own quiet pumping rhythm. Slowly growing in intensity, the natural animal instincts of both, aroused to the fullest, quickly agitated to a feverish pace. His legs tingled as his glands heightened their natural response to the stimulation of her slippery vaginal walls. He could feel her fingertips at the base of his neck, while her legs jerked spasmodically around his neck.

His passion growing, he increased the rhythmic speed of his buttocks and found himself pumping more demandingly than he had ever done before with anyone—even Eunice. It was like a new experience. The sensation of hands on his buttocks, pressing in direct cadence with his own increased tempo, brought him closer to climax. She held his face with both hands, kissing him, thrusting her tongue in and out of his mouth.

Myles stopped, frozen in position by the sudden realization that she was *holding* his face.

Then who was pressing on his buttocks?

At first, Nicole wasn't aware that he had stopped, passion carrying her to the brink of her own climax. Realizing after a moment that he wasn't moving, she asked huskily, "What's the matter, darling?"

When she freed his face, he turned his head as far as he could but saw nothing. The room was empty except for the two of them. He looked in the mirrors behind the bed—nothing. *They were alone.* Still, he could feel the pressure of two hands. Roughened hands. Calloused palms and fingers. Straining to one side, to see his rump better, he screamed when he made out the impressions of his own backside—five indentations half-surrounding a larger one where the palm of the hand should have rested on each cheek.

"What is it? Myles? Speak to me!"

Leaping from her, he grabbed her hand, roughly pulling her to her feet. "I . . . I could feel someone's hands on me. Helping me. Pushing my rear end to enter you even farther." Shuddering, he pulled back from her when she tried to embrace him.

"Myles. It'll be all right. Maybe you imagined it."

"Did you imagine the shower?" he snapped, reaching for his pants and slipping into them. "Get dressed. We're getting out of here. Now."

Both rushed to the closet, pulling clothing out. But try as they might, they could not dress in a hurry. Buttons seemed to be uncooperative, popping open as soon as they were done. Zippers stuck.

"Can you smell it?" she asked, throwing her bra aside when she could not get the hook to stay in place.

Myles sniffed deeply. "Yeah. God, that's awful."

The rancid stench continued to grow in intensity until it filled the room, pressing in on the fumbling couple. After what seemed an eternity, they stood facing each other, dressed but frantically apprehensive now that they were ready to leave.

"Should we take a bag or something?"

"No time. Grab your coat and let's go," he ordered.

The cloth coat she pulled from the closet

clung to its hanger, each button holding fast to the opposite side. Taking the time to open it, she tried to hurry but her fingers acted clumsily, not responding to her brain's simple commands. While she struggled, he fought with the zipper of his jacket. Again, an eternity seemed to pass before they were able to don their wraps. When they turned to leave the bedroom, they discovered they could only walk slowly, despite their instincts of survival and their desire to run as fast as possible.

"What's wrong with us?" Nicole asked, her words slurred, running together as if she were intoxicated.

"I . . . I don't know. Take my hand," Myles said, offering his and taking one of hers.

Together, they made their way to the hall door. When they reached it, the latch turned sluggishly as if the lock had not been turned for years. Myles reached out for the knob once the lock had yielded, and both froze when they heard the laugh. Low, evil, hoarse, it came from the bedroom, coursing down the hall toward them. Growing louder and louder, it filled the living room, flowing into the kitchen until the whole apartment rang with obscene hilarity.

Throwing their hands over their ears as the laughter stabbed at them threatening to break their eardrums, they half-fell, half-stepped into the hall. Instantly, the sound stopped and the door slammed shut of its own accord.

Unable to control her emotions, Nicole wept,

reaching out to Myles. "What . . . what's going on? I . . . I don't think I can stand much more of this sort of thing. Where'll we go now? Who can we call? How . . ."

"Whoa," he said, leading her away from the door of the apartment. "One thing at a time. There's an all night drugstore a couple of blocks over on Syracuse Avenue. Let's go there, and look up a church. There has to be one close by someplace."

"Then . . . then what?"

"Then we'll go there. I don't think there's a priest or minister who would not talk to a couple of people in trouble."

"Is . . . is that all there is to it? We're merely in trouble of some kind?" Her voice rang bitterly as they waited for the elevator. When it finally bumped to a stop and the door slid open, they got on.

"Call it what you will. I'm not quite certain as to what we should call our . . . our . . ."

"Pre . . . predicament? Situation?" she finished for him. "What about Gorkland? Couldn't we call him? He already . . ."

"No way. I've had it with that sanctimonious frustrated ass. We'll find someone else. And when we do find somebody who's willing to listen, I don't intend to hold back anything. And you had better not, either. Otherwise, who'll believe us if we tend to downplay it?"

As the doors slid open, she shrugged and sobbed once, following him into the small lobby.

He had anticipated his car being as stubborn as the lock and the clothing but it turned over on the first try, and they drove silently to the all night drugstore. Inside, they found a small bank of three telephones. Only the pharmacist on duty behind the locked lab cage peered out at them. When he saw they were going to use the telephone, he went about his own duties, looking up every so often to check on the late night visitors. The other employees, a woman behind the check-out counter and a heavily muscled man sweeping the floor, ignored them.

Flipping through the Yellow Pages, Myles ran a finger down the list of churches, quickly checking each for its address and proximity.

"The Holy Messiah Lutheran Church is only six blocks away. Let's try it." He jotted the name of the pastor down, along with the address, and pulling Nicole after him, hurried to the car.

In minutes they were standing in front of the main entrance to the parsonage of the church.

"This is crazy, Myles. He won't see us at this hour of the night."

"He'd better damn well plan on it, or I'll go in and drag him out," he said, jamming his finger onto the doorbell. After a half minute had passed, he did it again. As he pressed it for a third time, a light came on at the end of the hall and he smiled, satisfied that he would be talking with the Reverend Harvey Melssen in another minute or two.

The porch light flooded the entryway before

the curtains in the door's window were pulled back, allowing a sleep-puffed face, belonging to a middle aged man, to peer out. "Who's there?" he demanded groggily.

"We need your help, sir," Myles said.

"Can't it wait until tomorrow?"

"No," Myles said loudly. "We need help and we need it now. Tonight! Not tomorrow. Please?"

"Please, help us, Reverend," Nicole cried, stepping closer to Myles so she could see Melssen and he could see her.

"Give me a moment," he said, disappearing from sight when he dropped the curtain.

"Do you think he'll see us or is he calling the cops?" Nicole asked.

"We'll know that soon enough, won't we? Let's not anticipate the worst and only hope he'll see us."

Several long minutes crawled by before the sound of the door being unlocked soothed their rattled nerves and they stood facing Reverend Harvey Melssen.

"Come in," he said graciously. "I'm Reverend Melssen. How can I be of help to you?" He motioned for them to enter the living room off to one side of the hall, following them after he closed the front door.

"I hope you'll understand once I explain why we're here, Reverend," Myles said.

"I hope it's worth it," Melssen said, looking at his wristwatch. "I don't often get calls for help at my front door at three forty-five in the morning." Stifling a yawn, he said, "Please, sit down," and took a chair opposite the couch.

After Myles and Nicole sat down, Myles said, "Let me begin at the beginning and tell you everything. Nicole, you jump in anytime you feel I've overlooked something or haven't emphasized a point strongly enough. All right?"

She nodded—and Myles began their story.

If Melssen had been reluctant to listen to trouble so early in the day, his sleepiness and hesitency soon departed and he hung on every word that Myles uttered, turning his attention to Nicole whenever she spoke.

"Why have you waited so long to seek help?" Melssen asked when Myles finished telling of Nicole's ritual. Melssen looked at Nicole, who dropped her eyes from his, a gentle blush flowing onto her cheeks.

"We did."

"From whom?" Melssen asked, a more than quizzical look crossing his tired face.

"A Father Gorkland. Father DuWayne Gorkland."

"I don't believe I know him. Where is his parish? Is he Catholic or Episcopalian?"

"Catholic. And he's at Saint Timothy's over on Lanchester Avenue."

"What did he say? Are you two Catholic? If you are, why are you here?"

"First of all, Nicole isn't a Catholic but she attended a Catholic grade school at one time. I am . . . to some degree or other. I guess I haven't been practicing my faith too well lately. But the reason we're here is that Father Gorkland either didn't want to help us or couldn't help us. I still haven't figured out what it was. For some reason, I always felt he didn't believe anything I said . . . or maybe it was because he himself doesn't believe in the devil."

"That's pretty unfair when one considers our whole function as ministers of God is to fight the devil. Perhaps it was nothing more than a conflict of personality. Might that have been the case?"

Myles shrugged. "I don't know. All I do know is that he was ready to condemn Nicole and me for living together without the benefit of marriage and he seemed always to come back to that point. He said we were living in a state of sin and that our consciences were reacting to our guilt and making us believe all sorts of things."

"I wish he would have helped you, young man," Melssen said, running his hand through his thinning black hair.

"Wish he would have helped us? I don't understand."

"Why should I jeopardize my standing in the community and most especially in my own congregation by helping someone whose own priest wouldn't consider helping?"

"He's not my priest."

"He's of your religious persuasion, young man, and that makes him yours whether you want to accept him or not. Besides, I tend to agree with his appraisal of the situation."

Myles stared at him but said nothing.

"You both *are* living in a state of sin. Get your act straightened out for the sake of Jesus Christ, your Saviour. Now, please leave. You've already cost me enough sleep."

"I . . ." Nicole began but was stopped by Myles.

"Thank you for nothing, Reverend." He took Nicole's hand, leading her to the door before Melssen could stand.

When they reached the car, parked at the curb, Myles closed the door after she got in and went around to his side. Once the motor was running, he pulled away from the curb, driving aimlessly for several minutes before either spoke.

"What are we going to do, Myles? We're in real trouble. We need help, but no one is willing to listen to us or offer assistance."

"Right now, I'm beginning to remember why it was I stopped going to church. Pomposity of the individual. From the priests right down to the ushers who looked like they had a direct line to the Almighty themselves, and no one other than they and maybe the priest would ever make it to heaven."

"Do you know who I blame for tonight?"

"Who?" he asked, turning to her.

"Stacey. Stacey Ford and her rantings and ravings about . . ."

Myles slammed on the brakes and turned to

face her.

"*Stacey!*" they both chorused.

"Let's call her," he said, moving the car forward again.

"Maybe this Reverend Stangood or whatever his name is can help. What do you think?"

"I'm thinking exactly the same thing. Let's go back to that drugstore and call her."

"Right now? It's going on four forty-five. I'm not sure how she'll react to being called."

"If she's genuinely sincere and he's a real minister, they should have no objections whatsoever. Besides, the way you said she was— being so zealous and all—she'd probably welcome the call. Especially from you."

He parked the car in front of the drugstore and they both hurried inside. While Nicole looked up her telephone number, Myles stared at the colorful display of paperback books stretching for fifty feet down the aisle opposite the pay phones.

"Hi, Stacey?"

"Who's it?" the sleepy voice asked.

"It's Nicole. I . . . we . . . that is, Myles and I have a problem we thought Reverend Stangood might be able to help with."

"What kind of problem?" she asked, yawning.

"Listen carefully, Stacey, because it's sort of weird and way out." Nicole launched into her rendition of the phenomana and events that had plagued her and then Myles since she had performed the ritual. That in itself seemed to have taken place in another century—so far removed from reality as if it were merely a scene from a scary movie. She could hear nothing other than Stacey's even breathing in the earpiece and hoped that the woman hadn't fallen asleep. When she finished, she said, "That's about it, Stacey. Do you think he could help us?"

After a few seconds passed, Stacey said, "Where are you calling from? Your apartment?"

"No. We're in an all night drugstore. Why?"

"Give me the telephone number there and I'll call you back as soon as I talk with Reverend Eddie John. Okay?"

"That'll be fine, Stacey. Just a minute and I'll give the number to you." She read it from the little plate above the dial and hung up. She found Myles perusing the titles of the occult section of the paperback rack.

"Do you believe that people actually buy some of this crap?"

"Crap?" Nicole parroted.

"Yeah. Look at some of these titles. *Unto the Altar. Evil Dreams. Garden of the Incubus.* What sort of people read these? More importantly, what sort of weirdo writes them?"

"Never mind that now. Stacey'll call back and tell us if the Reverend Stangood will help us. She sounded as if she could convince him. At least I hope she can."

"That's great. Let's get a bottle of pop or can of juice to drink. I'm really thirsty."

"You get something. I'll wait by the telephone."

"Are you awake? Reverend? Reverend Eddie John? Are you awake? Wake up! We have to go out and help some people who are in trouble."

Eddie John Stangood moaned, breaking into another gutteral snore without awakening.

"Please, Eddie? Come on. Wake up. Nicole needs your help. Wake up. You can win her as a convert. She needs you."

"I need *you*," Eddie John Stangood said, reaching out to pull Stacey back into bed. "What are you doing up in the middle of the night?" He groped for her breasts.

"There was a telephone call from Nicole Kilton. She's got a problem. Sit up and let me tell you what it is. It might be just the thing to gain some attention to your cause. Our cause."

At the thought of promoting himself and his church, Reverend Stangood sat up in bed, ready to pay attention to whatever it was his lover, Stacey Ford, was about to tell him.

When she finished, he said, "That's about perfect. I'm sure she's only upset about something or other but if I can calm her down and make her see the light of *Gee*-zus and the *tru-ooth* as I present it, she should be willing to come into my flock. What about this man who's with her?"

"Myles? Myles in the anchorman on one of the TV stations here in town."

"That's even better. If we help her, we might get him to come along in with her. If that happens, the prestige of someone who's highly visible in the community and who is a member of my flock will be invaluable. Plus the fact that he might be able to help me launch a bigger television ministry right here. Call her, Stacey. Tell her *I* know my duty and obligation. *I* will help her. *I* will save her from this awful thing that has happened to her. Tell her, Stacey, tell her!"

He leaped from the bed and began dressing while Stacey hurried to the phone. "Tell her to meet us at the entrance of her apartment building. Oh, thank You *Lor-ud* above for this opportunity to gain her soul for You. Thank You! Thank You! Thank You! Thank You!"

"How long did Stacey say it would take them to get to the apartment?" Myles asked after Nicole had hung up the receiver.

"She said we should go there directly and that they'd get there as soon as possible."

Hurrying to the car, they got in and drove toward the complex several blocks away. When they turned the corner, they saw a large sedan parked in front of the entrance. After parking, they got out, and as they did so, Stacey Ford erupted from the back seat of the limousine. Reverend Eddie John Stangood, dressed in white from hat to shoes, followed her.

"The *Lor-ud* is my *shep-herd* and *I* shall not want. Yea, though I walk through the valley of death, *I* shall fear no *ev-eil*," he mumbled as Nicole and Myles approached.

"Reverend Eddie John, this is my friend, Nicole Kilton, and Myles Lawrence. They sincerely need your help. Will you help them?"

"I shall. I shall in-*deed* help them this night. And when *I* do, *I* know they shall be more than willing to sing the praises of the great *Lor-ud Gee-zus* and fall prostrate in His presence to thank Him. Of course, that can be done in the confines of my cathedral."

"I'll promise most anything if you can help us, Reverend Stangood," Nicole said softly. She was willing to compromise at the moment. Joining the man's church, or whatever it was he purported to have, would be small enough payment if she and Myles could get rid of the thing upstairs.

"And you, sir?" Reverend Eddie John asked, turning his attention to Myles.

Myles nodded brusquely, holding in reserve any vocal commitment at this point.

"Then come, my *chil-dren* and follow me, your leader. I will flush out the denizen of *hey-ell* and do battle with him. I shall drive him back to the fiery pit from whence he has dared venture."

He turned to lead them into the front entrance but was stopped by the locked door of the lobby. "Do you have a key, child?" he asked, turning to Nicole.

She stepped forward, her key already out, and unlocked the door. With a flourish, he held Nicole back and made his own entrance first. Stacey followed him and Nicole and Myles brought up the rear.

Upstairs, the lights in the third floor apartment flashed on, then off, then on, then off.

15

Saturday, December 6, 1986 5:50 A.M.

The small entourage made its way to the third floor, opting to walk instead of using the elevator. Reverend Eddie John Stangood moved slowly as if hesitant to meet whatever lurked in the apartment. Nicole followed him and Stacey preceded Myles who brought up the rear. When they stood on the third floor, Stangood stopped, waiting for Nicole to reach his side. When she did, he turned to her and said, "Which way does the *fow-ul* beast await?"

Without speaking and afraid she might break out into an impromptu laugh because of his way of speaking, Nicole pointed to her left, toward her apartment at the front of the building. She knew it was silly to want to giggle in such a situation. Myles would be upset if she took too light an attitude. Besides, she wanted the situation over and done with. If it meant having someone who talked in a weird way around for a short time, so be it. Nevertheless, his white suit and cloak seemed to make him even more ridiculous when he spoke. *Fow-ul beast, indeed!* She only hoped that something would happen when they entered and the Reverend Eddie John would be the one who would drive whatever was harassing her and Myles from the apartment and their lives.

When she stopped ten feet from her door, she motioned with one hand toward it. "That's it," she whispered.

"How close is your nearest neighbor?" he asked, looking first to the right and then to the left.

"Above me. Below me and on either side. Why?"

"I hope they're sound sleepers. One can never tell what one might encounter when facing a devil or demon from *hey-ell.*"

Nicole glanced at Myles, whose serious expression held rigid. Moving closer to him, she took his hand and then stepped closer to the door, unlocking it. She looked to Stangood who moved between her and it.

Reaching out, he opened the door, throwing it back with a flourish that seemed out of a nineteeth century melodrama.

The apartment, swathed in blackness, waited.

"Where is the light switch?" he whispered.

"To your right," Nicole answered, whispering in turn.

Reaching out a shaking hand, Stangood fumbled for a moment and then turned on the lights. Welcome, bright, revealing light flooded the entryway, spilling into the living room and down the short hall that led to the bath and bedroom.

"Shall we?" he asked, stepping in before anyone could answer.

Myles held Nicole back when she made a tentative step to go inside. Instead, he made way for Stacey to follow Stangood. After Stacey entered, her face whiter than usual, her mouth hanging agape, Myles stepped ahead of Nicole in a protective move, making her the last to enter.

"I think we should have the lights on all over the place," Stangood said, looking to Nicole and Myles for agreement.

Stretching out one hand, Myles reached around the corner of the living room and plunged it into light. The kitchen, bedroom and bath were taken care of before anyone said anything.

The stillness closed in on them. The mantel clock chimed six times.

"At least the devil's hour of three is past," Stangood said softly.

"The devil's hour?" Myles repeated, looking to the man for an explanation. "I always thought midnight was the bewitching hour."

"Old wives tale," Stangood said. "Think about it. There's three Gods that Christians believe in—*Gaw-ud* the Father, *Gaw-ud* the Son, who is *Gee-zus,* and the Holy Spirit. There are other things in the Bible that relate to the number three and the devil seems to be most active at that hour. At least, it seems to be, according to everything I've ever read about the subject."

Myles nodded but remained quiet. The awful silence crushed in on them. The only sound he could hear was the hissing of nothingness in his ears.

"Perhaps your consciences have been bothering you more than usual lately. Perhaps the other ministers to whom you spoke were right. I don't see anything or hear anything that would convince me that something is wrong here—out of the ordinary, that is."

At once, the door to the hall slammed shut and furniture began tipping over, one piece at a time. As if in slow motion, everything in the apartment turned over in a most careful manner—the chairs, the couch, the tables. Pillows from the couch floated through the apartment circling the four people, out to the kitchen, back again, down the hall where the doors to the bathroom and bedroom would open to them them fly in and close with a resounding bang when they returned to the living room. They swept by Reverend Eddie John Stangood, mussing his hair after knocking the white broad-brimmed fedora from his head. Ducking to one side, then the other, the pillows invariably touched him, bringing squeaky responses from the self-proclaimed minister of God.

"Oh, my God, look!" Stacey screamed, pointing to Nicole.

Myles turned, dropping her hand when he realized that she was horizontally floating in midair, next to him. Leaning away, he stared, too frightened to reach out and touch her, to try to bring her down to the floor, to help her. Slowly, deliberately turning counter-clockwise, Nicole's feet pointed to the north, to the west, to the south, to the east before she began gyrating at right angles to the floor. Her hair brushing the carpeting, she straightened and floated to the ceiling where she turned another 360 degrees. Then slowly, she wafted back to the floor, standing upright at the last minute next to Myles.

Books flew off the shelves in all directions before setting up a formation and attacking Stacey. Ducking behind the overturned couch, she screamed, swinging wildly at her attackers.

"De . . . de . . . demon?" Stangood cried shakily. "Get . . . get . . . out . . . of . . ."

"Welcome, Reverend Eddie John Stangood! Welcome!"

The voice boomed hollowly, echoing loudly, growing with each word until the windows shook. The stereo turned on, playing a John Phillips Sousa march, while the TV set displayed an early morning cartoon show.

Stangood stood frozen in the middle of the

living room. Color drained from his round, pudgy face and a wet spot blossomed in the front of his white pants at the base of the zipper, expanding and growing in an even larger circle as his bladder emptied.

"You do good work, you fucking phoney! Keep up the effort? You win more souls for me than you ever will for your God. Your god is money! You charlatan!"

The voice grew even louder and Stangood was buffeted about the head, his whole body reacting as it jostled from side to side as he was backhanded by the entity's unseen hands.

"But . . . I worship *Gee-zus! Gee-zus* will save me. *Gee-zus* is my savior. He will drive you back to *hey-ell. Gee-zus,* help me!" Stangood's voice barely whispered the words and when he saw clouds of steam ejecting from his mouth as he uttered the prayer, his face paled more.

Myles and Nicole watched, open-mouthed. What were they truly up against? Apparently Stangood would not be of much use to them. He needed an audience to put on his religious show. They needed a man of God who had the necessary weapons to fight something like this. Myles recalled his own childhood and the holy water that the priests had used on occasion. And the crucifix. Why didn't Stangood have something like that? At least Myles would feel as if they had some sort of armament on their side.

Stacey stood, yelling. "Get out, Eddie John.

Let's get out of here." Half-running, half-stumbling, she made her way toward the door, throwing it back. She dashed into the hall and didn't stop running until she reached the main floor. Reverend Eddie John Stangood, the only direct line to salvation, followed her and Nicole and Myles were in pursuit of him. As Myles plunged into the hall, the door slammed loudly, punctuated by a high-pitched laugh flooding the hall. The sound of the maniacal glee seemed to follow them to the first floor.

Once outside, Stangood and Stacey stood near their car. Myles and Nicole clutched each other some twenty feet away.

"I can't hardly wait until the neighbors call the cops," Myles said sarcastically.

Everyone looked up at the apartment building's front wall, expecting to see lights going on in each apartment. But the only thing out of the ordinary were the lights in Nicole's apartment, flashing on and off repeatedly. The sound of music continued from the stereo and voices boomed from the TV through the closed windows, but no one turned on lights in any of the adjoining apartments.

Myles walked over to the other couple, Nicole's hand tightly encased in his. "Well, Reverend?"

Stangood, swept the cloak around him in an effort to cover the yellowish stain, the tentacles of which streamed down both pant legs. Turning his back to them, Stacey stepped out, blocking Nicole and Myles.

"Reverend Eddie John doesn't want to speak to you."

"What?" Nicole and Myles cried together.

"He feels you purposely set this whole thing up just to embarrass him and he doesn't want anything more to do with you." She turned to Nicole. "I'm sorry, Nicole. Really I am. Why did you do such a thing?"

"Why . . . why did I . . . we . . . do such a thing?" Her anger mounted with each word.

Stacey nodded, a pained expression dominating her inanimate features.

"You really think we staged this whole thing just to make your Reverend Eddie John Stangood piss in his pants?" Nicole gasped the words out, unable to control her laughter that quashed her anger.

Stacey nodded.

Despite the serious aspects of what had happened upstairs, Nicole suddenly found it immensely funny that this pompous little ass would think that someone would want to embarrass him. She giggled uncontrollably.

"Laugh! Laugh, you whore!" Stangood screamed, turning around to shake a finger at Nicole and Myles. "*Gee-zus* does not let things like this go unpunished. *Gee-zus* will protect me. *Gee-zus* will heal me. *Gee-zus* will condemn you to everlasting *hey'ell's* fire unless you both repent and repent now. This instant. *Gee-zus* help them. *Gee-zus* give me the power to convince them to stop this chicanery."

Myles took Nicole's hand, leading her away.

Chicanery? That seemed to be his trump card, not theirs. How did Stangood think they could rig up some of the things that happened just a few minutes ago? He looked up. Lights were on in two of the apartments and he could see people peering out. Stangood's ravings must have awakened them although why they hadn't awakened earlier escaped him.

Off in the distance he could hear the wail of a siren. "We've got to get out of here, Nicole. Come on."

"Why?"

"Listen. A siren. Cops are coming."

"We haven't done anything wrong."

"I know that but we can be arrested for disturbing the peace. I don't want that to happen. Not for something like this. We've got to get help of some sort. Someplace."

"But what about my apartment? What will happen?"

"Why are you worried about that all of a sudden?"

"The book is up there. If the cops go in . . ."

"I don't think they'll notice that little book. Besides, I think we should get rid of it."

"I suppose you're right. I should have thrown it away a long time ago."

"Come on. The siren's getting closer. The cops will break in if they have to and turn off the stereo and lights. Tomorrow, we can act surprised if they contact us and ask questions. If we aren't here and no one other than *Geezus's* sword over there knows, we can bluff our way through. Somebody broke in and did it. We weren't anywhere near at the time."

Nicole got in the passenger's side while Myles went to the driver's. Reverend Eddie John Stangood's white Cadillac roared by and in seconds, Myles pulled into the street. He turned the first corner they came to, just as a squad car rounded another two blocks away.

7:30 A.M.

The sun drew a pencil line of gold across the bottom of the overcast eastern sky as Nicole and Myles made their way to the motel room they had rented. Unlocking the door, he hesitated for an instant before stepping in to turn on the light.

"What's the matter?" She looked at him furtively but still could not control her genuine concern.

"Nothing," he said, quickly adding, "that's not true. I was thinking what happened the last time we walked through a door."

"You mean at the apartment. A little while ago?"

He nodded. "If it weren't so goddamned serious and frightening, I would have laughed my ass off at Stangood. Whatever it is that's hanging around sure scared the be-*Geezus* out of God's right hand, didn't it?"

"I guess when I laughed, I was more hysterical than appreciating the humor of the situation." She moved closer to him and he took her in his arms. "Myles, what are we going to do? No one will help us."

"It sure seems that way. First Gorkland and then that Lutheran, Melssen. Why we thought that Stangood could help is beyond me."

"He is a minister, isn't he?"

"He's a phony. A real modern day marvel! One of the bible-thumping evangelists who are going to save the world, most especially your own individual neck and soul. And all for a small price. Of money, naturally." He pushed her back and threw himself on the bed, half-sitting, half-lying down.

His bitterness grated on Nicole. Most of the time, Myles was calm and laid back, almost passive in the things that went on around him. But he had been through an experience that most people seldom, if ever, face. He had been touched by the filthy evil that had caressed her in the shower. And no one would believe him or her about the things that had been going on. Weren't priests and preachers and even evangelists supposed to be ministers of God? Of Jesus? What were ordinary people expected to do under such circumstances? Run and hide their faces? Nicole and Myles were doing just that by being in the motel room. But there had to be more they could do—more that someone could do.

"Myles, I know you don't want to talk about it, but I think we have to." She dropped into one of the chairs.

He looked at her when she stopped talking.

What was she going to bring up? "I don't understand," he said, turning to face her from his position on the bed.

She sat forward in the chair next to the round table positioned under the hanging lamp. "About what happened. About your being touched."

"Oh," he said quietly. "What about it?"

"I think we had better get our stories together in the event we have to tell someone."

"Like who do you suggest?"

She shrugged. "What did the . . . hands feel like?"

"Rough. Very rough, as if they belonged to someone who did heavy, manual labor. Very calloused. Hardened skin. Am I making myself clear?"

Nodding, she said, "That's exactly the way I'd describe them."

"All right," he said, "our descriptions tally. Now what do we do?"

Tears created by the stinging reality of his question rose until they poured out. "There's got to be something we can do."

"Did you ever see *The Exorcist* or read the book?"

She shook her head.

"Any of the scary books? See any of the movies about possession?"

She shook her head again. "Just *Kiss Not the Child.*"

"I've seen *The Exorcist* and it was awful."

Wiping her eyes, she said, "Is that what you

think is happening? That I'm possessed? Or that you are? Or that . . ."

He held up his hand for her to stop. "I don't think you are, but I'm no expert. What I was going to say was that in the movie and in the book, too, they used holy water and a crucifix. I think if I remember correctly, they're supposed to have devastating effects on the devil."

"My God! Myles, what if I am possessed? What happens to me?"

Jumping from the bed, he crossed to her, falling to his knees in front of the chair. He held out his arms and she leaned forward until he could embrace her. "You're not possessed. I think you probably started something with that rite you performed but I don't think you're possessed."

"How can I tell?"

"Well, the little girl in the movie had open sores on her face and talked in a deep, rough voice and did all sorts of weird things like floating . . ." He stopped.

After a long minute went by, she said, "What's the matter?"

"You . . . you were floating in midair tonight and you did it once before. Remember?"

She slowly shook her head as the truth of his statement sunk home. "I . . . I don't remember actually flying around. Should I? Maybe because I don't remember means that I'm not possessed. Say that I'm not, Myles." Deep sobs racked her body and he held her tightly.

"I truly don't believe you're possessed, Nicole. I truly don't. But we do have to get some questions answered and answered damned soon. Or we have to be better equipped to fight whatever it is that's doing all of this stuff."

"Bet . . . ter equip . . . ped?" Her sobs grew in their intensity.

Holding her face in his hands, he stared deeply into her teary eyes. "I think we had better get some holy water and a crucifix. Maybe a little religion wouldn't hurt either."

"How . . . can that . . . help?"

"First of all, I don't mean the good old fashioned evangelical kind that the Reverend Eddie John Stangood puts out. I mean organized. Maybe I'll go back to the Catholic Church."

"What about . . . Gork . . ."

"Father Gorkland?" he finished for her.

She nodded, dabbing at her eyes.

"The man's human. He's going to have personal prejudices and likes and dislikes. So he can't see you and me living together and is blind to everything else where we're concerned. He's not the only priest around. Besides, maybe we should do something about our marital status anyway." He smiled gently.

Her eyes widened. Was he proposing? Were they going to be married? "What's . . . what's our . . . first . . . step?"

"First thing we'll do when we get up is go to a religious goods store and buy a crucifix.

Then, we'll find a priest who will bless it and get some holy water from him."

She looked at him, tilting her head.

"We won't necessarily tell him about our problem or what the crucifix and holy water are for. At least not right away. If we feel he likes us and we like him, maybe he'll be the one we unload our story on—again."

A look of relief crossed Nicole's face and she bravely forced a smile.

"I think we should at least lie down for a while and get some rest. It's been a long night." Standing, he held out his hand for her and she took it, allowing him to lead her to bed.

They both lay back, fully clothed, on top of the covers, staring at the ceiling. Reaching out, he took her hand in his, silently vowing to himself that somehow they would drive the demon who was in their lives back to hell. He knew they could beat the devil.

7:57 A.M.

Gray daylight seeped through the curtain of the apartment's living room. The TV, stereo, turntable and lights waited patiently, neither playing nor blinking. The furniture had been righted and everything had been straightened. The soft drumming of impatient fingers sounded through the rooms in accompaniment to the whispered words, *"Hurry! Hurry! Hurry!"*

PART FOUR

"You Are Mine Forever"

Saturday, December 6, 1986

16

Saturday, December 6, 1986   9:00 A.M.

To bolster their sagging physical condition,
Nicole and Myles had several cups of coffee at
the motel's dining room before going to the
nearest religious goods store. After a wait of
twenty minutes, the manager arrived,
unlocking the door just at the hour of nine.
They waited several minutes and then left
Myles' car, hurrying to the store's entrance
through the brisk morning air.

"What are we going to get other than a crucifix?" Nicole asked. For the first time since the
weird happenings had begun, she felt as if she
and Myles might gain the upper hand. But
what if all this, like everything else they'd
tried, was for nothing? Then what? Could they
look forward to spending their lives together?
Could they expect strange happenings forever?

"Let's look around but I don't think it's too

great an idea to ask for something to drive a devil out. He'd probably call the boys in the white coats.''

Nicole nodded, opening the door. The warmth of the store embraced them, which they welcomed. Without realizing it, they had been chilled waiting in the car without the heater running. She visibly shuddered, relaxing a bit in the heat.

"Good morning," the man said as he approached them. "May I help you?"

"Yes," Myles said, taking the initiative. "We'd like to look at some crucifixes."

"Right this way," he said, gesturing for them to follow. He went to the far side of the store, pointing to a glass counter that had the symbols of Christ's death displayed on several shelves. Behind the glass stand, more bare crosses and cruciforms adorned the wall. "Is there any one style or mode that you're looking for?"

"Not really," Myles offered absently, stepping closer to the counter. What would they need? As far as he could remember, a cross was a cross. Did it matter what the crucifix looked like when it came to driving the devil away? "Why don't you let us look these over? If we have any questions, we'll call you."

"Very well," the man said. "I'll be over at the cash register." He turned, walking away.

"What do we need?" Nicole asked as soon as the man was out of earshot.

"Just a crucifix. I don't think there's any

one type that's preferred. See anything you like?" His voice carried a hint of humor which he suppressed, refusing to make light of the situation.

"I like that one there," Nicole said, pointing to a silver one, which displayed the Crucifixion in modern design. The thin beams of the cross were barely big enough to support the slender, stylized figure of Christ.

"Okay," he said. "I can't see anything wrong with it."

"Is there anything else we could get?" She looked at him, her eyes pleading for something that would virtually guarantee their ultimate success.

"Other than holy water, I can't think of anything."

"Do they carry it here?" she asked.

"That you get in a church or from a priest."

Her look of understanding seemed like a little girl's, trusting and calm, as if being given a lesson in some facet of life. Before she could react he bent and kissed her mouth.

"What was that for?"

He smiled. "For just being you and the way you are."

It was Nicole's turn to smile. Myles' love for her seemed to be growing every day, every hour, and she enjoyed each expansion. "Are we going to go to a church and get some holy water?"

He nodded. "Let's ask the clerk if he can recommend someone—a priest. It can't be that all priests and ministers are like the turkeys we've encountered."

"Are you including Reverend Eddie John Stangood in that evaluation?" she asked, her eyes twinkling as she thought of the man's white suit pants adorned with the yellow splotch of urine.

"Especially that phony bastard. Let's not get started on him. I'll call the clerk."

After they indicated the silver crucifix, he withdrew it from the arrangement in the case, handing it to Myles for closer inspection.

"What else do you have to ward off evil?" he asked, handing the piece to Nicole.

Raising an inquisitive eyebrow, the man closely studied the couple for a long minute before answering. "I'm afraid I don't quite understand." He brought his fingertips together, tilting his head to one side while waiting for further explanation.

"Well, the cross or crucifix is a talisman to ward off the devil, isn't it?"

"In some respects, I imagine one might say that. However, it is primarily used as a reminder by Christians, Catholics most notably, of Christ's ignominious death and sufferings that He endured for all of mankind."

Myles sincerely hoped the man was not about to launch into some sort of religious tirade. "So, do you have anything that would fall into that category?" he said, quickly adding, "Of warding off evil, that is?"

Pursing his lips in thought, the man said, "I

suppose a medal or two would be in keeping with what you're describing. However, I feel things like that should be blessed by a priest before they're going to be of any use to the individual."

"Can you recommend someone?"

Again, he puckered up before speaking. "Well, there's Saint Mark's and Saint Peter's. Both of them are relatively close by. Of course, there are others. You can get a full listing of the different churches, Catholic, Protestant, Jewish Temples and what have you, in the Yellow Pages of the phone book."

Ignoring the man's generalized offer, Myles said, "Do you know the addresses of the two you just mentioned?"

"Of course," he said, taking the crucifix from Nicole, who held it out for him. "I'll write both of them down. What about the medals?"

Myles looked at Nicole, who nodded. Anything. If whatever the man suggested worked, they'd take anything.

"Put a couple in with the crucifix. Which of the two churches would you personally recommend?"

Stepping behind the counter holding the cash register, he withdrew a box, placing the silver item in it. He turned, opening a drawer in a small chest behind him. When he faced Myles and Nicole, he smiled and said, "Here are a couple of Miraculous Medals. They should fill the bill."

Myles thought he detected a note of sarcasm

in the man's voice, wondering if perhaps his decision in leaving the Church when he did had not been right all along. If everyone was cynical about faith and beliefs, then why should anyone simply give lip service to an unseen God?

"That'll be fourteen thirty-seven with tax," he said.

Myles studied him for a split second. Had he overreacted to the man's statement about the medals filling the bill? Was he becoming paranoid about this whole situation in which he and Nicole found themselves? That was all they'd need—jumping at every shadow, every move, reacting to every word said to them.

Instead of contemplating further, he reached for his billfold, pulling out two ten dollar bills and handing them to the man.

"Incidentally," the clerk said, "before those medals can do any good, they should be blessed. Here," he said, handing Myles a slip of paper, "are the addresses of St. Mark's and St. Peter's."

"Which of the two would you personally recommend?" he asked. "We're strangers in town."

The clerk leaned his head to one side. "I know you from someplace, don't I? Have you come in here before? No. That's not it. I've seen you though, I know I have. In the movie . . . No! On television! That's it! I seldom forget a face. Ever since you walked in here, I've been trying to place you. Aren't you on one of the local channels? News? Or weather or something to do with a news program? Sports?"

"I'm an anchorman," Myles said stiffly, hoping that the man would not pursue the subject or ask why he said they were not local.

"Well, then, you're not, are you?"

Myles looked at him, puzzled by the strange question. "I'm afraid I don't understand."

"You're not really a stranger in town, are you?"

"No, I guess not. You caught me there." Myles forced a harsh laugh. "However, which of the two churches would you recommend? Which has the most open, or should I say, laid back pastor?"

The clerk looked away for an instant, smothering a chuckle under his breath. "I think that would probably be Father Maskey at Saint Peter's, then. Father Willis at Saint Mark is pretty old and crotchety. Father Maskey is about forty years old or so. Real nice guy. Calm."

Miles looked at the slip, noting the address of Saint Peter's church and rectory. It was only a few blocks away. "Well, thank you very much for all the help you've given us," he said to the clerk.

"My pleasure, I'm sure."

Myles took Nicole's arm, steering her toward the door. He could feel the man's eyes on his back. If only he would forget about his TV anchorman customer of the morning. The last thing Myles needed was someone telling stories about him looking for religious articles that warded off evil. If the man knew the truth, he would never believe it, and the stories would more than likely stop before they started. But he seemed to Myles to be the imaginative type, and there was no telling what he might develop as a fanciful tale.

Once outside, he told Nicole of his fears where the clerk was concerned.

"Don't be silly," she said. "That's the price of fame. I think you're worrying needlessly."

"I hope you're right. Paranoia, I don't need."

They went to his car and in moments drove away from the curb, toward the rectory of Saint Peter's Roman Catholic Church.

9:30 A.M.

Myles and Nicole waited patiently at the door of the rectory. They had rung the bell, waiting for what seemed like minutes when in reality only a few seconds had slipped by. Presently, they could hear footsteps coming toward the entrance. Heavy footsteps. Myles quickly pictured a huge man, one capable of playing the line for a professional football team, storming toward the door, demanding to know who dared interrupt his holy revery so early in the day.

When the door opened, he breathed a sigh of relief. The man peering out at them smiled broadly and said, "Good morning. I'm Father Maskey. I don't think I know you. Do I?"

Shaking his head, Myles said, "No, you don't, Father. We've never met. I'm Myles Lawrence and this is Nicole Kilton. May we come in?"

"Judas Priest, I'm sorry," he said, jumping back from the opening to make a broad gesture with his free arm for them to enter. "The parish board would scalp me alive if they saw me standing here with the door wide open, trying to heat the great outdoors."

Covering her smile, Nicole followed the priest's motion, entering the warm hallway. Myles followed.

"What can I do for you?" the priest asked, peering first at one of his visitors, then at the other.

"We'd like this crucifix and these medals blessed, Father," Myles said, offering the package to the priest.

"Hey, no problem. Glad to be able to do it. Come with me," he said, motioning for them to follow him down the hall. He stopped at an open door, allowing them to enter first. "Take a seat. This'll only take a minute."

He laid the package on the desk, opening a drawer from which he pulled a small purple stole and vial of holy water.

Nicole elbowed Myles, nodding toward the small bottle. Taking her arm in his hand, he gently squeezed it.

When Father Maskey had draped the stole

around his neck after kissing it, he picked up the bottle and began praying softly but unintelligibly where Nicole and Myles were concerned. Then, he slowed the pace of the words and said, signing with the vial of holy water in the form of a cross, "I bless this crucifix and medals, in the name of the Father, and of the Son and of the Holy Spirit, Amen."

Taking the stole from around his neck, he kissed it again, before returning it, along with the container of blessed liquid, to the drawer. Myles and Nicole stood. "There," he said, smiling broadly, "that didn't hurt a bit, did it?" Handing the crucifix and medals to Myles, the priest studied his visitors' faces. "I must be slipping," he said slowly. "You two *are* Catholics, aren't you?"

"I am, Father," Myles said. "Nicole isn't. At least, she isn't now. I . . ."

"Does that mean the two of you are thinking of being married?"

Myles looked down at Nicole. "I guess you might say we're thinking along those lines."

An expression of relief crossed Father Maskey's face. "Let me explain what I meant when I said, 'I must be slipping.' " He walked casually into the hall, his guests following.

Myles shot an inquisitive look at Nicole, who returned one of her own.

"Every once in a while, some religious nut or member of an off-the-wall religious cult will stop at a rectory and ask for holy water or something that they can use in a rite or ritual of some sort. They always pose as Catholics. We've always been told to be on guard for just such a situation. Then, you two walk in, hand me a crucifix and a couple of medals and I obligingly bless them without so much as a question or howdydoo!'' Father Maskey smiled broadly. "Why do I feel as if I should know you, Mr. Lawrence? Do you belong to Saint Peter's or go to Mass here once in a while?"

"No, Father. I've never been in your church. You might have seen me on television. I give the newscast for KSLL-TV."

Snapping his fingers, he said, "Hey, that's it. Of course. Well, at any rate, I'm glad I could be of service." He waited as if expecting them to say thank you but fell silent when the couple did the same.

After several seemingly endless seconds passed, Myles said, "Holy water, Father. Could we get some from you?" He tried smiling but felt it must have looked forced and weak at best.

Father Maskey briefly glanced at Myles, then at Nicole and then back at Myles before speaking. "What is it, Myles? What's troubling you two?"

Myles coughed, embarrassed at the fact the priest could read his emotions so well. "I guess we didn't do so well at covering up, did we, Father?"

"After almost twenty years of being a priest, I guess one might say I can tell when peoople are happy and when they're not. You two are definitely not happy. What's wrong?''

"I don't think you'd be able to help us, Father,'' Myles said evenly. "From what we've learned so far, our problem is ours and no one else's. At least, no one we've talked with has been willing to offer a solution or help of any type.''

"Let's go back into my office,'' Father Maskey said, standing aside to allow them to enter.

"No,'' Nicole said. "You'll only listen and then tell us we're living in sin. I'm tired of hearing it.''

"Are you?''

"Are we what?'' Myles asked.

"Are you two living in sin, as the old saying goes?''

Myles turned to Nicole. "At least you have to give him credit for being laid back.''

"I've been accused of being just that,'' Father Maskey said. "Being laid back, that is. Come on, it can't hurt that much to talk it out with someone who's willing to listen. I'll bet you hit some other priest who was just itching for a fight because of some dumb experience and the two of you got the full brunt of his wrath. Am I right?'' He smiled, looking at both of them in turn.

"I suppose you're right, Father,'' Myles said, taking Nicole's arm, steering her back toward the man's office.

"How old are you, Myles?'' the priest asked.

Myles looked at him but didn't respond.

"I imagine you were raised Catholic and went off to college . . . or maybe the armed services . . . and found it was pretty easy to miss Sunday Mass. Then the next thing you knew, you just weren't going to any masses or fulfilling your obligatory duties to maintain your status as a Catholic." He stopped, looking up to find Myles nodding slowly.

Nicole looked at Myles. "Maybe he will help. Maybe he's the one we should have talked to in the first place."

"Well," Maskey said, "whatever the problem is, I'm willing to listen and if you want a suggested solution or help, I'll be more than happy to be of assistance, if I can."

Myles and Nicole relaxed, absorbing for the first time in hours the almost foreign sensation of calm.

"Well, who wants to start?" Maskey asked.

"I guess I should," Nicole said. She told him of Myles leaving her and her utter sense of desperation and loss, her hours of loneliness and her nightly rendevous with Myles when he gave the news. Then she hesitated for an instant about finding the book and looked to Myles for moral support.

"Go ahead. That's probably the most important part of the story."

Coughing to clear her throat, she continued, telling the priest of the antique book she had discovered. She described the rite she had performed before launching into the litany of weird events that had taken place since.

Without getting too explicit about the sensation of climaxing in the shower when the water took on the touch of rough hands, she nevertheless told of the calloused fingertips that seemed to touch her in the steam.

Maskey's eyes widened. "And you saw nothing?"

"Nothing," she said.

"I've felt the hands, too, Father," Myles offered, breaking in.

"Tell me about it," Maskey said brusquely, turning to Myles.

Myles recounted their evening up until they began making love and stopped.

"Go on, Myles," Maskey urged, "don't leave anything out. No matter how insignificant it might sound."

Myles laughed, embarrassed. "It's not that I don't want to, Father. It's just what was going on when I did feel the hands."

Father Maskey studied the two people sitting across from his position behind the desk. "Were the two of you being intimate? Making love?"

Myles nodded while Nicole looked away.

"Don't be ashamed. For heaven's sake, how do you think the human race is populated? If you two are in love, and I have every reason to believe you are, why wouldn't you be manifesting that love in a physical way?"

"But, Father," she stammered, "we're . . . we're not married."

"Let's not get involved in a battle of

336

semantics. Sometime in the future, the two of you will be married, I'm sure. Meanwhile, let's solve your problem or try to find a solution that'll work."

Relieved he would be able to tell the priest everything without being embarrassed, Myles continued. "I felt the hands on my bare rump, Father. So help me, I looked in the mirrored headboard and could see my image. We were all alone. There were no hands on me at all. That I could see, at least. Nicole's hands were holding my face. We were all alone in that room."

A thick silence fell over the office and Father Maskey did not speak immediately. Then, in a quiet voice, he said, "You *do* need help. Both of you."

"I hope you don't mean that in the way the others meant?" Myles said.

"No. They were only concerned with the surface of your beings. The problem you two have is something entirely different. At least, I have to say it sounds like it's extraordinary from what you've told me. However, I can only do so much."

Both their faces fell.

"What do you mean, Father?" she whispered.

"Right now, it's just your word. There has to be an investigation, of course. Someone will have to visit your apartment and witness some of the phenomena that you've described."

"But what if nothing happens while you're

there?'' Nicole asked.

"I didn't say I'd come to your apartment."
Maskey peered at them.

"Who, then, Father?" Myles asked.

"Let's slow down a bit. Let me tell you how
these things are handled normally."

A sense of disappointment visibly crossed
both their faces and Father Maskey smiled.
"This won't take forever. Still, it doesn't hurt
to know and learn something. Especially in
cases such as yours."

Their looks of unhappiness turned to expressions of puzzlement.

"What do you mean by 'cases such as
ours'?" Myles asked, sitting forward. "Do you
mean that what's happening to us is not that
uncommon or even happens frequently?"

"Suppose I take it one step at a time. If you
have a question, jump in."

Myles and Nicole nodded.

"Very well, then," Father Maskey said.
"First of all, try to forget everything that
you've ever heard about or read about such
things as possession. Most of them are not all
that accurate, and writers and novelists as
such usually take artistic liberties in dealing
with the devil."

Myles shrugged, smiling benignly.

"There are a couple of novels on the market
that were obviously well researched, but I
don't think that a person's imagination can
capture on paper the full fury and general
horror that is involved when one deals with the

forces of absolute evil."

"Have you been involved in anything like the novel *The Exorcist* told about, Father?" Myles asked quietly.

Father Maskey shook his head. "I'm not an exorcist, as such. There was a time in the past when all priests were considered exorcists but one of the results of Vatican II was the removal of several of the minor orders, one of which was the order of exorcism. When the priest blessed the congregation, it was a form of exorcism. But today, there are those priests who are designated as exorcists and they handle any and all cases of bona fide possession."

Nicole shuddered and Myles held up one hand for the priest to stop. "Are you saying that Nicole and I *are* possessed?"

Father Maskey shook his head. "Nothing of the kind. There are many steps that have to be satisfied or taken before such a decision is reached. First of all, I question whether or not either or both of you are or could be possessed. Based on what you've told me, it sounds as though you're describing disturbances caused by the Evil One—or Satan—or Lucifer—whatever you want to call him. Such disturbances are an interpretation that falls just short of what the Catholic Church defines as possession or actual control by the devil of a person's body and mind."

"How many steps are you talking about, Father? How long will it take to determine just what our problem is?" Myles turned to Nicole, who nodded, expressing her own sense of doubt and mixed emotions.

"In the past, hundreds of years ago, many times people who were suffering from common ordinary ailments were subjected to the awful rigors of exorcism. I . . ."

"Wait a minute, Father," Nicole said. "What do you mean by common ordinary ailments?"

"We'd think of them as being pretty commonplace by today's standards of medicine and psychiatry. But in the Dark Ages and before, right up to the introduction of modern psychiatry in the nineteeth century, people who suffered from some form of psychosis could have been diagnosed as being possessed by the devil."

Looks of astonishment crossed both their faces.

"Such as?" Myles asked.

"Such as impotence for example. If a man could not perform sexually, it was thought the devil had rendered him thus. Ordinary little fears, which would be ignored or at the worst handled during a visit to a psychiatrist today, would result in banishment or exorcism. Pretty scary stuff when viewed by today's standards."

"And you're saying," Myles said, "that psychiatry did away with all of that?"

"Let's say, the advances made by medicine and psychiatry caused the Church to fall back and reappraise the situation and condition of possession. Today, before anything can be done by the Church, medical and psychiatric evaluations must be made. There are certain conditions that have to be met before one can be officially declared by the Church as being possessed by the devil or an evil spirit. If a person expresses a knowledge of hidden things —by hidden I mean not generally known to the average person or unspoken thoughts of someone—it is classified as being extraordinary and one step or condition is more or less fulfilled. If the person suspected of being possessed suddenly speaks in a language that is completely unknown to that person, then something is obviously out of place, wouldn't you say? I don't mean just a few words. Someone could pick up a phrase or two of, say, German for example, just by watching a movie or television. What I'm saying is that a person who could carry on a conversation in a foreign language such as Greek or Iranian or Japanese without any prior knowledge or experience or memory of ever having spoken such a language, then . . ." His voice trailed off when he saw the people sitting opposite him understood.

Myles and Nicole looked at each other but remained quiet.

"Then, there is the phenomena of, how should I say, mind over matter? Unusual occurrences. Flying objects whenever the person is around. The person in question levitating or . . ."

"Oh, boy!" Myles groaned the two words.

"What is it, Myles?" Father Maskey asked.

"Nicole has levitated twice that I've seen. The furniture has been strewn around the apartment like a tornado went through."

"I remember Nicole saying that. But let's not go off jousting with windmills before we know what we're up against."

"But isn't that out of the ordinary, Father? Nicole floating around in midair?"

"Of course it is. But you're jumping to conclusions if you're saying that she is possessed because of it."

"What else could it be?"

"Saints have been known to levitate while praying intently. It's been documented. And that hardly seems to be the work of the devil. Besides, you have to remember there are quite a few steps to making a decision one way or the other. We must move slowly on this thing. At this point, we don't know what it is we're up against. That hasn't been determined. It could be possession but I doubt that very much. If I had to bet, I'd put my money on disturbances by the Evil One. Right now, I think we had best think in that direction. All right?"

Myles nodded and Nicole relaxed after glancing at him.

"What's our first step, then, Father?" he asked.

"First of all, I can only do so much. Remember, I'm not an exorcist and there will be someone a lot more qualified than I, who will

be involved. Of course, that's assuming that
what you have is a true case of possession, disturbances or something akin to it."

"Akin to it? What else could it be?" Nicole
asked.

"Other than disturbances by the Evil One,
which is I'm sure a new one to you, you've both
heard of poltergeists, haven't you? Playful
ghosts or however it is translated from
German. It could be something like that. It
could be a case of obsession, wherein Nicole's
subconscious mind would be responsible
because of her having performed the ritual. It
could be just a good old-fashioned ghost trying
to get your attention."

"A ghost?" Myles and Nicole said together.

"For lack of a better word. If one is to believe
in the immortal soul of man, one almost must
accept the possibility of a wayward soul once
in a while. But first we must determine if your
case is real."

"It's real, all right, Father," Myles said,
turning to Nicole for confirmation.

She nodded.

"I'm not doubting that you believe it's real.
What I'm saying is I have to witness something that will convince the chancery office to
have a full-fledged exorcist take a look. Then
both of you will have to have a complete
medical examination and consult with a
psychiatrist who will be chosen by the diocese.

"But, we *are* getting ahead of ourselves with
that sort of talk. First things first. When can I

visit your apartment? If I determine that a real entity of some sort is present in your home, I'll have to report the facts to the bishop.''

"Then what?" Myles asked.

"Then the Church starts doing the things I outlined before.''

"Just how long will all of this take, Father?" Myles asked, his voice failing to hide his frustration.

Maskey stood. "I suppose something like this could drag on for quite some time.''

"What? Days? Weeks? Months? What, Father?''

Maskey shrugged. "There have been instances I've read about that took only a few days. Others, though, took months and even,'' he paused, "years.''

"Oh, fine. And we're supposed to put up with all of this during that time?''

"If you don't like it, move," Father Maskey said.

Nicole's eyebrows shot up.

"What? Just like that? Move and leave the devil behind. Is that it?" Myles glared at the priest.

"To be quite honest,'' Maskey said, "it sounds as if the apartment you live in is more the victim than either of you. Neither one of you is suffering from malnutrition or loss of sleep to any great degree. You're not physically deteriorating in any way that I can see. It could very easily be just your apartment.''

"We've already tried to check out the lease.

We found it written in some foreign . . .
language," Myles said slowly when he realized
the full impact of his statement.

"Let's not panic," Father Maskey said. "Remember. First things first. Let's make that the
order of the day. All right?"

Myles and Nicole stood.

"Look, Father," Myles said as they moved
toward the front of the house. "Unless something happens darn soon, I'll drive the damn
thing out myself."

Maskey stopped, turning to face him. "And
how would you go about doing that?"

"I've got the crucifix you blessed and the
medals. I can get some holy water at any
Catholic Church. But I'll do it myself, if necessary. I don't want any delay on this. When are
you going to come over?"

"First," Father Maskey said, "I've got to
contact the chancery office and tell them that
I'm going to visit your home. I'll also tell them
everything that both of you have told me."

"Can we get together again today?" Myles
asked, persistent in his intent.

"Let me check," Father Maskey said, pulling
a small appointment book from his jacket
pocket. "I've got an appointment every hour
right up until noon. Suppose I come this afternoon about four. I'm free the rest of the day
and evening and we can have at it. Is that all
right with the two of you?"

Nicole nodded and Myles said, "Yes. But. . ."

"No buts about it, Myles," the priest said. "I

want your promise that you'll not do anything regarding this situation. Will you promise?''

Myles hesitated for a long minute before looking up at him. "I . . . I guess so, Father.''

"Fine.'' He handed Myles a small card and said, "Write down your address. I'll be there right at four, this afternoon.''

After giving him the address, Myles and Nicole went to the car and got in.

"For the first time, I think we might be getting somewhere,'' she said.

He turned the engine over and let it idle for several seconds before pulling away from the curb. "Yeah. I just hope he can do something for us.''

Father Maskey returned to his office after closing the front door. Picking up the telephone, he dialed a number and waited while it rang.

"Chancery office. Mrs. McPherson.''

"Mrs. McPherson, this is Father Maskey. Is Father Pins in?''

"One moment.'' The line went dead for several seconds before she came back on the line. "Go ahead, Father Maskey.''

"Joe? Chuck Maskey. How you doing?''

"Fine. What's up?''

"Let me tell you and then you decide if I should talk with the bishop.''

3:57 P.M.

Myles checked his watch again. Three minutes to four. Would the priest show up? Since leaving Maskey's office that morning, they had aimlessly driven around town, stopping several times for coffee, then lunch. By unspoken yet mutual agreement, they had not gone near the apartment building. At three forty-five, they had parked in front of the main entrance to wait for Father Maskey to arrive.

"I'm glad we didn't go in," she said. "I'm afraid you might have tried to do something."

"Like?"

She shrugged. "I don't know. I'm just glad that we waited for Father to come here."

"He's got one minute," he said, looking at his watch again. "If he doesn't . . ."

"Is that him?" she asked, interrupting him.

They watched the small Chevy turn into a parking place across the street. Both sighed when they saw the black-suited man get out. He half-ran, half-walked across the street toward their car and was about to walk by when he noticed them getting out.

"There you are. Haven't you gone inside?"

"We thought it better to wait for you," Nicole said.

"It's probably for the better. Shall we go?"

Myles took Nicole's arm and they hurried toward the lobby. Holding the door open after unlocking it, Myles stepped in after Nicole and the priest had entered. The smell of fresh paint assailed them, and when they saw the elevator was out of order, they began the climb to the third floor.

Just as they reached the entrance to Nicole's and Myles' home, the door to the next apartment opened and a woman stepped out. After locking her door, she noticed them for the first time and, startled, said, "Hello."

The trio answered in kind and then the woman stopped, peering at Nicole.

"Did you hear the commotion outside this morning?"

Nicole shot a quick look at Myles who stared at the woman. Would she accuse them of something now—in front of Father Maskey?

"Commotion?" Nicole asked, biding for time.

"Yes. Some fool in a white suit was yelling at the top of his voice in front of the building."

"No," Nicole lied. "I . . . we didn't hear anything like that. Did we, Myles?"

Myles shook his head.

"I have no idea who it was, but he sounded like he was preaching. There were several others there, too, but I couldn't make out who they were. At any rate, I called the police but the rascal got away before they arrived."

"Was that it?" Myles asked. "Nothing else?"

"No. But that was certainly enough. Ever since my Waldo died, I hear every little out-of-place noise in the building. Well, I must be going. 'Bye."

They watched the woman hurry toward the steps, muttering under her breath about the elevator being out of order.

"Are you ready, Father?" Myles asked, thrusting the key into the lock.

Father Maskey opened the book he carried, balancing it on one hand, while he withdrew a vial of holy water from his coat pocket. "Ready," he said softly.

Myles turned the key and opened the door. "Well, for crying out loud," he said hoarsely. "Look at that!"

Nicole stepped closer to Myles and looked over his shoulder. The furniture all sat in place. The books and papers were all back together, and the awful smell that had filled the room was not evident.

"What is it?" Father Maskey asked.

"Everything is in order. The place was a mess when we left this morning with Reverend Stangood," Nicole said.

"Was he the one the lady was talking about in the hall?" Father Maskey asked.

Myles nodded, stepping inside. Maskey followed and Nicole quietly closed the door behind her.

"Don't you find it strange that Mrs. Bellasco from next door hasn't heard anything out of the ordinary? Especially coming from my apartment?" Nicole asked.

"She must have heard the stereo and TV the times they blasted out," Myles said, looking to the priest for some sort of explanation.

Father Maskey shrugged. "These things can be pretty strange at times. I'm sure because the woman says she didn't hear something doesn't necessarily mean that it didn't take place."

"Then, too," Myles said, "she admitted calling the police this morning when Stangood was ranting and raving in front. More than likely she was the one who reported you that time when the police called when the TV and stereo acted up."

"Would you like to get that book for me, Nicole? I'd like to see it," Maskey asked, relaxing just a bit.

The sound of hissing punctuated his request and the three people exchanged quick glances at each other.

"What *is* that?" Nicole whispered. "I've never heard anything like that before. Have you, Myles?"

Myles nodded. "It sounds like water hissing on hot metal or steam escaping. What's it sound like to you, Father?"

Maskey was just about to speak when Nicole turned to face him. Her short scream pierced the quiet. Pointing behind the priest, she waited until the two men turned in that direction before crying out again. The door to the hall was fading from sight. The sizzling sound came from it, as the entrance disappeared.

Without waiting, Myles shouted, "Quick. To the kitchen." He dashed through the living room to the kitchenette, stopping in his tracks.

The door that led to the service hall and rear entrance was gone. Disappeared. He turned to face Nicole and the priest. Before he could say anything, the slamming of doors, of clanging metal plates being driven home, banged through the apartment. When they entered the living room, they found heavy, steel plates materializing from nothing, jamming into the openings of the windows.

They were trapped in the darkened apartment.

17

Saturday, December 6, 1986   4:07 P.M.

The awful quiet complemented the heavy darkness pressing in on Father Maskey, Nicole and Myles. No one moved. No one uttered a sound for fear of arousing the entity's wrath. How could such things as disappearing doors and steel plates that formed from nothing suddenly happen? How powerful was this demon? Barely breathing, the three stood their ground, unable to move because of the Stygian blackness enveloping them.

Nicole's stomach heaved. She wanted to cry but bit her lip. All of this was her fault. If she had not performed that stupid ceremony, none of this would be happening right now.

The full implication of Myles' return and the way it was connected to the book and the ritual and with the black space she found herself standing in right now overwhelmed her, and she lost the battle to keep from crying. Her plaintive wail wormed its way through the dark.

"Nicole?" Myles whispered hoarsely. "Are you all right?"

"Ye . . . yes," she sobbed. "All . . . of this is . . . is my . . . my fault!"

"I don't think it's the right time to hang blame for any of this on anyone," Father Maskey said quietly.

"Take my hand," Myles said, groping in the dark for Nicole's. When they touched, she grabbed his in a tight, vise-like grip. Pulling her closer, he put an arm around her shoulder, pulling her sobbing body to his.

She must have felt vulnerable in the dark, weak, helpless. How could Nicole accept the blame for any of this? If he, Myles, had not walked out on her the way he did, she would not have felt compelled to resort to some magical perversion—some bit of evil, black magic from a dark, bygone era. If anyone was to blame, it was he. When he drew that conclusion, he pulled Nicole even closer and she responded by throwing both arms around him.

"Father is right, Nicole," Myles said gently. "I feel strongly that you are *not* to blame for this. If anyone gets that particular honor, it's me. I walked out on you and . . ."

"I don't know about you two," Father Maskey said, breaking into Myles' admission, "but I'm tired of standing around in the dark.

Why don't one of you try turning on the lights?''

"Oh, for crying out loud," Myles said. "Why didn't we think of that? Nicole, turn on the lights. You're standing right by the switch, aren't you?''

Without a word, he released his hold and she pulled away from him. When he heard the click of the switch and the room was plunged into light, he uttered a short gasp. Nicole stood next to the light switch, but he was at the far end of the living room, next to where the windows were covered with steel plates. Who had he been embracing?

Nicole screamed when she saw Myles at the opposite end of the living room. "Myles? How did . . . did you get there? You . . . you were standing . . . next to me, holding me . . ." she stopped, the full impact of the situation hammering at her. Turning to the priest, she desperately swallowed the screams she felt rising within her.

Myles hurried to her side, throwing both arms about her.

"Don't be concerned right now," Father Maskey said. He sniffed the air. "What *is* that?''

Myles and Nicole followed his example, inhaling deeply. The awful stench, which had hounded them over the last weeks, filled the air. The redolent stink of decaying flesh, of something rotten and dead, washed over them. One moment it seemed to be alleviating but would increase tenfold the next instant.

"That's worse . . . worse than it's ever been,"
Nicole said, gagging.

A wailing laugh threaded its way through
the apartment, ebbing and flowing as it
undulated in volume. The lights went off, then
as quickly back on. The rhythm established,
the flickering lent an unreal, almost surreal-
istic atmosphere to the living room and that
part of the kitchen that was visible from where
the trio stood, rooted to their spots.

Then the darkness took hold again, while the
laugh rose and fell in direct proportion to the
smell of death that filled the apartment.

"Candles?" Myles cried. "Have we got any
candles?"

"I . . . I'm not certain," Nicole said.

"Here," Father Maskey said, "I've got a
lighter." He spun the wheel on the small
cigarette lighter, and when the flame danced
on the invisible stream of gas, the odor increased. Then, the rooms plunged back into a
sea of light, then dark, then light—and the
flashing continued unabated.

*"You filthy, rotten, non-fucking cocksucker.
Get out of this apartment right now, or I'll take
this weak-willed sow for my own!"* The words
boomed from the stereo speakers as the tuner
went on. The television set glowed with a life of
its own and the picture began changing from
one station to the next as it traversed its way
around the dial, the cable-converter box
spinning flashing red digits as some unseen
finger pressed the button.

"Come on, Maskey, you worthless bastard. Get out of my apartment! You don't belong here. This cunt is mine. She asked for a favor and I granted it. Now she owes me. Isn't that the way things are supposed to be, you worthless faggot-fucker?"

Nicole sucked in her breath and Myles looked away from the priest. Father Maskey opened his breviary to the prayers for exorcism and calmly said, "Don't pay him any attention. From what I've been told and from what I've read about such situations, the devil or demon tries to discredit the religious person present and shake up those who are in attendance."

"I . . . I'm sorry, Father," Nicole whispered.

"Don't be. Not for what he's saying at least. Remember, the devil is the champion liar of all times. Believe just the opposite of whatever he does say, and you'll be all right. I don't think he's capable of telling the truth about anything."

"Is there anything we can do to help you, Father?" Myles asked softly, stepping closer to him. Why did he feel he had to be close to the man and practically whisper?

"It's not necessary, you stupid asshole. You think you're so great because you're on television. Watch the set. This is what I think of you, Myles Lawrence!" The voice boomed so loudly that the lamps on the end tables bounced while the knick-knacks on the shelves above the TV set jiggled toward the edges.

The three people turned to the TV set, as if forced by some remote control. The picture tube's flipping images slowed, until it went blank. Then, the studio setting as used by the KSLL-TV news staff appeared. An image of Myles sat behind the large desk and he smiled at the camera.

"Good evening," the image said and was instantly greeted with a load of what appeared to be animal waste dumped over his head. The smell of manure filled the room. Maniacal laughter bellowed through the apartment. Eggs pelted Myles from off-camera, and a nude woman, grossly overweight, sashayed across the front of the desk, lightly jumping to the top of it. Bending her knees and thrusting her lower abdomen forward, she stood over the unperturbed image of Myles, urinating on his head.

Myles turned away from the picture and Nicole embraced him.

"Stop!" the priest shouted at the top of his voice. "Stop in the name of Jesus Christ!"

The scene on the tube disappeared, instantly replaced by a face, hideous in its make-up of jaundiced skin erupting with pustules and running sores. The triangular shape of the head paralleled along the two sides the shape of the mouth and nose, while the eyes were squinted into "V" shapes of their own. The mouth opened and the visage growled, "*Who are you to tell me to do anything, Priest!*"

Nicole stared at the visage. It was the same evil countenance that she had seen standing at the foot of her bed. Good God! What had she started?

Father Maskey raised his hand concealing the small bottle of holy water from sight and threw several drops on the television set. The first second the blessed liquid touched the tube and cabinet, a high-pitched scream, louder than anything yet unleashed by the demon, rent the air. The picture went blank, then dark as the set turned off.

A heavy silence hung in the air for several minutes. Father Maskey coughed. "Myles, if you know and recall the responses to the Litany of the Saints, please say them. We must, for our own protection, begin the rite of exorcism."

"Very well, Father."

"Go fuck it on the mountain—Go fuck it on the plain—Go fuck anything that's fuckable— try fucking on a train," the voice sang from the stereo speakers.

"In the name of the Father and of the Son and of the Holy Spirit," Father Maskey began.

"Amen," Myles said.

"Amen," Nicole repeated after Myles. Even though she had no idea what a Litany of the Saints might be, she intended to say as best she could the prayers along with Myles and the priest.

"Lord have mercy on us."

"Ah . . . Christ have mercy on us," Myles said, hesitating at the response, familiar and yet remote by the passage of time since he had helped say the prayer at a church service.

"Lord have mercy on us. Christ hear us," Maskey said.

Myles could not think of the appropriate response. Later in the prayer, when the names of the Saints were intoned, he would be able to answer with the correct, "Pray for us."

"Christ graciously hear us," Maskey said, before continuing with the next summons, "Holy Trinity, One God."

"Pray for us," Myles said, an expression of doubt covering his face.

"Have mercy on us," Maskey corrected.

"Have mercy on us," Myles said, turning when Nicole whispered it immediately after him.

Maskey intoned saint after saint, imploring their help in this hour of need. When he loudly said, "Saint Michael, the Archangel," the lights flashed on and off and the TV set turned on, joining in a deafening battle for supremacy with the stereo set that boomed with the sounds of cannon.

"Pray for us!" Myles shouted along with Nicole who quickly had learned the repetitious response, saying it with renewed fervor each time.

Realizing that the name had upset the entity, Father Maskey continued.

Myles answered each supplication with "Pray for us!" failing to notice immediately that Nicole had stopped answering with him. When he turned to her, he gasped. Nicole was gone. Looking up, he saw her body parallel to the ceiling, hovering in midair.

"Father! Father Maskey! Look!"

Maskey stopped the recitation of names, his eyes following Myles outstretched arm. Blessing himself, he said, "We must get her down. NOW!"

Myles reached up, just able to touch the pants leg around Nicole's ankle. When he pulled, she moved as if pivoting on a fulcrum. "She feels as if she weighs tons," Myles said, when Maskey reached up to help him.

Pulling with all their strength, the two men brought Nicole's feet down toward them and little by little, returned her down to the floor.

Nothing more happened, other than the putrid mist continuously filling the air along with a drastic drop in the room's temperature. When Maskey finished the Litany of Saints, he continued into the next prayer, a psalm.

"Save me, O God," he intoned, "by Thy Name, and judge me in Thy Strength. O God, hear my prayer: give ear to the words of my mouth. For strangers have risen up against . . ."

"I'm no stranger, you stupid fucker of old women!" the voice screamed. *"That prayer will not help you one iota's worth of fly-shit! Forget it, Maskey. Go get fucked someplace and leave me in peace!"*

Father Maskey continued reciting the psalm, raising his voice when he came to the last lines. "For Thou hast delivered me out of all trouble: and my eye hath looked down upon my enemies."

Turning the page, the priest continued. "I adjure Your Grace, Oh, heavenly Father, to aid me in this battle against the wicked dragon who possesses this dwelling. Drive him back to hell when it is right to do so. You, demon of the dark, tell me your name! Tell me the day and the hour and the manner of your leaving this place. Do this with some sign!"

Laughter was the priest's only response along with an increase in the degree of vile fetidness filling the rooms.

"The Lord be with you," Maskey continued, his breath's vapor condensing in the cold air, then read a gospel of John. Opening his coat a trifle when he finished with the words of the evangelist, Maskey exposed a purple stole hanging around his neck. He reached into a side pocket, withdrawing a small crucifix.

When Myles saw the cross, he opened the package he had been carrying when they entered the apartment. Withdrawing the silver crucifix, he held it up not unlike the priest, waiting to see what would happen next.

Nicole stared wide-eyed at the two men, both holding the symbols of Christ's death high in front of them.

Maskey held the cross and breviary in one hand and the bottle of holy water in his right. "I exorcise you, most vile of spirits, the embodiment of our dreaded enemy, Lucifer, the entire specter, the whole legion, in the name of Jesus Christ, to get out." He made the sign of the cross with the bottle, splashing droplets of the liquid about the room. "Flee this place, leaving these creatures of God." He made two more signs of the cross and was instantly slapped across the face by an invisible hand.

"Are you all right, Father?" Nicole asked when she realized what had happened.

Undaunted by the attack, Father Maskey continued the prayers of exorcism. The demon shrieked when he finished the first prayer of the ritual. "Fear Him who was immolated in Isaac, sold in Joseph, slain in the lamb, crucified in man and then was triumphant over hell!"

The high-pitched cry spiraled into laughter, seeming to take root in the kitchenette. Nicole tugged on Myles' sleeve and they both turned to Father Maskey, the unasked question on their faces.

Maskey shrugged, stepping back to peer into the next room. The door of the refrigerator flew open and eggs, fruit, vegetables, bottles of milk and salad dressing floated out into the kitchen, making a large circle in the air. The cupboards flew open and the contents of the refrigerator were joined by cups, saucers, plates, silverware and boxes of dried food. The circle grew more crowded and a second one formed beneath the first. Both turned more rapidly, and when it was difficult for the priest to distinguish the different items, he suddenly realized what was about to happen.

"Hit the floor," he cried just as the carton of milk sailed into the living room, smashing against the far wall. The milk splashed a white flower-pattern against the wall, fingers from each petal flowing toward the floor. Glasses and vegetables, pots and pans, fruits and eggs

—everything that had been in the cupboards and refrigerator—followed the milk carton, sailing into the living room, over their heads, crashing into the wall. Shards of glass sailed about after the tumblers had disintegrated. Food smeared the painted walls in a bizarre pattern as the remainder of eggs and oranges mixed with the milk and butter.

Nicole pressed herself to the floor in a desperate attempt to squeeze into the carpeting, her hands over the back of her head to protect herself. Myles lay half on her, shielding her from the assault. Father Maskey raised his head every second or so to see if the barrage had ended. Each time, he ducked as a new missile dove toward him before swooping back up to smash into the wall.

After several long minutes dragged into an eternity, the attack ceased. The only sound in the apartment was Nicole letting out sobs each time she could catch her breath.

Then Myles said in a hoarse whisper, "Is it over, Father?"

"That particular trick is probably finished because he ran out of ammunition in the kitchen," Father Maskey whispered.

"Trick?" Myles wheezed the word. Was the priest enjoying this or was it merely a poor choice of words on his part?

"Call it what you will, Myles. Manifestation. Phenomena. Hallucination. Of course if it were an hallucination, we'd all be suffering from the same delusion, wouldn't we?"

"Are you saying, then, that it *is* over?"

"I'm not too well versed in this sort of thing," Maskey said quietly. "I rather doubt that he'd quit so easily. Usually there's quite a confrontation between the exorcist and the demon. And I'm no exorcist."

Myles coughed as he stood, helping Nicole to her feet. Father Maskey followed suit and when they stood in the middle of the living room, Myles stared at him.

"What do you mean you're not an exorcist?"

"Not as such. Remember the minor order of exorcism has been done away with and the Church appoints those priests who are to act as official exorcists."

"So, in . . . in the meantime, what do . . . do we do?" Nicole asked, a slight tremor in her voice. The sobs diminished noticeably when she spoke.

"I'm going to have to report this to the chancery office, when and if we get out of here."

"When and *if*?" Myles asked.

"Right now, I don't see any means of leaving, do you?" Maskey asked.

Myles and Nicole shook their heads.

"Do you think we'll get out of here?" Myles asked.

The priest shrugged. "Right now, all I can say is we'll have to pray to that end since the demon has trapped us in here. When and if we can subdue him, to some degree at least, then perhaps with his power weakened, we'll be able to leave."

"This whole thing seems like a bad dream,"

Myles said, squeezing Nicole's hand.

"This whole thing is my fault . . . regardless of what you say, Myles. If I hadn't been such a romantic ninny, I would have accepted your decision to leave. I . . ."

The stereo blasted the apartment with a John Phillip Sousa march accompanying a high-pitched laugh.

"In the name of the Father and of the Son and of the Holy Spirit," Father Maskey intoned, opening his breviary. "I adjure thee, thou old serpent, by the judge of the quick and the dead, by thy Maker and the Maker of the whole world and universe, by Him Who has power to send thee to hell, that thou depart quickly from this place and leave these servants of God . . ."

"They're adulterers and fornicators, you fuckhead! They don't give a good healthy shit about your fucking Church. They'll not . . ."

"Quiet, you hound of hell," the priest shouted over the loud voice coming from the speakers of the stereo. "They will return to the bosom of God and his Son, Jesus Christ. They will do this with fear and affliction of thy terror. I adjure thee again . . ." Father Maskey made the sign of the cross on his own forehead, ". . . not in my weaknesses and infirmities, but by the virtue of the Holy Spirit, that thou depart from this place and these people of God, who were made in His image and likeness.

"Yield therefore. Yield not to me but to the ministry of Christ. For his power urges thee, who subjugated thee to His cross. Tremble at His arm, Who led the souls to light after the lamentations of hell had been subdued. May the body of man be a terror to thee." Maskey blessed his chest with the sign of the cross. "Let the image of God the Father be terrible to thee." He blessed his own forehead again. "Resist not, nor delay in fleeing from this place and these people, since it pleases Christ, the Almighty, to want this man and this woman to be of His Body here on earth. And although thou knowest me to be none the less a sinner, do not think me contemptible. For it is God Who commands Thee."

Father Maskey blessed the room and a scream pierced the air with an immediate response. Where the liquid fell to the floor, tiny puffs of smoke curled up while burnt spots singed the carpet, making the outline of a large double circle with a five pointed figure in the center.

Nicole winced, looking away when she recognized the pattern. An instant vision of herself, nude, standing in the center of the inverted Pentagon, formed. *Please, God, help me!* she prayed to herself. The image left.

"The Majesty of Christ commands thee."

Again, Maskey threw holy water about creating more smoke when it struck the rug. Wisps spiraled upward.

"God, the Father, commands thee. God, the Son, commands thee. God, the Holy Spirit, commands thee." After each order, Maskey threw water about and the stench of burning rug filled the air, entwining with the rancid aroma of decay and death.

Holding the cross high over his head, the priest threw water with his other hand after checking the next lines of exorcism from his book. "The sacred cross commands thee!"

Continuing thereafter to intone the names of Peter and Paul and calling on the martyrs to help in the battle against the demon, Father Maskey intoned the prayers, all during which Myles held his silver crucifix high with one hand and pulled Nicole tightly to him with the other.

When Father Maskey finished the second prayer of excorcism, he turned in a small circle blessing everything in the room. When he faced the wall and shelves whereon the TV, stereo components and books rested, he threw extra holy water.

His efforts were rewarding with laughter turning to shrieks of pain. When he finished, he turned to Nicole and said, "Where is that book?"

A sense of panic tore at Nicole. Myles' arm about her felt so comforting, so warm, so right. What would happen if she gave up the book? Surrendered it to this man of God? What would happen between her and Myles? Would he leave or disappear? After all, right now, she wasn't certain if he was real or if he was a conjuration of the demon she had summoned. If he had come back because of the paganistic ritual she had performed, would it not be likely that he would be gone once she gave the book to the priest?

"What's wrong?" Myles asked when he felt

her tense.

"No . . . nothing," she managed. "I love you, darling. Please don't leave me. I . . ." She stopped, crossing the few feet to the shelf where the book rested. Turning, she faced the priest and Myles. "No! I won't give it to you. Myles will leave if I do. He's here because of the book. He never would have come back to me if I had not performed the ceremony."

"Are you saying you wish to continue with the demon always present in your life?" Father Maskey asked, his look of astonishment barely concealed.

"Nicole! You've got to give it to him," Myles pleaded. "I'm not going to leave. I've learned that I love you. I want to be with you forever. I'm yours forever. You're mine forever. We belong together, you and me. Give it to Father or I *will* leave and then you'll have nothing but the demon and that Goddamned book! Give it to him!"

"I . . . I love you, Myles. Don't leave me . . . ever!"

"I promise you," Myles cried impatiently. "Please, darling, give Father Maskey the book. I will *not* leave you. I'll be yours forever. I promise."

After a long moment of deliberation, Nicole reached over the stereo equipment, pulling down the small gold-trimmed red book. When she faced the men again, it lurched in her hand before flying away to circle the room, diving at the priest, then at Myles before swiping at Nicole. Father Maskey threw holy water at it.

When it fell to the floor, an ear-splitting howl filled the apartment, dying away in minutes until there was nothing but its awful memory lingering in the ears of the three people.

Maskey bent down, picking up the book and laying it on an end table. Opening the breviary he prayed the last prayer of exorcism. Myles held Nicole in a tight embrace while the priest finished.

Nicole looked up into Myles' eyes. There was nothing there that said he had lied to her. They *would* be together forever. She smiled. The whole thing had been so foolish.

"He expels thee, from Whose Eye nothing is secret. He expels thee, to Whose Power all things are subject. He excludes thee, Who has prepared for thee and thy angels everlasting hell. Out of Whose Mouth the sharp sword will go, He shall come to judge the quick and the dead and the world by fire." Maskey blessed the room once more.

A dense silence filled the apartment. Nothing happened. Only the breathing of the captives could be heard above the roar of silence hammering their eardrums.

Then, the furniture wiggled, dancing about until each piece was flipping from side to side, each time rising higher in the air until the living room furnishings became airborne, flying about the apartment. The doors still had not reappeared nor had the windows. Still trapped, they watched horror-struck when the chairs, tables and couch deftly avoiding each other, attacked in formation, each taking a

turn to dive at them. Father Maskey stepped
between the first chair and Myles and Nicole,
holding up the crucifix, splashing a few drops
of holy water on it. As it fell, the squeal inten-
sified once more, growing louder each time he
blessed a piece of furniture that attacked them.

Covering their ears with both hands, Nicole,
Myles and when he could no longer stand it,
Father Maskey, dropped to their knees to
avoid being hit. The last piece of furniture
settled to the floor and again the silence held
sway.

A sound from the direction of the bedroom
filtered down the short hallway until it formed
into the sound of shuffling feet. Someone was
coming toward the living room from the
bedroom. Nicole looked first to Myles, then to
Father Maskey, asking, pleading her unspoken
questions. *What was that? What was coming
down the hall? Who was coming toward them?*

Turning the corner, the doll collection that
had filled the top of Nicole's chest of drawers
came marching into the living room, two
abreast, row after row after row. Marking time
until the rest of the dolls reached the living
room, the first ranks formed a solid line across
the far wall, waiting. When the company of
animated dolls had formed a phalanx, they
began moving forward, toward the wide-eyed
man, woman and priest.

"Remember Oh, most gracious Virgin
Mary," Father Maskey prayed, raising his
hand to splash holy water, "that never was it
known that anyone who fled to your

373

protection, implored your help or sought your supplication was left unaided. Inspired . . ." he threw the water " . . . by this confidence, we fly unto you, Oh Virgin of virgins, our heavenly Mother. To you do we send up our sighs from this vale of tears. Help us oh, Mother of Jesus."

As the water touched the dolls, the bellow of pain came once more, louder than anything they had heard before and the dolls fell over in their tracks.

Horrified, the trio stood their ground, staring at the pile of toys littering the floor. Slowly, the moldy odor of decay and rot dissipated until it was completely gone.

A death-like quiet gripped the warming apartment as Nicole's eyes roamed about searching for some sign of activity. When she focused on Myles, she smiled. He was still there. He was still with her. He hadn't left. But then, he had promised to stay with her forever.

A quiet hum brought them around to face the windowed wall of the living room. Not unlike clouds breaking up in a summer breeze, the plates over the windows dissolved and when they turned about, they found the door to the hallway.

Several minutes passed before Father Maskey blessed himself with the sign of the cross. Then he blessed Nicole and Myles.

Nicole smiled weakly. "Is it over, Father?"

"I'm not really certain. I think so. I hope so," Maskey said softly.

18

Saturday, December 6, 1986   4:38 P.M.

"Doesn't it seem rather light out for this time of night?" Myles asked, moving toward the windows.

"I don't understand," Nicole said, walking to his side and peering out with him.

"We came in here a little after four this afternoon. How long have we been in here? Three hours? Maybe four?" Myles looked, first at Nicole then to Father Maskey for agreement.

"It seemed like a lifetime," she said, "now that I think back on everything that happened. It must have been hours. Four at least."

Father Maskey smiled when he looked up. Pointing to his wristwatch, he said, "What time do you have, Myles?"

Myles glanced at his own, his attention frozen when the truth of the time registered. "It can't be. *Thirty minutes?* That's not possible. I don't believe it. How do you explain it, Father? What time do you have?"

"My watch apparently matches yours, since I have four thirty-nine. I imagine that the time seemed to go fast because there was so much going on, so many things happening. Other than that I have no explanation. I don't know if the devil can fool with time or not."

"I find thirty minutes unbelievable," Nicole said, "but your watches agree and so does the clock here in the living room. You said that it was over, Father. Is it?"

Shrugging, the priest said, "I hope so. I sincerely hope so. I don't know if it is or not. Remember I don't have too much experience in things of this nature."

"I hope it is. I've certainly learned my lesson. No more fooling around with stuff I know nothing about. Right, Myles?"

Myles nodded, reaching out for one of her hands, squeezing it gently when they touched. "If it is over, is it over for good, Father?"

Nicole stared at the priest until he answered.

"All I can say for now is that it seems to be over. However, it could occur again."

"*What?*" Myles and Nicole chorused.

"Let me explain," Maskey said. "There have been instances when the person afflicted with possession has been reinfested later by the same demon. Perhaps the person who was exorcized weakened later in his faith or dwelt too long on the situation, recalling the previous experiences with the unholy. I don't know. I'm no expert. Still, I do know of one or two well-documented cases wherein that very thing happened."

"I'm not sure I want to know about any of this," Nicole said sharply.

Myles looked at her but said nothing, turning back instead to Father Maskey.

"I think you should listen if for no other reason than to be aware of what not to do," the priest said, smiling kindly at the couple.

When Nicole nodded slowly, she looked up at Myles and found him smiling warmly at her.

"There was a famous case in Iowa wherein the woman who was possessed had been cursed by her father when she refused to have sexual relations with him. For many years, she found it impossible to go to Church, receive the sacraments, even though she wanted to, or do anything remotely holy or responsible in that area. When she was successfully exorcized, she was repossessed later in life. In fact, there was a lady in Germany who suffered with the stigmata of Christ, who predicted quite accurately that the woman in the Iowa case would be possessed by the unholy again."

"Then you're saying, Father, that this demon, even if he's gone now, could come back?"

"I'm saying that in as precise a way as I can. There was an incident involving a young girl who was allowed by the demon to enter the convent and was possessed when she did so. As I recall, she was killed in a fall from a church steeple or something. But the point I'm trying to make is, do *NOT* take any of this lightly. If the devil could invade the sacred confines of a convent, then actually no one is really safe, are they?" Maskey peered at Nicole before shifting his gaze to Myles.

As the truth of his statement sank home, their understanding reflected on their faces.

"As far as the two of you are concerned, I think Myles should get right with God. And you, Nicole, if you should want to visit me about any of this or if you have any questions pertaining to the Catholic Church, I'd be happy to answer them. The truth is, I'd feel a whole lot more comfortable answering that type of question than any about possession. Think about what I've said. It won't hurt you, you know. In fact, it'll take a lot more guts to go to Church and be a good Christian Catholic than it does to stay in bed on Sunday morning and try leading a life without Christ."

Myles looked down at the floor and said, "I guess I'll have to do something like you suggest after seeing what we've seen here this afternoon."

"Right now," Maskey said lightly, "why don't we try putting the apartment back together."

"That's really not necessary, Father," Nicole said.

Tipping the easy chair upright, the priest said, "Hey, come on. You and Myles can't handle that couch alone. Myles," he said, indicating the couch with one hand and stepping toward it.

Myles followed his example and betweeen them brought it to its correct position. In a few minutes the tables and other chairs had been righted, and Father Maskey stepped toward the kitchen.

"That's it, Father," Nicole said, moving quickly in front of the priest. "We can handle it from here on. Thank you so much for everything."

"I'm only glad that we had the opportunity to meet and weather the awful incident that took place this afternoon. Myles?" he said, turning toward him and extending his hand.

Myles accepted it and they shook firmly.

When he stood at the doorway to the hall, Maskey said, "Considering what the three of us have been through, maybe I'll be the one to help bring Nicole into the Church. Incidentally, when the two of you are ready, I'd be honored if you'd ask me to perform the marriage ceremony for you."

Nicole offered her hand to him and said, "That would be nice, Father. When we're ready, you can be assured that we'll be in touch with you."

"Whenever you're ready," Maskey said, turning to the door where he hesitated for a split second before spinning about once more. "The book. May I have it?"

Nicole looked at Myles for an anxious moment. Perhaps Myles was still here because the book was still here. Could she risk the chance of his leaving or disappearing once the book was taken away? Foolishness! Claptrap!

"One moment, Father," she said, turning to hurry to the shelves above the TV and stereo. She had put it back without even thinking while the men were arranging the furniture. Reaching up, she half expected the small volume to give a reluctant jerk, as if it wanted to stay. Grasping it firmly, she hurried back to Father Maskey.

"Isn't it amazing," the priest said, taking the book, "how people scoff at the idea of a devil in today's highly sophisticated world? You two certainly know better now, don't you?"

Wide smiles showed their agreement.

"Some people have the faith to move mountains and the same degree of faith can conjure up something horrible such as we witnessed here. And yet look at all of the unhappiness in the world—most of it because of misdirected faith. Lord, why doesn't man learn to get his priorities in order? Again, goodbye Nicole. Myles. I'll expect to hear from you."

Myles reached around Maskey to open the hall door and the priest stepped out. The hallway appeared the same, and when they heard the normal sound of footsteps coming down the hall, they all smiled.

Mrs. Bellasco mumbling under her breath, turned the corner, her face contorted by angry frustration.

"Oh, hello, Father," she said when she saw the priest. "Haven't you three gone in yet? Or are you leaving, Father?" She peered at the three, her own fit of unhappiness forgotten for a moment.

"What is it, Mrs. Bellasco?" Nicole asked, when she realized the woman was upset about something. Had she heard some of the commotion inside the apartment? Was she about to launch into a tirade directed at them about making too much noise for an apartment building?

"I walked all the way to the drugstore in the shopping center to buy some of the specials they have advertised in this bulletin," she said, waving the gaudily colored tabloid, "and I forgot my billfold."

Suppressing her grin, Nicole watched the woman storm by toward her own door.

"Goodbye, Father," Nicole and Myles said in unison.

"Goodbye," he said, turning to walk down the hall in the direction from which Mrs. Bellasco had come.

Nicole closed the door, the latch falling into place with a quiet click. "At last we're alone."

Myles embraced her and said, "Isn't it strange that ever since I came back, we thought we were alone a lot of the time but we really weren't."

"That's the scary part," she said. "But right now, my friend, we have to clean up that wall full of food, and the dolls have to be taken back to their place in the bedroom."

"Which do you want me to do?" Myles said, before adding, "I should tell you I don't do windows or walls." He smiled.

"I'll do the walls and you take care of the dolls. All right?"

"Fine with me."

Nicole went to the kitchen and Myles stood in the center of the living room, rubbing his hands. Why did they feel rough? He stared at them, looking closely to see if he had developed some callouses. His palms appeared as smooth as always but when he ran one over the other, he found them both to be rough.

His breath came in short, puffy gasps. A wave of horror splashed through his trembling body. Staring at the backs of his hands, he focused on hair—more hair than had ever been there before. When he stroked it, he found it to be more coarse than usual. A peculiar sensation corkscrewed through him, leaving a dizzy, nauseated sensation whipping at him.

What was wrong? What was wrong with him?

He rubbed his hands together again, finding them even rougher and the hair more coarse than just seconds before.

What was happening?

His eyes swept over the room, locking onto the dolls laying in a pile where they had fallen. An antique Little Annie Rooney doll's head turned by itself, staring at him, and then winked.

"Before you get started, darling," Nicole called from the kitchen, "can you come here and help me for a moment?"

A smile—an evil smile—crossed Myles' lips. "Coming, darling."